To Robin, for breathing life into Amilia, giving comfort to Modina, and saving two others from death

To the members of goodreads.com and the book blogging community, both of which have supported the series and invited others to join the adventure

And to the members of the Arlington Writers Group, for their generous support, assistance, and feedback

RISE OF EMPIRE

Royce watched the courier ride out of sight before taking off his imperial uniform. Turning to face Hadrian, he said, "Well, that wasn't so hard."

"Will?" Hadrian asked as the two slipped into the forest.

Royce nodded. "Remember yesterday you complained that you'd rather be an actor? I was giving you a part: Will, the Imperial Checkpoint Sentry. I thought you did rather well with the role."

"You know, you don't need to mock *all* my ideas." Hadrian frowned as he pulled his own tabard over his head. "Besides, I still think we should consider it. We could travel from town to town performing in dramatic plays, even a few comedies." Hadrian gave his smaller partner an appraising look. "Though maybe you should stick to drama—perhaps tragedies."

Royce glared back.

"What? I think I would make a superb actor. I see myself as a dashing leading man. We could definitely land parts in *The Crown Conspiracy*. I'll play the handsome swordsman that fights the villain, and you—well, you can be the other one."

BY MICHAEL J. SULLIVAN

The Ryria Chronicles

The Crown Tower

The Rose and Thorn

The Riyria Revelations

Theft of Swords

Rise of Empire

Heir of Novron

RISE OF EMPIRE

MICHAEL J. SULLIVAN

THE RIYRIA
REVELATIONS
VOLUME 2

www.orbitbooks.net

ORBIT

First published in Great Britain in 2011 by Orbit
Reprinted 2012 (three times), 2013

A CIP catalogue record for this book
is available from the British Library.

ISBN 978-0-356-50107-9

Printed and bound in Great Britain by
Clays Ltd, St Ives plc

Papers used by Orbit are from well-managed forests
and other responsible sources.

Orbit
An imprint of
Little, Brown Book Group
100 Victoria Embankment
London EC4Y 0DY

An Hachette UK Company
www.hachette.co.uk

www.orbitbooks.net

Contents

Known Regions of the World of Elan

Estrendor: Northern wastes
Erivan Empire: Elvenlands
Apeladorn: Nations of man
Ba Ran Archipelago: Islands of goblins
Westerlands: Western wastes
Dacca: Isle of south men

Nations of Apeladorn

Avryn: Central wealthy kingdoms
Trent: Northern mountainous kingdoms
Calis: Southeastern tropical region ruled by warlords
Delgos: Southern republic

Kingdoms of Avryn

Ghent: Ecclesiastical holding of the Nyphron Church
Melengar: Small but old and respected kingdom
Warric: Most powerful of the kingdoms of Avryn
Dunmore: Youngest and least sophisticated kingdom
Alburn: Forested kingdom
Rhenydd: Poor kingdom
Maranon: Producer of food. Once part of Delgos, which was lost when Delgos became a republic
Galeannon: Lawless kingdom of barren hills, the site of several great battles

The Gods

Erebus: Father of the gods
Ferrol: Eldest son, god of elves
Drome: Second son, god of dwarves
Maribor: Third son, god of men
Muriel: Only daughter, goddess of nature
Uberlin: Son of Muriel and Erebus, god of darkness

Political Parties

Imperialists: Those wishing to unite mankind under a single leader who is the direct descendant of the demigod Novron
Nationalists: Those wishing to be ruled by a leader chosen by the people
Royalists: Those wishing to continue rule by individual, independent monarchs

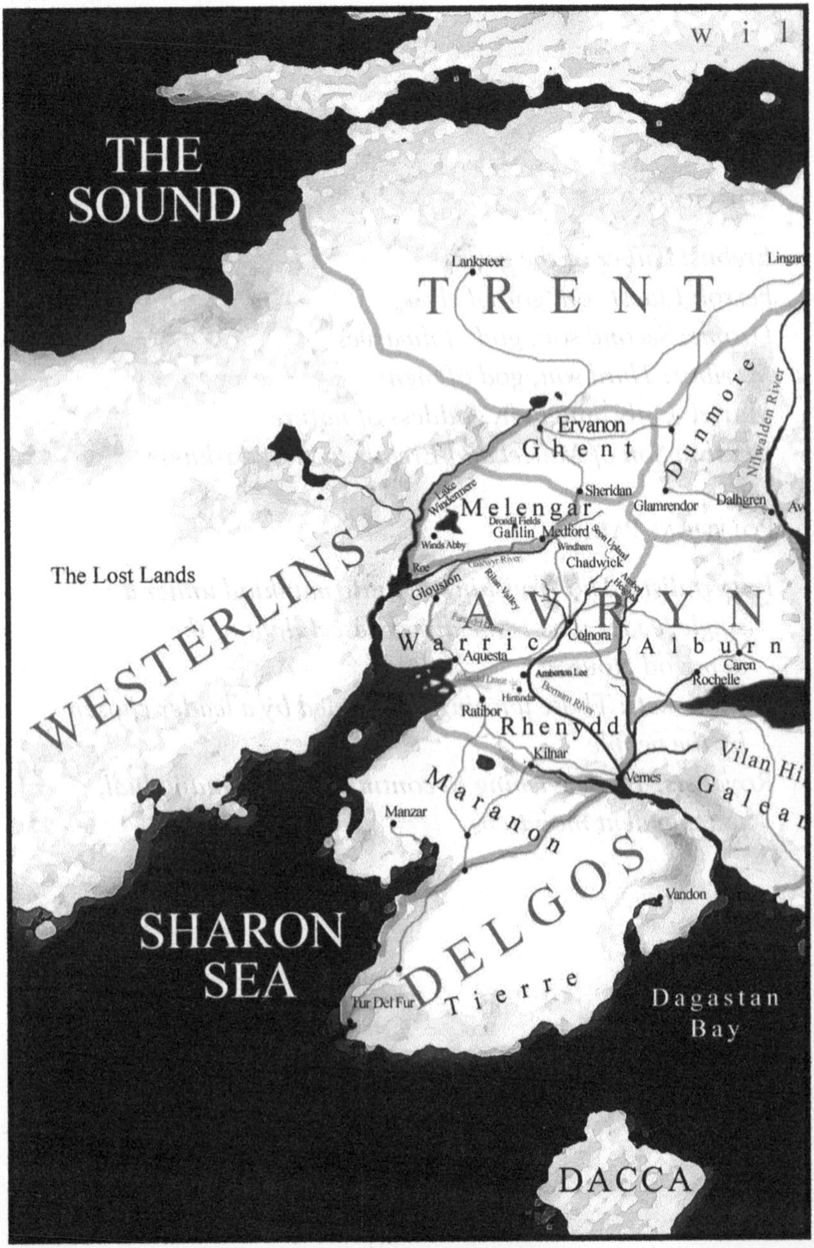

THE SOUND
TRENT
Lanksteer
Ervanon
Ghent
Dunmore
Nilwalden River
Sheridan
Glamrendor
Dalhgren
Lake Windermere
Melengar
Drondil Fields
Galilin
Medford
Winds Abby
Windham
Chadwick
Roe
Glouston
Rilan Valley
Amber Heights
WESTERLINS
The Lost Lands
AVRYN
Colnora
Warric
Aquesta
Alburn
Caren
Rochelle
Amberton Lee
Hintindar
Bernum River
Ratibor
Rhenydd
Kilnar
Vernes
Maranon
Manzar
DELGOS
Vandon
SHARON SEA
Fur Del Fur
Tierre
Dagastan Bay
DACCA

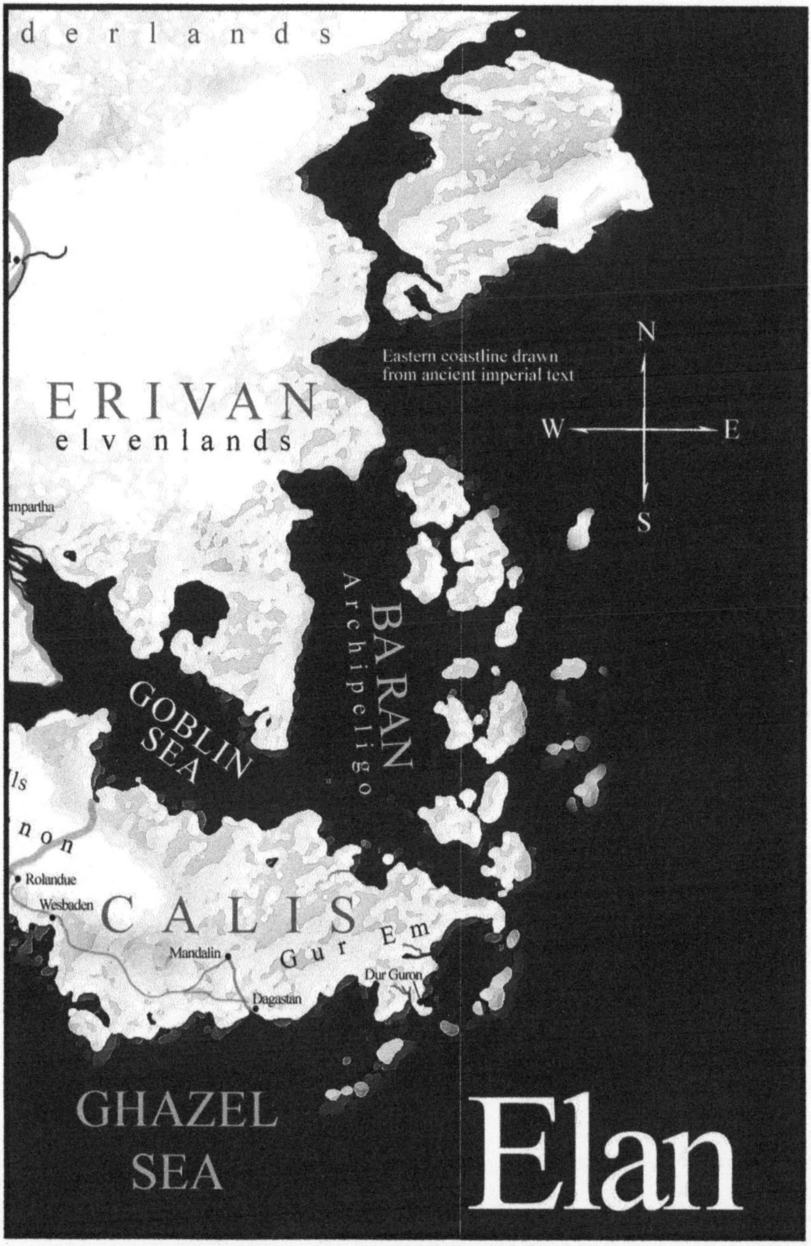

d e r l a n d s

Eastern coastline drawn
from ancient imperial text

N
W
E
S

ERIVAN
elvenlands

mpartha

BARAN
Archipeligo

GOBLIN
SEA

ls
n o n

Rolandue
Wesbaden

CALIS

Mandalin
Gur Em
Dur Guron
Dagastan

GHAZEL
SEA

Elan

BOOK III

NYPHRON RISING

BOOK III

NYPHRON RISING

Chapter 1

The Empress

Amilia made the mistake of looking back into Edith Mon's eyes. She had never meant to—she had never planned on raising her stare from the floor—but Edith startled her and she looked up without thinking. The head maid would consider her action defiance, a sign of rebellion in the ranks of the scullery. Amilia had never looked into Edith's eyes before, and doing so now, she wondered if a soul lurked behind them. If so, it must be cowering or dead, rotting like a late-autumn apple; that would explain her smell. Edith had a sour scent, vaguely rancid, as if something had gone bad.

"This will be another tenent withheld from yer pay," the rotund woman said. "Yer digging quite a hole, ain't you?"

Edith was big and broad and missing any sign of a neck. Her huge anvil of a head sat squarely on her shoulders. By contrast, Amilia barely existed. Small and pear-shaped, with a plain face and long, lifeless hair, she was part of the crowd, one of the faces no one paused to consider—neither pretty nor grotesque enough to warrant a second glance. Unfortunately, her invisibility failed when it came to the palace's head maid, Edith Mon.

"I didn't break it." *Mistake number two*, Amilia thought.

A meaty hand slapped Amilia's face, ringing ears and

watering eyes. "Go on," Edith enticed her with a sweet tone, and then whispered, "lie to me again."

Gripping the washbasin to steady herself, Amilia felt heat blossom on her cheek. Her gaze now followed Edith's hand, and when it rose again, Amilia flinched. With a snicker, Edith ran her plump fingers through Amilia's hair.

"No tangles," Edith observed. "I can see how ya spend yer time, instead of doing yer work. Ya hoping to catch the eye of the butcher? Maybe that saucy little man who delivers the wood? I saw ya talking to him. Know what they sees when they looks at ya? They sees an ugly scullery maid is what. A wretched filthy guttersnipe who smells of lye and grease. They would rather pay for a whore than get ya for nothing. You'd be better off spending more time on yer tasks. If ya did, I wouldn't have to beat ya so often."

Amilia felt Edith winding her hair, twisting and tightening it around her fist. "It's not like I enjoy hurting ya." She pulled until Amilia winced. "But ya have to learn." Edith continued pulling Amilia's hair, forcing her head back until only the ceiling was visible. "Yer slow, stupid, and ugly. That's why yer still in the scullery. I can't make ya a laundry maid, much less a parlor or chambermaid. You'd embarrass me, understand?"

Amilia remained quiet.

"I said, do ya understand?"

"Yes."

"Say yer sorry for chipping the plate."

"I'm sorry for chipping the plate."

"And yer sorry for lying about it?"

"Yes."

Edith roughly patted Amilia's burning cheek. "That's a good girl. I'll add the cost to yer tally. Now as for punishment..." She let go of Amilia's hair and tore the scrub brush from her hand, measuring its weight. She usually used a belt;

the brush would hurt more. Edith would drag her to the laundry, where the big cook could not see. The head cook had taken a liking to Amilia, and while Edith had every right to discipline her girls, Ibis would not stand for it in his kitchen. Amilia waited for a fat hand to grab her wrist, but instead Edith stroked her head. "Such long hair," she said at length. "It's yer hair that's getting in the way, isn't it? It's making ya think too much of yerself. Well, I know just how to fix both problems. Yer gonna look real pretty when I—"

The kitchen fell silent. Cora, who had been incessantly plunging her butter churn, paused in mid-stroke. The cooks stopped chopping and even Nipper, who was stacking wood near the stoves, froze. Amilia followed their gaze to the stairs.

A noblewoman adorned in white velvet and satin glided down the steps and entered the steamy stench of the scullery. Piercing eyes and razor-thin lips stood out against a powdered face. The woman was tall and—unlike Amilia, who had a hunched posture—stood straight and proud. She moved immediately to the small table along the wall, where the baker was preparing bread.

"Clear this," she ordered with a wave of her hand, speaking to no one in particular. The baker immediately scooped his utensils and dough into his apron and hurried away. "Scrub it clean," the lady insisted.

Amilia felt the brush thrust back into her hand, and a push sent her stumbling forward. She did not look up and went right to work making large swirls of flour-soaked film. Nipper was beside her in an instant with a bucket, and Vella arrived with a towel. Together they cleared the mess while the woman watched with disdain.

"Two chairs," the lady barked, and Nipper ran off to fetch them.

Uncertain what to do next, Amilia stood in place watching

the lady, holding the dripping brush at her side. When the noblewoman caught her staring, Amilia quickly looked down and movement caught her eye. A small gray mouse froze beneath the baker's table, trying to conceal itself in the shadows. Taking a chance, it snatched a morsel of bread and disappeared through a small crack.

"What a miserable creature," she heard the lady say. Amilia thought she was referring to the mouse until she added, "You're making a filthy puddle on the floor. Go away."

Before retreating to her washbasin, Amilia attempted a pathetic curtsy. A flurry of orders erupted from the woman, each announced with perfect diction. Vella, Cora, and even Edith went about setting the table as if for a royal banquet. Vella draped a white tablecloth, and Edith started setting out silverware only to be shooed away as the woman carefully placed each piece herself. Soon the table was elegantly set for two, complete with multiple goblets and linen napkins.

Amilia could not imagine who could be dining there. No one would set a table for the servants, and why would a noble come to the kitchen to eat?

"Here now, what's all this about?" Amilia heard the deep familiar voice of Ibis Thinly. The old sea cook was a large barrel-chested man with bright blue eyes and a thin beard that wreathed the line of his chin. He had spent the morning meeting with farmers, yet he still wore his ever-present apron. The grease-stained wrap was his uniform, his mark of office. He barged into the kitchen like a bear returning to his cave to find mischief afoot. When he spotted the lady, he stopped.

"I am Lady Constance," the noblewoman informed him. "In a moment I will be bringing Empress Modina here. If you are the cook, then prepare food." The lady paused a moment to study the table critically. She adjusted the positions of a few items, then turned and left.

"Leif, get a knife on that roasted lamb," Ibis shouted. "Cora, fetch cheese. Vella, get bread. Nipper, straighten that woodpile!"

"The empress!" Cora exclaimed as she raced for the pantry.

"What's she doing coming here?" Leif asked. There was anger in his voice, as if an unwelcome, no-account relative was dropping by and he was the inconvenienced lord of the manor.

Amilia had heard of the empress but had never seen her—not even from a distance. Few had. She had been coronated in a private ceremony over half a year earlier on Wintertide, and her arrival in Aquesta had changed everything.

King Ethelred no longer wore his crown, and was addressed as "Regent" instead of "Your Majesty." He still ruled over the castle, only now it was referred to as the imperial palace. The other one, Regent Saldur, had made all the changes. Originally from Melengar, the former bishop had taken up residence and set builders working day and night on the great hall and throne room. Saldur had also declared new rules that all the servants had to follow.

The palace staff could no longer leave the grounds unless escorted by one of the new guards, and all outgoing letters were read and needed to be approved. The latter edict was hardly an issue, as few servants could write. The restriction on going outside the palace, however, was a hardship to almost everyone. Many with families in the city or surrounding farms chose to resign, because they could no longer return home each night. Those remaining at the castle never heard from them again. Regent Saldur had successfully isolated the palace from the outside world, but inside, rumors and gossip ran wild. Speculations flourished in out-of-the-way corridors that giving notice was as unhealthy as attempting to sneak away.

The fact that no one ever saw the empress ignited its own

set of speculations. Everyone knew she was the heir of the original, legendary emperor, Novron, and therefore a child of the god Maribor. This had been proven when she had been the only one capable of slaying the beast that had slaughtered dozens of Elan's greatest knights. That she had previously been a farm girl from a small village confirmed that in the eyes of Maribor, all were equal. Rumors concluded that she had ascended to the state of a spiritual being, and only the regents and her personal secretary ever stood in her divine presence.

That must be who the noblewoman is, Amilia thought. The lady with the sour face and perfect speech was the imperial secretary to the empress.

They soon had an array of the best food they could muster in a short time laid out on the table. Knob, the baker, and Leif, the butcher, disputed the placement of dishes, each wanting his wares in the center. "Cora," Ibis said, "put your pretty cake of cheese in the middle." This brought a smile and blush to the dairymaid's face and scowls from Leif and Knob.

Being a scullion, Amilia had no more part to play and returned to her dishes. Edith was chatting excitedly in the corner near the stack of oak kegs with the tapster and the cupbearer, and all the servants were straightening their outfits and running fingers through their hair. Nipper was still sweeping when the lady returned. Once more everyone stopped and watched as she led a thin young girl by the wrist.

"Sit down," Lady Constance ordered in her brisk tone.

Everyone peered past the two women, trying to catch the first glimpse of the god-queen. Two well-armored guards emerged and took up positions on either side of the table. But no one else appeared.

Where is the empress?

"Modina, I said sit down," Lady Constance repeated.

Shock rippled through Amilia.

Modina? This waif of a child is the empress?

The girl did not appear to hear Lady Constance and stood limp with a blank expression. She looked to be a teenager, delicate and deathly thin. Once she might have been pretty, but what remained was an appalling sight. The girl's face was white as bone, her skin thin and stretched, revealing the detailed outline of her skull beneath. Her ragged blonde hair fell across her face. She wore only a thin white smock, which added to the girl's ghostly appearance.

Lady Constance sighed and forced the girl into one of the chairs at the baker's table. Like a doll, the girl allowed herself to be moved. She said nothing and her eyes stared blankly.

"Place the napkin in your lap this way." Lady Constance carefully opened and laid the linen with deliberate movements. She waited, glaring at the empress, who sat, oblivious. "As empress, you will never serve yourself," Lady Constance went on. "You will wait as your servants fill your plate." She was looking around with irritation when her eyes found Amilia. "You—come here," she ordered. "Serve Her Eminence."

Amilia dropped the brush in the basin and, wiping her hands on her smock, rushed forward. She lacked experience with serving but said nothing. Instead, she focused on recalling the times she had watched Leif cutting meat. Taking up the tongs and a knife, she tried her best to imitate him. Leif always made it look effortless, but Amilia's fingers betrayed her and she fumbled miserably, managing to place only a few shredded bits of lamb on the girl's plate.

"Bread." Lady Constance snapped the word like a whip and Amilia sliced into the long twisted loaf, nearly cutting herself in the process.

"Now eat."

For a brief moment, Amilia thought this was another order

for her and reached out in response. She caught herself and stood motionless, uncertain if she was free to return to her dishes.

"Eat, I said." The imperial secretary glared at the girl, who continued to stare blankly at the far wall.

"*Eat, damn you!*" Lady Constance bellowed, and everyone in the kitchen, including Edith Mon and Ibis Thinly, jumped. She pounded the baker's table with her fist, knocking over the stemware and bouncing the knives against the plates. "*Eat!*" Lady Constance repeated, and slapped the girl across the face. Her skin-wrapped skull rocked with the blow and came to rest on its own. The girl did not wince. She merely continued her stare, this time at a new wall.

In a fit of rage, the imperial secretary rose, knocking over her chair. She took one of the pieces of meat and tried to force it into the girl's mouth.

"What's going on?"

Lady Constance froze at the sound of the voice. An old white-haired man descended the steps into the scullery. His elegant purple robe and black cape looked out of place in the hot, messy kitchen. Amilia recognized Regent Saldur immediately.

"What in the world..." Saldur began as he approached the table. He looked at the girl, then at the kitchen staff, and finally at Lady Constance, who at some point had dropped the meat. "What were you thinking...bringing her down here?"

"I—I thought if—"

Saldur held up his hand, silencing her, then slowly squeezed it into a fist. He clenched his jaw and drew a deep breath through his sharp nose. Once more he focused on the girl. "Look at her. You were supposed to educate and train her. She's worse than ever!"

"I—I tried, but—"

"Shut up!" the regent snapped, still holding up his fist. No one in the kitchen moved. The only sounds were the faint crackle of the fire in the ovens and the bubbling of broth in a pot. "If this is the result of a professional, we may as well try an amateur. They couldn't possibly do worse." The regent pointed at Amilia. "You! Congratulations, you are now the imperial secretary to the empress." Turning his attention back to Lady Constance, he said, "And as for you—your services are no longer required. Guards, remove her."

Amilia saw Lady Constance falter. Her perfect posture evaporated as she cowered and stepped backward, nearly falling over the upended chair. "No! Please, no," she cried as a palace guard gripped her arm and pulled her toward the back door. Another guard took her other arm. She grew frantic, pleading and struggling as they dragged her out.

Amilia stood frozen in place, holding the meat tongs and carving knife, trying to remember how to breathe. Once the pleas of Lady Constance faded, Regent Saldur turned to her, his face flushed red, his teeth revealed behind taunt lips. "Don't fail me," he told her, and returned up the stairs, his cape whirling behind him.

Amilia looked back at the girl, who continued to stare at the wall.

⁂

The mystery of why no one saw the empress was solved when a soldier escorted the girls to Modina's room. Amilia expected to travel to the eastern keep, home of the regents' offices and the royal residence. To her surprise, the guard remained on the service side and headed for a curved stair across from the laundry. Chambermaids used this stairwell to service rooms on the upper floors. But here, the soldier went down.

Amilia did not question the guard, her thoughts preoccupied with the sword that hung at his side. His dark eyes were embedded in a stone face, and the top of her head reached the bottom of his chin. Each of his hands was the size of two of hers. He was not one of the guards who had taken Lady Constance away, but Amilia knew he would not hesitate when her time came.

The air turned cool and damp as they descended into darkness cut only by three mounted lanterns. The last dripped wax from an unhinged faceplate. At the bottom of the stairs a wooden door stood open, which led to a tiny corridor with more doors on either side. In one room Amilia spotted several casks and a rack of bottles dressed in packs of straw. Large locks sealed two other doors, and a third door stood open, revealing a small stone room, empty except for a pile of straw and a wooden bucket. When they reached it, the soldier stood to one side, his back to the wall.

"I'm sorry..." Amilia began, confused. "I don't understand. I thought we were going to the empress's bedchamber."

The guard nodded.

"Are you saying this is where Her Eminence sleeps?"

Again the soldier nodded.

As Amilia stared in shock, Modina wandered forward into the room and curled up on the pile of straw. The guard closed the heavy door and began fitting a large lock through the latch.

"Wait," Amilia said, "you can't leave her here. Can't you see she's sick?"

The guard snapped the lock in place.

Amilia stared at the oak door.

How is this possible? She's the empress. She's the daughter of a god and the high priestess of the church.

"You keep the empress in an old cellar?"

"It's better than where she was," the soldier told her. He had not spoken until then, and his voice was not what she expected. Soft, sympathetic, and not much louder than a whisper, his tone disarmed her.

"Where was she?"

"I've said too much already."

"I can't just leave her in there. She doesn't even have a candle."

"My orders are to keep her here."

Amilia stared at him. She could not see his eyes. The visor of his helm and the way the shadows fell cast darkness on everything above his nose. "Fine," she said at last, and walked out of the cellar.

She returned a moment later carrying the wax-laden lantern from the stairwell. "May I at least keep her company?"

"Are you sure?" He sounded surprised.

Amilia was not but nodded anyway. The guard opened the door.

The empress was lying huddled on the bed of straw, her eyes open, staring but not seeing. Amilia spotted a blanket wadded up in the corner. She set the lantern on the floor, shook out the wool covering, and draped it over the girl.

"They don't treat you very well, do they?" she said, carefully brushing back the mass of hair that lay across Modina's face. The strands felt as stiff and brittle as the straw that littered them. "How old are you?"

The empress did not answer, nor did she stir at Amilia's touch. Lying on her side, the girl clutched her knees to her chest and pressed her cheek against the straw. She blinked occasionally and her chest rose and fell with each breath but nothing more.

"Something bad happened, didn't it?" Amilia ran her fingers lightly over Modina's bare arm. She could circle the girl's wrist with her thumb and index finger with room to spare. "Look, I don't know how long I'm going to be here. I don't expect it'll be too long. See, I'm not a noble lady. I'm just a girl who washes dishes. The regent says I'm supposed to educate and train you, but he made a mistake. I don't know how to do any of that." She petted Modina's head and let her fingers run lightly over her hollow cheek, still blotchy where Lady Constance had struck her. "But I promise I won't ever hurt you."

Amilia sat for several minutes searching her mind for some way to reach the girl. "Can I tell you a secret? Now don't laugh...but...I'm really quite afraid of the dark. I know it's silly but I can't help myself. I've always been that way. My brothers tease me about it all the time. If you could chat with me a bit, maybe it would help me. What do you say?"

There was still no reaction.

Amilia sighed. "Well, tomorrow I'll bring some candles from my room. I've a whole bunch saved up. That will make things a bit nicer. You just try to rest now."

Amilia had not been lying about her fear of the dark. But that night it had to stand in line behind a host of new fears as she struggled to find sleep huddled beside the empress.

❧

The soldiers did not come for Amilia that night and she woke when breakfast was brought in—or rather was skipped across the floor on a wooden plate that spun to a stop in the middle of the room. On it were a fist-sized chunk of meat, a wedge of cheese, and thick-crusted bread. It looked wonderful and was similar to Amilia's standard meals, courtesy of Ibis. Before coming to the palace, she had never eaten beef or venison, but now it was commonplace. Being friends with the head cook had other advantages as well. People didn't want to offend the man who controlled their diet, so Amilia was generally well treated, except by Edith Mon. Amilia took a few bites and loudly voiced her appreciation. "This is sooooo good. Would you like some?"

The empress did not respond.

Amilia sighed. "No, I don't suppose you would. What would you like? I can get you whatever you want."

Amilia got to her feet, grabbed up the tray, and waited. Nothing. After a few minutes, she rapped on the door and the same guard opened it.

"Excuse me, but I have to see about getting a proper meal for Her Eminence." The guard looked at the plate, confused, but stepped aside, leaving her to trot up the stairs.

The kitchen was still buzzing over the events of the previous night, but it stopped the moment Amilia entered the kitchen. "Sent ya back, did they?" Edith grinned. "Don't worry, I done saved yer pile of pots. And I haven't forgotten about that hair."

"Hush up, Edith," Ibis reprimanded with a scowl. Returning his attention to Amilia, he said, "Are you all right? Did they send you back?"

"I'm fine, thank you, Ibis, and no, I think I'm still the empress's secretary—whatever that means."

"Good for you, lassie," Ibis told her. He turned to Edith and added, "And I'd watch what you say now. Looks like you'll be washing that stack yourself." Edith turned and stalked off with a *humph*.

"So, my dear, what does bring you here?"

"I came about this food you sent to the empress."

Ibis looked wounded. "What's wrong with it?"

"Nothing, it's wonderful. I had some myself."

"Then I don't see—"

"Her Eminence is sick. She can't eat this. When I didn't feel well, my mother used to make me soup, a thin yellow broth that was easy to swallow. I was wondering, could you make something like that?"

"Sure," Ibis told her. "Soup is easy. Someone shoulda told me she was feeling poorly. I know exactly what to make. I call it Seasick Soup. It's the only thing the new lads kept down their first few days out. Leif, fetch me the big kettle."

Amilia spent the rest of the morning making trips back and forth to Modina's small cell. She removed all her possessions from the dormitory: a spare dress, some underclothing, a nightgown, a brush, and her treasured stash of nearly a dozen candles. From the linen supply, she brought pillows, sheets, and blankets. She even snuck a pitcher, some mild soap, and a basin from an unoccupied guest room. Each time she passed, the guard gave her a small smile and shook his head in amusement.

After removing the old straw and bringing in fresh bundles from the stable, she went to Ibis to check on the soup. "Well, the next batch will be better, when I have more time, but this should put some wind in her sails," he said.

Amilia returned to the cell and, setting down the steaming pot of soup, helped the empress to sit up. She took the first sip to check the temperature, then lifted the spoon to Modina's lips. Most of the broth dribbled down her chin and dripped onto the front of her smock.

"Okay, that was my fault. Next time I'll remember to bring one of those napkins that lady was all excited about." With her second spoonful, Amilia cupped her hand and caught most of the excess. "Aha!" she exclaimed. "I got some in. It's good, isn't it?" She tipped another spoonful and this time saw Modina swallow.

When the bowl was empty, Amilia guessed most of the soup was on the floor or soaked into Modina's clothes, but she was certain at least some got in. "There now, that must be a little better, don't you think? But I see I've made a terrible mess of you. How about we clean you up a bit, eh?" Amilia washed Modina and changed her into her own spare smock. The two girls were similar in height; however, Modina swam in the dress until Amilia fashioned a belt from a bit of twine.

Amilia continued to chatter while she made two makeshift beds with the straw and purloined blankets, pillows, and sheets. "I would have liked to bring us some mattresses but they were heavy. Besides, I didn't want to risk too much attention. People were already giving me strange looks. I think these will do nicely, don't you?" Modina continued her blank stare. When everything was in order, Amilia sat Modina on her newly sheeted bed in the glow of a handful of cheery candles and began gently brushing her hair.

"So, how does one get to be empress, anyway?" she asked. "They say you slew a monster that killed hundreds of knights. You know, you really don't look like the monster-slaying type—no offense." Amilia paused and tilted her head. "Still not interested in talking? That's okay. You want to keep your past a secret. I understand. After all, we've only just met.

"So, let's see... What can I tell you about myself? Well, I come from Tarin Vale. Do you know where that is? Probably not. It's a tiny village between here and Colnora. Just a little town people sometimes pass through on their way to more exciting places. Nothing much happens in Tarin. My father makes carriages and he's really good at it. Still, he doesn't make much money." She paused and studied the girl's face to try to determine if she heard any of what Amilia was saying.

"What does your father do? I think I heard he was a farmer; is that right?"

Nothing.

"My da doesn't make much money. My mother says it's

because he does *too good* of a job. He's pretty proud of his work, so he takes a long time. It can take him a whole year to make a carriage. That makes it hard, because he only gets paid when it's done. What with buying the supplies and all, we sometimes run out of money.

"My mother does spinning and my brother cuts wood, but it never seems like enough. That's why I'm here, you see. I'm not a very good spinner but I can read and write." One side of the girl's head was now free of tangles and Amilia switched to the other.

"I can see you're impressed. It hasn't done me much good, though. Well, except I guess it did get me a foot in the door, as it were.

"Hmm, what's that? You want to know where I learned to read and write? Oh well, thank you for asking. Devon taught me. He's a monk that came to Tarin Vale a few years ago." Her voice lowered conspiratorially. "I liked him a lot and he was cute and smart—*very smart*. He read books and told me about faraway places and things that happened long ago. Devon thought either my dad or the head of his order would try to split us up, so he taught me so we could write each other. Devon was right, of course. When my da found out, he said, 'There's no future with a monk.' Devon was sent away and I cried for days."

Amilia paused to clear a particularly nasty snarl. She tried her best to be gentle, but was sure it caused the girl pain, even if she did not show it. "That was a rough one," she said. "For a minute I thought you might have a sparrow hiding in there.

"Anyway, when Da found out I could read and write, he was so proud. He bragged about me to everyone who came to the shop. One of his customers, Squire Jenkins Talbert, was impressed and said he could put in a good word for me here in Aquesta.

"Everyone was so excited when I was accepted. When I found out the job was just to wash dishes, I didn't have the heart to tell my family, so I've not been home since. Now, of course, they won't let me go." Amilia sighed but then put on a bright smile. "But that's okay, because now I'm here with you."

There was a quiet knock and the guard stepped in. He took a minute to survey the changes in the cell and nodded his approval. His gaze shifted to Amilia and there was a distinct sadness in his eyes. "I'm sorry, miss, but Regent Saldur has ordered me to bring you to him."

Amilia froze, then slowly put the brush down and with a trembling hand draped a blanket around the young girl's shoulders. She rose, kissed Modina on the cheek, and in a quivering voice managed to whisper, "Goodbye."

Chapter 2

The Messenger

He always feared he would die this way, alone on a remote stretch of road far from home. The forest pressed close from both sides, and his trained eyes recognized that the debris barring his path was not the innocent result of a weakened tree. He pulled on the reins, forcing his horse's head down. She snorted in frustration, fighting the bit—like him, she sensed danger.

He glanced behind him and to either side, scanning the trees standing in summer gowns of deep green. Nothing moved in the early-morning stillness. Nothing betrayed the tranquil facade except the pile before him. The deadfall was unnatural. Even from this distance, he saw the brightly colored pulp of fresh-cut wood—a barricade.

Thieves?

A band of highwaymen no doubt crouched under the cover of the forest, watching, waiting for him to draw near. He tried to focus his thoughts as his horse panted beneath him. This was the shortest route north to the Galewyr River, and he was running out of time. Breckton was preparing to invade the kingdom of Melengar, and he must deliver the dispatch before the knight launched the attack. Before he had embarked, his commander, as well as the regents, had personally expressed the importance of this mission. They were counting on him—*she* was counting on him. Like thousands of others, he had stood in the freezing square on Coronation Day just to catch a glimpse of Empress Modina. To the crowd's immense disappointment, she never appeared. An announcement came after many hours, explaining she was occupied with the affairs of the New Empire. Recently ascended from the peasant class, the new ruler obviously had no time for frivolity.

He removed his cloak and tied it behind the saddle, revealing the gold crown on his tabard. They might let him pass. Surely they knew the imperial army was nearby, and Sir Breckton would not stand for the waylaying of an imperial messenger. Highwaymen might not fear that fool Earl Ballentyne, but even desperate men would think twice before offending Ballentyne's knight. Other commanders might ignore a bloodied or murdered dispatch rider, but Sir Breckton would take it as a personal assault on his honor, and insulting Breckton's honor was tantamount to suicide.

He refused to fail.

Brushing the hair from his eyes, he took a fresh grip on the reins and advanced cautiously. As he neared the barricade, he saw movement. Leaves quivered. A twig snapped. He pivoted his mount and prepared to bolt. He was a good rider—fast and agile. His horse was a well-bred three-year-old, and once she was spurred, no one would catch them. He tensed in the saddle and leaned forward, preparing for the lurch, but the sight of imperial uniforms stopped him.

A pair of soldiers trudged to the road from the trees and grudgingly peered at him with the dull expression common to foot soldiers. They were dressed in red tabards emblazoned with the crest of Sir Breckton's command. As they approached, the larger one chewed a stalk of rye while the smaller man licked his fingers and wiped them on his uniform.

"You had me worried," the rider said with a mix of relief and irritation. "I thought you were highwaymen."

The smaller one smiled. He took little care with his uniform. Two shoulder straps were unfastened, causing the leather tongues to stand up like tiny wings on his shoulders. "Did ya hear that, Will? He thoughts we was thieves. Not a bad idea, eh? We should cut us some purses—charge a toll, as it were. At least we'd make a bit o' coin standin' out here all day. Course Breckton would skin us alive if'n he heard."

The taller soldier, most likely a half-wit mute, nodded in silent agreement. At least he wore his uniform smartly. It fit him better and he took the time to fasten everything properly. Both uniforms were rumpled and stained from sleeping outdoors, but such was the life of an infantryman—one of the many reasons he preferred being a courier.

"Clear this mess. I have an urgent dispatch. I need to get through to the imperial army command at once."

"Here now, we've orders too, ya know? We're not to let anyone pass," the smaller said.

"I'm an imperial courier, you fool!"

"Oh," the sentry responded with all the acumen of a wooden post. He glanced briefly at his partner, who maintained his dim expression. "Well, that's a different set of apples, now ain't it?" He petted the horse's neck. "That would explain the lather you've put on this here girl, eh? She looks like she could use a drink. We got a bucket and there's a little stream just over—"

"I've no time for that. Just get that pile out of the road and be quick about it."

"Certainly, certainly. You don't have to be so rough. Just tell us the watchword, and Will and me, we'll haul it outta yer way right fast," he said as he dug for something caught in his teeth.

"Watchword?"

The soldier nodded. He pulled his finger out and sniffed at something with a sour look before giving it a flick. "You know, the password. We can't be lettin' no spies through here. There's a war on, after all."

"I've never heard of such a thing. I wasn't informed of any password."

"No?" The smaller soldier raised an eyebrow as he took hold of the horse's bridle.

"I spoke to the regents themselves, and I—"

The larger of the two pulled him from his horse. He landed on his back, hitting the ground hard and banging his head. A jolt of pain momentarily blinded him. When he opened his eyes, he found the soldier straddling him with a blade to his throat.

"Who do you work for?" the large sentry growled.

"Whatcha doin', Will?" the smaller one asked, still holding his horse.

"Tryin' to get this spy to talk, that's what."

"I—I'm not a spy. I'm an imperial courier. Let me go!"

"Will, our orders says nothin' about interrogatin' them. If'n they don't know the watchword, we cuts they's throats and tosses them in the river. Sir Breckton don't have time to deal with every fool we get on this here road. Besides, who ya think he works for? The only ones fightin' us is Melengar, so he works for Melengar. Now slit his throat and I'll help you drag him to the river as soon as I ties up this here horse."

"But I *am* a courier!" he shouted.

"Sure ya is."

"I can prove it. I have dispatches for Sir Breckton in the saddlebag."

The two soldiers exchanged dubious looks. The smaller one shrugged. He reached into the horse's bags and proceeded to search. He pulled out a leather satchel containing a wax-sealed parchment, and breaking the seal, he examined it.

"Well, if'n that don't beat all. Looks like he's tellin' the truth, Will. This here looks like a real genuine dispatch for His Lordship."

"Oh?" the other asked as worry crossed his face.

"Sure looks that way. Better let him up."

His face downcast, the soldier sheathed his weapon and extended a hand to help the courier to his feet. "Ah—sorry about that. We were just followin' orders, ya know?"

"When Sir Breckton sees this broken seal, he'll have your heads!" the courier said, shoving past the large sentry and snatching the document from the other.

"Us?" The smaller one laughed. "Like Will here said, we was just followin' his orders. You were the one who failed to get the watchword afore ridin' here. Sir Breckton, he's a stickler for rules. He don't like it when his orders ain't followed. Course ya'll most likely only lose a hand or maybe an ear fer yer mistake. If'n I was you, I'd see if'n I could heat the wax up enough to reseal it."

"That would ruin the impression."

"Ya could say it was hot and, what with the sun on the pouch all day, the wax melted in the saddlebag. Better than losin' a hand or an ear, I says. Besides, busy nobles like Breckton ain't gonna study the seal afore openin' an urgent dispatch, but he will notice if'n the seal is broken. That's fer sure."

The courier looked at the document flapping in the breeze and felt his stomach churn. He had no choice, but he would not do it here with these idiots watching. He remounted his horse.

"Clear the road!" he barked.

The two soldiers dragged the branches aside. He kicked his horse and raced her up the road.

~

Royce watched the courier ride out of sight before taking off his imperial uniform. Turning to face Hadrian, he said, "Well, that wasn't so hard."

"Will?" Hadrian asked as the two slipped into the forest.

Royce nodded. "Remember yesterday you complained that you'd rather be an actor? I was giving you a part: Will, the Imperial Checkpoint Sentry. I thought you did rather well with the role."

"You know, you don't need to mock *all* my ideas." Hadrian frowned as he pulled his own tabard over his head. "Besides, I still think we should consider it. We could travel from town to town performing in dramatic plays, even a few comedies." Hadrian gave his smaller partner an appraising look. "Though maybe you should stick to drama—perhaps tragedies."

Royce glared back.

"What? I think I would make a superb actor. I see myself as a dashing leading man. We could definitely land parts in *The Crown Conspiracy*. I'll play the handsome swordsman that fights the villain, and you—well, you can be the other one."

They dodged branches while pulling off their coifs and gloves, rolling them in their tabards. Walking downhill, they reached one of the many small rivers that fed the great Galewyr. Here they found their horses still tied and enjoying the river grass. The animals lazily swished their tails, keeping the flies at bay. "You worry me sometimes, Hadrian. You really do."

"Why not actors? It's safe. Might even be fun."

"It would be neither safe nor fun. Besides, actors have to travel and I'm content with the way things are. I get to stay near Gwen," Royce added.

"See, that's another reason. Why not find another line of

work? Honestly, if I had what you do, I would never take another job."

Royce removed a pair of boots from a saddlebag. "We do it because it's what we're good at, and with the war, Alric is willing to pay top fees for information."

Hadrian released a sarcastic snort. "Sure, top fees for us, but what about the other costs? Breckton might work for that idiot Ballentyne, but he's no fool himself. He'll certainly look at the seal and won't buy the story about it softening in the saddlebag."

"I know," Royce began as he sat on a log, exchanging the imperial boots for his own, "but after telling one lie, his second tale about sentries breaking the seal will sound even more outlandish, so they won't believe anything he says."

Hadrian paused in his own efforts to switch boots and scowled at his partner. "You realize they'll probably execute him for treason?"

Royce nodded. "Which will neatly eliminate the only witness."

"You see, that's exactly what I'm talking about." Hadrian sighed and shook his head.

Royce could see the familiar melancholy wash over his partner. It appeared too often lately. He could not fathom his friend's moodiness. These strange bouts of depression usually followed successes and frequently led to a night of heavy drinking.

He wondered if Hadrian even cared about the money anymore. He took only what was needed for drinks and food and stored the rest. Royce could have understood his friend's reaction if they had been making a living by picking pockets or robbing homes, but they worked for the king now. Their jobs were almost too clean for Royce's taste. Hadrian had no real concept of filth. Unlike Royce, he had not grown up in the muddy streets of Ratibor.

Royce decided to try to reason with Hadrian. "Would you rather they find out and send a detachment to hunt us down?"

"No, I just hate being the cause of an innocent man's death."

"No one is innocent, my friend. And you aren't the cause... You're more like"—he searched for words—"the grease beneath the skids."

"Thanks. I feel *so* much better."

Royce folded the uniform and placed it, along with the boots, neatly into his saddlebag. Hadrian still struggled to rid himself of his black boots, which were too small. With a mighty tug, he jerked the last one off and threw it down in frustration. He gathered it up and wrestled his uniform into the satchel. Cramming everything as deep as possible, he strapped the flap down and buckled it as tight as he could. He glared at the pack and sighed once more.

"You know, if you organized your pack a little better, it wouldn't be so hard to fit all your gear," Royce said.

Hadrian looked at him with a puzzled expression. "What? Oh—no, I'm... It's not the gear."

"Then what is it?" Royce pulled on his black cloak and adjusted the collar.

Hadrian stroked his horse's neck. "I don't know," he replied mournfully. "It's just that... I thought by now I'd have done something more—with my life, I mean."

"Are you crazy? Most men work themselves to death on a small bit of land that isn't even theirs. You're free to do as you choose and go wherever you want."

"I know, but when I was young, I used to think I was... well... special. I imagined that I would triumph in some great purpose, win the girl, and save the kingdom, but I suppose every boy feels that way."

"I didn't."

Hadrian scowled at him. "I just had this idea of who I would become, and being a worthless spy wasn't part of that plan."

"We're hardly worthless," Royce said, correcting him. "We've been making a good profit, especially lately."

"That's not the point. I was successful as a mercenary too. It's not about money. It's the fact that I survive like a leech."

"Why is this suddenly coming up now? For the first time in years, we're making good money with a steady stream of *respectable* jobs. We're in the employ of a king, for Maribor's sake. We can actually sleep in the same bed two nights in a row and not worry about being arrested. Just last week I passed the captain of the city watch and he gave me a nod."

"It's not the amount of work. It's the *kind* of work. It's the fact that we're always lying. If that courier dies, it'll be our fault. Besides, it's not sudden. I've felt this way for years. Why do you think I'm always suggesting we do something else? Do you know why I broke the rules and took that job to steal Pickering's sword? The one that nearly got us executed?"

"For the unusual sum of money offered," Royce replied.

"No, that's why *you* took it. I wanted to go because it seemed like the right thing to do. For once I had the chance to help someone who really deserved to be helped, or so I thought at the time."

"And becoming an actor is the answer?"

Hadrian untied his horse. "No, but as an actor, I could at least *pretend* to be virtuous. I suppose I should just be happy to be alive, right?"

He did not answer. The nagging sensation was surfacing again. Royce hated keeping secrets from Hadrian, and it weighed heavily on his conscience, which was amazing, because he had never known he had one. Royce defined right and wrong by the moment. Right was what was best for him—wrong was everything else. He stole, lied, and even killed when necessary. This was his craft and he was good at it. There was no reason to apologize, no need to pause or reflect. The world was at war with him and nothing was sacred.

Telling Hadrian what he had learned ran too great a risk. Royce preferred his world constant, with each variable accounted for. Lines on maps were shifting daily and power slipped from one set of hands to another. Time flowed too fast and events were too unexpected. He felt like he was crossing a frozen lake in late spring. He tried to pick a safe path, but the surface cracked beneath his feet. Even so, there were some changes he could still control. He reminded himself that the secret he kept from Hadrian was for his friend's own good.

Climbing onto his short gray mare, Mouse, Royce thought a moment. "We've been working pretty hard lately. Maybe we should take a break."

"I don't see how we can," Hadrian replied. "With the imperial army preparing to invade Melengar, Alric is going to need us now more than ever."

"You'd think that, wouldn't you? But you didn't read the dispatch."

CHAPTER 3

THE MIRACLE

Princess Arista Essendon slouched on the carriage seat, buffeted by every rut and hole in the road. Her neck was stiff from sleeping against the armrest and her head throbbed from the constant jostling. Rising with a yawn, she wiped her eyes and rubbed her face. An attempt to straighten her hair trapped her fingers in a mass of auburn knots.

The ambassadorial coach was showing as much wear as its passenger, having traveled too many miles over the past year. The roof leaked, the springs were worn, and the bench was becoming threadbare in places. The driver had orders to push hard to return to Medford by midday. He was making good time, but at the expense of hitting every rut and rock along the way. As Arista drew back the curtain, the morning sun flashed through gaps in the leafy wall of trees lining the road.

She was almost home.

The flickering light revealed the interior of the coach; dust entering the windows coated everything. A discarded cheesecloth and several apple cores covered a pile of parchments spilling from a stack on the opposite bench. Soiled footprints patterned the floor where a blanket, a corset, and two dresses nested along with three shoes. She had no idea where the fourth was, and only hoped it was in the carriage and not left in Lanksteer. Over the past six months, she had felt as if she had left bits of herself all over Avryn.

Hilfred would have known where her shoe was.

She picked up her pearl-handled hairbrush and turned it over in her hands. Hilfred must have searched the wreckage for days. This one came from Tur Del Fur. Her father had given her a brush from every city he had traveled to. He had been a private man and saying *I love you* had not come easy, even when speaking to his own daughter. The brushes were his unspoken confessions. Once, she had owned dozens—now this was the last. When her bedroom tower had collapsed, she had lost them and it had felt as if she had lost her father all over again. Three weeks later this single brush appeared. It must have been Hilfred, but he never said a word or admitted a thing.

Hilfred had been her bodyguard for years, and now that he was gone, she realized just how much she had taken him for granted.

She had a new bodyguard now. Alric had personally picked him from his own castle guards. His name began with a T—Tom, Tim, Travis—something like that. He stood on the wrong side of her, talked too much, laughed at his own jokes, and was always eating something. He was likely a brave and skilled soldier, but he was no Hilfred.

The last time she had seen Hilfred had been over a year ago in Dahlgren, when he had nearly died from the Gilarabrywn attack. That had been the second time he had suffered burns trying to save her. The first had been when she was only twelve—the night the castle caught fire. Her mother and several others had died, but a boy of fifteen, the son of a sergeant-at-arms, had braved the inferno to pull her from her bed. At Arista's insistence, he went back for her mother. He never reached her, but nearly died trying. He suffered for months afterward, and Arista's father rewarded the boy by appointing him her bodyguard.

His wounds back then had been nothing like what he had suffered in Dahlgren. Healers had wrapped him from head to toe and he had lain unconscious for days. To her shock he had refused to see her upon awaking and left in the back of a wagon without saying goodbye. At Hilfred's request, no one would tell her where he had gone. She could have pressed. She could have ordered the healers to talk. For months, she looked over her shoulder expecting to see him, waiting to hear the familiar clap of his sword against his thigh. She often wondered if she had done the right thing in letting him go. She sighed at yet another regret added to a pile that had been building over the past year.

Taking stock of the mess around her increased her melancholy. This is what came from refusing to have a handmaid along, but she could not imagine being cooped up in the carriage with anyone for so long. She picked up her dresses and laid them across the far seat. When she spied a document crushed into a ball and hanging in the folds of the far window curtain, her stomach churned with guilt. With a frown, she plucked the crumpled parchment and smoothed it out by pressing it in her lap.

It contained a list of kingdoms and provinces with a line slashed through each and the notation *IMP* scrawled beside them. That the Earl of Chadwick and King Ethelred were the first in line to kiss the empress's ring was no surprise. But she shook her head in disbelief at the long list. The shift in power had occurred virtually overnight. One day nothing, the next—*bang!* There was a New Empire and the Avryn kingdoms of Warric, Ghent, Alburn, Maranon, Galeannon, and Rhenydd had all joined. They pressured the small holdouts, like Glouston, then invaded and swallowed them. She ran her finger over the line indicating Dunmore. His Highness King Roswort had graciously decided it was in his kingdom's best interest to accept the imperial offer of extended landholdings in return for becoming part of the New Empire. Arista would not be surprised if Roswort had been promised Melengar as part of his payment. Of all the kingdoms of Avryn, only Melengar refused to join.

It all happened so fast.

A year ago, the New Empire was merely an idea. She had spent months as ambassador trying to strike alliances. Without support, without allies, Melengar could not hope to stand against the growing colossus.

How long do we have before the empire marches north, before—

The carriage came to a sudden halt, throwing her forward, jerking the curtains, and creaking the tired springs. She looked out the window, puzzled. They were still on the old Steward's Road. The wall of trees had given way to an open field of flowers, which she knew placed them on the high meadow just a few miles outside Medford.

"What's going on?" she called out.

No response.

Where in Elan is Tim, or Ted, or whatever the blazes his name is?

She pulled the latch and, hiking up her skirt, pushed out the door. Warm sunlight met her, making her squint. Her legs were stiff and her back ached. At only twenty-six, she already felt ancient. She slammed the carriage door and, holding a hand to protect her eyes, glared as best she could up at the silhouettes of the driver and groom. They glanced at her, but only briefly, then looked back down the slope of the road ahead.

"Daniel! Why—" she started, but stopped after seeing what they were looking at.

The high meadowlands just north of Medford provided an extensive view for several miles south. The land sloped gently down, revealing Melengar's capital city, Medford. She saw the spires of Essendon Castle and Mares Cathedral and, farther out, the Galewyr River, marking the southern border of the kingdom. In the days when her mother and father had been alive, the royal family had come here in the summer to have picnics and enjoy the cool breeze and the view. Only that day the sight was quite different.

On the far bank, in the clear morning light, Arista saw rows and rows of canvas tents, hundreds of them, each flying the red-and-white flags of the Nyphron Imperial Empire.

"There's an army, Highness." Daniel found his voice. "An army is a stone's throw from Medford."

"Get me home, Daniel. Beat the horses if you must, but get me home!"

❧

The carriage had barely stopped when Arista punched open the door, nearly hitting Tommy—or Terence, or whoever he was—in the face when he foolishly attempted to open it for her. The servants in the courtyard immediately stopped their early-morning chores to bow reverently. Melissa spotted the coach and rushed over. Unlike Tucker—or Tillman—the small redheaded maid had served Arista for years and knew to expect a storm.

"How long has that army been there?" Arista barked at her even as she trotted up the stone steps.

"Nearly a week," Melissa replied, chasing after the princess and catching the traveling cloak as Arista discarded it.

"A week? Has there been fighting?"

"Yes, His Majesty launched an attack across the river just a few days ago."

"Alric attacked them? Across the river?"

"It didn't go well," Melissa replied in a lowered voice.

"I should think not! Was he drunk?"

Castle guards hastily pulled back the big oak doors, barely getting them open before the princess barreled through, her gown whipping behind her.

"Where are they?"

"In the war room."

She stopped.

They stood in the northern foyer. A wide gallery of polished stone pillars displayed suits of armor and hallways led to sweeping staircases.

"Missy, fetch my blue audience gown and shoes to go with it and prepare a basin of water—oh, and send someone to bring me something to eat. I don't care what."

"Yes, Your Highness." Melissa made a curt bow and raced up the stairs.

"Your Highness," her bodyguard called, chasing after her. "You almost lost me there."

"Imagine that. I'll just have to try harder next time."

❧

Arista watched as her brother, King Alric, stood up from the great table. Normally this would require everyone else to rise as well, but Alric had suspended that tradition inside the council chamber, as he had a habit of rising frequently and pacing during meetings.

"I don't understand it," he said, turning his back on all of them to begin his slow, familiar walk between the table and the window. As he moved, he stroked his short beard the way another man might wring his hands. Alric had started the beard just before Arista left on her trip. It still had not filled in. She guessed he grew it to look more like their father. King Amrath had worn a dark, full beard, but Alric's light brown wisps only underscored his youth. He made matters worse by drawing attention to it with his constant stroking. Arista recalled how their father used to drum his fingers during state meetings. Under the weight of the crown, pressures must build up until action sought its own means of escape.

Her brother was two years her junior, and she knew he had never expected to wear the crown so soon. For years she had heard Alric's plans to roam the wilds with his friend Mauvin Pickering. The two wanted to see the world and have grand adventures that would involve nameless women, too much wine, and too little sleep. They had even hoped to find and explore the ancient ruins of Percepliquis. She had suspected that when he tired of the road, he would be happy to return home and marry a girl half his age and father several strong sons. Only then, as his temples grayed and when all of life's other ambitions were accomplished, would he expect the crown to pass to him. All that changed the night their uncle Percy arranged the assassination of their father and left Alric king.

"It could be a trick, Your Majesty," Lord Valin suggested. "A plan to catch you off your guard."

Lord Valin, an elderly knight with a bushy white beard, was known for his courage, but not for his strategic skills.

"Lord Valin," Sir Ecton addressed the noble respectfully, "after our failure on the banks of the Galewyr, the imperial army can overrun Medford with ease, whether we are on or off our guard. We know it and they know it. Medford is their prize for the taking whenever they decide to get their feet wet."

Alric walked to the tall balcony window, where the afternoon light spilled into the royal banquet hall of Essendon Castle. The hall served as the royal war room out of the need for a large space to conduct the defense of the kingdom. Where once festive tapestries hung, great maps now covered the walls, each slashed with red lines illustrating the tragic retreat of Melengar's armies.

"I just don't understand it," Alric repeated. "It's so peculiar. The imperial army outnumbers us ten to one. They have scores of heavy cavalry, siege weapons, and archers—everything they need. So why are they sitting across the river? Why stop now?"

"It makes no sense from a military standpoint, Sire," Sir Ecton said. A large powerful man with a fiery disposition, he was Alric's chief general and field commander. Ecton was also Count Pickering's most accomplished vassal and regarded by many as the best knight in Melengar. "I would venture it's political," he continued. "It's been my experience that the most foolish decisions in combat are the result of political choices made by those with little to no field experience."

Earl Kendell, a potbellied fussy man who always dressed in a bright green tunic, glared at Ecton. "Careful with your tongue and consider your company!"

Ecton rose to his feet. "I held my tongue, and what was the result?"

"Sir Ecton!" Alric shouted. "I'm well aware of your opinion of my decision to attack the imperial encampment."

"It was insanity to attempt an assault across a river without even the possibility to flank," Ecton shot back.

"Nevertheless, it was my decision." Alric squeezed his hands into fists. "I felt it was...necessary."

"Necessary? Necessary!" Ecton spat the word as if it were a vile thing in his mouth. He looked like he was about to speak again but Count Pickering rose to his feet and Sir Ecton sat down.

Arista had seen this before. Too often Ecton looked to Count Pickering before acting on an order Alric had given. He was not the only one, and it was clear that although her brother was king, Alric had failed to earn the respect of his nobles, his army, or his people.

"Perhaps Ecton is right." Young Marquis Wymar spoke up. "About it being political, I mean." He then hastily added, "We all know what a pompous fool the Earl of Chadwick is. Isn't it possible that Ballentyne ordered Breckton to hold the final attack until Archibald could arrive? It would certainly raise his standing in the imperial court to claim he personally led the assault that conquered Melengar for the New Empire."

"That would explain the delay in the attack," Pickering replied in his fatherly tone, which she knew Alric despised. "But our scouts are reporting that large numbers of men are pulling out and by all accounts are heading south."

"A feint, perhaps?" Alric asked.

Pickering shook his head. "As Sir Ecton pointed out, there would be no need."

Several of the other advisors nodded thoughtfully.

"Something must be going on for the empress to recall her troops like this," Pickering said.

"But what?" Alric asked no one in particular. "I wish I knew what kind of person she was. It's impossible to guess the actions of a total stranger." He turned to his sister. "Arista, you met Modina, spent time with her in Dahlgren. What's she like? Do you have any idea what would cause her to pull the army back?"

A memory flashed in Arista's mind of her and a young girl trapped at the top of a tower. Arista had been frozen in fear, but Thrace had rummaged through a pile of debris and human limbs, looking for a weapon to fight an invincible beast. Had it been bravery or had she been too naive to understand the futility? "The girl I knew as Thrace was a sweet, innocent child who wanted only the love of her father. The church may have changed her name to Modina, but I can't imagine they changed her. She didn't order this invasion. She wouldn't want to rule her tiny village, much less conquer the world." Arista shook her head. "She's not our enemy."

"A crown can change a person," Sir Ecton said while glaring at Alric.

Arista rose. "It's more likely we are dealing with the church and a council of conservative Imperialists. I highly doubt a child from rural Dunmore could influence the archaic attitudes and inflexible opinions of so many stubborn minds who would strive to resist, rather than work with, a new ruler," she said while glaring at Ecton. Over the knight's shoulder, she noticed Alric cringe.

The door to the hall opened and Julian, the elderly lord chamberlain, entered. With a sweeping bow, he tapped his staff of office twice on the tiled floor. "The royal protector Royce Melborn, Your Majesty."

"Show him in immediately."

"Don't get your hopes too high," Pickering said to his king. "They're spies, not miracle workers."

"I pay them enough for miracles. I don't think it unreasonable to get what I pay for."

Alric employed numerous informants and scouts, but none were as effective as Riyria. Arista had originally hired Royce and Hadrian to kidnap her brother the night their father had been assassinated. Since then, their services had proved invaluable.

Royce entered the banquet hall alone. The small man with dark hair and dark eyes always dressed in layers of black. He wore a knee-length tunic and a long flowing cloak and, as always, carried no visible weapons. Carrying a blade in the presence of the king was unlawful, but given he and Hadrian had twice saved Alric's life, Arista surmised the royal guards did not thoroughly search him. She was certain Royce carried his white-bladed dagger and regarded the law as merely a suggestion.

Royce bowed before the assembly.

"Well?" her brother asked a bit too loudly, too desperately. "Did you discover anything?"

"Yes, Your Majesty," Royce replied, but his face remained so neutral that nothing more could be determined for good or ill.

"Well, out with it. What did you find? Are they really leaving?"

"Sir Breckton has been ordered to withdraw all but a small containment force and march south immediately with the bulk of his army."

"So it really is true?" Marquis Wymar said. "But why?"

"Yes, why?" Alric added.

"Because Rhenydd has been invaded by the Nationalists out of Delgos."

A look of surprise circulated the room.

"Degan Gaunt's rabble is invading Rhenydd?" Earl Kendell said in bewilderment.

"And doing quite well from the dispatch I read," Royce informed them. "Gaunt has led them up the coast, taking every village and town. He's managed to sack Kilnar and Vernes."

"He sacked Vernes?" Ecton asked, shocked.

"That's a good-sized city," Wymar mentioned.

"It's also only a few miles from Ratibor," Pickering observed. "From there it's what—maybe a hard day's march to the imperial capital itself?"

"No wonder the empire is recalling Breckton." Alric looked at the count. "What were you saying about miracles?"

❧

"I can't believe you couldn't find anyone to ally with." Alric berated Arista as he collapsed on his throne. The two were alone in the reception hall, the most ornate room in the castle. This room, the grand ballroom, the banquet hall, and the foyer were all that most people generally ever saw. Tolin the Great had built the chamber to be intimidating. The three-story ceiling was an impressive sight and the observation balcony that circled the walls provided a magnificent view of the parquet floor, inlaid with the royal falcon coat of arms. Double rows of twelve marble pillars formed a long gallery similar to that of a church, yet instead of an altar there was the dais. On seven pyramid-shaped steps sat the throne of Melengar—the only seat in the vast chamber. When they had been children, the throne had always appeared so impressive, but now, with Alric slouched in it, Arista realized it was just a gaudy chair.

"I tried," she offered, sitting on the steps before the throne as she had once done with her father. "Everyone had already sworn allegiance to the New Empire." Arista gave her brother the demoralizing report on her past six months of failure.

"We're quite a pair, you and I. You've done little as ambassador and I nearly destroyed us with that attack across the river. Many of the nobles are being more vocal. Soon Pickering won't be able to control the likes of Ecton."

"I must admit I was shocked when I heard about your attack. What possessed you to do such a thing?" she asked.

"Royce and Hadrian had intercepted plans drafted by Breckton himself. He was about to launch a three-pronged assault. I had to make a preemptive strike. I was hoping to catch the Imperialists by surprise."

"Well, it looks like it worked out after all. It delayed their attack just long enough."

"True, but what good will that do if we can't find more help? What about Trent?"

"Well, they haven't said no, but they haven't said yes either. The church's influence has never been strong that far north, but they also don't have any ties to us. All they want is to be on the winning side. They're at least willing to wait and watch. They won't join us because they don't think we have a chance. But if we can show them some success, they could be persuaded to side with us."

"Don't they realize the empire will be after them next?"

"I said that, but..."

"But what?"

"They really weren't very amenable to what I had to say. The men of Lanksteer are brutish and backward. They respect only strength. I would have fared better if I'd beaten their king senseless." She hesitated. "I don't think they quite knew what to make of me."

"I should never have sent you," Alric said, running a hand over his face. "What was I thinking, making a woman an ambassador?"

His words felt like a slap. "I agree that I was at a disadvantage in Trent, but in the rest of the kingdoms I don't think the fact that I am a woman—"

"A witch, then," Alric said, lashing out. "Even worse. All those Warric and Alburn nobles are so devoted, and what do I do? I send them someone the church tried for witchcraft."

"I'm not a witch!" she snapped. "I wasn't convicted of anything, and everyone with a brain between their ears knows that trial was a fabrication of Braga and Saldur to get their hands on our throne."

"The truth doesn't matter. Everyone believes what the church tells them. They said you're a witch, so that makes it so. Look at Modina. The Patriarch proclaims that she's the Heir of Novron, so everyone believes. I should have never made an enemy of the church. But between Saldur's betrayal and their sentinel killing Fanen, I just couldn't bring myself to bend my knee.

"When I evicted the priests and forbade Deacon Tomas from preaching about what happened in Dahlgren, the people revolted. They set shops in Gentry Square on fire. I could see the flames from my window, for Maribor's sake. The whole city could have burned. They were calling for my head—people right in front of the castle burning stuffed images of me and shouting, 'Death to the godless king!' Can you imagine that? Just a few years ago they were calling me a hero. People toasted to my health in every tavern, but now...well, it's amazing how fast they can turn on you. I had to use the army to restore order." Alric reached up and pulled his crown off, turning the golden circlet over in his hands.

"I was in Alburn at the court of King Armand when I heard about that," Arista said, shaking her head.

Alric laid the crown on the arm of the throne, closed his eyes, and softly banged his head against the back of the chair. "What are we going to do, Arista? The Imperialists will return. As soon as they deal with Gaunt's rabble, the army will come back." His eyes opened and his hand drifted absently toward his throat. "I suppose they'll hang me, won't they? Or do they use the axe on kings?" His tone was one of quiet acceptance, which surprised her.

The carefree boy she had once known was vanishing before

her eyes. Even if the New Empire failed and Melengar stood strong, Alric would never be the same. In many ways, their uncle had managed to kill him after all.

Alric looked at the crown sitting on the chair's arm. "I wonder what Father would do."

"He never had anything like this to deal with. Not since Tolin defeated Lothomad at Drondil Fields has any monarch of Melengar faced invasion."

"Lucky me."

"Lucky us."

Alric nodded. "At least we've got some time now. That's something. What do you think of Pickering's idea to send the *Ellis Far* down the coast to Tur Del Fur and contact the Nationalist leader—this Gaunt fellow?"

"Honestly, I think establishing an alliance with Gaunt is our only hope. Isolated, we don't stand a chance against the empire," Arista agreed.

"But the Nationalists? Are they any better than the Imps? They're as opposed to monarchies as much as the empire. They don't want to be ruled at all."

"Alone and surrounded by enemies is not the time to be choosy about your friends."

"We aren't completely alone," Alric said, correcting her. "Marquis Lanaklin joined us."

"A lot of good that does. The empire took his holdings. He's nothing more than a refugee now. He only came here because he has no place else to go. If we get more help like that, we'll go broke just feeding them. Our only chance is to contact Degan Gaunt and form an alliance. If Delgos joins with us, that may be enough to persuade Trent to side in our favor. If that happens, we could deal a mortal blow to this new Nyphron Empire."

"Do you think Gaunt will agree?"

"Don't know why not," Arista said. "It's to our mutual benefit. I'm certain I can talk him into it, and I must say I'm looking forward to the trip. A rolling ocean is a welcome change from that carriage. While I'm away, have someone work on it, or better yet order a new one. And put extra padding—"

"You aren't going," Alric told her as he put his crown back on.

"What's that?"

"I'm sending Linroy to meet with Gaunt."

"But I'm the ambassador and a member of the royal family. He can't negotiate a treaty or an alliance with—"

"Of course he can. Linroy is an experienced negotiator and statesman."

"He's the royal financier. That doesn't qualify him as a statesman."

"He's handled dozens of trade agreements," Alric interjected.

"The man's a bookkeeper!" she shouted, rising to her feet.

"It may come as a surprise to you, but other people are capable of doing things too."

"But why?"

"Like you said, you're a member of the royal family." Alric looked away and his fingers reached up to stroke his beard. "Do you have any idea what kind of position it would put me in if you were captured? We're at war. I can't risk you being held for ransom."

She stared at him. "You're lying. This isn't about ransom. You think I can't handle the responsibility."

"Arista, it's my fault. I shouldn't have—"

"Shouldn't have what? Made your witch-sister ambassador?"

"Don't be that way."

"I'm sorry, Your Majesty, what way would you like me to

be? How should I react to being told I'm worthless and an embarrassment and that I should go sit in my room and—"

"I didn't say any of that. Stop putting words in my mouth!"

"It's what you're thinking—it's what all of you think."

"Have you become clairvoyant now too?"

"Do you deny it?"

"Damn it, Arista, you were gone six months!" He struck the arm of the throne with his fist. The dull thud sounded loudly off the walls like a bass drum. "Six months, and not a single alliance. You barely got a maybe. That's a pretty poor showing. This meeting with Gaunt is too important. It could be our last chance."

She stood up. "Forgive me, Your Majesty. I apologize for being such an utter failure. May I please have your royal permission to be excused?"

"Arista, don't."

"Please, Your Majesty, my frail feminine constitution can't handle such a heated debate. I feel faint. Perhaps if I retire to my room, I could brew a potion to make myself feel better. While I'm at it, perhaps I should enchant a broom to fly around the castle for fresh air."

She pivoted on her heel and marched out, slamming the great door behind her with a resounding *boom!*

She stood with her back against the door, waiting, wondering if Alric would chase after her.

Will he apologize and take back what he said and agree to let me go?

She listened for the sound of his heels on the parquet.

Silence.

She wished she did know magic, because then no one could stop her from meeting with Gaunt. Alric was right: this was their last chance. And she was not about to leave the fate of Melengar to Dillnard Linroy, statesman extraordinaire.

Besides, she had failed and that made it her responsibility to correct the situation.

She looked up to see Tim—or Tommy—leaning against the near wall, biting his fingernails. He glanced up at her and smiled. "I hope you're planning on heading to the kitchens. I'm starved—practically eating my fingers here." He chuckled.

She pushed away from the door and quickly strode down the corridor. She almost did not see Mauvin Pickering sitting on the broad sill of the courtyard-facing window. Feet up, arms folded, back against the frame, he crouched in a shaft of sunlight like a cat. He still wore the black clothes of mourning.

"Troubles with His Majesty?" he asked.

"He's being an ass."

"What did he do this time?"

"Replaced me with that sniveling little wretch Linroy. He's sending him on the *Ellis Far* in my place to contact Gaunt."

"Dillnard Linroy isn't a bad guy. He's—"

"Listen, I really don't want to hear how wonderful Linroy is at the moment. I'm right in the middle of hating him."

"Sorry."

She glanced at his side and he immediately turned his attention back to the window.

"Still not wearing it?" she asked.

"It doesn't go with my ensemble. The silver hilt clashes with black."

"It's been over a year since Fanen died."

He turned back sharply. "Since he was killed by Luis Guy, you mean."

Arista took a breath. She was not used to the new Mauvin. "Aren't you supposed to be Alric's bodyguard now? Isn't that hard to do without a sword?"

"Hasn't been a problem so far. You see, I have this plan. I sit here and watch the ducks in the courtyard. Well, I suppose it's not really so much a plan as a strategy, or maybe it's more of a scheme. Anyway, this is the one place my father never thinks to look, so I can sit here all day and watch those ducks walking back and forth. There were six of them last year. Did you know that? Only five now. I can't figure out what happened to the other one. I keep looking for him, but I don't think he's coming back."

"It wasn't your fault," she told him gently.

Mauvin reached up and traced the lead edges of the window with his fingertips. "Yeah, it was."

She put her hand on his shoulder and gave a soft squeeze. She did not know what else to do. First her mother, then her father and Fanen, and finally Hilfred—they were all gone. Mauvin was slipping away as well. The boy who loved his sword more than Wintertide presents, sweet chocolate cake, or swimming on a hot day refused to touch it anymore. The eldest son of Count Pickering, who had once challenged the sun to a duel because it had rained on the day of a hunt, spent his days watching ducks.

"Doesn't matter," Mauvin remarked. "The world is coming to an end, anyway." He looked up at her. "You just said Alric is sending that bastard Linroy on the *Ellis Far*—he'll kill us all."

As hard as she tried, she could not help laughing. She punched his shoulder, then gave him a peck on the cheek. "That's the spirit, Mauvin. Keep looking on the bright side."

She left him and continued down the hall. As she passed the office of the lord chamberlain, the old man hurried out. "Your Highness?" he called, looking relieved. "The royal protector Royce Melborn is still waiting to see if there is something else needed of him. Apparently he and his partner are thinking of taking some time off, unless there is something pressing the king requires. Can I tell him he's excused?"

"Yes, of course you— No, wait." She cast a look at her bodyguard. "Tommy, you're right. I'm hungry. Be a dear and fetch us both a plate of chicken or whatever you can find that's good in the kitchen, will you? I'll wait here."

"Sure, but my name is—"

"Hurry before I change my mind."

She waited until he was down the corridor, then turned back to the chamberlain. "Where did you say Royce was waiting?"

CHAPTER 4

THE NATURE OF RIGHT

The Rose and Thorn Tavern was mostly empty. Many of its patrons had left Medford, fearful of the coming invasion. Those who remained were the indentured or those simply too poor, feeble, or stubborn to leave. Royce found Hadrian sitting alone in the Diamond Room—his feet up on a spare chair, a pint of ale before him. Two empty mugs sat on the table, one lying on its side while Hadrian stared at it with a melancholy expression.

"Why didn't you come to the castle?" Royce asked.

"I knew you could handle it." Hadrian continued to stare at the mug, tilting his head slightly as he did.

"Looks like our break will have to be postponed," Royce told him while pulling over a chair and sitting down. "Alric has another job. He wants us to make contact with Gaunt and the Nationalists. They're still working out the details. The princess is going to send a messenger here."

"Her Highness is back?"

"Got in this morning."

Royce reached into his vest, pulled out a bag, and set it in front of Hadrian. "Here's your half. Have you ordered dinner yet?"

"I'm not going," Hadrian said, rocking the fallen mug with his thumb.

"Not going?"

"I can't keep doing this."

Royce rolled his eyes. "Now don't start that again. If you haven't noticed, there's a war going on. This is the best time to be in our business. Everyone needs information. Do you know how much money—"

"That's just it, Royce. There's a war on and what am I doing? I'm making a profit off it rather than fighting in it." Hadrian took another swallow of ale and set the mug back on the table a little too heavily, rattling its brothers. "I'm tired of collecting money for being dishonorable. It's not how I'm built."

Royce glanced around. Three men eating a meal looked over briefly and then lost interest.

"They haven't all been just for money," Royce pointed out. "Thrace, for example."

Hadrian displayed a bitter smile. "And look how that turned out. She hired us to save her father. Seen him lately, have you?"

"We were hired to obtain a sword to slay a beast. She got the sword. The beast was slain. We did our job."

"The man is dead."

"And Thrace, who was nothing but a poor farm girl, is now empress. If only all our jobs ended so well for our clients."

"You think so, Royce? You really think Thrace is happy? See, I'm thinking she'd rather have her father than the imperial throne, but maybe that's just me." Hadrian took another swallow and wiped his mouth with his sleeve.

They sat in silence for a moment. Royce watched his friend staring at a distant point beyond focus.

"So you want to fight in this war, is that it?"

"It would be better than sitting on the sidelines like scavengers feeding off the wounded."

"Okay, so tell me, for which side will you be fighting?"

"Alric's a good king."

"Alric? Alric's a boy still fighting with the ghost of his father. After his defeat at the Galewyr, his nobles look to Count Pickering instead of him. Pickering has his hands full dealing with Alric's mistakes, like the riots here in Medford. How long before the count tires of Alric's incompetence and decides Mauvin would be better suited to the throne?"

"Pickering would never turn on Alric," Hadrian said.

"No? You've seen it happen plenty of times before."

Hadrian remained silent.

"Oh hell, forget about Pickering and Alric. Melengar is already at war with the empire. Have you forgotten who the empress is? If you fought with Alric and he prevailed, how will you feel the day poor Thrace is hanged in the Royal Square in Aquesta? Would that satisfy your need for an honorable cause?"

Hadrian's face had turned hard, his jaw clenched stiffly.

"There are no honorable causes. There is no good or evil. Evil is only what we call those who oppose us."

Royce took out his dagger and drove it into the table, where it stood upright. "Look at the blade. Is it bright or dark?"

Hadrian narrowed his eyes suspiciously. The brilliant surface of Alverstone was dazzling as it reflected the candlelight. "Bright."

Royce nodded.

"Now move your head over here and look from my perspective."

Hadrian leaned over, putting his head on the opposite side of the blade, where the shadow made it black as chimney soot.

"It's the same dagger," Royce explained, "but from where you sat it was light while I saw it as dark. So who is right?"

"Neither of us," Hadrian said.

"No," Royce said. "That's the mistake people always make, and they make it because they can't grasp the truth."

"Which is?"

"That we're both right. One truth doesn't refute another. Truth doesn't lie in the object, but in how we see it."

Hadrian looked at the dagger, then back at Royce.

"There are times when you are brilliant, Royce, and then there are times when I haven't a clue as to what you're babbling about."

Royce's expression turned to one of frustration as he pulled his dagger from the table and sat back down. "In the twelve years we've been together, I've never once asked you to do anything I wouldn't do, or didn't do with you. I've never lied or misled you. I've never abandoned or betrayed you. Name a single noble you even suspect you could say the same about twelve years from now."

"Can I get another round here?" Hadrian shouted.

Royce sighed. "So you're just going to sit here and drink?"

"That's my plan at present. I'm making it up as I go."

Royce stared at his friend a moment longer, then finally stood up. "I'm going to Gwen's."

"Listen." Hadrian stopped him. "I'm sorry about this. I guess I can't explain it. I don't have any metaphors with daggers I can use to express how I feel. I just know I can't keep doing what I've been doing anymore. I've tried to find meaning in it. I've tried to pretend we achieved some greater good, but in the end, I have to be honest with myself. I'm not a thief, and I'm not a spy. So I know what I'm not. I just wish I knew what I am. That probably doesn't make much sense to you, does it?"

"Do me a favor at least." Royce purposely ignored the question, noticing how the little silver chain Hadrian wore peeked out from under his collar. "Since you're going to be here anyway, keep an eye out for the messenger from the castle while I'm at Gwen's. I'll be back in an hour or so."

Hadrian nodded.

"Give Gwen my love, will ya?"

"Sure," Royce said, heading for the door and feeling that miserable sensation creeping in, the dull weight. He paused and looked back.

It won't help to tell him. It will just make matters worse.

⁂

It had been only a day and a half but Royce found himself desperate to see Gwen. While Medford House was always open, it did not do much business until after dark. During the day, Gwen encouraged the girls to use their free time learning how to sew or spin, skills they could use to make a bit of coin in their old age.

All the girls at the brothel, better known as the House, knew and liked Royce. When he came in, they smiled or waved, but no one said a word. They knew he enjoyed surprising Gwen. That night they pointed toward the parlor, where she was concentrating on a pile of parchments, a quill pen in hand and her register open. She immediately abandoned it all when he walked through the door. She sprang from her chair and ran to him with a smile so broad her face could hardly contain it and an embrace so tight he could barely breathe.

"What's wrong?" she whispered, pulling back and looking into his eyes.

Royce marveled at Gwen's ability to read him. He refused to answer, preferring instead to look at her, drinking her in.

She had a lovely face, her dark skin and emerald eyes so familiar, yet mysterious. Throughout his entire life and in all his travels he had never met anyone else like her.

Gwen provided use of a private room at The Rose and Thorn, where he and Hadrian conducted business, and she never blinked at the risks. They no longer used it. Royce was too concerned that Sentinel Luis Guy might track them there. Still, Gwen continued banking their money and watching out for them, just as she had done from the start.

They had met twelve years ago, the night soldiers had filled the streets and two strangers had staggered into the Lower Quarter covered in their own blood. Royce still remembered how Gwen had appeared as a hazy figure to his clouding eyes. "I've got you. You'll be all right now," she told him before he passed out. He never understood what had motivated her to take them in when everyone else had shown the good sense in closing their doors. When he had woken, she had been giving orders to her girls like a general marshaling troops. She sheltered Royce and Hadrian from the mystified authorities and nursed them back to health. She pulled strings and made deals to ensure no one talked. As soon as they were able, they left, but he always found himself returning.

He had been crushed the day she refused to see him. It did not take long for him to discover why. Clients often abused prostitutes, and the women of Medford House were not exempt. In Gwen's case the attacker had been a powerful noble. He had beaten her so badly she did not want anyone to see. Regardless of whether the client was a gentleman or a thug, the town sheriff never wasted his time on complaints by whores.

Two days later the noble had been found dead. His body hung in the center of Gentry Square. City authorities had closed Medford House and arrested the prostitutes. They had been told to identify the killer or face execution themselves. To everyone's surprise, the women spent only one night in jail. The next day Medford House had reopened and the sheriff of Medford personally delivered a public apology for their arrest, adding that swift punishment would follow any future abuse of the women, regardless of rank. From then on, Medford House prospered under unprecedented protection. Royce had never spoken of the incident, and Gwen never asked, but he was certain she knew—just as she had known about his heritage before he had told her.

When he had returned from Avempartha the previous summer, he had decided to reveal his secret to her, to be completely open and honest. Royce had never told anyone about being an elf, not even Hadrian. He expected that she would hate him, either for being a miserable *mir* or for deceiving her. He had taken Gwen for a walk down the bank of the Galewyr, away from people to lessen the embarrassment of her outrage. He had braced himself, said the words, and waited for her to hit him. He had decided to let her. She could scratch his eyes out if she wanted. He owed her at least that much.

"Of course you're elven," she had said while touching his hand kindly. "Was that supposed to be a secret?"

How she had known, she never explained. He had been so overwhelmed with joy to bother asking. Gwen just had a way of always knowing his heart.

"What is it?" she asked again now.

"Why haven't you packed?"

Gwen paused and smiled. That was her way of letting him know he would not get away with it. "Because there is no need. The imperial army isn't attacking us."

Royce raised an eyebrow. "The king himself has his things packed and his horse at the ready to evacuate the city on a moment's notice, but you know better?"

She nodded.

"And how is that?"

"If there was the slightest chance that Medford was in danger, you wouldn't be here asking me why I haven't packed. I'd be on Mouse's back holding on for dear life as you spurred her into a run."

"Still," he said, "I'd feel better if you moved to the monastery."

"I can't leave my girls."

"Take them with you. Myron has plenty of room."

"You want me to take whores to live in a monastery with monks?"

"I want you to be safe. Besides, Magnus and Albert are there too, and I can guarantee you *they're* not monks."

"I'll consider it." She smiled at him. "But you're leaving on another mission, so it can wait until you get back."

"How do you know these things?" he asked, amazed. "Alric ought to hire you instead of us."

"I'm from Calis. It's in our blood," she told him with a wink. "When do you leave?"

"Soon…tonight, perhaps. I left Hadrian at The Rose and Thorn to watch for a messenger."

"Have you decided to tell Hadrian yet?"

He looked away.

"Oh, so that's it. Don't you think you should?"

"No, just because a lunatic wizard—" He paused. "Listen, if I tell him what I saw, his reason will disappear. If Hadrian were a moth, he'd fly into every flame he could find. He'll sacrifice himself if necessary, and for what? Even if it's true, all that stuff with the heir happened centuries ago and has nothing to do with him. There's no reason to think that Esrahaddon wasn't just— Wizards toy with people, okay? It's what they do. He tells me to keep quiet, makes a big stink about how I have to take this secret to my grave. But you know damn well he expects me to tell Hadrian. I don't like being used, and I won't let Hadrian get himself killed at the whim of some wizard's agenda."

Gwen said nothing but looked at him with a knowing smile.

"What?"

"Sounds like you're trying to convince yourself and you're not doing very well. I think it might help if you consider you're one kind of person and Hadrian is another. You are trying to look out for him, but you're using *cat's eyes*."

"I'm doing what?"

Puzzled for a moment, Gwen looked at Royce, then chuckled quietly. "Oh, I suppose that must be a common saying only in Calis. Okay, let's say you're a cat and Hadrian's a dog and you want to make him happy. You give him a dead mouse and are surprised when he isn't thrilled. The problem is that you need to see the world through the eyes of a dog to understand what's best for him. If you did, you would see that a nice juicy bone would be a better choice, even though to a cat it's not very appealing."

"So you think I should let Hadrian go off and get himself killed?"

"I'm saying that for Hadrian, maybe fighting—even dying—for something or someone is the same as a bone is to a dog. Besides, you have to ask yourself, is keeping quiet really for his sake—or yours?"

"First daggers, now dogs and cats," Royce muttered.

"What?"

"Nothing." He let his hands run through her hair. "How did you get so wise?"

"Wise?" She looked at him and laughed. "I'm a thirty-four-year-old prostitute in love with a professional criminal. How wise can I possibly be?"

"If you don't know, perhaps you should try seeing with my eyes."

He kissed her warmly, pulling her tight. He recalled what Hadrian had said and wondered if he was being stupid for not settling down with Gwen. He had noticed for some time a growing pain whenever he said goodbye and a misery that dogged him whenever he left. Royce had never meant for it to happen. He always tried to keep her at a distance, for her own good as well as his. His life was dangerous and only possible so long as he had no ties, nothing others could use against him.

Winters had caused him to crack. Deep snows and brutal cold kept Riyria idle in Medford for months. Huddled before the warmth of hearth fires through the long dark nights, they had grown close. Casual chats had turned into long intimate conversations, and conversations had changed to embraces and confessions. Royce found it impossible to resist her open kindness and generosity. She was so unlike anyone, an enigma that flew in the face of all he had come to expect from the world. She made no demands and asked for nothing but his happiness.

His feelings for Gwen had led to Royce and Hadrian's longest imprisonment, six years earlier. They had taken a job in the spring, sending them all the way to Alburn. The thought of leaving her dragged on him like a weight, especially because she was not feeling well. Gwen had contracted the flu and looked miserable. She claimed it was nothing, but she looked pale and barely ate. He almost did not go but she insisted. He could still remember her face with that brave little smile that had quivered oh so slightly at the edges as he had left her.

The job had gone badly. Royce's concentration had suffered, mistakes had been made, and they had been left rotting in the dungeons of Blythin Castle. All he could do was sit and think about Gwen and wonder whether she was all right. As the months stretched out, he had begun to realize that if he survived, he would need to end their relationship. He resolved never to see her again, for both of their sakes. But the moment he had returned, the moment he had seen her again, felt her hands and smelled her hair, he knew leaving her would never be possible. Since that time, his feelings had only increased. Even now, the thought of leaving her, even for a week, was agony.

Hadrian was right. He should quit and take her away somewhere, perhaps get a small bit of land where they could raise a family. Somewhere quiet where no one knew Gwen as a prostitute or him as a thief. They could even go to Avempartha, that ancient citadel of his people. The tower stood vacant, far beyond the reaches of anyone who did not know its secrets, and would likely remain that way indefinitely. The thought was appealing, but he pushed it back, telling himself he would revisit it soon. For now, he had people waiting, which brought his mind back to Hadrian.

"I suppose I could look into Esrahaddon's story. Hadrian would be a fool for dedicating his life to someone else's dream, but at least I'd know it was genuine and not some kind of wizard's trick."

"How can you find out?"

"Hadrian grew up in Hintindar. If his father was a Teshlor Knight, maybe he left behind some indication. At least then I would have someone else's word instead of just Esrahaddon's. Our job is taking us south. I could make a stop in Hintindar and see if I can find something out. By the way," he told her gently, "I'll be gone a good deal longer than I have been. I want you to know so you don't worry needlessly."

"I never worry about you," she told him.

Royce's face reflected his pain.

Gwen smiled. "I *know* you'll return safely."

"And how do you know this?"

"I've seen your hands."

Royce looked at her, confused.

"I've read your palms, Royce," she told him without a trace of humor. "Or have you forgotten I also make a living as a fortune-teller?"

Royce had not forgotten, but had assumed it was just a way of swindling the superstitious. Not until that moment did he realize how inconsistent it would be for Gwen to deceive people.

"You have a long life ahead of you," she went on. "Too long—that was one of the clues that you weren't completely human."

"So I have nothing to worry about in my future?"

Gwen's smile faded abruptly.

"What is it?"

"Nothing."

"Tell me," he persisted, gently lifting her chin until she met his eyes.

"It's just that... you need to watch out for Hadrian."

"Did you look at his palms too?"

"No," she said, "but your lifeline shows a fork, a point of decision. You'll head either into darkness and despair or virtue and light. This decision will be precipitated by a traumatic event."

"What kind of event?"

"The death of the one you love the most."

"Then shouldn't you be worried about yourself?"

Gwen smiled warmly at him. "If only that were so, I'd die a happy woman. Royce, I'm serious about Hadrian. Please watch out for him. I think he needs you now more than ever. And I'm frightened for you if something were to happen to him."

❧

When Royce returned to The Rose and Thorn, he found Hadrian still seated at the same table, only he was no longer alone. Beside him sat a small figure hooded in a dark cloak. Hadrian sat comfortably. Either the person sitting next to him was safe, or he was too drunk to care.

"Take it up with Royce when he gets here," Hadrian was saying and looking up, added, "Ah! Perfect timing."

"Are you from—" Royce stopped as he sat down and saw the face beneath the hood.

"I do believe that is the first time I've ever surprised you, Royce," Princess Arista said.

"Oh no, that's not true," Hadrian said, chuckling. "You caught him way off guard when we were hanging in your dungeon and you asked us to kidnap your brother. That was *much* more unpredictable, trust me."

Royce was not pleased with meeting the princess in the open tavern room, and Hadrian was speaking far too loudly for his liking. Luckily, the room was empty. Most of the limited clientele preferred to cluster around the bar, where the door hung open to admit the cool summer breeze.

"That seems a lifetime ago," Arista replied thoughtfully.

"She has a job for you, Royce," Hadrian told him.

"For *us*, you mean."

"I told you." Hadrian looked at him but allowed a glance at the princess as well. "I'm retired."

Royce ignored him. "What's been decided?"

"Alric wants to make contact with Gaunt and his Nationalists," Arista began. "He feels, as the rest of us do, that if we can coordinate our efforts, we can create a formidable assault. Also, an alliance with the Nationalists could very well be the advantage we need to persuade Trent to enter the war on our side."

"That's fine," Royce replied. "I expected as much, but did you have to deliver this information yourself? Don't you trust your messengers?"

"One can never be too careful. Besides, I'm coming with you."

"What?" Royce asked, stunned.

Hadrian burst into laughter. "I knew you'd love that part," he said, grinning with the delight of a man blessed with immunity.

"I am the Ambassador of Melengar, and this is a diplomatic mission. Events are transpiring rapidly and negotiations may need to be altered to suit the situation. I've got to go because neither of you can speak for the kingdom. I can't trust anyone, not even you two, with such an important mission. This meeting will likely determine whether or not Melengar survives another year. I hope you understand the necessity of having me along."

Royce considered the proposal for a few minutes. "You and your brother understand that I cannot guarantee your safety?"

She nodded.

"You also understand that between now and the time we reach Gaunt, you'll be required to obey Hadrian and myself and you won't be provided any special treatment because of your station?"

"I expect none. However, it must also be understood that I'm Alric's representative and, as such, speak with his voice. So where safety and methods are concerned, you're granted authority, and I'll follow your direction, but as far as overall mission goals are concerned, I reserve the right to redirect or extend the mission if necessary."

"And do you also possess the power to guarantee additional payment for additional services?"

"I do."

"I now pronounce you client and escort," Hadrian said with a grin.

"As for you," Royce told him, "you'd better have some coffee."

"I'm not going, Royce."

"What's this all about?" Arista asked.

Royce scowled and shook his head at her.

"Don't shut her up," Hadrian said. He turned to the princess and added, "I've officially resigned from Riyria. We're divorced. Royce is single now."

"Really?" Arista said. "What will you do?"

"He's going to sober up and get his gear."

"Royce, listen to me. I mean it. I'm not going. There is nothing you can say to change my mind."

"Yes, there is."

"What, have you come up with another fancy philosophical argument? It's not going to work. I told you I'm done. It's over. I'm not kidding. I've had it." Hadrian watched his partner suspiciously.

Royce simply looked back with a smug expression. At last, Hadrian asked, "Okay, what is it? I'm curious now. What do you think you could possibly say to change my mind?"

Royce hesitated a moment, glancing uncomfortably at Arista, then sighed. "Because I'm asking you to—as a favor. After this mission, if you still feel the same way, I won't fight you and we can part as friends. But I'm asking you now—as my friend—to please come with me just one last time."

Just then, the barmaid arrived at the table.

"Another round?"

Hadrian did not look at her. He continued to stare at Royce, then sighed.

"Apparently not. I guess I'll take a cup of coffee, strong and black."

Chapter 5

Sheridan

Trapped in her long dress and riding cloak, Arista baked as the heat of summer arrived early in the day. Making matters worse, Royce insisted she travel with her hood up. She wondered at its value, as she guessed she was just as conspicuous riding so heavily bundled as she would be if riding naked. Her clothes stuck to her skin and it was difficult to breathe, but she said nothing.

Royce rode slightly ahead on his gray mare, which, to Arista's surprise, they called Mouse. A cute name—not at all what she had expected. As always, Royce was dressed in black and grays, seemingly oblivious to the heat. His eyes scanned the horizon and forest eaves. Perhaps his elven blood made him less susceptible to the hardships of weather. Even after finding out a year ago, she still marveled at his mixed race.

Why had I never noticed?

Hadrian followed half a length behind on her right—exactly where Hilfred used to position himself. It gave her a familiar feeling of safety and security. She glanced back at him and smiled under her hood. He was not immune to the heat. His brow was covered in sweat and his shirt clung to his chest. His collar lay open. His sleeves were rolled up, revealing strong arms.

A noticeable silence marked their travel. Perhaps it was the heat or a desire to avoid prying ears, but the lack of conversation denied her a natural venue to question their direction. After slipping out of Medford before sunrise, they had traveled north across fields and deer paths into the highlands before swinging east and catching the road. Arista understood the need for secrecy, and a roundabout course would help confuse any would-be spies, but instead of heading south, Royce led them north, which made no sense at all. She had held her tongue as hours had passed and they continued to ride out of Melengar and into Ghent. Arista was certain Royce took this route for a reason, and after she agreed to follow their leadership, it would be imprudent to question his judgment so early in their trip.

Arista was back in the high meadowlands where only the day before she had caught her first sight of the imperial troops gathered against Melengar. A flurry of activity was now under way on the far side of the Galewyr as the army packed up. Tents collapsed, wagons lined up, and masses of men started forming columns. She was fascinated by the sheer number and guessed there could be more imperial soldiers than citizens remaining in the city of Medford.

The meadowlands gave way to forest and the view disappeared behind the crest. The shade brought little relief from the heat.

If only it would rain.

The sky was overcast but rain was not certain. Arista knew, however, that it was possible to *make* it rain.

She recalled at least two ways. One involved an elaborate brewing of compounds and burning the mixture out of doors. This method should result in precipitation within a day but was not entirely reliable and failed more often than it succeeded. The other approach was more advanced and instantaneous, requiring great skill and knowledge. It could be accomplished with only hand movements, a focused mind, and words. The first technique she had learned as part of her studies at Sheridan University, where the entire class had attempted it without producing a single drop. The latter Esrahaddon had tried to teach her, but because the church had amputated his hands, he could not demonstrate the complex finger movements. This had always been the major obstacle in studying with him. Arista had nearly given up trying when one day, almost by accident, she made a guard sneeze.

Feeling the power of the Art for the first time had been an odd sensation, like flipping a tiny lever and sliding a gear into place. She had succeeded, not due to Esrahaddon's instructions, but rather because she had been fed up with him. To alleviate her boredom during a state dinner, Arista had been running Esrahaddon's instructions through her head. She purposely ignored his directions and instead tried something on her own. Doing so had felt easier, simpler. Discovering the right combination of movements and sounds had been like plucking the perfect note of music at exactly the right time.

That sneeze, and a short-lived curse placed on Countess Amril, had been her only magical successes during her apprenticeship with Esrahaddon. Arista had failed the rain spell hundreds of times. After her father had been murdered, she stopped attempting magic altogether. She had become too busy helping Alric with their kingdom to waste time on such childish games.

Arista glanced skyward and thought, *What else do I have to do?*

She recalled the instructions, and letting the reins hang limp on her horse's neck, she practiced the delicate weaving patterns in the air. The incantation she recalled easily enough, but the motions were all wrong. She could feel the awkwardness in the movements. There needed to be a pattern to the motion—a rhythm, a pace. She tried different variations and discovered she could tell which motions felt right and which felt wrong. The process was like fitting puzzle pieces together while blindfolded, or working out the notes of a melody by ear. She would simply guess at each note until, by sheer chance, she hit upon the right one. Then after adding it to the whole, she moved on to the next. Doing it this way was tedious, but it kept her mind occupied. She caught a curious glance from Hadrian, but she did not explain, nor did he ask.

Arista continued to work at the motions as the miles passed, until, mercifully, it began to rain on its own. She looked up so that the cool droplets hit her face and wondered if boredom had prompted her recollection of her magical studies, or if it was because they had steered off the Steward's Highway and were now on the road to Sheridan University.

Sheridan existed for the sons of merchants and scribes who needed to know mathematics and writing. Nobility rarely attended, and certainly not future rulers. Kings had no need for mathematics or philosophy. For that, he employed advisors. All he needed to know was the correct way to swing a sword, the proper tactics of military maneuvers, and the hearts of men. School could not teach these things. While it had been rare for a prince or a duke's son to attend the university, the thought of a princess going there was unheard of.

Arista had spent some of her happiest years within the sheltered valley of Sheridan. Here the world had opened up to her, and she had escaped the suffocating vacuum of courtly life. In Melengar her only purpose had been the same as the statues', an adornment for the castle halls. At Sheridan she could forget that she would eventually be a commodity—married for the benefit of the kingdom.

Arista's father had not been pleased with her abnormal interest in books, but he had never forbidden her from reading them. She had kept her habit discreet, which had caused her to spend more and more time alone. She had taken books from the scribe's collection and scrolls from the clergy. Most often she *borrowed* tomes from Bishop Saldur, who had left behind stacks of them after visits with her father. She had spent hours reading in the sanctuary of her tower, whisked away to far-off lands, where for a time she was happy. Books filled her head with ideas, thoughts of a larger world, of adventures beyond the halls, and the dream of a life lived bravely, heroically. Through these treasures she learned about Sheridan and later about Gutaria Prison.

Arista remembered the day she had asked her father for permission to attend the university. At first, he had adamantly refused and laughed, patting her head. She had cried herself to sleep, feeling trapped. All her ideas and ambitions sealed forever in a permanent prison. When her father had changed his mind the next day, it had never occurred to her to ask him why.

What are we doing here?

It irked her not knowing—patience was a virtue she still wrestled with. As they descended into the university's vale, she felt a modest inquiry would not hurt. She opened her mouth but Hadrian beat her to it.

"Why are we going to Sheridan?" he asked, trotting up closer to Royce.

"Information," Royce replied in his normal curt manner, which betrayed nothing else.

"It's your party. I'm just along for the ride."

No, no, no, she thought, *ask more*. Arista waited. Hadrian let his horse drift back. This was her opening. She had to say something. "Did you know I attended school there? You should speak to the master of lore, Arcadius. The chancellor is a pawn of the church, but Arcadius can be trusted. He's a wizard and used to be my professor. He'll know or be able to find out whatever it is you're interested in."

That was perfect. She straightened up in her saddle, pleased with herself. Common politeness would demand Royce reveal his intentions now that she had shown an interest, demonstrated some knowledge on the subject, and offered to help. She waited. Nothing. The silence returned.

I should have asked a question. Something to force him to respond. Damn.

Gritting her teeth, she slumped forward in frustration. Arista considered pressing further, but the moment had passed and now it would be difficult to say anything more without sounding critical. Being an ambassador had taught her the value of timing and of being conscious of other people's dignity and authority. Since she had been born a princess, it was a lesson not easily learned. She opted for silence, listening to the rain drum on her hood and the horses plod through the mud as they descended into the valley.

❧

The stone statue of Glenmorgan, holding a book in one hand and a sword in the other, stood in the center of the university. Walkways, benches, trees, and flowers surrounded the statue on all sides, as did numerous school buildings. A growing enrollment had required the addition of several lecture halls and dormitories, each reflecting the architectural style of its time. In the gray sheets of rain, the university looked like a mirage, a whimsical, romantic dream conceived in the mind of a man who spent his entire life at war. That an institution of pure learning existed in a world of brutish ignorance was more than a dream; it was a miracle, a testament to the wisdom of Glenmorgan.

Glenmorgan had intended the school to educate laymen at a time when hardly anyone but ecclesiastics could read. Its success was unprecedented. Sheridan achieved eminence above every other seat of learning, winning the praises of patriarchs, kings, and sages. Early on, Sheridan also established itself as a center for lively controversy, with scholars involved in religious and political disputes. Handel of Roe, a master of Sheridan, had campaigned for Ghent's recognition of the newly established republic of Delgos against the wishes of the Nyphron Church. Also, the school had been decidedly pro-Royalist in the civil wars following the Steward's Reign. That had come to be an embarrassment to the church, which had retained control of Ghent. The humiliation led to the heresy trials of the three masters Cranston, Landoner, and Widley, all burned at the stake on the Sheridan commons. This quieted the school's political voice for more than a century, until Edmund Hall, professor of geometry and lore at Sheridan, claimed to use clues gleaned from ancient texts to locate the ruins of Percepliquis. He disappeared for a year and returned with books and tablets revealing arts and sciences long lost, spurring an interest in all things imperial. At this time, a greater orthodoxy had emerged within the church and it outlawed owning or obtaining holy relics, as all artifacts from the Old Empire had been deemed. They arrested Hall and locked him in Ervanon's Crown Tower along with his notes and maps. The church later declared that Hall had never found the city and that the books were clever fakes, but no one ever heard from Edmund Hall again.

The traditions of Cranston, Landoner, Widley, and Hall were embodied in the present master of lore—Arcadius

Vintarus Latimer. Arista's old magic teacher had never appeared to notice the boundaries of good taste, much less those of political or religious significance. Chancellor Lambert was the school's head, because the church found his political leanings satisfactory to the task, but Arcadius was Sheridan's undisputed heart and soul.

"Should I take you to Master Arcadius?" Arista asked as they left their horses in the charge of the stable warden. "He really is very smart and trustworthy."

Royce nodded and she promptly led them through the now driving rain into Glen Hall, as most students referred to the original Grand Imperial College building in deference to Glenmorgan. An elaborate cathedral-like edifice, it embodied much of the grandeur of the Steward's Reign that was sadly missing from the other university buildings. Neither Royce nor Hadrian said a word as they followed her up the stairs to the second floor, shaking the water from their travel cloaks and their hair. Inside it was quiet, the air stuffy and hot. Because several people could easily recognize her, Arista remained in the confines of her hood.

"So as you can see, it would be possible to turn lead into gold, but it would require more than the gold's resulting worth to make the transformation permanent, thus causing the process to be entirely futile, at least using this method."

Arista heard Arcadius's familiar voice booming as they approached the lecture hall.

"There are some, of course, who take advantage of the temporary transformation to dupe the unwary, creating a very realistic fool's gold that hours later reveals itself to be lead."

The lecture room was lined with tiers of seats, all filled with identically gowned students. At the podium stood the lore master, a thin elderly man with a blue robe, a white beard, and spectacles perched on the end of his nose.

"The danger here is that once the ruse has been discovered, the victim is often more than mildly unhappy about it." This comment drew laughter from the students. "Before you put too much thought into the idea of amassing a fortune based on illusionary gold, you should know that it's been tried. This crime—and it *is* a crime—usually results in the victim taking out his anger on the perpetrator of the hoax in the form of a rather unceremonious execution. This is why you don't see your master of lore, dressed in the finest silks from Vandon, traveling about in an eight-horse carriage with an entourage of retainers."

More laughter.

Arista was unclear whether the lecture was at an end or if Arcadius spotted the party on the rise and cut the class short. In any case, the lore master closed his instruction for the day with reminders about homework and dates of exams. As most of the students filed out, a few gathered around their professor with questions, which he patiently addressed.

"Give me a chance to introduce you," Arista said as they descended the tiers. "I know Arcadius looks a little…odd, but he's really very intelligent."

"And the frog exploded, didn't it?" the wizard was saying to a young man wearing a sober expression.

"Made quite a mess too, sir," his companion offered.

"Yes, they usually do," Arcadius said in a sympathetic tone.

The lad sighed. "I don't understand. I mixed the nitric acid, sulfuric acid, and the glycerin and fed it to him. He seemed fine. Just as you said in class, the blackmuck frog's stomach held the mixture, but then when he hopped…" The boy's shoulders slumped while his friend mimicked an explosion with his hands.

The lore master chuckled. "Next time, dissect the frog first and remove the stomach. There's a lot less chance of it jumping then. Now run along and clean up the library before Master Falquin gets back."

The two boys scampered off. Royce closed the door to the lecture hall after them, at which point the princess felt it was safe to remove her cloak.

"Princess Arista!" Arcadius exclaimed in delight, walking toward her with his arms wide. The two exchanged a fond embrace. "Your Highness, what a wonderful surprise! Let me look at you." He stepped back, still holding her hands. "A bit disheveled, soaking wet, and tracking mud into my classroom. How nice. It's as if you're a student here again."

"Master Arcadius," the princess began formally, "allow me to introduce Royce Melborn and Hadrian Blackwater. They have some questions for you."

"Oh?" he said, eyeing the two curiously. "This sounds serious."

"It is," Hadrian replied. He took a moment to search the room for any remaining students while Royce locked the doors.

Arista saw the puzzled expression on her instructor's face and explained, "You have to understand they're cautious people by trade."

"I can see that. So I'm to be interrogated, is that it?" Arcadius asked accusingly.

"No," she said. "I think they just want to ask a few questions."

"And if I don't answer? Will they beat me until I talk?"

"Of course not!"

"Are you so sure? You said that you *think* they're here to ask questions. But I think they're here to kill me, isn't that right?"

"The fact is you know too much," Royce told the wizard,

his tone abruptly turning vicious. He reached into his cloak and drew out his dagger as he advanced on the old man. "It's time we silenced you permanently."

"Royce!" Arista shouted in shock. She turned to Hadrian, who sat relaxed in the front row of the lecture hall, casually eating an apple plucked from the lore master's table. "Hadrian, do something," she pleaded.

The old man shuffled backward, trying to put more distance between him and Royce. Hadrian did not respond, eating the apple like a man without a worry in the world.

"Royce! Hadrian!" Arista screamed at them. She could not believe what she was seeing.

"Sorry, Princess," Hadrian finally said, "but this old man has caused us a great deal of trouble in the past, and Royce is not one to forgive debts easily. You might want to close your eyes."

"She should leave," Royce said. "Even if she doesn't see, she'll hear the screams."

"So you're not going to be quick?" the old man whispered.

Hadrian sighed. "I'm not cleaning the mess up this time."

"But you can't! I—I—" Arista stood frozen in terror.

Royce closed the distance between him and Arcadius in a sudden rush.

"Wait." The wizard's voice quavered as he held up a hand to ward him off. "I think I'm entitled to ask at least one question before I'm butchered."

"What is it?" Royce asked menacingly, his dagger raised and gleaming.

"How is your lovely Gwen doing?"

"She's fine," Royce replied, lowering his blade. "She told me to be certain to tell you she sends her love."

Arista glared at each of them. "But what—I—you know each other?"

Arcadius chuckled as Hadrian and Royce snickered sheepishly. "I'm sorry, my dear." The professor held up his hands and cringed slightly. "I just couldn't resist. An old man has so few opportunities to be whimsical. Yes, I've known these two surly characters for years. I knew Hadrian's father before Hadrian was born, and I met Royce when he was..." The lore master paused briefly. "Well, younger than he is today."

Hadrian took another bite of the apple and looked up at her. "Arcadius introduced me to Royce and gave us our first few jobs together."

"And you've been inseparable ever since." The wizard smiled. "It was a sound pairing. You have been a good influence on each other. Left on your own, the two of you would have fallen into ruin."

There was a noticeable exchange of glances between Royce and Hadrian. "You only say that because you don't know what we've been up to," Hadrian mentioned.

"Don't assume too much." Arcadius shook a menacing finger at him. "I keep tabs on you. So what brings you here?"

"Just a few questions I thought you would be able to shed some light on," Royce told him. "Why don't we talk in your study while Hadrian and Arista settle in and get out of their wet things? Is it all right if we spend the night here?"

"Certainly. I'll have dinner brought up, although you picked a bad day; the kitchen is serving meat pies." He made a grimace.

Arista stood stiffly, feeling her heart still racing. She narrowed her eyes and glared. "I hate all of you."

Barrels, bottles, flasks, exotic instruments, jars containing bits of animals swimming in foul-smelling liquids, and a vast array of other oddities cluttered the small office and spilled out into the hallway. Shelves of web-covered books lined the walls. Aquariums displayed living reptiles and fish. Cages stacked to the ceiling housed pigeons, mice, moles, raccoons, and rabbits, filling the cramped office with the sounds of chirps, chatters, and squeaks, which accompanied the musky scent of books, beeswax, spices, and animal dung.

"You cleaned up," Royce said with feigned surprise as he carefully entered and stepped around the books and boxes scattered on the floor.

"Quiet, you," the wizard scolded, looking over the top of his glasses, which rested at the end of his nose. "You hardly ever visit anymore, and you don't need to be impertinent when you do."

Royce closed the door and slid the bolt, which drew another look from the wizard. Then from his cloak he pulled out a silver amulet hanging from a thin chain. "What can you tell me about this?"

Arcadius took the jewelry from him and moved to his desk, where he held it near the flame of a candle. He looked at it only briefly, then lifted his spectacles. "This is Hadrian's medallion. The one his father gave him when he turned thirteen. Are you trying to test me for senility?"

"Did you know Esrahaddon made it?"

"Did he?"

"Remember when I spoke with him in Dahlgren last summer? I didn't mention it before, but according to him, the church instigated a coup against the emperor nine hundred years ago. He insists that he remained loyal and made two amulets. One he gave to the emperor's son and the other to the boy's bodyguard. He claimed to have sent them into hiding while he stayed behind. These amulets are supposed to be enchanted so only Esrahaddon could find them. When Arista and I were with him in Avempartha, he conjured images of the people wearing his necklaces.

"And you saw Hadrian?"

Royce nodded.

"As the guardian or the heir?"

"Guardian."

"And the heir?"

"Blond hair, blue eyes, no one I recognized."

"I see," Arcadius said. "But you haven't told Hadrian what you saw."

"What makes you say that?"

The wizard let the amulet and the chain fall into his palm. "You're here alone."

Royce nodded. "Hadrian's been moody lately. If I tell him, he'll want to fulfill his destiny—go find this long-lost heir and be his whipping boy. He won't even question it, because he'll want it to be true, but I don't think it is. I think Esrahaddon is up to something. I don't want either of us to be pawns in his effort to bring his choice for emperor to the throne."

"You think Esrahaddon is lying? That he conjured false images to manipulate you?"

"That's what I came here to find out. Is it even possible to make enchanted amulets? If so, is it possible to locate the wearers by magic? And you knew Hadrian's father. Did he ever say anything to you about being the guardian to the Heir of Novron?"

Arcadius turned the amulet over in his hand. "*I* don't have the Art to enchant objects to resist magic, nor can I use magic to seek people, but a lot was lost when the Old Empire crumbled. Preserving him in that prison for nearly a thousand years makes Esrahaddon unique in his knowledge, so I can't intelligently say what he is or isn't capable of. As for Danbury Blackwater, I don't recall him ever telling me he was the

Guardian of the Heir. That isn't the kind of thing I would likely forget."

"So I'm right. This is all a lie."

"It may not be a lie, per se. You realize it's possible—even likely—that Danbury could have the amulet and not be anyone special. Nine hundred years is a long time to expect an heirloom to stay in the possession of one family. The odds are weighed heavily against it. Personal effects are lost every day. This is made of silver, and a poor man, in a moment of desperation and convinced any story he was told is just a myth, could be tempted to sell it for food. Moreover, what should happen if the owner died—killed in an accident—and this medallion was taken from the dead body and sold? This has likely passed through hundreds of hands before ever reaching Danbury. If what you say is true, Esrahaddon's incantation merely revealed the wearer of the amulet and not the identity of the original owner's descendants. So it's possible Esrahaddon may be sincere and still be wrong.

"Even if Danbury was the descendant of the last Teshlor, he might not have known any more than Hadrian does. His father, or his father before him, could have failed to mention it because it didn't matter anymore. The line of the heir may have died out, or the two became separated centuries ago."

"Is that what you think?"

Arcadius took off his glasses and wiped them.

"For centuries people have searched for the descendants of Emperor Nareion and no one has ever found them. The empire itself searched for Nareion's son, Nevrik, with all the power of great wizards and questing knights at a time when they could identify him by sight. They failed—unless you accept the recent declaration that they found the heir in the form of this farm girl from Dahlgren."

"Thrace is not the heir," Royce said simply. "The church

orchestrated that whole incident as theatrics to anoint their choice for ruler. They botched the job and she accidently caught the prize."

The wizard nodded. "So I think common sense decrees that an heir no longer exists... if he ever existed to begin with. Unless..." He trailed off.

"Unless what?"

"Nothing." Arcadius shook his head.

Royce intensified his stare until the wizard relented.

"Just supposition, really, but, well... it just seems too romantic that the heir and a bodyguard could have lived all alone on the run for so long, managing to hide while the entire world hunted them."

"What are you suggesting?" Royce asked.

"After the emperor's death, when Nevrik fled with his bodyguard, the Teshlor Jerish, wouldn't they have had friends? Wouldn't there have been hundreds of people loyal to the emperor's son willing to help conceal him? Support him? Organize an attempt to put him back on the throne? Of course this organization would have to act in secrecy, given that the bulk of the dying empire was in control of the church."

"Are you saying such a group exists?" Royce asked.

Arcadius shrugged. "I'm only speculating here."

"You're doing more than just speculating. What do you know?"

"Well, I've come across some odd references in various texts to a group known only as the Theorem Eldership. I first discovered them in a bit of historical text from 2465, about the time of the Steward's Reign of Glenmorgan the Second. Some priest made a brief notation about a sect by that name. Of course, at that time, anyone who opposed the church was considered heretical, so I didn't give it much thought. Then I spotted another reference to the same group in a very old letter sent from Lord Darius Seret to Patriarch Venlin dating back to within the first twenty years after the death of Emperor Nareion."

"Lord Seret?" Royce asked. "As in, Seret Knights?"

"Indeed," Arcadius said. "The duke was commanded by the Patriarch to locate the whereabouts of Nevrik, Emperor Nareion's missing son. He formed an elite band of knights who swore an oath to find the heir. A hundred years after the death of Darius the knights adopted their official name, the Order of Seret Knights, which was later shortened out of convenience. Quite ironic, actually, as their responsibilities and influence broadened dramatically. You would hardly know it, as the seret work mostly in secret—hidden so they can perform their duties invisibly. They still report directly to the Patriarch. It's really just a matter of perceptive logic. Given that there is a pseudo-invisible order of knights seeking to hunt down the heir, doesn't it seem sensible to conclude that there is another unseen group to protect him?"

Arcadius stood up and, with no trouble navigating his way through the room's debris, reached the far wall. There a slate hung and with a bit of chalk he wrote:

Theorem Eldership

Then he crossed out each letter and underneath wrote:

Shield the Emperor

He returned to his desk and sat back down.

"If you decide to search for the heir," Arcadius told Royce in a grave tone, "be very careful. This is not some bit of jewelry you seek and he may be protected and hunted by men who will sacrifice their lives and use any means against you. If any of this is true, then I fear you'll be entering into a world of shadows and lies where a silent, secret war has been waging for nearly a thousand years. There will be no honor and no quarter given. It's a place where people disappear without a trace and martyrs thrive. No price will be too great, no sacrifice too awful. What's at stake in this struggle—at least in their eyes—is the very future of Elan."

⁂

The number of students at Sheridan always diminished in summer, so Arcadius arranged for them to sleep in the vacated top floor, known as Glen's Attic. The fourth-floor dormitory in Glen Hall lacked even a single window and was oven hot in summer. Home to the sons of affluent farmers, the upper dorm was deserted this time of year, as students returned home to tend crops. This left the entire loft to them, a single long room with a slanted ceiling so low even Arista had to watch her head or risk hitting a rafter. Cots jutted out from the wall where the ceiling met the floor, each nothing more than a straw mattress on simple wooden frames. Personal belongings were absent, but every inch of wood was etched with a mosaic of names, phrases, or drawings—seven centuries of student memoirs.

Arista and Hadrian worked at drying their wet gear. They laid everything made of cloth across the floor, and damp stains spread across the ancient timbers. Everything was soaked, and smelled of horse.

"I'll get a drying line up," Hadrian told her. "We can use the blankets to create a bit of privacy for you at the same time." He gave her a quizzical look.

"What?"

He shook his head. "I've just never seen a soaking-wet

princess before. You sure you want to do this? It's not too late. We can still head back to Medford and—"

"I'll be fine." She headed for the stairs.

"Where are you going?"

"To bring up the rest of the bags."

"It's probably still raining and I can get those just as soon—"

Arista interrupted him. "You have ropes to tie and, as you pointed out, I'm already soaked." She descended the steps. Her shoes squished and her wet dress hung with added weight.

No one thinks I can handle this.

Arista knew she had led a pampered life. She was no fool, but neither was she made of porcelain.

How much fortitude does it take to live like a peasant?

She was the Princess of Melengar and daughter of King Amrath Essendon—she could rise to any occasion. They all had her so well defined, but she was not like Lenare Pickering. She did not sit all day considering which dress went best with her golden locks. Arista stroked her still dripping head and felt her flat tangled hair. Lenare would have fainted by now.

Outside, the rain had stopped, which left the air filled with the earthy smell of grass, mud, and worms. Everything glistened, and breezes touched off showers beneath trees. Arista had forgotten her cloak. It lay four flights up. She was going only a short distance and would be quick, but by the time she reached the carriage house, she regretted her decision. Three gown-draped students stood in the shadows, talking about the new horses.

"They're from Melengar," the tallest said with the confident, superior tone of a young noble speaking to lesser men. "You can tell by the Medford brand on that one."

"So, Lane, you think Melengar has fallen already?" the shortest of them asked.

"Of course. I'll wager Breckton took it last night or maybe early this morning. That's why the owners of these horses are here. They're probably refugees, cowards fleeing like rats from a sinking ship."

"Deserters?"

"Maybe," Lane replied.

"If Melengar really did fall last night, it might have been the king himself who fled," the short one speculated.

"Don't be a rube!" the second tallest told him. "A king would never ride on nags like these."

"Don't be too sure about that." Lane came to the little one's defense. "Alric isn't much of a *real* king. They say he and his witch sister killed their father and stole the throne just as he was about to name Percy Braga his successor. I even heard that Alric has taken his sister as his mistress, and there's talk of her becoming queen."

"That's disgusting!"

"The church would never allow that," said the other.

"Alric kicked the church out of Melengar months ago because he knew it would try to stop him," Lane explained. "You have to understand that the Melengarians aren't civilized people. They're still mostly barbarians and slip further back into their tribal roots every year. Without the church to watch over them, they'll be drinking the blood of virgins and praying to Uberlin before the year is out. They allow elves to run free in their cities, for Maribor's sake. Did you know that?"

Arista could not see their faces as she stood beyond the doorway, carefully keeping herself hidden.

"So perhaps this *is* the nag the king of Melengar escaped on. He could be staying in one of the dorm rooms right now, plotting his next move."

"Do you think Chancellor Lambert knows?"

"I doubt it," Lane replied. "I don't think a good man like Lambert would allow a menace like Alric to stay here."

"Should we tell him?"

"Why don't you tell him, Hinkle?" Lane said to the short fellow.

"Why me? You should do it. After all, you're the one that noticed them."

"Me? I don't have time. Lady Chastelin sent me another letter today and I need to work on my reply lest she drives a dagger into her chest for fear I've forgotten her."

"Don't look at me," said the remaining one. "I'll admit it—Lambert scares me."

The others laughed.

"No, I'm serious. He scares the wax out of me. I was sent to his office last semester because of that rabid rat stunt Jason pulled. I'd rather he'd just cane me."

Together they walked off, continuing their chatter, which drifted to Lady Chastelin and doubts of her devotion to Lane.

Arista waited a moment until she was certain they were gone, then found the bags near the saddles and stuffed one under her arm. She grabbed the other two and quickly, but carefully, returned across the commons and slipped back up the stairs of Glen Hall.

Hadrian was not in the loft when she returned, but he had the lines up and blankets hanging from them to divide the room. She slipped through the makeshift curtain and began the miserable task of stringing out her wet things. She changed into her nightgown and robe. They had been near the center of her bag and only slightly damp. Then she began throwing the rest of her clothes over the lines. Hadrian returned with a bucket of water and paused when he spotted Arista brazenly hanging her petticoats and corset. She felt her face flush as she imagined what he was thinking. Not only did she travel unescorted with two men, but she was bedding down in the same room—albeit a large and segmented hall—and now she hung her undergarments for them to see. She was surprised they had not questioned her more intently. She knew the unusual circumstances she traveled under would eventually come up. Royce was not the type to miss something as suspicious as a maiden princess traveling alone in the company of two rogues, no matter how highly esteemed by the crown. As for her clothes, there was no other way or place to dry them safely, so it was this or wear them wet in the morning. There was no sense being prissy about it.

Royce entered the dorm as she finished her work. He was wearing his cloak with the hood up. It dripped a puddle on the floor.

"We'll be leaving well before dawn," he pronounced.

"Is something wrong?" Hadrian asked.

"I found a few students snooping around the carriage house when I made my rounds."

"He does that," Hadrian explained to Arista. "Sort of an obsession he has. Can't sleep otherwise."

"You were there?" she asked.

Royce nodded. "They won't be troubling us anymore."

Arista felt the blood drain from her face. "You... you killed them?" she asked in a whisper. As she said it, she felt sick. A few minutes earlier, listening to their horrible discussion, she had found herself wishing them harm, but she had not meant it. They were little more than children. She knew, however, that Royce might not see it that way. She had come to realize that for him, a threat was a threat no matter the package.

"I considered it." No tone of sarcasm tempered his words. "If they had turned left toward the chancellor's residence, instead of right toward the dormitories... But they didn't. They went straight to their rooms. Nevertheless, we'll not be waiting until morning. We'll be leaving in a few hours. That way even if they do start a rumor about horses from Melengar, we'll be long gone by the time it reaches the right ears. The empire's spies will assume we're heading to Trent to beg their aid. We'll need to get you a new mount, though, before heading to Colnora."

"If we're leaving as soon as that, I should go see Arcadius about that meal he promised," Hadrian said.

"No!" Arista told him hastily. They looked at her, surprised. She smiled, embarrassed by her outburst. "I'll go. It will give you two a chance to change out of your wet things without me here." Before they could say anything, she slipped out and down the hallway to the stairs.

It had been nearly a year since that morning on the bank of the Nidwalden River when Esrahaddon had put a question in her head. The wizard had admitted using her to orchestrate the murder of her father to facilitate his escape, but he had also suggested there was more to the story. This could be her only chance to speak with Arcadius. She took a right at the bottom of the stairs and hurried to his study.

Arcadius sat on a stool at a small wooden desk on the far side of the room, studying a page of a massive tome. Beside him was a brazier of hot coals and an odd contraption she had never seen before—a brown liquid hung suspended above the heat of the brazier in a glass vial as a steady stream of bubbles rose from a small stone immersed in the liquid. The steamy vapors rose through a series of glass tubes and passed through another glass container, filled with salt crystals. From the end of that tube, a clear fluid slowly dripped into a small flask. A yellow liquid also hung suspended above the flask, and through a valve one yellow drop fell for each clear one. As these two liquids mixed, white smoke silently rose into the air. Occasionally he adjusted a valve, added salt, or pumped bellows, causing the charcoal to glow red hot. At her entrance, Arcadius looked up.

He removed his glasses, wiped them with a rag from the desk, and put them back on. He peered at her through squinting eyes.

"Ah, my dear, come in." Then, as if remembering something important, he hastily twisted one of the valves. A large puff of smoke billowed up, causing several of the animals in the room to chatter. The stone fell to the bottom of the vial, where it lay quietly. The animals calmed down, and the elderly master of lore turned and smiled at Arista, motioning for her to join him.

This was no easy feat. Arista searched for open floor to step on and, finding little, grabbed the hem of her robe and opted to step on the sturdiest-looking objects in the shortest path to the desk.

The wizard waited patiently with a cheery smile, his high rosy cheeks causing the edges of his eyes to wrinkle like a bedsheet held in a fist.

"You know," he began as she made the perilous crossing, "I always find it interesting what paths my students take to reach me. Some are direct, while others take more of a roundabout approach. Some end up getting lost in the clutter and others find the journey too much trouble and give up altogether without even reaching me."

Arista was certain he implied more than he said, but she had neither the time nor the inclination to explore it further. Instead, she replied, "Perhaps if you straightened up a bit, you wouldn't lose so many students."

The wizard tilted his head. "I suppose you're right, but where would be the fun in that?"

Arista stepped over the rabbit cage, around the large pestle and mortar, and stood before the desk on a closed cover of a book no less than three feet in height and two in width.

The lore master looked down at her feet, pursed his lips, and nodded his approval. "That's Glenmorgan the Second's biography, easily seven hundred years old."

Arista looked alarmed.

"Not to worry, not to worry," he told her, chuckling to himself. "It's a terrible book written by church propagandists. The perfect platform for you to stand on, don't you think?"

Arista opened her mouth, thought about what she was going to say, and then closed it again.

The wizard chuckled once more. "Ah yes, they've gone and made an ambassador out of you, haven't they? You've learned to think before you speak. I suppose that's good. Now tell me, what brings you to my office at this hour? If it's about dinner, I apologize for the delay, but the stoves were out and I needed to fetch a boy to get them fired again. I also had to drag the cook away from a card game, which he wasn't at all pleased about. But a meal is being prepared as we speak and I'll have it brought up the moment it is finished."

"It's not that, Master—"

He put up a hand to stop her. "You are no longer a student here. You are a princess and Ambassador of Melengar. If you call me Arcadius, I won't call you Your Highness, agreed?" The grin of his was just too infectious to fight. She nodded and smiled in return.

"Arcadius," she began again, "I've had something on my mind and I've been meaning to visit you for some time, but so much has been happening. First there was Fanen's funeral. Then, of course, Tomas arrived in Melengar."

"Oh yes, the Wandering Deacon of Dahlgren. He came here as well, preaching that a young girl named Thrace is the

Heir of Novron. He sounded very sincere. Even I was inclined to believe him."

"A lot of people did and that's part of the reason Melengar's fate is so precarious now."

Arista stopped. There was someone at the door—a pretty girl, perhaps six years old. Long dark hair spilled over her shoulders, and her hands were clasped together, holding a length of thin rope that she played with, spinning it in circles.

"Ah, there you are. Good," the wizard told the girl, who stared apprehensively at Arista. "I was hoping you'd turn up soon. He's starting to cause a fuss. It's as if he can tell time." Arcadius glanced at Arista. "Oh, forgive me. I neglected to introduce you. Arista, this is Mercy."

"How do you do?" Arista asked.

The little girl said nothing.

"You must forgive her. She's a bit shy with strangers."

"A bit young for Sheridan, isn't she?"

Arcadius smiled. "Mercy is my ward. Her mother asked me to watch over her for a while until her situation improved. Until then I try my best to educate her, but as I learned with you, young ladies can be most willful." He turned to the girl. "Go right ahead, dear. Take Mr. Rings outside with you before he rips up his cage again."

The girl moved across the room's debris as nimbly as a cat and removed a thin raccoon from his cage. He was a baby by the look of it, and she carried him out the door, giggling as Mr. Rings sniffed her ear.

"She's cute," Arista said.

"Indeed she is. Now, you said you had something on your mind?"

Arista nodded and considered her words. The question Esrahaddon had planted she now presented to her old teacher. "Arcadius, who approved my entrance into Sheridan?"

The lore master raised a bristled eyebrow. "Ah," he said. "You know, I always wondered why you never asked before. You are perhaps the only female to attend Sheridan University in its seven-hundred-year history, and certainly the only one to study the arcane arts at all, but you never questioned it once."

Arista's posture tightened. "I'm questioning it now."

"Indeed... indeed," the wizard replied. He sat back, removed his glasses, and rubbed his nose briefly. "I was visited by Chancellor Ignatius Lambert, and asked if I would be willing to accept a gifted young lady into my instructions on arcane theory. This surprised me. You see, I didn't teach a class on arcane theory. I had wanted to, and I requested to have it added to the curriculum on many occasions, but I was always turned down by the school's patrons. It seemed they didn't feel that teaching magic was a respectable pursuit. Magic uses power not connected to a spiritual devotion to Maribor and Novron. At best, it was subversive and possibly outright evil in their minds. The fact that I practiced the arcane arts at all has always been an embarrassment."

"Why haven't they replaced you?"

"It could be that my reputation as the most learned wizard in Avryn lends such prestige to this school that they allow me my hobbies. Or it may be that anyone who has tried to force my resignation has been turned into the various toads, squirrels, and rabbits you see about you."

He appeared so serious that Arista looked around the room at the various cages and aquariums, at which point the wizard began to chuckle.

She scowled at him—which only made him laugh harder.

"As I was saying," Arcadius went on once he regained control of himself, "Ignatius was in one sentence offering me my desire to teach magic if I was willing to accept you as a student.

Perhaps he thought I would refuse. Little did he know that unlike the rest of them, I harbor no prejudices concerning women. Knowledge is knowledge, and the chance to instruct and enlighten a princess—a potential leader—with the power to help shape the world around us was not a deterrent at all. On the contrary, I saw it as a bonus."

"So you're saying I was allowed entrance because of a plan of the school's headmaster that backfired?"

"Not at all. That is merely how it happened, not why. *Why* is a much more important question. You see, School Chancellor Ignatius Lambert was not alone in my office that morning. With him was another man. He remained silent and stood over there, just behind and to the left of you, where the birdcage is now. The cage wasn't there then, of course. Instead, he chose to stand on a discarded old coat and a dagger. As I mentioned, it's always interesting to see the paths people take when they enter this office, and where they choose to stand."

"Who was he?"

"Percy Braga, the Archduke of Melengar."

"So it *was* Uncle Percy."

"He certainly was involved, but even an archduke of Melengar wasn't likely to have influence over those running Sheridan University, especially on a matter as volatile as teaching magic to young noble ladies. Sheridan is in the ecclesiastical realm of Ghent, where secular lords have no sway. There was, however, another man with them. He never entered my office but stood in the doorway, in the shadows."

"Could you tell who it was?"

"Oh yes." Arcadius smiled. "These are reading glasses, my dear. I can see long distances just fine, but then, I can see that is a common mistake people make."

"Who was it, then?"

"A close friend of your family, I believe. Bishop Maurice Saldur of Medford's Mares Cathedral, but you probably already knew that, didn't you?"

Good to his word, Arcadius sent steaming meat pies and red wine. Arista recalled the pies from her days as a student. They were never very good, even when fresh. Usually they were made from the worst cuts of pork, because the school saved lamb for the holidays. The pies were heavy on onions and carrots and thin on gravy and meat. Students actually gambled on how many paltry shreds of pork they would find in their pies—a mere five stood as the record. Despite their complaints, the other students wolfed down their meals, but she never had. Most of the other students' indignation she guessed was only bluster—they likely ate no better at home. Arista, however, was accustomed to three or four different meats roasted on the bone, several varieties of cheese, freshly baked breads, and whatever fruits were in season. To get her through the week, she had servants bring deliveries from home, which she had kept in her room.

"You could have mentioned that you knew Arcadius," Arista told them as they sat down together at the common table, an old bit of furniture defaced like everything else. It wobbled enough to make her glad the wine was in a jug with cups instead of a bottle and stemmed glasses.

"And ruin the fun?" Hadrian replied with a handsome grin. "So Arcadius was your professor?"

"One of them. The curriculum requires you to take several classes, learning different subjects from the various teachers. Master Arcadius was my favorite. He was the only one to teach magic."

"So you learned magic from Arcadius as well as Esrahaddon?" Royce asked, digging into his pie.

Arista nodded, poking her pie with a knife and letting the steam out.

"That must have been interesting. I'm guessing their teaching styles were a bit different."

"Like night and day." She took a sip of wine. "Arcadius was formal in his lessons. He followed a structured course, using books and lecturing very professorially, like you saw this evening. His style made the lessons seem right and proper, despite the stigma associated with them. Esrahaddon was haphazard, and he seemed to teach whatever came to his mind. Oftentimes he had trouble explaining things. Arcadius is clearly the better teacher, but..." She paused.

"But?" Royce asked.

"Well, don't tell Arcadius," she said conspiratorially, "but Esrahaddon seems to be the more skilled and knowledgeable. Arcadius is the expert on the history of magic, but Esrahaddon *is* the history, if you follow me."

She took a bite of pie and got a mouthful of onions and burnt crust.

"Having learned from both, doesn't that make you the third most skilled mage in Avryn?"

Arista smirked bitterly and washed the mouthful down with more wine. While she suspected Royce was correct, she had cast only two spells since leaving their tutelage.

"Arcadius taught me many important lessons. Yet his classes concerned themselves with using knowledge as a means to broaden his students' understanding of their world. It's his way of getting us to think in new directions, to perceive what is around us in terms that are more sensible. Of course, this didn't make his students happy. We all wanted the secrets to power, the tools to reshape the world to our liking. Arcadius doesn't really give answers, but rather forces his students to ask questions.

"For instance, he once asked us what makes noble blood different from a commoner's blood. We pricked our fingers and ran tests, and as it turns out, there is no detectable difference. This led to a fight on the commons between a wealthy merchant's son and the son of a low-ranking baron. Master Arcadius was reprimanded and the merchant's son was whipped."

Hadrian finished eating, and Royce was more than halfway through his pie, but he had left his wine untouched after grimacing with the first sip. Arista chanced another bite and caught a mushy carrot, still more onions, and a soggy bit of crust. She swallowed with a sour look.

"Not a fan of meat pie?" Hadrian asked.

She shook her head. "You can have it if you like." She slid it over.

"So how was studying with Esrahaddon?"

"He was a completely different story," she went on after another mouthful of wine. "When I couldn't get what I wanted from Arcadius, I went to him. You see, all of Arcadius's teachings involved elaborate preparations, alchemic recipes that are used to trigger the release of nature's powers and incantations to focus it. He also stressed observation and experimentation to tap the power of the natural world. Arcadius relied on manual techniques to derive power from the elements, but Esrahaddon explained how the same energy could be summoned through more subtle enticement, using only motion, harmonic sound, and the power of the mind.

"The problem was Esrahaddon's technique relied on hand movements, which explains why the church cut his off. He tried to talk me through the motions, but without the ability to demonstrate, it was very frustrating. Subtle differences can separate success from failure, so learning from him was hopeless. All I ever managed to do was make a man sneeze. Oh, and once I cursed Countess Amril with boils." Hadrian poured the last of the wine into his and Arista's cups after Royce waved him off. "Arcadius was angry when he found out about the curse and lectured me for hours. He was always against using magic for personal gain or for the betterment of just a few. He often said, 'Don't waste energy to treat a single plague victim; instead, search to eliminate the illness and save thousands.'

"So yes, you're right. I'm likely the most tutored mage in all of Avryn, but that's really not saying much. I would be hard-pressed to do much more than tickle someone's nose."

"And you can do that just with hand movements?" Royce asked skeptically.

"Would you like a demonstration?"

"Sure, try it on Hadrian."

"Ah no, let's not," Hadrian protested. "I don't want to be accidently turned into a toad or rabbit or something. Didn't you learn anything else?"

"Well, he tried to teach me how to boil water, but I never got it to work. I would get close, but there was always something missing. He used to..." She trailed off.

"What?" Hadrian asked.

She shrugged. "I don't know. It's just that I was practicing gestures on the ride here and I—" She squinted in concentration as she ran through the sequence in her mind. They should be similar. Both the rain and the boiling spell used the same element—water. The same motion should be found in each. Just thinking about it made her heart quicken.

That is it, isn't it? That is the missing piece. If I have the rest of the spell correct, then all I need to do is...

Looking around for the bucket that Hadrian had brought up, she closed her eyes and took several deep breaths. Boiling water, while harder than making a person sneeze, took a short, simple incantation, one she had attempted without success hundreds of times. She cleared her mind, relaxed, then reached out, sensing the room—the light and heat emanating from the candles, the force of the wind blowing above the roof, the dripping of water from their wet clothes. She opened her eyes and focused on the bucket and the water inside. Lukewarm, it lay quiet, sleeping. She felt its place in the world, part of the whole, waiting for a change, wanting to please.

Arista began to hum, letting the sounds follow the rhythm that spoke to the water. She sensed its attention. Her voice rose, speaking the few short words in a melody of a song. She raised a single hand and made the motions, only this time she added a simple sweep of her thumb. It felt perfect—the hole that evaded her in the past. She closed her hand into a fist and squeezed. The moment she did, she could feel the heat, and across the room steam rose.

Hadrian stood up, took two steps, and then stopped. "It's bubbling," he said, his voice expressing his amazement.

"Yeah, and so are our clothes." Royce pointed to the pieces of wet clothing hanging on the line, which were beginning to hiss as steam rose from them.

"Oops." Arista opened her hand abruptly. The wash water stopped boiling and the clothes quieted.

"By Mar, that's unbelievable." Hadrian stood grinning. "You really did it."

Royce remained silent, staring at the steaming clothes.

"I know. Can you believe it?" she said.

"What else can you do?"

"Let's not find out," Royce interrupted. "It's getting late and we'll be leaving in a few hours, so we should get to sleep."

"Killjoy," Hadrian replied. "But he's probably right. Let's turn in."

Arista nodded, walked behind the wall of blankets, and only then allowed herself a smile.

It worked! It really worked.

Lying on the little cot without bothering with a blanket, she stared at the ceiling and listened to the thieves moving about.

"You have to admit that was impressive," she heard Hadrian say.

If Royce made a reply, she did not hear it. She had frightened him. The expression on his face had said more than words ever could. Lying there, looking up at the rafters, she realized she had seen that look before—the day Arcadius had reprimanded her. She had been leaving his office when he had stopped her. "I never taught curses in this class, boils or otherwise. Did you cause them by mixing a draft that she drank?"

"No," she recalled saying. "It was a verbal curse."

His eyes widened and his mouth gaped, but he said nothing more. At the time, she had thought his look was one of amazement and pride in a student exceeding expectations. Looking back, Arista realized she had seen only what she had wanted to see.

Chapter 6

The Word

As Amilia watched, the playful flicker of candlelight caught the attention of the empress, which briefly replaced her blank stare.

Is that a sign?

Amilia often played this game with herself, looking for any improvement. A month had passed since Saldur had summoned her to his office to explain her duties. She knew she could never do half of what he wanted, but his main concern was the empress's health, and Amilia was doing well in that regard. Even in this faint light, she could see the change. Modina's cheeks were no longer hollow, her skin no longer stretched. The empress was now eating some vegetables and even bits of meat hidden in the soup. Still, Amilia feared the progress would not be good enough.

Modina still had not said a word—at least, not while awake. Often when the empress slept, she mumbled, moaned, and tossed about restlessly. Upon awakening, the girl cried, tears running down her cheeks. Amilia held her, stroked her hair, and tried to keep her warm, but the empress did not seem to notice her presence.

To pass the time, Amilia continued to tell Modina stories,

hoping it might prompt her into speaking, perhaps to ask a question. After telling her everything she could think of about her family, she moved on to fairy tales from her childhood. There was Gronbach, the evil dwarf who kidnapped a milkmaid and imprisoned her in his subterranean lair. The maiden solved the riddle of the three boxes, snipped off his beard, and escaped.

She even recounted scary stories told by her brothers in the dark of the carriage workshop. She knew they had been purposefully trying to frighten her, and even now the tales gave Amilia chills. But anything was worth a try to snap Modina back to the land of the living. The most disturbing of these were about elves, who put their victims to sleep with music before eating them.

When she ran out of fairy tales, she turned to stories she remembered from church, like the epic tale of how, in their hour of greatest need, Maribor sent the divine Novron to save mankind. Wielding the wondrous Rhelacan, he defeated the elves.

Thinking Modina would like the similarities to her own life, Amilia told the romantic account of the farmer's daughter Persephone, whom Novron took to be his queen. When she refused to leave her simple village, he built the great imperial capital right there and named the city Percepliquis after her.

"So what story shall we have this evening?" Amilia asked as the two girls lay across from each other, bathed in the light of the candles. "How about *Kile and the White Feather*? Our monsignor used it from time to time when he wanted to make a point about penance and redemption. Have you heard that one? Do you like it? I do.

"Well, you see, the father of the gods, Erebus, had three sons: Ferrol, Drome, and Maribor; the gods of elves, dwarves, and men. He also had a daughter, Muriel, who was the loveliest being ever created, and she held dominion over all the plants and animals. Well, one night Erebus became drunk and raped his own daughter. In anger, her brothers attacked their father and tried to kill him, but of course, gods can't die."

Amilia saw the candles flicker from a draft. It was always colder at night, and she got up and brought them each another blanket.

"So, where was I?"

Modina merely blinked.

"Oh, I remember, racked with guilt and grief, Erebus returned to Muriel and begged for her forgiveness. She was moved by her father's remorse but still could not look at him. He pleaded for her to name a punishment. Muriel needed time to let the fear and pain pass, so she told him, 'Go to Elan to live. Not as a god, but as a man, to learn humility.' To repent for his misdeeds, she charged him to do good works. Erebus did as she requested and took the name of Kile. It's said that he walks the world of men to this day, working miracles. For each act that pleases her, she bestows a white feather to him from her magnificent robe, which he places in a pouch kept forever by his side. On the day when all the feathers have been awarded, Muriel promised to call her father home and forgive him. The legend says that when the gods are reunited, all will be made right, and the world will transform into a paradise."

This really was one of Amilia's favorite stories and she told it hoping for miraculous results. Perhaps the father of the gods would hear her and come to their aid. Amilia waited. Nothing happened. The walls were the same cold stone, the flickering flames the only light. She sighed. "Well, maybe we'll just have to make our own miracles," she told Modina as she blew out all but a single candle, then closed her eyes to sleep.

⁂

Amilia woke with a newfound purpose. She resolved to free Modina from her room, if only for a short while. The cell reeked of the scent of urine and mildew, which lingered even after scrubbing and fresh straw. She wanted to take Modina outside but knew that would be asking too much. Amilia tried to convince herself that Lady Constance had been dragged away because of Modina's failing health, and not because she had taken her to the kitchen. But even so, no matter the consequences, Amilia had to try.

Amilia changed both herself and Modina into their day clothing and, taking her gently by the hand, led her to the door and knocked. When it opened, she faced the guard straight and tall and announced, "I'm taking the empress to the kitchen for her meal. I was appointed the imperial secretary by Regent Saldur himself, and I'm responsible for her care. She can't remain in this filthy cell. It's killing her."

She waited.

He would refuse and she would argue. She tried to organize her rebuttals: noxious vapors, the healing power of fresh air, the fact that they would kill her if the empress did not show improvement. Why that last one would persuade him she had not worked out, but it was one of the thoughts pressing on her mind.

The guard looked from Amilia to Modina and back to Amilia again. She was shocked when he nodded and stepped aside. Amilia hesitated; she had not considered the possibility he would relent. She led the empress up the steps while the soldier followed.

She made no announcement like Lady Constance. She simply walked in with the empress in tow, bringing the kitchen once more to a halt. Everyone stared. No one said a word.

"The empress would like her meal," Amilia told Ibis, who

nodded. "Could you please put some extra bread at the bottom of the bowl, and could she get some fruit today?"

"Aye, aye," the big man acknowledged. "Leif, get on it. Nipper, go to the storage and bring up some of those berries. The rest of you, back to work. Nothing to see here."

Nipper bolted outside, leaving the door open. Red, one of the huntsman's old dogs, wandered in. Modina dropped Amilia's hand.

"Leif, get that animal out of here," Ibis ordered.

"Wait," Amilia said. Everyone watched as the empress knelt down next to the elkhound. The dog, in turn, nuzzled her.

Red was old, and his muzzle had gone gray, and his eyes clouded with blindness. Why the huntsman kept him was a mystery, as all he did was sleep in the courtyard and beg for handouts from the kitchen. Few took notice of his familiar presence, but he commanded the empress's attention. She scratched behind his ears and stroked his fur.

"I guess Red gets to stay." Ibis chuckled. "Dog's got important friends."

Edith Mon entered the kitchen, halting abruptly at the sight of Amilia and the empress. She pursed her lips, narrowed her eyes, and without a word pivoted and exited the way she had come.

ఆ

Amidst the sound of pounding hammers, Regent Maurice Saldur strode through the palace reception hall, where artisans were busy at work. A year ago this had been King Ethelred's castle, the stark stone fortress of Avryn's most powerful monarch. Since the coronation of the empress, it had become the imperial palace of the Nyphron Empire and the home of the Daughter of Maribor. Saldur had insisted on the renovations: a grand new foyer, complete with the crown seal etched in white marble on the floor; several massive chandeliers to lighten the dark interior; a wider ornate balcony from which Her Eminence could wave to her adoring people; and of course, a complete rework of the throne room.

Ethelred and the chancellor had balked at the expense. The new throne cost almost as much as a warship, but they did not understand the importance of impressions the way Saldur did. He had an illiterate, nearly comatose child for an empress, and the only thing preventing disaster was that no one knew. Saldur's edict restricting servants from leaving the castle had been issued to contain most of the gossip. Brute-force opulence would further the misdirection.

How much silk, gold, and marble does it take to blind the world?

More than he had access to, he was certain, but he would do what he could.

These past few weeks, Saldur had felt as if he had been balancing teacups on his head while standing on a stool, strapped to the back of a runaway horse. The New Empire had manifested itself in just a matter of weeks. Centuries of planning had finally coalesced, but as with everything, there were mistakes and circumstances for which they could not possibly account.

The whole fiasco in Dahlgren had been only the start. The moment they had declared the establishment of the New Empire, Glouston had gone into open revolt. Alburn had decided to haggle over terms, and of course, there was Melengar. The humiliation was beyond words. Every other Avryn kingdom had fallen in step as planned, all except his. He had been the bishop of Melengar and close personal advisor to the king, as well as the king's son, and yet Melengar remained independent. Saldur's clever solution to the Dahlgren problem had kept him from fading into obscurity. He had drawn victory from ashes, and for that the Patriarch had appointed him the church's representative, making him co-regent alongside Ethelred.

The old king of Warric maintained the existing systems, but Saldur was the architect of the new world order. His vision would define the lives of thousands for centuries to come. Although it was a tremendous opportunity, Saldur felt as if he were rolling a massive boulder up a hill. If he should trip or stumble, the rock would roll back and crush him and everything else with it.

When Saldur reached his office, he found Luis Guy waiting. The church sentinel had just arrived, hopefully with good news. The Knight of Nyphron waited near the window, as straight and impeccable as ever. He stood looking out at some distant point with his hands clasped behind his back. As usual, he wore the black and scarlet of his order, each line clean, his beard neatly trimmed.

"I assume you've heard," Saldur said, closing the door behind him and ignoring any greeting. Guy was not the type to bother with pleasantries—something Saldur appreciated about the man. Over the past several months, he had seen little of Guy, whom the Patriarch kept occupied searching for the real Heir of Novron and the wizard Esrahaddon. This was also to his liking, as Guy, who was one of only two men in the world with direct access to the Patriarch, could be a formidable rival. Strangely, Guy appeared to have little interest in carving out a place for himself in the New Empire—something else to be grateful for.

"About the Nationalists? Of course," Guy responded, turning away from the window.

"And?"

"And what?"

"And I would like to know what—" Saldur halted when he noticed another man in the room.

The office was comfortable in size, large enough to accommodate a desk, bookshelves, and a table with a chessboard between two soft chairs, where the stranger sat.

"Oh yes." Guy motioned to the man. "This is Merrick Marius. Merrick, meet Bishop—forgive me—*Regent* Saldur."

"So this is him," Saldur muttered, annoyed that the man did not rise.

He remained sitting comfortably, leaning back with casual indifference, staring in a manner too direct, too brazen. Merrick wore a thigh-length coat of dark red suede—an awful shade, Saldur thought—the color of dried blood. His hair was short, his face pale, and aside from his coat, his attire was simple and unadorned.

"Not very impressive, are you?" Saldur observed.

The man smiled at this. "Do you play chess, Your Grace?"

Saldur's eyebrows rose and he glanced at Guy. This was his man, after all. Guy had been the one who dug him up, unearthing him from the fetid streets, and praised his talents. The sentinel said nothing and showed no outward sign of outrage or discontent with his pet.

"I'm running an empire, young man," Saldur replied dismissively. "I don't have time for games."

"How strange," Merrick said. "I've never thought of chess as a game. To me it's really more of a religion. Every aspect of life, distilled into sixteen pieces within sixty-four black and white squares, which from a distance actually appear gray. Of course, there are more than a mere sixty-four squares. The smaller squares taken in even numbers form larger ones, creating a total of two hundred and four. Most people miss that. They see only the obvious. Few have the intelligence to look deeper to see the patterns hidden within patterns. That's part of the beauty of chess—it is much more than it first appears, more complicated, more complex. The world at your fingertips, so manageable, so defined. It has such simple rules, a near infinite number of possible paths, but only three outcomes.

"I've heard some clergy base sermons on the game, explaining the hierarchy of pieces and how they represent the classes of society. They correlate the rules of movement to the duties that each man performs in his service to Maribor. Have you ever done that, Your Grace?" Merrick asked, but he did not wait for an answer. "Amazing idea, isn't it?" He leaned over the board, his eyes searching the field of black and white.

"The bishop is an interesting piece." He plucked one off the board and held it in his hand, rolling the polished stone figure back and forth across his open palm. "It's not a very well-designed piece, not as pretty perhaps as, say, the knight. It's often overlooked, hiding in the corners, appearing so innocent, so disarming. But it's able to sweep the length of the board at sharp, unexpected angles, often with devastating results. I've always thought that bishops were underutilized through a lack of appreciation for their talents. I suppose I'm unusual in this respect, but then, I'm not the type of person to judge the value of a piece based on how it looks."

"You think you're a very clever fellow, don't you?" Saldur challenged.

"No, Your Grace," Merrick replied. "Clever is the man who makes a fortune selling dried-up cows, explaining how it saves the farmers the trouble of getting up every morning to milk them. I'm not clever—I'm a genius."

At this, Guy interjected, "Regent, at our last meeting I mentioned a solution to the Nationalist problem. He sits before you. Mr. Marius has everything worked out. He merely needs approval from the regents."

"And certain assurances of payment," Merrick added.

"You can't be serious." Saldur whirled on Guy. "The Nationalists are sweeping north on a rampage. They've taken

Kilnar. They're only miles from Ratibor. They will be marching on this palace by Wintertide. What I need are ideas, alternatives, solutions—not some irreverent popinjay!"

"You have some interesting ideas, Your Grace," Merrick told Saldur, his voice calm and casual, as if he had not heard a word. "I like your views on a central government. The benefits of standardizations in trade, laws, farming, even the widths of roads are excellent. It shows clarity of thought that I would not expect from an elderly church bishop."

"How do you know anything of my—"

Merrick raised his hand to halt the regent. "I should explain right away that how I obtain information is confidential and not open for discussion. The fact is, I know it. What's more—I like it. I can see the potential in this New Empire you're struggling to erect. It may well be exactly what the world needs to get beyond the petty warfare that weakens our nations and mires the common man in hopeless poverty. At present, however, this is still a dream. That is where I come in. I only wish you came to me earlier. I could have saved you that embarrassing and now burdensome problem of Her Eminence."

"That was the result of an unfortunate error on the part of my predecessor, the archbishop. Something he paid for with his life. I was the one who salvaged the situation."

"Yes, I know. Some idiot named Rufus was supposed to slay the mythical beast and thereby prove he was the fabled Heir of Novron, the descendant of the god Maribor himself. Only instead, Rufus was devoured and the beast laid waste to everything in the vicinity. Everything except a young girl, who somehow managed to slay it, and in front of a church deacon, no less—oops. But you're right. That wasn't your fault. You were the smart one with the brilliant idea to use her as a puppet—a girl so bereft from losing everything and everyone that she went mad. Your solution is to hide her in the depths of the palace and hope no one notices. In the meantime, you and Ethelred run a military campaign to take over all of Avryn, sending your best troops north to invade Melengar just as the Nationalists invade from the south. Brilliant. I must say, with things so well in hand it's a wonder I was contacted at all."

"I'm not amused," Saldur told him.

"Nor should you be, for at this moment King Alric of Melengar is setting into motion plans to form an alliance with the Nationalists, trapping you in a two-front war, and bringing Trent into the conflict on their side."

"You know this?"

"It is what I would do. And with the wealth of Delgos and the might of Trent, your fledgling empire, with its insane empress, will crumble as quickly as it rose."

"More impressed now?" Guy asked.

"And what would you have us do to stave off this impending cataclysm?"

Merrick smiled. "Pay me."

⁂

The grand, exalted empress Modina Novronian, ruler of Avryn and high priestess of the Church of Nyphron, sat sprawled on the floor, feeding her bowl of soup to Red, who expressed his gratitude by drooling on her dress. He rested his head on her lap and slapped his tail against the stone, his tongue sliding lazily in and out. The empress curled up beside the dog and laid her head on the animal's side. Amilia smiled. She was encouraged by seeing Modina interact with something, anything.

"Get that disgusting animal out of here and get her off the floor!"

Amilia jumped and looked up, horrified. Regent Saldur

entered the kitchen with Edith Mon, wearing a sinister smile. Amilia could not move. Several scullery maids rushed to the empress's side and gently pulled her to her feet.

"The very idea." He continued to shout as the maids busied themselves with smoothing out Modina's dress. "You," the regent growled, pointing at Amilia, "this is your doing. I should have known. What was I expecting when I put a common street urchin in charge of... of..." He trailed off, looking at Modina with an exasperated expression. "At least your predecessors didn't have her groveling with animals!"

"Your Grace, Amilia was—" Ibis Thinly began.

"Shut up, you oaf!" Saldur snapped at the stocky cook, and then returned his attention to Amilia. "Your service to the empress has ended, as well as your employment at this palace."

Saldur motioned to the empress's guard and then said, "Take her out of my sight."

The guard approached Amilia, unable to meet her eyes.

Amilia breathed in short, stifled gasps and realized she was trembling as the soldier approached. Not normally given to crying, Amilia could not help it, and tears began streaming down her cheeks.

"No," Modina said.

Spoken with no force, barely above a whisper, the single word cast a spell on the room. One of the cooking staff dropped a metal pot, which rang loudly on the stone floor. They all stared. The regent turned in surprise and then began to circle the empress, studying her with interest. The girl had a focused, challenging look as she glared at Saldur. The regent glanced from Amilia to Modina several times. He cocked his head from side to side, as if trying to work out a puzzle. The guard stood by awkwardly.

At length, Saldur put him at ease. "As the empress commands," Saldur said without taking his eyes off Modina. "It seems that I may have been a bit premature in my assessment of..." Saldur glanced at Amilia, annoyed. "What's your name?"

"A-Amilia."

He nodded as if approving the correct answer. "Your techniques are unusual, but certainly one can't argue with results."

Saldur looked back at Modina as she stood within the circle of maids, who parted at his approach. "She does look better, doesn't she? Color's improved. There's"—he motioned toward her face—"a fullness to her cheeks." He was nodding. He crossed his arms and with a final nod of approval said, "Very well, you can keep the position, as it seems to please Her Eminence."

The regent turned and headed out of the scullery. He paused at the doorway to look over his shoulder, saying, "You know, I was really starting to believe she was mute."

Chapter 7

The Jewel

Arista had always thought of herself as an experienced equestrian. Most ladies had never even sat in a saddle, but she had ridden since childhood. The nobles mocked, and her father scolded, but nothing could dissuade her. She loved the freedom of the wind in her hair and her heart pounding with the beat of the hooves. Before setting out, she had looked forward to impressing the thieves with her vast knowledge of horsemanship. She knew they would be awed by her skill.

She was wrong.

In Sheridan, Royce had found her a spirited bay mare to replace her exquisite palfrey. Since setting out, he had forced them over rough ground, fording streams, jumping logs, and dodging low branches—often at a trot. Clutching white-knuckled to the saddle, she had used all her skills and strength just to remain on the horse's back. Gone were her illusions of being praised as a skilled rider, and all that remained was the hope of making it through the day without the humiliation—not to mention the physical pain—of falling.

They rode south after leaving the university, following trails only Royce could find. Before dawn, they crossed the narrow headwaters of the Galewyr and proceeded up the embankment on the far side. Briars and thickets lashed at them. Unseen dips caught the horses by surprise, and Arista cried out once when her mount made an unexpected lunge across a washed-out gap. Their silence added to her humiliation. If she had been a man, they would have commented.

They climbed steadily, reaching such a steep angle that their mounts panted for air in loud snorts and on occasion uttered deep grunts as they struggled to scramble up the dewy slope. At last, they crested the hill, and Arista found herself greeting a chilly dawn atop the windswept Senon Uplands.

The Senon was a high, barren plateau of exposed rock and scrub bushes with expansive views on all sides. The horses' hooves clacked loudly on the barefaced granite until Royce brought them to a stop. His cloak fluttered with the morning breeze. To the east, the sunrise peered at them over the mist-covered forests of Dunmore. From this height, the vast wood looked like a hazy blue lake as it fell away below them, racing toward the dazzling sun. Arista knew that beyond it lay the Nidwalden River, the Parthaloren Falls, and the tower of Avempartha. Royce stared east for several minutes, and she wondered if his elven eyes could see that tiny pinnacle of his people in the distance.

In front of them and to the southwest lay the Warric province of Chadwick. Like everything else west of the ridge, it remained submerged in darkness. Down in the deep rolling valley, the predawn sky would only now be separating from the dark horizon. It would have appeared peaceful, a world tucked in bed before the first cock's crow, except for the hundreds of lights flickering like tiny fireflies.

"Breckton's camp," Hadrian said. "The Northern Imperial Army is not making very good time, it seems."

"We'll descend before Amber Heights and rejoin the road

well past Breckton," Royce explained. "How long do you figure before they reach Colnora?"

Hadrian rubbed the growing stubble of his beard. "Another three, maybe four, days. An army that size moves at a snail's pace, and I'm guessing Breckton isn't pleased with his orders. He's likely dragging his feet, hoping they'll be rescinded."

"You sound as if you know him," Arista said.

"I never met the man, but I fought under his father's banner. I've also fought against him, when I served in the ranks of King Armand's army in Alburn."

"How many armies have you served in?"

Hadrian shrugged. "Too many."

They pushed on, traversing the crest into the face of a fierce wind, which tugged at her clothes and caused her eyes to water. Arista kept her head down and watched her horse's hooves pick a path across the cracked slabs of lichen-covered rock. She clutched her cloak tight about her neck as the damp of the previous day's rain and sweat conspired with the wind to make her shiver. When they plunged back into the trees, the slow descent began. Once more the animals struggled. This time Arista bent backward, nearly to her horse's flanks, to keep her balance.

Although it was mercifully cooler than the day before, the pace was faster and more challenging. Finally, several hours after midday, they stopped on the bank of a small stream, where the horses gorged themselves on cool water and river grass. Royce and Hadrian grabbed packs and gathered wood. Exhausted, Arista as much fell as sat down. Her legs and backside ached. There were insects and twigs in her hair and a dusting of dirt covering her gown. Her eyes stared at nothing, losing their focus as her mind stalled, numb from fatigue.

What have I gotten myself into? Am I up to this?

They were below the Galewyr, in imperial territory. She had thrown herself into the fire, perhaps foolishly. Alric would be furious when he found her missing, and she could just imagine what Ecton would say. If they caught her— She stopped herself.

This is not helping.

She turned her attention to her escorts.

As during the hours on horseback, Royce and Hadrian remained quiet. Hadrian unsaddled the horses and gave them a light brushing while Royce set up a small cook fire. Watching the two of them was entertaining. Without a word, they would toss tools and bags back and forth. Hadrian blindly threw a hatchet over his shoulder and Royce caught it just in time to begin breaking up branches for the fire. Just as Royce finished the fire, Hadrian had a pot of water ready to place on it. For Arista, who had lived her life in public, among squabbling nobles and chattering castle staff, such silence was strange.

Hadrian chopped carrots and dropped them into the dented, blackened pot on the coals. "Are you ready to eat the best meal you've ever had, Highness?"

She wanted to laugh but did not have the strength. Instead, she said, "There are three chefs and eighteen cooks back at Essendon Castle that would take exception to that remark. They spend their whole lives perfecting elaborate dishes. You would be amazed at the feasts I've attended, filled with everything from exotic spices to ice sculptures. I highly doubt you'll be able to surpass them."

Hadrian smirked. "That might be," he replied, struggling to cut chunks of dry brine-encrusted pork into bite-sized cubes, "but I guarantee this meal will put them all to shame."

Arista removed the pearl-handled hairbrush from a pouch that hung at her side, and she tried in vain to untangle her hair. Eventually giving up, she sat and watched Hadrian drop wretched-looking meat into the bubbling pot. Ash and bits of twigs thrown up by the crackling fire landed in the mix.

"Master chef, debris is getting in your pot."

Hadrian grinned. "Always happens. Can't help it. Just be careful not to bite down too hard on anything or you might crack a tooth."

"Wonderful," she told him, then turned her attention to Royce, who was busy checking the horses' hooves. "We've come a long way today, haven't we? I don't think I've ever traveled so far so quickly. You keep a cruel pace."

"That first part was over rough ground," Royce mentioned. "We'll cover a lot more miles after we eat."

"After we eat?" Arista felt her heart sink. "We aren't stopping for the day?"

Royce glanced up at the sky. "It's hours until nightfall."

They mean for me to get back into the saddle?

She did not know if she could stand, much less ride. Virtually every muscle in her body was in pain. They could entertain any thoughts they wished, but she would not travel any farther that day. There was no reason to move this fast, or over such rough ground. Why Royce was taking such a difficult course, she did not understand.

She watched as Hadrian dished the disgusting soup he had concocted into a tin cup and held it out to her. There was an oily film across the top, through which green meat bobbed, everything seasoned with bits of dirt and tree bark. Most assuredly, it was the worst thing anyone had ever presented her to eat. Arista held the hot cup between her hands, grimacing and wishing she had eaten more of the meat pie back at Sheridan.

"Is this a...stew?" she asked.

Royce laughed quietly. "He likes to call it that."

"It's a dish I learned from Thrace," Hadrian explained with a reminiscent look on his face. "She's a much better cook than I am. She did this thing with the meat that— Well, anyway, no, it's not stew. It's really just boiled salt pork and vegetables. You don't get a broth, but it takes away the rancid taste of the salt and softens the meat. And it's hot. Trust me, you're going to love it."

Arista closed her eyes and lifted the cup to her lips. The steamy smell was wonderful. Before she realized it, she had devoured the entire thing, eating so quickly she burned her tongue. A moment later, she was scraping the bottom with a bit of hard bread. She looked for more and was disappointed to see Hadrian already cleaning the pot. Lying in the grass, she let out a sigh as the warmth of the meal coursed through her body.

"So much for ice sculptures." Hadrian chuckled.

Despite her earlier reluctance, she found new strength after eating. The next leg of the trip was over level ground, along the relative ease of a deer trail. Royce drove them as fast as the terrain allowed, never pausing or consulting a map.

After many hours, Arista had no idea where they were, nor did she care. The food faded into memory and she found herself once more near collapse. She rode bent over, resting on the horse's neck and drifting in and out of sleep. She could not discern between dream and reality and would wake in a panic, certain she was falling. Finally, they stopped.

Everything was dark and cold. The ground was wet and she stood shivering once more. Her guides went back into their silent actions. This time, to Arista's immense disappointment, no fire was made, and instead of a hot meal, they handed her strips of smoked meat, raw carrots, an onion quarter, and a triangle of hard, dry bread. She sat on the wet grass, feeling the moisture soak into her skirt and dampen her legs as she devoured the meal without a thought.

"Shouldn't we get a shelter up?" she asked hopefully.

Royce looked up at the stars. "It looks clear."

"But..." She was shocked when he spread out a cloth on the grass.

They mean to sleep right here—on the ground without even a tent!

Arista had three handmaids who dressed and undressed her daily. They bathed her and brushed her hair. Servants fluffed pillows and brought warm milk at bedtime. They tended the fireplace in shifts, quietly adding logs throughout the night. Sleeping in her carriage had been a hardship, sleeping on that ghastly cot in the dorm a torment—this was insane. Even peasants had hovels.

She wrapped her cloak tight against the night's chill.

Will I even get a blanket?

Tired beyond memory, she got on her hands and knees and feebly brushed a small pile of dead leaves together to act as a mattress. Lying down, she felt them crunch and crinkle beneath her.

"Hold on," Hadrian said, carrying over a bundle. He unrolled a canvas tarp. "I really need to make more of these. The pitch will keep the damp from soaking through." He handed her a blanket as well. "Oh, there's a nice little clearing just beyond those trees, just in case you need it."

Why in the world would I need a—

"Oh," she said, and managed a nod. Surely they would come upon a town soon. She could wait.

"Good night, Highness."

She did not reply as Hadrian went a few paces away and assembled his own bed from pine boughs. Without a tent, there was no choice but to sleep in her dress, which left her trapped in a tight corset. Arista spread out the tarp, removed her shoes, and lay down while pulling the thin blanket up to her chin. Though utterly miserable, she stubbornly refused to show it. After all, common women lived every day under similar conditions, so she could as well. The argument was noble but gave little comfort.

The instant she closed her eyes, she heard the faint buzzing. She was blinded by darkness, but the sound was unmistakable—a horde of mosquitoes descended. Feeling one on her cheek, she slapped at it and pulled the blanket over her head, exposing her feet. Curling into a ball, she buried herself under the thin wool shield. Her tight corset made breathing a challenge and the musty smell of the blanket, long steeped in horse sweat, nauseated her. Arista's frustration overflowed and tears slipped from her tightly squeezed eyes.

What was I thinking coming out here? I can't do this. Oh dear Maribor, what a fool I am. I always think I can do anything. I thought I could ride a horse—what a joke. I thought I was brave—look at me. I think I know better than anyone—I'm an idiot!

What a disappointment she was to those who loved her. She should have listened to her father and served the kingdom by marrying a powerful prince. Now that she was tarnished with the stain of witchery, no one would have her. Alric had stuck his neck out and given her a chance to be an ambassador. Her failure had doomed the kingdom. Now this trip—this horrible trip was just one more mistake, one more colossal error.

I'll go home tomorrow. I'll ask Royce to take me back to Medford and I'll formally resign as ambassador. I'll stay in my tower and rot until the empire takes me to the gallows.

Tears ran down her cheeks as she lay smothered by more than just the blanket until—mercifully in the cold, unforgiving night—she fell asleep.

❧

The songs of birds woke her.

Arista opened her eyes to sunlight cascading through the green canopy of leafy trees. Butterflies danced in brilliant shafts of golden light. The beams revealed a tranquil pond so placid it appeared as if a patch of sky had fallen. A delicate white mist hovered over the pool's mirrored surface like a scene from a fairy story. Circled by sun-dappled trees, cattails, and flowers, the pool was perfect—the most beautiful thing she had ever seen.

Where'd that come from?

Royce and Hadrian still slept under rumpled blankets, leaving her alone with the vision. She got up quietly, fearful of shattering the fragile beauty. Walking barefoot to the water's edge, she caught the warmth of the sun, melting the night's chill. She stretched, feeling the unexpected pride in the ache of a well-worked muscle. Crouching, Arista scooped a handful of water and gently rinsed away the stiff tears of the night before. In the middle of the pond, a fish jumped. She saw it only briefly as it flashed silver, then disappeared with a *plop!* Another followed and, delighted by the display, Arista stared in anticipation for the next leap, grinning like a child at a puppet show.

The mist burned away before sounds from the camp caught her attention, and Arista walked over to find the clearing Hadrian had mentioned. She returned to camp, brushed out her hair, and ate the cold pork breakfast waiting for her. When finished, she folded the blankets and rolled up the tarps, then stowed the food and refilled the water pouches. Arista mounted her mare, deciding at that moment to name her Mystic. Only after Royce had led them out of the little glade did she realize that no one had spoken a single word all morning.

They reached the road almost immediately, which explained the lack of a fire the night before and the unusual way Royce and Hadrian were dressed—in doublets and hose. Hadrian's swords were also conspicuously missing, stowed somewhere out of sight. How Royce had known the road was nearby baffled her. As they traveled with the warm sun overhead and the birds singing in the trees, Arista could scarcely understand what had troubled her the night before. She was still sore but felt a satisfaction in the dull pain that owed nothing to being a princess.

They had not gone far when Royce brought Mouse to a stop. A troop of imperial soldiers came down the road escorting a line of four large grain wagons—tall, solid-sided boxes with flat bottoms. Riders immediately rode forward, bringing a cloud of dust in their wake. An intimidating officer in bright armor failed to give his name but demanded theirs, as well as their destination and reason for traveling. Soldiers of his vanguard swept around behind the three with spears at the ready, horses puffing and snorting.

"This is Mr. Everton of Windham Village and his wife, and I am his servant," Royce explained quickly as he politely dismounted and bowed. His tone and inflections were formal and excessive, his voice nasal and high-pitched. Arista was amazed by how much like her fussy day steward he sounded. "Mr. Everton was—I mean, is—a respected merchant. We are on our way to Colnora, where Mrs. Everton has a brother whom they hope will provide temporary…er, I mean…they will be visiting."

Before they had left The Rose and Thorn, Royce had coached Arista on this story and the part she might have to play. In the safety of the Medford tavern, it had seemed like a plausible tale. But now that the moment had come and soldiers surrounded her, she doubted its chances of success. Her palms began to sweat and her stomach churned. Royce continued to play his part masterfully, supplying answers in his nonthreatening effeminate voice. The responses were specific-sounding, but vague on crucial details.

"It's *your* brother in Colnora?" The officer confronted Arista, his tenor harsh. No one had ever spoken to her in such a tone. Even when Braga had threatened her life, he had been more polite than this. She struggled to conceal her emotion.

"Yes," she said simply. Arista was remembering Royce's instructions to keep her answers as short as possible and her face blank. She was certain the soldiers could hear the pounding of her heart.

"His name?"

"Vincent Stapleton," she answered quickly and confidently, knowing the officer would be looking for hesitation.

"Where does he live?"

"Bridge Street, not far from the Hill District," she replied. This was a carefully rehearsed line. It would be typical for the wife of a prominent merchant to boast about how near the affluent section of the city her family lived.

Hadrian now played his part.

"Look here, I've had quite enough of you, and your imperial army. The truth of the matter is my estate has been overrun, used to quarter a bunch of brigands like you who I'm sure will destroy my furniture and soil the carpets. I have some questions of my own. Like when will I get my home back?" he bellowed angrily. "Is this the kind of thing a merchant can expect from the empress? King Ethelred never treated us like this! Who's going to pay for damages?"

To Arista's great relief, the officer changed his demeanor. Just as they had hoped, he avoided getting involved in complaints from evicted patrons and waved them on their way.

As the wagons passed, she was revolted by the sight visible

through the bars on the rear gates. The wagons did not hold captured soldiers, but elves. Covered in filth, they were packed so tightly they were forced to stand, jostling into each other as the wagon dipped and bounced over the rutted road. There were females and children alongside the males, all slick with sweat from the heat. Arista heard muffled cries as the wagons crawled by at a turtle's pace. Some reached through the bars, pleading for water and mercy. Arista was so sickened at the sight she forgot her fear, which only a moment before had consumed her. Then a sudden realization struck her—she looked for Royce.

He stood a few feet away on the roadside, holding Mouse's bridle. Hadrian was at his side, firmly gripping Royce's arm and whispering in his ear. Arista could not hear what he said, but guessed at the conversation. A few tense moments passed, but then they turned and continued toward Colnora.

⁂

The street below drifted into shadow as night settled in. Carriages raced to their destinations, noisily bouncing along the cobblestone. Lamplighters made their rounds in zigzag patterns, moving from lamp to lamp. Lights flickered to life in windows of nearby buildings and silhouettes passed like ghosts behind curtains. Shopkeepers closed their doors and shutters while cart vendors covered their wares and harnessed horses as another day's work ended.

"How long do you think?" Hadrian asked. He and Royce had donned their usual garb and Hadrian once more wore his swords. While Arista was used to seeing them this way, their change in appearance and Royce's constant vigilance at the window put her on edge.

"Soon," Royce replied, not altering his concentration on the street.

They waited together in the small room at The Regal Fox Inn, the least expensive of the five hotels in the affluent Hill District. Once they had arrived, Royce had continued to pose as their servant by renting two rooms—one standard, the other small. He avoided inquiries about luggage and arrangements for dinner. The innkeeper had not pursued the matter.

When they were upstairs, Royce insisted they all remain in the standard room together. Arista noticed a pause after he said this, as if he expected an argument. This amused her, because the idea of sharing a comfortable room was infinitely better than any accommodations she had experienced so far. Still, she had to admit, if only to herself, that a week ago she would have been appalled by the notion.

Even the standard room was luxurious by most boardinghouse standards. The beds were made of packed feathers and covered in smooth, clean sheets, overstuffed pillows, and heavy quilts. There were a full-length mirror, a large dresser, a wardrobe, a small writing table and chair, and an adjoining room for the washbasin and chamber pot. The room was equipped with a fireplace and lamps, but Royce left them unlit and darkness filled the space. The only illumination was from the outside streetlamps, which cast an oblong checkerboard image on the floor.

Now that they were off the road and in a more familiar setting, the princess gave in to curiosity. "I don't understand. What are we doing here?"

"Waiting," Royce replied.

"For what?"

"We can't just ride into the Nationalists' camp. We need a go-between. Someone to set up a meeting," Hadrian said. He sat at the writing desk across the room from her. In the growing darkness, he was fading into a dim ghostly outline.

"I didn't see you send any messages. Did I miss something?"

"No, but the messages were delivered nonetheless," Royce mentioned.

"Royce is kind of a celebrity here," Hadrian told her. "When he comes to town—"

Royce coughed intentionally.

"Okay, maybe not a celebrity, but he's certainly well known. I'm sure talk started the moment he arrived."

"Then we wanted to be seen?"

"Yes," Royce replied. "Unfortunately, the Diamond wasn't the only one watching the gate. Someone's watching our window."

"And he's not a Black Diamond?" Hadrian asked.

"Too clumsy. Has about the same talent for delicate work as a draft horse. The Diamond would laugh if he applied."

"Black Diamond is the thieves' guild?" she asked.

They both nodded.

While supposedly a secret organization, the Diamond was nevertheless well known. Arista heard of it from time to time in court and at council meetings. They were always spoken about with disdain by haughty nobles, even though they often used their services. The black market was virtually controlled by the Diamond, who supplied practically any commodity for anyone willing to pay the price.

"Can he see you?"

"Not unless he's an elf."

Hadrian and Arista exchanged glances, wondering if he had meant it as a joke.

Hadrian joined Royce at the window and looked out. "The one near the lamppost with his hand on his hilt? The guy shifting his weight back and forth? He's an imperial soldier, a veteran of the Vanguard Scout Brigade," Hadrian said.

Royce looked at him, surprised.

The light from the street spilled across Hadrian's face as he grinned. "The way he's shifting his weight is a technique taught to soldiers to keep from going footsore. That short sword is standard issue for a lightly armed scout and the gauntlet on his sword hand is an idiosyncrasy of King Ethelred, who insists all his troops wear them. Since Ethelred is now part of the New Empire, the fellow below is an Imp."

"You weren't kidding about serving in a lot of armies, were you?" Arista asked.

Hadrian shrugged. "I was a mercenary. It's what I did. I served anywhere the pay was good." Hadrian took his seat back at the table. "I even commanded a few regiments. Got a medal once. But I would fight for one army only to find myself going against them a few years later. Killing old friends isn't fun. So I kept taking jobs farther away. Ended up deep in Calis fighting for Tenkin warlords." Hadrian shook his head. "Guess you could say that was my low point. You really know you've—"

Hadrian was interrupted by a knock. Without a word, Royce crossed the room, taking up position on one side of the door while Hadrian carefully opened it. Outside, a young boy stood dressed in the typical poor clothing of a waif.

"Evening, sirs. Your presence is requested in room twenty-three," he said cheerily, and then, touching his thumb to his brow, he walked away.

"Leave her here?" Hadrian asked Royce.

Royce shook his head. "She comes along."

"Must you speak about me as if I'm not in the room?" Arista asked, but only with feigned irritation. She sensed the seriousness of the situation from the look on Royce's face and was not about to interfere. She was behind enemy lines. If she was caught, it was not certain what would happen. If she tried to claim a diplomatic status, it was doubtful the New Empire would honor it. Ransoming Arista for Alric's compliance was not out of the question—nor was a public execution.

"We're just going to walk in?" Hadrian asked skeptically.

"Yes, we need their help, and when one goes begging, it's best to knock on the front door."

They lodged in room nineteen, so it was a short trip down the hall and around a corner to room twenty-three. It was conveniently isolated. There were no other doors off this hall, only a stair, which likely led to the street. Royce rapped twice, paused, then added three more.

The door opened.

"Come in, Duster."

The room was a larger, more luxurious suite with a chandelier brightly lighting the interior. No beds were visible as they entered a parlor. Against the far wall were two doors, which no doubt led to sleeping quarters. Dark green damask fabric adorned the walls, and carpet covered the entire floor except for the area around the marble fireplace. Four tall windows, each shrouded with thick velvet curtains, decorated the outside wall. Several ornate pieces of furniture lined the room. In the center stood a gaunt man with sunken cheeks and accusing eyes. Two more men stood slightly behind him, while another two waited near the door.

"Everyone, please take a seat," the thin man told them. He remained standing until they all had sat. "Duster, let me get right to the point. I made it clear on your last visit that you are not welcome here, didn't I?"

Royce was silent.

"I was unusually patient then, but seeing as how you've returned, perhaps politeness is not the proper tack to take with you. Personally, I hold you in the highest regard, but as First Officer, I simply cannot allow you to blatantly walk into this city after having been warned." He paused, but when no reaction came from Royce, he continued. "Hadrian and the princess are welcome to leave. Point of fact, I must insist the lady leave, as the death of a noblewoman would make things awkward. Shall I assume Hadrian will refuse?"

Hadrian glanced at Royce, who did not return his look, and then Hadrian shrugged. "I would hate to miss whatever show is about to start."

"In that case, Your Highness..." The man made a sweeping hand motion toward the door. "If you'll please return to your room."

"I'm staying," Arista said. It was only two words, but spoken with all the confidence of a princess accustomed to getting her way.

He narrowed his eyes at her.

"Shall I escort her, sir?" one of the men near the door offered with a menacing tone.

"Touch her and this meeting will end badly," Royce said barely above a whisper.

"Meeting?" The thin man laughed. "This is no meeting. This is retribution, and it'll most assuredly end very badly."

He looked back at Arista. "I've heard about you. I'm pleased to see the rumors are true."

Arista had no idea what he meant, but did not like a thug *knowing* about her. She was even more disturbed by his approval.

"Nevertheless, my men *will* escort you." He clapped his hands and the two doors to the adjoining rooms opened, as did the one behind them, leading to the hallway. Many well-armed men poured in.

"We're here to see the Jewel," Royce quietly said.

Immediately the thin man's expression changed. Arista watched as, in an instant, his face followed a path from confidence to confusion, then suspicion, and finally curiosity. He ran a bony hand through his thin blond hair. "What makes you think the Jewel will see you?"

"Because there's profit in it for him."

"The Jewel is already very wealthy."

"It's not that kind of profit. Tell me, Price, how long have you had the new gate guards? The ones in the imperial uniforms. For that matter, when did Colnora get a gate? How many others like them are roaming the city?" Royce sat back and folded his hands across his lap. "I should have been stopped the moment I entered Colnora, and under farmer Oslow's field over two hours ago. Why the delay? Why are there no watches posted on the Arch or Bernum Bridge? Are you really getting that sloppy, Price? Or are the Imps running the show?"

Now it was the thin man's turn to remain silent.

"The Diamond can't be happy with the New Empire flexing its muscle. You used to have full rein, and the Jewel his own fiefdom. But not anymore. Now he must share. The Diamond has been forced back into the shadows while the new landlord kicks up his heels in front of the fire in the house they built. Tell Cosmos I'm here to help with his little problem."

Price stared at Royce, and then his eyes drifted to Arista. He nodded and stood up. "You will, of course, remain here until I return."

"Why not?" Hadrian remarked, apparently undisturbed by the tension radiating in the room. "This is a whole lot better than our room. Are those walnuts over there?"

During the exchange and while Price was gone, Royce never moved. Four men who were the most menacing of those present watched him intently. There seemed to be a contest of wills going on, each waiting to see who would flinch first. Hadrian, in contrast, casually strode around the room, examining the various paintings and furnishings. He selected a chair with a padded footstool, put up his feet, and began eating from a bowl of fruits and nuts.

"This stuff is great," he said. "We didn't get anything like this in our room. Anyone else want some?" They ignored him. "Suit yourself." He popped another handful of walnuts into his mouth.

Finally, Price returned. He had been gone for quite a while, or perhaps it had just seemed that way to Arista as she had quietly waited. The Jewel had consented to the meeting.

A carriage waited for them in front of The Regal Fox. Arista was surprised when Royce and Hadrian surrendered their weapons before boarding. Price joined them in the carriage, while two of the guild members sat up top with the driver. They rolled south two blocks, then turned west and traveled farther up the hill, past the Tradesmen's Arch, toward the Langdon Bridge. Through the open window, Arista could hear the metal rims of the coach and the horses' hooves clattering on the cobblestone. Across from her the glare of tavern lights crawled across the face of Price, who sat eyeing her with a malevolent smile. The man was all limbs, with fingers that were too long and eyes sunk too deep.

"It would seem you're doing better these days, Duster," he said with his hands folded awkwardly in his lap, a jackal pretending to be civilized. "At least your clientele has improved." The Diamond's First Officer smiled a toothy grin and nodded at Arista. "Although rumor has it that Melengar might not be the best investment these days. No offense intended, Your Highness. The Diamond is as a whole—and I personally am—rooting for you, but as a businessman, one does have to face facts."

Arista presented him a pleasant smile. "The sun will rise tomorrow, Mr. Price. That is a fact. You have horrid breath and smell of horse manure. That is also a fact. Who will win this war, however, is still a matter of opinion, and I put no weight in yours."

Price raised his eyebrows.

"She's an ambassador and a woman," Hadrian told him. "You'd be cut less fencing with a Pickering, and stand a better chance of winning."

Price smiled and nodded.

Arista was unsure whether it was in approval or resentment; such was the face of thieves. "Who exactly are we going to see, or is that a secret?"

"Cosmos Sebastian DeLur, the wealthiest merchant in Avryn," Royce replied. "Son of Cornelius DeLur of Delgos, who's probably the richest man alive. Between the two of them, the DeLur family controls most of the commerce and lends money to kings and commoners alike. He runs the Black Diamond and goes by the moniker of the Jewel."

Price's hands twitched slightly.

As they reached the summit of the hill, the carriage turned into a long private brick road that ascended Bernum Heights, a sharply rising bluff that overlooked the river below. Protecting the palatial DeLur estate was a massive gate wider than three city streets, which opened at their approach. Elegantly dressed guards stood rigid while a stuffy administrative clerk with white gloves and a powdered wig marked their passing on a parchment. Then the carriage began its long serpentine ascent along a hedge- and lantern-lined lane. Unexpected breaks in the foliage revealed glimpses of an elegant garden with elaborate sculpted fountains. At the top of the bluff stood a magnificent white marble mansion. Three stories in height, it was adorned with an eighteen-pillar colonnade forming a half-moon entrance illuminated by a massive chandelier suspended at its center. This estate was built to impress, but what caught Arista's attention was the huge bronze fountain of three nude women pouring pitchers of water into a pool.

A pair of gold doors were opened by two more impeccably dressed servants. Another man, dressed in a long dark coat, led the way into the vestibule, filled with tapestries and more sculptures than Arista had ever seen in one place. They were led through an archway outside to an expansive patio. Ivy-covered lattices lined an open-air terrace decorated with a variety of unusual plants and two more fountains—once more of nude women, only these were much smaller and wrought of polished marble.

"Good evening, Your Highness, gentlemen. Welcome to my humble home."

Seated on a luxurious couch, a large man greeted them. He was not tall but of amazing girth. He looked to be in his early fifties and well on his way to going bald. He tied what little hair he had left with a black silk ribbon and let it fall in a tail down his back. His chubby face remained youthful, showing lines of age only at the corners of his eyes when he smiled, as he was doing now. He dressed in a silk robe and held a glass of wine, which threatened to spill as he motioned them over.

"Duster, how long has it been, my old friend? I can see now that I should have made you First Officer when I had the chance. It would have saved so much trouble for the both of us. Alas, but I couldn't see it then. I hope we can put all that unpleasantness behind us now."

"My business was settled the day Hoyte died," Royce replied. "Judging from our reception, I would say it was the Diamond that was having trouble putting the past behind them."

"Quite right, quite right." Cosmos chuckled. Arista determined he was the kind of man who laughed the way other people twitched, stammered, or bit their nails. "You won't let me get away with anything, will you? That's good. You keep me honest—well, as honest as a man in my profession can be." He chuckled again. "It's that pesky legend that keeps the guild on edge. You're quite the bogeyman. Not that Mr. Price here buys into any of that, you understand, but it's his responsibility to keep the organization running smoothly. Allowing you to stroll about town is like letting a man-eating tiger meander through a crowded tavern. As the tavern keeper, they expect me to maintain the peace."

Cosmos motioned toward Price with his goblet. "You knew Mr. Price only briefly when you were still with us, I think. A pity. You would like him if you met under different circumstances."

"Who said I didn't like him?"

Cosmos laughed. "You don't like anyone, Duster, with the exception of Hadrian and Miss DeLancy, of course. There are only those you put up with and those you don't. By the mere fact that I'm here, I can at least deduce I'm not on your short list."

"Short list?"

"I can't imagine your slate of targets stays full for very long."

"We both have lists. Names get added and names get erased all the time. It would appear Price added me to yours."

"Consider it erased, my friend. Now tell me, what can I get you to drink? Montemorcey? You always had a fondness for the best. I have a vintage stock in the cellar. I'll have a couple bottles brought up."

"That'd be fine," Royce replied.

Cosmos gave a slight glance to his steward, who bowed abruptly and left. "I hope you don't mind meeting in my little garden. I do so love the night air." Closing his eyes and tilting his head up, he took a deep breath. "I don't manage to get out nearly as often as I would like. Now please sit and tell me about this offer you bring."

They took seats opposite Cosmos on elaborate cushioned benches, the span between taken up by an ornate table whose legs were fashioned to look like powerful snakes, each different from the next, facing out with fanged mouths open. Behind them Arista could hear the gurgling of fountains and the late breeze shifting foliage. Below that was the deeper, menacing roar of the Bernum River, hidden from view by the balcony.

"It's more of a proposition, really," Royce replied. "The princess here has a problem you might be able to help with, and you have a problem she may be able to solve."

"Wonderful, wonderful. I like how this is starting. If you had said you were offering me the chance of a lifetime, I would have been doubtful, but arrangements of mutual benefit show you're being straightforward. I like that, but you were always blunt, weren't you, Duster? You could afford to lay your cards on the table, because you always had such excellent cards."

A servant with white gloves identical to those worn by the gate clerk arrived and silently poured the wine, then withdrew to a respectful distance. Cosmos waited politely for them each to take a taste.

"Montemorcey is one of the finest vineyards in existence, and my cellar has some of their very best."

Royce nodded his praise.

Hadrian sniffed the dark red liquid skeptically, then swallowed the contents in a single mouthful. "Not bad for old grape juice."

Cosmos laughed once more. "Not a wine drinker. I should have known. Wine is no potable for a warrior. Gibbons, bring Hadrian a pull from the Oak Cask and leave the head on it. That should be more to your liking. Now, Duster, tell me about our mutual problems?"

"Your problem is obvious. You don't like this New Empire crowding you."

"Indeed, I do not. They're everywhere and spreading. For each one you see in uniform, you can expect three more you don't. Tavern keepers and blacksmiths are secretly working for the Imperialists, passing information. It's impossible to run a proper guild as extensive and elaborate as the Black Diamond in such a restrictive environment. There is even evidence they have spies in the Diamond itself, which is most unsettling."

"I also happen to know that Degan Gaunt is your boy."

"Well, not mine, per se."

"Your father's, then. Gaunt is supported by Delgos, Tur Del Fur is the capital of Delgos, and your father is the ruler of Tur Del Fur."

Cosmos laughed again. "No, not the ruler. Delgos is a republic, remember. He's but one of a triumvirate of businessmen elected to lead the government."

"Ah-huh."

"You don't sound convinced."

"It doesn't matter. The DeLurs are backing Gaunt in the hopes of breaking the empire, so something that might help Gaunt would help you as well."

"True, true, and what are you bringing me?"

"An alliance with Melengar. The princess here is empowered to negotiate on behalf of her brother."

"Word has it Melengar is helpless and about to fall to Ballentyne's Northern Imperial Army."

"Word is mistaken. The empress recalled the northern army to deal with the Nationalists. We passed it near Fallon Mire. Only a token force remains to watch the Galewyr River. The army moves slowly but it'll reach Aquesta before Gaunt does. That will tip the scales in favor of the empire."

"What are you suggesting?"

Royce looked at Arista, indicating that she should speak now.

Arista set down her glass and gathered her thoughts as best she could. She was still befuddled from the day's ride and now the wine on an empty stomach caused her head to fog. She took a short breath and focused.

"Melengar still has a defensive force," the princess began. "If we use it to attack across the river and break into Chadwick, there would be nothing to stop us from sweeping across into Glouston. Once there, Marquis Lanaklin could raise an army from his loyal subjects and together we could march on Colnora. We can catch the empire in a vise with Melengar pushing from the north and the Nationalists from the south. The empire would have to either recommit the northern army, leaving the capital to Gaunt, or let us sweep across northern Warric unopposed."

Cosmos said nothing, but there was a smile on his face. He took a drink of his wine and sat back to consider their words.

"All we need you to do"—Royce spoke again—"is to set up a meeting between Gaunt and the princess."

"Once a formal agreement is struck between the Nationalists and Melengar," Arista explained, "I can take that to Trent. With the Nationalists on Aquesta's doorstep, and my brother ravaging northern Warric, Trent will be more than happy to join us. And with their help, the New Empire will be swept back into history, where it belongs."

"You paint a lovely picture, Your Highness," Cosmos said. "But is it possible for Melengar to break out of Medford? Will Lanaklin be able to raise a force quickly enough to fend off any counterattack the empire sends? I suspect you would say yes to both, but without the conviction that comes from knowing. Fortunately, these are not my concerns so much as they're yours. I'll contact Gaunt's people and arrange a meeting. It'll take a few days, however, and in the meantime it's not safe for you to stay in Colnora."

"What do you mean?" Royce asked.

"As I said, I fear it's possible the guild has been compromised. Mr. Price tells me imperial scouts were on hand when you passed through the gate, so it would only be wishful thinking to suppose your visit here was not observed. Given the situation, it'll not take a genius to determine what's happening. The next logical step will be to eliminate the threat. And, Duster, you're not the only Diamond alumnus passing through Warric."

Royce's eyes narrowed as he stared at Cosmos and studied the fat man carefully. Cosmos said nothing more on the subject, and strangely, Royce did not inquire further.

"We'll leave immediately," Royce said abruptly. "We'll head south into Rhenydd, which will carry us closer to Gaunt. I'll expect you to contact us with the meeting's place and time in three days. If by the morning of the fourth day we don't hear from you, we'll find our own way to Gaunt."

"If you don't hear from me by then, things will be very bad indeed," Cosmos assured them. "Gibbons, see that they have whatever is needed for travel. Price, arrange for them to slip out of town unnoticed, and get that message to Gaunt's people. Will you need to send a message back to Medford?" Cosmos asked the princess.

She hesitated briefly. "Not until I've reached an agreement with Gaunt. Alric knows the tentative plan and has already begun preparing the invasion."

"Excellent," Cosmos said, standing up and draining his glass. "What a pleasure it is to work with professionals. Good luck to all of you and may fortune smile upon us. Just remember to watch your back, Duster. Some ghosts never die."

"Your horses and gear will be taken to Finlin's windmill by morning," Price told them as he rapidly led them out through the rear of the patio. His long gangly legs gave him the appearance of a wayward scarecrow fleeing across a field. Noticing Arista had trouble keeping up, he paused for her to catch her breath. "However, you three will be leaving by boat down the Bernum tonight."

"There'll be a watch on the Langdon and the South Bridge," Royce reminded him.

"Armed with crossbows and hot pitch, I imagine," Price replied, grinning. His face looked even more skull-like in the darkness. "But no worries, arrangements have been made."

The Bernum started as a series of tiny creeks that cascaded from Amber Heights and the Senon Uplands. They converged, creating a swift-flowing river that cut through a limestone canyon, forming a deep gorge. Eventually it spilled over Amber Falls. The drop took the fight out of the water, and from there on the river flowed calmly through the remaining ravine that divided the city. This put Colnora at the navigable headwater of the Bernum—the last stop for goods coming up the river, and a gateway for anyone traveling to Dagastan Bay.

After Arista had regained her breath, Price resumed rushing them along at a storm's pace. They ducked under a narrow ivy-covered archway and passed through a wooden gate, which brought them to the rear of the estate. A short stone wall, only a little above waist high, guarded the drop to the river gorge. Looking down, she could see only darkness, but across the expanse she could make out points of light and the silhouette of buildings. Price directed them to an opening and the start of a long wooden staircase.

"Our neighbor, Bocant, the pork mogul, has his six-oxen hoist," Price said, motioning to the next mansion over. Arista could just make out a series of cables and pulleys connected to a large metal box. Two lanterns, one hung at the top and another at the bottom, revealed the extent of the drop, which appeared to be more than a hundred feet. "But we have to make do with our more traditional, albeit more dangerous, route. Try not to fall. The steps are steep and it's a long way down."

The stairs were indeed frightening—a plummeting zigzag of planks and weathered beams bolted to the cliff's face. It looked like a diabolical puzzle of wood and rusting metal, which quaked and groaned the moment they stepped on it. Arista was certain she felt it sway. Memories of a tower collapsing while she clutched on to Royce flooded back to her. Taking a deep breath, she gripped the handrail with a sweaty palm and descended, sandwiched between Royce and Hadrian.

A narrow dock sat at the bottom and a shallow-draft rowboat banged dully against it with the river's swells. A lantern mounted on the bow illuminated the area with a yellow flicker.

"Put that damn light out, you fools!" Price snapped at the two men readying the craft.

A quick hand snuffed out the lantern and Arista's eyes adjusted to the moonlight. From previous trips to Colnora, she knew that the river was as congested as Main Street on Hospitality Row during the day, but in the dark it lay empty, the vast array of watercraft bobbing at various piers.

When the last of the supplies were aboard, Price returned their weapons. Hadrian strapped his on and Royce's white-bladed dagger disappeared into the folds of his cloak. "In you go," Price told them, putting one foot on the gunwale to steady the boat. A stocky, shirtless boatman stood in the center of the skiff and directed them to their seats.

"Which one of ya might be handy with a tiller?" he asked.

"Etcher," Price said, "why don't you take the tiller?"

"I'm no good with a boat," the wiry youth with a thin mustache and goatee replied as he adjusted the lay of the gear.

"I'll take the rudder," Hadrian said.

"And grateful I am to you, sir," the boatman greeted him cheerily. "Name's Wally... You shouldn't need to use it much. I can steer fine with just the oars, but in the current it's sometimes best not ta paddle a'tall. All ya needs to do is keep her in the center of the river."

Hadrian nodded. "I can do that."

"But of course you can, sir."

Royce held Arista's hand as she stepped aboard and found a seat beside Hadrian on a shelf of worn planking. Royce followed her and took up position near the bow next to Etcher.

"When did you order the supplies brought down?" Royce asked Price, who still stood with his foot on the rail.

"Before returning to pick you up at The Regal Fox. I like to stay ahead of things." He winked. "Duster, you might remember Etcher here from the Langdon Bridge last time you were in Colnora. Don't hold that against him. Etcher volunteered to get you safely to the mills when no one else cared for the idea. Now off you go." Price untied the bowline and shoved them out into the black water.

"Stow those lines, Mr. Etcher, sir," Wally said as he waited until they cleared the dock to lock the two long oars into place. With each stroke, the oars creaked quietly, and the skiff glided into the river's current.

The boatman sat backward as he pulled on the oars. Little effort was required as the current propelled them downstream. Wally pulled on one side or the other, correcting their course as needed. Occasionally he stroked both together, to keep them moving slightly faster than the water's flow.

"Blast," Wally cursed softly.

"What is it?" Hadrian asked.

"The lantern went out on the Bocant dock. I use it to steer by. Just my luck, any other night they leave it on. They use that hoisting contraption to unload boats. Sometimes the barges are late rounding the point, and in the darkness that lantern is their marker. They never know when the barges will arrive, so they usually just leave it on all night and—oh wait, it's back. Must have just blown out or something."

"Quiet down," Etcher whispered from the bow. "This is no pleasure cruise. You're being paid to row, not be a river guide."

Royce peered into their dark wake. "Is it normal for small boats to be on the river at night?"

"Not unless you're smuggling," Wally said in a coy tone that made Arista wonder if he had firsthand experience.

"If you don't keep your traps shut, someone will notice us," Etcher growled.

"Too late," Royce replied.

"What's that?"

"Behind us, there's at least one boat following."

Arista looked but could see nothing except the line the moon drew on the black surface of the water.

"You've got a fine pair of eyes, you do," Wally said.

"You're the one that saw them," Royce replied. "The light on the dock didn't go out. The other boat blocked it when they passed in your line of sight."

"How many?" Hadrian asked.

"Six, and they're in a wherry."

"They'll be able to catch us, then, won't they?" Arista questioned.

Hadrian nodded. "They race wherries down the Galewyr and here on the Bernum for prize money. No one races skiffs."

Despite this, Wally stroked noticeably harder, which, combined with the current, moved the skiff along at a brisk pace, raising a breeze in their faces.

"Langdon Bridge approaching," Etcher announced.

Arista saw it towering above them as they rushed toward it.

Massive pillars of stone blocks formed the arches supporting the bridge, whose broad span straddled the river eight stories above. She could barely make out the curved heads of the decorative swan-shaped streetlamps that lit the bridge, creating a line of lights against the starry sky.

"There are men up there," Royce said, "and Price wasn't kidding about them having crossbows."

Wally glanced over his shoulder and peered up at the bridge before regarding Royce curiously. "What are ya, part owl?"

"Stop paddling and shut up!" Etcher ordered, and Wally pulled his oars out of the water.

They floated silently, propelled by the river's current. In the swan lights, the men on the span soon became visible, even to Arista. A dark boat on a black river would be hard, but not impossible, to spot. The skiff started to rotate sideways as the current pushed the stern. A nod from Wally prompted Hadrian to compensate with the tiller and the boat straightened.

Light exploded into the night sky. A bright orange-and-yellow glow spilled onto the bridge from somewhere on the left bank. A warehouse was on fire. It burst into flame, spewing sparks skyward like a cyclone of fireflies. Silhouetted figures ran the length of the bridge and harsh shouts cut the stillness of the night.

"Now paddle!" Etcher ordered, and Wally put his back into it.

Arista used the opportunity to glance aft and now she also saw the wherry, illuminated by the fire from above. The approaching boat was a good fifteen feet in length and she guessed barely four feet across. Four men sat in two side-by-side pairs, each manning an oar. Besides the oarsmen, there were a man sitting in the stern and another at the bow with a grappling hook.

"I think they mean to board us," Arista whispered.

"No," Royce said. "They're waiting."

"For what?"

"I'm not sure, but I don't intend to find out. Give us as much distance as you can, Wally."

"Slide over, pal. Let me give you a hand," Hadrian told the boatman as he took up a seat beside him. "Arista, take the tiller."

The princess replaced Hadrian, grabbing hold of the wooden handle. She had no idea what to do with it and opted for keeping it centered. Hadrian rolled up his sleeves and, bracing his feet against the toggles, took one of the oars. Royce slipped off his cloak and boots and dropped them onto the floor of the boat.

"Don't do anything stupid," Etcher told him. "We've still got another bridge to clear."

"Just make sure you get them past the South Bridge and we'll be fine," Royce said. "Now, gentlemen, if you could put a little distance between us."

"On three," Wally announced, and they began stroking together, pulling hard and fast, so that the bow noticeably rose and a wake began to froth. Caught by surprise, Etcher stumbled backward and nearly fell.

"What the blazes are—" Etcher started when Royce leapt over the gunwale and disappeared. "Damn fool. What does he expect us to do, wait for him?"

"Don't worry about Royce," Hadrian replied as he and Wally stroked in unison. To Arista, the wherry did seem to drop farther back but perhaps that was only wishful thinking.

"South Bridge," Etcher whispered.

As they approached, Arista saw another fire blazing. This time it was a boat dock burning like well-aged kindling. The old South Bridge, which marked the city's boundary, was not nearly as high as the Langdon, and Arista could easily see the guards.

"They aren't going for it this time," Hadrian said. "They're staying at their posts."

"Quiet. We might slip by," Etcher whispered.

With oars held high, they all sat as still as statues. Arista found herself in command of the skiff as it floated along in the current. She quickly learned how the rudder affected the boat. The results felt backward to her. Pulling right made the bow swing left. Terrified of making a mistake, she concentrated on keeping the boat centered and straight. Up ahead, something odd was being lowered from the bridge. It looked like cobwebs or tree branches dangling. She was going to steer around it when she realized it stretched the entire span.

"They draped a net!" Etcher said a little too loudly.

Wally and Hadrian back paddled, but the river's current was the victor and the skiff flowed helplessly into the fishnet. The boat rotated, pinning itself sideways. Water frothed along the length, threatening to tip them.

"Shore your boat and don't move from it!" A shout echoed down from above.

A lantern lowered from the bridge revealed their struggles to free themselves from the mesh. Etcher, Wally, and Hadrian slashed at the netting with knives, but before they could clear it, two imperial soldiers descended and took up position on the bank. Each was armed with a crossbow.

"Stop now or we'll kill you where you stand," the nearest soldier ordered with a harsh, anxious voice. Hadrian nodded and the three dropped their knives.

Arista could not take her eyes off the crossbows. She knew those weapons. She had seen Essendon soldiers practicing with them in the yard. They pierced old helms placed on dummies, leaving huge holes through the heavy metal. These were close enough for her to see the sharp iron heads of the bolts—

the power to pierce armor held in check by a small trigger and pointed directly at them.

Wally and Hadrian maneuvered the boat to the bank and one by one they exited, Hadrian offering Arista his hand as she climbed out. They stood side by side, Arista and Hadrian in front, Wally and Etcher behind.

"Remove your weapons," one of the soldiers ordered, motioning toward Hadrian. Hadrian paused, his eyes shifting between the two bowmen, before slipping off his swords. One of the soldiers approached, while the other stayed back, maintaining a clear line of sight.

"What are your names?" the foremost soldier asked.

No one answered.

The lead guard took another step forward and intently studied Arista. "Well, well, well," he said. "Look what we have here, Jus. We done caught ourselves a fine fish, we have."

"Who is it?" Jus asked.

"This here is that Princess of Melengar, the one they say is a witch."

"How do you know?"

"I recognize her. I was in Medford the year she was on trial for killing her father."

"What's she doing here, ya think?"

"Don't know... What are you doing here?"

She said nothing, her eyes locked on the massive bolt heads. Made of heavy iron, the points looked sharp. Knight killers, Sir Ecton called them.

What will they do to me?

"The captain will find out," the soldier said. "I recognize these two as well." He motioned to Wally and Etcher. "I seen them around the city afore."

"Course you have." Wally spoke up. "I've piloted this river for years. We weren't doing nothin' wrong."

"If you've been on this river afore, then you knows we don't allow transports at night."

Wally did not say anything.

"I don't know that one, though. What's yer name?"

"Hadrian," he said, taking the opportunity to step forward as if to shake hands.

"Back! Back!" the guard shouted, bringing his bow to bear at Hadrian's chest. Hadrian immediately stopped. "Take one more step and I'll punch a hole clear through you!"

"So what's your plan?" Hadrian asked.

"You and your pals just sit tight. We sent a runner to fetch a patrol. We'll take you over to see the captain. He'll know what to do with the likes of you."

"I hope we don't have to wait long," Hadrian told them. "This damp night air isn't good. You could catch a cold. Looks like you have already. What do you think, Arista?"

"I ain't got no cold."

"Are you sure? Your eyes and nose look red. Arista, you agree with me, don't you?"

"What?" Arista said, still captivated by the crossbows. She could feel her heart hammering in her chest and barely heard Hadrian addressing her.

"I bet you two been coughing and sneezing all night, haven't you?" Hadrian continued. "Nothing worse than a summer cold. Right, Arista?"

Arista was dumbfounded by Hadrian's blathering and his obsession with the health of the two soldiers. She felt obligated to say something. "I—I suppose."

"Sneezing, that's the worst. I hate to *sneeze.*"

Arista gasped.

"Just shut up," the soldier ordered. Without taking his eyes off Hadrian, he called to Jus behind him. "See anyone coming yet?"

"Not yet," Jus replied. "All of them off dealing with that fire, I 'spect."

Arista had never tried this under pressure before. Closing her eyes, she fought to remember the concentration technique Esrahaddon had taught her. She took deep breaths, cleared her mind, and tried to calm herself. Arista focused on the sounds around her—the river lapping against the boat, the wind blowing through the trees, and the chirping of the frogs and crickets. Then slowly she blocked each out, one by one. Opening her eyes, she stared at the soldiers. She saw them in detail now, the three-day-old whiskers on their faces, their rumpled tabards, even the rusted links in their hauberks. Their eyes showed their nervous excitement and Arista thought she even caught the musky odor of their bodies. Breathing rhythmically, she focused on their noses as she began to hum, then mutter. Her voice slowly rose as if in song.

"I said no—" The soldier stopped suddenly, wrinkling his nose. His eyes began to water and he shook his head in irritation. "I said no—" he began again, and stopped once more, gasping for air.

At the same time, Jus was having similar problems, and the louder Arista's voice rose, the greater their struggle. Raising her hand, she moved her fingers as if writing in the air.

"I—said—I—I—"

Arista made a sharp clipping motion with her hand and both of them abruptly sneezed in unison.

In that instant, Hadrian lunged forward and broke the closest guard's leg with a single kick to his knee. He pulled the screaming guard in front of him just as the other fired. The crossbow bolt caught the soldier square in the chest, piercing the metal ringlets of his hauberk and staggering both of them backward. Letting the dead man fall, Hadrian picked up his bow as the other guard turned to flee. *Snap!* The bow launched the bolt. The impact made a deep resonating *thwack!* and drove the remaining guard to the ground, where he lay dead.

Hadrian dropped the bow. "Let's move!"

They jumped back in the skiff just as the wherry approached.

It came out of the darkness, its long pointed shape no longer slicing through the water. Instead, it drifted aimlessly, helpless to the whims of the current. As it approached, it became apparent why. The wherry was empty. Even the oars were gone. As the boat passed by, a dark figure crawled out of the water.

"Why have you stopped?" Royce admonished, wiping his wet hair away from his face. "I would have caught up." Spotting the bodies halted his need for explanation.

Hadrian pushed the boat into the river, leaping in at the last instant. From above, they could hear men's voices. They finished cutting loose the net and, once free, slipped clear of the bridge. The current, combined with Wally's and Hadrian's pulling hard on the oars, sent them flying downriver in the dark of night, leaving the city of Colnora behind them.

—

Chapter 8

Hintindar

Arista woke feeling disoriented and confused. She had been dreaming about riding in her carriage. She sat across from both Sauly and Esrahaddon. Only, in her dream, Esrahaddon had hands and Sauly was wearing his bishop's robes. They were trying to pour brandy from a flask into a cup and were discussing something—a heated argument, but she could not recall it.

A bright light hurt her eyes, and her back ached from sleeping on something hard. She blinked, squinted, and looked around. Her memory returned as she realized she was still in the skiff coasting down the Bernum River. Her left foot was asleep, and dragging it from under a bag started the sensation of pins and needles. The morning sun shone brightly. The limestone cliffs were gone, replaced by sloping farmlands. On either side of the river, lovely green fields swayed gently in the soft breeze. The tall spiked grass might have been wheat, although it could just as easily have been barley. Here the river was wider and moved slower. There was hardly any current, and Wally was back to rowing.

"Morning, milady," he greeted her.

"Morning," Hadrian said from his seat at the tiller.

"I guess I dozed off," she replied, pulling herself up and adjusting her gown. "Did anyone else get any sleep?"

"I'll sleep when I get downriver," Wally replied, hauling on the oars, rocking back, then sitting up again. The paddle blades dripped and plunged. "After I drop you fine folks off, I'll head down to Evlin, catch a nap and a meal, then try to pick up some travelers or freight to take back up. No sense fighting this current for nothing."

Arista looked toward Hadrian.

"Some," he told her. "Royce and I took turns."

Her hair was loose and falling in her face. Her blue satin ribbon had been lost somewhere during the night's ride from Sheridan. Since then, she had been using a bit of rawhide provided by Hadrian. Even that was missing now, and she poked about her hair and found the rawhide caught in a tangle. While she worked to free it, she said, "You should have woken me. I would have taken a shift at the tiller."

"We actually considered it when you started to snore."

"I don't snore!"

"I beg to differ," Hadrian chided while chewing.

She looked around the skiff as each of them, even Etcher, nodded. Her face flushed.

Hadrian chuckled. "Don't worry about it. You can't be held accountable for what you do in your sleep."

"Still," she said, "it's not very ladylike."

"Well, if that's all you're worried about, you can forget it," Hadrian informed her with a wicked smirk. "We lost all illusions of you being prissy back in Sheridan."

How much better it was when they were silent.

"That's a compliment," he added hastily.

"You don't have much luck with the ladies, do you, sir?" Wally asked, pausing briefly and letting the paddles hang out like wings, leaving a tiny trail of droplets on the smooth surface of the river. "I mean, with compliments like that, and all."

Hadrian frowned at him, then turned back to her with a concerned expression. "I really did mean it as a compliment. I've never met a lady who would—well, without complaining you've been—" He paused in frustration, then added, "That little trick you managed back there was really great."

Arista knew Hadrian only brought up the sneezing spell to try to smooth things over, but she had to admit a sense of pride that she had finally contributed something of value to their trip. "That was the first practical application of hand magic I've ever performed."

"I really wasn't sure you could do it," Hadrian said.

"Who would have thought such a silly thing would come in handy?"

"Travel with us long enough and you'll see we can find a use for just about anything." Hadrian extended his hand. "Cheese?" he asked. "It's really quite good."

Arista took the cheese and offered him a smile but was disappointed he did not see it. His eyes had moved to the riverbank, and her smile faded as she ate self-consciously.

Wally continued to paddle in even strokes and the world passed slowly by. They rounded bend after bend, skirting a fallen tree, then a sandy point. It took Arista nearly an hour with her brush to finally work all the knots out of her hair. She retied its length with the rawhide into a respectable ponytail. Eventually a gap opened in the river reeds to reveal a small sandy bank that showed signs of previous boat landings.

"Put in here," Etcher ordered, and Wally deftly spun the boat to land beneath the shadow of a massive willow tree. Etcher leapt out and tied the bowline. "This is our stop. Let's get the gear off."

"Not yet," Royce said. "You want to check the mill sails first?"

"Oh yeah." Etcher nodded, looking a little embarrassed and a tad irritated. "Wait here," he said before trotting up the grassy slope.

"Sails?" Hadrian asked.

"Just over this rise is the millwright Ethan Finlin's windmill," Royce explained. "Finlin is a member of the Diamond. His windmill is used to store smuggled goods and also serves as a signal that can be seen from the far hills. If the mill's sails are spinning, then all is clear. If furled, then there's trouble. The position of the locked sails indicates different things. If straight up and down, like a ship's mast, it means he needs help. If the sails are cockeyed, it means stay away. There are other signals as well, but I'm sure they've changed since I was a member."

"All clear," Etcher notified them as he strode back down the hill.

They each took a pack, waved goodbye to Wally, and climbed up the slope.

Finlin's mill was a tall weathered tower that sat high on the crest of a grassy knoll. The windmill's cap rotated and currently faced into the wind, which blew steadily from the northeast. Its giant sails of cloth-covered wooden frames rotated slowly, creaking as they turned the great mill's shaft. Around the windmill were several smaller buildings, storage sheds, and wagons. The place was quiet and absent of customers.

They found their horses, as well as an extra one for Etcher, along with their gear in a nearby barn. Finlin briefly stuck his nose out of the mill and waved. They waved back, and Royce had a short talk with Etcher as Hadrian saddled their animals and loaded the supplies. Arista threw her own saddle on her mare, which garnered a smile from Hadrian.

"Saddle your own horse often, do you?" he asked as she reached under the horse's belly for the cinch. The metal ring at the end of the wide band swung back and forth, making catching it a challenge without crawling under the animal.

"I'm a princess, not an invalid."

She caught the cinch and looped the leather strap through it, tying what she thought was a fine knot, exactly like the one she used to tie her hair.

"Can I make one minor suggestion?"

She looked up. "Of course."

"You need to tie it tighter and use a flat knot."

"That's two suggestions. Thanks, but I think it'll be fine."

He reached up and pulled on the saddle's horn. The saddle easily slid off and came to rest between the horse's legs.

"But it *was* tight."

"I'm sure it was." Hadrian pulled the saddle back up and undid the knot. "People think horses are stupid—dumb animals, they call them—but they're not. This one, for instance, just out-smarted the Princess of Melengar." He pulled the saddle off, folded the blanket over, and returned the saddle to the animal's back. "You see, horses don't like to have a saddle bound around their chest any more than I suspect you enjoy being trussed up in a corset. The looser, the better, they figure, because they don't really mind if you slide off." He looped the leather strap through the ring in the cinch and pulled it tight. "So what she's doing right now is holding her breath, expanding her chest and waiting for me to tie the saddle on. When she exhales, it'll be loose. Thing is, I know this. I also know she can't hold her breath forever." He waited with two hands on the strap, and the moment the mare exhaled, he pulled, gaining a full four inches. "See?"

She watched as he looped the strap across, then through and down, making a flat knot that laid comfortably against the horse's side. "Okay, I admit it. This is the first time I've saddled a horse," she confessed.

"And you're doing wonderfully," he mocked.

"You are aware I can have you imprisoned for life, right?"

Royce and Etcher entered the barn. The younger thief grabbed his horse and left without a word.

"Friendly sorts, those Diamonds are," Hadrian observed.

"Cosmos seemed hospitable," Arista pointed out.

"Yeah, but that's how you might expect a spider to talk to a fly as she wraps him up."

"What an interesting metaphor," Arista noted. "You could have a future in politics, Hadrian."

He glanced at Royce. "We never considered that as one of the options."

"I'm not sure how it differs from acting."

"He never likes my ideas," Hadrian told her, then turned his attention back to Royce. "Where to now?"

"Hintindar," Royce replied.

"Hintindar? Are you serious?"

"It's out of the way and a good place to disappear for a while. Problem?"

Hadrian narrowed his eyes. "You know darn well there's a problem."

"What's wrong?" Arista asked.

"I was born in Hintindar."

"I've already told Etcher that's where we'll wait for him," Royce said. "Nothing we can do about it now."

"But Hintindar is just a tiny manorial village—some farms and trade shops. There's no place to stay."

"Even better. After Colnora, lodging in a public house might not be too smart. There must be a few people there that still know you. I'm sure someone will lend a hand and put us up for a while. We need to go somewhere off the beaten track."

"You don't honestly think anyone is still following us. I know the empire would want to stop Arista from reaching Gaunt, but I doubt anybody recognized her in Colnora—at least no one still alive."

Royce did not answer.

"Royce?"

"I'm just playing it safe," he snapped.

"Royce? What did Cosmos mean back there about you not being the only ex-Diamond in Warric? What was that talk of ghosts all about?" Royce remained silent. Hadrian glared at him. "I came along as a favor to you, but if you're going to keep secrets..."

Royce relented. "It's probably nothing, but then again—Merrick could be after us."

Hadrian lost his look of irritation and replied with a simple, "Oh."

"Anyone going to tell me who Merrick is?" Arista asked. "Or why Hadrian doesn't want to go home?"

"I didn't leave under the best of circumstances," Hadrian answered, "and haven't been back in a long time."

"And Merrick?"

"Merrick Marius, also known as Cutter, was Royce's friend once. They were members of the Diamond together, but they..." He glanced at Royce. "Well, let's just say they had a falling out."

"So?"

Hadrian waited for Royce to speak and, when he did not, answered for him. "It's a long story, but the gist of the matter is that Merrick and Royce seriously don't get along." He paused, then added, "Merrick is an awful lot like Royce."

Arista continued to stare at Hadrian until the revelation dawned on her.

"Still, that doesn't mean Merrick is after us," Hadrian

went on. “It’s been a long time, right? Why would he bother with you now?”

“He’s working for the empire,” Royce said. “That’s what Cosmos meant. And if there’s an imperial mole in the Diamond, Merrick knows all about us by now. Even if there isn’t a spy, Merrick could still find out about us from the Diamond. There are plenty who think of him as a hero for sending me to Manzant. I’m the evil one in their eyes.”

“You were in Manzant?” Arista asked, stunned.

“It’s not something he likes to talk about.” Hadrian again answered for him. “So if Merrick is after us, what do we do?”

“What we always do,” Royce replied, “only better.”

❧

The village of Hintindar lay nestled in a small sheltered river valley surrounded by gentle hills. A patchwork of six cultivated fields, outlined by hedgerows and majestic stands of oak and ash, decorated the landscape in a crop mosaic. Horizontal lines of mounded green marked three of the fields with furrows, sown in strips, to hold the runoff. Animals grazed in the fourth field and the fifth was cut for hay. The last field lay fallow. Young women were in the fields, cutting flax and stuffing it in sacks thrown over their shoulders, while men weeded crops and threw up hay.

The center of the village clustered along the main road near a little river, a tributary of the Bernum. Wood, stone, and wattle-and-daub buildings with shake or grass-thatched roofs lined the road, beginning just past the wooden bridge and ending halfway up the hillside toward the manor house. Between them were a variety of shops. From several buildings smoke rose, the blackest of which came from the smithy. Their horses announced their arrival with a loud hollow *clop clip clop* as they crossed the bridge. Heads turned, each villager nudging the next, fingers pointing in their direction. Those they passed stopped what they were doing to follow, keeping a safe distance.

"Good afternoon," Hadrian offered, but no one replied. No one smiled.

Some whispered in the shelter of doorways. Mothers pulled children inside and men picked up pitchforks or axes.

"This is where *you* grew up?" Arista whispered to Hadrian. "Somehow it seems more like how I would imagine Royce's hometown to be."

This brought a look from Royce.

"They don't get too many travelers here," Hadrian explained.

"I can see why."

They passed the mill, where a great wooden wheel turned with the power of the river. The town also had a leatherworker's shop, a candlemaker, a weaver, and even a shoemaker. They were halfway up the road when they reached the brewer.

A heavyset matron with gray hair and a hooked nose worked outside beside a boiling vat next to a stand of large wooden casks. She watched their slow approach, then walked to the middle of the road, wiping her hands on a soiled rag.

"That'll be fer enough," she told them with a heavy south-province accent.

She wore a stained apron tied around her shapeless dress and a kerchief tied over her head. Her feet were bare and her face was covered in dirt and sweat.

"Who are ya and what's yer business here? And be quick afore the hue and cry is called and yer carried to the bailiff. We don't stand fer troublemakers here."

"Hue and cry?" Arista softly asked.

Hadrian looked over. "It's an alarm that everyone in the

village responds to. Not a pretty sight." His eyes narrowed as he studied the woman. Then he slowly dismounted.

The woman took a step back and grabbed hold of a mallet used to tap the kegs. "I said I'd call the hue and cry and I meant it!"

Hadrian handed his reins to Royce and walked over to her. "If I remember correctly, *you* were the biggest troublemaker in the village, Armigil, and in close to twenty years, it doesn't seem much has changed."

The woman looked surprised, then suspicious. "Haddy?" she said in disbelief. "That can't be, can it?"

Hadrian chuckled. "No one's called me Haddy in years."

"Dear Maribor, how you've grown, lad!" When the shock wore off, she set the mallet down and turned to the spectators now lining the road. "This here is Haddy Blackwater, the son of Danbury the smithy, come back home."

"How are you, Armigil?" Hadrian said with a broad smile, stepping forward to greet her.

She replied by making a fist and punching him hard in the jaw. She had put all her weight into it, and winced, shaking her hand in pain. "Oww! Damned if ya haven't got a hard bloody jaw!"

"Why did you hit me?" Hadrian held his chin, stunned.

"That's fer running out on yer father and leaving him to die alone. I've been waiting to do that fer nearly twenty years."

Hadrian licked blood from his lip and scowled.

"Oh, get over it, ya baby! An' ya better keep yer eyes out fer more round here. Danbury was a damn fine man and ya broke his heart the day ya left."

Hadrian continued to massage his jaw.

Armigil rolled her eyes. "Come here," she ordered, and grabbed hold of his face. Hadrian flinched as she examined him. "Yer fine, for Maribor's sake. Honestly, I thought yer father made ya tougher than that. If I had a sword in me hand, yer shoulders would have less of a burden to carry, and the wee ones would have a new ball to kick around, eh? Here, let me get ya a mug of ale. This batch came of age this morning. That'll take the sting out of a warm welcome, it will."

She walked to a large cask, filled a wooden cup with a dark amber draft, and handed it to him.

Hadrian looked at the drink dubiously. "How many times have you filtered this?"

"Three," she said unconvincingly.

"Has His Lordship's taster passed this?"

"Of course not, ya dern fool. I just told ya it got done fermenting this morning. Brewed it day afore yesterday, I did, a nice two days in the keg. Most of the sediment ought to have settled and it should have a nice kick by now."

"Just don't want to get you into trouble."

"I ain't selling it to ya, now am I? So drink it and shut up or I'll hit ya again for being daft."

"Haddy? Is it really you?" A thin man about Hadrian's age approached. He had shoulder-length blond hair and a soft doughy face. He was dressed in a worn gray tunic and a faded green cowl, his feet wrapped in cloth up to his knees. A light brown dust covered him as if he had been burrowing through a sand hill.

"Dunstan?"

The man nodded and the two embraced, clapping each other on the shoulders. Wherever Hadrian patted Dunstan, a puff of brown powder arose, leaving the two in a little cloud.

"You used to live here?" a little girl from the gathering crowd asked, and Hadrian nodded. This touched off a wave of conversations among those gathering in the street. More people rushed over and Hadrian was enveloped in their midst. Eventually he was able to get a word in and motioned toward Royce and Arista.

"Everyone, this is my friend Mr. Everton and his wife, Erma."

Arista and Royce exchanged glances.

"Vince, Erma, this is the village brew mistress, Armigil, and Dunstan here is the baker's son."

"Just the baker, Haddy. Dad's been dead five years now."

"Oh—sorry to hear that, Dun. I've nothing but fond memories of trying to steal bread from his ovens."

Dunstan looked at Royce. "Haddy and I were best friends when he lived here—until he disappeared," he said with a note of bitterness.

"Will I have to endure a swing from you too?" Hadrian feigned fear.

"You should, but I remember all too well the last time I fought you."

Hadrian grinned wickedly as Dunstan scowled back.

"If my foot hadn't slipped..." Dunstan began, and then the two broke into spontaneous laughter at a joke no one else appeared to understand.

"It's good to have you back, Haddy," he said sincerely. He watched Hadrian take a swallow of beer, and then to Armigil he said, "I don't think it fair that Haddy gets a free pint and I don't."

"Let me give ya a bloody lip and ya can have one too." She smiled at him.

"Break it up! Break it up!" bellowed a large muscular man making his way through the crowd. He had a bull neck, a full dark beard, and a balding head. "Back to work, all of ya!"

The crowd groaned in displeasure but quickly quieted down as two horsemen approached. They rode down the hill, coming from the manor at a trot.

"What's going on here?" the lead rider asked, reining his horse. He was a middle-aged man with weary eyes and a strong chin. He dressed in light tailored linens common to a favored servant and on his chest was an embroidered crest of crossed daggers in gold threading.

"Strangers, sir," the loud bull-necked man replied.

"They ain't strangers, sir." Armigil spoke up. "This here's Haddy Blackwater, son of the old village smith—come fer a visit."

"Thank you, Armigil," he said. "But I wasn't speaking to you. I was addressing the reeve." He looked down at the bearded man. "Well, Osgar, out with it."

The burly man shrugged his shoulders and stroked his beard, looking uncomfortable. "She might be right, sir. I haven't had a chance to ask, what with getting the villeins back to work and all."

"Very well, Osgar, see to it that they return to work, or I'll have you in stocks by nightfall."

"Yes, sir, right away, sir." He turned, bellowing at the villagers until they moved off. Only Armigil and Dunstan quietly remained behind.

"Are you the son of the old smithy?" the rider asked.

"I am," Hadrian replied. "And you are?"

"I'm His Lordship's bailiff. It's my duty to keep order in this village and I don't appreciate you disrupting the villeins' work."

"My apologies, sir." Hadrian nodded respectfully. "I didn't mean—"

"If you're the smithy's son, where have you been?" The other rider spoke this time. Much younger-looking, he was better dressed than the bailiff, wearing a tunic of velvet and linen. His legs were covered in opaque hose, and his feet in leather shoes with brass buckles. "Are you aware of the penalty for leaving the village without permission?"

"I'm the son of a freeman, not a villein," Hadrian declared. "And who are you?"

The rider sneered at Hadrian. "I'm the imperial envoy to this village, and you would be wise to watch the tone of your voice. Freemen can lose that privilege easily."

"Again, my apologies," Hadrian said. "I'm only here to visit my father's grave. He died while I was away."

The envoy's eyes scanned Royce and Arista, then settled on Hadrian, looking him over carefully. "Three swords?" he asked the bailiff. "In this time of war an able-bodied man like this should be in the army fighting for the empress. He's likely a deserter or a rogue. Arrest him, Siward, and take his associates in for questioning. If he hasn't committed any crimes, he will be properly pressed into the imperial army."

The bailiff looked at the envoy with annoyance. "I don't take my orders from you, Luret. You forget that all too frequently. If you have a problem, take it up with the steward. I'm certain he will speak to His Lordship the moment he returns from loyal service to the empire. In the meantime, I'll administer this village as best I can for my lord—not for you."

Luret jerked himself upright in indignation. "As imperial envoy, I am addressed as *Your Excellency*. And you should understand that my authority comes directly from the empress."

"I don't care if it comes from the good lord Maribor himself. Unless His Lordship, or the steward in his absence, orders me otherwise, I only have to put up with you. I don't have to take orders from you."

"We'll see about that." The envoy spun and spurred his horse back toward the manor, kicking up a cloud of dust.

The bailiff shook his head with irritation, waiting for the dust to settle.

"Don't worry," he told them. "The steward won't listen to him. Danbury Blackwater was a good man. If you're anything like him, you'll find me a friend. If not, you had best make your stay here as short as possible. Keep out of trouble. Don't interfere with the villeins' work, and stay away from Luret."

"Thank you, sir," Hadrian said.

The bailiff then looked around the village in irritation. "Armigil, where did the reeve get off to?"

"Went to the east field, I think, sir. There is a team he has working on drainage up that way."

The bailiff sighed. "I need him to get more men working on bringing in the hay. Rain's coming and it'll ruin what's been cut if he doesn't."

"I'll tell him, sir, if he comes back this way."

"Thank you, Armigil."

"Sir?" She tapped off a pint of beer and handed it up to him. "While you're here, sir?" He took one swallow, then poured the rest out and tossed her back the cup.

"A little weak," he said. "Set your price at two copper tenents a pint."

"But, sir! It's got good flavor. At least let me ask three."

He sighed. "Why must you always be so damn stubborn? Let it be three, but make them brimming pints. Mind you, if I hear one complaint, I'll fine you a silver and you can take your case to the Steward's Court."

"Thank you, sir," she said, smiling.

"Good day to you all." He nodded and trotted off toward the east.

They watched him go, and then Dunstan started chuckling. "A fine welcome home you've had so far—a belt in the mouth and threat of arrest."

"Actually, outside the fact that everything looks a lot smaller, not much has changed here," Hadrian observed. "Just some new faces, a few buildings, and, of course, the envoy."

"He's only been here a week," Dunstan said, "and I'm sure the bailiff and the steward will be happy when he leaves. He travels a circuit covering a number of villages in the area and has been showing up here every couple of months since the New Empire annexed Rhenydd. No one likes him, for obvious reasons. He's yet to meet Lord Baldwin face to face. Most of us think Baldwin purposely avoids being here when the envoy comes. So Luret's list of complaints keeps getting longer and longer and the steward just keeps writing them down.

"So are you really here just to see your father's grave? I thought you were coming back to stay."

"Sorry, Dun, but we're just passing through."

"In that case, we had best make the most of it. What say you, Armigil? Roll a keg into my kitchen and I'll supply the bread and stools for toasts to Danbury and a proper welcome for Haddy?"

"He don't deserve it. But I think I have a keg round here that is bound to go bad if'n I don't get rid of it."

"Hobbie!" Dunstan shouted up the street to a young man at the livery. "Can you find a place for these horses?"

Dunstan and Hadrian helped Armigil roll a small barrel to the bakery. As they did, Royce and Arista walked their animals over to the stables. The boy cleared three stalls, then ran off with a bucket to fetch water.

"Do you think the envoy will be a problem?" Arista asked Royce once Hobbie had left.

"Don't know," he said, untying his pack from the saddle. "Hopefully we won't be here long enough to find out."

"How long will we be here?"

"Cosmos will move fast. Just a night or two, I imagine." He threw his bag over his shoulder and crossed to Hadrian's horse. "Have you decided what you'll say to Gaunt when you meet him? I hear he hates nobility, so I wouldn't start by asking him to kiss your ring or anything."

She pulled her own gear off Mystic and then, holding out

her hands, wiggled her bare fingers. "Actually, I thought I'd ask him to kidnap my brother." She smiled. "It worked for you. And if I can gain the trust and aid of a Royce Melborn, how hard can it be to win over a Degan Gaunt?"

They carried the gear across the street to the little whitewashed shop with the signboard portraying a loaf of bread. Inside, a huge brick oven and a large wooden table dominated the space. The comforting scent of bread and wood smoke filled the air, and Arista was surprised the bakery wasn't broiling. The wattle-and-daub walls and the good-sized windows managed to keep the room comfortable. As Arista and Royce entered, they were introduced to Dunstan's wife, Arbor, and a host of other people whose names Arista could not keep up with.

Once word spread, freemen, farmers, and other merchants dropped by, grabbing a pint and helping themselves to a hunk of dark bread. There were Algar, the woodworker; Harbert, the tailor; and Harbert's wife, Hester. Hadrian introduced Wilfred, the carter, and explained how he used to rent Wilfred's little wagon four times every year to travel to Ratibor to buy iron ingots for his father's smithy. There were plenty of stories of the skinny kid with pimples who used to swing a hammer beside his father. Most remembered Danbury with kindness, and there were many toasts to his good name.

Just as the bailiff had predicted, it started to rain, and soon the villeins, released from work due to weather, dropped by to join the gathering. They slipped in, quietly shaking off the wetness. Each got a bit of bread, a pint to drink, and a spot to sit on the floor. Some brought steaming crocks of vegetable pottage, cheese, and cabbage for everyone to share. Even Osgar, the reeve, pressed himself inside and was welcomed to share the community meal. The sky darkened, the wind whipped up, and Dunstan finally closed the shutters as the rain poured.

They all wanted to know what had happened to Hadrian—where he had gone and what he had done. Most of them had spent their whole lives in Hintindar, barely crossing the river. In the case of the villeins, they were bound to the land and, by law, could not leave. For them, generations passed without their ever setting foot beyond the valley.

Hadrian kept them entertained with stories of his travels. Arista was curious to hear tales of the adventures he and Royce had shared over the years, but none of those came out. Instead, he told harmless stories of distant lands. Everyone was spellbound by stories about the far east, where the Calian people supposedly interbred with the Ba Ran Ghazel to produce the half-goblin Tenkin. Children gathered close to the skirts of their mothers when he spoke about the oberdaza—Tenkin who worshiped the dark god Uberlin and blended Calian traditions with Ghazel magic. Even Arista was captivated by his stories of far-off Dagastan.

With Hadrian the center of attention, few took notice of Arista, which was fine with her. She was happy just to be off her horse and in a safe place. The tension melted away from her.

The hot bread and fresh-brewed beer were wonderful. She was comfortable for the first time in days and reveled in the camaraderie of the bakery. She drank pints of beer until she lost track of the number. Outside, night fell and the rain continued. They lit candles, giving the room an even friendlier charm. The beer was infecting the group with mirth, and soon they were singing loudly. She did not know the words but found herself rocking with the rhythm, humming the chorus, and clapping her hands. Someone told a bawdy joke and the room burst into laughter.

"Where are you from?" Although it had been asked three times, this was the first instance that Arista had realized it was meant for her. Turning, she found Arbor, the baker's wife, sitting beside her. She was a petite woman with a plain face and short-cropped hair.

"I'm sorry," Arista apologized. "I'm not accustomed to beer. The bailiff said it was weak, but I think I would take exception to that."

"From yer mouth to his ears, darling!" Armigil said loudly from across the room. Arista wondered how she had heard from so far away, especially when she had thought she had spoken so softly.

Arista remembered Arbor had asked her a question. "Oh—right, ah... Colnora," the princess said at length. "My husband and I live in Colnora. Well, actually we are staying with my brother now, because we were evicted from our home in Windham Village by the Northern Imperial Army. That's up in Warric, you know—Windham Village, I mean, not the army. Of course, it could be—the army, I mean this time—not the village—because they could be there. Does that answer your question?"

The room was spinning slowly and it gave Arista the feeling she was falling, though she knew she was sitting still. The whole sensation made it difficult for her to concentrate.

"You were evicted? How awful." Arbor looked stricken.

"Well, yes, but it's not that great of a hardship, really. My brother has a very nice place in the Hill District in Colnora. He's quite well off, you know?" She whispered this last part into Arbor's ear. At least, she thought she did, but Arbor pulled back sharply.

"Oh really? You come from a wealthy family?" Arbor asked, rubbing her ear. "I thought you did. I was admiring your dress. It's very beautiful."

"This? Ha!" She pulled at the material of her skirt. "I got this old rag from one of my servants, who was about to throw it out. You should see my gowns. Now those are something, but yes, we're very wealthy. My brother has a virtual *army* of servants," she said, and burst out laughing.

"Erma?" someone said from behind her.

"What does your brother do?" Arbor asked.

"Hmm? Do? Oh, he doesn't *do* anything."

"He doesn't work?"

"Erma *dear*?"

"My brother? He calls it work, but it's nothing like what *you* people do. Did you know I slept on the ground just two nights ago? Not indoors either, but out in the woods. My brother never did that, I can tell you. You probably have, haven't you? But he hasn't. No, he gets his money from taxes. That's how all kings get their money. Well, some can get it from conquest. Glenmorgan got *loads* from conquest, but not Alric. He's never been to war—until now, of course, and he's not doing well at all, I can tell you."

"*Erma!*" Arista looked up to see Royce standing over her, his face stern.

"Why are you calling me that?"

"I think my wife has had a little too much to drink," he said to the rest of them.

Arista looked around to see several faces smirking in an effort to suppress laughter.

"Is there anywhere I can take her to sleep it off?"

Immediately several people offered the use of their homes, some even the use of their beds, saying they would sleep on the floor.

"Spend the night here," Dunstan said. "It's raining out. Do you really want to wander around out there in the dark? You can actually make a fine bed out of the flour sacks in the storeroom."

"How would you know that, Dun?" Hadrian asked,

chuckling. "The wife's kicked you out a few times?" This brought a roar of laughter from the crowd.

"Haddy, *you*, my friend, can sleep in the rain."

"Come along, Wife." Royce pulled Arista to her feet.

Arista looked up at him and winked. "Oh right, sorry. Forgot who I was."

"Don't apologize, honey," Armigil told her. "That's why we're drinking in the first place. Ya just got there quicker than the rest of us, is all."

❧

The next morning, Arista woke up alone and could not decide which hurt more, her head from the drink, or her back from the lumpy flour bags. Her mouth was dry, her tongue coated in some disgusting film. She was pleased to discover her saddlebags beside her. She pulled them open and grimaced. Everything inside smelled of horse sweat and mildew. She had brought only three dresses: the one worn through the rain, which was a wrinkled mess; the stunning silver receiving gown she planned to wear when she met Degan Gaunt; and the one she presently wore. Surprisingly, the silver gown was holding up remarkably well and was barely even wrinkled. She had brought it hoping to impress Gaunt, but recalling her conversation with Royce about how the Nationalist leader felt about royalty, she realized it was a poor choice. She would have been much better off with something simpler. It would at least have given her something decent to change into. She pulled off her dirt-stained garment, removed her corset, and pulled on the dress she had worn at Sheridan.

She stepped out of the storeroom and found Arbor hard at work kneading dough surrounded by dozens of cloth-covered baskets. Villagers entered and set either a bag of flour or a sackcloth of dough on the counter along with a few copper coins. Arbor gave them an estimated pickup time of either midday or early evening.

"You do this every day?" Arista asked.

Arbor nodded with sweat glistening on her brow as she used the huge wooden paddle to slide another loaf into the glowing oven. "Normally Dun is more helpful, but he's off with your husband and Haddy this morning. It's a rare thing, so I'm happy to let him enjoy the visit. They're down at the smithy if you're interested, or would you rather have a bite to eat?"

Arista's stomach twisted. "No, thank you. I think I'll wait a bit longer."

Arbor worked with a skilled hand born of hundreds, perhaps thousands, of repetitions.

How does she do it?

She knew the baker's wife got up every morning and repeated the same actions as the day before.

Where is the challenge?

Arista was certain Arbor could not read and probably had few possessions, yet she seemed happy. She and Dunstan had a pleasant home, and compared to that of those toiling in the fields, her work was relatively easy. Dunstan seemed a kind and decent man and their neighbors were good, friendly folk. While not terribly exciting, it was nonetheless a safe, comfortable life, and Arista felt a twinge of envy.

"What's it like to be wealthy?"

"Hmm? Oh—well, actually, it makes life easier but perhaps not as rewarding."

"But you travel and can see the world. Your clothing is so fine and you ride horses! I'll bet you've even ridden in a carriage, haven't you?"

Arista snorted. "Yes, I've certainly ridden in a carriage."

"And been to balls in castles where musicians played and the ladies dressed in embroidered gowns of velvet?"

"Silk, actually."

"Silk? I've heard of that but never seen it. What's it like?"

"I can show you." Arista went back into the storeroom and returned with the silver gown.

At the sight of the dress, Arbor gasped, her eyes wide. "I've never seen anything so beautiful. It's like—it's like..." Arista waited but Arbor never found her words. Finally, she said, "May I touch it?"

Arista hesitated, looking first at Arbor, then at the dress.

"That's okay," Arbor said quickly with an understanding smile. She looked at her hands. "I would ruin it."

"No, no," Arista told her. "I wasn't thinking that at all." She looked down at the dress in her arms once more. "What I was thinking was it was stupid for me to have brought this. I don't think I'll have a chance to wear it, and it's taking up so much space in my pack. I was wondering—would you like to have it?"

Arbor looked like she was going to faint. She shook her head adamantly, her eyes wide as if with terror. "No, I—I couldn't."

"Why not? We're about the same size. I think you'd look beautiful in it."

A self-conscious laugh escaped Arbor and she covered her face with her hands, leaving flour on the tip of her nose. "Oh, I'd be a sight, wouldn't I? Walking up and down Hintindar in *that*. It's awfully nice of you, but I don't go to grand balls or ride in carriages."

"Maybe one day you will, and then you'll be happy you have it. In the meantime, if you ever have a bad day, you can put it on and perhaps it'll make you feel better."

Arbor laughed again, only now there were tears in her eyes.

"Take it—really—you'd be doing me a favor. I do need the space." She held out the dress. Arbor reached toward it and gasped at the sight of her hands. She ran off and scrubbed them red before taking the dress in her quivering arms, cradling it as if it were a child.

"I promise to keep it safe for you. Come back and pick it up anytime, all right?"

"Of course," Arista replied, smiling. "Oh, and one more thing." Arista handed her the corset. "If you would be so kind, I never wish to see this thing again."

Arbor carefully laid the dress down and put her arms around Arista, hugging her close as she whispered, "Thank you."

❧

When Arista stepped out of the bakery into the sleepy village, her head throbbed, jolted by the brilliant sunlight. She shaded her eyes and spotted Armigil working in front of her shop, stoking logs under her massive cooker.

"Morning, Erma," Armigil called to her. "Yer looking a mite pale, lassie."

"It's your fault," Arista growled.

Armigil chuckled. "I try my best. I do indeed."

Arista shuffled over. "Can you direct me to the well?"

"Up the road four houses. You'll find it in front of the smithy."

"Thank you."

Following the unmistakable clanging of a metal hammer, Arista found Royce and Hadrian under the sun canopy in the smithy's yard, watching another man beating a bit of molten metal on an anvil. He was muscular and completely bald-headed, with a bushy brown mustache. If he had been in the bakery the previous night, Arista did not remember. Beside him was a barrel of water, and not far away was the well, a full bucket resting on its edge.

The bald man dropped the hot metal into his barrel, where it hissed. "Your father taught me that," the man said. "He was a fine smith—the finest."

Hadrian nodded and recited, "Choke the hammer after stroke, grip it high when drilling die."

This brought laughter from the smith. "I learned that one too. Mr. Blackwater was always making up rhymes."

"So this is where you were born?" Arista asked, dipping a community cup into the bucket of water and taking a seat on the bench beside the well.

"Not exactly," Hadrian replied. "I lived and worked here. I was actually born across the street there at Gerty and Abelard's home." He pointed at a tiny wattle-and-daub hovel without even a chimney. "Gerty was the midwife back then. My father kept pestering her so much that she took Mum to her house and Da had to wait outside in the rain during a terrible thunderstorm, or so I was told."

Hadrian motioned to the smith. "This is Grimbald. He apprenticed with my father after I left—does a good job too."

"You inherited the smithy from Danbury?" Royce asked.

"No, Lord Baldwin owns the smithy. Danbury rented from him, just as I do. I pay ten pieces of silver a year, and in return for charcoal, I do work for the manor at no cost."

Royce nodded. "What about personal belongings? What became of Danbury's things?"

Grimbald raised a suspicious eyebrow. "He left me his tools and if'n you're after them, you'll have to fight me before the steward in the manor court."

Hadrian raised his hands and shook his head, calming the burly man. "No, no, I'm not here after anything. His tools are in good hands."

Grimbald relaxed a bit. "Ah, okay, good, then. I do have something for you, though. When Danbury died, he made a list of all his things and who they should go to. Almost everyone in the village got a little something. I didn't even know the man could write until I saw him scribbling it. There was a letter and instructions to give it to his son, if he ever returned. I read it, but it didn't make much sense. I kept it, though."

Grimbald set down his hammer and ducked inside the shop, then emerged a few minutes later with the letter.

Hadrian took the folded parchment and, without opening it, stuffed the note into his shirt pocket and walked away.

"What's going on?" Arista asked Royce. "He didn't even read it."

"He's in one of his moods," Royce told her. "He'll mope for a while. Maybe get drunk. He'll be fine tomorrow."

"But why?"

Royce shrugged. "Just the way he is lately. It's nothing, really."

Arista watched Hadrian disappear around the side of the candlemaker's shop. Picking up the hem of her dress, she chased after him. When she rounded the corner, she found him seated on a fence rail, his head in his hands. He glanced up.

Is that annoyance or embarrassment on his face?

Biting her lip, she hesitated, then walked over and sat beside him. "Are you all right?" she asked.

He nodded in reply but said nothing. They sat in silence for a while.

"I used to hate this village," he offered at length, his tone distant and his eyes searching the side of the shop. "It was always so small." He lowered his head again.

She waited.

Does he expect me to say something now?

From down the street, she heard the rhythmic hammering

of metal as Grimbald resumed his work, the blows marking the passage of time. She pretended to straighten her skirt, wondering if it would be better if she left.

"The last time I saw my father, we had a terrible fight," Hadrian said without looking up.

"What about?" Arista gently asked.

"I wanted to join Lord Baldwin's men-at-arms. I wanted to be a soldier. He wanted me to be a blacksmith." Hadrian scuffed the dirt with his boot. "I wanted to see the world, have adventures—be a hero. He wanted to chain me to that anvil. And I couldn't understand that. I was good with a sword; he saw to that. He trained me every day. When I couldn't lift the sword anymore, he just made me switch arms. Why'd he do that if he wanted me to be a smith?"

A vision swept back to her of two faces in Avempartha: the heir she had not recognized—but Hadrian's face had been unmistakable as the guardian.

Royce didn't tell him? Should I?

"When I told him my plans to leave, he was furious. He said he didn't train me to gain fame or money. That my skills were meant for *greater things*, but he wouldn't say what they were.

"The night I left, we had words—lots of them—and none good. I called him a fool. I might even have said he was a coward. I don't remember. I was fifteen. I ran away and did just what he didn't want me to. I was gonna show him—prove the old man wrong. Only he wasn't. It's taken me this long to figure that out. Now it's too late."

"You never came back?"

Hadrian shook his head. "By the time I returned from Calis, I heard he'd died. I didn't see any point in returning." He pulled the letter out. "Now there's this." He shook the parchment in his fingers.

"Don't you want to know what it says?"

"I'm afraid to find out." He continued to stare at the letter as if it were a living thing.

She placed a hand on his arm and gave a soft squeeze. She did not know what else to do. She felt useless. Women were supposed to be comforting, consoling, nurturing, but she did not know how. She felt awful for him, and her inability to do anything to help just made her feel worse.

Hadrian stood up. With a deep breath, he opened the letter and began reading. Arista waited. He lowered his hand slowly, holding the letter at his side.

"What does it say?"

Hadrian held out the letter, letting it slip from his fingers. Before she could take it, the parchment drifted to the ground at her feet. As she bent to pick it up, Hadrian walked away.

❧

Arista rejoined Royce at the well.

"What was in the letter?" he asked. She held it out to Royce, who read it. "What was his reaction?"

"Not good. He walked off. I think he wants to be alone. You never told him, did you?"

Royce continued to study the letter.

"I can't believe you never told him. I mean, I know Esrahaddon told us not to, but I guess I just expected that you would anyway."

"I don't trust that wizard. I don't want me or Hadrian wrapped up in his little schemes. I couldn't care less who the guardian is, or the heir, for that matter. Maybe it *was* a mistake coming here."

"You came here on purpose? You mean this had nothing to do with— You came here for proof, didn't you?"

"I wanted something to confirm Esrahaddon's claim. I really didn't expect to find anything."

"He just told me his father trained him night and day in sword fighting and said his skills were *for greater things*. Sounds like proof to me. You know, you would have discovered that if you had just talked to him. He deserves the truth, and when he gets back, one of us needs to tell him."

Royce nodded, carefully refolding the letter. "I'll talk to him."

Chapter 9

The Guardian

The oak clenched the earth with a massive hand of gnarled roots unchanged by time. In the village, houses were lost to fires. New homes were built to accommodate growing families, and barns were raised on once vacant land, but on this hill time stood as still as the depths of Gutaria Prison. Standing beneath the tree's leaves, Hadrian felt young again.

Here, at this tree, Haddy had first kissed Arbor, the shoemaker's daughter. He and Dunstan had been competing for years for her favor, but Haddy kissed her first. That had been what started the fight. Dun had known better. He had seen Haddy spar with his father, and witnessed Haddy beat the old reeve for whipping Willie, a villein friend of theirs. The reeve had been too embarrassed to report to the bailiff that a fourteen-year-old boy had bested him. Haddy's skill was no secret to Dunstan, but rage had overcome reason.

When Dunstan found out about Arbor, he had charged at Haddy, who instinctually sidestepped and threw him to the ground. Misfortune landed Dun's head on a fieldstone. He had lain unconscious with blood running from his nose and ears. Horrified, Haddy had carried him back to the village, convinced he had just killed his best friend. Dun recovered, but Haddy never would. He never spoke to Arbor again. Three days later, the boy known as Haddy had left for good.

Hadrian slumped to the ground and sat in the shade of the tree with his back to the old oak's trunk. When he had been a boy, this had been where he had always come to think. From here, he could see the whole village below and the hills beyond—hills that had called to him, and a horizon that had whispered of adventure and glory.

Royce and Arista would be wondering where he had gone. Hadrian was not usually self-indulgent on the job.

The job!

He unconsciously shook his head. This was Royce's job, not his. He had kept his part of the bargain, and all that remained was for Arista to reach the rendezvous. When she did, that would end the assignment and his career in the world of intrigue. Strange how the end brought him back to the beginning. Coming full circle could be a sign for him to make a fresh start.

Near the center of the village he could see the smithy, which was easy to pick out by its rising black smoke. He had worked those bellows for hours each day. Hadrian remembered the sound of the anvil and the ache in his arms. That had been a time when all he had known of the world had stopped at this tree, and Hadrian could not help wondering how different his life might have been if he had stayed. One thing was certain; he would have more calluses and less blood on his hands.

Would I've married Arbor? Had children of my own? A stout, strong son who would complain about working the bellows and come to this tree to kiss his first girl? Could I've found contentment making plowshares and watching Da smile as he taught his grandson fencing, like a commoner's version of the Pickerings? If I'd stayed, at this very moment, would I be sitting here thinking of my happy family below? Would Da have died in peace?

He sighed heavily. Regret was a curse without a cure, except to forget. He closed his eyes. He did not want to think. He fell asleep to the sound of songbirds and woke to the thunder of horses' hooves.

❧

As night approached, Royce became worried. Once more they enjoyed the hospitality of the Bakers. Arbor was making a dinner of pottage while Dunstan ran a delivery of loaves to the manor. Arista offered assistance but appeared more a hindrance than a help. Arbor did not seem to mind. The two were inside, chatting and laughing, while Royce stood outside, watching the road with an uneasy feeling.

The village felt different to him. The evening had an edge, a tension to the air. Somewhere in the distance, a dog barked. He felt a nervous energy in the trees and an apprehension rising from the earth and rock. Before Avempartha, he had considered it intuition, but now he wondered. Elves drew power from nature. They understood the river's voice and the chatter of the leaves.

Did that pass to me?

He stood motionless, his eyes panning the road, the shops, the houses, and the dark places between. He was hoping to spot Hadrian returning, but felt something else.

"The cabbage goes in last," Arbor was telling Arista, her voice muffled by walls. "And cut it up into smaller pieces than that. Here, let me show you."

"Sorry," Arista said. "I don't have a lot of experience in a kitchen."

"It must be wonderful to have servants. Dun could never make that much money here. There aren't enough people to buy his bread."

Royce focused on the street. The sun had set and the twilight haze had begun to mask the village. He was looking at the candlemaker's shop when he spotted movement by the livery. When he looked closer, nothing was there. It could have been Hobbie coming to check the animals, but the fact that the image had vanished so quickly made him think otherwise.

Royce slipped into the shadows behind Armigil's brew shop and crept toward the livery. He entered from the rear, climbing to the loft. A fresh pile of hay cushioned his movements and muted his approach. In the dark, he could clearly see the back of a figure standing by the doorway, peering at the street.

"Move and die," Royce whispered softly in his ear.

The man froze. "Duster?" he asked.

Royce turned the man to face him. "Etcher, what are you doing here?"

"The meeting has been set. I've been sent to fetch you."

"That was fast."

"We got word back this morning and I rode hard to get here. The meeting is set for tonight at the ruins of Amberton Lee. We need to get going if we're going to make it in time."

"We can't leave right now. Hadrian is missing."

"We can't wait. Gaunt's people are suspicious—they think it could be an imperial trap. They'll back off if we don't stick to the plan. We need to leave now or the opportunity will pass."

Royce silently cursed to himself. It was his own fault for not having chased after Hadrian that afternoon. He almost had. Now there was no telling where he was. Etcher was right—the mission had to come first. He would leave word for Hadrian with the Bakers and get the princess to her meeting with Gaunt.

The moist, steamy smell of the boiling cabbage and wood smoke filled the bakery. The candles Arista lit flickered with the opening of the door. Arbor was stirring the pot while Arista set the table. Both looked up, startled.

"Hadrian hasn't shown?"

"No," Arista replied.

"We need to get going," Royce told her.

"Now? But what about Hadrian?"

"He'll have to catch up. Get your things."

Arista hesitated only a moment and then crossed to the flour storage to gather her bags.

"Can't you even stay for dinner?" Arbor asked. "It's almost ready."

"We need to get moving. We have a—" Royce stopped as he heard the noisy approach of a horse and cart being driven fast down the road. It stopped just out front, so close they could hear the driver pull the hand brake. Dunstan came through the door a moment later.

"Hadrian's been arrested!" he announced hurriedly, and then he pointed at Royce and Arista. "The steward ordered your arrests as well."

"Their arrests?" Arbor said, shocked. "But why?"

"The bailiff was wrong. It looks like Luret has more influence than he thought," Royce muttered. "Let's get the horses."

"His Lordship's soldiers were just behind me as I started down the hill. They will be here in minutes," Dunstan said.

"My horse is down by the river," Etcher said. "It can carry two."

Royce was thinking quickly, calculating risks and outcomes. "You take her to the rendezvous on your horse, then," he told Etcher. "I'll see what I can do to help Hadrian. With any luck, we'll catch up to you. If we don't, it shouldn't matter." He looked at Arista. "From what I've heard of your *contact*, he will see to your safety even if he ultimately declines your offer."

"Don't worry about me." The princess rushed toward the door with her bags. "I'll be fine. Just make sure that Hadrian is okay."

Taking a bag and the princess's hand, Etcher pulled her out into the night and dodged into the shadows of the buildings.

Royce followed them out, caught hold of the eaves, and climbed up on the Bakers' shake roof, where he crouched in the shadow of the chimney, listening. He watched about half a dozen men with torches moving fast down the main street from the direction of the manor. They stopped first at the livery, then went to the Bakers'.

"Where are the strangers that rode in with the old blacksmith's son?" a loud voice he had not heard before demanded.

"They left hours ago," Dunstan replied.

Royce heard a grunt and a crash, followed by a scream from Arbor and the sound of furniture falling over.

"Their horses are still in the livery. We saw you race from the manor to warn them! Now where are they?"

"Leave him alone!" Arbor shouted. "They ran out when they heard you coming. We don't know where. They didn't tell us anything."

"If you're lying, you'll be arrested for treason and hanged, do you understand?"

There was a brief silence.

"Fan out in pairs. You two cover the bridge. You and you search the fields, and you two start going door-to-door. Until further notice, all citizens of Hintindar are to remain in their homes. Arrest anyone outside. Now move!"

The men, marked conveniently by their flaming torches,

scattered out of the bakery in all directions, leaving Royce to watch them scurrying about. He glanced across the dark fields. Etcher would have no trouble avoiding the foot search. Once they reached his horse, they would be gone. Arista was safely on her way, his job done. All he had to worry about now was Hadrian.

❧

The manor house's jail was less a dungeon and more an old well. Forced to descend by a rope, Hadrian was left trapped at the bottom. He waited in silence, looking up at the stars. The rising moon cast a shaft of pale light that descended the wall, marking the slow passage of the night.

Cold spring water seeped in through the walls, leaving them damp and creating a shallow pool at the base. With his feet tiring, Hadrian eventually sat in the cold puddle. Jagged rocks hidden under the water added to his misery. In time, he was forced to stand again to fight the cold.

The moonlight was more than halfway down the wall when Hadrian heard voices and movement from above. Dark silhouettes appeared and the iron grate scraped as it slid clear. A rope lowered and Hadrian thought they had reconsidered. He stood up to take hold of it, but stopped when he saw another figure coming down.

"In ya go," someone at the top ordered, and laughed, his voice echoing. "We keep all our rats down there!"

The figure was nimble and descended quickly.

"Royce?" Hadrian asked. "They—they *captured you*?"

The rope was pulled up and the grate slid back in place.

"More or less," he replied, glancing around. "Not much on accommodations, are they?"

"I can't believe they caught you."

"It wasn't as easy as you'd think. They aren't very bright." Royce reached out and let his fingers run over the glistening walls. "Was this just a well that went dry?"

"Hintindar doesn't have much need for a big prison." Hadrian shook his head. "So you *let* them capture you?"

"Ingenious, don't you think?"

"Oh, brilliant."

"I figured it was the easiest way to find you." Royce shuffled his feet in the water, grimacing. "So what's your excuse? Did they come for you with an army of twenty heavily armored men?"

"They caught me sleeping."

Royce shot him a skeptical look.

"Let's just say I was put in a position where I'd have to kill people and I chose not to. This is my home, remember. I don't want to be known as a killer here."

"So it *is* good I didn't slit throats. I'm smarter than I thought."

"Oh yes, I can see the genius in your plan." Hadrian looked up. "How do you suggest we get out now?"

"Eventually, Luret will haul us out and hand us over to a press-gang, just as he threatened. We'll serve in the imperial army for a few days, learn what we can, and then slip away. We can report what we discover to Alric for an added bonus."

"What about Arista?"

"She's safely on her way to the rendezvous with Gaunt. Etcher arrived just before dark and I sent her with him. She'll likely stay with Gaunt, sending dispatches back to Melengar via messengers until Alric's forces join with the Nationalists."

"And if Gaunt turns her down?"

"It's in Gaunt's best interest to see to her safety. It's not like he's going to turn her over to the empire. She'll probably end up returning to Melengar by sea. Actually, it's better we aren't with her. If Merrick *is* out there, I'm sure he'll be more interested in me than her. So that job is complete."

"I guess there is that to be thankful for, at least."

Royce chuckled.

"What?"

"I'm just thinking about Merrick. He'll have no idea where I am now. My disappearance will drive him crazy."

Hadrian sat down.

"Isn't that water cold?" Royce asked, watching him and making an unpleasant face.

He nodded. "And the bottom has sharp rocks coated in a disgusting slime."

Royce looked up at the opening once more, then gritted his teeth and slowly eased himself down across from Hadrian. "Oh yeah, real comfortable."

They sat in silence for a few minutes, listening to the breeze flutter across the grating. It made a humming noise when it blew just right. Occasionally, a droplet of water would drip into the pool with a surprisingly loud *plop!* magnified by the chamber.

"You realize that with this job over, I'm officially retired."

"I assumed as much." Royce fished beneath him, withdrew a rock, and tossed it aside.

"I was thinking of returning here. Maybe Grimbald could use a hand, or Armigil. She's getting older now and probably would welcome a partner. Those barrels can be heavy and brewing beer has its perks."

Moonlight revealed Royce's face. He looked tense.

"I know you're not happy with this, but I really need a change. I'm not saying I'll stay here. I probably won't, but it's a start. I consider it practice for a peaceful life."

"And that's what you want, a peaceful life? No more dreams of glory?"

"That's all they were, Royce, just dreams. It's time I faced that and got on with my life."

Royce sighed. "I've something to tell you. I should have told you a long time ago, but...I guess I was afraid you'd do something foolish." He paused. "No, that's not true either. It's just taken me a while to see that you have the right to know."

"Know what?"

Royce looked around him. "I never thought I'd be telling you in a place like this, but I must admit it could be a benefit that they took your weapons." He pulled out Danbury's letter.

"How do you have that?" Hadrian asked.

"From Arista."

"Why didn't they take it when they grabbed you?"

"Are you kidding? I practically had to remind them to take my dagger. They don't seem too accustomed to thieves, much less ones that turn themselves in." Royce handed the note to Hadrian. "What did you think of when you read this?"

"That my father died filled with pain and regret. He believed the words of a selfish fifteen-year-old that he was a coward and wasted his life. It's bad enough I left him, but I had to paint that stain on him before leaving."

"Hadrian, I don't think this letter had anything to do with your leaving. I think it's due to your heritage. I think your father was trying to tell you something about your past."

"How would you know? You never met my father. You're not making any sense."

Royce sighed. "Last year in Avempartha, Esrahaddon was using a spell to find the heir."

"I remember. You told me that before."

"But I didn't tell you everything. The spell didn't find the heir exactly, but rather magical amulets worn by him and his guardian. Esrahaddon made the necklaces so he could locate the wearers and prevent other wizards from finding them. As

I told you, I didn't recognize the face of the heir. He was some guy with blond hair and blue eyes I'd never seen before."

"And this is important why?"

"I didn't know, at least not for certain, not really. I always thought Esra was using us. That's mainly why I never told you. I wanted to be sure it was true, and that's why I asked you to come and why I led us here."

Royce paused a moment, then asked, "Where did you get that necklace, the amulet you wear under your shirt?"

"I told you, my father..." Hadrian paused, staring at Royce, his hand unconsciously rising to his neck to feel the necklace.

"I didn't recognize the heir... but I did recognize the guardian. Your father had a secret, Hadrian—a *big* secret."

Hadrian continued to stare at Royce. His mind flashed back to his youth, to his gray-haired father, spending day after day toiling humbly on the anvil and forge, making harrows and plowshares. He recalled Danbury growling at him to clean the shop.

"No," Hadrian said. "My father was a blacksmith."

"How many blacksmiths teach their sons ancient Teshlor combat skills, most of which have been lost for centuries? Where did you get that big spadone sword you've carried on your back since I first met you? Was that your father's too?"

Hadrian slowly nodded and felt a chill raise the hairs on his arms. He had never told Royce about that. He had never told anyone. He had taken the sword the night he had left. He had needed his own blade. Da often had several weapons in his shop, but taking them would have cost his father money. Instead, he had taken the only weapon he felt his father would not miss. Da had kept the spadone hidden in a small compartment under the shop's fifth floorboard. Danbury had taken it out only once, a long time ago, when Hadrian's mother had still been alive. At the time, Hadrian was very young, and now the memory was hard to recall. His mother was asleep and Hadrian should have been as well, but something had woken him. Crawling out of bed, he had found his father in the shop. Da had been drinking Armigil's ale and was sitting on the floor in the glow of the forge. In his hands, he cradled the huge two-handed sword, talking to it as if it were a person. He was crying. In fifteen years of living with the man, Hadrian had seen him cry only that one time.

"I want you to do me a favor. Read this again, only this time pretend you hadn't run away. Read it as if you and your father were on great terms and he was proud of you."

Hadrian held the parchment up to the moonlight and read it again.

> Haddy,
>
> I hope this letter will find you. It's important that you know there is a reason why you should never use your training for money or fame. I should have told you the truth, but my pain was too great. I can admit to you now I'm ashamed of my life, ashamed of what I failed to do. I suppose you were right. I'm a coward. I let everyone down. I hope you can forgive me, but I can never forgive myself.
>
> love, Da
>
> Before you were born, the year ninety-two,
> lost what was precious, and that what was new.
> The blink of an eye, the beat of a heart,
> Out went the candle, and guilt was my part.
>
> A king and his knight went hunting a boar,
> A rat and his friends were hunting for love.

Together they fought, till one was alive.
The knight sadly wept, no king had survived.

The answers to riddles, to secrets and more,
Are found in the middle of legends and love.
Seek out the answer, and learn if you can
The face of regret, the life of a man.

"You realize a spadone is a knight's weapon?" Royce asked.

Hadrian nodded.

"And yours is a very old sword, isn't it?"

Hadrian nodded again.

"I would venture to guess it's about nine hundred years old. I think you're the descendant of Jerish, the Guardian of the Heir," Royce told him. "Although maybe not literally. The way I heard it, the heir has a direct bloodline but the guardian just needed to pass down his skills. The next in line didn't need to be his son, although I guess it's possible."

Hadrian stared at Royce. He did not know how to feel about this. Part of him was excited, thrilled, vindicated, and part of him was certain Royce was insane.

"And you kept this from me?" Hadrian asked, astonished.

"I didn't want to tell you until I knew for sure. I thought Esrahaddon might be playing us."

"Don't you think I would have thought of that too? What do you take me for? Have you worked with me for twelve years because you think I'm stupid? How conceited can you be? You can't trust me to make my own decisions, so you make them for me?"

"I'm telling you now, aren't I?"

"It took you a whole damn year, Royce!" Hadrian shouted at him. "Didn't you think I'd find this important? When I told you I was miserable because I felt my life lacked purpose—

that I wanted a cause worth fighting for—you didn't think that protecting the heir qualified?" Hadrian shook his head in disbelief. "You stuck-up, manipulative, lying—"

"I *never* lied to you!"

"No, you just concealed the truth, which to me is a lie, but in *your* twisted little mind is a virtue!"

"I knew you were going to take it this way," Royce said in a superior tone.

"How else would you expect me to take it? Gee, pal, thanks for thinking so little of me that you couldn't tell me the truth about my own life."

"That's not the reason I didn't tell you," Royce snapped.

"You just said it was!"

"I know I did!"

"So you're lying to me again?"

"Call me a liar one more time—"

"And what? What? You going to fight me?"

"It's dark in here."

"But there's no room for you to hide. You're only a threat until I get my hands on you. I just need to grab your spindly little neck. For all your quickness, once I get a grip on you, it's all over."

Without warning, cold water poured down on them. Looking up, Hadrian saw silhouetted figures.

"You boys, be quiet down there!" shouted a voice. "His Excellency wants a word with you."

One head disappeared from view and another replaced it at the opening's edge.

"I'm Luret, the imperial envoy of Her Eminence, the grand imperial empress Modina Novronian. Because of your involvement in escorting a member of the royal court of Melengar to Her Eminence's enemy, the Nationalists, the two of you are hereby charged with espionage and hitherto will be put to death by hanging in three days' time. Should, however, you wish to attempt to rescind that sentence to life in prison, I'd be willing to do so under the condition that you reveal to me the whereabouts of Princess Arista Essendon of Melengar."

Neither said a word.

"Tell me where she is, or you'll be hanged as soon as the village carpenter can build a proper gallows."

Again, they were silent.

"Very well, perhaps a day or two rotting in there will change your mind." He turned away and spoke to the jailor. "No food or water. It might help to loosen their tongues. Besides, there's really no sense in wasting it."

They waited in silence as the figures above moved away.

"How does he know?" Hadrian whispered.

A ghastly look stole over Royce's face.

"What is it?"

"Etcher. He's the mole in the Diamond."

Royce kicked the wall, causing a splash. "How could I've been so blind? He was the one who lit the lamp on the river, alerting the wherry behind us. The only reason he never thought to check the mill's sails was because it didn't matter to him. I bet he never even told Price where we were, so there would be no way for the Diamond to find us. There must be an ambush waiting at Amberton Lee, or somewhere along the way."

"But why take her there? Why not just turn Arista over to Luret?"

"I'd wager this is Merrick's game. He doesn't want some imperial clown like Luret getting the prize. She's a commodity which can be sold to the empire, or ransomed to Melengar for a profit. If Luret grabs her, he gets nothing."

"So why tell Luret about us at all?"

"Insurance. With the manor officials after us, we'd be

pressed for time and wouldn't question Etcher's story. I'm sure it was to hasten our departure and have us unprepared, but it turned out even better, because you were captured and I decided to stay behind to help you."

"And you sent Arista off alone with Etcher."

"She's on her way to Merrick, or Guy, or both. Maybe they'll keep her and demand Alric surrender Medford. He won't, of course. Pickering won't let him."

"I can't believe Alric sent her in the first place. What an idiot! Why didn't he pick a representative outside the royal court? Why did he have to send *her*?"

"He didn't send her," Royce said. "I doubt anyone in Medford has a clue where she is. She did this on her own."

"What?"

"She arrived at The Rose and Thorn unescorted. Have you *ever* seen her go anywhere without a bodyguard?"

"So why did you—"

"Because I needed an excuse to bring you here, to find out if what Esrahaddon showed me was true."

"So this is *my* fault?" Hadrian asked.

"No, it's everyone's fault: you for pushing so hard to retire, me for not telling you the truth, Arista for being reckless, even your father for never having told you who you really are."

They sat in silence a moment.

"So what do we do now?" Hadrian said at last. "Your original plan isn't going to work so well anymore."

"Why do I always have to come up with the plans, Mr. I'm-Not-So-Stupid?"

"Because when it comes to deciding how I should live my own life, I should be the one to choose—but when getting out of a prison, even as pathetic as it is, that's more your area of expertise."

Royce sighed and began to look around at the walls.

"By the way," Hadrian began, "what was the *real* reason you didn't tell me?"

"Huh?"

"A bit ago you said—"

"Oh." Royce continued to study the walls. He seemed a little too preoccupied by them. Just as Hadrian was sure he would not answer, Royce said, "I didn't want you to leave."

Hadrian almost laughed at the comment, thinking it was a joke, and then nearly bit his tongue. Thinking of Royce as anything but callous was difficult. Then he realized Royce never had a family and precious few friends. He had grown up an orphan on the streets of Ratibor, stealing his food and clothes and likely receiving his share of beatings for it. He had probably joined the Diamond as much from a desire to belong as a means to profit. After only a few short years, they had betrayed him. Hadrian realized at that moment that Royce did not see him as just his partner, but his family. Along with Gwen and perhaps Arcadius, Hadrian was the only one he had.

"You ready?" Royce asked.

"For what?"

"Turn around. Let's go back-to-back and link arms."

"You're kidding. We aren't going to do that again, are we?" Hadrian said miserably. "I've been sitting in cold water for hours. I'll cramp."

"You know another way to get up there?" Royce asked, and Hadrian shook his head. Royce looked up. "It isn't even as high as the last time and it's narrower, so it'll be easier. Stand up and stretch a second. You'll be fine."

"What if the guard is up there with a stick to poke us with?"

"Do you want to get out of here or not?"

Hadrian took a deep breath. "I'm still mad at you," he said, turning and linking arms back-to-back with Royce.

"Yeah, well, I'm not too happy with me either right now."

They began pushing against each other as they walked up the walls of the pit. Immediately Hadrian's legs began to protest the effort, but the strain on his legs was taken up some by the tight linking of their arms and the stiff leverage it provided.

"Push harder against me," Royce told him.

"I don't want to crush you."

"I'm fine. Just lean back more."

Initially the movement was clumsy and the exertion immense, but soon they fell into a rhythm.

"Step," Royce whispered. The pressure against each other was sufficient to keep them pinned.

"Step." They slid another foot up, scraping over the stony sides.

The water running down the walls gave birth to a slippery slime and Hadrian carefully placed his feet on the drier bricks and used the cracks for traction. Royce was infinitely better at this sort of thing, and likely impatient with their progress. Hadrian was far less comfortable and often pushed too hard. His legs were longer and stronger and he had to keep remembering to relax.

They finally rose above the level of the slime to where the rock was dry, and they moved with more confidence. They were now high enough that a fall would break bones. He started to perspire with the effort, and his skin was slicked with sweat. A droplet cascaded down his face and hung dangling on the tip of his nose. Above, he could see the grate growing larger, but it was still a maddening distance away.

What if we can't make it? How can we get back down besides falling?

Hadrian had to push the thought out of his mind and concentrate. Nothing good would come from anticipating failure.

Instead, he forced himself to think of Arista riding to her death or capture. They had to make it up—and quickly—before his legs lost all their strength. Already they shook from fatigue, buckling under the strain.

As they neared the top, Royce stopped calling steps. Hadrian kept his eyes on the wall where he placed his feet, but felt Royce tilting his head back, peering up. "Stop," Royce whispered. Panting for air, they steadied themselves, unlinked arms, and grabbed the grating. Letting their tortured legs fall loose, they hung for a minute. The release of the strain was wonderful, and Hadrian closed his eyes with pleasure as he gently swayed.

"Good news and bad news," Royce said. "No guards, but it's locked."

"You can do something about that, right?"

"Just give me a second."

He could feel Royce shifting around behind him. "Got it." There was another brief pause and Hadrian's fingers were starting to hurt. "Okay, we'll slide it to your left, ready? Feet up."

The grate was lighter than Hadrian had expected, and it easily slid clear. They hauled themselves out, rolling on the damp grass of the manor's lawn, and lay for a second catching their breath. They were alone in a darkened corner of the manor's courtyard.

"Weapons?" Hadrian asked.

"I'll check the house. You see about getting horses."

"Don't kill anyone," Hadrian mentioned.

"I'll try not to, but if I see Luret—"

"Oh yeah, kill him."

Hadrian worked his way carefully toward the courtyard stable. The horses started at his approach, snorting and bumping loudly into the stall dividers. He grabbed the first saddle and bridle he found and discovered they were familiar. Arista's bay mare, his horse, and Mouse were corralled with the rest.

"Easy, girl," Hadrian whispered softly as he threw the blankets on two of them. He buckled the last bridle around Mouse's neck when Royce came in carrying a bundle of swords.

"Your weapons, sir knight."

"Luret?" Hadrian asked, strapping his swords on.

Royce made a disappointed sound. "Didn't see him. Didn't see hardly anyone. These country folk go to bed early."

"We're a simple lot."

"Mouse?" Royce muttered. "I just can't seem to get rid of this horse, can I?"

Arista discovered riding on the back of a horse was significantly less comfortable than riding in a saddle. Etcher added to her misery by keeping the horse at a trot. The hammering to Arista's body caused her head to ache. She asked for him to slow down but was ignored. Before long, the animal slowed to a walk on its own. It frothed and Arista could feel its sweat soaking her gown. Etcher kicked the beast until it started again. When the horse once more returned to a walk, Etcher resorted to whipping it with the ends of the reins. He missed and struck Arista hard across the thigh. She yelped, but that was also ignored. Eventually Etcher gave up and let the horse rest. She asked where they were going and why they needed to rush. Still, he said nothing—he never even turned his head. After a mile or two, he drove the animal into a trot once more. He acted as if she was not there.

With each jarring clap on the horse's back, Arista became increasingly aware of her vulnerability. She was alone with a strange man somewhere in the backwoods of Rhenydd, where any authority of law would seize her rather than him, regardless of what he did. All she knew about him—the only thing she could be certain of—was that he was morally dubious. While it was one thing to trust herself to Royce and Hadrian, it was quite another to leap onto the back of a horse with a stranger who took her off into the wilds. If she had thought about it, if there had been time to think, she might have declined to go, but now it was too late. She rode trusting the mercy of a dangerous man in a hostile land.

His silence did nothing to alleviate her fear. When it came to silence, Etcher put Royce to shame. He said nothing at all. The profession of thievery was not likely to attract gregarious types, but Etcher seemed an extreme case. He even refused to look at her. This was perhaps better than some alternatives. A man such as Etcher was likely acquainted only with sun-baked, easy women in dirty dresses. How appealing must it be to have a young noblewoman clutching to him alone in the wilderness—and a royal princess, at that.

If he attacks me, what can I do?

A good high-pitched scream would draw a dozen armed guards in Essendon Castle, but since leaving Hintindar, she had not seen a house or a light. Even if someone heard her, she would probably spend her life in an imperial prison once her identity was discovered. He could do anything he wanted with her. When he was done, he could either kill her or hand her over to imperial authorities, who would no doubt pay richly. No one would care if he delivered her bruised and bloodied. She regretted her fast escape without taking the time to think. She had nothing to defend herself with. Her small side pouch held only her father's hairbrush and a bit of coin. Her dagger was somewhere in the bundle of her bedding.

How long will it take me to find it in the dark?

She sighed.

Why must I always focus on the negative? The man has done nothing at all. So he's quiet, so what? He's risking his own life smuggling me to this meeting. He's nervous, watchful. Perhaps he's frightened too. Is it so odd he's not making small talk? I'm just scared, that's all. Everything looks bad when you're scared. Isn't it possible he's just shy around women? Cautious around noble ladies? Concerned anything he says or does could be misconstrued and lead to dangerous accusations? Obviously he has good cause to be concerned. I've already practically convicted him of a host of crimes he hasn't committed! Royce and Hadrian are honorable thieves. Why not Etcher as well?

The trail disappeared entirely and they rode across unmarked fields of windswept grass. They seemed to be heading toward a vague and distant hill. She spotted some structures silhouetted against the pallid sky. They entered yet another forest, this time through a narrow opening in the dense foliage, where Etcher was content to let the horse walk. Away from the wind it was quiet. Fireflies blinked around them and Arista listened to the clacking steps of their mount.

We're on a road?

Although it was too dark to see anything clearly, Arista recognized the sound of hooves on cobblestone.

Where are we?

When at last they cleared the trees, she could see the slope of a bald hill where the remains of buildings sat. Giant stones spilled and scattered to the embrace of grass, forming dark heaped ruins of arched doorways and pylons of rock. Like grave markers, they thrust skyward at neglected angles, the lingering cadavers and bleached bones of forgotten memories.

"What is this place?" Arista asked.

She heard a horse whinny and spotted the glow of a fire up the slope. Without a word, Etcher kicked the horse once more into a trot. Arista took solace in knowing the end of her ordeal was at hand.

Near the top, two men sat huddled amidst the ruins. A campfire flickered, sheltered from the wind by a corner section of weathered stone and rubble. One man was hooded, the other hatless, and immediately Arista thought of Royce and Hadrian.

Did they somehow arrive ahead of us?

As they drew closer, Arista realized she was wrong. These men were younger and both as large as, if not larger than, Hadrian. They stood at the horse's approach and Arista saw dark shirts, leather tunics, and broadswords hanging from thick belts.

"Running late," the hooded one said. "Thought you weren't going to make it."

"Are you Nationalists?" she asked.

The men hesitated. "Of course," the other replied.

They approached, and the hooded one helped her down from the horse. His hands were large and powerful. He showed no strain taking her weight. He had two days of beard and smelled of sour milk.

"Is one of you Degan Gaunt?"

"No," the hooded one replied. "He sent us ahead to see if you were who you said you were. Are you Princess Arista Essendon of Melengar?"

She looked from one face to the next, all harsh expressions. Even Etcher glared at her.

"Well, are you or aren't you?" he pressed, moving closer.

"Of course she is!" Etcher blurted out. "I have a long ride back, so I want my payment, and don't try to cheat me."

"Payment?" Arista asked.

Etcher once more ignored her.

"I don't think we can pay you for delivery until we know it's her, and we certainly aren't taking *your* word for it. She could be a whore from the swill yards of Colnora that you washed and dressed up—and did a piss-poor job of it, at that."

"She's pretending to be a commoner and she's dirty on account of the ride here."

The hooded man advanced even closer to study her. She backed up instinctively but not fast enough as he grabbed her roughly at the chin and twisted her face from side to side.

Infuriated, she kicked at him and managed to strike his shin.

The man grunted and anger flashed in his eyes. "You bloody little bitch!" He struck her hard across the face with the flat of his hand.

The explosion of pain overwhelmed her. She found herself on her hands and knees, gripping a spinning world with fists full of grass. Her face ached and her eyes watered.

The men laughed.

The humiliation was too much. "How dare you strike me!" she screamed.

"See?" Etcher said, pointing at her.

The hooded man nodded. "All right, we'll pay you. Danny, give him twenty gold."

"Twenty? The sentinel agreed to fifty!" Etcher protested.

"Keep your mouth shut or it'll be ten."

Arista panted on the ground, her breath coming in short stifled gasps. She was scared and rapidly losing herself to panic. She needed to calm down—to think. Through bleary eyes, she looked at Etcher and his horse. There was no chance of grabbing the animal and riding away. Etcher's feet were in the stirrups and her weight could never pull him off.

"Guy won't appreciate you pocketing thirty of the gold he sent with you."

They laughed. "Who do you really think he'll believe? You or us?"

Arista considered the fire. She could try to run to it and grab a stick. She concluded she would never make the distance. Even if she did, a stick would be useless against swords. They would only laugh at her.

"Take the twenty and keep your damn mouth shut, or you can ride away with nothing."

She thought about running. *It's downhill, and in the dark I could— No, I'm not fast enough and the hill has no cover.*

Arista would have to make it all the way to the forest before having the slightest hope of getting away, and Etcher could ride after her and drag her back. Afterward, they would beat and tie her, and then all hope would be lost.

"Don't even think about it, you little git," the hooded one was saying to Etcher.

Etcher spat in anger. "Give me the twenty."

The hooded man tossed a pouch that jingled and Etcher caught it with a bitter look.

Arista started to cry. Time was running out. She was helpless and there was nothing at all she could do. For all her royal rank, she could not defend herself. Nor was her education in the art of magic any help. All she could do was make them sneeze and that was not going to save her this time.

Where are Royce and Hadrian? Where is Hilfred? How could I be so stupid, so reckless? Isn't there anyone to save me?

Not surprisingly, Etcher left without a word to her.

"So this is what a princess looks like?" the hooded one said. "There's nothing special about you, is there? You look just as dirty as any wench I've had."

"I don't know," the other said. "She's better than I've seen. Throw me the rope over there. I wanna enjoy myself, not get scratched up."

She felt her blood go cold. Her body trembled. Tears streamed down her cheeks as she watched the man set off to fetch the rope.

No man had ever touched her before. No one dared to think in such terms. Doing so would mean death in Melengar. She had no midnight rendezvous, no casual affairs or castle romances. No boy had ever chanced so much as a kiss, but now... She watched as the man with the stubble beard came at her with a length of twine.

If only I'd learned something more useful than tickling noses and boiling water, I could—

Arista stopped crying. She did not realize it, but she had stopped breathing as well.

Can it work?

There was nothing else to try.

The man grinned expectantly as Arista closed her eyes and began to hum softly.

"Look at that. I think she likes the idea. She's serenading us."

"Maybe it's a noble ritual or something?"

Arista barely heard them. Once more, using the concentration method Esrahaddon had taught her, she focused her mind. She listened to the breeze swaying the grass, the buzz of the fireflies, the whine of the mosquitoes, and the song of the crickets. She could feel the stars and sense the earth below. There was power there. She pulled it toward her, breathing it in, sucking it into her body, drawing it to her mind.

"How you want her?"

"Wrists behind the back works for me, but maybe we should ask her how *she* likes it?" They laughed again. "Never know what might tickle a royal's fancy."

She was muttering, forming the words, drawing in the power, giving it form. She focused elements, giving them purpose and direction. She built the incantation as she had before, but now varied it. She pushed, altering the tone to shift the focus just enough.

The crickets stopped their song and the fireflies ceased their mating flashes. Even the gentle wind no longer blew. The only sound now was Arista's voice as it grew louder and louder.

Arista felt herself pulled to her feet as the man spun her and maneuvered her arms behind her back. She ignored him, concentrating instead on moving her fingers as if she were playing an invisible musical instrument.

Just as she felt the rough, scratchy rope touch her wrists, the men began to scream.

The ruins of Amberton Lee stood splintered on the hilltop. Pillars, steps of marble, and slab walls lay fractured and fallen. Only three trees stood near the summit of the barren hill, all of them dead, leafless corpses, like the rest of the ruins, still standing long after their time.

"There's a fire up there, but I only see Arista," Royce said.

"Bait?"

"Probably. Give me a head start. Maybe I can free her before they know something is up. If nothing else, I should spring whatever trap is waiting and then hopefully you can rush in and save the day."

It bothered Royce how quiet the hill was. He could hear the distant snorting and hoofing of horses and the crackle of the campfire, but nothing else. They had raced as fast as their horses could manage, and still Royce was afraid they would be too late. When riding, he had been certain she was dead.

Now he was confused. There was no doubt that the woman near the fire was Arista.

So where is Etcher? Where are those they intended to meet?

He crept carefully, slipping nimbly around a holly tree and up the slope. Half-buried stones and tilted rocks lay hidden beneath grass and thorns, making the passage a challenge. He circled once and found no sentries or movement.

He climbed higher and happened upon two bodies. The men were dead, yet still warm to the touch—more than warm, they felt...hot. There were no wounds, no blood. Royce proceeded up the last of the hill, advancing on the flickering fire. The princess sat huddled near it, quietly staring into the flames. She was alone and lacked even her travel bags.

"Arista?" he whispered.

She looked up lazily, drunkenly, as if her head weighed more than it should. The glow of the fire spilled across her face. Her eyes appeared red and swollen. A welt stood out on one of her cheeks.

"It's Royce. You all right?"

"Yes," she replied. Her voice sounded distant and weak.

"Are you alone?"

She nodded.

He stepped into the firelight and waited. Nothing happened. A light summer breeze gently brushed the hill's grass and breathed on the flames. Above them, the stars shone, muted only by the white moon, which cast nighttime shadows. Arista sat with the stillness of a statue, except for the hairbrush she turned over and over in her hands. As tranquil as the scene appeared, Royce's senses were tense. This place made him uneasy. The odd marble blocks, toppled and broken, rose out of the ground like teeth. Once more he wondered if somehow he was tapping into his elven heritage, sensing more than could be seen, feeling a memory lost in time.

He caught sight of movement down the slope and spotted Hadrian climbing toward them. He watched him pause for a moment near the bodies before continuing up.

"Where's Etcher?" Royce asked the princess.

"He left. He was paid by Luis Guy to bring me here, to deliver me to some men."

"Yeah. We found that out a bit late. Sorry."

The princess did not look well. She was too quiet. He expected anger or relief, but her stillness was eerie. Something had happened—something bad. Besides the welt, there was no sign of abuse. Her clothes were intact. There were no rips or tears. He spotted several blades of dead grass and a brown leaf tangled in her hair.

"You all right?" Hadrian asked as he crested the hill. "Are you hurt?"

She shook her head and one of the bits of grass fell out.

Hadrian crouched down next to her. "Are you sure? What happened?"

Arista did not answer. She stared at the fire and started to rock.

"What happened to the men down on the hill?" Hadrian asked Royce.

"Wasn't me. They were dead when I found them. No wounds either."

"But how—"

"I killed them," Arista said.

They both turned and stared at her.

"You killed two Seret Knights?" Royce asked.

"Were they seret?" Arista muttered.

"They have broken-crown rings," Royce explained. "There's no wound on either body. How did you kill them?"

She started trembling, her breaths drawn in staggered bursts. Her hand went to her cheek, rubbing it lightly with her fingertips. "They attacked me. I—I couldn't think of—I didn't know what to do. I was so scared. They were going to—and I was alone. I didn't have a choice. I didn't have a choice. I couldn't run. I couldn't fight. I couldn't hide. All I could do was make them sneeze and boil water. I didn't have a choice. It was all I could do." She began sobbing.

Hadrian tentatively reached toward her. She dropped the brush and took his hands, squeezing them tightly. She pulled at him and he wrapped his arms around her while she buried her face into the folds of his shirt. He gently stroked her hair.

Hadrian looked up at Royce with a puzzled expression and whispered, "She made them sneeze to death?"

"No," Royce said, glancing back over his shoulder in the direction of the bodies. "She boiled water."

"I didn't know—I didn't know if it would really work," she whispered between hitching breaths. "I—I had to change it. Switch the focus. Fill in the blanks on my own—invent a whole new spell. I was only guessing, but—but it felt right. The pieces fit. I felt them fit—I *made* them fit."

Arista lifted her head, wiped her eyes, and looked down the slope of the hill. "They screamed for a very long time. They were on the ground—writhing. I—I tried to stop it then, but I didn't know how and they just kept—they kept on screaming, their faces turning so red. They rolled around on the ground and clawed the dirt, they cried and their screams—they—they got quieter and quieter, then they didn't make any noise except—except they were hissing—hissing and I could see steam rising from their skin."

Tears continued to slip down her cheeks as she looked up at them. Hadrian wiped her face.

"I've never killed anyone before."

"It's okay," Hadrian told her, stroking the back of her head and clearing away the remainder of the grass and leaves. "You didn't want to do it."

"I know. It's just—just that I've never killed anyone before, and you didn't hear them. It's horrible, like part of me was dying with them. I don't know how you do it, Royce. I just don't know."

"You do it by realizing that if the situation was reversed and they succeeded, they wouldn't be crying."

Hadrian slipped a finger under her chin and tilted her face. He cleared the hair stuck to her cheeks and brushed his thumbs under her eyes. "It's okay. It wasn't your fault. You did what you had to. I'm just sorry I wasn't here for you."

Arista looked into his eyes for a moment, then nodded and took a clear deep breath and wiped her nose. "I'm really ruining your impression of me, aren't I? I get drunk, I wolf down food, I think nothing of sharing a room with you, and now I…"

"You've nothing to be ashamed of," Hadrian told her. "I only wish more princesses were as worthy of their title as you."

Royce made another survey of the hill and a thorough check of the seret, their horses, and their gear. He found symbol-emblazoned tunics, confirming their knightly identities, and a good-sized bag of gold, but no documents of any sort. He pulled the saddle and bridle off one horse and let it go.

"There's only the two?" Hadrian asked when he returned. "I expected more." He stirred the coals of the fire with a stick, brightening the hilltop. Arista looked better. She was eating a bit of cheese. Her face was washed, her hair brushed. She certainly was showing more resilience than he had expected.

"Gives you a whole new respect for Etcher, doesn't it?" Royce said.

"How do you mean?"

"He never planned to bring all of us here, just her. He's a lot brighter than I gave him credit for."

"He wasn't too smart," Arista told them. "The seret cheated him out of thirty gold Luis Guy had promised."

"So this was Guy's operation, not Merrick's," Hadrian said.

"Not sure," Royce responded. "Seems too sophisticated for Guy, but Merrick's plans don't fail." He looked at the princess. "Of course, not even Merrick could have anticipated what she did."

Hadrian stood up and threw away the stick, then looked at the princess. "You gonna be okay? Can you ride?"

She nodded rapidly and followed it with a sniffle. "I was pretty scared—really missed you two. You have no idea—no idea how happy I am to see you again." She blew her nose.

"I get that from a lot of women," Hadrian replied, grinning. "But I'll admit, you're the first princess."

She managed a slight smile. "So what do we do now? I haven't a clue where we are, and I'm pretty sure there isn't any meeting with Gaunt."

"There could be," Royce said. "But Cosmos doesn't know where we are to tell us. I'm sure Etcher never carried any message about Hintindar back to Colnora. I should have told Price before we left, but I didn't want to take chances. Just stupid, really. I was being too cautious."

"Well, you know I'm not going to argue," Hadrian told him. "It was withholding information that got us into this."

Arista looked at Royce questioningly.

"I told him," Royce said.

"No bruises?" she asked. "Not even a black eye?"

"We never got that far, but maybe later when we have more time," Hadrian said. "Turned out we had to hurry to save a woman who didn't need saving."

"I'm real glad you did."

"We should head to Ratibor," Royce said. "We aren't too far. We can reestablish connection with the Diamond there."

"*Ratibor?*" Hadrian said suddenly.

"Yeah, you know, dirty, filthy rat hole—the capital of Rhenydd? We've seen where you grew up, so we might as well stop by my hometown as well."

Hadrian started searching his clothing. "Hunting a boar!" he exclaimed as he pulled out the note from his father. He rushed toward the firelight. "'A king and his knight went hunting a boar; a rat and his friends were hunting for lore.' A rat and a boar—Ratibor! The king and his knight are my father and the heir, who must have traveled to Ratibor and were attacked by lore hunters." Hadrian pointed over his shoulder in the direction of the dead men. "Seret."

"What's the rest of it?" Royce asked, intrigued.

"'Together they fought, till one was alive. The knight sadly wept; no king had survived.'"

"So they fought, but only your father survived the battle and the heir was killed."

"No king had survived," Hadrian said. "An odd way to put that, isn't it? Why not say 'The king died'?"

"Because it doesn't rhyme?" Royce suggested.

"Good point."

"What comes next?" Arista asked.

"'The answers to riddles, to secrets and more, are found in the middle of Legends and Lore.'"

"There's more to the story, apparently," she said, "and you can find the answers in ancient lore? Maybe you should ask Arcadius."

"I think not," Royce said. "There's a street in Ratibor called Legends Avenue and another named Lore Street."

"Do they intersect?"

Royce nodded. "Just a bit south of Central Square."

"And what's there?"

"A church, I think."

"Royce is right. We need to get to Ratibor," Hadrian announced.

Arista stood up. "Trust me, I'm more than ready to leave this place. When I—" She stopped herself. "When I used the Art, I sensed something unpleasant. It feels..."

"Haunted," Royce provided, and she nodded.

"What is this place?" Royce asked Hadrian.

"I don't know."

"It's only a few miles from where you grew up."

Hadrian shrugged. "Folks in Hintindar never talked about it much. There are a few ghost stories and rumors of goblins and ghouls that roam the woods, that kind of thing."

"Nothing about what it was?"

"There was a children's rhyme I remember, something like,

Ancient stones upon the Lee,
dusts of memories gone we see.
Once the center, once the all,
lost forever, fall the wall."

"What's that supposed to mean?"

Hadrian shrugged again. "We used to sing it when playing Fall-the-Wall—it's a kids' game."

"I see," Royce lied.

"Whatever it used to be, I don't like it," Arista declared.

Royce nodded. "It almost makes me look forward to Ratibor—almost."

Chapter 10

Rewards

The midday bell rang and Amilia stopped, uncertain of which way to go. As a kitchen servant, she was unfamiliar with areas reserved for nobles. Only on rare occasions had she filled in for sick chambermaids by servicing bedrooms on the third floor. She had worked as fast as possible to finish before the guests returned. Working with a noble present was a nightmare. They usually ignored her, but she was terrified of drawing attention. Invisibility was her best defense and it was easy to remain unseen in the steam and bustle of the scullery. In the open corridors, anyone could notice her.

This time she had no choice. Saldur had ordered her to his office. A soldier had found her on the way to breakfast and told her to report to His Grace at the midday bell. She lost her appetite and spent the rest of the morning speculating on what horrible fate awaited her.

The bell rang for the second time and Amilia began to panic. She had visited the regent's office only once, and since she had been under armed escort at the time, the route had been the last thing on her mind. She remembered going upstairs, but didn't recall the number of flights.

Oh, why didn't I leave earlier?

She passed the great hall, filled with long tables set with familiar plates and shining goblets, which she had washed each day—old companions all. They were friends of a simpler time, when the world had made sense. Back then she had woken each morning knowing every day would be as the one before. Now each day was filled with the fear of being discovered a failure.

On the far side of the hall, men entered, dressed in embroidered clothing rich in colors—nobles. They took seats, talking loudly, laughing, rocking back in chairs, and shouting for stewards to bring wine. She held the door for Bastion, who carried a tray of steaming food. He smiled gratefully at her as he rushed by, wiping his forehead with his sleeve.

"How do I get to the regent's office?" she whispered.

Bastion did not pause as he hurried past, but called back, "Go around the reception hall, through the throne room."

"Then what?"

"Just ask the clerk."

She headed down the corridor and around the curved wall of the grand stair toward the palace entrance. Workers propped the front doors open, granting entry to three stories of daylight, which revealed the cloud of dust they were building. Sweat-oiled men hauled in timber, mortar, and stone. Teams cut wood and marble. Workers scrambled up and down willowy ladders while pulleys hoisted buckets to scaffold-perched masons. All of them were working hard to reshape visitors' first impressions. She noticed with amazement that a wall had been moved and the ceiling was higher than the last time she had been here. The entrance was now more expansive and impressive than the darkened chamber it once had been.

"Excuse me?" a voice called. A thin man stood in the open doorway to the courtyard. He hesitated on the steps, dodging the passing workers. "May I enter?" He coughed, waving a handkerchief before his face.

Amilia looked at him and shrugged. "Why not? Everyone else is."

He took several tentative steps, glancing up fearfully, his arms partially raised as if to ward off a blow. A thin, brittle-looking man wearing a powdered wig, a brilliant yellow tunic, and striped orange britches, he stood taller than Amilia.

"Good day to you, my lady," he greeted her with a bow as soon as he had cleared the activity. "My name is Nimbus of Vernes and I have come to offer my services."

"Oh," she said with a blank stare. "I don't think—"

"Oh please, I beg of you, hear me out. I am a courtier formerly of King Fredrick and Queen Josephine of Galeannon. I am well versed in all courtly protocol, procedures, and correspondence. Prior to that, I was chamberlain to Duke Ibsen of Vernes, so I am capable of managing—" He paused. "Are you all right?"

Amilia swallowed. "I'm just in a hurry. I'm on my way to a very important meeting with the regent."

"Please forgive me, then. It is just that—well, I have—" He slouched his shoulders and sighed. "I am embarrassed to say that I am a refugee of the Nationalists' invasion and have nothing more than the clothes on my back and what little I have in this satchel. I have walked my way here and... I am a bit hungry. I was hoping I could find employment at the palace court. I am not suited for anything else," he said, dusting his shoulders clear of the snowy debris that drifted down from the scaffolds.

"I'm sorry to hear that, but I'm not—" She stopped when she saw his lip tremble. "How long has it been since you've eaten?"

"Quite some time, I am afraid. I have actually lost track."

"Listen," she told him. "I can get you something to eat, but you have to wait until after my meeting."

She thought he would cry then as he bit his lip and nodded several times, saying, "Thank you ever so much, my lady."

"Wait here. I'll be back soon...I hope."

She headed off, dodging the lathered men in leather aprons, and slipped past three others in robes, holding measuring sticks like staffs and arguing over lines on huge parchments spread across a worktable.

The throne room, which also showed signs of renovation, was nearly finished and only a few towers of scaffolding remained. The marble floor glistened with a luster, as did the mammoth pillars that held up the domed ceiling. Near the interior wall rose the dais, upon which stood the golden imperial throne, sculpted in the shape of a giant bird of prey. The wings spread into a vast circle of splayed feathers, which formed the chair's back. She passed through the arcade behind it to the administration offices.

"What do you want?" the clerk asked Amilia. She had never liked him. His face looked like a rodent's, with small eyes, large front teeth, and a brief smattering of black hair on a pale, balding head. The little man sat behind a formidable desk, his fingers dyed black from ink.

"I'm here to see Regent Saldur," she replied. "He sent for me."

"Upstairs, fourth floor," he said, dismissing her by looking back down at his parchments.

On the second floor, plaster covered the walls. On the third floor, she found paneling, and by the fourth level the paneling was a richly carved dark cherry wood. Lanterns became elegant chandeliers, a long red carpet ran the length of the corridor, and glass windows let in light from outside. She recalled how out of place Saldur had seemed when he had visited the kitchen. She looked down at her dirty smock and recognized the irony.

The door lay open and Regent Saldur stood before an arched window built from three of the largest pieces of glass she had ever seen. Birdsongs drifted in from the ward below as the regent read a parchment he held in the sunlight.

"You're late," he said without looking up.

"I'm sorry. I didn't know how to get here."

"Something you should understand: I'm not interested in excuses or explanations. I'm only interested in results. When I tell you to do something, I expect it'll be done exactly as I dictate, not sooner, not later, not differently, but *exactly* how I specify. Do you understand?"

"Yes, Your Grace." She felt considerably warmer than she had a moment earlier.

The regent walked to his desk and laid the parchment on it. He placed his fingertips together, tapping them against each other while studying her. "What's your name again?"

"Amilia of Tarin Vale."

"Amilia—a pretty name. Amilia, you impressed me. That is not easy to do. I appointed five separate women to the task of imperial secretary—ladies of breeding, ladies of pedigree. You are the first to show an improvement in Her Eminence. You have also presented me with a unique problem. I can't have a common scullery maid working as the personal assistant to the empress. How will that look?" He took a seat behind his desk, brushing out the folds of his robe. "It's conceivable that the empress could have died if not for whatever magic you performed. For this, you deserve a reward. I'm bestowing on you the diplomatic rank equal to a baroness. From this moment on, you will be known as Lady Amilia."

He dipped a quill into ink and scribbled his name. "Present

this to the clerk downstairs and he will arrange for you to obtain the necessary material for a better—Well, for a dress."

Amilia stared at him, unable to move, taking shallow breaths, not wanting to disturb anything. She was riding a wave of good fortune and feared the slightest movement could throw her into an unforgiving sea. He was not punishing her after all. The rest she could think about later.

"Have you nothing to say?"

Amilia hesitated. "Could the empress get a new dress as well?"

"You are now Lady Amilia, imperial secretary to Empress Modina Novronian. You can take whatever measures you feel are necessary to ensure the well-being of the empress."

"Can I take her outside for walks?"

"No," he said curtly. He then softened his tone and added, "As we both know, Modina is not well. I personally feel she may never be. But it's imperative that her subjects believe they have a strong ruler. Through her name, Ethelred and I are doing great things for the people out there." He pointed at the window. "But we can't hope to succeed if they discover their beloved empress does not have her wits about her. It's a difficult task that Novron has laid before us, to build a better world while concealing the empress's incapacitation, which brings me to your first assignment."

Amilia blinked.

"Despite all my efforts, word is getting out that the empress is not well. Since the public has never seen her, there is a growing rumor that she doesn't exist. We need to calm the people's fear. To this end, it will be your task to prepare Modina to give a speech upon the Grand Balcony in three days' time."

"What?"

"Don't worry, it's only three sentences." He picked up the

parchment he had been reading and held it out to her. "It should be a simple task. You got her to say one word. Now get her to say a few more. Have her memorize the speech and train her to deliver it—like an empress."

"But I—"

"Remember what I said about excuses. You are part of the nobility now, a person of privilege and power. I've given you means and with that comes responsibility. Now out with you. I've more work to do."

Taking the parchments, she turned and walked toward the door.

"And, Lady Amilia, don't forget that there were five imperial secretaries before you, and all of them were noble as well."

❧

"Well, if that don't put a stiff wind in your main," Ibis declared, looking at the patent of nobility Amilia showed him. Most of the kitchen staff gathered around the cook as he held the parchment up, grinning.

"It's awfully pretty," Cora pointed out. "I love all the fancy writing."

"Never had a desire to read before," Ibis said. "But I sure wish I could now."

"May I?" Nimbus asked. He carefully wiped his hands on his handkerchief and, reaching out, gently took the parchment. "It reads 'I, Modina, who am right wise empress, appointed to this task by the mercy of our lord Maribor, through my imperial regents, Maurice Saldur and Lanis Ethelred, decree that in recognition of faithful service and commission of charges found to our favor, Amilia of Tarin Vale, daughter of Bartholomew the carriage maker, be raised from her current station and shall belong to the unquestionable nobles of the Novronian Empire and will henceforth and forever be known as Lady Amilia of Tarin Vale.'" Nimbus looked up. "There is a good deal more, concerning the limitations of familial inheritance and nobility rights, but that is the essence of the writ."

They all stared at the cornstalk of a man.

"This is Nimbus," Amilia said, introducing him. "He's in need of a meal, and I was hoping you could give him a little something."

Ibis grinned and made a modest bow.

"Yer a lady now, Amilia. There isn't a person in this room who can say no to you. You hear that, Edith?" he shouted at the head maid as she entered. "Our little Amilia is a noble lady now."

Edith stood where she was. "Says who?"

"The empress and Regent Saldur, that's who. Says so right on this here parchment. Care to read it?"

Edith scowled.

"Oh, that's right. You can't read any more than I can. Would you like *Lady* Amilia to read it to you? Or how about her personal steward? He has an excellent reading voice."

Edith grabbed up a pile of linens from the bin and headed for the laundry, causing the cook to burst into laughter. "She's never given up spouting how you'd be back scrubbing dishes—or worse." Clapping his big hands, he turned his attention to Nimbus. "So, what would you like?"

"Anything, actually," Nimbus replied, his hands quivering, shaking the parchment he still held. "After several days, even shoe leather looks quite appetizing."

"Well, I'll get right on that, then."

"Can we clear a place for Nimbus to sit?" Amilia asked, and immediately Cora and Nipper were cleaning off the baker's table and setting it just as they had before.

"Thank you," Amilia said. "You don't need to go to this much trouble—but thank you, everyone."

"Pardon me, my lady," Nimbus addressed her. "If I may be so bold, it is not entirely proper for a lady of nobility to convey appreciation for services rendered by subordinates."

Amilia sat down beside him and sighed. She dropped her chin into her hands and grimaced. "I don't know how to be noble. I don't know anything, but I'm expected to teach Modina how to be an empress?" The contrast of fortune and pending disaster left her perplexed. "His Grace might as well kill me now." She took the parchment from Nimbus and shook it in her hand. "At least now that I'm noble, I might get a quick beheading."

Leif delivered a plate of stew. Nimbus looked down at the bowl and the scattering of utensils arrayed around him. "The kitchen staff is not very experienced in setting a table, are they?" He picked up a small two-prong fork and shook his head. "This is a shellfish fork, and it should be on the left of my plate...assuming I was eating shellfish. What I do not have is a spoon."

Amilia felt stupid. "I don't think anyone here knows what a fork is." She looked down incredulously at the twisted spindle of wire. "Even the nobility don't use them. At least, I've never washed one before."

"That would depend on where you are. They are popular farther south."

"I'll get you a spoon." She started to get up when she felt his hand on hers.

"Again," he said, "forgive my forwardness, but a lady does not fetch flatware from the pantry. And you *are* now in the nobility. You there!" He shouted at Nipper as the boy flew by with a bucket. "Fetch a spoon for Her Ladyship."

"Right away," the boy replied, setting the bucket down and running to the pantry.

"See?" he said. "It is not difficult, and takes just a bit of confidence and the right tone of voice."

Nipper returned with the spoon. It never touched the table. Nimbus took it right from his hand and began to eat. Despite his ravenous state, he ate slowly, occasionally using one of the napkins that he placed neatly on his lap to dab the corners of his mouth. He sat straight, in much the same way Lady Constance had—his chin up, his shoulders squared, his fingers placed precisely on the spoon. She had never seen anyone eat so... perfectly.

"You need not stay here," he told her. "While I appreciate the company, I am certain you have more important things to attend to. I can find my way out when I am finished, but I do wish to thank you for this meal. You saved my life."

"I want you to work for me," she blurted out. "To help me teach Modina to act like an empress."

Nimbus paused with a spoonful halfway to his mouth.

"You know all about being noble. You even said you were a courtier. You know all the rules and stuff."

"Protocol and etiquette."

"Yeah, those too. I don't know if I can arrange for you to be paid, but I might. The regent said I could take whatever steps necessary. Even if I can't, I can find you a place to sleep and see that you get meals."

"At the moment, my lady, that is a fortune, and I would consider it an honor if I could assist Her Eminence in any way."

"Then it's settled. You are officially the..."

"Imperial Tutor to Her Eminence, the Empress Modina?" Nimbus supplied.

"Right. And our first job is to teach her to give a speech on the Grand Balcony in three days."

"That does not sound too difficult. Has she done much public speaking?"

Amilia forced a smile. "A week ago she said the word *no*."

CHAPTER 11

RATIBOR

Entering the city of Ratibor at night, Arista thought it the most filthy, wretched place she could ever imagine. Streets lay in random, confusing lines, crisscrossing at intersections as they ran off at various odd angles. Refuse was piled next to every building, and narrow dirt thoroughfares were appalling mires of mud and manure. Wooden planks created a network of haphazard paths and bridges over the muck, forcing people to parade in lines like tightrope walkers. The houses and shops were as miserable as the roads. Constructed to fit in the spaces left by the street's odd, acute corners, buildings were shaped like wedges of cheese, giving the city a strange, splintered appearance. The windows, shut tight against the city's stench, were opaque with thick grime repeatedly splashed by passing wagons.

Ratibor reveled in its filth like a poor man who is proud of the calluses on his hands. Arista had heard of its reputation, but until experiencing it firsthand, she had not truly understood. This was a workingman's town, a struggling city where no quarter was expected or given. Here men bore poverty and misfortune as badges of honor, deriving dubious prestige from contests of woe over tankards of ale.

Idlers and vagabonds, hawkers and thieves moved along the plank ways, appearing and disappearing again into the shadows. There were children on the street—orphans, by the look—ragged and pitiful waifs covered in filth, crouching under porches. Small families also moved among the crowds. Tradesmen with their wives and children carried bundles or wheeled overfilled carts loaded with all their worldly possessions. All looked exhausted and destitute as they trudged through the city's maze.

The rain had started not long after they had left Amberton Lee, and poured the entire trip. She was soaked through. Her hair lay matted to her face, her fingers were pruned, and her hood collapsed about her head. Arista followed Royce as he led them through the labyrinth of muddy streets. The cool night wind blew the downpour in sheets, making her shiver. During the trip, she had looked forward to reaching the city. Although it was not what she had expected, anything indoors would be welcomed.

"Care for a raincoat, mum?" a hawker asked, holding up a garment for Arista to see. "Only five silver!" he continued as she showed no sign of slowing her horse. "How about a new hat?"

"Either of you gentlemen looking for companionship for the night?" called a destitute woman standing on a plank beneath the awning of a closed dry-goods shop. She flipped back her hair and smiled alluringly, revealing missing teeth.

"How about a nice bit of poultry for an evening meal?" another man asked, holding up a dead bird so thin and scraggly it was hardly recognizable as a chicken.

Arista shook her head, saying nothing except words to urge her horse forward.

Signs were everywhere—nailed to porch beams or attached to tall stakes driven into the mud. They advertised things like

ALE, CIDER, MEAD, WINE, NO CREDIT! and THREE-DAY-OLD PORK — CHEAP! But some were more ominous, such as BEGGARS WILL BE JAILED! and ALL ELVES ENTERING THE CITY MUST REGISTER AT THE SHERIFF'S OFFICE. This last poster's paint was still bright.

Royce stopped at a public house with a signboard of a grotesque cackling face and a scripted epitaph that read THE LAUGHING GNOME. The tavern stood three stories, a good size even by Colnora's standards, yet people still struggled to squeeze in the front door. Inside, the place smelled of damp clothes and wood smoke. A large crowd filled the common room such that Hadrian had to push his way through.

"We're looking for the proprietor," Royce told a young man carrying a tray.

"That would be Ayers. He's the gray-haired gent behind the bar."

"It's true, I tell you!" a young man with fiery red hair was saying loudly as he stood in the center of the common room. To whom he was speaking, Arista was not certain. It appeared to be everyone. "My father was a Praleon Guard. He served on His Majesty's personal retinue for twenty years."

"What does that prove? Urith and the rest of them died in the fire. No one knows how it started."

"The fire was set by Androus!" shouted the red-haired youth with great conviction. Abruptly, the room quieted. The young man was not content with this, however, and he took the stunned pause to press his point. "He betrayed the king, killed the royal family, and took the crown so he could hand the kingdom over to the empress. Good King Urith would never have accepted annexation into the New Empire, and those loyal to his name shouldn't either."

The crowd burst into an uproar of angry shouts.

In the midst of this outburst, the three of them reached the bar, where a handful of men stood watching the excitement with empty mugs in hand.

"Mr. Ayers?" Royce asked of a man and a boy as they struggled to hoist a fresh keg onto the rear dock.

"Who wants to know?" asked the man in a stained apron. A drop of sweat dangled from the tip of his red nose, his face flushed from exertion.

"We're looking to rent a pair of rooms."

"Not much luck of that. We're full up," Ayers replied, not pausing from his work. "Jimmy, jump up and shim it." The young lad, filthy with sweat and dirt, leapt up on the dock and pushed a wooden wedge under the keg, tilting it forward slightly.

"Do you know of availability elsewhere in the city?" Hadrian asked.

"Gonna be the same all over, friend. Every boardinghouse is full—refugees been coming in from the countryside for weeks."

"Refugees?"

"Yeah, the Nationalists have been marching up from the coast sacking towns. People been running ahead of them and most come here. Not that I mind—been great for business."

Ayers pulled a tap out of the old keg and hammered it into the face of the new barrel with a wooden mallet. He turned the spigot and drained a pint or two to clear the sediment. Wiping his hands on his apron, he began filling the demands of his customers.

"Is there no place to find lodging for the night?"

"I can't say that, just no place I know of," Ayers replied, and finally took a moment to wipe a sleeve over his face and clear the drop from his nose. "Maybe some folks will rent a room in their houses, but all the inns and taverns are packed. I've even started to rent floor space."

"Is there any left?" Hadrian asked hopefully.

"Any what?"

"Floor space. It's raining pretty hard out there."

Ayers lifted his head up and glanced around his tavern. "I've got space under the stairs that no one's taken yet. If you don't mind the people walking on top of you all night."

"It's better than the gutter," Hadrian said, shrugging at Royce and Arista. "Maybe tomorrow there will be a vacancy."

Ayers's face showed he doubted this. "If you want to stay, it'll be forty-five silver."

"Forty-five?" Hadrian exclaimed, stunned. "For space under the stairs? No wonder no one has taken it. A room at The Regal Fox in Colnora is only twenty!"

"Go there, then, but if you want to stay here, it'll cost you forty-five silver—in tenents. I don't take those imperial notes they're passing now. It's your choice."

Hadrian scowled at Ayers but counted out the money just the same. "I hope that includes dinner."

Ayers shook his head. "It doesn't."

"We also have three horses."

"Lucky you."

"No room at the stable either? Is it okay to leave them out front?"

"Sure...for another...five silver a horse."

They pushed and prodded their way through the crowd with their bags until they came to the wooden staircase. Beneath it, several people had discarded their wet cloaks on nail heads or on the empty kegs and crates stored there. Royce and Hadrian stacked the containers to make a cubby and threw the coats and cloaks on them. A few people shot them harsh looks—the owners of the cloaks, no doubt—but no one said anything, as it appeared most understood the situation. Looking around, Arista saw others squatting in corners and along the edge of the big room. Some were families with children trying to sleep, their little heads resting on damp clothes. Mothers rubbed their backs and sang lullabies over the racket of loud voices, shifting wooden chairs, and the banging of pewter mugs. These were the lucky ones. She wondered about the families who could not afford floor space.

How many are cowering outside under a boardwalk or in a muddy alley somewhere in the rain?

As they settled, Arista noticed the noise of the inn was not simply the confusing sounds of forty unrelated conversations, but rather one discussion voiced by several people with various opinions. From time to time one speaker would rise above the others to make a point, and then drown in the response from the crowd. The most vocal was the red-haired young man.

"No, he's not!" he shouted once more. "He's not a blood relative of Urith. He's the brother of Urith's second wife."

"And I suppose you think his first wife was murdered so he could be pushed into marrying Amiter, just so Androus could become duke?"

"That's exactly what I'm saying!" the youth declared. "Don't you see? They planned this for years, and not just here either. They did it in Alburn, Warric... They even tried it in Melengar, but they failed there. Did anyone see that play last year? You know, *The Crown Conspiracy*. It was based on real events. Amrath's children outsmarted the conspirators. That's why Melengar hasn't fallen to the New Empire. Don't you see? We're all the victims of a conspiracy. I've even heard that the empress might not exist. The whole story of the Heir of Novron is a sham, invented to placate the masses. Do you really think a farm girl could kill a great beast? It is men like Androus who control us—evil, corrupt murderous men without an ounce of royal blood in their veins, or honor in their hearts!"

"So what?" a fat man in a checked vest asked defiantly. "What do we care who rules us? Our lot is always the same. You speak of matters between blue bloods. It doesn't affect us."

"You're wrong! How many men in this city were pressed into the army? How many are off to die for the empress? How many sons have gone to fight Melengar, who has never been our enemy? Now the Nationalists are coming. They're only a few miles south. They will sack this city, just as they did Vernes, and why? Because we are now joined to the empire. Do you think your sons, brothers, and fathers would be off dying if Urith were still alive? Do you want to see Ratibor destroyed?"

"They won't destroy Ratibor!" the fat man shouted back. "You're just spouting rumors, trying to scare decent people and stir up trouble. Armies will fight, and maybe the city will change hands, but it won't affect *us*. We'll still be poor and still struggling to live, as we always have. King Urith had his wars and Viceroy Androus will have his. We work, fight, and die under both of them. That's our lot and treasonous talk like this will only get people killed."

"They will burn the city," an older woman in a blue kerchief said suddenly. "Just as they burned Kilnar. I know. I was there. I saw them."

All eyes turned to her.

"That's not true! It can't be," the fat man protested. "It doesn't make sense. The Nationalists have no cause to burn the cities. They would want them intact."

"The Nationalists didn't burn it," she said. "The empire did." This statement brought the room to stunned silence. "When the imperial government saw that the city would be lost, they ordered Kilnar to be torched to leave nothing for the Nationalists."

"It's true," said a man seated with his family near the kitchen. "We lived in Vernes. I saw the city guards burning the shops and homes there too."

"The same will happen here." The youth caught the crowd's attention once more. "Unless we do something about it."

"What can we do?" a young mother asked.

"We can join the Nationalists. We can give the city to them before the viceroy has a chance to torch it."

"This is treason," the fat man said. "You'll bring death to us all!"

"The empire took Rhenydd through deceit, murder, and trickery. I don't speak treason. I speak loyalty—loyalty to the monarchy. To sit by and let the empire rape this kingdom and burn this city *is* treason and, what's more, it's foolhardy cowardice!"

"Are you calling me a coward?"

"No, sir, I'm calling you a fool *and* a coward."

The fat man stood up indignantly and drew a dagger from his belt. "I demand satisfaction."

The youth stood and unsheathed a long sword. "As you wish."

"You would duel me sword against dagger and call me the coward?"

"I also called you a fool, and a fool it is who holds a dagger and challenges a man with a sword."

Several people in the room laughed at this, which only infuriated the fat man more. "Do you have no honor?"

"I'm but a poor soldier's son from a destitute town. I can't afford honor." Again, the crowd laughed. "I'm also a practical man, who knows it's more important to win than to die—for honor is something that concerns only the living. But understand this: if you choose to fight me, I'll kill you any way I can, the same way that I'll try to save this city and its people any way I can. Honor and allegiance be damned!"

The crowd applauded now, much to the chagrin of the fat man. Red-faced, he stood for a moment, then shoved his dagger back in his belt and abruptly stalked out the door into the rain.

"But how can we turn the city over to the Nationalists?" the old woman asked.

The youth turned to her. "If we raise a militia, we can raid the armory and storm the city garrison. After that, we'll arrest the viceroy. That will give us the city. The imperial army is camped a mile to the south. When the Nationalists attack, they will expect to retreat to the safety of the city walls. But when they arrive, they will find the gates locked. In disarray and turmoil, they will be routed and the Nationalists will destroy them. After that, we'll welcome the Nationalists in as allies. Given our assistance in helping them take the city, we can expect fair treatment and possibly even self-rule, as that is the Nationalists' creed.

"Imagine that," he said dreamily. "Ratibor, the whole city—the whole kingdom of Rhenydd—being run by a people's council, just like Tur Del Fur!"

This clearly caught the imagination of many in the room.

"Craftsmen could own their own shops instead of renting. Farmers would own their land and be able to pass it tax-free to their sons. Merchants could set their own rates and taxes wouldn't be used to pay for foreign wars. Instead, that money can be used to clean up this town. We could pave the roads, tear down the vacant buildings, and put all the people of the city to work doing it. We would elect our own sheriffs and bailiffs, but they would have little to do, for what crime could there be in a free city? Freemen with their own property have no cause for crime."

"I would be willing to fight for that," a man seated with his family near the windows said.

"For paved roads, I would too," said the elderly woman.

"I'd like to own my own land," another said.

Others voiced their interest and soon the conversation turned more serious. The level of the voices dropped and men clustered together to speak in small groups.

"You're not from Rhenydd, are you?" someone asked Arista.

The princess nearly jumped when she discovered a woman had slipped in beside her. She was not immediately certain that it was a woman, as she was oddly dressed in dark britches and a man's loose shirt. Arista initially thought she was an adolescent boy, due to her short blonde hair and dappled freckles, but her eyes gave her away. They were heavy and deep, as if stolen from a much older person.

"No," Arista said apprehensively.

The woman studied Arista, her old eyes slowly moving over her body as if she were memorizing every line of her figure and every crease in her dress. "You have an odd way about you. The way you walk, the way you sit. It's all very . . . *precise*, very . . . proper."

Arista was over being startled now and was just plain irritated. "You don't strike me as the kind of person who should accuse others of being odd," she replied.

"There!" the woman said excitedly, and wagged a finger. "See? Anyone else would have called me a mannish little whore. You have manners. You speak in subtle innuendo, like a . . . *princess*."

"Who are you?" Hadrian abruptly intervened, moving between the two. Royce also appeared from the shadows behind the strange woman.

"Who are *you*?" she replied saucily.

The door to The Laughing Gnome burst open and uniformed imperial guards poured in. Tables were turned over and drinks hit the floor. Customers nearest the door fell back in fear, cowering in the corners, or were pushed aside.

"Arrest everyone!" a man ordered in a booming voice. He was a big man with a potbelly, dark brows, and sagging cheeks. He kept his weight on his heels and his thumbs in his belt as he glared at the crowd.

"What's this all about, Trenchon?" Ayers shouted from behind the bar.

"You would be smart to keep your hole shut, Ayers, or I'll close this tavern tonight and have you in stocks by morning—or worse. Harboring traitors and providing a meeting place for conspirators will buy you death at the post!"

"I didn't do nothing!" Ayers cried. "It was the kid. He's the one that started all the talk, and that woman from Kilnar. They're the ones. I just served drinks like every night. I'm not responsible for what customers say. I'm not involved in this. It was them and a few of the others who were going along with it."

"Take everyone in for questioning," Trenchon ordered. "We'll get to the bottom of this. I want the ringleaders!"

"This way," the mannish woman whispered. Grabbing Arista's arm, she began to pull the princess away from the soldiers toward the kitchen.

Arista pulled back.

The woman sighed. "Unless you want to have a long talk with the viceroy about who you are and what you're doing here, you'll follow me now."

Arista looked at Royce, who nodded, but there was concern on his face. They grabbed up their bags and followed.

Starting at the main entrance, the imperial soldiers began hauling people out into the rain and mud. Women screamed and children cried. Those who resisted were beaten and thrown out. Some near the rear door tried to run, only to find more soldiers waiting.

The mannish woman plowed through the crowd into the tavern's kitchen, where a cook looked over, surprised. "Best look out," their guide said. "Trenchon is looking to arrest everyone."

The cook dropped her ladle in shock as they pressed by her, heading to the walk-in pantry. Closing the door, the woman revealed a trapdoor in the pantry's floor. They climbed down a short wooden stair into The Laughing Gnome's wine cellar. Several dusty bottles lined the walls, as did casks of cheese and containers of butter. The woman took a lantern that hung from the ceiling and, closing the door above, led them behind the wine racks to the cellar's far wall. There was a metal grate in the floor. She wedged a piece of old timber in the bars and pried it up.

"Inside, all of you," she ordered.

Above, they could still hear the screams and shouts, then the sound of heavy boots on the kitchen floor.

"Hurry!" she whispered.

Royce entered first, climbing down metal rungs that formed a ladder. He slipped into darkness and Hadrian motioned for the princess to follow. She took a deep breath as if going underwater and climbed down.

The ladder continued far deeper than Arista would have expected, and instead of the tight, cramped tunnel she anticipated, she found herself dropping into a large gallery. It was completely dark, except around the lantern, and the smell was unmistakable. Without pause or a word of direction, the woman walked away. They had no choice but to follow her light.

They were in a sewer far larger and grander than Arista had imagined possible after seeing the city above. Walls of brick and stone rose twelve feet to a roof of decorative mosaic tiles. Every few feet grates formed waterfalls that spilled from the ceiling, raining down with a deafening roar. Storm water frothed and foamed in the center of the tunnel as it churned around corners and broke upon dividers, spraying walls and staining them dark.

They chased the woman with the lantern as she moved quickly along the brick curb near the wall. Like ribs supporting the ceiling, thick stone archways jutted out at regular intervals, blocking their path. The woman skirted around these easily, but it was much harder for Arista in her gown to traverse the columns and keep her footing on the slick stone curb. Below her, the storm's runoff created a fast-flowing river of dirty water and debris that echoed in the chamber.

The corridor reached a four-way intersection. In the stone at the top corners were chiseled small notations. These read HONOR WAY going one direction and HERALD'S STREET going the other. The woman with the lantern never wavered, and turned without a pause, leading them down Honor Way at a breakneck pace. Abruptly, she stopped.

They stood on a curb beside the sewer river, which was like any other part of the corridor they had traveled except a bit wider and quieter.

"Before we go further, I must be certain," she began. "Allow me to make things easier by guessing the lady here is actually Princess Arista Essendon of Melengar. You are Hadrian Blackwater, and you're Duster, the famous Demon of Colnora. Am I correct?"

"That would make you a Diamond," Royce said.

"At your service." She smiled, and Arista thought how catlike her face was, in that she appeared both friendly and sinister at the same time. "You can call me Quartz."

"In that case, you can assume you're correct."

"Thanks for getting us out of there," Hadrian offered.

"No need to thank me. It's my job and, in this particular

case, my happy pleasure. We didn't know where you were since leaving Colnora, but I was hoping you would happen by this way. Now follow me."

Off she sprang again, and Arista once more struggled to follow.

"How is this here?" Hadrian asked from somewhere behind Arista. "This sewer is incredible but the city above has dirt roads."

"Ratibor wasn't always Ratibor," Quartz shouted back. "Once it was something bigger. All that's been forgotten—buried like this sewer under centuries of dirt and manure."

They moved on down the tunnel until they came to an alcove, little more than a recessed area surrounded by brick. Quartz leaned up against a wooden panel and gave a strong shove. The back shifted inward slightly. She put her fingers in the crack and slid the panel sideways, exposing a hidden tunnel. They entered and traveled up a short set of steps to a wooden door. Light seeped around its cracks and voices could be heard from the other side. Quartz knocked and opened it, revealing a large subterranean chamber filled with people.

Tables, chairs, desks, and bunk beds stacked four high filled the room, lit by numerous candles that spilled a wealth of waxy tears. A fire burned in a blackened cooking hearth, where a huge iron pot was suspended by a swivel arm. Several large chests lay open, displaying sorted contents of silverware, candlesticks, clothes, hats, cloaks, and even dresses. Still other chests held purses, shoes, and rope. At least one was partially filled with coins, mostly copper, but Arista spotted a few silver and an occasional gold tenent sparkling in the firelight. This last chest they closed the moment the door opened.

A dozen people filled the room, all young, thin predators, each dressed in an odd assortment of clothing.

"Welcome to the Rat's Nest," Quartz told them. "Rats, let

me introduce you to the three travelers from Colnora." Shoulders settled, hands pulled back from weapons, and Arista heard a number of exhales. "The older gent back there is Polish." Quartz pointed over some heads at a tall, thin man with a scraggly beard and drooping eyes. He sported a tall black hat and a dramatic-looking cloak, like something a bishop would wear. "He's our fearless leader."

This comment drew a round of laughter.

"Damn you, Quartz!" a boy no older than nine cursed her.

"Sorry, Carat," she told him. "They just walked into the Gnome while I was there."

"We heard the Imps just crashed the Gnome," Polish said.

"Aye, they did." Quartz gleamed.

Eyes left them and focused abruptly on Quartz, who allowed herself a dramatic pause as she took a seat on a soft, beat-up chair, throwing her legs over the arm in a cavalier fashion. She obviously enjoyed the attention as the members of the room gathered around her.

"Emery was speeching again," she began like a master storyteller addressing an eager audience. "This time people were actually listening. He might have gotten something started, but he got under Laven's skin. Laven challenged him to a duel, but Emery says he'll fight sword to dagger, which really irks Laven and he storms out of the Gnome. Emery shoulda known to beat it then, but the dispute with Laven gets him in real good with the crowd, see, so he keeps going."

Arista noticed the thieves hanging on every word. They were enthralled as Quartz added to her tale's drama with sweeping arm gestures.

"Laven, being the bastard that he is, goes to Bailiff Trenchon, right? And returns with the town garrison. They bust in and start arresting everyone for treason."

"What'd Ayers do?" Polish asked excitedly.

"What could he do? He says, 'What's going on?' and they tell him to shut up, so he does."

"Anyone killed?" Carat asked.

"None that I saw, but I had to beat it out of there real quick like to save our guests here."

"Did they take Emery?"

"I suppose so, but I didn't see it."

Polish crossed the room to face them up close. He nodded as if in approval and pulled absently on his thin beard.

"Princess Arista," he said formally, and tipped his hat as he made a clumsy bow. "Please excuse the place. We don't often entertain guests of your stature here, and quite frankly, we didn't know when, or even if, you'd be coming."

"If we had known, we'd have at least washed the rats!" someone in the back shouted, bringing more laughter.

"Quiet, you reprobate. You must forgive them, milady. They're the lowest form of degenerates and their lifestyle only aggravates their condition. I try to elevate them, but as you can see, I've been less than successful."

"That's because you're the biggest blackguard here, Polish," Quartz shot at him.

Polish ignored the comment and moved to face Royce. "Duster?" he said, raising an eyebrow.

At the mention of that name, the whole room quieted and everyone pushed forward to get a better look.

"I thought he was bigger," someone said.

"That's not Duster," Carat declared, bravely stepping forward. "He's just an old man."

"Carat," Quartz said dismissively, "the cobbler's new puppy is old compared to you."

This brought forth more laughter and Carat kicked Quartz's feet off the chair's arm. "Shut up, freckle face."

"The lad makes a good point," Polish said.

"I don't have that many freckles," Quartz countered.

Polish rolled his eyes. "No, I meant just how do we really know this *is* Duster and the princess? Could be the Imps knew we were looking and are setting us up. Do you have any proof about who you are?"

As he said this, Arista noticed Polish let his hand drift casually to the long black dagger at his belt. Others in the room began to spread out, making slow but menacing movements. Only Quartz remained at ease on her chair.

Hadrian looked a bit concerned as Royce cast off his cloak, letting it fall to the floor. Eyes narrowed on him as they stared at the white-bladed dagger in his belt. Everyone waited anxiously for his next move. Royce surprised them by slowly unbuttoning his shirt and pulling it down to expose his left shoulder, revealing a scarred brand in the shape of an *M*.

Polish leaned forward and studied the scar. "The Mark of Manzant," he said, and his expression changed to one of wonder. "Duster is the only living man known to have escaped that prison."

They all nodded and murmured in awed tones as Royce put his cloak back on.

"He still doesn't look like no monster to me," Carat said with disdain.

"That's only because you've never seen him first thing in the morning," Hadrian told him. "He's an absolute fiend until he's had breakfast."

This brought a chuckle from the Diamonds and a reluctant smile from Carat.

"Now that that's settled, can we get to business?" Royce asked. "You need to send word to the Jewel that Etcher is a traitor and find out if a meeting has been set up with Gaunt."

"All in good time," Polish said. "First we have a very important matter to settle."

"That's right." Quartz came to life, leapt to her feet, and took a seat at the main table. "Pay up, people!"

There were irritated grumblings as the thieves reluctantly pulled out purses and counted coins. They each set stacks of silver in front of Quartz. Polish joined her and they started counting together.

"You too, Set," Quartz said. "You were down for half a stone."

When everyone was finished, Polish and Quartz divided the loot into two piles.

"And for being the one to find them?" she said, smiling at Polish.

Polish scowled and handed her a stack of silver, which she dropped into her own purse, now bulging and so heavy she needed to use two hands to hold it.

"You bet we wouldn't make it here?" Arista asked.

"Most everyone did, yes," Polish replied, smiling.

"'Cept Polish and I," Quartz said happily. "Not that I thought you'd make it either. I just liked the odds and the chance for a big payoff if you did."

"Great minds, my dear," Polish told her as he also put his share away. "Great minds, indeed."

Once his treasure was safely locked in a chest, Polish turned with a more serious look on his face. "Quartz, take Set and visit the Nationalists' camp. See if you can arrange a meeting. Take Degan Street. It'll be the safest now."

"Not to mention poetic," Quartz said, smiling at her own insight. She waved at Set, who grabbed his cloak. "I know exactly how much is in my trunk," Quartz told everyone as she dropped her purse in a chest. "It had best be there when I come back or I'll make sure *everyone* pays."

No one scoffed or laughed. Apparently, when it came to money, thieves did not make jokes.

"Yes, yes, now out with you two." Polish shooed them into the sewer, then turned to face the new guests. "Hmm, now what to do with you? We can't move around tonight with the city watch in a frenzy, besides which, the weather has been most unfriendly. Perhaps in the morning we can find you a safe house, but for tonight I'm afraid you'll all have to stay here in our humble abode. As you can see, we don't have the finest accommodations for a princess."

"I'll be fine," she said.

Polish looked at her, surprised. "Are you sure you *are* a princess?"

"She's becoming more human every day," Hadrian said, smiling at her.

"You can sleep over here," Carat told them, bouncing on one of the bunks. "This is Quartz's bed and the one below is Set's. They'll be out all night."

"Thank you," Arista told him, taking a seat on the lower berth. "You're quite the gentleman."

Carat straightened up at the comment and puffed up his chest, smiling back at Arista fondly.

"He's a miserable thief, behind on his accounts, is what he is," Polish admonished, pointing a finger. "You still owe me, remember?"

The boy's proud face dropped.

"I'm surprised they already named a street after Degan Gaunt," Arista mentioned, changing the subject. "I had no idea he was that popular."

Several people snickered.

"You got it backward," an older man with a craggy face said.

"The street wasn't named after Gaunt," Polish explained. "Gaunt's mother named him after the street."

"Gaunt is from Ratibor?" Hadrian asked.

Polish looked at him as if he had just questioned the existence of the sun. "Born on Degan Street. They say he was captured by pirates and that's where his life changed and the legend began."

Hadrian turned to Royce. "See? Being raised in Ratibor isn't always such a bad thing."

"Duster is from Ratibor? Where 'bouts did you live?"

Royce kept his eyes on his pack. "Don't you think you should send someone with that message about Etcher back to Colnora? The Jewel will want to know about him immediately, and any delay could get people killed."

Polish wagged a finger at Royce. "I remember you, you know. We never met, but I was in the Diamond back when you were. You were quite the bigwig, telling everyone what to do." Polish allowed himself a snicker. "I suppose that's a hard habit to break, eh? Still, practice makes perfect," Polish said, turning away. "There are dry blankets here you can use. We'll see about better arrangements in the morning."

Royce and Hadrian rooted around in their bags. Arista watched them enviously. Etcher had taken her bundle with him. Maybe he needed it as proof, or perhaps he had thought there could have been something of value in it. In any case, he had known she would not need it. Most likely, he had forgotten her pack was still on the horse. The loss was not great, a mangled and dirty dress, her nightgown and robe, her kris dagger, and a blanket. The only thing she still had with her was the only thing she cared about—the hairbrush from her father, which she took out. She attempted to tame the tangled mess that was her hair.

"You have such a way with people, Royce," Hadrian mentioned as he opened another pack.

Royce growled something Arista could not make out, and seemed overly focused on his gear.

"Where *did* you live, Royce?" Arista asked. "When you were here."

There was a long pause. Finally, he replied, "This isn't the first time I've slept in these sewers."

❧

The sun had barely peeked over the horizon and already the air was hot, heavy with a stifling blanket of humidity. The rain had stopped but clouds lingered, shrouding the sun in a milky haze. The streets were filled with puddles, great pools of brown water, still as glass. A mongrel dog—thin and mangy—roamed the market, sniffing garbage. Flushing a rat, the mutt chased it to the sewers. Having lost it, he lapped from the brown water, then collapsed, panting. Insects appeared. Clouds of gnats formed over the larger puddles and biting flies circled the tethered horses. They fought them as best they could with a shake of the head, a stomp of the hooves, or a swish of the tail. Before long, people appeared. Most were women clad in plain dresses. The few men were shirtless, and everyone went about barefoot, their legs caked with mud to their knees. They opened shops and stands displaying a meager assortment of fruits, eggs, vegetables, and some meat, laid bare, to the flies' delight.

Royce had barely slept. Too wary to close his eyes for more than a few minutes at a time, he had given up. He rose sometime before dawn and made his way to the surface. He climbed on the bed of a wagon left abandoned in the mud and watched East End Square come alive. He had seen the sight before, only the faces were different. He hated this city. If it were a man, he would have slit its throat decades ago. The thought appealed to him as he stared at the muddy, puddle-filled square. Some problems were easily fixed by the draw of a knife, but others…

He was not alone.

Not long after first light, Royce spotted a boy lying under a cart in the mud, only his head visible above the ruts. For hours, the two remained aware of each other, but neither acknowledged it. When the shops began to open, the boy slipped from his muddy bed, crawled to one of the larger puddles, and washed some of the muck off. His hair remained caked with the gray clay, because he did not submerge his head. As the boy moved down the road, Royce saw he was nearly naked and kept a small pouch tied around his neck. Royce knew the pouch held all the boy's possessions. He imagined a small bit of glass for cutting, string, a smooth rock for hammering and breaking, and perhaps even a copper coin or two—it was a king's ransom that he would defend with his life, if it came to that.

The boy moved to an undisturbed puddle and drank deeply from the surface. Untouched rainwater was the best. Cleaner, fresher than well water, and much easier to get—much safer.

The boy kept a keen eye on him, constantly glancing over.

With his morning wash done, the lad crept around the cooper's shop, which was still closed. He hid himself between two tethered horses, rubbing their muddy legs. He glanced once more at Royce with an irritated look and then threw a pebble in the direction of the grocer. Nothing happened. The boy searched for another, paused, then threw again. This time the stone hit a pitcher of milk, which toppled and spilled. The grocer howled in distress and rushed to save what she could. As she did, the boy made a dash to steal a small sour apple and an egg. He made a clean grab and was back around the corner of the cooper's barn before the grocer turned.

His chest heaved as he watched Royce. He paused only a moment, then cracked the egg and spilled the gooey contents into his mouth, swallowing with pleasure.

Over the waif's right shoulder, Royce saw two figures

approaching. They were boys like him, but older and larger. One wore a pair of men's britches that extended to his ankles. The other wore a filthy tunic tied around his waist with a length of twine and a necklace made from a torn leather belt. The boy did not see them until it was too late. The two grabbed him by the hair and dragged him into the street, where they forced his face into the mud. The bigger boys wrenched the apple from his hand and ripped the pouch from his neck before letting go.

Sputtering, gasping, and blind, the boy struggled to breathe. He came up swinging and found only air. The kid wearing the oversized britches kicked him in the stomach, crumpling the boy to his knees. The one wearing the tunic took a turn and kicked the boy once, striking him in the side and landing him back in the mud. They laughed as they continued up Herald's Street, one holding the apple, the other swinging the neck pouch.

Royce watched the boy lying in the street. No one helped. No one noticed. Slowly the boy crawled back to his shelter beneath the wheel cart. Royce could hear him crying and cursing as he pounded his fist in the mud.

Feeling something on his cheek, Royce brushed away the wetness. He stood up, surprised his breathing was so shallow. He followed the plank walkway to the grocer, who smiled brightly at him.

"Terribly hot today, ain't it, sir?"

Royce ignored her. He picked out the largest, ripest apple he could find.

"Five copper if you please, sir."

Royce paid the woman without a word, then pulled a solid gold tenent from his pouch and pressed it sideways into the fruit. He walked back across the square. This time he took a different path, one that passed by the cart the boy lay under, and as he did, the apple slipped from his fingers and fell into the mud. Royce muttered a curse at his clumsiness and continued his way up the street.

~

As the day approached midmorning, the temperature grew oppressive. Arista was dressed in a hodgepodge of boyish clothes gleaned from the Diamond's stash. A shapeless cap hid most of her hair. A battered, oversized tunic and torn trousers gave her the look of a hapless urchin. In Ratibor, this nearly guaranteed her invisibility. Hadrian guessed it was more comfortable than her heavy gown and cloak.

The three of them arrived at the intersection of Legends and Lore. There had been a brief discussion about leaving Arista in the Rat's Nest, but after Hintindar, Hadrian was reluctant to have her out of his sight.

The thoroughfares of the two streets formed one of the many acute angles so prevalent in the city. Here a pie-shaped church dominated. Made of stone, the building stood out among its wooden neighbors, a heavy, overbuilt structure more like a fortress than a place of worship.

"Why a Nyphron church of all things?" Hadrian asked as they reached the entrance. "Maybe we got it wrong. I don't even know what I'm looking for."

Royce nudged Hadrian and pointed at the cornerstone. Chiseled into its face, the epitaph read:

ESTABLISHED 2992

"'Before you were born, the year ninety-two,'" he whispered. "I doubt it's a coincidence."

"Churches keep accounts concerning births, marriages,

and deaths in their community," Arista pointed out. "If there was a battle in which people died, there could be a record."

Pulling on the thick oak doors, Hadrian found them locked. He knocked and, when no response came, knocked again. He pounded with his fist, and then, just as Royce began looking for another way in, the door opened.

"I'm sorry, but services aren't until tomorrow," an elderly priest announced. He was dressed in the usual robes. He had a balding head and a wrinkled face that peered through the small crack of the barely opened door.

"That's okay. I'm not here for services," Hadrian replied. "I was hoping I could get a look at the church records."

"Records?"

Hadrian glanced at Arista. "I heard churches keep records on births and deaths."

"Oh yes, but why do you want to see them?"

"I'm trying to find out what happened to someone." The priest looked skeptical. "My father," he added.

Understanding washed over the priest's face and he beckoned them in.

As Hadrian had expected, it was oppressively dark. Banks of candles burned on either side of the altar and at various points around the worship hall, each doing more to emphasize the darkness than provide illumination.

"We actually keep very good records here," the priest mentioned as he closed the door behind them. "By the way, I'm Monsignor Bartholomew. I'm watching over the church while His Reverence Bishop Talbert is away on pilgrimage to Ervanon. And you are?"

"Hadrian Blackwater." He gestured to Royce and Arista. "These are friends of mine."

"I see. Then if you'll please follow me..." Bartholomew said.

Hadrian had never spent much time in churches. The darkness, opulence, and staring eyes of the sculptures unnerved him. He was at home in a forest or a field, a hovel or a fortress, but the interior of a church always made him uneasy. This one had a vaulted ceiling supported by marble columns and cinquefoil-shaped stonework and blind-tracery moldings common to Nyphron churches. The altar itself was an ornately carved wooden cabinet with three broad doors and a blue-green marble top. His mind flashed back to a similar cabinet in Essendon Castle that had concealed Magnus, a dwarf waiting to accuse him and Royce of Amrath's death. That incident had started his and Royce's long-standing employment with Medford's royal family.

On this one, more candles burned, and three large gilded tomes lay sealed. The sickly-sweet fragrance of salifan incense was strong. On the altar stood the obligatory alabaster statue of Novron. As always, he knelt, sword in hand, while the god Maribor loomed over him, placing a crown on his head, anointing his son the ruler of the world. All the churches Hadrian had visited had one, each a replica of the original sculpture preserved in the Crown Tower of Ervanon. They varied only in size and material.

Taking a candle, the priest led them down a narrow, curling stair. At the base, they stopped at a door, beside which hung an iron key on a peg. The priest lifted it off and twisted it in the large square lock until it clanked. The door creaked open and the priest replaced the key.

"Doesn't make much sense, does it? To keep the key there?" Royce pointed out.

The priest glanced back at it blankly. "It's heavy and I don't like carrying it."

"Then why lock the door?"

"Only way to keep it closed. And if left open, the rats eat the parchments."

Inside, the cellar was half the size of the church above and divided into aisles of shelves that stretched to the ceiling and were filled with thick leather-bound books. The priest took a moment to light a lantern that hung near the door.

"They're all in chronological order," he told them as the lantern revealed a low ceiling and walls made of small stacked stones quite unlike the larger blocks and bricks used in the rest of the church.

"About what time period are you looking for? When did your father die?"

"Twenty-nine ninety-two."

The priest hesitated. "Ninety-two? That was forty-two years ago. You age remarkably well. How old were you?"

"Very young."

The priest looked skeptical. "Well, I'm sorry. We have no records from ninety-two."

"The cornerstone outside says this church was built then," Royce said.

"And yet we do not have the records for which you ask."

"Why is that?" Hadrian pressed.

The priest shrugged. "Maybe there was a fire."

"*Maybe* there was a fire? You don't know?"

"Our records cannot help you, so if you'll please follow me, I'll show you out." The priest took a step toward the exit.

Royce stepped in his path. "You're hiding something."

"I'm doing nothing of the sort. You asked to see records from ninety-two—there are none."

"The question is, why?"

"Any number of reasons. How should I know?"

"The same way you knew there aren't any records here for

that date without even looking," Royce replied, his voice lowering. "You're lying to us, which again brings up the question of why."

"I'm a monsignor. I don't appreciate being accused of lying in my own church."

"And I don't appreciate being lied to." Royce took a step forward.

"Neither do I," Bartholomew replied. "You're not looking for anyone's father. Do you think I'm a fool? Why are you back here? That business ended decades ago. Why are you still at it?"

Royce glanced at Hadrian. "We've never been here before."

The priest rolled his eyes. "You know what I mean. Why is the seret still digging this up? You're Sentinel Thranic, aren't you?" He pointed at Royce. "Talbert told me about the interrogation you put him through—a bishop of the church! If only the Patriarch knew what his pets were up to, you would all be disbanded. Why do you still exist, anyway? The Heir of Novron is on her throne, isn't she? Isn't that what we're all supposed to believe? At long last, you found the seed of Novron and all is finally right with the world. You people can't accept that your mandate is over, that we don't need you anymore—if we ever did."

"We aren't seret," Hadrian told him, "and my friend here is definitely not a sentinel."

"No? Talbert described him perfectly—small, wiry, frightening, *like Death himself*. But you must have shaved your beard."

"I'm not a sentinel," Royce told him.

"We're just trying to find out what happened here forty-two years ago," Hadrian explained. "And you're right. I'm not looking for a record of my father's death, because I know he didn't die here. But he was here."

The monsignor hesitated, looking at Hadrian and shooting

furtive glances at Royce. "What was your father's name?" he asked at length.

"Danbury Blackwater."

The priest shook his head. "Never heard of him."

"But you know what happened," Royce said. "Why don't you just tell us?"

"Why don't you just get out of my church? I don't know who you are, and I don't want to. What happened, happened. It's over. Nothing can change it. Just leave me alone."

"You were there," Arista muttered in revelation. "Forty-two years ago—you were there, weren't you?"

The monsignor glared at her, his teeth clenched. "Look through the stacks if you want," he told them in resignation. "I don't care. Just lock up when you leave. And be sure to blow out the light."

"Wait." Hadrian spoke quickly as he fished his medallion out of his shirt and held it up toward the light. Bartholomew narrowed his eyes and then stepped closer to examine it.

"Where did you get that?"

"My father left it to me. He also wrote me a poem, a sort of riddle, I think. Maybe you can help explain it." Hadrian took out the parchment and passed it to the cleric.

After reading, the cleric raised a hand to his face, covering his mouth. Hadrian noticed his fingers tremble. His other hand sought and found the wall and he leaned heavily against it. "You look like him," the priest told Hadrian. "I didn't notice it at first. It's been over forty years and I only knew him briefly, but that's his sword on your back. I should have recognized that if nothing else. I still see it so often in my nightmares."

"So you knew my father, you knew Danbury Blackwater?"

"His name was Tramus Dan. That's what he went by, at least."

"Will you tell us what happened?"

He nodded. "There's no reason to keep it secret, except to protect myself, and perhaps it's time I faced my sins."

The monsignor looked at the open door to the stairs. "Let's close this." He stepped out, then returned, puzzled. "The key is gone."

"I've got it," Royce volunteered, revealing the iron key in his hand. Pulling the door shut, he locked it from the inside. "I've never cared for rooms I can be locked in."

Bartholomew took a small stool from behind one of the stacks and perched himself on it. He sat bent over with his head between his knees, as if he might be sick. They waited as the priest took several steadying breaths.

"It was forty-two years ago, next week, in fact," he began, his head still down, his voice quiet. "I had been expecting them for days and was worried. I thought they had been discovered, but that wasn't it. They were traveling slowly because she was with child."

"Who was?" Hadrian asked.

The monsignor looked up, confused. "Do you know the significance of that amulet you wear?"

"It once belonged to the Guardian of the Heir of Novron."

"Yes," the old man said simply. "Your father was the head of our order—a secret organization dedicated to protecting the descendants of Emperor Nareion."

"The Theorem Eldership," Royce said.

Bartholomew looked at him, surprised. "Yes. Shopkeepers, tradesmen, farmers—people who preserved a dream handed down to them."

"But you're a priest in the Nyphron Church."

"Many of us were encouraged to take vows. Some even tried to join the seret. We needed to know what the church was doing, where they were looking. I was the only one in Ratibor to receive the would-be emperor and his guardian.

The ranks of the Eldership had dwindled over the centuries. Few believed in it anymore. My parents raised me to believe in the dream of seeing the heir of Nareion returned to an imperial throne, but I never expected it would happen. I often questioned if the heir even existed, if the stories were just a myth. You see, the Eldership only contacted members if needed. You had a few meetings and years could go by without a word. Even then, messages were only words of encouragement reminding us to stay strong. We never heard a thing about the heir. There were no plans to rise up, no news of sightings, victories, or defeats.

"I was only a boy, a young deacon, recently arrived in Ratibor, assigned to the old South Square Church, when my father sent a letter saying simply 'He is coming. Make preparations.' I didn't know what to think. It took several readings before I even understood what 'he' meant. When I realized, I was dumbstruck. The Heir of Novron was coming to Ratibor. I didn't know exactly what I should do, so I rented a room at the Bradford's boardinghouse and waited. I should have found a better place. I should have..." He paused for a moment, dropped his head again to look at the floor, and took a breath.

"What happened?" Hadrian asked, keeping his voice calm, not wanting to do anything to stop the cleric from revealing his tale.

"They arrived late, around midnight, because his wife was about to give birth and their travel was slow. His name was Naron and he traveled with his guardian, Tramus Dan, and Dan's young apprentice, whose name I sadly can't recall. I saw them to their rooms at the boardinghouse and your father sent me in search of a midwife. I found a young girl and sent her ahead while I set out to find what supplies were needed.

"By the time I returned with my arms full, I saw a company of Seret Knights coming up the street, searching door-to-door.

I was horrified. I had never seen seret in Ratibor. They reached the boardinghouse before I could.

"They found it locked and beat on the door. There was no answer. When they tried to break in, your father refused them entry and the fight began. I watched from across the street. It was the most amazing thing I ever saw. Your father and his apprentice stepped out and fought back-to-back, defending the entrance. Knight after knight died until as many as ten lay dead or wounded on the street, and then came a scream from inside. Some of the seret must have found a way into the building from the back.

"The apprentice ran inside, leaving your father alone at the door to face the remainder of the knights. There must have been a dozen or more. By wielding two swords in the shelter of the entrance, he kept them at bay. He held them off for what felt like an eternity, and then Naron appeared at the doorway. He was mad with rage and drenched in blood. He pushed past Dan into the street. Your father tried to stop him, but Naron kept screaming, 'They killed her!' and threw himself into the crowd of knights, swinging his sword like a man possessed.

"Your father tried to reach Naron—to protect him. The seret surrounded Naron and I watched him die on their swords. I fell to my knees, the blankets, needle, and thread falling to the street. Your father, surrounded by his own set of knights, cried out and dropped his two swords. I thought they had stabbed him too. I expected to see him fall, but instead he drew the spadone blade from his back. The bloodshed I witnessed up to that point did not compare to what followed. Tramus Dan, with that impossibly long sword, began cleaving the seret to pieces. Legs, arms, and heads—explosions of blood. Even across Lore Street, I felt the spray carried on the wind like a fine mist on my face.

"When the last seret fell, Dan ran inside and emerged a

moment later with tears streaking down his cheeks. He went to Naron and cradled the heir, rocking him. I admit that I was too frightened to approach or even speak. Dan looked like Uberlin himself, bathed slick from head to foot in blood, that sword still at his side, his body shaking as if he might explode. After a time, he gently laid Naron on the porch. A few of the knights were still alive, groaning, twitching. He picked up the sword again and cut through them as if he were chopping wood. Then he picked up his weapons and walked away.

"I was too scared to follow, too terrified to even stand up, and I did not dare approach the house. As time passed, others arrived, and together we found the courage to enter. We found the younger swordsman—your father's apprentice—dead in the upper bedroom, surrounded by several bodies of seret. In the bed was a woman stabbed to death, her newborn child murdered in her arms. I never saw or heard anything of your father again."

They sat in silence for a few minutes.

"It explains a lot I never understood about my father," Hadrian finally said. "He must have wandered to Hintindar after that and changed his name. Dan—bury. Even his name was a riddle. So the line of Novron is dead?"

The old priest said nothing at first. He sat perfectly still except for his lips, which began to tremble. "It's all my fault. The seed of Maribor is gone. The tree, so carefully watered for centuries, has withered and died. It was all my fault. If only I had found a better safe house, or if I had kept a better watch." He looked up. The light from the lantern glistened off tears.

"The next day, more seret came and burned the boarding-house to the ground. I petitioned for this church to be built. The bishops never realized I was doing it as a testament—a monument to their memory. They thought I was honoring the fallen seret. So here I remained, upon their graves, guarding still. Yet now I protect not hope but a memory, a dream that, because of me, will never be."

❧

At noon, the ringing of the town bell summoned the citizens to Central Square. On their way back from the church, Arista, Hadrian, and Royce entered the square, barely able to see due to the gathered crowd. There they found twelve people locked in stocks. They all stood bent over with head and wrists locked, their feet and lower legs sunk deep in mud. Above each hung a hastily scrawled sign with the word *Conspirator* written on it.

The young, red-haired Emery was not in a stock, but instead hung by his wrists from a pole. Naked to the waist, his body was covered in numerous dark bruises and abrasions. His left eye was puffed and sealed behind a purple bruise, and his lower lip was split and stained dark with dried blood.

Next to him hung the older woman from The Laughing Gnome, the one who had mentioned that the Imperialists had burned Kilnar. Above both of them were signs reading TRAITOR. Planks circled the prisoners, and around them paced the sheriff of Ratibor. In his hands he held a short whip comprising several strands knotted at the ends, which he wagged threateningly as he walked. The whole city garrison had turned out to keep the angry crowd at bay. Archers were poised on roofs, and soldiers armed with shields and unsheathed swords threatened any who approached too close.

Many of the faces in the stocks were familiar to Arista from the night before. She was shocked to see mothers, who had sung their children to sleep on the floor of the tavern, now locked in stocks beside their husbands, sobbing. The children reached out for their parents from the crowd. The treatment of the woman from Kilnar disturbed her the most. Her only crime was telling the truth, and now she hung before the entire city, awaiting the whip. The sight was all the more terrifying because Arista knew it could have been her up there if Quartz had not intervened.

A regally dressed man in a judge's robe and a scribe approached the stocks. When they reached the center of the square, the scribe handed a parchment to the judge. The sheriff shouted for silence, and then the judge held up the parchment and began to read.

"'For the crimes of conspiracy against Her Royal Eminence the empress Modina Novronian, the New Empire, Maribor, and all humanity; for slander against His Excellency the empress's imperial viceroy; and for the general agitation of the lower classes to challenge their betters, it is hereby proclaimed good and right that punishment be laid immediately upon these criminals. Those guilty of conspiracy are hereby ordered to be flogged twenty lashes and spend one day in stocks, not to be released until sunset. Those guilty of treason will receive one hundred lashes and, if they remain alive, will be left hanging until they expire from want of food and water. Anyone attempting to help or lend comfort to any of these criminals will be likewise found guilty and receive similar punishment.'" He rolled up the parchment. "Sheriff Vigan, you may commence."

With that, he thrust the scroll into the hands of the scribe and promptly walked back the way he had come. With a nod from the sheriff, a soldier approached the first stock and ripped open the back of the young mother's dress. From somewhere in the crowd, a child screamed, yet without pause the sheriff swung his whip, even as the poor woman cried for mercy. The knots bit into the pale skin of her back and she howled and danced in pain. Stroke after stroke fell with the scribe standing by, keeping careful track. By the time it was done, her back was red and slick with blood. The sheriff took a break and handed the whip to a soldier, who performed similar punishment on her husband as the sheriff sat by, leisurely drinking from a cup.

The crowd, already quiet, grew deadly still as they came to the woman from Kilnar, who began screaming as they approached. The sheriff and his deputies took turns whipping her, as the day's heat made such work exhausting. The fatigue in their arms was evident by the wild swings that struck the woman high on her shoulders as well as low on her back, and even occasionally as low as her thighs. After the first thirty lashes, the woman stopped screaming and only whimpered softly. The whipping continued, and by the time the scribe counted sixty, the woman merely hung limp. A physician approached the post, lifted her head by her hair, and pronounced her dead. The scribe made a note of this. They did not remove her body.

The sheriff finally moved to Emery. The young man was not daunted after seeing the punishment carried out on the others, and made the bravest showing of all. He stood defiant as the soldier with the whip approached him.

"Killing me will not change the truth that Viceroy Androus is the real traitor and guilty of killing King Urith and the royal family!" he managed to shout before the first strokes of the whip silenced him. He did not cry out but gritted his teeth and only dully grunted as the knots turned his back into a mass of blood and pulpy flesh. By the last stroke, he also hung limp and silent, but everyone could see him breathing. The physician indicated such to the scribe, who dutifully jotted it down.

"Those people didn't do anything," Arista said as the crowd began to disperse. "They're innocent."

"You, of all people, know that isn't the point," Royce replied.

Arista whirled. She opened her mouth, hesitated, and then shut it.

"Alric had twelve people publicly flogged for inciting riots when the church was kicked out of Melengar," he reminded her. "How many of them were actually guilty of anything?"

"I'm sure that was necessary to keep the peace."

"The viceroy will tell you the same."

"This is different. Mothers weren't whipped before their children, and women weren't beaten to death before a crowd."

"True," Royce said. "It was only fathers, husbands, and sons who were whipped bloody and left scarred for life. I stand corrected. Melengar's compassion is astounding."

Arista glared at him but could say nothing. As much as she hated it, as much as she hated him for pointing it out, she realized what Royce said was true.

"Don't punish yourself over it," Royce told her. "The powerful control the weak. The rich exploit the poor. It's the way it's always been and how it always will be. Just thank Maribor you were born both rich and powerful."

"But it's not right," she said, shaking her head.

"What does *right* have to do with it? With anything? Is it right that the wind blows or that the seasons change? It's just the way the world is. If Alric hadn't flogged those people, maybe they would have succeeded in their revolt. Then you and Alric might have found yourselves beaten to death by a cheering crowd, because they would hold the power and you two would be weak."

"Are you really that indifferent?" she asked.

"I like to think of it as practical, and living in Ratibor for any length of time has a tendency to make a person *very* practical." He glanced sympathetically at Hadrian, who had been quiet since leaving the church. "Compassion doesn't make house calls to the streets of Ratibor—now or forty years ago."

"Royce..." Hadrian said, then sighed. "I'm going to take a walk. I'll see you two back at the Nest in a little while."

"Are you all right?" Arista asked.

"Yeah," he said unconvincingly, and moved away with the crowd.

"I feel bad for him," she said.

"Best thing that could have happened. Hadrian needs to understand how the world really works and get over his childish affection for ideals. You see Emery up there? He's an idealist and that's what eventually happens to idealists, particularly those that have the misfortune of being born in Ratibor."

"But for a moment he might have changed the course of this city," Arista said.

"No, he would only have changed who was in power and who wasn't. The course would remain the same. Power rises to the top like cream and dominates the weak with cruelty disguised as—and often even believed to be—benevolence. When it comes to people, there is no other possibility. It's a natural occurrence, like the weather, and you can't control either one."

Arista thought for a moment and glanced skyward. Then she said defiantly, "I wouldn't be so sure of that."

Chapter 12

Making It Rain

By the time Hadrian returned to the Rat's Nest, he could see Quartz had returned and there was trouble. Arista stood in the middle of the room with arms folded stubbornly, a determined look on her face. The rest watched her, happily entertained, while Royce paced with a look of exasperation.

"Thank Maribor you're back!" Royce said. "She's driving me insane."

"What's going on?"

"We're going to take control of the city," Arista announced.

Hadrian raised an eyebrow. "What happened to the meeting with Gaunt?"

"Not going to happen," Quartz answered. "Gaunt's gone."

"Gone?"

"Officially, he's disappeared," Royce explained. "Likely he's dead or captured. I'm certain Merrick is behind this somehow. It feels like him. He stopped us from contacting Gaunt and used both sides as bait for the other. Brilliant, really. Degan went to meet with Arista just as Arista went to meet him, and both walked into a trap. Arista avoided hers but it would appear that Gaunt was not so fortunate. The Nationalists are blaming Her Highness and Melengar, convinced that she's responsible. Even though the plan failed to catch the princess, there is no chance for an alliance. Definitely Merrick."

"Which is exactly why we need to prove ourselves to the Nationalists," Arista explained while Royce shook his head. She turned to face Hadrian. "If we take the city from the inside and hand it over to them, they'll trust us and we'll be able to get them to agree to an alliance. When you took this job, I reserved the right to change the objectives, and I'm doing so now."

"And how, *exactly*, do we *take* the city?" Hadrian asked carefully, trying to keep his tone neutral. He was usually inclined to side with Royce, and at face value Arista's idea did seem more than a little insane. On the other hand, he knew Arista was no fool and Royce often made choices based solely on self-interest. Beyond all that, he could not help admiring Arista, standing in a room full of thieves and opportunists, proclaiming such a noble idea.

"Just like Emery said at The Laughing Gnome," Arista began. "We storm the armory. Take weapons and what armor we can find. Then attack the garrison. Once we defeat them, we seal the city gates."

"The garrison in Ratibor is made up of what?" Hadrian asked. "Fifty? Sixty experienced soldiers?"

"At least that," Royce muttered disdainfully.

"Going up against hastily armed tailors, bakers, and grocers? You'd need to have half the population of the city backing you," he pointed out.

"Even if you could raise a rabble, scores of people will die and the rest will break and run," Royce added.

"They won't run," Arista said. "There's no place for them to go. We're trapped in a walled city. There can be no retreat. Everyone will have to fight to the death. After this afternoon's demonstration of the empire's cruelty, I don't think anyone will chance surrender."

Hadrian nodded. "But how do you expect to incite the city to fight for you? They don't even know you. You're not like Emery, with lifelong friends who will lay their lives on the line on your behalf. I doubt not even Polish here has a reputation that will elicit that kind of devotion—no offense."

Polish smiled at him. "You are quite right. The people rarely see me, and when they do, I'm thought of as a despicable brigand—imagine that."

"That's why we need Emery," Arista said.

"The kid dying in the square?"

"You saw the way the people listened," she said earnestly. "They believe in him."

"Right up until they were flogged at his side," Royce put in.

Arista stood straighter and spoke in a louder voice. "And even when they were, did you see the look in the faces of those people? In The Laughing Gnome, they already saw him as something of a hero—standing up for them against the Imperialists. When they flogged him, when he faced death and yet stood by his convictions, it solidified their feelings for him and his ideals. The Imperialists left Emery to die today. When they did, they made him a martyr. Just imagine how the people will feel if he survives! If he slipped out of the Imperialists' grasp just as everyone felt certain he was dead, it could be the spark that can ignite their hopes."

"He's probably already dead," Quartz said indifferently as she cleaned her nails with a dagger.

Arista ignored her. "We'll steal Emery from the post, spread the news that he's alive and that he asks everyone to stand up with him and fight—to fight for the freedom he promised them."

Royce scoffed but Hadrian considered the idea. He wanted

to believe. He wanted to be swept along with her passion, but his practical side, which had waged dozens of battles, told him there was little chance for success. "It won't work," he finally stated. "Even if you managed to take the city, the imperial army will just take it back. A few hundred civilians could overwhelm the city garrison, but they aren't going to stop an army."

"That's why we have to coordinate our attack with the Nationalists'. Remember Emery's plan? We'll shut the gates and lock them out. Then the Nationalists can crush them."

"And if you don't manage to close the gates in time? If the battle against the garrison doesn't go perfectly to plan?" Royce asked.

"It still won't matter," Arista said. "If the Nationalists attack the imperial army at the same time that we launch our rebellion, they won't be able to bother with us."

"Except the Nats won't attack without Gaunt," Polish said. "That's the reason they're still out there. Well, that and the three hundred heavy cavalry Lord Dermont commands along with the rest of his army. The Nats haven't ever faced an organized force. Without Gaunt, they have no one to lead them. They aren't disciplined troops. Just townsfolk and farmers Gaunt picked up along the way here. They'll run the moment they see armored knights."

"Who's in charge of Gaunt's army?" Hadrian asked. He had to admit Arista's plans were at least thought out.

"Some fat chap who goes by the name of Parker. Rumor has it he was a bookkeeper for a textile business. He used to be the Nats' quartermaster before Gaunt promoted him," Quartz said. "Not the brightest coin in the purse, if you understand me. Without Gaunt planning and leading the attack, the Nats don't stand a chance."

"You could do it," Arista said, looking squarely at Hadrian. "You've commanded men in battle before. You got a medal."

Hadrian rolled his eyes. "It wasn't as impressive as it sounds. They were only small regiments. Grendel's army was, well, in a word, pathetic. They refused to even wear helms, because they didn't like the way their voices echoed in their heads."

"But you led them in battle?"

"Yes, but—"

"And did you win or lose?"

"We won but—"

"Against a larger or smaller force?"

Hadrian stood silent, a beaten look on his face.

Royce turned toward him. "Tell me you aren't considering this nonsense."

Am I? But three hundred heavy cavalry!

Desperation slipped into Arista's voice. "Breckton's Northern Imperial Army is marching here. If the Nationalists don't attack now, the combined imperial forces will decimate them. That's what Lord Dermont is waiting for—that's his plan. If he sits and waits, then he will win. But if the Nationalists attack first, if he has no support, and nowhere to run... This may be our only chance. It's now or all will be lost.

"If the Nationalists are destroyed, nothing will stop the empire. They'll retake and punish all of Rhenydd for its disobedience, and that will include Hintindar." She paused, letting him consider this. "Then they will take Melengar. After that, nothing will stop them from conquering Delgos, Trent, and Calis. The empire will rule the world once more, but not like it once did. Instead of an enlightened rule uniting the people, it will be one of cruelty dividing them, headed not by a noble, benevolent emperor, but by a handful of greedy, power-hungry men who pull strings while hiding behind the shield of an innocent girl.

"And what about you, Royce?" She turned toward him.

"Have you forgotten the wagons? What do you think the fate of those and others like them will be when the New Empire rules all?

"Don't you see?" She addressed the entire room. "We either fight here and win, or die trying, because there won't be anything left if we fail. This is the moment. This is the crucial point where the future of yet unborn generations will be decided either by our action or inaction. For centuries to come, people will look back at this time and rejoice at our courage or curse our weakness." She looked directly at Royce now. "For we have the power. Here. Now. In this place. We have the power to alter the course of history and we will be forever damned should we not so much as try!"

She stopped talking, exhausted and out of breath.

The room was silent.

To Hadrian's surprise, it was Royce who spoke first. "Making Emery disappear isn't the hard part. Keeping him hidden is the problem."

"They'll tear the city apart looking, that's certain," Polish said.

"Can we bring him here?" Arista asked.

Polish shook his head. "The Imps know about us. They leave us alone because we don't cause much trouble and they enjoy the black market we provide. No, they'll most certainly come down here looking. Besides, without orders from the Jewel or the First Officer, I couldn't expose our operation to that much risk."

"We need a safe house where the Imps won't dare look," Royce said. "Someplace they won't even want to look. Is the city physician an Imperialist or a Royalist?"

"He's a friend of Emery, if that's any indication," Quartz explained.

"Perfect. By the way, Princess, conquering Ratibor wasn't

in our contract. This will most certainly cost you extra," Royce said.

"Just keep a tally," she replied, unable to suppress her smile.

"If this keeps up, we're going to own Melengar," Hadrian mentioned.

"What's this *we* stuff?" Royce asked. "You're retired, remember?"

"Oh? So *you'll* be leading the Nationalist advance, will you?"

"Sixty-forty?" Royce proposed.

⁂

Despite the recent rain, the public stable on Lords Row caught fire just after dark. More than two dozen horses ran through the streets. The city's inhabitants responded with a bucket brigade. Those unable to find a place in line stood in awe as the vast wooden building burned with flames reaching high into the night's sky.

With no chance of saving the stable, the town fought to save the butcher's shop next door. Men climbed on the roof and, braving the rain of sparks, soaked the shake shingles. Bucket after bucket doused the little shop as the butcher's wife watched from the street, terrified. Her face glowed in the horrific light. The townsfolk, and even some imperial guards, fought the fire for hours, until, at last, deprived of the shop next door, it burned itself out. The stable was gone. All that remained of it was charred and smoking rubble, but the butcher's shop survived with one blackened wall to mark its brush with disaster. The townsfolk, covered in soot and ash, congratulated themselves on a job well done. The Gnome filled with patrons toasting their success. They clapped their neighbors on the back and told jokes and stories of near death.

No one noticed Emery Dorn was missing.

The next morning, the city bell rang with the news. A stuffed dummy hung in his place. Guards swore they had not left their stations, but had no explanation. Sheriff Vigan, the judge, and various other city officials were furious. They stood in Central Square, shouting and pointing fingers at the guards, then at each other. Even Viceroy Androus interrupted his busy schedule to emerge from City Hall and personally witness the scene.

By midmorning, the Gnome filled with gossipers and happy customers, as if the town had declared a holiday, and Ayers was happily working up a sweat filling drinks.

"He was still breathing at sunset!" the cooper declared.

"He's definitely alive. Why free him if he was dead?" the grocer put forth.

"Who did it?"

"What makes you think *anyone* did it? That boy likely got away himself. Emery is a sly one, he is. We shoulda known the Imps couldn't kill the likes of him."

"He's likely down in the sewers."

"Naw, he's left the city. Nothing for him here now."

"Knowing Emery, he's in the viceroy's house right now, drinking the old man's brandy!"

This brought laughter to go with the round of ales Ayers dispensed. Ayers had his own thoughts on the matter—he guessed the guards had freed him. Emery was a great talker. Ayers had heard him giving speeches in the Gnome dozens of times, and the lad had always won over the crowd. He could easily imagine the boy talking all night to the men who were charged to watch him and convincing them to let him go. He wanted to mention his idea, but the keg was nearly empty and he was running low on mugs. He did not care much for the Imps personally, but they were great for business.

A loud banging at the tavern's entrance killed the laughter and people turned sharply. Ayers nearly dropped the keg he was lifting, certain the sheriff was leading another raid, but it was only Dr. Gerand. He stood at the open door, hammering the frame with his shoe to get their attention. Everyone breathed again.

"Come in, Doctor!" Ayers shouted. "I'll have another keg brought up."

"Can't," he replied. "Need to be keeping my distance from everyone for a while. Just want to let people know to stay clear of the Dunlaps' house. They've got a case of pox there."

"Is it bad?" the grocer asked.

"Bad enough," the physician said.

"All these new immigrants from down south are bringing all kinds of sickness with them," Ayers complained.

"Aye, that's probably what did it," Dr. Gerand said. "Mrs. Dunlap took in a boarder a few days back, a refugee from Vernes. It was that fella who first come down with the pox. So don't be going near the Dunlaps' place until you hear it's safe from me. In fact, I'd steer clear of Benning Street altogether. I'm gonna see if I can get the sheriff to put up some signs and maybe a fence or something to let people know to keep out. Anyway, I'm just going around telling folks, and I would appreciate it if you helped me spread the word before this gets out of hand."

By noon, the city guard was turning all the townsfolk out of their houses and shops, searching for the escaped traitor, and the very first place they looked was the Dunlaps' home. The five guards on duty the night Emery had disappeared were forced to draw lots, and one lone soldier went in. He came out after finding nothing but a couple of sick people, neither of whom was Emery. After making his report from a distance, he returned to the Dunlaps' to remain under quarantine.

The soldiers then tore through The Laughing Gnome, the marketplace, the old church, and even the scribe's office, leaving them all a mess. Squads of soldiers entered the sewers and came up soaked. They did not find the escaped traitor, but they did find a couple of chests that some said were filled with stolen silver.

There was no sign of Emery Dorn.

By nightfall, a makeshift wooden fence stood across Benning Street and a large whitewashed sign read

KEEP OUT!

Quarantined by order of the Viceroy!

Two days later, the soldier who had searched the Dunlaps' house died. He was seen covered with puss-filled boils in the yard. The doctor dug a hole while people watched from a distance. After that, no one went near Benning Street.

The city officials and those at the Gnome concluded Emery had left town or died—and was secretly buried somewhere.

⁂

Arista, Hadrian, and Royce waited silently just outside the entrance to the bedroom until the doctor finished. "I've taken the bandages off him," Dr. Gerand said. He was an elderly man with white hair, a hooknose, and bushy eyebrows that managed to look sad even when he smiled. "He's much better today. A whipping like he took..." He paused, unsure how to explain. "Well, you saw what it did to the poor lady that hung alongside him. He should have died, but he's young. He'll bounce back once he wakes up and starts eating. Of course, his back will be scarred for life and he'll never be as strong as he was—too much damage. The only concern I have is noxious humors causing an imbalance in his body, but honestly, that doesn't look like it'll be a problem. Like I said, the boy is young and strong. Let him continue to rest and he should be fine."

They followed the doctor downstairs, escorting him to the front door of the Dunlaps' home, where he bid them good night.

Pausing in the doorway, he looked back. "Emery is a good lad. He was my son's best friend. James was taken into the imperial army and died in some battle up north." He glanced at the floor. "Watching Emery on that post was like losing him all over again. Whatever happens now, I just wanted to say thank you." With that, the doctor left.

Arista had seen the insides of more commoners' homes over the past week than she had in her entire life. After visiting with the Bakers of Hintindar, she had assumed all families lived in identical houses, but the Dunlaps' home was nothing like the Bakers'. This one was two stories tall, with a solid wooden floor on both levels. The upper story created a thick-beamed ceiling to the lower one. While still modest and a bit cramped, it showed touches of care and a dash of prosperity, which Hintindar lacked. The walls were painted and decorated with pretty designs of stars and flowers, and the wood surfaces were buffed and stained. Knickknacks of glazed pottery and wood carvings lined shelves above the fireplace. Unlike Dunstan and Arbor's sparse home, the Dunlaps' house had a lot of furniture. Wooden chairs with straw seats circled the table. Another pair bookended a spinning wheel surrounded by several wicker baskets. Little tables held vases of flowers, and on the wall hung a cabinet with small doors and knobs. Kept neat, clean, and orderly, it was a house loved by a woman whose husband had been a good provider, but had rarely been home.

"Are you sure you don't want anything else?" Mrs. Dunlap

asked while clearing the dinner plates. She was an old, plump woman who always wore an apron and a matching white scarf and had a habit of wringing her wrinkled hands.

"We're fine," Arista told her. "And thank you again for letting us use your home."

The old woman smiled. "It's not so much a risk as you might think. My husband has been dead six years now. He proudly served as His Majesty Urith's coachman. Did you know that?" Her eyes sparkled as she looked off as if seeing him once more. "He was a handsome man in his driver's coat and hat with that red plume and gold broach. Yes, sir, a mighty fine-looking man, proud to serve the king, and had for thirty years."

"Was he killed with the king?"

"Oh no." She shook her head. "But he died soon after, of heartbreak, I think. He was very close to the royal family. Drove them everywhere they went. They gave him gifts and called him by his given name. Once, during a storm, he even brought the princes here to spend the night. The little boys talked about it for weeks. We never had children of our own, you see, and I think Paul—that's my husband—I think he thought of the royals as his own boys. It devastated him when they died in that fire—that horrible fire. Emery's father died in it too, did you know that? He was one of the king's bodyguards. There was so much death that terrible, terrible night."

"Urith was a good king?" Hadrian asked.

She shrugged. "I'm just an old woman, what do I know? People complained about him all the time when he was alive. They complained about the high taxes, and some of the laws, and how he would live in a castle with sixty servants, dining on deer, boar, and beef all at the same meal while people in the city were starving. I don't know that there is such a thing as a good king. Perhaps there are just kings that are good enough." She looked at Arista and winked. "Perhaps what we need is less kings and more womenfolk running things."

Mrs. Dunlap went back to the work of straightening as they sat at the round dining table.

"Well," Royce began, looking at Arista, "step one of your rebellion is complete. So now what?"

She thought a moment, then said, "We'll need to circulate the story of Emery leading the coming attack. Play him up as a hero, a ghost that the empire can't kill."

"I've heard talk like that around town already," Royce said. "You were right about that, at least."

Arista smiled. Such a compliment from Royce was high praise.

"We need to use word of mouth," she continued, "to get the momentum for the revolt started. I want everyone to know it's coming. I want them to think of it as inevitable as the coming of dawn. I want them to believe it can't fail. I'll need leaders as well. Hadrian, keep an eye out for reliable men who can help lead the battle. Men others listen to and respect. I'll also need you to devise a battle plan to take the armory and the garrison for me. Unlike my brother, I never studied the art of war. They made me learn needlepoint instead. Do you know how often I've used needlepoint?"

Hadrian chuckled.

"It's also imperative that we get word to Alric to start the invasion from the north. Even if we take the city, Breckton can wait us out unless Melengar applies pressure. I would suggest asking the Diamond to send the message, but given how reliable they were last time and how utterly important this is—Royce, I need to ask you to carry the message for me. If anyone can get through and bring back help, it's you."

Royce pursed his lips, thinking, and then nodded. "I'll talk to Polish just the same and see if I can get him to part with one or two of his men to accompany me. You should write three messages to Alric. Each of us will carry one and split up if there's trouble. Three people will increase the odds that at least one will make it. And don't neglect to write an additional letter explaining how this trip south was all your idea. I don't want to bear the brunt of his anger when he finds out where you went. Oh, and, of course, an explanation of the fees to be paid," he said with a wink.

Arista sighed. "He'll want to kill me."

"Not if you succeed in taking the city," Hadrian said encouragingly.

"Speaking of which, after you complete the battle plan for the garrison, you'll need to see about reaching Gaunt's army and taking command of it. I'm not exactly sure how you're going to do that, but I'll write you a decree and declare you general-ambassador in proxy, granting you the power to speak on my behalf. I'll give you the rank of auxiliary marshal and the title of lord. That might just impress them and at least give you the legal right to negotiate and the credentials to command."

"I doubt royal titles will impress Nationalists much," Hadrian said.

"Maybe not, but the threat of the Northern Imperial Army should give you a good deal of leverage. Desperate men might be willing to cling to an impressive title in the absence of anything else."

Hadrian chuckled again.

"What?" she asked.

"Oh, nothing," he said. "I was just thinking that for an ambassador, you're a very capable general."

"No you weren't," she told him bluntly. "You're thinking that I'm capable for a *woman*."

"That too."

Arista smiled. "Well, it's lucky that I am, because so far I'm pretty lousy at being a woman. I honestly can't stand needlepoint."

"I suppose I should set out tonight for Melengar," Royce said. "Unless there's something else you need before I go?"

Arista shook her head.

"How about you?" he asked Hadrian. "Assuming you survive this stunt, what are you going to do now that you know the heir is dead?"

"Hang on, are you sure the heir is dead?" Arista broke in.

"You were there. You heard what Bartholomew said," Hadrian replied. "I don't think he was lying."

"I'm not saying that he was...It's just that...well, Esrahaddon seemed pretty convinced the heir was still alive when he left Avempartha. And then there's the church. They're after Esra, expecting him to lead them to the *real* heir. They so much as told me that when I was at Ervanon last year. So why is everyone looking if he's dead?"

"There's no telling what Esrahaddon is up to. As for the church, they pretended to look for the heir just as they're pretending they found her," Royce said.

"Perhaps, but there's still the image that we saw in the tower. He seemed like a living, breathing person to me."

Royce nodded. "Good point."

Hadrian shook his head. "There couldn't have been another child. My father would have known and searched for him...or *her.* No, Danbury knew the line ended or he wouldn't have stayed in Hintindar."

He glanced at Royce, then lowered his eyes. "In any case, if I survive, I won't be returning to Riyria."

Royce nodded. "You'll probably get killed, anyway. But... I suppose you're okay with that—as happy as a dog with a bone."

"How's that?"

"Nothing."

There was a pause, then Hadrian said, "It's not completely hopeless. It's just that damn cavalry. They'll cut down the Nationalists in a heartbeat. If only it would rain again."

"Rain?" Arista asked.

"Charging horses carrying heavy armored knights need solid ground. After the last few days, the ground has already dried. If I could engage them over tilled rain-drenched farmland, the horses will mire themselves and Dermont would lose his best advantage. But the weather doesn't look like it's gonna cooperate."

"So you would prefer it to rain nonstop between now and the battle?" Arista asked.

"That would be one sweet miracle, but I don't expect we'll have that kind of luck."

"Perhaps luck isn't what we need." Arista smiled at him.

৵

The Dunlap household was dark except for the single candle Arista carried up the steps to the second floor. She had said her goodbyes to Royce and Hadrian. Mrs. Dunlap had gone to bed hours earlier and the house was quiet. This was the first time in ages she found herself alone.

How can this plan possibly work? Am I crazy?

She knew what her old handmaid, Bernice, would say. Then the old woman would offer her a gingerbread cookie as a consolation prize.

What will Alric say when Royce reaches him?

Even if she succeeded, he would be furious that she had disobeyed him and gone off without telling anyone. She pushed those thoughts away, deciding to worry about all that later. They could hang her for treason if they wished, so long as Melengar was safe.

All estimates indicated Breckton would arrive in less than four days. She would have to control the city by then. She planned to launch the revolt in two days and hoped she would have at least a few days to recover, pull in supplies from the surrounding farms, and set up some defenses.

Royce would get through with the message. If he could get to Alric quickly, and if her brother moved fast, Alric could attack across the Galewyr in just a few days, and it would take only two or three days for word to reach Aquesta and new orders to be sent to Sir Breckton. She would need to hold him off at least that long. All this assumed they successfully took the city and defeated Lord Dermont's knights to the south.

Two days. How long does it normally take to plan a successful revolution?

Longer than two days, she was certain.

"Excuse me. Hello?"

Arista stopped as she passed the open door of Emery's bedroom. They had put him in the small room at the top of the stairs, in the same bed where the princes of Rhenydd had once slept on a stormy night. Emery had remained unconscious since they had stolen him from the post. She was surprised to see his eyes open and looking back at her. His hair was pressed from sleep, and a puzzled look was on his face.

"How are you feeling?" she asked softly.

"Terrible," he replied. "Who are you? And where am I?"

"My name is Arista and you're at the Dunlaps' on Benning Street." She set the candle on the nightstand and sat on the edge of the bed.

"But I should be dead," he told her.

"Awfully sorry to disappoint, but I thought you would be more helpful alive." She smiled at him.

His brow furrowed. "Helpful with what?"

"Don't worry about that now. You need to sleep."

"No! Tell me. I won't be a party to the Imperialists, I tell you!"

"Well, of course you won't. We need your help to take the city back *from* them."

Emery looked at her, stunned. His eyes shifted from side to side. "I don't understand."

"I heard your speech at The Laughing Gnome. It's a good plan, and we're going to do it in two days, so you need to rest and get your strength back."

"Who are 'we'? Who are you? How did you manage this?"

Arista smiled. "Practice, I guess."

"Practice?"

"Let's just say this isn't the first time I've had to save a kingdom from a traitorous murderer out to steal the throne. It's okay. Just go back to sleep. It will—"

"Wait! You said your name is *Arista*?"

She nodded.

"You're the Princess of Melengar!"

She nodded again. "Yes."

"But…but how…Why?" He started to push up on the bed with his hands and winced.

"Calm down," she told him firmly. "You need to rest. I mean it."

"I shouldn't be lying down in your presence!"

"You will if I tell you to, and I'm telling you to."

"I—I just can't believe…Why…why would you come here?"

"I'm here to help."

"You're amazing."

"And you're suffering from a flogging that would have killed any man with the good sense to know he should be dead. Now you need to go back to sleep this instant, and that's an order. Do you understand?"

"Yes, Your Majesty."

She smiled. "I'm not a ruling queen, Emery, just a princess. My brother is the king."

Emery looked embarrassed. "Your Highness, then."

"I would prefer it if you just called me Arista."

Emery looked shocked.

"Go ahead, give it a try."

"It's not proper."

"And is it proper that you should deny a princess's request? Particularly one who saved your life?"

He shook his head slowly. "Arista," he said shyly.

She smiled at him and, on an impulse, leaned over and kissed him on the forehead. "Good night, Emery," she said, and stepped back out of the room.

She walked back down the steps through the dark house and out the front door. The night was still. Just as Hadrian had mentioned, the sky was clear, showing a bountiful banquet of stars spilling across the vast blackness. Benning Street, a short lane that dead-ended at the Dunlaps' carriage house, was empty.

It was unusual for Arista to be completely alone outdoors. Hilfred had always been her ever-present shadow. She missed him and yet it felt good to be on her own facing the night. It had been only a few days since she had ridden out of Medford, but she knew she was not the same person who had left. She had always feared her life would be no more than that of a woman of privilege, helpless and confined. She had escaped that fate and entered into the more prestigious, but equally restricted, role of ambassador, which was nothing more than a glorified messenger. Now, however, she felt for the first time she was finding her true calling.

She began to hum softly to herself. The spell she had cast on the Seret Knights had worked, yet no one had taught her how to do it. She had invented the spell, drawing from a similar idea and her general knowledge of the Art and altering the incantation to focus on the blood of their bodies.

That's what makes it an art.

There was indeed a gap in her education, but it was because what was missing could not be taught. Esrahaddon had not held back anything. The gap was the reality of magic. Instructors could teach the basic techniques and methods, but a mastery of mechanical knowledge could never make a person an artist. No one could teach creativity or invention. A spark needed to come from within. It must be something unique, something discovered by the individual, a leap of understanding, a burst of insight, the combining of common elements in an unexpected way.

Arista knew it to be true. She had known it since killing the knights. The knowledge both excited and terrified her. The horrible deaths of the seret had only compounded that terrible realization. Now, however, standing alone in the yard under the blanket of stars and in the stillness of the warm summer night, she embraced her understanding and it was thrilling. There was danger, of course, both intoxicating and alluring, and she struggled to contain her emotions. Recalling the death cries of the knights and the ghastly looks on their faces helped ground her. She did not want to get lost in that power. In her mind's eye, the Art was a great beast, a dragon of limitless potential that yearned to be set free, but a mindless beast let loose upon the world would be a terrible thing. She understood the wisdom of Arcadius and the need to restrain the passion she now touched.

Arista set the candle down before her and cleared her mind to focus.

She reached out and pressed her fingers in the air as if gently touching the surface of an invisible object. Power vibrated like the strings of a harp as her humming became a chant. They were not the words that Esrahaddon had taught her. Nor was it an incantation from Arcadius. The words were her own. The fabric of the universe was at her fingertips, and she fought to control her excitement. She plucked the strings on her invisible harp. She could play individual notes or chords, melodies, rhythms, and a multitude of combinations of each. The possibilities of creation were astonishing, and so numerous were the choices that she was equally overwhelmed. It would clearly take a lifetime, or more, to begin to grasp the potential she now felt. That night, however, her path was simple and clear. A flick of her wrist and a sweep of her fingers, almost as if she were motioning farewell, and at that moment the candle blew out.

A wind gusted. The dry soil of the street whirled into a dust devil. Old leaves and bits of grass were buffeted about. The stars faded as thick, full clouds crept across the sky. She heard the sound ring off the tin roof. It sang on the metal, the chorus of her song, and then she felt the splatter of rain on her upturned and laughing face.

Chapter 13

Modina

The ceiling of the grand imperial throne room was a dome painted robin's egg blue interspersed with white puffy clouds mimicking the sky on a gentle summer's day. The painting was heavy and uninspired, but Modina thought it was beautiful. She could not remember the last time she had seen the real sky.

Her life since Dahlgren had been a nightmare of vague unpleasant people and places she could not, and did not care to, remember. She had no idea how much time had passed since the death of her father. It did not matter. Nothing did. Time was a concern of the living, and if she knew anything, it was that she was dead. A ghost drifting dreamlike, pushed along by unseen hands, hearing disembodied voices—but something had changed.

Amilia had come, and with her, the haze and fog that Modina had been lost in for so long had begun to lift. She started to become aware of the world around her.

"Keep your head up, and do not look at them," Nimbus was telling her. "You are the empress and they are beneath you, contemptible and not worthy of even the slightest glance from your imperial eyes. Back straight. Back straight."

Modina, dressed in a formal gown of gold and white, stood on the imperial dais before an immense and gaudy throne. She scratched it once and discovered the gold was a thin veneer over dull metal. The dais itself was five feet from the ground, with sheer sides except for where the half-moon stairs provided access. The stairs were removable, allowing her to be set on display, the perfect unapproachable symbol of the New Empire.

Nimbus shook his head miserably. "It is not going to work. She is not listening."

"She's just not used to standing straight all the time," Amilia told him.

"Perhaps a stiff board sewn into her corset and laced tight?" a steward proposed timidly.

"Actually, that's not a bad idea," Amilia replied. She looked at Nimbus. "What do you think?"

"Better make it a *very* stiff board," Nimbus replied sardonically.

They waved over the royal tailor and seamstress and an informal meeting ensued. They droned on about seams, stays, and ties while Modina looked down from above.

Can they see the pain in my face?

She did not think so. There was no sympathy in their eyes, just awe—awe and admiration. They simultaneously marveled and quaked when in her presence. She had heard them whispering about *the beast* she had slain, and how she was the daughter of a god. To thousands of soldiers, knights, and commoners, she was something to worship.

Until recently, Modina had been oblivious to it all, her mind shut in a dark hole where any attempt to think caused such anguish she recoiled back into the dull safety of the abyss. Time dulled the pain, and slowly the words of nearby conversations seeped in. She began to understand. According to what she had overheard, she and her father were descendants of some legendary lost king. This was why only they could harm the beast. She had been anointed empress, but she was not certain what that meant. So far, it had meant pain and isolation.

Modina stared at those around her without emotion. She was no longer capable of feeling. There was no fear, anger, or hate, nor was there love or happiness. She was a ghost haunting her own body, watching the world with detached interest. Nothing that transpired around her held any importance—except Amilia.

Previously the people hovering around her were vague gray faces. They had spoken to her of ridiculous notions, the vast majority she could not begin to comprehend even if she wanted to. Amilia was different. She had said things to Modina that she could understand. Amilia had told stories of her own family and reminded Modina of another girl—a girl named Thrace—who had died and was just a ghost now. It was a painful memory, but Amilia managed to remind her about times before the darkness, before the pain, when there had been someone in the world who loved her.

When Saldur had threatened to send Amilia away, Modina had seen the terrible fear in the girl's eyes. She had recognized that fear. Saldur's voice was the screech of the beast, and at that moment, she had awoken from her long dream. Her eyes had focused, seeing clearly for the first time since that night. She would not allow the beast to win again.

Somewhere in the chamber, out of sight of the dais, a door slammed. The sound echoed around the marbled hall. Loud footsteps followed with an even louder conversation.

"I don't understand why I can't launch an attack against Alric on my own." The voice came from an agitated well-dressed man.

"Breckton's army will dispatch the Nationalists in no time.

Then he can return to Melengar, and you can have your prize, Archie," replied the voice of an older man. "Melengar isn't going anywhere, and it's not worth the risk."

The younger voice she did not recognize, but the older one she had heard many times before. They called him Regent Ethelred. The pair of nobles and their retinue came into view. Ethelred was dressed as she usually had seen him—in red velvet and gold silk. His thick mustache and beard betrayed his age, as both were steadily going gray.

The younger man walking beside him dressed in a stylish scarlet silk tunic with a high-ruffed collar, an elegant cape, and an extravagant plumed hat that matched the rest of his attire perfectly. He was taller than the regent, and his long auburn hair trailed down his back in a ponytail. They walked at the head of a group of six others: personal servants, stewards, and court officials. Four of the six Modina recognized, as she had seen the little parade before.

There was the court scribe, who went everywhere carrying a ledger. He was a plump man with long red cheeks and a balding head, and he always had a feathered quill behind each ear, making him look like a strange bird. His staunchly straight posture and odd strut reminded her of a quail parading through a field, and because she did not know the scribe's name, in her mind she dubbed him simply *The Quail.*

There was also Ethelred's valet, whom she labeled *The White Mouse*, as he was a thin, pale man with stark white hair, and his fastidious pampering seemed rodent-like. She never heard him speak except to say, "Of course, my lord." He continuously flicked lint from Ethelred's clothes and was always on hand to take a cloak or change the regent's footwear.

Then there was *The Candle*, so named because he was a tall, thin man with wild red curly hair and a drooping mouth that sagged like tallow wax.

The last of the entourage was a soldier of some standing. He wore a uniform that had dozens of brightly colored ribbons pinned to it.

"I would appreciate you using a formal address when we are in public," Archie pointed out.

Ethelred turned as if surprised to see they were not alone in the hall.

"Oh," he said, quickly masking a smile. Then, in a tone heavy with sarcasm, he proclaimed, "Forgive me, *Earl of Chadwick*. I didn't notice them. They're more like furniture to me. My point was, however, that we only suspect the extent of Melengar's weakness. Attacking them would introduce more headaches than it is worth. As it is, there is no chance Alric will attack us. He's a boy, but not so foolhardy as to provoke the destruction of his little kingdom."

"Is that..." Archibald stared up at Modina and stopped walking so that Ethelred lost track of him for a moment.

"The empress? Yes," Ethelred replied, his tone revealing a bit of his own irritation that the earl had apparently not heard what he had just said.

"She's...she's...beautiful."

"Hmm? Yes, I suppose she is," Ethelred responded without looking. Instead, he turned to Amilia, who, along with everyone else, was standing straight, her eyes looking at the floor. "Saldur tells me you're our little miracle worker. You got her eating, speaking, and generally cooperating. I'm pleased to hear it."

Amilia curtsied in silence.

"She'll be ready in time, correct? We can ill afford another fiasco like the one we had at the coronation. She couldn't even make an appearance. You'll see to that, won't you?"

"Yes, my lord." Amilia curtsied again.

The Earl of Chadwick's eyes remained focused on Modina,

and she found his expression surprising. She did not see the awe-inspired look of the palace staff, nor the cold, callous countenance of her handlers. His face bore a broad smile.

A soldier entered the hall, walking briskly toward them. The one with the pretty ribbons left the entourage and strode forward to intercept him. They spoke in whispers for a brief moment and then the other soldier handed over some parchments. Ribbon Man opened them and read them silently to himself before returning to Ethelred's side.

"What is it?"

"Your Lordship, Admiral Gafton's blockade fleet succeeded in capturing the *Ellis Far*, a small sloop, off the coast of Melengar. On board, they found parchments signed by King Alric granting the courier permission to negotiate with the full power of the Melengar crown. The courier and ship's captain were unfortunately killed in the action. The coxswain, however, was taken and persuaded to reveal the destination of the vessel as Tur Del Fur."

Ethelred nodded his understanding. "Trying to link up with the Nationalists, but that was expected. So the sloop sailed from Roe?"

"Yes."

"You're sure no other ship slipped past?"

"The reports indicate it was the only one."

While Ethelred and the soldier spoke and the rest of the hall remained still as statues, the Earl of Chadwick stared at the empress. Modina did not return his gaze, and it made her uncomfortable the way he watched her.

He ascended the steps and knelt. "Your Eminence," he said, gently taking her hand and kissing the ring she wore. "I am Archibald Ballentyne, twelfth Earl of Chadwick."

Modina said nothing.

"Archibald?" Ethelred's voice once more.

"Forgive my rude approach," the earl continued, "but I find I can't help myself. How strange it is that we haven't met before. I've been to Aquesta many times but never had the pleasure. Bad luck, I suppose. I'm certain you're very busy, and as I command a substantial army, I'm busy as well. Recent events have seen fit to bring my command here. It's not something I was pleased with. That is, until now. You see, I was doing very well conquering new lands for your growing empire, and having to stop I considered unfortunate. But my regret has turned to genuine delight as I've been blessed to behold your splendor."

"Archie!" Ethelred had been calling out to him for some time, but it was not until he used that name that the well-dressed man's attention finally left her. "Stop with that foolishness, will you? We need to get to the meeting."

The earl frowned in irritation.

"Please forgive me, Your Eminence, but duty calls."

❧

The moment the practice had ended, they changed Modina back into her simple dress and she had been escorted to her cell. She thought there had been a time when two palace soldiers had walked with her everywhere, but now there was only one. His name was Gerald. That was all she knew about him, which was strange, because she saw him every day. Gerald escorted her wherever she went and stood guard outside her cell door. She assumed he took breaks, most likely late at night, but in the mornings, when she and Amilia went to breakfast, he was always there. She never heard him speak. They were quite a quiet pair.

When she reached the cell door, it was open, the dark interior waiting. He never forced her in. He never touched her. He merely stood patiently, taking up his post at the entrance. She hesitated before the threshold, and when she looked at Gerald, he stared at the floor.

"Wait." Amilia trotted up the corridor toward them. "Her Eminence is moving today."

Both Gerald and Modina looked puzzled.

"I've given up talking to the chamberlain," Amilia declared. She was speaking quickly and seemed to address them both at once. "Nimbus is right—I'm the secretary to the empress, after all." She focused on Gerald. "Please escort Her Eminence to her new bedroom on the east wing's fifth floor."

The order was weak, not at all in the voice of a noblewoman. It lacked the tenor of confidence, the power of arrogance. There was a space of time, a beat of uncertainty, when no one moved and no one spoke. Committed now, Amilia remained awkwardly stiff, facing Gerald. For the first time, Modina noticed the largeness of the man, the sword at his side, and the castle guard uniform. He was meticulous, every line straight, every bit of metal polished.

Gerald nodded and moved aside.

"This way, Your Eminence," Amilia said, letting out a breath.

The three of them walked to the central stairs as Amilia continued to speak. "I got her eating, I got her to talk—I just want a better place for her to sleep. How can they argue? No one is even on the fifth floor."

As they reached the main hall, they passed several surprised servants. One young woman stopped, stunned.

"Anna." Amilia caught her attention. "It is Anna, isn't it?"

The woman nodded, unable to take her eyes off Modina.

"The empress is moving to a bedroom on the fifth floor. Run and get linens and pillows."

"Ah—but Edith told me to scrub the—"

"Forget Edith."

"She'll beat me."

"No, she won't," Amilia said, and thought for a moment. With sudden authority, she continued. "From now on, you're working for the empress—her personal chambermaid. From now on, you report directly to me. Do you understand?"

Anna looked shocked.

"What do you want to do?" Amilia asked. "Defy Edith Mon or refuse the empress? Now get those linens and get the best room on the fifth floor in order."

"Yes, Your Eminence," she said, addressing Modina, "right away."

They climbed the stairs, moving quickly by the fourth floor. In the east wing, the fifth floor was a single long hall with five doors. Light entered from a narrow slit at the far end, revealing a dust-covered corridor.

Amilia looked at the doors for a moment. Shrugging, she opened one and motioned for them to wait as she entered. When she returned, she grimaced and said, "Let's wait for Anna."

They did not have to wait long. The chambermaid, chased by two young boys with rags, a broom, a mop, and a bucket, returned with an armload of linens. Anna panted for breath and her brow glistened. The chambermaid traversed the corridor and selected the door at the far end. She and the boys rushed in. Amilia joined them. Before long, the boys raced back out and returned hauling various items: pillows, a blanket, more water, brushes. Modina and Gerald waited in the hallway, listening to the grunts and bumps and scrapes. Before long, Anna exited covered in dirt and dust, dragging armloads of dirty rags. Then Amilia reappeared and motioned for Modina to enter.

Sunlight. She spotted the brilliant shaft spilling in, slicing across the floor, along a tapestry-covered wall, and over a massive bed covered in satin sheets and a host of fluffy pillows. There was even a thick carpet on the floor. A mirror and a washbasin sat on a small stand. A little writing desk stood next to a fireplace, and on the far wall was the open window.

Modina walked forward and looked out at the sky. Breathing in the fresh air, she fell to her knees. The window was narrow, but Modina could peer down into the courtyard below or look up directly into the blue of the sky—the real sky. She rested her head on the sill, reveling in the sunshine like a drought victim might douse herself with water. Until that moment, she had not noticed how starved she had been for fresh air and sunlight. Amilia might have spoken to her, but she was too busy looking at the sky to notice.

Smells were a treat. A cool breeze blew in, tainted by the stables below. For her, this was a friendly, familiar scent, hearty and comforting. Birds flew past. A pair of swallows darted and dove in aerial acrobatics as they chased each other. They had a nest in a crevice above one of the other windows that dotted the exterior wall.

She did not know how long she had knelt there. At some point, she realized she was alone. The door behind her had been closed and a blanket had been draped over her shoulders. Eventually she heard voices drifting up from below.

"We've spent more than enough time on the subject, Archibald. The case is closed." It was Ethelred's voice, coming from one of the windows just below hers.

"I know you're disappointed." She recognized the fatherly tone of Regent Saldur. "Still, you have to be mindful of the big picture. This isn't just some wild landgrab. This is an empire we are building."

"Two months at the head of an army and he acts as if he were a war-hardened general!" Ethelred laughed.

Another voice spoke, too softly or too distant from the window for her to hear. Then she heard the earl once again. "I've taken Glouston and the Rilan Valley through force of arms and thereby secured the whole northern rim of Warric. I think I've proved my skill."

"Skill? You let Marquis Lanaklin escape to Melengar and you failed to secure the wheat fields in Rilan, which burned. Those crops would have fed the entire imperial army for the next year, but now they're lost because you were preoccupied with taking an empty castle."

"It wasn't empty..." There was more said but the voices were too faint to hear.

"The marquis was gone. The reason for taking it went with him," the bellowing voice of Ethelred thundered. The regent must be standing very near the window, as she could hear him the best.

"Gentlemen," Saldur said, intervening, "water under the bridge. What's past is past. What we need to concern ourselves with is the present and the future, and at the moment both go by the same name—Gaunt."

Again, there were other voices speaking too faintly, their sounds fading to silence. All Modina could hear was the hoeing of servants weeding the vegetable garden below.

"I agree," Ethelred suddenly said. "We should have killed that bastard years ago."

"Calm yourself, Lanis," Saldur's voice boomed. Modina wasn't certain if he was using Ethelred's first name or addressing someone else whose voice was too distant for her to catch. "Everything has its season. We all knew the Nationalists wouldn't give up their freedom without a fight. Granted, we had no idea Gaunt would be their general or that he would prove to be such a fine military commander. We had assumed he was nothing more than an annoying anarchist, a lone voice in the wilderness, like our very own Deacon Tomas. His transformation into a skilled general was—I will admit—a bit unexpected. Nevertheless, his successes are not beyond our control."

"And what does that mean?" someone asked.

"Luis Guy had the foresight to bring us a man who could effectively deal with the problems of Delgos and Gaunt and I present him to you today. Gentlemen, let me introduce Merrick Marius." His voice began to grow faint. "He's quite a remarkable man...been working for us these...on a..." Saldur's voice drifted off, too far from the window.

There was a long silence, and then Ethelred spoke again. "Let him finish. You'll see."

Again, the words were too quiet for her to hear.

Modina listened to the wind as it rose and rustled distant leaves. The swallows returned and played again, looping in the air. From the courtyard below came the harsh shouts of soldiers in the process of changing guards. She had nearly forgotten about the conversation from below when she heard an abrupt communal gasp.

"Tur Del Fur? You're not serious?" an unknown voice asked in a stunned tone.

More quiet murmurings.

"...and as I said, it would mark the end of Degan Gaunt and the Nationalists forever." Saldur's voice returned.

"But at what cost, Sauly?" another voice floated in. Normally too far, it was now loud and clear.

"We have no other choice," Ethelred put in. "The Nationalists are marching north toward Ratibor. They must be stopped."

"This is insane. I can't believe you're even contemplating it!"

"We've done much more than contemplate. Nearly everything is in place. Isn't that so?" Saldur asked.

Modina strained to hear, but the voice that replied was too faint.

"We'll send it by ship after we receive word that all is set," Saldur explained. There was another pause, and then he spoke again. "I think we all understand that."

"I see no reason to hesitate any longer," Ethelred said. "Then we're all in agreement?"

A number of voices spoke their acknowledgment.

"Excellent. Marius, you should leave immediately..."

"There's just one more thing..." She had not heard this voice before and it faded, probably because the man speaking was walking away from the window.

Saldur's voice returned. "You have? Where? Tell us at once!"

More muffled conversation.

"Blast, man! I can assure you that you'll get paid," Ethelred said.

"If he's led you to the heir, he's no longer of any use. That's right, isn't it, Sauly? You and Guy have a greater interest in this, but unless you have an objection, I say be done with him at your earliest convenience."

Another long pause.

"I think the Nyphron Empire is good for it, don't you?" Saldur said.

"You're quite the magician, aren't you, Marius?" said Ethelred. "We should have hired your services earlier. I'm not a fan of Luis Guy or any of the Patriarch's sentinels, but it seems his decision to employ you was certainly a good one."

The voices drifted off, growing fainter until it was quiet.

Most of what she had heard held no interest for Modina—too many unknown names and places. She had only the vaguest notions of the terms *Nationalist*, *Royalist*, and *Imperialist*. Tur Del Fur was a famous city—someplace south—that she had heard of before, but Degan Gaunt was only a name. She was glad the talking was over. She preferred the quiet sounds of the wind, the trees, and the birds. They took her back to an earlier time, a different place. As she sat looking out at her sliver of the world, she found herself wishing she could still cry.

Chapter 14

The Eve

Gill had a hard time seeing anything clearly in the pouring rain, but he was certain that a man was walking right at him. He felt for the horn hanging at his side and regretted trapping it underneath his rain smock that morning. During thirty watches, he had never needed it. He peered through the gray curtain—no army, just the one guy.

He was dressed in a cloak that hung like a soaked rag, his hood cast back, his hair slicked flat. No armor or shield, but two swords hung from his belt, and Gill spotted the two-handed pommel of a great sword on his back. The man walked steadily through the muddy field. He seemed to be alone and could hardly pose a threat to the nearly one thousand men bivouacked on the hill. If Gill sounded the alarm without cause, he would never hear the end of it. He was confident he could handle one guy.

"Halt!" Gill shouted over the drumming rain as he pulled his sword from its sheath and brandished it at the stranger. "Who are you, and what do you want?"

"I'm here to see Commander Parker," the man said, not showing any signs of slowing. "Take me to him at once."

Gill laughed. "Oh, aren't you the bold one?" he said,

extending the sword. The stranger walked right up to the tip, as if he meant to impale himself. "Stop or I'll run—"

Before Gill could finish, the man hit the flat face of the sword. The vibration ran down the blade, breaking Gill's grip. A second later, the man had the weapon and was pointing it at him.

"I gave you an order, picket," the stranger snapped. "I'm not accustomed to repeating myself to my troops. Look sharp or I'll have you flogged."

Then the man returned his sword, which only made matters worse.

"What's your name, picket?"

"Gill, ah, sir," he said, adding the *sir* in case this man was an officer.

"Gill, in the future when standing watch, arm yourself with a crossbow and never let even one man approach to within one hundred feet without putting a hole through him, do you understand?" The man did not wait for an answer. He walked past him and continued striding up the hill through the tall wet grass.

"Umm, yes, sir, but I don't have a crossbow, sir," Gill said as he jogged behind him.

"Then you had best get one, isn't that right?" the man called over his shoulder.

"Yes, sir." Gill nodded even though the man was ahead of him.

The man walked past scores of tents, heading toward the middle of the camp. Everyone was inside, away from the rain, and no one saw him pass. The tents were a haphazard array of rope and stick-propped canvas. No two were alike, as the soldiers had scrounged supplies as they moved. Most were cut from ship sails grabbed at the port in Vernes and again in Kilnar. Others made do with nothing but old bed linens, and in a few rare cases, actual tents were used.

The stranger paused at the top of the hill. When Gill caught up, he asked, "Which of these tents belongs to Parker?"

"Parker? He's not in a tent, sir. He's in the farmhouse down that way," Gill said, pointing.

"Gill, why are you off your post?" Sergeant Milford growled at him as he came out of his tent, blinking as the rain stung his eyes. He was wrapped in a cloak, his pale bare feet showing beneath it.

"Well, I—" Gill began, but the stranger interrupted.

"Who is this now?" The stranger walked right up to Milford and, scowling, stood with his hands on his hips.

"This here is Sergeant Milford, sir," Gill answered, and the sergeant looked confused.

The stranger inspected him and shook his head. "Sergeant, where in Maribor's name is your sword?"

"In my tent, but—"

"You don't think it necessary to wear your sword when an enemy army stands less than a mile away and could attack at any minute?"

"I was sleeping, sir!"

"Look up, sergeant!" the man said.

The sergeant tilted his head up, wincing as rain hit his face.

"As you can see, it's nearly morning."

"Ah—yes, sir. Sorry, sir."

"Now get dressed and get a new picket on Gill's post at once, do you understand?"

"Yes, sir. Right away, sir!"

"Gill!"

"Yes, sir!" Gill jumped.

"Let's get moving. I'm late as it is."

"Yes, sir!" Gill set off following once more, offering the sergeant a flummoxed shrug as he passed.

The main body camped on what everyone called Bingham

Hill, apparently after farmer Bingham, who grew barley and rye in the fields below. Gill heard there had been quite the hullabaloo when Commander Gaunt had informed Bingham the army would be using his farm and Gaunt would take his house for a headquarters. The pastoral home with a thatched roof and wooden beams found itself surrounded by a sea of congested camps. Flowers that had once lined the walkway had been crushed beneath a hundred boots. The barn housed the officers and the stable provided storage and was also used as a dispensary and tavern for those with rank. There were tents everywhere and a hundred campfires burned rings into the ground.

"Inform Commander Parker I'm here," the stranger told one of the guards on the porch.

"And who are you?"

"Marshal Lord Blackwater."

The sentry hesitated only a moment, then disappeared inside. He reemerged quickly and held the door open.

"Thank you, Gill. That will be all," the stranger said as he stepped inside.

⁂

"You're Commander Parker?" Hadrian asked the portly man before him, who was sloppily dressed in a short black vest and dirty white britches. An upturned nose sat in the middle of his soft face, which rested on a large wobbly neck.

He was seated before a rough wooden table littered with candles, maps, dispatches, and a steaming plate of eggs and ham. He stood up, pulling a napkin from his neck, and wiped his mouth. "I am, and you are Marshal Blackwater? I wasn't informed of—"

"Marshal *Lord* Blackwater," he said, correcting the man with a friendly smile, and handed over his letter of reference.

Parker took the letter, roughly unfolding it, and began reading.

Wavy wooden beams edged and divided the pale yellowing walls. Along these hung pots, sacks, cooking tools, and what Hadrian guessed to be Commander Parker's sword and cloak. Baskets, pails, and jugs huddled in corners, stacked out of the way on the floor, which listed downhill toward the fireplace.

After reading the letter, Parker returned to his seat and tucked his napkin back into his collar. "You're not really a lord, are you?"

Hadrian hesitated briefly. "Well, technically I am, at least for the moment."

"What are you when you're not a lord?"

"I suppose you could call me a mercenary. I've done a lot of things over the years."

"Why would the Princess of Melengar send a mercenary to me?"

"Because I can win this battle for you."

"What makes you think I can't win it?"

"The fact that you're still in this farmhouse instead of the city. You're very likely a good manager and quartermaster, and I'm certain a wonderful bookkeeper, but war is more than numbers in ledgers. With Gaunt gone, you might be a bit unsure of what to do next. That's where I can help you. As it happens, I have a great deal of combat experience."

"So you know about Gaunt's disappearance."

Hadrian did not like the tone in his voice. There was something there, something coy and threatening. Aggression was still his best approach. "This army has been camped here for days, and you've not launched a single foray at the enemy."

"It's raining," Parker replied. "The field is a muddy mess."

"Exactly," Hadrian said. "That's why you should be attacking. The rain will give you the upper hand. Call in your captains and I can explain how we can turn the weather to our advantage, but we must act quickly—"

"You'd like that, wouldn't you?" There was that tone again, this time more ominous. "I have a better idea. How about you explain to me why Arista Essendon would betray Degan?"

"She didn't. You don't understand. She's—"

"Oh, she most certainly did!" Parker rose to his feet and threw his napkin to the floor as if it were a gauntlet of challenge. "And you needn't lie any further. I know why. She did it to save her miserable little kingdom." He took a step forward and bumped the table. "By destroying Degan, she hopes to curry favor for Melengar. So what are your real orders?" He advanced, pointing an accusatory finger. "To gain our confidence? To lead this army into an ambush like you did with Gaunt? Was it you? Were you there? Were you one of the ones that grabbed him?"

Parker glanced at Hadrian's swords. "Or is it to get close enough to kill me?" he said, staggering backward. The commander knocked his head on a low-hanging pot, which fell with a brassy clang. The noise made Parker jump. "Simms! Fall!" he cried, and the two sentries rushed in.

"Sir!" they said in unison.

"Take his swords. Shackle him to a stake. Get him out of—"

"You don't understand. Arista isn't your enemy," Hadrian interrupted.

"Oh, I understand perfectly."

"She was set up by the empire, just as Gaunt was."

"So she's missing too?"

"No, she's in Ratibor right now planning a rebellion to aid your attack."

Parker laughed aloud at that. "Oh please, sir! You do need lessons in lying. A *princess* of Melengar organizing an uprising in Ratibor? Get him out of here."

One of the soldiers drew his sword. “Remove your weapons—now!”

Hadrian considered his options. He could run, but he would never get another opportunity to persuade them. Taking Parker prisoner would require killing Simms and Fall and destroy any hope of gaining their trust. With no other choice, he sighed and unbuckled his belt.

⁂

“Exactly how confident are you that Hadrian will succeed in persuading the Nationalists to attack tomorrow morning?” Polish asked Arista as they sat at the Dunlaps’ table. Outside, it continued to storm.

“I have the same level of confidence in his success as I do in ours,” Arista replied.

Polish smirked. “I keep forgetting you’re a diplomat.”

Eight other people sat around the little table, where the city lay mapped out with knickknacks borrowed from Mrs. Dunlap’s shelves. Those present had been handpicked by Hadrian, Dr. Gerand, Polish, or Emery, who was back on his feet and eating everything Mrs. Dunlap put under his nose.

With Royce and Hadrian gone, Arista spent most of her time talking with the young Mr. Dorn. While he no longer stumbled over using her first name, the admiration in his eyes was unmistakable, and Arista caught herself smiling self-consciously. He had a nice face—cheerful and passionate—and while he was younger even than Alric, she thought him more mature. Perhaps that came from hardship and struggle.

Since he had regained consciousness, she had babbled on about the trials that had brought her there. He told her about how his mother’s death had given him life and what it had been like to grow up as a soldier’s son. They both shared memories of the fires that had robbed them of the ones they loved. She listened as he poured out his life's story of being an orphan with such intensity that it filled her eyes with tears. He had such a way with words, a means of inciting emotion and empathy. She realized Emery could have changed the world if only he had been born noble. Listening to him, to his ideals, to his passion for justice and compassion, she realized this was what she could expect from Degan Gaunt, a common man with the heart of a king.

"You must understand it's not entirely up to me," Polish told them. "I don't issue policy in the guild. I simply don't have the authority to sanction an outright attack, particularly when there is nothing to be gained. Even if victory were assured, instead of a rather wild gamble, my hands would still be tied."

"Nothing to be gained?" Emery said, stunned. "There is a whole city to be gained! Furthermore, if the imperial army is routed from the field, it's possible that all Rhenydd might fall under the banner of the Delgos Republic."

"I would also add," Arista said, "that defeating the Imperialists here would leave Aquesta open for assault by the remainder of the Nationalists, Melengar, and possibly even Trent—if I can swing their alliance. If Aquesta falls, Colnora will be a free city and certain powerful merchants could find themselves in legitimate seats of power."

"You are good. I'll grant you that, milady," Polish replied. "But there are many *ifs* in that scenario, and the Royalists won't allow Colnora to be ruled by a commoner. Lanaklin would assume the throne of Warric and likely appoint his own duke to run the city."

"Well, the Diamond's position will certainly continue to decline if you fail to aid us and the New Empire's strength grows," Arista shot back.

Polish frowned and shook his head. "This is far beyond the

bounds of my mandate. I simply can't commit without orders from the Jewel. The Imps leave the Diamond alone, for the most part. They see us as inevitable as the rats in any sewer. As long as we don't make too much of a nuisance, they leave us to our scurrying. But if we do this, they will declare war. The Diamond will no longer be neutral. We'll be a target in every Imp city. Hundreds could be imprisoned or executed."

"We could keep your involvement a secret," Emery offered.

Polish laughed. "The winner chooses which secrets are kept, and which remain hidden, so I would have to insist on proof of your success before I could help you. We both know that is not possible. If your chances were that good, then you would not need my assistance in the first place. No, I'm sorry. My rats will do what we can, but joining in the assault is not possible."

"Can you at least see that the armory door is unlocked?" Emery asked.

Polish thought a moment and nodded. "That I can do."

"Can we get back to the plan?" Dr. Gerand asked.

Before leaving, Hadrian had outlined the details for a strategy to take the city. Emery's idea was a good one, but an idea simply was not the same as a battle plan and they were all thankful for Hadrian's advice. He had explained that surprise was their greatest tool and catching the armory unaware was their best tactic. After that, things would be more difficult. Their greatest adversary would be time. Securing the armory would be essential, and they must be quick in order to prepare for the attack by the garrison.

"I'll lead the men into the armory," Emery declared. "If I survive, I'll take my place in the square with the men at the weak point of the line."

Everyone nodded grimly.

Hadrian's plan further called for the men to form two straight lines—one before the other—outside the armory and to purposely leave a gap as a weak point. Professional soldiers would look for this kind of vulnerability, so the rebels could predetermine where the attack would fall the hardest. He warned that the men stationed there would suffer the highest number of casualties, but it would also allow the townsfolk to fold the line and generate a devastating envelopment maneuver, which would best utilize their superior numbers.

"I'll lead the left flank," Arista said, and everyone looked at her, stunned.

"My lady," Emery began, "you understand I hold you in the highest esteem, but a battle is no place for a woman and I would be sorely grieved should your life come into peril."

"My life will be in peril no matter where I am, so I may as well be of some use. Besides, this is all my idea. I can't stand by while all of you risk your own lives."

"You need fear no shame," Dr. Gerand told her. "You have already done more than we can hope to repay you for."

"Nevertheless," she said resolutely, "I'll stand with the line."

"Can you wield a sword too?" Perin the grocer asked. His tone was not mocking or sarcastic, but one of expectant amazement, as if he anticipated she would reply that she was a master sword fighter of some renown.

The miraculous survival of Emery was only one of the rallying points of the rebellion. Arista had overlooked the power of her own name. Emery pointed out that she and her brother were heroes to those wishing to fight the New Empire. Their victory over Percy Braga, immortalized in the traveling theater play, had inspired many throughout Apeladorn. All the recruiters had to do was whisper that Arista Essendon had come to Ratibor and that she had stolen Emery from death at the hands of the empire, and most people simply assumed victory was assured.

"Well," she said, "I certainly have just as much experience as most of the merchants, farmers, and tradesmen that will be fighting alongside me."

No one said anything for a long while, and then Emery stood up.

"Forgive me, Your Highness, but I cannot allow you to do this."

Arista gave him a harsh, challenging stare and Emery's face cringed, exposing that a mere unpleasant glance from her was enough to hurt him.

"And how do you plan to stop me?" she snapped, recalling all the times her father, brother, or even Count Pickering, had shooed her out of the council hall, insisting she would spend her time more productively with a needle in her hand.

"If you insist on fighting, I will not fight," he said simply.

Dr. Gerand stood up. "Neither will I."

"Nor I," Perin said, also rising.

Arista scowled at Emery. Again, her glare appeared to hurt the man, but he remained resolute. "All right. Sit down. You win."

"Thank you, my lady," Emery said.

"Then I'll lead the left flank, I suppose," Perin volunteered. He was one of the larger men at the table, stocky and strong.

"I'll take the right flank," Dr. Gerand said.

"That is very brave of you, sir," Emery told him, "but I'll ask Adam the wheeler to take that responsibility. He has fighting experience."

"And he's not an old man," the doctor said bitterly.

Arista knew the helplessness that he was feeling. "Doctor, your services will be required to tend to the injured. Once the armory is taken, you and I will do what we can for those that are wounded."

They went over the plan once more from beginning to end. Arista and Polish came up with several potential problems: What if too few people came? What if they could not secure the armory? What if the garrison did not attack? They made contingency plans until they were certain everything was accounted for.

As they concluded, Dr. Gerand drew forth a bottle of rum and called for glasses from Mrs. Dunlap. "Tomorrow morning we go into battle," he said. "Some of us at this table will not survive to see the sunset again." He lifted his glass. "To those who will fall and to our victory."

"And to the good lady who made it possible," Emery added as they all raised their glasses and drank.

Arista drank with the rest but found the liquor to have a bitter taste.

❧

The princess lay awake in the tiny room across the hall from Mrs. Dunlap's bedroom. Smaller than her maid's quarters in Medford, it had just a small window and a tiny shelf to hold a candle. There was so little room between the walls and the bed that she was forced to crawl over the mattress to enter. She could not sleep. The battle to take the city would start in just a few hours and she was consumed by nervous energy. Her mind raced through precautions, running a checklist over and over again.

Have I done all I can to prepare?

Everything was about to change, for good or ill.

Will Alric forgive me if I die? She gave a bitter laugh. *Will he forgive me if I live?*

She stared at the ceiling, wondering if there was a spell to help her sleep.

Magic.

She considered using it in the coming battle. She toyed with the idea while tapping her feet together, anxiously listening to the rain patter the roof.

If I can make it rain, what else can I do? Could I conjure a phantom army? Rain fire? Open the earth to swallow the garrison?

She was certain of only one thing—she could boil blood. The thought sobered her.

What if I lose control? What if I boiled the blood of our men...or Emery?

When she had boiled the water at Sheridan, the nearby clothing had sizzled and hissed. Magic was not easy. Perhaps with time she could master it, but already she sensed her limitations. Now it was clear why Esrahaddon had given her the task of making it rain. Previously she had thought it an absurd challenge to attempt such an immense feat. Now she realized that making it rain was easy. The target was as broad as the sky and the action was natural—it was the equivalent of a marksman throwing a rock and trying to hit the ground. The process would be the same, she guessed, for any spell—the drawing of power, the focus, and the execution through synchronized movement and sound—but the idea of pinpointing such an unruly force to a specific target was daunting. She realized with a shudder that if Royce and Hadrian had been on the hill that night, they would have died along with the seret. There was no doubt she could defeat the garrison, but she might kill everyone in Ratibor in the process. She could possibly use the Art to draw down lightning or summon fire to consume the soldiers, but it would be like a first-year music student trying to compose and orchestrate a full symphony.

No, I can't take such a risk.

She turned her mind to more practical issues. Did they have enough bandages prepared? She had to remember to get a fire going to have hot coals for sealing wounds.

Is there anything else I can do?

She heard a soft rapping and pulled the covers up, as she wore only a thin nightgown borrowed from Mrs. Dunlap. "Yes?"

"It's me," Emery said. "I hope I didn't wake you."

"Come in, please," she told him.

Emery opened the door and stood at the foot of the bed, wearing only his britches and an oversized shirt. "I couldn't sleep and I thought maybe you couldn't either."

"Who would have guessed that waiting to see if you'll live or die would make it so hard to sleep?" She shrugged and smiled.

Emery smiled back and looked for a means to enter the room.

She sat up and propped two pillows behind her. "Just crawl on the bed," she told him, folding her legs and slapping the covers. He looked awkward but took her offer and sat at the foot of the mattress, which sank with his weight.

"Are you scared?" she inquired, and realized too late that it was not the kind of question a woman should ask a man.

"Are you?" he parried, pulling his knees up and wrapping his arms around them. He was barefoot and his toes shone pale in the moonlight.

"Yes," she said. "I'm not even going to be on the line and I'm terrified."

"Would you think me a miserable coward if I said I was frightened too?"

"I would think you a fool if you weren't."

He sighed and let his head rest on his knees.

"What is it?"

"If I tell you something, do you promise to keep it a secret?" he asked, keeping his head down.

"I'm an ambassador. I do that sort of thing for a living."

"I've never fought in a battle before. I've never killed a man."

"I suspect that is the case for nearly everyone fighting tomorrow," she said, hoping he would assume she included herself in that statement. She could not bear to tell him the truth. "I don't think most of these people have ever used a sword."

"Some have." He lifted his head. "Adam fought with Ethelred's army against the Ghazel when Lord Rufus won his fame. Renkin Pool and Forrest, the silversmith's son, also fought. That's why I have them as leaders in the line. The thing is, everyone is looking to me like I'm a great war hero, but I don't know if I'll stand and fight or run like a coward. I might faint dead away at the first sight of blood."

Arista reached out, taking his hand in hers. "If there is one thing I'm certain of"—she looked directly into his eyes—"it's that you'll stand and fight bravely. I honestly don't think you could do anything else. It just seems to be the way you're made. I think your innate courage is what everyone sees and why they look up to you—like I do."

Emery bowed his head. "Thank you, that was very kind."

"I wasn't being kind, just honest." Suddenly feeling awkward, she released his hand and asked him, "How is your back?"

"It still hurts," he said, raising his arm to test it. "But I'll be able to swing a sword. I really should let you get to sleep." He scrambled off the bed.

"It was nice that you came," she told him, and meant it.

He paused. "I'll only have one regret tomorrow."

"And what is that?"

"That I'm not noble."

She gave him a curious look.

"If I were even a lowly baron and survived the battle, I would ride to Melengar and ask your brother for your hand. I would pester him until he either locked me up or surrendered you. I know that is improper. I know you must have dukes and princes vying for your affections, but I would try just the same. I would fight them for you. I would do anything...if only."

Arista felt her face flush and fought an urge to cover it with her hands. "You know, a common man whose father died in the service of his king, who was so bold as to take Ratibor and Aquesta, could find himself knighted for such heroics. As ambassador, I would point out to my brother that such an act would do well for our relationship with Rhenydd."

Emery's eyes brightened. They had never looked so vibrant or so deep. There was joy on his face. He took a step back toward the bed, paused, then slowly withdrew.

"Well, then," Emery said at last, "I shall need my sleep if I'm to be knighted."

"You shall indeed, *Sir* Emery."

"My lady," he said, and attempted a sweeping bow but halted partway with a wince and a gritting of his teeth. "Good night."

After he had left her room, Arista discovered her heart was pounding, her palms moist. How shameful. In a matter of hours, men would die because of her. By noon, she could be hanging from a post, yet she was flushed with excitement because a man showed an interest in her. How horribly childish...how infantile...how selfish...and how wonderful. No one had ever looked at her the way he just had. She remembered how his hand felt and the rustle of his toes on her bed covers—what awful timing she had.

She lay in bed and prayed to Maribor that all would be well. They needed a miracle, and immediately she thought of Hadrian and Royce. Isn't that what Alric always called them...his miracle workers? Everything would be all right.

Chapter 15

The Speech

Amilia sat biting her thumbnail, or what little was left of it. "Well?" she asked Nimbus. "What do you think? She seems stiff to me."

"Stiff is good," the thin man replied. "People of high station are known to be reserved and inflexible. It lends an air of strength to her. It is her chin that bothers me. The board in her corset fixed her back, but her chin—it keeps drooping. She needs to keep her head up. We should put a high collar on her dress, something stiff."

"A little late for that now," Amilia replied, irritated. "The ceremony is in less than an hour."

"A lot can be done in that time, Your Ladyship," he assured her.

Amilia still found it awkward, even embarrassing, to be referred to as "Your Ladyship" or "my lady." Nimbus, who had always followed proper protocol, insisted on referring to her formally. His mannerisms rubbed off on the other members of the castle staff. Maids and pages, who only months earlier had laughed and made fun of Amilia, took to bowing and curtsying to her. Even Ibis Thinly had begun addressing Amilia as *Her Ladyship*. The attention was flattering, but it could also be fleeting. Amilia was a noble in name only. She could lose her title just as easily as it had been won—and that was exactly what would happen in less than an hour.

"All right, wait outside," she ordered. "I'll hand you the dress to take to the seamstress. Your Eminence, can I please have the gown?"

Modina raised her arms as if in a trance and two handmaidens immediately went to work undoing the numerous buttons and hooks.

Amilia's stomach churned. She had done everything possible in the time allotted. Modina had been surprisingly cooperative and easily memorized and repeated the speech Saldur had provided, which was mercifully short and easy to remember. Modina's role was remarkably simple. She would step onto the balcony, recite the words, and withdraw. The whole process would only take a few minutes, yet Amilia was certain of an impending disaster.

Despite all the preparations, Modina simply was not ready. The empress had only recently showed signs of lucidity and managed to follow directions, but no more than that. In many ways, she reminded Amilia of a dog. Trained to sit and stay, a pup would do as it was told when the master was around, but how many could maintain their composure when left on their own? A squirrel passing by would break their discipline and off they would go. Amilia was not permitted on the balcony, and if anything unexpected happened, there was no telling how the empress would react.

Amilia took the elaborate gown to Nimbus. "Make it quick. I don't want to be here with an empress clad only in her undergarments when the bell strikes."

"I will run like the wind, my lady," he said with a forced smile.

"What are you doing out here?" Regent Saldur asked.

Nimbus made a hasty bow, then ran off with the empress's gown.

The regent was lavishly dressed for the occasion, which made him even more intimidating than usual. "Why aren't you in with the empress? There is less than an hour before the presentation."

"Yes, Your Grace, but there are some last-minute prep—"

Saldur took her angrily by the arm and dragged her inside the staging room. Modina was wrapped in a robe and the two handmaidens fussed with her hair. They both stopped abruptly and curtsied. Saldur took no notice.

"Must I waste my time impressing on you the importance of this day?" he said while roughly releasing her. "Outside this palace, all of Aquesta is gathering, as well as dignitaries from all over Warric and even ambassadors from as far away as Trent and Calis. It's paramount that they see a strong, competent empress. Has she learned the speech?"

"Yes, Your Grace," Amilia replied with a bowed head.

Saldur examined the empress in her disheveled robe and unfinished hair. He scowled and whirled on Amilia. "If you ruin this—if she falters—I'll hold you personally responsible. A single word from me and you'll never be seen again. Given your background, I won't even have to create an excuse. No one will question your disappearance. No one will even notice you're gone. Fail me, Amilia, and I'll see you deeply regret it."

He left, slamming the door behind him and leaving Amilia barely able to breathe.

"Your Ladyship?" the maid Anna addressed her.

"What is it?" she asked weakly.

"It's her shoe, milady. The heel has come loose."

What else could go wrong?

On any ordinary day, nothing like this would happen, but

that day, because her life depended on it, problems followed one upon another. “Get it to the cobbler at once and tell him if it isn’t fixed in twenty minutes, I’ll—I’ll—”

“I will tell him to hurry, milady.” Anna ran from the room, shoe in hand.

Amilia began to pace. The room was only twenty feet long, causing her to turn frequently, which made her dizzy, but she continued it anyway. Her body was reacting unconsciously while her mind flew over every aspect of the ceremony.

What if she leaps off the balcony?

The thought hit her like a slap. As absurd as it seemed, it was possible. The empress was not of sound mind. With the noise and confusion of thousands of excited subjects, Modina could become overwhelmed and simply snap. The balcony was not terribly high, only thirty feet or so. The fall might not kill the empress if she landed well. Amilia, on the other hand, would not survive the incident.

Sweat broke out on her brow as her pacing quickened.

There was no time to put up a higher rail.

Perhaps a net at the bottom? No, that won’t help.

The problem was not the injury. It was the spectacle.

A rope?

She could tie a length around Modina’s waist and hold it from behind. That way if she made any forward movement, Amilia could stop her.

Nimbus returned, timidly peeking into the room. “What is it, my lady?” he asked, seeing her expression.

“Hmm? Oh, everything. I need a rope and a shoe—but never mind that. What about the dress?”

“The seamstress is working as fast as she can. Unfortunately, I don’t think there will be time for a test dressing.”

“What if it doesn’t fit? What if it chokes her so she can’t even speak?”

"We must think positively, my lady."

"That's easy for you to say. Your life isn't dangling by a thread—perhaps literally."

"But surely, Your Ladyship, you cannot fear such repercussions merely from a dress alteration? We are civilized people, after all."

"I'm not certain what civilization you're from, Nimbus, but this one can be harsh to those who fail."

Amilia looked at Modina, sitting quietly, oblivious to the importance of the speech she was about to give. They would do nothing to her. She was the empress and the whole world knew it. If she disappeared, there would be an inquiry and the people would demand justice for the loss of their god-queen. Even people as well placed as Saldur could hang for such a crime.

"Shall I bring the headdress?" Nimbus asked.

"Yes, please. Anna fetched it from the milliner's this morning and likely left it in the empress's bedroom."

"And how about I bring a bite for you to eat, my lady? You haven't had anything all day."

"I can't eat."

"As you wish. I will be back as soon as I can."

Amilia went to the window. From this vantage point, she could just see the east gate, through which scores of people poured. Men, women, and children of all classes entered the outer portcullis. The gathering throng emitted a low murmur, like some gigantic beast growling just out of sight. There was a knock at the door and in stepped the seamstress with the gown in her arms as if it were a newborn baby.

"That was fast," Amilia said.

"Forgive me, Your Ladyship, it's not quite done, but the royal tutor just stopped by and said I should finish up here, where I can size it to Her Eminence's neck. It's not how things are done, you see. It's not right to make the great lady sit and wait on me like some dress dummy. Still, the tutor said if I didn't do as he said, then he—" She paused and lowered her voice to a whisper. "He said he'd have me horsewhipped."

Amilia put a hand over her mouth to hide a smile. "He was not serious about the whipping, I can assure you, but he was quite right. This is too important to worry about inconveniencing Her Eminence. Get to work."

They dressed her once more in the gown and the seamstress worked feverishly, stitching in the rest of the collar. Amilia had begun to resume her pacing when there was another knock on the door. With the seamstress and maids occupied, Amilia opened it herself and was startled to find the Earl of Chadwick.

"Good evening, Lady Amilia," he said, bowing graciously. "I was hoping for a word with Her Eminence prior to the commencement."

"This is not a good time, sir," she said. Amilia could hardly believe she was saying no to a noble lord. "The empress is indisposed at the moment. Please understand."

"But of course. My apologies. Perhaps I could have a word with you, then?"

"Me? Ah, well—yes, I suppose that would be all right." Amilia stepped outside, closing the door behind her.

Amilia expected the earl would make his issue known right then, but instead, he began to walk down the corridor, and it took a moment for her to realize he expected her to follow.

"The empress is well, I trust?"

"Yes, my lord," she said, glancing back at the door to the dressing room, which was getting farther and farther away.

"I'm pleased to hear that," the earl said, and then suddenly added, "How rude of me. How are *you* feeling, milady?"

"I'm as well as can be expected, sir."

If Amilia had not been so consumed with thoughts of the empress, she would have found it funny that an earl was embarrassed by not immediately inquiring about her own health.

"And it's beautiful weather for the festivities today, is it not?"

"Yes, sir, it is." She forced her voice to remain calm.

Nimbus, Anna, and the cobbler all appeared and rushed down the hall. Nimbus paused briefly, giving her a worried look before entering the dressing room.

"Allow me to be blunt," the earl said.

"Please do, sir." Amilia's anxiety neared the breaking point.

"Everyone knows you're the closest to the empress. She confides in no one but you. Can you—Have you—Does the empress ever speak of me?"

Amilia raised her eyebrows in surprise. Under ordinary circumstances, the earl's hesitancy could have seemed quaint and even charming, but at that moment, she prayed he would just get it out and be done with it.

"Please, I know I'm being terribly forward, but I'm a forward man. I would like to know if she has ever thought of me, and if so, is it to her favor?"

"My lord, I can honestly say she has never once mentioned you to me."

The earl paused to consider this.

"I'm not sure how I should interpret that. I'm certain she sees so many suitors. Can you do me a favor, milady?"

"If it is in my power, sir."

"Could you speak to her about gracing me with a dance this evening at the ball after the banquet? I would be incredibly grateful."

"Her Eminence won't be attending the ball or the banquet, sir. She never dines in public and has many matters that require her attention."

"Never?"

"I'm afraid not, sir."

"I see." The earl paused in thought as Amilia rapidly drummed the tips of her fingers together.

"If you please, sir, I do need to be seeing to the empress."

"Of course. Forgive me for taking up your valuable time. Still, if you should perhaps mention me to Her Eminence and let her know I would very much like to visit with her..."

"I will, Your Lordship. Now, if you'll excuse me..."

Amilia hurried back and found that the seamstress had finished the collar, which was tall and did indeed keep her chin up. The addition looked horribly uncomfortable. Modina, of course, didn't seem to care. The cobbler, however, was still working on her shoe.

"What's going on here?" she asked.

"The new heel he put on was taller than the other," Nimbus told her. "He tried to resize, but in his haste he overcompensated and now it is shorter."

Amilia turned to Anna. "How long do we have?"

"About fifteen minutes," she replied gloomily.

"What about the headdress? I don't see it."

"It was not in the bedroom, or hall, my lady."

Anna's face drained of color. "Oh dear Maribor, forgive me. I forgot all about it!"

"You forgot? Nimbus!"

"Yes, my lady?"

"Run to the milliner and fetch the headdress, and when I say run, I mean sprint, do you hear me?"

"At once, my lady, but I don't know where the milliner shop is."

"Get a page to escort you."

"The pages are all busy with the ceremony."

"I don't care! Grab one at sword point if necessary. Find one who knows the way and tell him it's by order of the empress and don't let anyone stop you. Now move!"

"Anna!" Amilia shouted.

"Yes, milady." The maid was trembling, in tears. "I'm so sorry, milady, truly I am."

"We don't have time for apologies or tears. Go to the empress's bedroom and fetch her day shoes. She'll have to wear them instead. Do it now!"

Amilia slammed the door behind them and gave it a solid kick in frustration. She leaned her forehead against the oak as she concentrated on calming down. The gown would cover the shoes. No one would know the difference. The headdress was another matter. They had worked on it for weeks and the regents would notice its absence. The milliner's shop was out in the city proper, and she had left it to Anna to pick up. She could really blame only herself. She should have asked about it earlier and was furious at her incompetence. She kicked the door once more, then turned around and slumped to the floor, her gown ballooning about her.

The ceremony would begin in minutes but there was still time. Modina's speech was scheduled to be last and Amilia was certain she would have at least another twenty, perhaps even thirty, minutes while the others addressed the crowd. Across from her, Modina sat stiff and straight in her royal gown of white and gold, her long neck held high by the new collar. There was something different about Modina. She was watching Amilia with interest. She was actually studying her.

"Are you going to be all right?" she asked the empress.

Immediately, the light in her eyes vanished and the blank stare returned.

Amilia sighed.

Regent Ethelred spoke for nearly an hour from the balcony, which was decorated in colorful bunting, although Amilia hardly heard a word of what he said. Something about the grandness and might of the New Empire and how Maribor had ordained that it would unite all of humanity once again. He spoke of the New Empire's military successes in the north and the bloodless annexation of Alburn and Dunmore. He followed this with the news of an expected surplus in wheat and barley and an end to the elven problem. They would no longer be allowed to roam free, and instead of being turned into useless slaves, they would simply disappear. The New Empire was gathering wayward elves from all over the realm. How they would be disposed of, he did not say. The massive crowd below cheered their approval and their combined voices roared.

Amilia sat in the staging room, her arms wrapped about her waist. She could not even pace now. The empress herself appeared unconcerned by the approaching presentation and sat calmly as ever in her shimmering gown and massive headdress, which mimicked a fanning peacock.

Nimbus had managed excellent time reaching the milliner, although in the process he had apparently terrified a young page with threats. They also had good fortune in that the ceremony had started late due to a last-minute dispute about the order of speakers. Amilia had managed to secure the headdress on Modina just minutes before the first started.

The chancellor had spoken first, then Ethelred, and finally Saldur. With each word, Amilia felt it harder and harder to breathe. Finally, Ethelred's speech concluded and Saldur stepped forward for the formal introduction. The crowd hushed, as they knew the expected moment was at hand.

"Nearly a thousand years have passed since the breaking of the great Empire of Novron," he told the multitude below. "We stand here today as witnesses to the enduring power of Maribor and his promise to Novron that his seed will reign forever. Neither treachery nor time can break this sacred covenant. Allow me to introduce to you proof of this. Welcome with me now the once simple farm maid, the slayer of the elven beast, the Heir of Novron, the high priestess of the Nyphron Church, Her Most Serene and Royal Grand Imperial Eminence, Empress Modina Novronian!"

The crowd erupted in cheers and applause. Amilia could feel the vibration of their voices even where she sat. She looked at Modina, pleading and hopeful. The empress's face was calm as she stood up straight and gracefully walked forward, the train of her dress trailing behind her.

When she stepped upon the balcony—when the people finally saw her face—the noise of the crowd did the impossible. It exploded. The unimaginably boisterous cheering was deafening, like a continuous roll of thunder that vibrated the very stone of the castle. It went on and on and Amilia wondered if it would ever stop.

In the face of the tumult, surely Modina could not endure. What effect would this have on her fragile countenance? Amilia wished Saldur had allowed her to use the rope or accompany her onto the balcony. Amilia's only consolation was knowing that Modina was likely frozen, her mind retreating to that dark place she had so long lived in, the place she crawled to hide from the world.

Amilia prayed the crowd would quiet. She hoped Ethelred or Saldur would do something to silence them, but neither moved and the crowd continued to roar with no end in sight. Then something unexpected happened. Modina slowly raised her hands, making a gentle quieting motion. Almost immediately, the crowd fell silent. Amilia could not believe her eyes.

"My beloved and cherished loyal subjects." She spoke with a loud, clear, almost musical voice that Amilia had not heard at practice. "It is wonderful to finally meet you."

The crowd roared anew, even louder than before. Modina allowed them to cheer for a full minute before raising her hands and silencing them again.

"As some of you may have heard, I have not been well. The battle with Rufus's Bane left me weakened, but with the help of my closest friend, the grand imperial secretary, Lady Amilia of Tarin Vale, I am feeling much better."

Amilia stopped breathing at the mention of her name. That was not in the speech.

"I owe Amilia the greatest debt of gratitude for her efforts on my behalf, for I should not be here at all if not for her strength, wisdom, and kindness."

Amilia closed her eyes and cringed.

"While I am feeling better, I am still easily exhausted and I must keep my strength in order to devote it to ensuring our defense against invaders, a bountiful harvest, and our return to the glory and prosperity that was Novron's Empire," she finished with an elaborate wave of her hand, turned, and left the balcony with elegant grace and poise.

The crowd erupted once more into cheers, which continued long after Modina had returned inside.

"I swear I didn't tell her to say that." Amilia pleaded with Saldur.

"Because the empress publicly named you her friend and the hero of the realm, you've become famous," Saldur replied. "This will make it almost impossible for me to replace you—*almost.* But don't worry," he continued thoughtfully. "With such a fine display, I would be a fool to do anything other than praise you. I'm once more impressed. I wouldn't have expected this from you. You're more clever than I thought, but I should have guessed that already. I'll have to remember this. Good work, my dear. Good work, indeed."

"Yes, that was excellent!" Ethelred said. "We can now put the fiasco of the coronation behind us. I can't say I approve of the self-aggrandizement, Amilia, but seeing what you've done with her, I can't begrudge you a little recognition. In fact, we should consider rewarding her for a job well done, Sauly."

"Indeed," he replied. "We'll have to consider what that should be. Come, Lanis, let's proceed to the banquet." The two of them left, talking back and forth about the ceremony as they went.

Amilia moved to the empress's side, took her hand, and escorted her back to her quarters. "You'll be the death of me yet," she told her.

Chapter 16

The Battle of Ratibor

Hadrian sat in the rain. Heavy chains shackled his ankles and wrists to a large metal stake driven into the ground. All day, and throughout the night, he waited in the mud, watching the lazy movements of the Nationalist army. They were just as slow to decide his fate as they were to attack. Horses walked past, meals were called, and men grumbled about the rain and the mud. The gray light faded into night and regret consumed him.

He should have escaped, even if it had meant shedding blood. He might have been able to save Arista's life. He could have warned her that the Nationalists would not cooperate and would have her call off the attack. Now even if she succeeded, the victory would be short-lived and she would face the gallows or a beheading.

"Gill!" he shouted as he saw the sentry walking by in his soaked cloak.

"Ah yes!" Gill laughed, coming closer with a grin. "If it isn't the *grand marshal.* Not so grand now, are you?"

"Gill, you have to help me," he shouted over the roar of the rain. "I need you to get a message to—"

Gill bent down. "Now why would I help the likes of you? You made a fool out of me. Sergeant Milford weren't too pleased neither. He has me running an all-night shift to show his displeasure."

"I have money," Hadrian told him eagerly. "I could pay you."

"Really? And where is this money, in some chest buried on some distant mountain, or merely in another pair of pants?"

"Right here in the purse on my belt. I have at least ten gold tenents. You can have it all if you just promise me to take a message to Ratibor."

Gill looked at Hadrian's belt curiously. "Sure," he said. Reaching down, he untied the purse. He weighed it in his hands. The bouncing produced a jingle. He pulled open the mouth and poured out a handful of coins. "Whoa! Look at that. You weren't joshing. There's really gold in here. One, two, three...damn! Well, thank you, Marshal." He made a mock salute. "This will definitely take the sting out of having to stand two watches." He started to walk away.

"Wait!" Hadrian told him. "You need to hear the message."

Gill kept walking.

"You need to tell Arista not to attack," he shouted desperately, but Gill continued on his way, swinging the purse, until his figure was obscured by the rain.

Hadrian cursed and kicked the stake hard. He collapsed on his side, lost in frustration. He remembered the look on Arista's face, how hopeful she had been. It had never crossed her mind that he could fail. When he had first met the princess, he had thought she was arrogant and egotistical, like all nobles—grown-up brats, greedy and self-centered.

When did that change?

Images flooded back to him. He remembered her hanging out her wet undergarments at Sheridan. How stubbornly she had slept under the horse blanket that first night outside, crying herself to sleep. He and Royce had both been certain she would cancel the mission the next day. He saw her sleeping in the skiff that morning when they had drifted down the Bernum, and remembered how she had practically announced her identity to everyone when drunk in Dunstan's home. She had always been their patron and their princess, but somewhere along the way she had become more than that.

As he sat there, pelted with rain and helpless in the mud, he was tormented with visions of her death. He saw her lying facedown in the filthy street, her dress torn, her pale skin stained red with blood. The Imperialists would likely hoist her body above Central Square or perhaps drag it behind a horse to Aquesta. Maybe they would cut her head off and send it to Alric as a warning.

In a flash of anger and desperation, he began digging in the mud, trying to dislodge the stake. He dug furiously, pulled hard, then dug again—wrenching the stake back and forth. A guard spotted him and used a second stake on the chains connected to his wrists to stretch him out flat.

"Still trying to get away and cause mischief, are ya?" the guard said. "Well, that ain't gonna happen. You killed Gaunt. You'll die for that, but until then, you'll stay put." The guard spat in his face, but the effect was hardly what he sought, as the rain rinsed it away. It crushed Hadrian to know that it was Arista's rain washing him clean. Lying there, he saw the first sign of dawn lightening the morning sky and his heart sank further.

⁂

Emery could see the horizon as the faint light of dawn separated sky from building and tree. Rain still fell and the sound of crickets was replaced by early-morning stirrings. Merchants appeared on the street far earlier than usual, pushing carts and rolling wagons toward the West End Square. They neglectfully left them blocking the entrances from King's Street and Legends Avenue.

Other men came out of their homes and shops. Emery watched them appear out of the gray morning rain, coming one and two at a time, then gathering into larger groups as they wandered aimlessly around the square, drifting slowly, almost hesitantly, toward the armory. They wore heavy clothes and carried hoes, pitchforks, shovels, and axes. Most had knives tucked into their belts.

A pair of city guards working the end of the night shift—dressed only in light summer uniforms—had just finished their last patrol circuit. They stopped and looked around at the growing crowd with curious expressions. "Say there, what's going on here?"

"I dunno," a man said, and then moved away.

"Listen, what are you all doing here?" the other guard asked, but no one answered.

Barefoot and dressed in a white oversized shirt and a pair of britches that left his shins bare, Emery strode forward, feeling the clap of the sword at his side. "We're here to avenge the murder of our lord and sovereign, King Urith of Rhenydd!"

"It's him. It's Emery Dorn," the guard shouted. "Grab the bastard!"

The guards rushed forward, but they were too late to realize their peril as the groups closed around them, sweeping together like a flock of birds.

The soldiers hastily drew their swords and swung them. "Back! Get back! All of you! Back or we'll have the lot of you arrested!"

Hatred filled the faces of the crowd and excitement crept into their eyes. They jabbed at the soldiers with pitchforks and hoes. The guards knocked them away with swords.

For several minutes the crowd taunted with feints and

threats, and then Emery drew his blade. Mrs. Dunlap had found the sword for him. It had once belonged to her husband. In all his years of service, Paul Dunlap, carriage driver for King Urith, had never had occasion to draw it. The steel scraped as Emery pulled the blade from the metal sheath. With a grim expression and a set jaw, he pushed his way through the circle and faced the guards.

They were sweating. He could see the wetness on the upper lip of the closest man. The guard lunged, thrusting. Emery stepped to the side and hit the soldier's blade with his own, hearing the solid *clank* and feeling the impact in his hand. He took a step forward and swung. It felt good. It felt perfect, just the right move. The tip of his sword hit something soft and Emery watched as he sliced the man, cutting him across the chest. The soldier screamed, dropping his sword. He fell to his knees, his eyes wide in shock, clutching himself as blood soaked his clothes. The other guard tried to run, but the crowd held him back. Emery pushed past the wounded man and, with one quick thrust, stabbed the remaining guard through the kidney. Several cheered and began beating the wounded men, hacking them with axes and shovels.

"Enough," Emery shouted. "Follow me!"

The guards' weapons were taken and the crowd chased Emery to the flagstone building with the iron gate. By the time they arrived, Carat was already picking the lock. They killed those on duty only to discover most of the rest were still in their beds. A few had gotten to their feet before the mob arrived. They stabbed the first confused man through the ribs with a pitchfork, which he took with him when he fell. Emery stabbed another and an axe took a third's shoulder partway off, lodging there so that the owner had to kick his victim to pull the axe free. Swords and shields lined the walls and lay in pine boxes. Steel helms and chain hauberks sat on shelves.

The mob grabbed these as they passed, discarding their

tools of trade for tools of war. Only ten men guarded the armory and all died quickly, most beaten to death in their beds. The men cheered when they realized they had taken the armory without a single loss of life from their side. They laughed, howled, and jumped on tables, breaking plates and cups and whatever else they could find as they gleefully tested out their new weapons.

All around him, Emery could see the wild looks in the eyes of the men and realized he must wear a similar expression. His heart was pounding, his lungs pumping air. He felt no pain at all from his back now. He felt powerful, elated, and a little nauseous all at the same time.

"Emery! Emery!" He turned to see Arista pushing through the men. "You're too slow," she screamed at him. "The garrison is coming. Get them armed and formed up in the square."

As if pulled from a dream, Emery realized his folly. "Everyone out!" he shouted. "Everyone out—now! Form up on the square!"

Arista had already begun organizing those men who remained outside into two lines with their backs to the armory and their faces to the square.

"We need to get weapons!" Perin shouted at the princess.

"Stay in line!" she barked. "We'll have them brought out. You have to maintain the lines to stop the garrison from charging."

The men who stood in line holding only farm tools looked at her, terrified, as across the square, the first of the soldiers struggled to push away the wagons and carts that had been rutted in the mud. Before long, the men Emery had shooed out began taking their place in front of the line.

"Form up!" Emery shouted. "Two straight lines."

Arista ran back into the armory and began grabbing

swords and dragging them out. She spotted Carat stealing coins from a dead man's purse and shoved him against a wall. "Help me carry swords and shields out!"

"But I'm not allowed to," he said.

"You're not allowed to fight, but you can carry some swords, damn it. Just like you unlocked the door. Now do it!"

Carat seemed like he would say something and then gave in. He started pulling shields down from the walls. Dr. Gerand entered carrying bandages but discarded them quickly to help deliver weapons. On her way out, Arista saw a woman running in, her dress soaked from the rain, her long blonde hair pasted to her face so that she could barely see. The blonde stopped abruptly at Arista's approach.

"Let me help," she said to Arista. "You get more while I pass these out."

Arista nodded and handed over the weapons, then ran back inside.

Carat handed her the stack of shields he was carrying and she ran them down to the young woman, who in turn took them to the waiting line. When Arista came out again, she found that a line of older men and some women had formed up, and they were passing the weapons like a bucket brigade, with the young blonde adding more people to the line.

"More swords!" Arista shouted. "Helms and mail last."

Carat assembled weapons into manageable piles for the others to grab.

"No more swords!" The call soon came. "Send shields!"

The bell in Central Square began to ring, its tone sounding different that morning than on any other, perhaps due to the heavy rain or the pounding of blood in Arista's ears. Most men on the line held only a sword. Arista could see fear in every face.

She could hear Emery's voice drifting above the rain with each delivery. "Steady! Dress those lines. Tighten that formation." He barked the orders like a veteran commander. "No more than a fist's distance between your shoulders. Those with spears or pikes to the rear line. Those with shields to the front. Wait! Halt!" he shouted. "Forget that. Back in line. Just pass the spears back and hand the shields forward."

With the next delivery of weapons, Arista paused at the armory doorway and looked out across the square. The garrison had cleared the wagons from King's Street and a few soldiers entered. They looked briefly at the lines of townsfolk, then went to work to clear the other carts.

Emery stood in front of the troops. Everyone had a sword or a spear but most did not know how to wield them properly. Nearly every man in the front row had a wooden shield, but most simply held them in their hands. At least one man had his shield upside down.

"Adam the wheeler, front and center!" Emery shouted, and the middle-aged wheelwright stepped forward. "Take the left side and see that the men know how to wear their shields and hold their swords." Emery likewise called Renkin Pool and Forrest into action and set them to dressing the line.

"Keep your shield high," Adam was shouting. "Don't swing your sword—thrust it instead. That way you can maintain closer formations. Keep the line tight. The man next to you is a better shield than that flimsy bit of wood in your hands! Stay shoulder to shoulder!"

"Don't let them turn the flank!" Renkin was shouting on the other side of the line. "Those on the ends, turn and hold your shields to defend from a side assault. Everyone must move and work together!"

Helms and hauberks were coming out now and there were a few in the front row hastily pulling chain mail netting over their heads.

A surprising number of imperial soldiers had already

formed themselves into rows on the far side of the square. Each one was impeccably dressed in hauberk, helm, sword, and shield. They stood still, straight, and confident. Looking at Emery's men, Arista saw nervous movements and fear-filled eyes.

Four knights rode into the square. Two bore the imperial pennant at the ends of tall lances. On the foremost horse rode Sheriff Vigan. Beside him came Trenchon, the city's bailiff, splashing through the puddles. Hooked to Vigan's belt, in addition to his sword, was the whip. Vigan's face was stern and unimpressed by the hastily assembled, slightly skewed lines of peasants. He rode up and down, trotting menacingly, his mount throwing up clods of mud into the air.

"I know why you're here," Vigan shouted at them. "You're here because of one man." He pointed at Emery. "He has incited you to perform criminal acts. Normally, I would have each one of you executed for treason, but I can see it's the traitor Emery Dorn, and not you, who has caused this. You are victims of his poison, so I'll be lenient. Put down those stolen weapons, return to your homes, and I'll only hang the leaders that led you astray. Continue this and you'll be slaughtered to the last man."

"Steady, men," Emery shouted. "He's just trying to frighten you. He's offering you a deal because he's scared—scared of us because we stand before him, united and strong. He's scared because we do not cower before his threats. He's scared because, for the first time, he does not see sheep, he does not see slaves, he does not see victims to beat, but men. Men! Tall and proud. Men who are still loyal to their king!"

Vigan raised his hand briefly, then lowered it. There was a harsh crack followed immediately by a muffled *thwack!* Emery staggered backward. Blood sprayed those near him. A crossbow bolt was lodged in his chest. An instant later, the fiery red-haired boy fell into the mud.

The line wavered at the sight.

"No!" Arista screamed, and shoved through the men and collapsed in the mud beside Emery. Frantically she struggled to turn him over, to pull his face out of the muck. She wiped the mud away while blood vomited from his mouth. His eyes rolled wildly. He wheezed in short, halting gasps.

Everyone was silent. The whole world stopped.

Arista held Emery in her arms. She could see a pleading in his eyes as they found hers. She could feel his breath shortening with each wretched gasp. With each jerk of his body, she felt her heart breaking.

This can't be happening!

She looked into his eyes. She wanted to say something—to give him a part of her to take with him—but all she could do was hold on. As she squeezed him tightly, he stopped struggling. He stopped moving. He stopped breathing.

Arista cried aloud, certain her body would break.

Above her the sheriff's horse snorted and stomped. Behind her the men of the rebellion wavered. She heard them dropping weapons, discarding shields.

Arista took in a shuddering breath of her own and turned her face toward the sky. She raised one leg, then the other, pushing herself—willing herself—to her feet. As her shaking body rose from the mud, she drew Emery's sword in a tight fist, lifted the blade above her head, and glared at the sheriff.

She cried in a loud voice, "Don't—you—dare—break! *Hold the line!*"

As Hadrian lay on his back, chained and stretched out in the mud, a shadow fell across his face and the rain stopped hitting him. He opened his eyes and, squinting, saw a man outlined in the morning light.

"What in Maribor's name are you doing here?"

The voice was familiar and Hadrian struggled to see the face lost in the folds of a hooded robe. All around him, rain continued to pour, splashing the mud puddles and grass, forcing him to blink.

The figure standing over him shouted, "Sergeant! Explain what goes on here. Why is this man chained?"

Hadrian could hear boots slogging through the mud. "It's Commander Parker's orders, sir." There was nervousness in his voice.

"I see. Tell me, Sergeant, do you enjoy being human?"

"What's that, sir?"

"I asked if you liked the human form. For example, do you find it useful to have two hands and two legs?"

"I, ah—well, I don't think I quite understand your meaning."

"No, you don't, but you will if this man isn't freed immediately."

"But, Lord Esrahaddon, I can't. Commander Parker—"

"Leave Parker to me. Get those chains off him, get him out of that mud, and escort him to the house immediately, or I swear you'll be walking on all fours within the hour, and for the rest of your life."

"Wizards!" the sergeant grumbled after Esrahaddon had left him. He pulled a key from his belt and struggled to open the mud-caked locks. "Get up," he ordered.

The sergeant led Hadrian back to the house. The chains were gone but his wrists were still bound by two iron manacles. Hadrian was cold and hungry and felt nearly drowned, but only one thought filled his mind as he watched the sun rising in the east.

Is there still time?

"And what about the wagons on the South Road?" Esrahaddon growled as Hadrian entered. The wizard stood in his familiar robe, which was, at that moment, gray and perfectly dry despite the heavy rain. Esrahaddon looked the same as he had in Dahlgren except for the length of his beard, which now reached to his chest, giving him a more wizardly appearance.

Parker was seated behind his table, a napkin tucked into his collar, another plate of ham and eggs before him.

Does he have the same meal brought to him each morning?

"It's the mud. They can't be moved, and I don't appreciate—" He paused when he spotted Hadrian. "What's going on? I ordered this man staked. Why are you bringing him here?"

"I ordered it," Esrahaddon told him. "Sergeant, remove those restraints and fetch his weapons."

"You?" Parker replied, stunned. "You are here only as an advisor. You forget I'm in command."

"Of what?" the wizard asked. "A thousand lazy vagabonds? This was an army when I left. I come back and it's a rabble."

"It's the rain. It doesn't stop."

"It's not supposed to stop," Hadrian burst out in frustration. "I tried to tell you. We need to attack Dermont now. Arista is launching a rebellion this morning in Ratibor. She'll seal the city so he can't retreat. We have to engage and defeat Dermont before he's reinforced by Sir Breckton and the Northern Imperial Army. They will be here any day now. If we don't attack, Dermont will enter the city and crush the rebellion."

"What nonsense." Parker pointed an accusing finger. "This man entered the camp claiming to be a marshal-at-arms who was taking command of *my* troops."

"He is, and he will," the wizard told him.

"He will not! He and the Princess of Melengar are both

responsible for the treachery that probably cost Degan his life. And we have had no news of any Northern—"

"Degan is alive, you idiot. Neither Hadrian nor Arista had anything to do with his abduction. Do as this man instructs or everyone will likely be dead or captured by the imperium in two days. You, of course"—the wizard glared at Parker—"will die much sooner."

Parker's eyes widened.

"I don't even know who he is!" Parker exclaimed. "I can't turn over command to a stranger I know nothing about. How do I know he's capable? What are his qualifications?"

"Hadrian knows more about combat than any living man."

"And am I to take your word? The word of a—a—sorcerer?"

"It was on my word that this army was formed—my direction that produced its victories."

"But you've been gone. Things have changed. Degan left me in charge and I don't think I can—"

Esrahaddon stepped toward the commander. As he did, his robe began to glow. A bloodred radiance filled the interior of the house, making Parker's face look like a plump beet.

"All right! All right!" Parker shouted abruptly to the sergeant, "Do as he says. What do I care!"

The sergeant unlocked Hadrian's hands, then exited.

"Now, Parker, make yourself useful for once," Esrahaddon said. "Go round up the regiment captains. Tell them that they will now be taking their orders from Marshal Blackwater, and have them gather here as soon as possible."

"Marshal *Lord* Blackwater," Hadrian said with a smile.

Esrahaddon rolled his eyes. "Do it now."

"But—"

"Go!"

Parker grabbed up his cloak and his sword and pulled his boots from under the table. He retreated out the door still holding them.

"Is he going to be a problem?" Hadrian asked, watching the ex-commander hop into the rain, grumbling.

"Parker? No. I just needed to remind him that he's terrified of me." Esrahaddon looked at Hadrian. "Marshal *Lord* Blackwater?"

"*Lord* Esrahaddon?" he replied, rubbing feeling back into his wrists.

The wizard smiled and nodded. "You still haven't said what you're doing here."

"A job—for Arista Essendon. She hired us to help her contact the Nationalists."

"And now she has you seizing control of my army."

"Your army? I thought this was Gaunt's."

"So did he. And the moment I'm away, Degan gets himself captured after putting that thing in charge. Royce with you?"

"Was—Arista sent him to contact Alric about invading Warric."

While eating Parker's ham and eggs, Hadrian provided Esrahaddon with further details about the rebellion and his plans for attacking Dermont. Just as he had finished the meal, there was a knock on the door. Five officers and the harried-looking sergeant who carried Hadrian's swords entered.

Esrahaddon addressed them. "As Parker no doubt informed you, this is Marshal Lord Blackwater, your new commander. Do anything he says, as if he were Gaunt himself. I think you'll find him a very worthy replacement for your general."

They nodded and stood at attention.

Hadrian got up, walked around the table, and announced, "We will attack the imperial position immediately."

"Now?" one said, astonished.

"I wish there was more time, but I've been tied up elsewhere. We'll launch our attack directly across that muddy field, where the Imps' three hundred heavy cavalry can't ride, and where their longbow archers can't see in this rain. Our lightly armored infantry must move quickly to overwhelm them. We'll close at a run and butcher them man to man."

"But they'll—" a tall gruff-looking soldier with a partial beard and mismatched armor started, then stopped himself.

"They'll what?" Hadrian asked.

"I was just thinking. The moment they see us advance, won't they retreat within the city walls?"

"What's your name?" Hadrian asked.

The man looked worried but held his ground. "Renquist, sir."

"Well, Renquist, you're absolutely right. That's exactly what they will try to do. Only they won't be able to get in. By then our allied forces will own the city."

"Allied forces?"

"I don't have time to explain. Don't strike camp, and don't use horns or drums to assemble. With luck, there's a good chance we can catch them by surprise. By now, they probably think we'll never attack. Renquist, how long do you estimate to have the men assembled and ready to march?"

"Two hours," he replied with more confidence.

"Have them ready in one. Each of you form up your men on the east slope, out of their sight. Three regiments of infantry in duel lines, senior commanders located at the center, left, and right flanks in that order. And I want light cavalry to swing to the south and await the call of the trumpet to sweep their flank. I want one contingent of cavalry—the smallest—that I'll command and hold in reserve to the north, near the city. At the waving of the blue pennant, begin crossing the field as quietly as possible. When you see the green flag, relay the signal and charge. We move in one hour. Dismissed!"

The captains saluted and ran back out into the rain. The sergeant handed over Hadrian's weapons and started to slip out quietly.

"Wait a moment." Hadrian halted him. "What's your name?"

The sergeant spun. "I was just following orders when I chained you up. I didn't know—"

"You've just been promoted to adjutant general," Hadrian told him. "What's your name?"

The ex-sergeant blinked. "Bently…sir."

"Bently, from now on you stick next to me and see that my orders are carried out, understand? Now, I'll need fast riders to work as messengers—three should do—and signal flags, a blue and a green one, as big as possible. Mount them on tall sticks and make certain all the captains have identical ones. Oh, and I need a horse!"

"Make that two," the wizard said.

"Make that three," Hadrian added. "You'll need one too, Bently."

The soldier opened his mouth, closed it, then nodded and stepped out into the rain.

"An hour," Hadrian muttered as he strapped on his weapons.

"You don't think Arista can hold out that long?"

"I was supposed to take control of this army yesterday. If only I had more time…I could have…I just hope it's not too late."

"If anyone can save Ratibor, it's you," the wizard told him.

"I know all about being the guardian to the heir," Hadrian replied.

"I had a feeling Royce would tell you."

Hadrian picked up the large spadone sword and looped the baldric over his head. He reached up and drew it out, testing the position of the sheath.

"I remember that weapon." The wizard pointed to the blade. "That's Jerish's sword." He frowned, then added, "What have you done to it?"

"What do you mean?"

"Jerish loved that thing—had a special cloth he kept in his gauntlet that he used to polish it—something of an obsession, really. That blade was like a mirror."

"It's seen nine hundred years of use," Hadrian told him, and put it away.

"You look nothing like Jerish," Esrahaddon said, then paused when he saw the look on Hadrian's face. "What is it?"

"The heir is dead—you know that, don't you? Died right here in Ratibor forty years ago."

Esrahaddon smiled. "Still, you hold a sword the same way Jerish did. Must be in the training somehow. Amazing how much it defines both of you. I never really—"

"Did you hear me? The bloodline ended. Seret caught up to them. They killed the heir—his name was Naron, by the way—and they killed his wife and child. My father was the only survivor. I'm sorry."

"My teacher, old Yolric, used to insist the world has a way of righting itself. He was obsessed with the idea. I thought he was crazy, but after living for nine hundred years, you perceive things differently. You see patterns you never knew were there. The heir isn't dead, Hadrian, just hidden."

"I know you'd like to think that, but my father failed and the heir died. I talked to a member of the Theorem Eldership who was there. He saw it happen."

Esrahaddon shook his head. "I've seen the heir with my own eyes, and I recognize the blood of Nevrik. A thousand years cannot mask such a lineage from me. Still, just to be sure, I performed a test that cannot be faked. Oh yes, the heir is alive and well."

"Who is it, then? I'm the guardian, aren't I? Or I'm supposed to be. I should be protecting him."

"At the moment, anonymity is a far better protection than swords. I cannot tell you the heir's identity. If I did, you would rush off and be a beacon to those watching." The wizard sighed. "And trust me, I know a great deal about being watched. In Gutaria they wrote down every word I uttered. Even now, at this very moment, every word I say is being heard."

"You sound like Royce." Hadrian looked around. "We're alone, surrounded by an army of Nationalists. Do you think Saldur or Ethelred have spies pressing an ear against this farmhouse?"

"Saldur? Ethelred?" Esrahaddon chuckled. "I'm not concerned with the imperial regents. They're pawns in this game. Haven't you wondered how the Gilarabrywn escaped Avempartha? Do you think Saldur or Ethelred could manage such a trick? My adversary is much more dangerous, and I'm certain he spends a great deal of time listening to what I say, no matter where I am. You see, I do not have the benefit of that amulet you wear."

"Amulet?" Hadrian touched his chest, feeling the metal circle under his shirt. "Royce said it prevents wizards like you from finding the wearer."

The wizard nodded. "Preventing clairvoyant searches was the primary purpose, but they are far more powerful than that. The amulets protect the wearers from all effects of the Art and have a dash of good fortune added in. Flip a coin wearing that, and it will come up the way you need it to more often than not. You've been in many battles and I'm sure in plenty of dangerous situations with Royce. Have you not considered yourself lucky on more than one occasion? That little bit of jewelry is extremely powerful. The level of the Art that went into making it was beyond anything I'd ever seen."

"I thought you made it."

"I did, but I had help. I could never have built them on my own. Yolric showed me the weave. He was the greatest of us. I could barely understand his instructions and wasn't certain I had performed the spell properly, but it appears I was successful."

"Still, you're the only one left in the world who can really do magic, right? So there's no chance anyone is magically listening."

"What about this rain? It's not *supposed* to stop? It would seem I'm not the only one."

"You're afraid of Arista?"

"No, just making a point. I'm not the only wizard in the world and I've already been far too careless. In my haste, I took chances that maybe I should not have, drawing too much attention, playing into others' hands. With so little time left—only a matter of months—it would be foolhardy to risk more now. I fear the heir's identity has already been compromised, but there is a chance I'm wrong and I'll cling to that hope. I'm sorry, Hadrian. I can't tell you just yet, but trust me, I will."

"No offense, but you don't seem too trustworthy."

The wizard smiled. "Maybe you *are* Jerish's descendant after all. Very soon I'll need Riyria's help with an extremely challenging mission."

"Riyria doesn't exist anymore. I've retired."

The wizard nodded. "Nevertheless, I'll require both of you, and as it concerns the heir, I presume you'll make an exception."

"I don't even know where I'll be."

"Don't worry, I'll find you both when the time comes. But for now, we have the little problem of Lord Dermont's army to contend with."

There was a knock at the door. "Horses ready, sirs," the new adjutant general reported.

As they stepped out, Hadrian spotted Gill walking toward him with his purse. "Good morning, Gill," Hadrian said, taking his pouch back.

"Morning, sir," he said, looking sick but making an effort to smile. "It's all there, sir."

"I'm a bit busy at the moment, Gill, but I'm sure we'll have a chance to catch up later."

"Yes, sir."

Hadrian mounted a brown-and-white gelding that Bently held for him. He watched as Esrahaddon mounted a smaller black mare by hooking the stub of his wrist around the horn. Once in the saddle, the wizard wrapped the reins around his stubs.

"It's strange. I keep forgetting you don't have hands," Hadrian commented.

"I don't," the wizard replied coldly.

Overhead, heavy clouds swirled as boys ran about the camp spreading the order to form up. Horses trotted, kicking up clods of earth. Carts rolled, leaving deep ruts. Half-dressed men darted from tents, slipping in the slick mud. They carried swords over their shoulders, dragged shields, and struggled to fasten helms. Hadrian and Esrahaddon rode through the hive of soggy activity to the top of the ridge, where they could see the lay of the land for miles. The city to the north, with its wooden spires and drab walls, stood as a ghostly shadow. To the south lay the forest, and between them a vast plain stretched westward. What had once been farmland was now a muddy soup. The field was shaped like a basin, and at its lowest point a shallow pond had formed. It reflected the light of the dreary gray sky like a steel mirror. On the far side, the hazy encampment of the imperial army was just visible through a thick curtain of rain. Hadrian stared but could make out only faint, shadowy shapes. Nothing indicated they knew what was about to happen. Below them on the east side of the slope, hidden from imperial view, the Nationalist army assembled into ranks.

"What is it?" Esrahaddon asked.

Hadrian realized he was grimacing. "They aren't very good soldiers," he replied, watching the men wander about, creating misshapen lines. They stood listless, shoulders slumped, heads down.

Esrahaddon shrugged. "There are a few good ones. We pulled in some mercenaries and a handful of deserters from the Imperialists. That Renquist you were so taken with, he was a sergeant in the imperial forces. Joined us because he heard nobility didn't matter in the Nationalist army. We got a few of those, but mostly they're farmers, merchants, or men who lost their homes or families."

Hadrian glanced across the field. "Lord Dermont has trained foot soldiers, archers, and knights—men who devoted their whole lives to warfare and trained since an early age."

"I wouldn't worry about that."

"Of course *you* wouldn't. I'm the one who has to lead this ugly rabble. I'm the one who must go down there and face those lances and arrows."

"I'm going with you," he said. "That's why you don't need to worry about it."

Bently and three other young men carrying colored flags rode up beside them. "Captains report ready, sir."

"Let's go," Hadrian told them, and trotted down to take

his place with a small contingent of cavalry. The men on horseback appeared even less capable than those on foot. They had no armor and wore torn, rain-soaked clothes. Except for the spears they held across their laps, they looked like vagabonds or escaped prisoners.

"Raise your lances!" he shouted. "Stay tight, keep your place, wheel together, and follow me." He turned to Bently. "Wave the blue flag."

Bently swung the blue flag back and forth until the signal was mimicked across the field, and then the army began moving forward at a slow walk. Armies never moved at a pace that suited Hadrian. When attacking with him, they crept with agonizing slowness. But when he was defending, they seemed to race at an unnatural speed. He patted the neck of his horse, which was larger and more spirited than old Millie. Hadrian liked to know his horse better before a battle. They needed to work as a team in combat, but he did not even know this one's name.

With the wizard riding at his right side, and Bently on his left, Hadrian crested the hill and began the long descent into the wet field. He wheeled his cavalry to the right, sweeping toward the city, riding the rim of the basin and avoiding the middle of the muck, which he left to the infantry. He would stay to the higher ground and watch the army's northern flank. This would also place him near the city gate, able to intercept any imperial retreat. After his company made the turn, he watched as the larger force of light-mounted lancers broke and began to circle left, heading to guard the southern flank. The swishing tails of their horses soon disappeared into the rain.

The ranks of the infantry came next. They crested the hill, jostling each other, some still struggling to get their helms on and shields readied. The lines were skewed, broken and wavy, and when they hit the mud, whatever mild resemblance they had to a formation was lost. They staggered and slipped forward as a mob. They were at least quiet. He wondered if it might be because most of them were half-asleep.

Hadrian felt his stomach twist.

This will not go well. If only I had more time to drill the men properly, then they would at least look like soldiers.

Success or failure in battle often hinged on impressions, decided in the minds of men before the first clash. Like bullies casting insults in a tavern, it was a game of intimidation—a game the Nationalists did not know how to play.

How did they ever win a battle? How did they take Vernes and Kilnar?

Unable to see the Imperialists' ranks clearly, he imagined them lined up in neat straight rows, waiting, letting his troops exhaust themselves in the mud. He expected a wall of glistening shields peaked with shining helms locked shoulder to shoulder, matching spears foresting above. He anticipated hundreds of archers already notching shafts to string. Lord Dermont would hold back the knights. Any fool could see the futility of ordering a charge into the muck. Clad in heavy metal armor, their pennants fluttering from their lances, the knights probably waited in the trees or perhaps around the wall of the city. They would remain hidden until just the right moment. That is what Hadrian would have done. When the Nationalists tried to flank, only Hadrian and his little group would stand in the way. He would call the charge and hope those behind him followed.

They were more than halfway across the field when he was finally able to see the imperial encampment. White tents stood in perfect rows, horses were corralled, and no one was visible.

"Where are they?"

"It's still very early," the wizard said, "and in a heavy rain no one likes to get up. It's so much easier to stay in bed."

"But where are the sentries?"

Hadrian watched in amazement as the mangled line of infantry cleared the muddy ground and closed in on the imperial camp, their lines straightening out a bit. He saw the heads of his captains. There was still no sign of the enemy.

"Have you ever noticed," Esrahaddon said, "how rain has a musical quality about it sometimes? The way it drums on a roof? It's always easier to sleep on a rainy night. There's something magical about running water that is very soothing, very relaxing."

"What did you do?"

The wizard smiled. "A weak, thin enchantment. Without hands it's very hard to do substantive magic anymore, but—"

They heard a shout. A tent flap fluttered, then another. More shouts cascaded, and then a bell rang.

"There, see?" Esrahaddon sighed. "I told you. It doesn't take much to break it."

"But we have them," Hadrian said, stunned. "We caught them sleeping! Bently, the green flag. Signal the charge. Signal the charge!"

Sheriff Vigan scowled at Arista. Behind her, men picked up weapons and shuffled back into position.

"I told you to lay down your arms and leave," the sheriff shouted. "Not more than a few of you will be punished in the stocks, and only your leaders will be executed. The first has already fallen. Will you stand behind a woman? Will you throw away your lives for her sake?"

No one moved. The only sounds were those of the rain and the sheriff's horse and the jangling of his bridle.

"Very well," he said. "I'll execute the leading agitators one at a time if that's what it takes." He glanced over his shoulder and ominously raised his hand again.

The princess did not move.

She stood still and tall with Emery's sword above her head, his blood on her dress, and the wind and rain lashing her face. She glared defiantly at the sheriff.

Thwack!

The sound of a crossbow.

Phhump!

A muffled impact.

Arista felt blood spray her face, but there was no pain. Sheriff Vigan fell sideways into the mud. Polish stood in front of the blacksmith's shop, an empty crossbow in his hands.

Renkin Pool grabbed Arista by the shoulder and jerked her backward. Off balance, she fell. He stood over her, his shield raised. Another telltale *thwack* and Pool's shield burst into splinters. The bolt continued into his chest. The explosion of blood and wood rained on her.

Another crossbow fired, this one handled by Adam. Trenchon screamed as the arrow passed through his thigh and continued into his horse, which collapsed, crushing Trenchon's leg beneath it. Another bow fired, then another, and Arista could see that during the pause, the blonde woman had hauled crossbows out of the armory and passed them throughout the ranks.

The garrison captain assumed command of the Imperialists. He gave a shout and the remainder of their bowmen fired across the square. Men in the line fell.

"Fire!" Adam shouted, and rebel bows gave answer. A handful of imperial soldiers dropped in the mud.

"Tighten the line!" Adam shouted. "Fill in the gaps where people fall!"

They heard a shout from across the field, then a roar as the garrison drew their swords and rushed forward. Arista felt the vibration of charging men. They screamed like beasts, their faces wild. They struck the line in the center. There was no prepared weak point—Emery and Pool were dead, the tactic lost.

She heard cries, screams, the clanging of metal against metal, and the dull thumps of swords against wooden shields. Soldiers pushed forward and the line broke in two. Perin was supposed to lead the left flank in a folding maneuver. He lay in the mud, blood running down his face. His branch of the line disconnected from the rest and quickly routed. The main line also failed, disintegrated, and disappeared. Men fought in a swirling turmoil of swords, broken shields, blood, and body parts.

Arista remained where she had collapsed. She felt a tugging on her arm and looked up to see the blonde woman again. "Get up! You'll be killed!" She had a hold on her wrist and dragged Arista to her feet. All around them men screamed, shouted, and grunted. Water splashed, mud flew, and blood sprayed. The hand squeezing her wrist hauled her backward. She thought of Emery lying in the mud and tried to pull away.

"No!" the blonde snapped, jerking her once more. "Are you crazy?" The woman dragged her to the armory entrance, but once she reached the door, Arista refused to go in any farther and remained at the opening, watching the battle.

The skill and experience of the garrison guards overwhelmed the citizens. They cut through the people of Ratibor and pushed them against the walls of the buildings. Every puddle was dark with blood, every shirt and face stained red. Mud and manure mixed and churned with severed limbs and blood. Everywhere she looked lay bodies. Dead men with open, lifeless eyes and those writhing in pain lay scattered across the square.

"We're going to lose," Arista said. "I did this."

The candlemaker, a tall thin man with curly hair, dropped his weapons and tried to run. Arista watched as six inches of sword came out of his stomach. She did not even know his name. A young bricklayer called Walter had his head crushed. Another man she had not met lost his arm.

Arista still held Emery's sword in one hand and clutched the doorframe with the other as the world spun around her. She felt sick and wanted to vomit. She could not move or turn away from the carnage. They would all die, and it was her fault. "I killed us all."

"Maybe not." The blonde caught Arista's attention and pointed at the far end of the square. "Look there!"

Arista saw a rush of movement coming up King's Street and heard the pounding of hooves. They came out of the haze of falling rain. Riding three and four abreast, horsemen charged into the square, shouting. One carried the pennant of the Nationalists, but the foremost brandished a huge sword, and she recognized him instantly.

Throwing up a spray of mud, Hadrian crossed the square. As he closed on the battle, he led the charge into the thickest of the soldiers. The garrison heard the cry and turned to see the band of horsemen rushing at them. Out front, Hadrian came at them like a demon, whirling his long blade, cleaving a swath through their ranks, cutting them down. The garrison broke and routed before the onslaught. When they found nowhere to retreat to, they threw down their weapons and pled for mercy.

Spotting Arista, Hadrian leapt to the ground and ran to her. Arista found it hard to breathe, and the last of her strength gave out. She fell to her knees, shaking. Hadrian reached down, surrounding her in his arms, and pulled her up.

"The city is yours, Your Highness," he said.

She dropped Emery's sword, threw her arms around his neck, and cried.

Chapter 17

Degan Gaunt

The rain stopped. The sun, so long delayed, returned full face to a bright blue sky. The day quickly grew hot as Hadrian made his way around the square through the many mud-covered bodies, searching for anyone who was still alive. Everywhere seemed to be the muffled wails and weeping of wives, mothers, fathers, and sons. Families pulled their loved ones from the bloody mire and carried them home to wash them for a proper burial. Hadrian stiffened when he spotted Dr. Gerand gently closing the lifeless eyes of Carat. Not far from him, Adam sat slumped against the armory. He looked as if he had merely walked over and sat down for a moment to rest.

"Over here!"

He spotted a woman with long blonde hair motioning to him. Hadrian quickly crossed to where she squatted over the body of an imperial soldier.

"He's still alive," she said. "Help me get him out of the mud. I can't believe no one saw him."

"Oh, I think they saw him," Hadrian replied as he gripped the soldier under his back and knees and lifted him.

He carried the man to the silversmith's porch and laid him

down gently as the woman ran to the well for a bucket of clean water.

Hadrian shed his own bloodstained shirt. "Here," he said, offering the linen to the woman.

"Thank you," she replied. She took the shirt and began rinsing it in the bucket. "Are you certain you don't mind me using this to help an imperial guard?"

"My father taught me that a man is only your enemy until he falls."

She nodded. "Your father sounds like a wise man," she said, and wrung the excess water from the shirt, then began to clean the soldier's face and chest, looking for the wound.

"He was. My name is Hadrian, by the way."

"Miranda," she replied. "Pleased to meet you. Thank you for saving our lives. I assume the Nationalists defeated Lord Dermont?"

Hadrian nodded. "It wasn't much of a battle. We caught them sleeping."

Pulling up the soldier's hauberk and tearing back his tunic, she wiped his skin and found a puncture streaming blood.

"I hope you aren't terribly attached to this shirt," she told Hadrian as she tore it in two. She used half as a pad, and the other half to tie it tight about the man's waist. "Let's hope that will stop the bleeding. A few stitches would help, but I doubt a needle could be spared for him right now."

Hadrian looked the man over. "I think he'll live, thanks to you."

This brought a shallow smile to her lips. She dipped her blood-covered hands in the bucket and splashed water on her face. Looking out across the square, she muttered, "So many dead."

Hadrian nodded.

Her eyes landed on Carat, a hand went to her mouth, and

her eyes started to tear. "He was such a help to us," she said. "Someone said he was a thief, but he proved himself a hero today. Who would have thought that thieves would stick out their necks? I saw their leader, Polish, shoot the sheriff."

Hadrian smiled. "If you ask him, he'll tell you you're mistaken."

"Thieves with hearts, who'd have thought?" she said.

"I'm not so sure I would go that far."

"No? Then where are the vultures?"

Hadrian looked up at the sky, then, realizing his own stupidity, shook his head. "You mean the looters?" He looked around. "You're right. I didn't even notice until now."

She nodded. Hadrian's medallion reflected the sunlight, catching her eye. Miranda pointed. "That necklace, where did you get it?"

"My father."

"Your father? Really? My older brother has one just like it."

Hadrian's heart raced. "Your brother has a necklace like this?"

She nodded.

Hadrian looked around the square, suddenly concerned. "Is he..."

She thought a moment. "I don't think so," she said. "At least, my heart tells me he's still alive."

Hadrian tried to control his racing thoughts. "How old is your brother?"

"I think he'd be about forty now, I guess."

"You guess?"

She nodded. "We never celebrated his birthday, which was always kind of strange. You see, my mother adopted him. She was the midwife at his birth and..." She hesitated. "Things didn't go well. Anyway, my mother kept an amulet just like yours and gave it to my brother as his inheritance the day he left home."

"What do you mean things didn't go well with the birth?" Hadrian asked.

"The mother died—that sort of thing happens, you know. Mothers die all the time in childbirth. It's not at all uncommon. It just happens. We should probably look for other wounded—"

"You're lying," Hadrian shot back.

She started to stand but Hadrian grabbed her arm. "This is very important. I must know everything you can tell me about the night your brother was born."

She hesitated but Hadrian held her tight.

"It wasn't her fault. There was nothing she could do. They were all dead. She was just scared. Who wouldn't be!"

"It's okay. I'm not accusing your mother of anything. I just need to know what happened." He held up his amulet. "This necklace belonged to my father. He was there that night."

"Your father, but no one..." He saw realization in her eyes. "The swordsman covered in blood?"

"Yes." Hadrian nodded. "Does your mother still live in the city? Can I speak to her?"

"My mother died several years ago."

"Do you know what happened? I have to know. It's very important."

She looked around, and when she was sure no one could overhear, she said, "A priest came to my mother one night looking for a midwife and took her to a boardinghouse, where a woman was giving birth. While my mother worked to deliver the baby, a fight started on the street. My mother had just delivered the first child—"

"First child?"

Miranda nodded. "She could see another was on the way, but men in black broke into the room. My mother hid in a wardrobe. The husband fought, but they killed his wife, child, and another man who came to help. The father took off his necklace—like the one you wear—and put it around the neck of the dead baby. There was still fighting on the street out front and the husband ran out of the room.

"My mother was terrified. She said there was blood everywhere, and the poor woman and her baby... But she summoned the courage to slip out of the wardrobe. She remembered the second child and knew it would die if she didn't do something. She picked up a knife and delivered it.

"From the window she saw the husband die, and the street was filled with a dozen bodies. A swordsman covered in blood was killing everyone. She didn't know what was happening. She was terrified and certain he would kill her too. With the second child in her arms, she took the necklace from the dead baby and fled. She pretended the baby was hers and never told anyone what really happened until the night she died—when she told me."

"Why did she take the necklace?"

"She said it was because the father meant it for his child."

"But you don't believe that?"

She shrugged. "Look at it." She pointed at his amulet. "It's made of silver. My mother was a very poor woman. But it's not like she sold it. In the end, she did give it to him."

"What's your brother's name?"

She looked puzzled. "I thought you knew. I mean, you were with the Nationalists, weren't you?"

"How would being with—"

"My brother is the leader of the Nationalist army."

"Oh." Hadrian's hopes sank. "Your brother is Commander Parker?"

"No, no, my name is Miranda Gaunt. My brother is Degan."

❧

She had not fought or taken blows, but Arista felt battered and beaten. She sat in what until that morning had been the viceroy's office. A huge, gaudy chamber, it contained all that had survived the burning of the old royal palace. Night had fallen, heralding a close to the longest day she could recall. Memories of that morning were already distant, from another year, another life.

Outside, the flicker of bonfires bloomed in the square, where they had sentenced Emery to die. Die he did, but his dream survived, his promise fulfilled. She could hear the citizens of Ratibor singing and saw their shadows dance. They toasted Emery with mugs of beer and celebrated his victory with lambs on spits. A decidedly different gathering than the one the sheriff had planned.

Inside, Arista sat with a dozen men with concerned faces.

"We insist you take the crown of Rhenydd," Dr. Gerand repeated, his voice carrying over the others.

"I agree," Perin said. Since the battle, the big grocer, who had been designated to lead the failed left flank and was wounded in the fight, had become a figure of legend. He found himself thrust into the ad hoc city council, hastily composed of the city's most revered surviving citizens.

Several other heads nodded. She did not know them but guessed they owned large farms or businesses—commoners all. None of the former nobility remained after the imperial takeover and all the Imperialists were either dead or imprisoned. Viceroy Androus, evicted from his office, was relocated to a prison cell along with the city guards who had surrendered. A handful of other city officials and Laven, the man who had argued with Emery in the Gnome, waited to stand trial for crimes against the citizenry.

After the battle had ended, Arista had helped organize the treatment of the wounded. People kept returning to her, asking what to do next. She directed them to bury the bodies of those without families outside the city. There was a brief ceremony presided over by Monsignor Bartholomew.

The wounded and dying overwhelmed the armory, and makeshift hospitals were created in the Dunlaps' barn and rooms commandeered at the Gnome. People also volunteered their private homes, particularly those with beds recently made empty. With the work of cleaning up the dead and wounded under way, the question of what to do with the viceroy and the other imperial supporters arose, along with a dozen other inquiries. Arista suggested they form a council to decide what should be done. They did, and their first official act was to summon her to the viceroy's old office.

The decision was unanimous. The council had voted to appoint Arista ruling queen of the kingdom of Rhenydd.

"There is no one else here of noble blood," Perin said. He wore a bloodstained bandage around his head. "No one else who even knows how to govern."

"But Emery envisioned a republic," Arista told them. "A self-determining government, like they have in Delgos. This was his dream—the reason he fought, the reason he died."

"But we don't know how to do that," Dr. Gerand said. "We need experience and you have it."

"He's right." Perin spoke up again. "Perhaps in a few months we could hold elections, but Sir Breckton and his army are still on their way. We need action. We need the kind of leadership that won us this city, or come tomorrow, we'll lose it again."

Arista sighed and looked over at Hadrian, who sat near the window. As commander of the Nationalist army, he had also received an invitation.

"What do you think?" she asked.

"I'm no politician."

"I'm not asking you to be. I just want to know what you think."

"Royce once told me two people can argue over the same point and both can be right. I thought he was nutty, but I'm not so sure anymore, because I think you're both right. The moment you become queen, you'll destroy any chance of this becoming the kind of free republic Emery spoke of, but if someone doesn't take charge—and fast—that hope will die anyway. And they're right. If I were going to choose anyone to rule, it would be you. As an outsider, you have no bias, no chance of favoritism—you'll be fair. And everyone already loves you."

"They don't love me. They don't even know me."

"They think they do, and they trust you. You can give directions and people will listen. And right now, that's what is needed."

"I can't be queen. Emery wanted a republic, and a republic he will have. You can appoint me temporary mayor of Ratibor and steward of the kingdom. I'll administer only until a proper government can be established, at which time I'll resign and return to Melengar." She nodded more to herself than to any of them. "Yes, that way I'll be in a position to ensure it gets done."

The men in the room muttered in agreement. After addressing a few of the more pressing matters, the council filed out of City Hall into the square, leaving Arista and Hadrian alone. Outside, the constant noise of the crowd grew quiet and then exploded with cheers.

"You're very popular, Your Highness," Hadrian told her.

"Too popular. They want to commission a statue of me."

"I heard that. They want to put it in the West End Square, one of you holding up that sword."

"It's not over yet. Breckton is almost here, and we don't even know if Royce got through. What if he never made it? What if he did and Alric doesn't listen? He might not think it possible to take Ratibor, and refuse to put the kingdom at risk. We need to be certain."

"You want me to go?"

"No," she said. "I want you here. I *need* you here. But if Breckton lays siege, we'll eventually fall, and by then it'll be too late for you to get away. Our only hope is if Alric's forces can turn Breckton's attention away from us."

He nodded and his hand played with the amulet around his neck. "I suppose it doesn't matter where I go for a while."

"What do you mean?"

"Esrahaddon was in Gaunt's camp. He's been helping the Nationalists."

"Did you tell him about the heir?"

Hadrian nodded. "And you were right. The heir is alive. I think he's Degan Gaunt."

"Degan Gaunt is the heir?"

"Funny, huh? The voice of the common man is also the heir to the imperial throne. There was another child born that night. The midwife took the surviving twin. No one else knew. I've no idea how Esrahaddon figured it out, but that explains why he's been helping Gaunt."

"Where is Esrahaddon now?"

"Don't know. I haven't seen him since the battle started."

"You don't think..."

"Hmm? Oh no. I'm sure he's fine. He hung back when we engaged Dermont's forces. I suspect he's off to find Gaunt and will contact me and Royce once he does." Hadrian sighed. "I wish my father could have known he didn't fail after all.

"Anyway, I'll take care of things tonight before I leave. I'll put one of the regiment captains in charge of the army. There's a guy named Renquist who seems intelligent. I'll have him see to the walls, patch up the stonework, ready gate defenses, put up sentries, guards, and archers. He should know how to do all of that. And I'll put together a list of things you'll want to do, like bring the entire army and the surrounding farmers within the city walls and seal it up. You should do that right away."

"You'll be leaving in the morning, then?"

He nodded. "Doubt I'll see you again before I go, so I'll say goodbye now. You've done the impossible, Arista—excuse me—Your Highness."

"Arista is just fine," she told him. "I'm going to miss you." It was all she could say. Words were too small to express gratitude so immense.

He opened his mouth but hesitated. He smiled then and said, "Take care of yourself, Your Highness."

❧

In her dream, Thrace could see the beast coming for her father. He stood smiling warmly at her, his back to the monster. She tried to scream for him to run, but only a soft muffled moan escaped. She tried to wave her arms and draw his attention to the danger, but her limbs were heavy as lead and refused to move. She tried to run to him, but her feet were stuck, frozen in place.

The beast had no trouble moving.

It charged down the hill. Her poor father took no notice, even though the beast shook the ground as it ran. It consumed him completely with a single swallow, and she fell, as if pierced through the heart. She collapsed onto the grass, struggling to breathe. In the distance, the beast was coming for her now, coming to finish the job, coming to swallow her up—his legs squeaking louder and louder as he advanced.

She woke up in a cold sweat.

She was sleeping on her stomach in her feather bed with the pillow folded up around her face. She hated sleeping. Sleep always brought nightmares. She stayed awake as long as possible, many nights sitting on the floor in front of the little window, watching the stars and listening to the sounds outside. There was a whole symphony of frogs that croaked in the moat and a chorus of crickets. Fireflies sometimes passed by her tiny sliver of the world. But eventually, sleep found her.

The dream had been the same every night. She was on the hill, her father unaware of his impending death, and there was never anything she could do to prevent it. However, tonight's dream had been different. Usually it ended when the beast devoured her, but this time she had woken early, and something else was different. When the beast came that night, it had made a squeaking sound. Even for a dream, that seemed strange.

Then she heard it again. The sound entered through her window.

Squeak...squeak...squeak!

There were other noises too, sounds of men talking. They spoke quietly but their voices drifted up from the courtyard below. She went to the window and peered out. As many as a dozen men with torches drew a wagon whose large wooden wheels squeaked once with each revolution. The wagon was a large box with a small barred window cut in the side, like the kind that would hold a lion for a traveling circus. The men were dressed in black-and-scarlet armor. She had seen that armor before, while in Dahlgren.

One man stood out. He was tall and thin with long black hair and a short, neatly trimmed beard.

The wagon came to a stop and the knights gathered.

"He's chained, isn't he?" she heard one of them say.

"Why? Are you frightened?"

"He's not a wizard," the tall man scolded. "He can't turn you into a frog. His powers are political, not mystical."

"Come now, Luis, even Saldur said not to underestimate him. Legends speak of strange abilities. He's part god."

"You believe too much in church doctrine. We're the protectorate of the faith. We don't have to wallow in superstition like ignorant peasants."

"That sounds blasphemous."

"The truth can never be blasphemous, so long as it's tempered with an understanding of what's good and right. The truth is a powerful thing, like a crossbow. You wouldn't hand a child a loaded crossbow and say, 'Run and play,' would you? People get killed that way, tragedies occur. The truth must be kept safe, reserved only for those capable of handling it. This—this sacrilegious treasure in a box—is one truth above all that must be kept a secret. It must never again see the light of day. We will bury it deep beneath the castle. We will seal it in for all time and it will become the cornerstone on which we will build a new and glorious empire that will eclipse the previous one and wash away the sins of our forefathers."

She watched as they opened the rear of the wagon and pulled out a man. A black hood covered his face. Chains bound his hands and ankles, yet the men treated him carefully, as if he could explode at any minute.

With four men on either side, they marched him across the courtyard out of the sight of her narrow window.

She watched as they rolled the wagon back out and closed the gate behind them. Modina stared at the empty courtyard for more than an hour, until, at last, she fell asleep again.

❧

The carriage bounced through the night on the rough, hilly road, following a sliver of open sky between walls of forest. The jangle of harnesses, the thudding of hooves, and the crush of wheels dominated this world. The night's air was heavily scented with the aroma of pond water and a skunk's spray.

Arcadius, the lore master of Sheridan University, peered out the open window and hammered on the roof with his walking stick until the driver brought the carriage to a halt.

"What is it?" the driver shouted.

"This will be fine," the lore master replied, grabbing up his bag and slipping it over his shoulder.

"What is?"

"I'm getting out here." Arcadius popped open the little door and carefully climbed out onto the desolate road. "Yes, this is fine." He closed the door and lightly patted the side of the carriage as if it were a horse.

The lore master walked to the front of the coach. The driver sat on the raised bench with his coat drawn up around his neck, a formless sack hat pulled down over his ears. Between his thighs he trapped a small corked jug. "But there's nothing here, sir," he insisted.

"Don't be absurd; of course there is. You're here, aren't you? And so am I." Arcadius pulled open his bag. "And look, there are some nice trees and this excellent road we've been riding on."

"But it's the middle of the night, sir."

Arcadius tilted his head up. "And just look at that wonderful starry sky. It's beautiful, don't you think? Do you know your constellations, good man?"

"No, sir."

"Pity." He measured out some silver coins and handed them up to the driver. "It's all up there, you know. Wars, heroes, beasts, and villains, the past and the future spread above us each night like a dazzling map." He pointed. "That long, elegant set of four bright stars is Persephone, and she, of course, is always beside Novron. If you follow the line that looks like Novron's arm, you can see how they just barely touch—lovers longing to be together."

The driver looked up. "Just looks like a bunch of scattered dust to me."

"It does to a great many people. Too many people."

The driver looked down at him and frowned. "You sure you want me to just leave you? I can come back if you want."

"That won't be necessary, but thank you."

"Suit yourself. Good night." The carriage driver slapped the reins and the coach rolled out, circled in a field, and returned the way it had come. The driver glanced up at the sky twice, shaking his head each time. The carriage and the team rode away, the horses' clopping became softer and softer until it faded below the harsh shrill of nightly noises.

Arcadius stood alone, observing the world. It had been some time since the old professor had been out in the wild. He had forgotten how loud it was. The high-pitched trill of crickets punctuated the oscillating echoes of tree frogs, which peeped with the regular rhythm of a human heart. Winds rustled a million leaves, fashioning the voice of waves at sea.

Arcadius walked along the road, crossing the fresh grooves of the carriage wheels. His shoes on the dirt made a surprisingly large amount of noise. The dark had a way of drawing attention to the normally invisible, silent, and ignored. That was why nights were so frightening. Without the distraction of light, the doors to other senses were unlocked. To children, the dark spoke of the monster beneath the bed. To adults, it spoke of the intruder. To old men, it was the herald of death on its way.

"Long, hard, and rocky is the road we walk in old age," he muttered to his feet.

He stopped when he reached a post lurching at a crossroad. The sign declared RATIBOR to the right and AQUESTA to the left. He stepped off the road into the tall grass and found a fallen log to sit on. He pulled the shoulder strap of the sack over his head and set it down. Rummaging through the bag, he found a honeyed muffin, one of three he had pilfered from the dinner table at the inn. He was old, but his sleight of hand was still impressive. Royce would have been proud—less so if he found out that Arcadius had paid for the meal, which had included the muffins. Still, the big swarthy fellow at his elbow would have poached them if he had not acted first. Now it looked as if they would come in handy, as he had no idea when—

He heard hoofbeats long before he saw the horse. The sound came from the direction of Ratibor. As unlikely as it was for anyone else to be on that road at that hour, the lore master's heart nevertheless increased until, at last, the rider cleared the trees. A woman rode alone in a dark hood and cloak. She came to a stop at the post.

"You're late," he said.

She whirled around, relaxing when she recognized him. "No, I'm early. You are just earlier."

"Why are you alone? It's too dangerous. These roads are—"

"And who would you suggest I trust to escort me? Have you added to our ranks?"

She dismounted and tied her horse to the post.

"You could have paid some young lad. There must be a few in the city you trust."

"Those I trust would be of no aid, and those that could help, I don't trust. Besides, this isn't far. I couldn't have been on the road for more than two hours. And there's not much between Ratibor and here." Before she reached him, he started to rise. "You don't have to get up."

"How else can I give you a hug?" He embraced her. "Now tell me, how have you been? I was very worried."

"You worry too much. I'm fine." She drew back her hood, revealing long blonde hair, which she wore scooped back.

"The city has been taken?" Arcadius asked.

"The Nationalists have it now. They attacked and defeated Lord Dermont's forces in the field and the princess led a revolt against Sheriff Vigan in the city. Sir Breckton and the Northern Imperial Army arrived too late. With the city buttoned up and Dermont dead, Breckton's army turned around and headed back north."

"I passed part of his supply train. He's taking up a defensive position around Aquesta, I think. Hadrian and Arista? How are they?"

"Not a scratch on either," she replied. "Hadrian turned command of the Nationalist army over to a man named Renquist—one of the senior captains—and left the morning after the battle. I'm not sure where to."

"Did you have a chance to talk with him?"

She nodded. "Yes, I told him about my brother. Arcadius, do you know where Degan is?"

"Me?" He looked surprised. "No. The seret have him, I'm certain of that, but where is anyone's guess. They have gotten a whole lot smarter recently. It's like Guy has sprouted another head, and this one has a brain in it."

"Do you think they killed him?"

"I don't know, Miranda." The wizard paused, regretting his curt words, and looked at her sympathetically. "It's hard to fathom the imperial mind. We can hope they want him alive. Now that we've unleashed Hadrian, there's a good chance that he and Royce will save him. It could even be that Esrahaddon will connect the dots and send them."

"Esrahaddon already knows," Miranda said. "He's been with Degan for months."

"So he found out. Excellent. I thought he might. When he visited Sheridan, it was obvious he knew more than he let on."

"Maybe he and Hadrian are looking together—planned a place to meet up after the battle?"

The wizard stroked his chin thoughtfully. "Possible... probable, even. So those two are off looking for your brother. What about Arista? What is she doing?"

Miranda smiled. "She's running the city. The citizens of Ratibor were ready to proclaim her queen of Rhenydd, but she settled for mayor pro tem until elections can be held. She intends to honor Emery's dream of a republic in Rhenydd."

"A princess establishing the first republic in Avryn." Arcadius chuckled. "Quite the turn of events."

"The princess has cried a lot since the battle. I've watched her. She works constantly, settling disputes, inspecting the walls, appointing ministers. She falls asleep at her desk in City Hall. She cries when she thinks no one is looking."

"All that violence after so privileged a life."

"I think she might have been in love with a young man who was killed."

"In love? Really? That's surprising. She's never showed an interest in anyone. Who was he?"

"No one of note—the son of the dead bodyguard to King Urith."

"That's too bad," the wizard said sadly. "For all her privilege, she's not had an easy life."

"You didn't ask about Royce," she noted.

"I know about him. He arrived back in Medford not long before I set out. The next day, Melengar's army crossed the Galewyr. Alric has enlisted every able-bodied man and even a good deal of the boys. He's put Count Pickering, Sir Ecton, and Marquis Lanaklin in command. They broke through the little imperial force and at last report were sweeping south, causing a great deal of havoc. Another obstacle I had to travel around. Getting back to the university will take a month, I expect."

The wizard sighed and a look of concern passed over his face. "Two things still trouble me. First, Aquesta is threatened by an enemy army resting in Ratibor, and they aren't negotiating or evacuating. Second, there's Marius."

"Who?"

"Merrick Marius, also known as Cutter."

"Isn't he the one who put Royce in Manzant?"

"Yes, and now he's working for the New Empire. He's a wild card I hadn't expected." The old man paused. "You're certain that Hadrian believed everything you said?"

"Absolutely. His eyes nearly fell out of his head when I told him Degan was the heir." She sighed. "Are you sure we—"

"I'm sure, Miranda. Make no mistake. We're doing what's absolutely right and necessary. It's imperative that Royce and Hadrian never find out the truth."

BOOK IV

The Emerald Storm

Chapter 1

Assassin

Merrick Marius fitted a bolt into the small crossbow before slipping the weapon beneath the folds of his cloak. Smoke-thin clouds drifted across the sliver of moon, leaving him and Central Square shrouded in darkness. Looking for movement, he searched the filthy streets lined with ramshackle buildings, but found none. At this hour, the city was deserted.

Ratibor may be a pit, he thought, *but at least it's easy to work in.*

Conditions had improved since the Nationalists' recent victory. The imperial guards were gone, and without them the regular patrols had stopped. The town lacked even an experienced sheriff, as the new mayor refused to hire seasoned men or members of the military to administer so-called law and order. Instead, she had opted to make do with grocery clerks, shoemakers, and dairy farmers. Merrick thought her choices were ill-advised, but he expected such mistakes from an inexperienced noble. Not that he was complaining—he appreciated the help.

Despite this shortcoming, he admired Arista Essendon's accomplishments. In Melengar, her brother, King Alric, reigned, and as an unwed princess, she possessed no real power. Then she had come here and masterminded a revolt, and the surviving peasants had rewarded her with the keys to the city. She was a foreigner and a royal, yet they thanked her for taking rule over them. *Brilliant.* He could not have done better himself.

A slight smile formed at the edge of Merrick's lips as he watched her from the street. A candle still burned on the second floor of City Hall, even at this late hour. Her figure moved hazily behind the curtains as she left her desk.

It will not be long now, he thought.

Merrick shifted his grip on the weapon. Only a foot and a half long, with a bow span even shorter, it lacked the penetration strength of a traditional crossbow. Still, it would be enough. His target wore no armor, and he was not relying on the force of the bolt. Venden pox coated the serrated steel tip. A deplorable poison for assassination, it neither killed quickly nor paralyzed the victim. The concoction would certainly kill, but only after what he considered an unprofessional span of time. He had never used it before, and had only recently learned of its most important trait—venden pox was invulnerable to magic. Merrick had it on good authority that the most powerful spells and incantations would be useless against its venom. Given his target, this would prove to be essential.

Another figure entered Arista's room, and she sat abruptly. Merrick thought she had just received some interesting news and he was about to cross the street to listen at the window when the tavern door behind him opened. A pair of patrons exited, and by the sway of their steps and the volume of their voices, he could tell they had drained more than one mug that night.

"Nestor, who's that leaning against the post?" one said,

pointing in Merrick's direction. A plump man with a strawberry nose whose shape matched its color squinted in the dim light and staggered forward.

"How should I know?" said the other. The thin man's mustache still glistened with beer foam.

"What's he doing here at this time of night?"

"Again, how should I know, you git?"

"Well, ask him."

The tall man stepped forward. "Whatcha doing, mister? Holding up the post so the porch doesn't fall down?" Nestor snorted a laugh and doubled over with his hands on his knees.

"Actually," Merrick told them, his tone so serious it was almost grave, "I'm waiting to appoint the position of town fool to the person who asks me the stupidest question. Congratulations. You win."

The thin man slapped his friend on the shoulder. "See? I've been telling you all night how funny I am, and you haven't laughed once. Now I'm getting a new job...probably pays better than yours."

"Oh yeah, you're quite the entertainer," his friend assured him as they staggered off into the night. "You should audition at the theater. They're gonna be doing *The Crown Conspiracy* for the mayor. The day I see you on a stage—now *that* will be funny."

Merrick's mood turned sour. He had seen that play several years ago. While the two thieves depicted in it used different names, he was sure they portrayed Royce Melborn and Hadrian Blackwater. Royce had once been Merrick's best friend, back when the two of them were assassins for the Diamond. That friendship had ended seventeen years earlier on that warm summer night when Royce murdered Jade.

Although he had not been present, Merrick had imagined the scene countless times. That was before Royce had his white dagger, back when he had used a pair of curved, black-handled kharolls. Merrick knew Royce's technique well enough to picture him silently slicing through Jade with both blades at once. Merrick did not care that someone had set up Royce, or that he had not known his victim's identity when it happened. All Merrick knew was that the woman he loved was dead and his best friend had killed her.

Nearly two decades had passed, and still Jade and Royce haunted him. He could not think of one without the other, and he could not bear to forget. Love and hate welded together forever, intertwined in a knot too tight to untie.

Loud noises and shouts from Arista's room pulled Merrick back to the present. He checked his weapon, then crossed the street.

❧

"Your Highness?" the soldier asked, entering the mayoral office.

Her hair a tangled mess and eyes wreathed in shadow, Princess Arista looked up from her cluttered desk. She took a moment to assess her visitor. The man in mismatched armor displayed an expression of unabated annoyance.

This is not going to go well, she thought.

"You sent for me?" he asked with only partially restrained irritation.

"Yes, Renquist," she said, her mind catching up with his face. She had hardly slept in two days and was having difficulty concentrating. "I asked you here to—"

"Princess, you can't be summoning me like this. I have an army to run and a war to win. I don't have time to chat."

"Chat? I wouldn't call you here if it wasn't important."

Renquist rolled his eyes.

"I need you to remove the army from the city."

"What?"

"It can't be helped. Your men are causing trouble. I'm getting daily reports of soldiers bullying merchants and destroying property. There has even been an accusation of rape. You must take your men out of the city where they can be controlled."

"My men risked their lives against the Imperialists. The least this lousy city can do is feed and house them. Now you want me to take away their beds and the roof over their heads as well?"

"The merchants and farmers refuse to feed them because they can't," Arista explained. "The empire confiscated the city's reserves when the Imperialists took control. The rains and the war destroyed most of this year's crops. The city doesn't have enough to feed its citizens, much less an army. Fall is here, and cold weather is on its way. These people don't know how they will survive the winter. They can't take care of themselves with a thousand soldiers raiding their shops and farms. We're thankful for your contribution in taking the city, but your continued presence threatens to destroy what you risked your lives to liberate. You must leave."

"If I force them back into camps with inadequate food and leaky canvas shelters, half will desert. As it is, many are talking of going home for the harvest season. I shouldn't have to tell you that if this army disappears, the empire will take this city back."

Arista shook her head. "When Degan Gaunt was in charge, the Nationalist army lived under similar conditions for months without it being a problem. The soldiers are becoming complacent here in Ratibor. Perhaps it's time you pressed on to Aquesta."

Renquist stiffened at the suggestion. "Gaunt's capture makes taking Aquesta all the more difficult. I need time to gather information and I'm waiting for reinforcements and supplies from Delgos. Attacking the capital won't be like taking Vernes or Ratibor. The Imperialists will fight to the last man to defend their empress. No. We need to stay here until I'm fully prepared."

"Wait if you must, but not here," she replied firmly.

"What if I refuse?" His eyes narrowed.

Arista put the parchments she was holding on the desk but said nothing.

"My army conquered this city," he told her pointedly. "You hold authority only because *I* allow it. I don't take orders from you. You're not a princess here, and I'm not your serf. My responsibility is to my men, not to this city and certainly not to you."

Arista slowly rose.

"I'm the mayor of this city," she said, her voice growing in authority, "appointed by the people. Furthermore, I'm steward and acting administrator of all of Rhenydd, again by the consent of those who live here. You and your army are here by *my* leave."

"You are a princess from Melengar! At least *I* was born in Rhenydd."

"Regardless of your personal feelings toward me, you'll respect the authority of this office and do as I say."

"And if I don't?" he asked coldly.

Renquist's reaction did not surprise Arista. He had been a career soldier serving with King Urith, as well as the imperial army, before joining the rebel Nationalists when Kilnar fell. When Gaunt had disappeared, Renquist had been appointed commander in chief, a position far higher in rank than he could ever have hoped for. Now he was finally realizing the power he possessed and starting to assert himself. She had hoped he would demonstrate the same spirit Emery had shown, but Renquist was not a commoner with the heart of a nobleman. If she did not take action now, Arista could find herself facing a military overthrow.

"This city just liberated itself from one tyrant, and I won't allow it to fall under the heel of another. If you refuse to obey me, I'll replace you as commander."

"And how will you do that?"

Arista revealed a faint smile. "Think hard...I'm sure you can figure it out."

Renquist continued to stare at her, and then his eyes widened in realization and fear flashed across his face.

"Yes," she told him, "the rumors about me are true. Now take your army out of the city before I feel a need to prove it. You have just one day to remove them. Scouts found a suitable valley to the north. I suggest you camp where the river crosses the road. It's far enough away to prevent further trouble. By heading north, your men will feel they're progressing toward the goal of Aquesta, thus helping morale."

"Don't tell me how to run my army," he snapped, although not as loudly, nor as confidently, as before.

"My apologies," she said with a bow of her head. "That was only a suggestion. The order to leave the city, however, is not. Good evening to you, sir."

Renquist hesitated, his breath labored, his hands balled into fists.

"I said, good evening, sir."

He muttered a curse and slammed the door as he left.

Exhausted, Arista slumped in her chair.

Why does everything have to be so hard?

Everyone wanted something from her now: food, shelter, assurances that everything would be all right. The citizens looked at her and saw hope, but Arista could see little herself. Plagued by endless problems and surrounded by people, she felt oddly alone.

Arista laid her head on her desk and closed her eyes.

Just a few minutes' catnap, she told herself. *Then I'll get up and figure out how to deal with the shortage of grain and look into the reports of the mistreatment of prisoners.*

Since she had become mayor, a hundred issues had demanded her attention, such as who should be entitled to harvest the fields owned by farmers who had been lost in battle. With food in short supply, and harsh autumn weather threatening, she needed a quick solution. At least these problems distracted her from thinking about her own loss. Like everyone in town, Arista remained haunted by the Battle of Ratibor. She bore no visible injury—her pain came from a memory, a face seen at night, when her heart ached as if pierced. It would never fully heal. There would always be a wound, a deformity, a noticeable scar for the rest of her life.

When she finally fell asleep, thoughts of Emery, held at bay during her waking hours, invaded her dreams. He appeared, as always, sitting at the foot of her bed, bathed in moonlight. Her breath shortened in anticipation of the kiss as he leaned forward, a smile across his lips. Abruptly he stiffened, and a drop of blood slipped from the corner of his mouth—a crossbow bolt protruding from his chest. She tried to cry out but could not make a sound. The dream had always been the same, but this time Emery spoke. "*There's no time left*," he told her, his face intent and urgent. "*It's up to you now.*"

She struggled to ask what he meant when—

"Your Highness." She felt a gentle hand jostle her shoulder.

Opening her eyes, Arista saw Orrin Flatly. The city scribe, who had once kept track of the punishment of rebels in Central Square, had volunteered to be her secretary. His cold efficiency had given her pause but eventually she had realized that there was no crime in doing one's job well. Her decision had proved sound and he had turned out to be a loyal, diligent worker. Still, waking to his expressionless face was disturbing.

"What is it?" she asked, wiping her eyes and feeling for the tears that should have been there.

"Someone is here to see you. I explained you were occupied, but he insists. He's very..." Orrin shifted uncomfortably. "...hard to ignore."

"Who is he?"

"He refused to give his name, but he said you knew him and claims his business is of utmost importance. He insists that he must speak to you immediately."

"Okay." Arista nodded drowsily. "Give me a moment and then send him in."

Orrin left, and in his absence, she smoothed the wrinkles from her dress to ensure her appearance was at least marginally presentable. Having lived the life of a commoner for so long, what Arista deemed acceptable had reached an appallingly low level. Checking her hair in a mirror, she wondered where the Princess of Melengar had gone and if she would ever return.

While she was inspecting herself, the door opened. "How may I help—"

Esrahaddon stood in the doorway, wearing the same flowing robe whose color Arista could never determine. His arms, as always, were lost in its shimmering folds. His beard was longer, and gray streaked his hair, making him appear older than she remembered. She had not seen the wizard since that morning on the bank of the Nidwalden River.

"What are *you* doing here?" she asked, her warm tone icing over.

"I'm pleased to see you as well, Your Highness."

After admitting the wizard, Orrin had left the doors open. With a glance from Esrahaddon, they swung shut.

"I see you're getting along better without hands these days," Arista said.

"One adapts to one's needs," he replied, sitting opposite her.

"I didn't extend an invitation for you to sit."

"I didn't ask for one."

Arista's own chair slammed into the backs of her legs, causing her to fall into it.

"How are you doing that with no hands or sound?" she asked, disarmed by her own curiosity.

"The lessons are over, or don't you remember declaring that at our last meeting?"

Arista hardened her composure once more. "I remember. I also thought I made it clear I never wanted to see you again."

"Yes, yes, that's all well and good, but I need your help to locate the heir."

"Lost him again, have you?"

Esrahaddon ignored her. "We can find him with a basic location spell."

"I'm not interested in your games. I have a city to run."

"We need to perform the spell immediately. We can do it right here, right now. I've a good idea where he is, but time is short and I can't afford to run off in the wrong direction. So clear your desk and we can get started."

"I have no intention of doing anything of the sort."

"Arista, you know I can't do this alone. I need your help."

The princess glared at him. "You should have thought of that before you arranged my father's murder. What I should do is order your execution."

"You don't understand. This is important. Thousands of lives are at stake. This is larger than your loss. It's larger than the loss of a hundred kings and a thousand fathers. You are not the only one to suffer. Do you think I enjoyed rotting in a prison for a thousand years? Yes, I used you and your father to escape. I did so out of necessity—because what I protect is more important than any single person. Now stop this foolishness. We're running out of time."

"I'm so happy to be of no service to you." She smirked. "I can't bring my father back, and I know I could never kill you, nor would you allow yourself to be imprisoned again. This is truly a gift—the opportunity to repay you for what you took from me."

Esrahaddon sighed and shook his head. "You don't really hate me, Arista. It's guilt that's eating you. It's knowing that you had as much to do with your father's death as I. But the church is the one to blame. They orchestrated the events so I would escape and hopefully lead them to the heir. They enticed you to Gutaria, knowing I would use you."

"Get out!" Arista got to her feet, her face flushed red. "Orrin! Guards!"

The scribe struggled with the door, and it opened a crack, but a slight glance from Esrahaddon slammed it again. "Your Highness, I'll get help," Orrin said, his voice coming from behind the door.

"You need to forgive yourself, Arista."

"*Get out!*" she screamed. With a wave of her hand, the office door burst open, nearly coming free from the hinges.

Esrahaddon got up and moved toward the door, adding, "You need to realize you didn't kill your father any more than I did."

After he left the room, Arista slammed the door and sat on the floor with her back against it. She wanted to scream, *It wasn't my fault!* even though she knew that was a lie. In the years since her father's death, she had hid from the truth, but she could hide no longer. As difficult as it was to admit, Esrahaddon was right.

❧

Esrahaddon stepped out of City Hall into the darkness of Ratibor's Central Square. He looked back and sighed. He genuinely liked Arista. He wished he could tell her everything, but the risk was too great. Even though he was free of Gutaria Prison, he feared the church still listened to his conversations—not every word, as when he had been incarcerated, but Mawyndulë had the power to hear from vast distances. Therefore, Esrahaddon had to assume all conversations were suspect. A single slip, the casual mention of a name, and he could ruin everything.

Time was growing short but at least now there was no doubt that Arista *had* become a Cenzar. He had safely planted the seed, and the soil had proved fertile. He had begun to suspect her abilities on the morning of the Battle of Ratibor, when Hadrian had mentioned that the rain was not *supposed* to stop. He suspected Arista had cast the spell that had been instrumental to the Nationalists' victory. Since then, he had heard the rumors concerning the new mayor's *unnatural powers*. But it was only when she broke his locking charm, with just a simple wave of her hand, that he knew for certain that Arista finally understood the Art.

Aside from Arcadius and him, no human wizards remained, and the two of them were pitiful representatives of the craft. Arcadius was nothing but an old hack, what Cenzars used to refer to as a *faquin*, an elven term for the most inept magician—knowledge without talent. *Faquins* never managed to transition from materials-based alchemy to the kinetic true version of the Art.

Esrahaddon did not consider himself any better. Without his hands, he was as much a magical cripple as a physical invalid. Now, however, with Arista's birth into the world of wizardry, mankind once again possessed a true artist. She was still a novice, a mere infant, but given time, her talent would grow. One day she would become more powerful than any king, emperor, warrior, or priest.

Knowing that she could hold sway over all mankind was more than a little disturbing. During the Old Empire, safeguards had existed. The Cenzar Council had overseen wielders of the Art and ensured its proper use. They were all gone now. The other wizards, his brethren and even the lesser mages, were dead. With him essentially castrated, the church thought they had eliminated the Cenzar threat from the world. Now a true practitioner of the Art had returned, and he was certain no one understood the danger this simple princess posed.

He needed her, and though she did not know it yet, she needed him. He could explain the Art's source and how they had come to use it. The Cenzars had been the guardians, the preservers, and the defenders. They had kept secrets that would protect mankind when the *Uli Vermar* ended.

When Esrahaddon had learned the truth so long ago, he had felt relieved that it would not be his problem to face, as the day of reckoning was centuries away. How ironic that his imprisonment in the timeless vault of Gutaria had extended his life to this time. What had once been forever in the future was now but months away. He allowed himself a bitter laugh, then walked to the center of the square to sit and think.

His plan was so tenuous, so weak, but all the pieces were in their proper places. Arista just needed time to master her feelings and then she would come around. Hadrian knew he was the Guardian of the Heir, and he had proved himself worthy of that legacy. Then there was the heir, an unlikely choice to be sure, but one that somehow made perfect sense.

Yes, it'll be all right, he concluded. *Things always work out in the end. At least, that is what Yolric always used to say.*

Yolric had been the wisest of them all and had been passionate about the world's ability to correct itself. Esrahaddon's greatest fear when the Old Empire fell had been that Yolric might side with Venlin. That the emperor's descendant still lived proved Esrahaddon's master had not helped the Patriarch find the emperor's son when the boy had been taken into hiding. Esrahaddon allowed himself a grin. He missed old Yolric. His teacher would be dead now. He had been ancient even when Esrahaddon was a boy.

Esrahaddon stretched his legs and tried to clear his mind. He needed to rest, but rest had eluded him for centuries. Rest was enjoyed only by men of clear conscience, and he had too much innocent blood on his hands. Too many people had given their lives for him to fail now.

Remembering Yolric opened the door to his past, and through it emerged faces of people long dead: his family, his friends, and the woman he had hoped to marry. It seemed his life before the fall had been merely a dream, but perhaps his current state was the real dream, a nightmare that he was trapped in. Maybe one day he would wake and find himself back in the palace with Nevrik, Jerish, and his beloved Elinya.

Did she somehow survive the destruction of the city?

He wanted to believe so, no matter how unlikely. It pleased him to think that she had escaped the end, but even that thought gave him little comfort.

What if she believed what they said about me afterward? Did she marry someone else, feeling betrayed? Did Elinya die at an old age, hating me?

He needed to stop thinking this way. What he had told Arista was true: the sacrifices they made were insignificant when compared to the goal. He should try to get some sleep. He rose and headed back toward the inn. A cloud covered the moon, snuffing out what little light it cast. As it did,

Esrahaddon felt a stabbing pain in his back. Crying out in anguish, he fell to his knees. Twisting at the waist, he felt his robe stick to his skin with a growing wetness.

I'm bleeding.

"*Venderia*," he whispered, and instantly his robe glowed, lighting up the square. At the fringe of its radiance, he caught a glimpse of a man dressed in a dark cloak. At first he thought it might be Royce. He shared the same callous gait and posture, but this man was taller and broader.

Esrahaddon muttered a curse and four beams supporting the porch directly over the man exploded into splinters. The heavy roof collapsed just as the man stepped out from under it. The force of the crashing timbers merely billowed his cloak.

With sweat coating his face and a stabbing pain in his back, Esrahaddon struggled to rise and confront his attacker, who walked casually toward him. The wizard concentrated. He spoke again, and the dirt of the square whirled into a tornado, traveling directly toward his attacker. It engulfed the man, who burst into flames. Esrahaddon could feel the heat of the inferno as the pillar surged, bathing the square in a yellow glow. At its center, the figure stood wreathed in blue tongues of flame, but when the fire faded, the man continued forward, unharmed.

Reaching the wizard, he looked curiously at Esrahaddon—the way a child might study a strange bug before crushing it. He said nothing, but revealed a silver medallion that hung from a chain he wore around his neck.

"Recognize this?" the man asked. "Word is you made it. I'm afraid the heir won't need it any longer."

Esrahaddon gasped.

"If only you had hands, you might rip it from my neck. Then I'd be in real trouble, wouldn't I?"

The noise of the collapse, and the explosions of light, had

woken several people in nearby buildings. Candles were lit in windows and doors opened onto the square.

"The regents bid me to tell you that your services are no longer required." The man in the dark cloak smiled coldly. Without another word, he walked away, disappearing into the maze of dark streets.

Esrahaddon was confused. The bolt or dart lodged in his back did not feel fatal. He could breathe easily, so it had missed his lungs and was nowhere near his heart. He was bleeding but not profusely. The pain was bad, a deep burning, but he could still feel his legs and was certain he could walk.

Why did he leave me alive? Why would—poison!

The wizard concentrated and muttered a chant. It failed. He struggled with his handless arms to weave a stronger spell. It did not help. He could feel the poison now as it spread throughout his back. He was helpless without hands. Whoever the man in the cloak was, he knew exactly what he was doing.

Esrahaddon looked back at City Hall. He could not die—not yet.

❧

The noise from the street caught Arista's attention. She still sat against the office door as voices and shouts drifted from the square. What had happened was unclear, but the words *he's dying* brought Arista to her feet.

She found a small crowd gathered on the steps outside. Within their center, an eerie pulsating light glowed, as if a bit of the moon had landed in Central Square. Drawing closer, Arista saw the wizard. The light emitted from his robe, growing bright, then ebbing, then brightening again in pace with his slow and labored breath. The pale light revealed a pool of blood. As Esrahaddon lay on his back, a bolt beside him, his face was almost luminous with a ghostly pallor, his lips a dark shade of blue. His disheveled sleeves exposed the fleshy stumps of his wrists.

"What happened here?" she demanded.

"We don't know, Your Highness," someone from the crowd replied. "He's been asking to see you."

"Get Dr. Gerand," she ordered, and knelt beside him, gently pulling down his sleeves.

"Too late," Esrahaddon whispered, his eyes locked intently on hers. "Can't help me—poison—Arista, listen—there's no time." His words came hurriedly between struggles to take in air. On his face was a look of determination mixed with desperation, like that of a drowning man searching for a handhold. "Take my burden—find..." The wizard hesitated, his eyes searching the faces gathered. He motioned for her to draw near.

When she placed her ear close to his mouth, he continued. "Find the heir—take the heir with you—without the heir everything fails." Esrahaddon coughed and fought to breathe. "Find the Horn of Gylindora—need the heir to find it—buried with Novron in Percepliquis—" He drew in another breath. "Hurry—at Wintertide the *Uli Vermar* ends—" Another breath. "They will come—without the horn everyone dies." Another breath. "Only you know now—only you can save...Patriarch...is the same..." The next breath never came. The next words were never uttered. The pulsating brilliance of his robe faded, leaving them all in darkness.

Arista watched the foul-smelling, chalk-colored smoke drift as the strand of blond hair smoldered. There was no breeze or draft in her office, yet the smoke traveled unerringly toward the northern wall, where it disappeared against the stone and mortar.

A spell of location required burning a part of a person. Hair was the obvious choice, but fingernails or even skin would work. The day after Esrahaddon's death, she had requested delivery of any personal belongings left behind by the missing leader of the Nationalist army. Parker had sent over an old pair of Degan Gaunt's worn muddy boots, a tattered shirt, and a woolen cloak. The boots had been useless, but the shirt and cloak held many treasures. Scraping the surfaces, she had retrieved dozens of blond hairs and hundreds of flakes of skin, which she carefully gathered and placed in a velvet pouch. At the time, she had convinced herself she merely wanted to see if the spell would work. When she had started the incantation, she had no intention of acting on the results. Now she was unsure what to do next.

To Esrahaddon, the heir had meant everything. Since leaving Gutaria, the wizard had dedicated his life to finding the emperor's descendant, even coercing Arista to assist him by casting a spell in Avempartha to identify the heir and his guardian. The guardian she had recognized immediately as Hadrian; however, the heir she had never seen before. The blond-haired image of a middle-aged man had been just a face until after the Battle of Ratibor, when she learned that he was Degan Gaunt, the leader of the Nationalists. There was no doubt that the New Empire was responsible for Gaunt's disappearance, and the smoke's color confirmed he was alive and held somewhere to the north within a few days' travel. She stared at the wall where the smoke disappeared.

"This is crazy," she said aloud to the empty room. *I can't possibly go in search of the heir. The empire has him and they'll kill me on sight. Besides, I'm needed here. Why should I care about Esrahaddon's obsession?*

If Arista wanted, she could declare herself high queen of Rhenydd and the citizenry would welcome her. She could permanently reign over a kingdom larger than Melengar and be rich as well as beloved. Long after her death, her name would endure in stories and songs—her image immortalized on statues and in books.

She glanced at the neatly folded robe on the corner of her desk. It had been delivered after Esrahaddon's burial. The sum of all the wizard's worldly possessions amounted to just this piece of cloth. He had devoted everything to his quest, and after nine hundred years, he had died without fulfilling his mission. The question of exactly what that mission had been nagged at her. Loyalty to the descendant of a boy ruler from a millennium ago could not have driven Esrahaddon so fanatically—she was missing something.

"They will come."

What did that mean? Who is coming?

"Without the horn everyone dies."

Everyone? Who is everyone? He couldn't have meant everyone, everyone—could he? Maybe he was just babbling. People do that when they're dying, don't they?

She remembered his eyes, clear and focused, holding on like...*Emery. "There's no time left. It's up to you now."*

"Only you know now—only you can save..." When Esrahaddon had spoken those words, she had not really listened, but now she could hear nothing else. She could not ignore the fact that the wizard had used his last breath to deliver to her the secrets he had carried for a thousand years. She felt that he had presented her with sparkling gems of immeasurable worth, but without his knowledge, they were nothing more than dull pebbles. While she could not unravel what he had been trying to say, it was impossible to ignore what had to be done. She had to leave. Once she discovered where Gaunt was

being held, she could send word to Hadrian and leave the rest to him. After all, he was the guardian, and Gaunt was his problem, not hers.

Arista stuffed the only possession she cared about, a pearl-handled hairbrush from Tur Del Fur, into a sack. She hastily wrote a letter of resignation and left it on the desk. Reaching the door, she paused and glanced back. Somehow, taking it seemed appropriate... almost necessary. She crossed the office and picked up the old wizard's robe. It hung, gray and dull, in her hands. No one had cleaned it, yet she found no stain of blood. Even more surprising, no hole marked the passage of the bolt. She wondered at this puzzle—even in death the man continued to be a mystery. Slipping the robe over her dress, she was amazed that it fit perfectly—despite the fact that Esrahaddon had been more than a foot taller than her. Turning her back on her office, she walked out into the night.

The autumn air was cold. Arista pulled the robe tight and lifted the hood. The material was unlike anything she had ever felt before—light, soft, yet wonderfully warm and comforting. It smelled pleasantly of salifan.

She considered taking a horse from the stables. No one would begrudge her a mount, but wherever she was going, it could not be too far, and a long walk suited her. Esrahaddon had indicated a need for haste, but it would be imprudent to rush headlong into the unknown. Walking seemed a sensible way to challenge the mysterious and unfamiliar. It would give her time to think. She guessed Esrahaddon would have chosen the same mode of travel. It just felt right.

Arista filled a water skin at the square's well and packed some food. Farmers, who objected to providing for the soldiers, always placed a small tribute on the steps of City Hall. Most she gave to the city's poor, which only resulted in more food appearing. She helped herself to a few rounds of cheese, two loaves of bread, and a number of apples, onions, and turnips. Hardly a king's feast, but it would keep her alive.

She slipped the full water bag over her shoulder, adjusted her pack, and headed for the north gate. She was conscious of the sound of her feet on the road and the noises of the night. How dangerous, even foolhardy, leaving Medford had been, even in the company of Royce and Hadrian. Now, just a few weeks later, she set out into the darkness by herself. She knew her path would lead into imperial territory, but she hoped that by traveling alone she would avoid attention.

"Your Highness!" the north gate guard said with surprise when she approached.

She smiled sweetly. "Can you please open the gate?"

"Of course, milady, but why? Where are you going?"

"For a walk," she replied.

The guard stared at her incredulously. "Are you certain? I mean..." He looked over her shoulder. "Are you alone?"

She nodded. "I assure you I'll be fine."

The guard hesitated briefly before relenting and drew back the bar. Putting his back against the giant oak doors, he slowly pushed one open.

"You need to be careful, milady. There is a stranger about."

"A stranger?"

"A fellow came to the gate just a few hours after sunset, wanting in—a masked man in a hood. I could see he was up to no good, so I turned him away. Likely as not, he's out there somewhere waiting for me to open at sunrise. Please be careful, Your Highness."

"Thank you, but I'm sure I'll be fine," she said while slipping past him. Once she was through, the gate closed behind her.

Arista stayed to the road, walking as quickly and quietly as she could. Now on her way, she felt exhilarated despite the dangers that lay ahead. Leaving Ratibor without farewells was for the best. They would have insisted she appoint a successor and remain for a time to counsel whoever was selected. While she did not feel enough urgency for a horse, she worried that too long of a delay would be a mistake. Besides, she could not risk an imperial spy discovering her plan and placing sentries to capture her.

In one way she felt safer on the road than in her office—she was confident no one knew where she was or where she was going. This thought was as comforting as the old wizard's robe. In the days following Esrahaddon's death, she had been concerned that she too might be a target. His assassin had escaped capture, the only trace was an unusually small crossbow discovered in an East End Square rain barrel. She felt certain that the killer was an agent of the New Empire, sent to eliminate a lingering threat. She was Esrahaddon's apprentice, who had helped defeat the church's attempt to take Melengar, and led the revolt in Ratibor. Surely those in power wanted her dead as well.

Before long, she spotted the flicker of a light not far off the road—a simple campfire burning low.

The man turned away at the gate? Could he be the assassin?

She kept her eyes on the fire while carefully walking past. She soon cleared a hill and the light disappeared behind it. After a few hours, the excitement of the adventure waned and she found herself yawning. With several hours until dawn, she pulled a blanket from her bag and found a soft place to lie.

Is this what each night was like for Esrahaddon?

She had never felt so alone. In the past, Hilfred had been her ever-present shadow, but her bodyguard had disappeared more than two years earlier after having suffered burns in her service. Most of all, she missed Royce and Hadrian, a common thief and an ex-mercenary. To them, she was nothing more than a wealthy patron, but to her, they were nothing less than her closest friends. She imagined Royce disappearing into the trees to search the area as he had at every camp. Even more, she wanted Hadrian there by her side. She pictured him with a lopsided grin, making that awful stew of his. He always made her feel safe. She remembered how he had held her on the hill of Amberton Lee and at the armory after the Battle of Ratibor. She had been soaked in rain, mud, and Emery's blood, and his arms had held her up. She had never felt so horrible and no one's embrace had ever felt so good.

"I wish you were here now," she whispered.

Lying on her back, she looked up at the stars, scattered like dust over the immense heavens. Seeing them, she felt even more alone. She closed her eyes and drifted off to sleep.

Chapter 2

The Empty Castle

Above Hadrian's head the wooden sign displaying a thorny branch and a faded bloom rocked in the morning breeze. It was weathered and worn, and it took imagination to determine that the flower depicted was a rose. The tavern it announced displayed the same haphazard charm of necessity as the other buildings along Wayward Street. The crooked length of the narrow road was empty. Autumn leaves scattering in the wind and the rocking sign marked the only movement.

The lack of activity surprised Hadrian. At this time of year, Medford's Lower Quarter usually bustled with vendors selling apples, cider, pumpkins, and hardwood. The air should be scented with wood smoke. Chimney sweeps should be dancing across rooftops as children watched in awe. Instead, the doors of several stores were nailed shut—and to his dismay, even The Rose and Thorn Tavern lay dormant.

Hadrian sighed as he tethered his horse. Skipping breakfast in exchange for an early start had left him eager for a hot meal eaten indoors. He had expected the war to take its toll and Medford to be affected, but he had never expected The Rose and Thorn to—

"Hadrian!"

He recognized the voice before turning to see Gwen, the lovely Calian native, who, in her sky-blue day dress, looked more like an artisan's wife than a madam. She swept down the steps of Medford House, one of the few open businesses. Prostitutes were always the first to arrive and the last to leave. Hadrian hugged her, lifting her small body. "We were worried about you," she said. "What took you so long?"

"What are you doing back at all?" Royce called as he stepped out onto the porch. The lithe and slender thief stood barefoot, wearing only black pants and a loose unbelted tunic.

"Arista sent me to make sure you made it all right and were able to convince Alric to send the army south."

"Took you long enough. I've been back for weeks."

Hadrian shrugged. "Well, Alric's forces laid siege to Colnora right after I arrived. It took me a while to find a way out."

"So, how did—"

"Royce, shouldn't we let Hadrian sit and eat?" Gwen interrupted. "You haven't had breakfast, have you? Let me grab a shawl, and I'll have Dixon fire the stove."

"How long has the tavern been closed?" Hadrian asked as Gwen disappeared back inside.

Royce raised an eyebrow and shook his head. "Not closed. Business has just been slow, so she opens for the midday meal."

"It's like a ghost town around here."

"A lot of people left, expecting an invasion," Royce explained. "Most who stayed were called to serve when the army moved out."

Gwen reappeared with a wrap around her shoulders and led them across the street to The Rose and Thorn. In the shadows of an alley, Hadrian spotted movement. Figures slept huddled amid piles of trash. Unlike Royce, who easily passed for human, these shabbily dressed creatures bore the unmistakable angled ears, prominent cheekbones, and almond eyes characteristic of elves.

"The army didn't want them," Royce commented, seeing Hadrian's stare. "No one wants them."

Dixon, the bartender and manager, was taking chairs off the tables when Gwen unlocked the doors. A tall, stocky man, he had lost his right arm several years earlier in the Battle of Medford.

"Hadrian!" he shouted in his booming voice. Hadrian instinctively held out his left hand to shake Dixon's. "How are you, lad? Gave them what for in Ratibor, eh? Where you been?"

"I stayed to sweep up," Hadrian replied with a wink and a smile.

"Denny in yet?" Gwen asked Dixon, stepping past him and rummaging through a drawer behind the bar.

"Nope, just me. I figured, why bother? All of you want breakfast? I can manage if you like."

"Yes," Gwen told him, "and make some extra."

Dixon sighed. "You keep feeding them and they'll just keep hanging around."

She ignored the comment. "Did Harry deliver the ale last night?"

"Yup."

"Three barrels, right?"

As Gwen talked with Dixon, Royce slipped his arm around her waist and gave her a gentle squeeze. That he loved her was no secret, but Royce had never even held Gwen's hand in public before. Seeing him with her, Hadrian noticed that his friend looked different. It took him a moment to realize what it was—Royce was smiling.

When Gwen followed Dixon into the pantry to discuss inventory, Royce and Hadrian resumed the task of pulling chairs off tables. Throughout the years, Hadrian had likely sat in each one and drunk from every wooden cup and pewter tankard hanging behind the bar. For more than a decade The Rose and Thorn had been his home, and it felt odd to be *just visiting.*

"So, have you decided what you'll do now?" Royce asked.

"I'm going to find the heir."

Royce paused, holding a chair inches above the floor. "Did you hit your head during the Battle of Ratibor? The heir is dead, remember?"

"Turns out he's not. What's more, I know who he is."

"But the nice priest told us the heir was murdered by Seret Knights forty years ago," Royce countered.

"He was."

"Am I missing something?"

"Twins," Hadrian told him. "One was killed, but the midwife saved the other."

"So who's this heir?"

"Degan Gaunt."

Royce's eyes widened and a sardonic grin crossed his face. "The leader of the Nationalist army, who is bent on the New Empire's destruction, is the imperial heir destined to rule over it? How ironic is that? It's also pretty unfortunate for you, seeing as how the Imps snatched him up."

Hadrian nodded. "Yeah, it turns out Esrahaddon's been helping him win all those victories in Rhenydd."

"Esrahaddon? How do you know that?"

"I found him in Gaunt's camp right before the Battle of Ratibor. Looks like the old wizard was planning to put Gaunt on the throne by force."

The two finished with the chairs and took seats at a table near the windows. Outside, a lone apple seller wheeled a cart past, presumably on her way to the Gentry Quarter.

"I hope you're not taking Esrahaddon's word about Gaunt

being the heir. You can never be sure exactly what he's up to," Royce said.

"No—well, yes—he confirmed the heir was alive, but I discovered his identity through Gaunt's sister."

"So how do you plan to find Gaunt? Did either of them tell you where he is?"

"No. I'm pretty sure Esrahaddon knows, or has a good idea, but he wouldn't tell me, and I've not seen him since the battle. He did say he would need us for a job soon. I think he'll want help rescuing Gaunt. He hasn't been around here, has he?"

Royce shook his head. "I'm happy to say I haven't seen him. Is that why you're in town?"

"Not really. I'm sure he can find me wherever I am. After all, he found us in Colnora when he wanted us to come to Dahlgren. I'm on my way to see Myron at the abbey. If anyone knows about the history of the heir, he should. I was also given a letter to drop off to Alric."

"A letter?"

"When I was stuck in Colnora during the siege, your old friends helped get me out."

"The Diamond?"

Hadrian nodded. "Price arranged for me to slip away one night in exchange for delivering the letter. He preferred risking my neck rather than one of his boys."

"What did it say? Who was it from?"

Hadrian shrugged. "How would I know?"

"You didn't read it?" Royce asked incredulously.

"No, it was for Alric."

"Do you still have it?"

Hadrian shook his head. "Delivered it to the castle on the way in."

Royce dropped his face into his hands. "Sometimes, I just..." Royce shook his head. "Unbelievable."

"What's wrong?" Gwen asked as she joined them.

"Hadrian's an idiot," Royce replied, his voice muffled by his hands.

"I'm sure that's not true."

"Thank you, Gwen. See? At least *she* appreciates me."

"So, Hadrian, tell me about Ratibor. Royce told me about the rebellion. How did it go?" Gwen asked with an excited smile.

"Emery was killed. Do you know who he was?"

Gwen nodded.

"So were a lot of others, but we took the city."

"And Arista?"

"She survived the fight but took the aftermath hard. She's become something of a heroine there. They put her in charge of the whole kingdom."

"She's a remarkable woman," Gwen said. "Don't you think so, Hadrian?" Before he could answer, a loud crash from the kitchen made her sigh. "Excuse me while I help Dixon."

She started to stand but Royce reached his feet first. "Sit," he said, kissing the crown of her head. "I'll help him. You two get caught up."

Gwen looked surprised but simply said, "Thank you."

Royce hurried off, shouting in an unusually good-natured tone, "Dixon! What's taking you so long? You've still got one hand, haven't you?"

Gwen and Hadrian both laughed, mirroring surprised expressions.

"So, what's new around here?" Hadrian asked.

"Not a whole lot. Albert came by last week with a job from a nobleman to place the earrings of a married woman in the bedchambers of a priest, but Royce declined it."

"Really? He loves plant jobs. And a priest? That's just easy money."

She shrugged. "I think with you retired, he's—"

Outside, an approaching clatter of hooves halted abruptly. A moment later, a man dressed as a royal courier, and walking with a distinct limp, entered the tavern. He paused at the doorway, looking puzzled.

"Can I help you?" Gwen asked as she stood.

"I have a message from His Majesty for the royal protectors. I was told they were here."

"I'll take that," Gwen said, stepping forward.

The courier stiffened and shook his head. "It's for the royal protectors only."

Gwen halted and Hadrian noticed her annoyed expression.

"You must be new." Rising to his feet, Hadrian held out his hand to the courier. "I'm Hadrian Blackwater."

The courier nodded smartly and pulled a waxed scroll from his satchel. He handed over the dispatch and departed. Hadrian sat back down and broke the falcon seal.

"It's a job, isn't it?" Gwen's expression darkened and she stared at the floor.

"It's nothing. Alric just wants to see us," Hadrian said. She looked up, her eyes revealing a troubled mix of emotions Hadrian could not decipher. "Gwen, what's wrong?" he pressed, his voice softening.

At length she replied, almost in a whisper, "Royce asked me to marry him."

Hadrian sat back in his chair. "Seriously?"

She nodded and hastily added, "I guess he thought that since you retired from Riyria, he would too."

"That's—why, that's wonderful!" Hadrian burst out as he leapt to his feet and hugged her. "Congratulations! He didn't even say anything. We'll be like family! It's about time he got around to this. I would have asked for your hand myself years ago, except I knew if I did, I'd wake up dead the next morning."

"When he asked me, it was as if—well, as if a wish I never dared ask for had come true. So many problems solved, so much pain eased. Honestly, I didn't think he ever would."

Hadrian nodded. "That's only because he's not only an idiot, he's blind as well."

"No. I mean, well—he's Royce."

"Isn't that what I just said? But yeah, he's really not the marrying type, is he? Clearly, you've had tremendous influence on him."

"You have too," she said, reaching out and taking hold of his hand. "There are times I hear him say things I know come from you. Things like *responsibility* and *regret*, words that were never part of his vocabulary before. I wonder if he even knows where he found them. When I first met you two, he was so withdrawn, so guarded."

Hadrian nodded. "He has trust issues."

"But he's learning. His life has been so hard. I know it has, abandoned and betrayed by those who should have loved him. He doesn't talk about it, at least not to me. But I know."

Hadrian shook his head. "Me either. Occasionally something might come up, but he usually avoids mentioning anything about his past. I think he's trying to forget."

"He's built so many defenses, but every year it's as if another wall has fallen. He even summoned the courage to tell me he's part elven. His fortress is dissolving, and I can see him peering out at me. He wants to be free. This is the next step—and I'm so proud of him."

"When will the wedding be?"

"We were thinking in a couple of weeks at the monastery, so Myron can preside. But we'll have to postpone, won't we?"

"Why do you say that? Alric just wants to see us. It doesn't mean—"

"He needs the two of you for a job," Gwen interrupted.

"No. He might *want us*, but we're retired. I have other things to do and Royce... well, Royce needs to start a new life—with you."

"You'll go, and you must take Royce with you." Her voice was filled with sadness and a hint of regret, emotions so unlike her.

Hadrian smiled. "Listen, I can't think of anything Alric could say that would get me to go, but if he does, I'll do the job on my own—as a wedding present. We don't even have to tell Royce the courier was here."

"No!" she burst out. "He *has* to go. If he doesn't, you'll die."

Hadrian's first impulse was to laugh, but that thought evaporated when he saw her face. "I'm not as easy to kill as all that, you know?" He winked at her.

"I'm from Calis, Hadrian, and I know what I'm talking about." Her gaze drifted off toward the windows, but her eyes were unfocused, as if she were seeing another place. "I can't be the one responsible for your death. The life we would have after..." She shook her head. "No, he *must* go with you," she repeated firmly.

Hadrian was not convinced but knew there was no reason to argue further. Gwen was not the type for debate. Most women he knew invited discussion and even enjoyed arguments, but not Gwen. There was clarity to her thinking that let you know she had already made her own journey to the inevitable conclusion and was just politely waiting there for you to join her. In her own way, she was much like Royce—except for the polite waiting.

"With you two gone, I'll have time to organize a first-rate wedding," she said, her voice strained as she blinked frequently. "It will take that long just to decide what color dress a former prostitute should wear."

"You know something, Gwen?" Hadrian began as he reached out and took her hand. "I've known a lot of women, but I've met only two I admire. Royce is a very lucky man."

"Royce is a man on the edge," she replied thoughtfully. "He's seen too much cruelty and betrayal. He's never known mercy." She gave his hand a squeeze. "*You* have to do this, Hadrian. You have to be the one to show him mercy. If you can do that, I know it will save him."

Royce and Hadrian entered Essendon Castle's courtyard, once the site of Princess Arista's witchcraft trial. Nothing remained of that unfortunate day except a slightly raised patch of ground where the stake and woodpile had stood. It had been just three years earlier, and the weather had been turning cold then too. That had been a different time. Amrath Essendon had only recently been murdered and the New Empire had been little more than an Imperialist's dream.

The guards at the gate nodded and smiled at them.

"I hate that," Royce muttered as they passed.

"What?"

"They didn't even think to stop us, and they actually smiled. They know us by sight now—*by sight*. Alric used to have the decency to send word discreetly and receive us unannounced. Now uniformed soldiers knock on the door in daylight, waving and saying, 'Hello, we have a job for you.'"

"He didn't wave."

"Give it time, he will be—waving and grinning. One day Jeremy will be buying drinks for his soldier buddies at The Rose and Thorn. They'll all be there, the entire sentry squad, laughing, smiling, throwing their arms over our shoulders and asking us to sing 'Calide Portmore' with them—'Once more, with gusto!' And at some point one particularly sweaty ox will give me a hug and say how *honored* he is to be in our company."

"*Jeremy?*"

"What? That's his name."

"You know the name of the soldier at the gate?"

Royce scowled. "You see my point? Yes, I know his name and they know ours. We might as well wear uniforms and move into Arista's old room."

They climbed the stone steps to the main entrance, where a soldier quickly opened a door for them and gave a slight bow. "Master Melborn, Master Blackwater."

"Hey, Digby." Hadrian waved as he passed. When he caught Royce scowling, he added, "Sorry."

"It's a good thing we're both retired. You know, there's a reason there are no famous *living* thieves."

Hadrian's heels echoed on the polished floor of the corridor as they walked. Royce's footsteps made no sound at all. They crossed the west gallery past the suits of armor and the ballroom. The castle appeared as empty as the rest of the city. As they approached the reception hall, Hadrian spotted Mauvin Pickering heading their way. The young noble looked thinner than Hadrian had remembered. There was a hollow cast to his cheeks, shadows beneath his eyes, but his hair was the same wild mess.

"About time," Mauvin greeted them. "Alric just sent me to look for you."

Two years had passed since his brother Fanen's death, and Mauvin still dressed in black. The haunted look in his eyes would be unnoticeable to most. Only those who had known him before the contest in Dahlgren would see the difference. That had been when Sentinel Luis Guy attacked Hadrian with a force of Seret Knights, and Mauvin and Fanen had taken up arms with him. The brothers had fought masterfully, as was the nature of Pickerings. Yet Mauvin had been unable to save his brother from the killing stroke. Before that day, Mauvin Pickering had been bright, loud, and joyful. He had worn a permanent smile and challenged the world with a wink and a laugh. Now he stood with his shoulders slumped and his chin dipped.

"You're wearing it again?" Hadrian gestured toward Mauvin's sword.

"They insisted."

"Have you drawn it?"

Mauvin looked at his feet. "Dad says it doesn't matter. If the need arises, he's certain I won't hesitate."

"And what do you think?"

"Mostly I try not to." Mauvin opened the doors to the hall and let them swing wide. He led Royce and Hadrian past the clerk and the door guards into the reception hall. Tall windows let in the late-morning light, casting bright spears on the parquet floor. The great tapestries still lay rolled in bundles against the wall, stacked in hope of a better day. In their places, maps with red lines covered by blue arrows pointing south plastered the walls.

Alone, Alric paced near the windows, his crowned head bowed and his mantle trailing behind him like—*like a king*, Hadrian thought. Alric looked up as they entered, and pushed the rim of the royal diadem back with his thumb.

"What took you so long?"

"We ate breakfast, Your Majesty," Royce replied.

"You ate break— Never mind." The king held out a rolled parchment. "I'm told you delivered this dispatch to the castle this morning?"

"Not me," Royce said. Unrolling it, he found two parchments and began reading.

"I did," Hadrian admitted. "I just arrived from Ratibor. Your sister has matters well in hand, Your Majesty."

Alric scowled. "Who sent this?"

"I'm not sure," Hadrian replied. "I got it from a man named Price in Colnora."

Royce finished reading and looked up. "I think you're about to lose this war," he said without bothering to add the expected *Your Majesty*.

"Don't be absurd. This is likely a hoax. Ecton is probably behind it. He enjoys seeing me make a fool of myself. Even if it's authentic, it's simply someone making wild claims to extort a bit of gold from the New Empire."

"I don't think so." Royce handed the letter to Hadrian.

King Alric—
Found this on a courier traveling from Calis to Aquesta. Sweepers bumped him in Alburn but he was more than he seemed. Three Diamonds dead. Bucket men caught him and found this letter addressed to the regents. The Jewel thought you'd like to know.

Esteemed Regents,

The fall of Ratibor was unexpected and unfortunate but, as you know, not fatal. Thus far, I have delivered Degan Gaunt and eliminated the wizard Esrahaddon. This completes two-thirds of our contract, but the best is yet to come.

The Emerald Storm rests anchored in Aquesta Harbor, ready to sail. When you receive this message, place the payment on board along with the sealed orders I left. Once loaded, the ship will depart, the fortunes of war will shift, and your victory will be assured. With the Nationalists eliminated, Melengar is yours for the taking.

While I have all the time in the world, you, on the other hand, might wish to make haste, lest the flame you call the New Empire is snuffed out.

Merrick Marius

"Merrick?" Hadrian muttered, and looked at Royce. "Is this . . . ?"

Royce nodded.

"You know this Marius?" Alric asked.

Again, Royce nodded. "Which is why I know you're in trouble."

"And do you know who sent this?"

"Cosmos DeLur."

"Isn't Cosmos a wealthy merchant in Colnora?"

"He's also the leader of the thieves' guild known as the Black Diamond."

Alric paused to consider this, then paced once more. "Why would he send this to me?"

"The Diamond wants the Imps out of Colnora. I guess with Gaunt gone, Cosmos thought you could make the best use of this information."

Alric stroked his beard thoughtfully. "So who is this Merrick fellow? How do you know him?"

"We were friends when I was a member of the Diamond."

"Excellent. Find him and ask what this is all about."

Royce shook his head. "I have no idea where Merrick is, and we're not on good terms anymore. He won't tell me anything."

Alric sighed. "I don't care what kind of terms you're on.

Find him, resolve your differences, and get me the information I need."

Royce said nothing and Hadrian hesitantly added, "Merrick had Royce sent to Manzant after he mistakenly killed the woman Merrick loved."

Alric stopped pacing and stared. "Manzant Prison? But no one ever leaves Manzant."

"That was the plan. I was happy to disappoint him," Royce replied.

"Nowadays, Royce and Merrick have an unspoken agreement to stay out of each other's way."

"So how can I find out if this Merrick is just boasting, or if there is a real threat to Melengar?"

"Merrick doesn't boast. If he says he can turn the war in the New Empire's favor, he can. I suggest you take this seriously." Royce thought a moment. "If I were you, I'd send someone to deliver this message and then stow away on this ship and see where it leads."

"Fine. Do that, and let me know what you find out."

Royce shook his head. "We're retired. Only a week ago I came here and explained how—"

"Don't be ridiculous! You said to take his threat seriously, which is why I need my best—and that means you."

"Pick someone else," Royce said firmly.

"All right, how much do you want? It's land this time, right? Fine. As it happens, Baron Milborough of Three Fords was killed in battle a few weeks ago. He doesn't have any sons, so I'll grant you his estate if you succeed. Land, title—all of it."

"I don't want land. I don't want anything. *I'm retired.*"

"By Mar, man!" Alric shouted. "The future of the kingdom may depend on this. I'm the king and—"

Hadrian interrupted. "I'll do it."

"What?" Alric and Royce asked together.

"I said I'll go."

⁂

"You can't take this job," Royce told him as they walked back to The Rose and Thorn.

"I have to. If Esrahaddon is dead, Merrick is my only chance to find Gaunt. Do you think he really could have done it?"

"Merrick wouldn't lie to a client about a job."

"But Esrahaddon was a wizard. He's survived a thousand years—I can't imagine he could be murdered by a common killer."

"I just said it was Merrick. He's not common."

As the two walked through an empty Gentry Square, even the bells of Mares Cathedral were silent. Hadrian sighed. "Then I'm on my own in finding the heir now. If I follow the payment to Merrick, I'll be halfway to finding Gaunt."

"Hadrian." Royce placed a hand on his friend's arm, stopping them mid-step. "You're not up to this. You don't know Merrick. Think a minute. If he can kill a wizard, one who could create pillars of fire even without hands, what do you think your chances are? You're a good—no, you're a great—fighter, the best I've ever seen, but Merrick is a genius and he's ruthless. You go after him, he'll know, and he'll kill you."

They were across from Lester Furl's old haberdashery in Artisan Row, the shop that the monk Myron once worked in. The sign of the cavalier hat still hung out front, but the place was empty.

"Listen, I'm not asking you to come. I know you're marrying Gwen. Congratulations on that, by the way. And it's about time, I might add. This isn't your problem. It's mine. It's what

I was born to do. What my father trained me for. Protecting Gaunt, and finding a way to put him on the imperial throne—that's my destiny."

Royce rolled his eyes.

"I know you don't believe that, but I do."

"Gaunt could be dead already, you know? If Merrick killed Esrahaddon, he might have slit Gaunt's throat too."

"I still have to go. By now, even you must see that."

❧

When they reached The Rose and Thorn, Gwen was waiting with anxious eyes. She stood on the porch, her arms crossed, clutching her shawl. The autumn wind brushed her skirt and hair. Behind her, within the darkened interior, patrons talked loudly around the bar.

"It's okay," Hadrian reassured her as they approached. "I'm taking the job, but Royce is staying. With luck I'll be back for—"

"Go with him," Gwen told Royce firmly.

"No—really, Gwen," Hadrian said, "it's nothing—"

"You have to go with him."

"What's wrong?" Royce asked. "I thought we were getting married. Don't you want to?"

Gwen closed her eyes, shaken. Then her hands clenched into fists and she straightened. "You *must* go. Hadrian will be killed if you don't—and then you... you..."

Royce took her in his arms on the steps of the tavern and held her as she began to cry.

"You have to go," Gwen said, her voice muffled by Royce's shoulder. "Nothing will be right if you don't. I can't marry you—I *won't* marry you—if you don't. Tell me you'll go, please, Royce, please..."

Royce gave Hadrian a puzzled glance and whispered, "Okay."

❧

"Here, I made this for you," Gwen said to Royce, holding out a folded bit of knitted cloth. They were in Gwen's room at the top of the stairs of Medford House and he had just finished packing.

He held it up. "A scarf?"

Gwen smiled. "Since I'm going to be married, I thought I should take up knitting. I hear that's what proper wives do for their husbands."

Royce started to laugh but stopped when he saw her expression. "This is important to you, isn't it? You realize you've always been better than all those ladies in the Merchant Quarter. Having a husband doesn't make them special."

"It's not that. It's just...I know you had a less than perfect childhood, and so did I. I want something *better* for our children. I want their lives—our home—to be perfect, or as much as possible for a pair such as us."

"I don't know. I've met dozens of aristocrats who had ideal childhoods and they turned out to be horrors. You, on the other hand, are the best person I've ever met."

She smiled at him. "That's nice, but I highly doubt you would approve of our daughter working here. And would you really want our son living the way you did as a boy? We can raise them right. Just because they grow up in a proper home doesn't mean they will turn out to be *horrors*. You'll be firm, and I'll be loving. You'll spank little Elias when he acts disrespectfully, and I'll kiss his tears and give him cookies."

"Elias? You've named our son already?"

"Would you prefer Sterling? I can't decide between the two.

But the girl's name is not negotiable—it's Mercedes. I've always loved that name.

"I'll sell this house and my other holdings. Combined with the money I banked for you, we'll never want for anything. We can live peaceful, happy, simple lives—I mean, if you want to live like that. Do you?"

He looked into her eyes. "Gwen, if it means being with you, I don't care where we are or what I do."

"Then it's settled." Gwen grinned and her eyes brightened. "It's what I've always dreamed of…the two of us in a small cottage somewhere safe and warm, raising a family."

"You make us sound like squirrels."

"Yes, exactly! A family of squirrels tucked in our cozy nest in some tree trunk while the troubles of the world pass us by." Her lower lip quivered.

Royce pulled her close and held her tight as she buried her face in his shoulder. He stroked her head, feeling her hair linger on his fingertips. For all Gwen's strength and courage, he was forever amazed at how fragile she could be. He had never known anyone like her, and he considered telling Hadrian that he had changed his mind. "Gwen—"

"Don't even think it," she told him. "We can't build a new life until you're done with the old one. Hadrian needs you, and I won't be blamed for his death."

"I could never blame you."

"I couldn't bear it if I felt you hated me, Royce. I'd rather be dead than let that happen. Promise me you'll go. Promise me you'll take care of Hadrian. Promise me you won't despair, and that you'll set things right."

Royce let his head lower until it rested on hers. He stood there, smelling the familiar scent of her hair as his own breathing tightened. "All right, but you have to agree to go to the abbey if things get bad like they did before."

"I will," she said. Her arms tightened around him. "I'm so scared," she whispered.

Surprised, Royce said, "You've always told me you were never frightened when I left on missions."

She looked up at him with tears in her eyes and a guilty expression on her face. "I lied."

CHAPTER 3

THE COURIER

Hadrian stood in the anteroom, waiting in line to deliver the dispatch. The clerk was a short, plump, balding man with ink-stained fingers and a spare quill behind each ear. He sat behind a formidable desk, scribbling on documents and muttering to himself, unconcerned with the growing line of people.

Hadrian and Royce had ridden to Aquesta, and Hadrian had volunteered to deliver the dispatch while Royce waited at a rendezvous with horses at the ready. Although Hadrian had performed jobs for many of the nobility, few here would know him by sight. Riyria had always conducted business anonymously, working through third parties, such as Viscount Albert Winslow, who fronted the organization and preserved their anonymity. He doubted that Saldur would recognize him, but Luis Guy certainly would. As a result, Hadrian kept a clear map of the nearest exit in his head and a count of the imperial guards between him and freedom.

The seat of the New Imperial Empire was busy. Members of the palace staff hurried by, entering and exiting through the many doors around him. They ran or walked as briskly as need dictated and dignity allowed. Some turned his way, but only briefly. As he knew from experience, the degree of attention someone paid others was inversely proportional to his or her status. The lord chamberlain and high chancellor passed without a glance, while the serving steward ventured a long look, and a young page stared curiously for nearly a full minute. Although Hadrian was invisible to those at the highest levels, he was becoming uncomfortable.

This is taking too long.

Two dispatch riders reached the front of the line, quickly dropped off their satchels, and left. A city merchant was next and had come to file a complaint. This took some time, as the clerk asked numerous questions and meticulously recorded each answer.

Next came the young, plain-looking woman directly ahead of Hadrian. "Tell the chamberlain I wish an audience," she said, stepping forward. She wore no makeup, leaving her face dull. Her hair, pulled back and drawn up in a net, did nothing to accentuate her appearance. She was pear-shaped, a feature made even more evident by her gown, which flared at the hips into a great hoop.

"The lord chamberlain is in a meeting with the regents and cannot be disturbed, Your *Ladyship*."

The words were proper, but the tone was disrespectful. The inflection on *ladyship* sounded particularly sarcastic. The woman either did not notice or chose to ignore it.

"He's been ducking me for over a week," the woman said accusingly. "Something must be done. I need material for the empress's new dress."

"My records indicate that quite a large sum was spent on a gown for Modina recently. We're at war and have more important appropriations to make."

"That was for her presentation on the balcony. She can't walk around in that. I'm talking about a day dress."

"It was very expensive nonetheless. You don't want to take food from our soldiers' mouths just so the empress can have another pretty outfit, do you?"

"Another? She has two worn hand-me-downs!"

"Which is more than many of her subjects, isn't it?"

"The empire has spent a fortune remodeling this palace. Surely it won't break the imperial economy to buy a bit of cloth. She doesn't need silk. Linen will do. I'll have the seamstress—"

"I'm quite certain that if the lord chamberlain thought the empress needed another dress, he would provide one. Since he has not, she doesn't need it. Now, *Amilia*," he said brazenly, "if you don't mind, I have work to do."

The woman's shoulders slumped in defeat.

Footsteps echoed from behind them, and the small man's smug expression faltered. Hadrian turned and saw the farm girl he had once known as Thrace walking up, flanked by an armed guard. Her dress was faded and frayed, just as Amilia had said, but the young woman stood tall, straight, and unabashed. She motioned to the guard to wait as she moved to the front of the line to face the clerk.

"Lady Amilia speaks with my authority. Please do as she has requested," Thrace said.

The clerk looked confused. His bright eyes flickered nervously between the two.

Thrace continued, "I'm sure you do not wish to refuse an order from your empress, do you?"

The scribe lowered his voice, but his irritation still carried as he addressed Amilia. "If you think I'm going to kneel before your trained dog, you're mistaken. She's as insane as rumored. I'm not as ignorant as the castle staff, and I'm not going to be toyed with by common trash. Get out of here, both of you. I don't have time for foolishness this morning."

Amilia cringed openly, but Thrace did not waver. "Tell me, Quail, do you think the palace guards share your opinions of me?" She looked back at the soldier. "If I were to call him over and accuse you of... let's see... being a traitor, and then... let me think... order him to execute you right here, what do you think he would do?"

The clerk looked suspiciously at Thrace, as if trying to see behind a mask. "You wouldn't dare," he said, his eyes shifting between the two women.

"No? Why not?" Thrace replied. "You just said yourself that I'm insane. There's no telling what I might do, or why. From now on, you'll treat Lady Amilia with respect and obey her orders as if they come from the highest authority. Do you understand?"

The clerk nodded slowly.

As Thrace turned to leave, she caught sight of Hadrian and stopped as if she had run into an invisible wall. Her eyes locked on his and she staggered a step and stood, wavering.

Amilia reached out to support her. "Modina, what's wrong?"

Thrace said nothing. She continued to stare at him—her eyes filling with tears, her lips trembling.

The door to the main office opened.

"I don't want to hear another word about it!" Ethelred thundered as he, Saldur, and Archibald Ballentyne entered the anteroom together. Hadrian looked toward the hall window, estimating the number of steps it would take to reach it.

The old cleric focused on Thrace. "What's going on here?"

"I'm taking Her Eminence back to her room," Amilia replied. "I don't think she's feeling well."

"They were requesting material for a new dress," the clerk announced with an accusing tone.

"Well, obviously she needs one. Why is she still wearing that rag?" Saldur asked.

"The lord chamberlain refuses—"

"What do you need him for?" Saldur scowled. "Just tell the clerk to order what you require. You don't need to pester Bernard with such trivialities."

"Thank you, Your Grace," Amilia said, placing one arm around Thrace's waist and supporting her elbow with the other as she gently led her away. Thrace's eyes never left Hadrian, her head turning over her shoulder as they departed.

Saldur followed her gaze and looked curiously at Hadrian. "You look familiar," he said, taking a step toward him.

"Courier," Hadrian said, his heart racing. He bowed and held up the message like a shield.

"He's probably been here a dozen times, Sauly." Ethelred snatched the folded parchment and eyed it. "This is from Merrick!"

All three lost interest in Hadrian as Ethelred unfolded the letter.

"Your Lordships." Hadrian bowed, then turned and quickly walked away, passing Amilia and Thrace. With each step, he felt her stare upon his back, until he turned the corner, placing him out of her sight.

⁂

"Any problems?" Royce asked when Hadrian met him outside.

"Almost. I saw Thrace," Hadrian said as they walked. "She doesn't look good. She's thin—real thin—and pale. She was begging for clothes from some sniveling little clerk."

Royce looked back, concerned. "Did she recognize you?"

Hadrian nodded. "But she didn't say anything. She just stared."

"I guess if she was planning to arrest us, she'd have done it by now," Royce said.

"Arrest us? This is Thrace we're talking about, for Maribor's sake."

"They've had her for more than a year—she's Empress Modina now."

"Yeah, but..."

"What?"

"I don't know," Hadrian said, remembering the look on Thrace's face. "She doesn't look well. I'm not sure what's going on in the palace, but it's not good. And I promised her father I'd look out for her."

Royce shook his head in frustration. "Can we focus on one rescue at a time? For a man in retirement, you're really busy. Besides, Theron's idea of success was to get his eldest son a cooper's shop. I think he *might* settle for his daughter being crowned empress. Now, let's get rid of these horses and make our way down to the wharf. We need to find the *Emerald Storm*."

Chapter 4

The Race

While not as large or as wealthy as Colnora, the imperial capital of Aquesta was the most powerful city in Avryn. The palace dated back to before the age of Glenmorgan and had originally been a governor's residence in the ancient days of the Novronian Empire. Scholars pointed to the gray rock of the castle's foundation with pride and boasted about how imperial engineers from Percepliquis had laid it. Here, at Highcourt Fields, great tournaments were held each Wintertide. The best knights from all of Apeladorn arrived to compete in jousting, fencing, and other contests of skill. These weeklong events included an ongoing feast for the nobles and provided healthy revenue for the merchants, who showed their wares along the streets. The city became a carnival of sights and sounds that attracted visitors for hundreds of miles.

Much of Aquesta's economic success came from possessing the largest and busiest saltwater port in Avryn. The docks were awash with all manner of sailing watercraft. Brigs, trawlers, grain ships, merchant vessels, and warships all anchored in its harbor. To the south lay the massive shipyard, along with rope, net, and sail manufacturers. The northern end of the bay held the wharf and its fish houses, livestock pens, lumberyards, and tar boilers. All the industries of the sea and seafaring were represented.

"Which one is the *Emerald Storm*?" Hadrian asked, looking at the forest of masts and rigging that lined the docks.

"Let's try asking at the information office." Royce hooked his thumb at a tavern perched on the edge of the dock. The wooden walls were bleached white with salt, and the clapboards were warped like ocean waves. The door hung askew off leather hinges, and above it, a weathered sign in the shape of a fish announced THE SALTY MACKEREL.

The tavern had few windows, leaving the interior dim and smoky. Each tiny table had a melted candle, and a weak fire smoldered in a round brick hearth in the center of the room. Men, dressed in loose trousers, long checkered shirts, and wide-brimmed hats with glossy tops, packed the place. Many sat with pipes in their mouths and their feet on tables. Some stood leaning against posts. All heads turned when Hadrian and Royce entered, and Hadrian realized just how much they stood out in their tunics and cloaks.

"Hello." Hadrian smiled as he struggled to close the door. The wind whistled through and snuffed out the three candles nearest them. "Sorry, could use some better hinges."

"Iron hinges rust overnight here," the bartender said. The thin, crooked man wiped the counter with one hand while gathering empty mugs in the other. "What do you two want?"

"Looking for the *Emerald Storm*." Royce spoke up.

Neither took more than a step inside. None of the haggard faces looked friendly, and Hadrian liked the comfort of a nearby exit.

"Whatcha want with it?" another man asked.

"We heard it was a good ship, and we were wondering if there are any openings for sailors."

This brought a riotous round of laughter.

"And where be these sailors who be looking fer a job?" another voice bellowed from within the murky haze. "Certainly not two sand crabs like you."

More laughter.

"So what you're saying is you don't know anything about the *Emerald Storm*. Is that right?" Royce returned in a cutting tone that quieted the room.

"The *Storm* is an imperial ship, lad," the crooked man told them, "and it's all pressed up. They're only taking seasoned salts now—if there's any room left at all."

"If yer looking fer work, the fishery always needs gutters. That's about as close to seafaring work as is likely for you two."

Once more the room filled with boisterous laughter.

Hadrian looked at Royce, who shoved the door open and, with a scowl, stepped outside. "Thanks for the advice," Hadrian told everyone before following his partner.

They sat on the Mackerel's steps, staring at the line of ships across the street. Spires of wood draped with tethered cloth looked like ladies getting dressed for a ball. Hadrian wondered if that was why they always referred to ships as women.

"What now?" he asked softly.

Royce sat hunched with his chin on his hands. "Thinking," was all he said.

Behind them the door scraped open, and the first thing Hadrian noticed was a wide-brimmed hat with one side pinned up by a lavish blue plume.

The face beneath the hat was familiar, and Royce recognized the man immediately. "Wyatt Deminthal."

Wyatt hesitated as he locked eyes with Royce. He stood with one foot still inside. He did not look surprised to see them, but seemed to be merely questioning the wisdom of advancing, like a child who approached a dog that had unexpectedly growled. For a heartbeat no one said a word, and then Wyatt gritted his teeth and pulled the door shut behind him.

"I can get you on the *Storm*," he said quickly.

Royce narrowed his eyes. "How?"

"I'm the helmsman. They're short a cook and can always use another topman. She's ready to sail as soon as a shipment from the palace arrives."

"Why?"

Wyatt swallowed, and his hand absently drifted to his throat. "I know you saw me. You're here to collect, but I don't have the money I owe. Setting you up in Medford was nothing personal. We were starving, and Trumbul paid gold. I didn't know they were going to arrest you for the king's murder. I was just hiring you to steal the sword—that's all. A hundred gold tenents is a lot of money. And honestly—well, I've never saved that much in my life and I doubt I ever will."

"So you think getting us on the *Emerald Storm* is worth a hundred gold?"

Wyatt licked his lips, his eyes darting back and forth between them. "I don't know... is it?"

❧

Royce and Hadrian crossed the busy street, dodging carts, and stepped onto weathered decking suspended by ropes. The boards bobbed and weaved beneath their feet. The two were dressed in loose-fitting duck-trousers, oversized linen shirts, tarpaulin hats with a bit of ribbon, and neckerchiefs tied in some arcane way that Wyatt had fussed with for some time to get right. They both carried large, heavy cloth seabags, in which they stowed their old clothes and Hadrian hid his three swords. Being unarmed left him feeling off balance and naked.

They snaked through the crowded dock, following Wyatt's directions to the end of the pier. The *Emerald Storm* was a smart-looking, freshly painted ship, with three masts, four decks, and the figurehead of a golden winged woman ornamenting the bow. Its sails were furled, and green pennants flew from each mast. A small army of men hoisted bags of flour and barrels of salted pork onto the deck, where the crew stowed the supplies. Shouts came from what appeared to be an officer, who directed the work, and another man, who enforced the orders with a stout rattan cane. Two imperial soldiers guarded the ramp.

"Do you have business here?" one asked at their approach.

"Yeah," Hadrian replied with an innocent, hopeful tone. "We're looking for work. Heard this ship was short on hands. We were told to speak with Mr. Temple."

"What's this here?" asked a short, heavyset man with threadbare clothes, bushy eyebrows, and a gruff voice worn to gravel from years of yelling in the salt air. "I'm Temple."

"Word is you're looking to put on a cook," Hadrian said pleasantly.

"We are."

"Well then, this is your lucky day."

"Ah-huh." Temple nodded with a sour look.

"And my friend here is an able—ah—topman."

"Oh, he is, is he?" Temple eyed Royce. "We have openings, but only for *experienced* sailors. Normally, I'd be happy to take on green men, but we can't afford any more landlubbers on this trip."

"But we are sailors—served on the *Endeavor*."

"Are you, now?" the ship's master asked skeptically. "Let me see yer hands."

The master examined Hadrian's palms, looking over the various calluses and rough places while grunting occasionally.

"You must have spent most of your time in the galley. You've not done any serious rope work." He examined Royce's hands and raised an eyebrow at him. "Have you *ever* been on a ship before? It's certain you've never handled a sheet or a capstan."

"Royce here is a—you know—" Hadrian pointed up at the ship's rigging. "The guy who goes up there."

The master shook his head and laughed. "If you two are seamen, then I'm the Prince of Percepliquis!"

"Oh, but they are, Mr. Temple," a voice declared. Wyatt exited the forecastle and came jogging toward them. A bright white shirt offset his tawny skin and black hair. "I know these men, old mates of mine. The little one is Royce Melborn, as fine a topman as they come. And the big one is, ah..."

"Hadrian." Royce spoke up.

"Right, of course. Hadrian's a fine cook—he is, Mr. Temple."

Temple pointed toward Royce. "This one's a topman? Are you joking, Wyatt?"

"No, sir, he's one of the best."

Temple looked unconvinced.

"You can have him prove it to you, sir," Hadrian offered. "You could have him race your best up the ropes."

"You mean up the *shrouds*," Wyatt said, correcting him.

"Yeah."

"You mean *aye*."

Hadrian sighed and gave up.

The master did not notice as he had been focused on Royce. He sized him up, then shouted, "Derning!" His strong, raspy voice carried well against the ocean wind. Immediately, a tall, thin fellow with leathery skin jogged over.

"Aye, sir?" he responded respectfully.

"This fellow says he can beat you in a race to loose the topsail and back. What do you think?"

"I think he's mistaken, sir."

"Well, we'll find out." The master turned back to Royce. "I don't actually expect you to beat Derning. Jacob here is one of the best topmen I've seen, but if you put in a good showing, the two of you will have jobs aboard. If it turns out you're wasting my time, well, you'll be swimming back. Derning, you take starboard. Royce, you have port. We'll begin after Lieutenant Bishop gives permission for us to get under way."

Mr. Temple moved toward the quarterdeck and Wyatt slid down the stair rail to Royce's side. "Remember what I taught you last night... and what Temple said. You don't need to beat Derning."

Hadrian clapped Royce on the back, grinning. "So the idea is to just free the sail and get back down alive."

Royce nodded and looked apprehensively up at the towering mast before him.

"Not afraid of heights, I hope." Wyatt grinned.

"All right, gentlemen!" Mr. Temple shouted, addressing the crew from his new position on the quarterdeck. "We're having a contest." He explained the details to the crew as Royce and Jacob moved to the base of the mainsail. Royce looked up with a grimace that drew laughter from the rest.

"Seriously, he isn't afraid of heights, is he?" Wyatt asked, looking concerned. "I mean, it looks scary, and well—okay, it is the first few times you go aloft, but it really isn't that hard if you're careful and can handle heights."

Hadrian grinned at Wyatt, but all he said was, "I think you're going to like this."

An officer appeared on the quarterdeck and stood beside the master. "You may set sail, Mr. Temple."

The master turned to the main deck and roared, "Loose the topsail!"

Royce appeared caught by surprise, not realizing this was

the order to begin the competition. As a result, Jacob got the jump on him, racing up the ratlines like a monkey. Royce turned but did not begin climbing. Instead, he watched Jacob's ascent for several seconds. The majority of the crew rooted for Jacob, but a few, perhaps those who had heard they would win a ship's cook if the stranger won, urged Royce to get climbing and called to him like a dog: "Go on, boy! Climb, you damn fool!" Some laughed, and a few made disparaging comments about his mother.

Royce finally seemed to work something out in his head and leapt to the task. He sprang, clearing the deck by several feet, and began to run, rather than climb, up the ratlines. It appeared as if Royce was defying gravity as he pumped his legs up the netting, showing no more difficulty than if he were running up a staircase. He had nearly caught up to Jacob by the time he reached the futtock shrouds. Here the webbing extended away from the mast, reaching toward the small wooden platform known as the masthead. Both men were forced to hang upside down using the ratlines, and Royce lost momentum without the ability to go no-handed.

Jacob swung around the masthead and jumped to the topmast shroud, where he ascended rapidly once more in monkey form. By the time Royce cleared the masthead, he was well behind Derning. He made up time when he could once again advance without crawling inverted. They reached the yard together and both ran out along the top of the narrow beam like circus performers. Seeing them balance a hundred feet above the deck drew gasps from some of the crew, who gaped in amazement. Royce stopped, pivoting to watch his opponent. Derning threw himself down across the yard, lying on his belly. He reached below for the gaskets to free the buntlines. Royce quickly imitated him, and together they worked their way across the arm. As they did, the sail came free, revealing its bright white face and dark green crown. It spilled down, whipping in the wind. Royce and Jacob lifted themselves back to their feet and moved to the end of the beam. They each grabbed the brace, the rope connected to the far end of the yardarm, and slid to the deck with the cheers of the crew in their ears. The two touched down together.

Mr. Temple shouted to restore order of the unruly crew. It did not matter who had won. The skillful display by both men had been impressive enough to earn their approval. Even Hadrian found himself clapping, and he noticed Wyatt was staring with his mouth open. Temple nodded at Hadrian and Wyatt.

"Stand by at the capstan!" Lieutenant Bishop shouted, returning order. "Loose the heads'ls, hands aloft, loose the tops'ls fore and aft!"

The crew scattered to their duties. A ring of men surrounded the wooden spoke wheel of the capstan, ready to raise the anchor. Wyatt moved quickly toward the ship's helm while the rest, Jacob included, climbed the shrouds of the three masts.

"And what are you two waiting for?" Mr. Temple asked after Hadrian had joined Royce. "You heard the lieutenant—get those sails loosed. Hadrian, take station at the capstan."

As they trotted to their duties, Mr. Temple gestured in Royce's direction and remarked to Wyatt, "No wonder he doesn't have rough hands. He doesn't use them!"

The ship's captain appeared on the quarterdeck. He stood beside the lieutenant, his hands clasped behind his back, chest thrust out, and chin set against the salty wind that tugged at the edges of his uniform. Of slightly less than average height, he seemed the opposite of the lieutenant. While Bishop was tall and thin, the captain was short and plump, with a double chin and long hanging cheeks, which quickly flushed red with the wind. He watched the progress of the crew and then nodded to his first officer.

"Take her out, Mr. Bishop."

"Raise anchor!" the lieutenant bellowed. "Wheel hard over!"

Hadrian found a place among those at the capstan and pushed against the wooden spokes, rotating the large spool that lifted the anchor from the bottom of the harbor. With the anchor broken out, the wheel hard over, and the forecastle hands drawing at the headsail sheets, the *Emerald Storm* brought its bow around. As it gained steerage, it moved away from the dock and into the clear of the main channel, and the rigging crew dropped the remaining sails. The great canvases quivered and flapped, snapping in the wind like three violent white beasts.

"Hands to the braces!" Mr. Temple barked, and the men took hold of the ropes, pulling the yards around until they caught the wind. The sails plumed full as the sea breeze stretched them taut. Hadrian could feel the deck lurch beneath his feet as the *Emerald Storm* slipped forward through the water, rudder balanced against sail pressure.

They traveled down the coast, passing farmers and workers, who paused briefly to look at the handsome vessel flying by. At the helm, Wyatt spun the wheel, steering steadily out to sea. The men on the braces trimmed the yards so not a sail fluttered, sending the ship dashing through the waves as it raced from shore.

"Course sou'west by south, sir," Wyatt said, updating Temple, who repeated the statement to the lieutenant, who repeated it to the captain, who in turn nodded his approval.

The men at the capstan dispersed, leaving Hadrian looking around for something to do. Royce descended to the deck beside him, neither one certain of his duty now that the ship was under way. It did not matter much, as the lieutenant, the captain, and Temple were all busy on the quarterdeck. The other hands moved casually now, cleaning up the rigging, finishing the job of stowing the supplies, and generally settling in.

"Why didn't we ever consider sailing as a profession?" Hadrian asked Royce as he moved to the side and faced the wind. He took a deep, satisfying breath and smiled. "This is nice. A lot better than a sweaty, fly-plagued horse—and look at the land go by! How fast do you think we're going?"

"The fact that we're trapped here, with no chance of retreat except into the ocean, doesn't bother you?"

Hadrian glanced over the side at the heaving waves. "Well, not until now. Why do you always have to ruin everything? Couldn't you let me enjoy the moment?"

"You know me, just trying to keep things in perspective."

"Our course is south. Any clue where we might be going?"

Royce shook his head. "It only means we aren't invading Melengar, but we could be headed just about anywhere else." Someone arriving deck side caught his attention. "Who's this now?"

A man in red and black appeared from below and climbed the stair to the quarterdeck. He stood out from the rest of the crew by virtue of his pale skin and silken vestments, which were far too elegant for the setting and whipped about like streamers at a fair. He moved hunched over; his slumped shoulders reminded Hadrian of a crow shuffling along a branch. He sported a mustache and short goatee. His dark hair, combed back, emphasized a dramatically receding hairline.

"Broken-crown crest," Hadrian noted. "Seret."

"Red cassock," Royce added. "Sentinel."

"At least he's not Luis Guy. It'd be pretty hard to hide on a ship this size."

"If it was Guy"—Royce smiled wickedly—"we wouldn't need to hide."

Hadrian noticed Royce glance over the side of the ship at the water, which foamed and churned as it rushed past.

"If a sentinel is on board," Royce continued, "we can assume there are seret as well. They never travel alone."

"Maybe below."

"Maybe disguised in the crew," Royce cautioned.

To starboard, a sailor dropped his burden on the deck and wiped the sweat from his brow with a rag. Noticing them standing idle, he walked over.

"Yer good," he said to Royce. "No man's beaten Jacob aloft before."

The sailor was tan and thin, with a tattoo of a woman on his forearm and a ring of silver in his ear.

"I didn't beat him. We landed together," Royce said, correcting him.

"Aye, clever that. My name's Grady. What do they call you?"

"Royce, and this is Hadrian."

"Oh yeah, the cook." Grady gave Hadrian a nod, and then returned his attention. "Royce, huh? I'm surprised I haven't heard yer name before. With skills like you got, I woulda figured you'd be famous. What ships have you served on?"

"None around these waters," Royce replied.

Grady looked at him curiously. "Where, then? The Sound? Dagastan? The Sharon? Try me, I've been around a few places myself."

"Sorry, I'm really bad at remembering names."

Grady's eyebrows rose. "You don't remember the names of the ships you served on?"

"I would prefer not to discuss them."

"Aye, consider the subject closed." He looked at Hadrian. "You were with him, then?"

"We've worked together for some time."

Grady nodded. "Just forget I said anything. I won't be getting in the way. You can bank money on Grady's word, too." The man winked, then walked away, glancing back over his shoulder at them a few times as he went off, grinning.

"Seems like a nice sort," Hadrian said. "Strange and confusing, but nice. You think he knows why we're here?"

"Wish he did," Royce replied, watching Grady resume his work. "Then he could tell us. Still, I've found that when hunting Merrick, stranger things have been known to happen. One thing's for certain—this trip is going to be interesting."

CHAPTER 5

BROKEN SILENCE

Although it was early, Nimbus was already waiting outside the closed door of Amilia's office with armloads of parchments. He smiled brightly at her approach. "Good morning, Your Ladyship," he greeted her with as much of a bow as he could manage without spilling his burden. "Beautiful day, is it not?"

Amilia grunted in reply. She was not a morning person, and that day's agenda included a meeting with Regent Saldur. If anything was likely to ruin a day, that would do it. She opened her office door with a key kept on a chain around her neck. The office was a reward for the successful presentation of the empress nearly a month before.

Modina had been near death when Saldur had appointed Amilia imperial secretary to the empress. At that time, the young ruler had not spoken a word, was dangerously thin, and had an unwavering expression, which was never more than a blank stare. Amilia had provided her with better living conditions and worked hard to get her to eat. After several months, the girl had begun to improve. Modina had managed to memorize a short speech for the day of her presentation but abandoned the prepared text and publicly singled out Amilia, proclaiming her a hero.

No one had been more shocked than Amilia, but Saldur thought she had been responsible. Rather than exploding in anger, he congratulated her. Since that day, his attitude toward Amilia had changed—as if she had bought admission into the exclusive club of the deviously ambitious. In his eyes, she had not only been capable of manipulating the mentally unbalanced ruler, but willing to do so as well. This raised opinion of her had been followed by additional responsibilities and a new title: Chief Imperial Secretary to the Empress.

She took her directions from Saldur as Modina remained locked in the dark recesses of her madness. One of her new responsibilities was reading and replying to mail addressed to the empress. Saldur gave her the task as soon as he discovered she could read and write. Amilia also received the responsibility of being the empress's official gatekeeper. She decided who could, and who could not, have an audience with Modina. Normally a position of extreme power, hers was just a farce, because absolutely no one *ever* saw Modina.

Despite Amilia's grandiose new title, her office was a small chamber with nothing but an old desk and a pair of bookshelves. The room was cold, damp, and sparse—but it was hers. She was filled with pride each morning when she sat behind the desk, and pride was something Amilia was unaccustomed to.

"Are those more letters?" Amilia asked.

"Yes, I am afraid so," Nimbus replied. "Where would you like them?"

"Just drop them on the pile with the others. I can see now why Saldur gave me this job."

"It is a very prestigious task," Nimbus assured her. "You are the de facto voice of the New Empire as it relates to the people. What you write is taken as the word of the empress, and thus the voice of a god incarnate."

"So you're saying I'm the voice of god now?"

Nimbus smiled thoughtfully. "In a manner of speaking—yes."

"You have a crazy way of seeing things, Nimbus. You really do."

He was always able to cheer her up. His outlandishly colored clothes and silly powdered wig made her smile on even the bleakest of days. Moreover, the odd little courtier had a bizarre manner of finding joy in everything, blind to the inevitable disaster that Amilia knew lurked at every turn.

Nimbus deposited the letters in the bin beside Amilia's desk, then fished out a tablet and looked it over briefly before speaking. "You have a meeting this morning with Lady Rashambeau, Baroness Fargal, and Countess Ridell. They have insisted on speaking to you personally about their failed petitions to have a private audience with Her Supreme Eminence. You also have a dedication to make on behalf of the empress at the new memorial in Capital Square. That is at noon. Also, the material has arrived, but you still need to get specifications to the seamstress for the new dress. And, of course, you have a meeting this afternoon with Regent Saldur."

"Any idea yet what he wants to see me about?"

Nimbus shook his head.

Amilia slumped in her chair. She was certain Saldur's appointment had to do with Modina's berating of the clerk the previous day. She had no idea how to explain the empress's actions. That had been the only time since her speech that Modina had uttered a single word.

"Would you like me to help you answer those?" Nimbus asked with a sympathetic smile.

"No, I'll do it. Can't have both of us playing god, now can we? Besides, you have your own work. Tell the seamstress to meet me in Modina's chambers in four hours. That should give me time to reduce this pile some. Reschedule the ladies of the court meeting to just before noon."

"But you have the dedication at noon."

"Exactly."

"Excellent planning," Nimbus said, praising her. "Is there anything else I can do for you before I get to work?"

Amilia shook her head. Nimbus bowed and left.

The pile beside her got higher each day. She plucked a letter from the top and started working. While not a difficult job, the task was repetitious and boring, as she said the same thing in each reply.

The office of the empress regrets to inform you that Her Most Serene and Royal Grand Imperial Eminence, Empress Modina Novronian, will not be able to receive you due to time constraints caused by important and pressing matters of state.

She had replied to only seven of the letters when there was a soft knock at the office door. A maid hesitantly popped her head inside, the new girl. She had started only the day before, and she worked quietly, which Amilia appreciated. Amilia nodded an invitation, and the maid wordlessly slipped inside with her bucket, mop, and cleaning tools, taking great pains not to bang them against the door.

Amilia recalled her own days as a servant in the castle. As a kitchen worker, she had rarely cleaned rooms but occasionally had to fill in for a sick chambermaid. She used to loathe working in a room with a noble present. It always made her self-conscious and frightened. She could never tell what they might do. One minute they might seem friendly. The next they could be calling for you to be whipped. Amilia had never understood how they could be so capricious and cruel.

She watched the girl set about her work. The maid was on

her hands and knees, scrubbing the floor with a brush, the skirt of her uniform soaked with soapy water. Amilia had a stack of inquiries to attend to, but the maid distracted her. She felt guilty not acknowledging the girl's presence. It felt rude.

I should talk to her. Even as Amilia thought this, she knew it would be a mistake. This new girl saw her as a noble, the chief imperial secretary to the empress, and would be terrified if Amilia so much as offered a *good morning.*

Perhaps a few years older than Amilia, the girl was slender and pretty, although little could be determined, given her attire. She wore a loose-fitting dress with a canvas apron, her figure hidden, a mystery lost beneath the folds. All serving girls adopted the style except the foolish or ambitious. When you worked in the halls of those who took whatever they wanted, it was best to avoid notice.

Amilia tried to decide if the girl was married. After Modina's speech, the ban on servants leaving the castle had been lifted, and it was possible that the maid had a family in the city. She wondered if she went home to them each night, or, like Amilia, she had left everything, and everyone, to live in the castle. She likely had several children; pretty peasant girls married young.

Amilia chided herself for watching the maid instead of working, but something about the girl kept her attention. The way she moved and how she held her head seemed out of place. She watched her dab the brush in the water and stroke the floor, moving the brush from side to side like a painter. She spread water around but did little to free the dirt from the surface. Edith Mon would whip her for that. The headmistress was a cruel taskmaster. Amilia had found herself on the wrong end of her belt on a number of occasions for lesser infractions. For that reason alone, Amilia felt sorry for the poor girl. She knew all too well what she faced.

"Are they treating you well here?" Amilia found herself asking, despite her determination to remain silent.

The girl looked up and glanced around the room.

"Yes, you," Amilia assured her.

"Yes, milady," the maid replied, looking up.

She's looking right at me, Amilia thought, stunned. Even with her title, and a rank equivalent to baroness, Amilia still had a hard time returning the stare of even the lowest-ranking nobles, but this girl was looking right at her.

"You can tell me if they aren't. I know what it's like to—" She stopped, realizing the maid would not believe her. "I understand new servants can be picked on and belittled by the others."

"I'm getting along fine, milady," she said.

Amilia smiled, trying to set her at ease. "I didn't mean to suggest you weren't. I'm very pleased with you. I just know it can be hard sometimes when you start out in a new place. I want you to know that I can help if you're having trouble."

"Thank you," she said, but Amilia heard the suspicion in her voice.

Having a noble offer to help with bullying peers was probably a shock to the girl. If it had been her, Amilia would have thought it a trap of some kind, a test perhaps to see if she would speak ill of others. If she admitted to problems, the noble might have her removed from the palace. Under no circumstances would Amilia have admitted anything to a noble, no matter how kindly the woman might have presented herself.

Amilia instantly felt foolish. There was a division between nobles and commoners, and for good or ill, she was now on the other side. The conditioning that separated the two was far too entrenched for her to wipe away. She decided to stop tormenting the poor girl and return to her work. Just then, however, the maid put down the scrub brush and stood.

"You're Lady Amilia, is that right?"

"Yes," she replied, surprised at the sudden forwardness.

"You're the chief secretary to the empress?"

"How well informed you are. It's good that you're learning your way around. It took me quite some time to figure out—"

"How is she?"

Amilia hesitated. Interrupting was very inappropriate, and it was incredibly bold to inquire so bluntly about Her Eminence. Amilia was touched, however, by her concern for the welfare of Modina. Perhaps this girl was unaccustomed to interacting with the gentry. She was likely from some isolated village that had never seen a visiting noble. The unnerving way she held Amilia's stare revealed she had no experience with proper social etiquette. Edith Mon would waste no time beating those lessons into her.

"She's fine," Amilia replied. Then, as a matter of habit, she added, "She was ill, and still is, but getting better every day."

"I never see her," the maid went on. "I've seen you, the chancellor, the regents, and the lord chamberlain, but I never see her in the halls or at the banquet table."

"She guards her privacy. You have to understand that everyone wants time with the empress."

"I guess she gets around using secret passages?"

"Secret passages?" Amilia chuckled at the imagination of this girl. "No, she doesn't use secret passages."

"But I heard this palace is very old and filled with hidden stairs and corridors that lead to all kinds of secret places. Is that true?"

"I don't know anything about that," Amilia replied. "What got this into your head?"

The maid immediately put a hand over her mouth in embarrassment. Her eyes dropped to the floor in submission. "Forgive me, milady. I didn't mean to be so bold. I'll get back to my work now."

"That's all right," Amilia replied as the maid dunked her brush again. "What's your name, dear?"

"Ella, milady," the maid replied softly without pausing or looking up.

"Well, Ella, if you have problems or other questions, you have permission to speak to me."

"Thank you, milady. That is very kind of you."

Amilia returned to her own work and left the maid to hers. In a short time, the servant finished and gathered her things to leave.

"Goodbye, Ella," Amilia offered.

The maid smiled at the mention of her name and nodded appreciatively. As she walked out, Amilia glanced at her hands, which gripped the bucket handle and the mop, and was surprised to see long fingernails on them. Ella noticed her glance, shifted her grip to cover her nails, and promptly left the chamber.

Amilia stared after her awhile, wondering how a working girl could manage to grow nails as nice as hers. She put the thought out of her mind and returned to her letters.

"You realize they're going to get wise," Amilia said after the seamstress had finished taking Modina's measurements and left the chamber.

The chief secretary moved around the empress's bedroom, straightening up. Modina sat beneath the narrow window, in the only patch of sunshine entering the room. This was where Amilia found her most often. She would sit there for hours, just staring outside, watching clouds and birds. It broke Amilia's heart a little each time she saw her longing for a world barred to her.

The empress showed no response to Amilia's comment. Her lucidity from the day before had vanished. The empress heard her, though. She was quite certain of that now.

"They aren't stupid," she went on as she fluffed a pillow. "After your speech and that incident with the clerk yesterday, I think it's only a matter of time. You would have been wiser to stay in your room and let me handle it."

"He wasn't going to listen to you." The empress spoke.

Amilia dropped the pillow.

Turning as casually as she could, she stole a glance over her shoulder to see Modina still looking out the window with her traditional vague and distant expression. Amilia slowly picked up the pillow and resumed her straightening. Then she ventured, "It might have taken a little time, but I'm certain I could have persuaded him to provide us with the material."

Amilia waited, holding her breath, listening.

Silence.

Just when she was certain it had been only one of her rare outbursts of coherency, Modina spoke again. "He never would have given in to you. You're scared of him, and he knows that."

"And you aren't?"

Again silence. Amilia waited.

"I'm not afraid of anything anymore," the empress finally replied, her voice distant and thin.

"Maybe not afraid, but it would bother you if they took the window away."

"Yes," Modina said simply.

Amilia watched as the empress closed her eyes and turned her face full into the light of the sun.

"If Saldur discovers your masquerade—if he thinks you've been just acting insane and misleading the regents for over a year—it might frighten him into locking you up where you can't do any harm. They could put you in a dark hole somewhere and leave you there."

"I know," Modina said, her eyes still closed and head tilted upward. Immersed in the daylight, she appeared almost to glow. "But I won't let them hurt you."

The words took a moment to register with Amilia. She had heard them clearly enough, but their meaning came so unexpectedly that she sat on the bed without realizing it. As she thought back, it should have been obvious, but not until that moment did she realize what Modina had done. The empress's speech had been for Amilia's benefit—to ensure that Ethelred and Saldur could not have her removed or killed. Few people had ever gone out of their way for Amilia. The concept that Modina—the crazy empress—had risked herself in this way was unimaginable. Such an event was as likely as the wind changing direction to suit her, or the sun asking her permission to shine.

"Thank you," was all she could think to say. For the first time she felt awkward in Modina's presence. "I'm going to go now."

She headed for the door. As her hand touched the latch, Modina spoke again.

"It isn't completely an act, you know."

Waiting inside the regent's office, Amilia realized she had not heard a word in her meeting with the ladies or during the dedication later that morning. Dumbfounded by her conversation with Modina—by the mere fact that she had actually had a conversation with Modina—she registered little else. Her distraction, however, vanished the instant Saldur arrived.

The regent appeared imposing, as always, in his elegant

robe and cape of purple and black. His white hair and lined face lent him a grandfatherly appearance, but his eyes held no warmth.

"Afternoon, Amilia," he said, walking past her and taking a seat at his desk. The regent's office was dramatically opulent. Ten times larger than hers, it featured an elegant decor. A fine patterned rug covered the polished hardwood, and numerous end tables flanked couches and armchairs. On one table sat an elaborately carved chess set. The fireplace was an impressively wide hearth of finely chiseled marble. There were decanters of spirits on the shelves, along with thick books. Religious-themed paintings lined the spaces between the bookcases and windows. One illustrated the familiar scene of Maribor anointing Novron. The immense desk, behind which Saldur sat, was a dark mahogany polished to a fine luster and adorned with a bouquet of fresh flowers. The entire office was perfumed with the heady scent of incense, the kind Amilia had smelled only once before, when visiting a cathedral.

"Your Grace," Amilia replied respectfully.

"Sit down, my dear," Saldur said.

Amilia found a chair and mechanically sat. Every muscle in her body was tense. She wished Modina had not spoken to her that morning—then she could honestly plead ignorance. Amilia was no good at lying and had no idea how she should respond to Saldur's interrogation in order to bring the least amount of punishment to her and the empress. She was still debating what she might say when Saldur spoke.

"I've some news for you," he said, folding his hands on the surface of the desk and leaning forward. "It won't be public for several weeks, but you need to know now so you can begin preparations. I want you to keep this to yourself until I announce it, do you understand?"

Amilia nodded as if she understood.

"In almost four months, during the Wintertide celebrations, Modina will marry Regent Ethelred. I don't think I need to impress upon you the importance of this occasion. The Patriarch himself is personally coming to perform the ceremony. All eyes will be on this palace...and on the empress."

Amilia said nothing and barely managed another shallow nod.

"It's your charge to ensure that nothing embarrassing occurs. I've been very pleased with your work to date, and as a result I'm giving you an opportunity to excel further. I'm putting *you* in charge of arranging the ceremony. It'll be your responsibility to develop a guest list and prepare invitations. Go to the lord chamberlain for help with that. You'll also need to coordinate with the palace cooks for meals. I understand you have a good relationship with the head cook?"

Once more she nodded.

"Wonderful. There should be decorations, entertainment—music certainly, and perhaps a magician or a troupe of acrobats. The ceremony will take place here, in the great hall. That should make things a bit easier for you. You'll also need to have a wedding dress made—one worthy of the empress." Seeing the tension on her face, Saldur added, "Relax, Amilia, this time you only need to get her to say two words...*I do*."

CHAPTER 6

THE EMERALD STORM

As the ship lurched once more, Hadrian stumbled and nearly hit his head on the overhead beam. It would have been his third time that day. The lower decks of the *Emerald Storm* provided meager headroom and precious little light. An obstacle course of sea chests, ditty bags, crude wooden benches, tables that swung from ropes, and close to one hundred thirty men was crammed into the berth deck. Hadrian made his way aft, dodging the majority of the starboard watch, most of whom were asleep, swaying in hammocks strung from the same thick wooden crossbeams on which Hadrian had nearly cracked his skull. The clutter and the shifting of the ship were not the only things making Hadrian stagger. He had been feeling nauseated since sunset.

The *Emerald Storm* had been at sea for nearly fifteen hours, and the enigma of life aboard ship was slowly revealing itself. Hadrian had spent many years in the company of professional soldiers and recognized that each branch of the military held its own jargon, traditions, and idiosyncrasies, but he had never set foot on a ship. He knew he could be certain of only two things: he had a lot of learning to do, and he had little time to do it.

He had already picked up several important pieces of information, such as where to relieve himself, which, to his surprise, was at the head of the ship. A precarious experience, as he had to hang out over the sea at the base of the bowsprit. This might be second nature to sailors, and easy for Royce, but it gave Hadrian pause.

Another highly useful discovery was a cursory understanding about the chain of command. Hadrian determined that the officers—noblemen mostly—were skilled tradesmen and held a higher rank than the general seamen, but he could also tell there were substrata within these broad classes. There were different ranks of officers and even more subtle levels of seniority, influence, and jurisdiction. He could not expect to penetrate such a complex hierarchy on his first day, but he had managed to determine that the boatswain and his mates were the ones charged with making sure the seamen did their jobs. They were quite persuasive with their short rope whips and kept a keen eye on the crew at all times. Because of this, they were the ones he watched.

The ship's crew divided into two watches. While one worked the ship, the other rested, slept, or ate. Lieutenant Bishop had placed Royce on the starboard watch assigned to the maintop. His job was to work the rigging on the center mast. This put him under Boatswain Bristol Bennet and his three mates. Hadrian had seen their like before. Drunks, vagrants, and thugs, they would never have amounted to much on land, but aboard ship they held power and status. The chance to repay others for any mistreatment they had experienced made them cruel and quick to punish. Hadrian still waited to discover his watch assignment, but he hoped it would be the same as Royce's.

He had been lucky so far. This being the first day out, preparing meals had been little more than placing out fresh foods from the recent stay at port. Fruit, fresh bread, and salted meats were merely handed out with no cooking required. Consequently, Hadrian's talents remained untested, but time was running out. He knew how to cook, of course. He had prepared meals for years using little more than a campfire, but that had mainly been for him and Royce. He didn't know how to cook for an entire ship's crew. Needing to find out exactly what they expected drove him to wander in hopes of finding Wyatt.

"The Princess of Melengar rules there now," Hadrian heard a young lad say.

He didn't look to be much more than sixteen. He was a waif of a boy with thin whiskers, freckles darkened by days in the sun, and curly hair cut in a bowl-like fashion except for a short ponytail he tied with a black cord. He sat with Wyatt, Grady, and a few other men around a swaying table illuminated by a candle melted to the center of a copper plate. They were playing cards and the giant shadows they cast only made Hadrian's approach more disorienting.

"She doesn't rule Ratibor. She's the mayor," Wyatt said, correcting the boy as he laid a card on the pile before him.

"What's the difference?"

"She was appointed, lad."

"What's that mean?" the boy asked as he tried to decide which card to play, holding his hand so tight to his chest he could barely see the cards himself.

"It means she didn't just take over. The people of the city *asked* her to run things."

"But she can still execute people, right?"

"I suppose."

"Sounds like a ruler to me." With a wide grin, the boy laid a card indicating that he thought it was a surprisingly good play.

"Sounds like them people of Ratibor are dumb as dirt," Grady said gruffly. His expression betrayed his irritation at the boy's discard. "They finally get the yoke off their backs and right away they ask for a new one."

"Grady!" said a man with a white kerchief on his head. "I'm from Ratibor, you oaf!"

"Exactly! Thanks for proving me point, Bernie," Grady replied, slamming his play on the table so hard several surrounding seamen groaned in their hammocks. Grady laughed at his own joke and the rest at the table chuckled good-naturedly, except Bernie from Ratibor.

"Hadrian!" Wyatt greeted him warmly as the new cook staggered up to them like a drunk. "We were just talking about land affairs. Most of these poor sods haven't been ashore in over a year and we were filling them in on the news about the war."

"Which has been bloody cracking, seeing as how we didn't even know there was one," Grady said, feigning indignation.

"We were just in dock, though," Hadrian said. "I would have thought—"

"That don't mean nuttin'," one of the other men said. With next to no hair and few teeth, he appeared to be the oldest at the table, and possibly the entire ship. He had a silver earring that glinted with the candlelight and a tattoo of a mermaid that wrapped around his forearm. He too wore a white kerchief on his head. "Most of this here crew is pressed. The captain would be barmy to let them touch solid ground in a port. He and Mr. Bishop would be the only ones left to rig her!"

This brought a round of laughter and garnered irritated growls from those trying to sleep.

"You don't look so good," Wyatt mentioned to Hadrian.

He shook his head miserably. "It's been a long time since I've been on a ship. Does the *Storm* always rock so much?"

"Hmm?" Wyatt glanced at him, then laughed. "This? This here is nothing. You won't even notice it in a day or so." He watched the next man at the table play his card. "We're still in the sound. Wait until we hit the open sea. You might want to sit. You're sweating."

Hadrian touched his face and felt the moisture. "Funny, I feel chilled, if anything."

"Have a seat," Wyatt said. "Poe, give him your spot."

"Why me?" the young boy asked, insulted.

"Because I said so." Poe's expression showed that was not enough for him to give up one of the limited places. "And because I'm a quartermaster and you're a seaman, but even more importantly, because Mr. Bishop appointed you cook's mate."

"He did?" Poe asked, and blinked, a smile crossing his face.

"Congratulations," Wyatt said. "Now, you might want to make a good impression on your new boss and move your infernal arse!"

The boy promptly stood and pretended to clean the bench with an invisible duster. "After you, sir!" he said with an exaggerated bow.

"Does he know anything about cooking?" Hadrian asked dubiously, taking the seat.

"Sure, sure!" Poe declared exuberantly. "I know plenty. You just wait. I'll show ya."

"Good, I don't feel up to working with food yet." Hadrian let his head drop into his hands. The old man next to Wyatt tossed down his card and the whole group groaned in agony.

"You bloody bastard, Drew!" Grady barked at him, tossing what remained of his cards onto the pile. The others did the same.

Drew grinned, showing his few yellowed teeth, and

collected the tiny pile of silver tenents. "That's it for me, boys. Good night."

"Night, Drew, ya lousy Lanksteer!" Grady said, shooing him away as if he were a bug. "We can talk at breakfast, eh?"

"Sure, Grady," Drew said. "Oh, that reminds me. I heard something right funny tonight when I was reefing the tops'l. We're going to be taking on a passenger to help find the horn. How stupid are these landlubbers? It's only the most well-known point on the Sharon! Anyway, remind me at breakfast and I'll tell ya about it. It's a real hoot, it is. Night now."

Most of the rest of the men headed off, leaving just Wyatt, Grady, Poe, and Hadrian.

"You should turn in as well," Wyatt told Poe.

"I'm not tired," he protested.

"I didn't ask if you were tired, did I?"

"I want to stay up and celebrate my promotion."

"Off with ya before I report you for disobeying a superior."

Poe scowled and stomped off, looking for his hammock.

"You too, Grady," Wyatt told him.

The old seaman looked at Wyatt suspiciously, then leaned over and quietly asked, "Why you trying to get rid of me, Deminthal?"

"Because I'm tired of looking at that ugly scowl of yours, that's why."

"Codswallop!" he hissed. "You wanna be alone to talk about the you-know-what, don't ya? Both of you are in on it. I can tell, and that Royce fellow, he's in too. How many more you got, Wyatt? Room for another? I'm pretty good in a fight."

"Shut up, Grady," Wyatt told him. "Talk like that can get you hanged."

"Okay, okay," Grady said, holding up his palms. "Just letting you know, that's all." He got up and headed for his own hammock, casting several glances back over his shoulder, until he disappeared into the forest of swinging men.

"What was that all about?" Hadrian asked, hooking a thumb toward Grady's retreating figure.

"I don't know," Wyatt replied. "There's always one sailor on board any ship looking for a mutiny. Grady seems to be the *Emerald Storm's*. Ever since he signed on, he's been thinking there's a conspiracy going on—mostly because he wants there to be, I think. He has issues with authority, Grady does." Wyatt started gathering up the scattered deck of cards into a pile. "So, what's your story?"

"How do you mean?" Hadrian asked.

"Why are you and Royce here? I stuck my neck out getting you on board. I think I've a right to know why."

"I thought you got us aboard to pay off a debt."

"True, but I'm still curious why you wanted on the *Storm* in the first place."

"We're looking for a safer line of work and thought we'd try sailing," Hadrian offered. Wyatt's face showed he was not buying it. "We're on a job, but I can't tell you more than that."

"Does it have to do with the secret cargo?"

Hadrian blinked. "It's possible. What *is* the secret cargo?"

"Weapons. Steel swords, heavy shields, imperial-made crossbows, armor—enough to outfit a good-sized army. It came aboard at the last minute, hauled up in the middle of the night just before we sailed."

"Interesting," Hadrian mused. "Any idea where we're headed?"

"Nope, but that's not unusual. Captains usually keep that information to themselves, and Captain Seward doesn't even share that with me... and I'm the quartermaster."

"Quartermaster? I thought you were the helmsman."

"I'm guessing you've served in armies, haven't you?"

"A few, and the quartermaster is the supply officer."

"But on the sea, the quartermaster steers the ship, and as I mentioned, the captain hasn't even told me where we are going." Wyatt shuffled the cards absently. "So, you don't know where the ship is going, and you weren't aware of the cargo. This job didn't come with much in the way of information, did it?"

"What about you?" Hadrian turned the tables. "What are you doing here?"

"I could say I was working for a living, and for me it would actually make sense, but like you, I'm looking for answers."

"To what?"

"To where my daughter is." Wyatt paused a moment, his eyes glancing at the candle. "Allie was taken a week ago. I was out finding work, and while I was gone, the Imps grabbed her."

"Grabbed her? Why?"

Wyatt lowered his voice. "Allie is part elven, and the New Empire is not partial to their kind. Under a new law, anyone with even a drop of elf blood is subject to arrest. They've been rounding them up and putting them on ships, but no one can tell me where they've taken them. So here I am."

"But what makes you think this ship will go to the same place?"

"I take it you haven't ventured down to the waist hold yet?" He paused a second, then added, "That's the bottom of the ship, below the waterline. Ship stores are there, as well as livestock like goats, chickens, and cows. Sailors on report get the duty to pump the bilge. It's a miserable job on account of the manure mixing with the seawater that leaks in. It's also where—right now—more than a hundred elves are chained up in an area half this size."

Hadrian nodded with a grimace at the thought.

"You and Royce gave me a break once because of my daughter. Why was that?"

"That was Royce's call. You need to take that up with him. Although I wouldn't do it for a while. He's sicker than I am. I've never seen him so miserable, and this sea business is making him irritable. Well, more irritable than usual."

Wyatt nodded. "My daughter's the same way on water. Pitiful little thing, she's like a cat on a piece of driftwood. It takes her forever to get accustomed to the rocking." He paused a moment, looking at the candle.

"I'm sure you'll find her, don't worry." Hadrian glanced at the mass of men around him and lowered his voice to a whisper. "The job we're on is important, and we can't afford to be distracted, but if the situation presents itself, we'll help any way we can. Something tells me I won't have much trouble convincing Royce."

Hadrian felt the nausea rising in his stomach once more. His face must have betrayed his misery.

"Don't worry. Seasickness usually only lasts three days," Wyatt assured him as he put the cards in his breast pocket. "After that, both of you will be fine."

"If we can stay on board that long. I don't know anything about being a ship's cook."

Wyatt smiled. "Don't worry. I've got you covered. Poe will do most of the work. I know he looks young, but he'll surprise you."

"So how is it that I get an assistant?"

"As ship's cook, you rank as a petty officer. Don't get all excited, though. You're still under the boatswains and their mates, but it does grant you the services of Ordinary Seaman Poe. It also exempts you from the watches. That means so long as the ship's meals are on schedule, the rest of your time is your own. What you need to know is that breakfast is served promptly at the first bell of the forewatch." Wyatt paused. "That's the first time you'll hear a single bell toll after eight bells is rung just after the sun breaks above the horizon.

"So have Poe light the galley fires shortly after middle watch. He'll know when that is. Tell him to make skillygalee—that's oatmeal gruel. Don't forget biscuits. Biscuits get served at every meal. At eight bells, the men are piped to breakfast. Each mess will send someone to you with a messkid, sorta like a wooden bucket. Your job will be to dish out the food. Have Poe make some tea as well. The men will drink beer and rum at dinner and supper, but not at breakfast, and no one on board will risk drinking straight water."

"Risk?"

"Water sits in barrels for months, or years if a ship is on a long voyage. It gets rancid. Tea and coffee are okay 'cause they're boiled and have a little flavor. Coffee is expensive, though, and reserved for the officers. The crew and the midshipmen eat first. After that, Basil, the officers' cook, will arrive to make meals for the lieutenants and captain. Just stay out of his way.

"For dinner make boiled pork. Have Poe start boiling it right after Basil leaves. The salted meat will throw off a thick layer of fat. Half of that goes to the top captains to grease the rigging. The other half you can keep. You can sell it to tallow merchants at the next port for a bit of coin, but don't give it to the men. It will make you popular if you do, but it can also give them scurvy, and the captain won't like it. Have Poe boil some vegetables and serve them together as a stew, and don't forget the biscuits."

"So I tell Poe what to make and dish it out, but I don't actually do any cooking?"

Wyatt smiled. "That's the benefit of being a petty officer. Sadly, however, you only get a seaman's rate of pay. For supper, just serve what's left over from dinner, grog, and, of course, biscuits. After that, have Poe clean up, and like I said, the rest of the day is open to you. Sound easy?"

"Maybe, if I could stand straight and keep my stomach from doing backflips."

"Listen to Poe. He'll take good care of you. Now you'd best get back in your hammock. Trust me, it helps. Oh, and just so you know, you would have been wrong."

"About what?" Hadrian asked.

"About thinking sailing was a safer line of work."

❧

It was still dark when the captain called, "All hands!"

A cold wind had risen, and in the dark hours before dawn, a light rain sprayed the deck, adding a wet chill to the seasick misery that had already deprived Hadrian of most of his sleep. During the night, the *Emerald Storm* had passed by the Isle of Niel and now approached the Point of Man. The point was a treacherous headland shoal that marked the end of Avryn Bay and the start of the Sharon Sea. In the dark, it was difficult to see the shoal, but the sound was unmistakable. From somewhere ahead there came the rhythmic, thundering boom of waves crashing against the point.

The below decks emptied as the boatswain and his mates roused all the men from both watches with their starter ropes, driving them up to stations.

"Bring her about!" shouted the captain from his perch on the quarterdeck. The dignified figure of Lieutenant Bishop echoed the order, which Mr. Temple repeated.

"Helm-a-lee!" shouted the captain. Once more the order echoed across the decks. Wyatt spun the ship's great wheel.

"Tacks and sheets!" Lieutenant Bishop barked to the crew.

At the mizzen, main, and foremasts the other lieutenants shouted more orders, which the boatswains reinforced.

Hadrian stood on the main deck in the dark and the drizzling rain, unsure of his station or even if he had one. He was a cook, after all, but it seemed even a cook was expected to lend a hand on deck when necessary. He still felt ill, but Royce appeared worse. Hadrian watched as Boatswain Bristol, a big burly man, ordered him up the ropes, waving his short whip menacingly. Drained of color, Royce's face and hands stood out pale in the dark. His eyes were unfocused and empty. He reluctantly moved up the mainmast's ratlines, but he did not display any of the acrobatics of the previous day. Instead, he crawled miserably and hesitated partway up. He hovered in the wet rigging as if he might fall. From below, Bristol cursed at him until, at last, he moved upward once more. Hadrian imagined that the higher into the rigging Royce went, the more pronounced the sway of the ship would be. Between that, the slippery wet ropes, and the cold wind-driven rain, he did not envy his friend.

Several men were working the ropes that controlled the direction of the sails, but others, like him, remained idle, waiting in lines, which the boatswains formed. There was a tension evident in the silence of the crew. The booming of the headlands grew louder and closer, sounding like the pounding of a giant's hammer or the heartbeat of a god. They seemed to be flying blindly into the maw of some enormous unseen beast that would swallow them whole. The reality, Hadrian imagined, would not be much different should they come too close to the shoal.

Anticipating something, all eyes watched the figure of Captain Seward. Hadrian could tell by the feel of the wind and the direction of the rain that the ship was turning. The sails, once full and taut, began to flutter and collapsed as the bow crossed over into the face of the wind.

"Mains'l haul!" the captain suddenly shouted, and the crew cast off the bowlines and braces.

Seeing the movements, Hadrian realized the strategy. They were attempting a windward tack around the dangerous point, which meant the wind would be blowing the ship's hull toward the treacherous rocks even as they struggled to reset the sails to catch the wind from the other side. The danger came from the lack of maneuverability caused by empty sails during the tack. Without the wind driving the ship, the rudder could not push against the water and turn it. If the ship could not come about fully, it would not be able to catch the wind again, and it would drift into the shoal, which would shatter the timbered hull like an eggshell and cast the cargo and crew into a dark, angry sea.

Hadrian took hold of the rope in his line and, along with several others, pulled the yards round, repositioning the sails to catch the wind as soon as they were able. The rope was slick, and the wind jerked the coil so roughly that it took the whole line to pull the yards safely into position.

There was another deafening boom, and a burst of white spray shot skyward as the breaking water exploded over the port bow. The vessel was turning fast now, pulling away from the foam, struggling to get clear. No sooner had the bow cleared the wind than he heard the captain order: "Now! Meet her! Hard over!"

His voice was nearly lost as another powerful wave rammed the rocks just beside them, throwing the *Emerald Storm's* bow upward with a rough lurch that staggered them all. On the quarterdeck, Wyatt followed the order, spinning the wheel back, checking the swing before the ship could turn too far and lose its stern in the rocks.

Overhead, Hadrian heard a scream.

Looking up, he saw the figure of a man fall from the

mainsail rigging. His body landed a dozen steps away with a sickening thud. All eyes looked at the prone figure lying like a dark stain on the deck, but none dared move from their stations. Hadrian strained to see who it was. The man lay face-down, and in the dim light it was difficult to tell anything.

Is that Royce?

Normally he would never have questioned his friend's climbing skills, but with his sickness, the motion of the ship, and his inexperience, it was possible he could have slipped.

"Haul off all!" Mr. Temple shouted, ignoring the fallen man. The crew pulled on the sheets and braces, and once more captured the wind. The sails bloomed full, and Hadrian felt the lurch under his feet as the ship burst forward once more, heaving into the waves, now steering out to the open sea.

"Dr. Levy on deck!" Bishop shouted.

Hadrian rushed over the instant he could, but stopped short on seeing the tattoo of the mermaid on the dead man's forearm.

"It's Edgar Drew, sir. He's dead, sir!" Bristol shouted to the quarterdeck as he knelt next to the fallen man.

Several sailors gathered around the body, glancing upward at the mainsail shrouds, until the boatswain's mates took them to task. Hadrian thought he could see Royce up near the top yard, but in the dark he could not be sure. Still, he must have been close by when Drew fell.

The boatswain broke up the crowd and Hadrian, once more unsure of his duty, stood idle. The first light of dawn arrived, revealing a dull gray sky above a dull gray sea that lurched and rolled like a terrible dark beast.

"Cook!" a voice barked sharply.

Hadrian turned to see a young boy who was not much older than Poe but wearing the jacket and braid of an officer. He stood with a firm-set jaw and a posture so stiff he seemed made of wood. His cheeks were flushed red with the cool night air, and rainwater ran off the end of his nose.

"Aye, sir?" Hadrian replied, taking a guess it would be the right response.

"We are securing from all hands. You're free to fire the stove and get the meal ready."

Not knowing anything better to say, Hadrian replied, "Aye, aye." He turned to head for the galley.

"Cook!" the boy-officer snapped disapprovingly.

Hadrian pivoted as sharply as he could, recalling some of his military training. "Aye, sir?" he responded once more, feeling a bit stupid at his limited vocabulary.

"You neglected to salute me," he said hotly. "I'm putting you on report. What's your name?"

"Hadrian, sir. Blackwater, sir."

"I'll have the respect of you men even if I must flog you to obtain it! Do you understand? Now, let's see that salute."

Hadrian imitated the salute he had seen others perform by placing his knuckles to his forehead.

"That's better, seaman. Don't let it happen again."

"Aye, aye, sir."

It felt good to get down out of the rain and wind, and Poe met him on the way to the galley. The boy knew his way around the kitchen well, which was no doubt why Wyatt had suggested him. They fired up the stove and Hadrian watched Poe go to work cooking the morning oatmeal, adding butter and brown sugar in proper amounts and asking Hadrian to taste test it. Despite its name, the skillygalee was surprisingly good. Hadrian could not say the same about the biscuits, which were rock hard. Poe had not made them. He had merely fetched the round stones from the bread room, where boxes of them were stored. Hadrian's years of soldiering had made him familiar with hardtack, as they were known on land. The ubiquitous biscuits lasted forever but were never very filling. They were so hard that you had to soften them in tea or soup before eating them.

With the meal made, stewards from the mess arrived to gather their shares and carry them below.

Hadrian entered the berth deck, helping the mess steward carry the last of the servings. "Bloody show-off couldn't even make it up the lines," Jacob Derning was saying loudly. The men of the tops, and the petty officers, sat together at the tables as befitted their status on board, while others lay scattered with their copper plates amid the sacks and chests. Jacob looked like he was holding court at the center table. All eyes were on him as he spoke with grand gestures. On his head he wore a bright blue kerchief, as did everyone on the foretop crew.

"It's a different story with him when the sea's heaving and the lines are wet," Jacob went on. "You don't see him prancing then."

"He looked scared to me," Bristol the boatswain added. "Thought I was gonna have to go up and wallop him good to get him going again."

"Royce was fine," said a thin, gangly fellow with a white kerchief tied over his head and a thick blond walrus mustache. Hadrian did not know his name but recognized him as the captain of the maintop. "Just seasick, that's all. Once he was aloft, he reefed the tops'l just fine, albeit a bit oddly."

"Make excuses for him all ya want, Dime," Jacob told him, pointing a finger his way, "but he's a queer one, he is, and I find it more than a little dodgy that his first day aloft finds his fellow mate falling to his death."

"You suggesting Royce killed Drew?" Dime asked.

"I ain't saying nuttin', just think it's odd is all. Of course, you'd know better what went on up there, wouldn't you, Dime?"

"I didn't see it. Bernie was with him on the tops'l yard when he fell. He says Drew just got careless. I've seen it before. Fools like him skylarking in the sheets. Bernie says he was trying to walk the yard when the ship lurched 'cause of that burst from the shoal. He lost his footing. Bernie tried to grab him as he hung on to the yard, but the wetness made him slip off."

"Drew walking the yard in a rainstorm?" Jacob laughed. "Not likely."

"And where was Royce during all this?" Bristol asked.

Dime shook his head. "I dunno, didn't see him till later when he turned up at the masthead."

"Bernie was playing cards with him last night, wasn't he? I heard Drew walked away with a big pot."

"Now you're saying Bernie killed him?" a third fellow, with a red kerchief, asked. Hadrian had never seen him before but guessed he must be the captain of the mizzenmast, as the top captains, along with the boatswains, seemed to dine together at the same table.

"No, but I'm saying the cook was there and he and Royce are mates, aren't they? I think—" Jacob stopped short when he spotted Hadrian. "Bloody good thing you're a better cook than your mate is a topman or Mr. Temple's liable to chuck you both in the deep."

Hadrian said nothing. He looked around for Royce but did not find him, which was not too surprising, as he guessed his friend would not want to be anywhere near food.

"Might want to let your mate know I've asked Bristol here to have a word with Mr. Beryl about him."

"Beryl?" Bristol responded, puzzled. "I was gonna talk to Wesley."

"Bugger that," Jacob said. "Wesley's useless. He's a bleeding joke, ain't he?"

"I can't go over his head to Beryl," Bristol said defensively. "Wesley was watch officer when it happened."

"Are you barmy? What're you scared of? Think Wesley's gonna have at ya for going to Beryl? All Wesley will do is report you. That's all he ever does. He's a boy and hasn't grown a spine yet in that midshipman's uniform of his. Only reason he's on the *Storm* is 'cause his daddy is Lord Belstrad."

"We need to serve the midshipmen next," Poe reminded Hadrian, urgently tugging at his sleeve. "They mess in the wardroom aft."

Hadrian dropped off the messkid, hanging it from a hook the way he had seen Poe do, and gave Jacob one last glance only to find the fore captain grinning malevolently.

Far smaller and not much more comfortable than the crew's quarters, the midshipmen's mess was a tiny room aft on the berth deck that creaked loudly as the ship's hull lurched in the waves. Normally, Basil delivered the food he cooked for the officers, but this morning he was kept particularly busy working on the lieutenants' and captain's meal and had asked Poe and Hadrian for help in delivering the food to the midshipmen's mess.

"What are you doing in here?" the biggest midshipman asked abruptly as Hadrian and Poe entered. Hadrian almost answered when he realized the question was not addressed to him. Behind them, coming in late, was the young officer who had put Hadrian on report earlier. "You're supposed to be on watch, Wesley."

"Lieutenant Green relieved me a bit early so I could get some food while it was hot."

"So you've come to force yourself in on your betters, is that it?" the big man asked, and got a round of laughter from those with him. This had to be Beryl, Hadrian guessed. He was by far the oldest of the midshipmen—by ten years or more. "You're going to be nothing but a nuisance to the rest of us on this voyage, aren't you, boy? Here we thought we could have a quiet meal without you disturbing us. What did you do, whine to Green about how your stomach was hurting because we didn't let you have anything to eat last night?"

"No, I—" Wesley began.

"Shut it! I don't want to hear your sniveling voice. You there, cook!" Beryl snapped. "Don't serve Midshipman Wesley any food, not a biscuit crumb, do you understand?"

Hadrian nodded, guessing that Beryl somehow outranked Wesley despite both of them wearing midshipmen uniforms.

Wesley looked angry but said nothing. The boy turned away from the table toward his sea chest.

"Oh yes," Beryl said, rising from the table and walking across the room to Wesley. As he did, Hadrian noticed an old scar down the side of Beryl's face that looked to have nearly taken out his eye. "I've been meaning to go through your stuff to see if you had anything I might like."

Wesley turned, closing his chest abruptly.

"Open it, boy, and let me have a look."

"No, you have no right!"

Beryl's toadies at the table jeered the boy and laughed.

He took a step forward, and from his posture, Hadrian knew what was coming even if Wesley was oblivious. The big midshipman struck Wesley hard across the face. The boy fell over his sea chest onto his back. He rolled to his side, his face red with fury, but never got farther than his knees before Beryl struck him again, this time hard enough to spray blood from his nose. Wesley collapsed to the floor again with a wail of pain and lay crumbled in a ball, holding his face. The other midshipmen cheered.

Beryl sifted through the contents of Wesley's chest. "All that for nothing? I thought you were a lord's son. This is pathetic." He pulled a white linen shirt out and looked it over. "Well, this isn't too bad, and I could use a new shirt." He slammed the chest and returned to his breakfast.

Disgusted, Hadrian started to move to help Wesley but stopped when he saw Poe earnestly shaking his head. The young seaman took hold of Hadrian's arm and nearly dragged him back up to the main deck, where the sun had risen sufficiently enough to cause them to squint.

"Don't involve yourself in the affairs of officers," Poe told him earnestly. "They're just like nobles. Strike one and you'll hang for it. Trust me, I know what I'm talking about. My older brother Ned is the coxswain on the *Immortal.* The horror stories he's told me can turn one's stomach. Blimey, you act like you've never been on a ship before."

Hadrian did not say anything as he followed Poe back toward the galley.

"You haven't, have you?" Poe asked suddenly.

"So, who is this big fella? Is he Beryl?" Hadrian asked, changing the subject.

Poe scowled, then sighed. "Yep, he's the senior midshipman."

"So Beryl's a noble?"

"Don't know if he is or he ain't. Most are third or fourth sons, the ones not suited for the tournaments or monastic life who volunteer to serve, hoping they can one day manage a captain's rank, rule their own ship, and make some money. Most midshipmen only serve about five years before making lieutenant, but Beryl, he's been a midshipman for something like ten years now, I reckon. I guess it makes a man sorta cranky, being left behind like that. Even if he isn't a true blue-blooded noble, he's still an officer, and on this ship, that means the same thing."

⁂

"Royce?" Hadrian whispered.

Royce lay in his hammock near the bow of the ship, his

head still covered with the white kerchief—the insignia of the maintop crew. He was shivering and wet, lying in soaked clothes.

"Royce," he repeated. This time, he shook his partner's shoulder.

"Do that again and I'll cut your hand off," he growled, his voice garbled and sickly.

"I brought you some coffee and bread. I put raisins in the bread. You like raisins."

Royce peered out from under his thin blanket with a vicious glare. He eyed the meal and promptly looked away with a grimace.

"Sorry, I just knew you hadn't eaten since yesterday." Hadrian put the tray down away from him. "They gave you extra duty, didn't they? You seemed to be up there longer than anyone else."

"Bristol kept me on station as punishment for being slow yesterday. How long was I up there?"

"Twelve hours at least. Listen, I thought we'd have a look around the forward hold. Wyatt tells me the seret are hiding a special cargo up there. If you can get your stomach under control, maybe you can open a few locks for me?"

Royce shook his head. "Not until this ship stops rolling. I stand up and the world spins. I've got to sleep. How come you're not sick?"

"I am, but not like you. I guess elven blood and water don't mix."

"It might," Royce said, disappearing back under his blanket. "If I don't start feeling better soon, I'll slit my wrists."

Hadrian took his blanket, laid it over the shivering form of Royce, and was about to head back up topside when he paused and asked, "Any idea what happened to Edgar Drew?"

"The guy that fell?"

"Yeah, some of the crew think he might have been murdered."

"I didn't see anything. Spent most of my time hugging the mast. I was pretty sick—still am. Get out of here and let me sleep."

It was late and the port watch was on duty, but most of them slept on deck or in the rigging. Only a handful had to remain alert during the middle watch: three lookouts aloft at the masthead, the quartermaster's mate who manned the wheel in Wyatt's absence, and the officer of the watch. Hadrian nearly ran into this last man as he came on deck.

"Mr. Wesley, sir," Hadrian said, shifting the tray so he could properly perform the salute.

Wesley's face was blotchy, his nose and eyes black and blue. Hadrian knew he was standing an additional watch. On his way to Royce, Hadrian had overheard Lieutenant Bishop questioning the midshipman about a brawl, but because Wesley had refused to divulge the name of his adversary, the young man took the punishment alone.

"Mr. Wesley, I thought you might like something to eat. I'm guessing you haven't had much today."

The officer glared at him a moment, then looked at the tray. As he saw the steam rising from the coffee cup, his mouth opened and abruptly shut. "Who sent you here? Was it Beryl? Is this supposed to be funny?"

"No, sir. I just know you didn't get to eat breakfast, and you've been on duty through the rest of the meals today. You must be starved."

"You were ordered not to feed me."

Hadrian shrugged. "I've also been ordered by the captain to see that the crew is fed and fit for duty. You've been up a long time. A man could fall asleep without something to help keep his eyes open."

Wesley looked back down. "That's coffee, isn't it?" the young midshipman asked, astonished. "There's not more than a few pounds of that on the entire ship, most of which is reserved for the captain."

"I did a bit of trading this afternoon with the purser and managed to get a couple cups' worth."

"Why offer it to me?"

Hadrian looked up at the night sky. "It's a cold night, and punishment for falling asleep can be severe."

Wesley nodded gravely. "On this ship, a midshipman is flogged."

"Do you think that's Beryl's plan, sir? For standing up to him this morning in front of the other officers, I mean."

"Maybe. Beryl is a tyrant of the worst order, and a libertine who squandered his family's fortune. I suspect Beryl would not even notice me, if it were not for my brother. By beating me he thinks he is superior to our family."

"Your brother is Sir Breckton Belstrad?"

Wesley nodded. "But the joke is on him. I am nothing like my brother, so besting me is no great accomplishment. If I were like him, I would not allow myself to be bullied by a lout like Beryl."

"Take the coffee and bread, sir," Hadrian said. "I can't say I care for Beryl, and if keeping you awake tonight gets under his skin, it'll make tomorrow all the better in my book. The orders of the captain override a senior midshipman's."

"I'll still have to put you on report for this morning. This kindness will not change that."

"I didn't expect it to, sir."

The midshipman studied Hadrian, his face betraying a new curiosity. "In that case, thank you," he said, taking the food.

❧

Dovin Thranic walked through the waist hold. Dark and cramped, the ship's bottom deck reeked of animal dung and salt water. A good four inches of liquid slime pooled along the centerline gutter, forcing him to walk up the sides, hurdling the futtock rider beams to keep his shoes dry. The next day he would order Lieutenant Bishop to direct the detail of men to work the bilge pump in the evening to ensure he did not need to go through this every night. He was a sentinel of the Nyphron Church, presently one of only two men allowed to speak personally with His Holiness the Patriarch, and yet here he was crawling through sewage.

His unsettled stomach made the ordeal even more miserable. After several days of sleeping on board the *Emerald Storm* while it was in dock, he thought he had gained his sea legs. The initial wretchedness had subsided only to return now that the ship was rolling at a different cadence on the open sea. While not nearly as bad as before, his nausea was still a nuisance and would make his work less enjoyable.

Thranic carried no light but did not need one. The sentry's lanterns at the far end of the hold gave sufficient illumination for him to see. He passed several sentries, seret who stood rigidly at their stations, ignoring his approach.

"They seem quiet tonight. Have they been behaving?" Thranic asked as he approached the cages.

"Yes, sir," the senior guard replied, breaking his statuesque facade only briefly. "Seasickness. They're all under the weather."

"Yes," Thranic noted, not without a degree of revulsion. He watched them. "They can see me, you know, even in the dark. They have very good eyesight."

Because a response was not required, the seret remained silent.

"I can see recognition on their faces, recognition and fear. This is my first trip to visit them, but already they know me. They can sense the power of Novron within me, and the evil in them instinctually cowers. It's like I'm a candle, and the light I give off pushes back their darkness."

Thranic stepped closer to the cages, each so densely packed the elves were forced to take turns standing and lying. Those standing pressed their filthy naked bodies against each other for support. Males, females, and children were jammed together tightly, creating a repugnant quivering mass of flesh. He watched with amusement as they whimpered and whined, struggling to move away from his approach.

"See? I am light, and the putrid blackness of their souls retreats before me." Thranic studied their faces, each gaunt and hollow from starvation. "They're disgusting creatures—unnatural abominations that never should have been. Their very existence is an insult. You feel it, don't you? We need to purge the world of the stain they cause. We need to do our best to clear the offense. We need to prove ourselves worthy."

Thranic was no longer looking at the elves. He was staring at his own hands. "Purification is never easy, but always necessary," he muttered pensively. "Fetch me that tall male with the missing tooth," Thranic ordered. "I'll begin with him."

Following the sentinel's direction, the guards ripped the elf from his cage and bound his elbows behind his back. Using a spare rigging pulley, they hoisted the unfortunate prisoner by his arms to the overhead beam. The effort pulled the elf's limbs from their sockets, causing him to scream in agony. His wails and the wretched look on his face caused even the seret to look away, but Thranic watched stoically, his lips pursed approvingly.

"Swing him," he said. The elf howled anew from the motion.

The sentinel looked at the cages again. Inside, others were

weeping. At his glance, one female pushed forward. "Why can't you leave us alone?"

Thranic searched her face with a look of genuine pity. "Maribor demands that the mistake of his brother be erased. I'm merely his tool."

"Then why not—why not just kill us and get it over with?" she cried at him, eyes wild. Thranic paused. He stared once more at his hands. He turned them over, examining both sides with a distant expression. He was silent for so long that even the seret turned to face him. Thranic looked back at the female, his eyes blurring and lips trembling. "One must scrub very hard to remove *some* stains. Take her next."

Chapter 7

Rotten Eggs

For Empress Modina, everything had changed a month ago, after she had stood on the balcony and addressed the citizens of the New Empire. Due to Amilia's constant chipping away at the regents' resolve, the empress now enjoyed an unprecedented degree of freedom within the palace, and she wandered freely, dressed in fresh new clothing.

She never went anywhere in particular, and oftentimes after returning she could not recall where she had been. Although she longed to feel grass beneath her feet, her permitted boundary did not extend past the palace walls. She was certain no guard would stop her if she tried to leave, but she feared Amilia would suffer the regents' wrath if she did, so she remained inside the keep.

Now Modina walked gracefully in her new dress, silent and pensive, the way an empress should. As she descended the curved stair, she felt the hem of her gown drag along the stone steps. The new dresses had also been Amilia's doing. Her secretary had personally supervised the imperial seamstress in their construction and curtailed any attempts the woman had tried to make to embellish them with lace or embroidery. Each was brilliant white and patterned after a simple, yet eloquent, design. Amilia had told the seamstress that the main goal was to create clothing that would make Modina feel as comfortable as possible, so the dressmaker focused on constructing plain but well-fitted garments and dispensed with utilizing stiff collars, tight bodices, or stays.

While the freedom and new dresses had been welcome changes, the most dramatic difference had been the way people reacted when seeing the empress. Since leaving her bedroom, Modina had passed two young women carrying a pile of linens and a page with an armful of assorted boots. He had dropped one the moment he spotted her, and the two girls chatted excitedly to each other. She had seen in their faces the same look that everyone wore: the belief that she was the Chosen One of Maribor.

When she had first come to the palace, everyone had avoided her the way one evades a dog known to bite. After her speech, those few members of the palace staff she chanced upon had looked at her with affectionate admiration and an unspoken understanding, as if acknowledging that they finally comprehended her previous behavior. The new gowns had the unintended effect of turning admiration into adoration, as the white purity and modest simplicity gave Modina an angelic aura. She had transformed from the mad empress to the saintly—although troubled—high priestess.

Everyone attributed Modina's recovery to Amilia's healing powers. What she had said on the balcony was the truth. Amilia had saved her, if *saved* was the right word. Modina did not feel saved.

Ever since Dahlgren, she had been drowning in overwhelming terrors that she could not face. Amilia had pulled her to shore, but no one could call her existence living. There had been a time, long, long ago, when she would have said that life carried hope for a better tomorrow, but for her, hope was a dream that had blown away on a midsummer's night. The horrors were all that remained, calling to her, threatening to pull her under again. It would be easy to give in, to close her eyes and sink to the bottom once more, but if pretending to live could help Amilia, then she would. Amilia had become a tiny point of light in a sea of darkness, the singular star Modina steered by, and it did not matter where that light led.

Like most afternoons, Modina wandered the sequestered halls and chambers like a ghost searching for something long forgotten. She heard that people with missing limbs felt an itching in a phantom leg or arm. Perhaps it was the same for her, as she struggled to scratch at her missing life.

The smell of food indicated she was near the kitchen. Modina did not recall the last time she had eaten, but she was not hungry. Ghosts did not get hungry, at least not for food. She had come to the bottom of the stairs. To the right, cupboards lined a narrow room holding plates, goblets, candles, and utensils. To the left, folded linens were stacked on shelves. Filled with laboring servants and steam, the place was hot and noisy.

Modina spotted the big elkhound sleeping in the corner of the kitchen and immediately recalled that his name was Red. She had not been down this way in a long time, not since Saldur had caught her feeding the dog. That was the first day since her father had died that she could remember clearly. Before that—nothing—nothing but...*rotten eggs*.

She smelled the rancid stench as she stood at the bottom of the steps. Modina glanced around with greater interest. That awful smell triggered a memory. There was a place, a small room that was cold, dark, and lacked any windows. She could almost taste it.

Modina approached a small wooden door. With a shaking hand, she pulled it open. Inside was a small pantry filled with sacks of flour and grain. This was not the room, but the smell was stronger there.

There was another place—small like this—small, dark, and evil. The thought came at her with the force of a forgotten nightmare. Black, earthy, and cold, a splashing and a ratcheting that echoed ominously, the wails of lost souls crying for mercy and finding none. She had been one of them. She had cried aloud in the dark until she could cry no more, and always the smell of dirt penetrated her nostrils and the dampness of the dirt floor soaked into her skin. A sudden realization jolted her.

I'm remembering my grave! I am dead. I am a ghost.

She looked at her hands—this was not life. The darkness closed in all around her, growing deeper, swallowing her, smothering her.

⁂

"Are you all right, Your Eminence?"

"Ya think she's sick again?"

"Don't be daft. She's just upset. You can see that well enough, can't ya?"

"Poor thing, she's so fragile."

"Remember who you're speaking of. That lass slew Rufus's Bane!"

"*You* remember who *you're* speaking of, *that lass* indeed! By Maribor's beard, she's the empress!"

"Out of my way," Amilia growled as she shooed the crowd like a yard full of chickens.

She was in no mood to be polite. Fear made her voice harsh, and it lacked the familiar tone of a fellow kitchen worker—it was the voice of an angry noblewoman. The servants scattered. Modina sat on the floor with her back against the wall. She was weeping softly with her hands covering her face.

"What did you do to her?" Amilia snapped accusingly while glaring at the lot of them.

"Nothing!" Leif said, defending them.

Leif, the butcher and assistant cook, was a scrawny little man with thick dark hair covering his arms and chest but absent from his balding head. Amilia had never cared for him, and the thought that he, or any of them, might have hurt Modina made her blood boil.

"No one was even near her. I swear!"

"That's right," Cora confirmed. The dairymaid was a sweet, simple girl who churned the butter each morning and always added too much salt. "She just sat and started crying."

Amilia knew better than to listen to Leif, but Cora was trustworthy. "All right," she told them. "Leave her be. Back to work, all of you."

They were slow to respond until Amilia gave them a threatening glare.

"Are you all right? What's wrong?" she asked, kneeling beside Modina.

The empress looked up and threw her arms around Amilia's neck as she continued to sob uncontrollably. Amilia held her, stroking her hair. She had no idea what was wrong, but needed to get the empress to her room. If word reached Saldur, or worse, if he wandered in—She tried not to think of it.

"It's okay, it's all right. I've got you. Try to calm down."

"Am I alive?" Modina asked with pleading eyes.

For the briefest of moments, Amilia thought she might be joking, but there were two things wrong with that. First, there was the look in Modina's eyes, and second, the empress *never* joked.

"Of course you are," she reassured her. "Now come. Let's get you to bed."

Amilia helped her up. Modina stood like a newborn fawn,

weak and unsure. As they left, excited whispering rose. *I'll have to deal with that right away*, she thought.

She guided Modina upstairs. Gerald, the empress's personal guard, gave them a concerned look as he opened the chamber door.

"Is she all right?" Gerald asked.

"She's tired," Amilia said, closing the door on him.

The empress sat on the edge of her bed, staring at nothing. This was not her familiar blank stare. Amilia could see her thinking hard about something.

"Were you sleepwalking? Did you have a nightmare?"

Modina thought a moment, then shook her head. "I remembered something." Her voice was faint and airy. "It was something bad."

"Was it about the battle?" This was the first time Amilia had brought up the subject. Details of Modina's legendary combat with the beast that had destroyed Dahlgren were always vague or clouded by so much dogma and propaganda that it was impossible to tell truth from fiction. Like any imperial citizen, Amilia was curious. The stories claimed Modina had slain a powerful dragon with a broken sword. Just looking at the empress, she knew that could not be true, but Amilia was certain something terrible had happened.

"No," Modina said softly. "It was afterward. I woke up in a hole, a terrible place. I think it was my grave. I don't like remembering. It's better for both of us if I don't try."

Amilia nodded. Since Modina had begun speaking, most of their conversations had centered on Amilia's life in Tarin Vale. On the few occasions when she asked Modina about her own past, the empress's expression darkened and the light in her eyes faded. She would not speak any more after that, sometimes for days. The skeletons in Modina's closet were legion.

"Well, don't think about it, then," Amilia told her in a soothing voice. She sat next to Modina on the edge of the bed and ran her fingers through the empress's hair. "Whatever it was, it's over. You're here with me now. It's getting late. Do you think you can sleep?"

The empress nodded, but her eyes remained troubled.

Once she was certain the empress was resting peacefully, Amilia crept out of her room. Ignoring Gerald's questioning looks, she trotted downstairs to the kitchen. If left to themselves, the scullions would start a wave of rumors certain to engulf the entire palace, and she could not afford to have this getting back to Saldur.

Amilia had not visited the kitchens for quite some time. The moist steamy cloud that smelled of onions and grease, once so familiar, was now oppressive. Eight people worked the evening shift. There were several new faces, mostly young boys fresh off the street and girls still smelling of farm manure. All of them worked perfunctorily, as they were engrossed in the conversation that rose above the sound of the boiling kettles and the clatter of pans. That all stopped when she entered.

"Amilia!" Ibis Thinly boomed the moment he saw her. The old sea cook was a huge barrel-chested man with bright blue eyes and a beard that wreathed his chin. Blood and grease stained his apron. He held a towel in one hand and a spoon in the other. Leaving a large pot on the stove, he strode over to her, grinning. "Yer a fine sight for weathering eyes, lass! How's life treating you, and why don't you visit more often?"

She rushed to him. Ignoring his filthy garment and all courtly protocol, she hugged the big man tight.

The water boy dropped both buckets and gasped aloud.

Ibis chuckled. "It's as if they plum forgot you used to work here. Like they think their old Amilia died er sumptin' and the chief imperial secretary to the empress grew outta thin air."

He put down the spoon and took her by the hand. "So, how are you, lassie?"

"Really good, actually."

"I hear you got a fancy place up there in the east wing with all the swells. That's sumptin' to be proud of, that is. Yer moving up in the world. There's no mistaking that. I just hope you don't forget us down here."

"If I do, just burn my dinner and I'll remember who the really important people are."

"Oh, speaking of that!" Ibis quickly used the towel to lift the steaming pot from the stove. "Don't want to be ruining the sauce for the chamberlain's quail."

"How are things here?"

"Same as always." He hoisted the pot onto the stone bench and lifted the lid, freeing a cloud of steam. "Nuttin' changes in the scullery, and you picked a fine time to visit. Edith ain't here. She's upstairs hollering at the new chambermaid."

Amilia rolled her eyes. "They should have dismissed that woman years ago."

"Don't I know it, but I only run the kitchen and don't have no say over what she does. Course, you being a swell an' all now, maybe—"

She shook her head. "I don't have any real power. I just take care of Modina."

Ibis used the spoon to taste the sauce before replacing the lid.

"Well now, I know you didn't come here to jaw with me about Edith Mon. This have sumptin' to do with the empress crying down here a bit ago? It wasn't the pea soup I made for her, was it?"

"No," Amilia assured him. "She loves your cooking, but yes, I did sort of want to explain things." She turned to face the rest of the staff and raised her voice. "I just wanted everyone to know the empress is okay. She heard some bad news today and it saddened her is all. But she's fine now."

"Was it about the war?" Nipper asked.

"I bet it had to do with the prisoners in Ratibor," Knob, the baker, speculated. "The princess from Melengar done executed them, didn't she? Everyone knows she's a witch and a murderess. She'd think nothing of slaughtering defenseless folk. That's why she was weeping, wasn't it? 'Cause she couldn't save them?"

"The poor dear," the butcher's wife declared. "She cares so much, it's no wonder she's so upset with everything she has to deal with. Thank Maribor she has you taking care of her, Lady Amilia. You're a mercy and then some, you are."

Amilia smiled and turned to Ibis. "Didn't she always used to yell at me about the way I cleaned her husband's knives?"

Ibis chuckled. "She also accused you of taking that pork loin a year ago last spring. Said you ought to be whipped. I guess she forgot about that. They all have, I 'spect. It's the dress, I think. Seeing you in a gown like this, even I have to fight the impulse to bow."

"Don't do that," she told him, "or I'll never come back here."

Ibis grinned. "It's good to see you again."

❧

In her dream, Modina saw the beast coming up behind her father. She tried to scream, but only a muffled moan escaped. She tried to run to him, but her feet were stuck in mud—thick, green, foul-smelling mud. The beast had no trouble moving as it charged down the hill toward him. To Modina's anguished amazement, Theron took no notice of the ground shaking from the monster's massive bulk. It consumed him in a single bite, and Modina collapsed in the dirt. The musty smell filled her nostrils as she struggled to breathe. She could feel the damp earth against her body. In the darkness, the sounds of splashing told her that the beast came for her too. All around, men and women cried and howled in misery and fear. The beast came for them all. Splashing, cranking, splashing, cranking, it was coming to finish the job, coming to swallow her up as well.

It was hungry. Very hungry. It needed to eat.

They all needed to eat, but there was never enough food. What little they had was a putrid gruel that smelled awful—like rotten eggs. She was cold, shivering, and weeping. She had cried so hard and for so long that her eyes no longer teared. There was nothing left to live for…or was there?

Modina woke in her darkened room shivering in a cold sweat.

The same dream haunted her each night, making her afraid to close her eyes. She got up and moved toward the moonlight of her window. By the time she reached it, most of the dream was forgotten, but she realized something had been different. Sitting in her usual place, she looked out over the courtyard below. It was late and everyone was gone except the guards on watch. She tried to remember her nightmare, but the only thing she could recall was the smell of rotten eggs.

Chapter 8

The Horn

After the first few disorienting days, life aboard the *Emerald Storm* settled into a rigid pattern. Every morning began with the scrubbing of the upper deck, although it never had a chance to get dirty from one day to the next. Breakfast followed. The watches changed and the scrubbing continued, this time on the lower decks. At noon, Lieutenant Bishop or one of the other officers fixed their position using the sun and confirmed it with the captain. Afterward, the men drilled on the masts and yards, launching longboats, boarding and repelling, and practicing archery, the ballista, and hand-to-hand combat. Not surprisingly, Hadrian won high marks in sword fighting and archery, his display of skill not lost on Grady, who nodded knowingly.

From time to time, the men were drummed to the main deck to witness punishment. So far, there had been four floggings, but Hadrian knew the victims only by name. In the afternoon, the men received their grog, a mixture of rum and sugar water, and in the evening, the master-at-arms went about making certain all fires were out.

Most days were the same as the one before, with only a few exceptions. On make 'n' mend day, the captain granted the crew extra time in the afternoon to sew up rips in their clothing or indulge in hobbies such as wood carving or scrimshaw. On wash day, they cleaned their clothes. Because using freshwater was forbidden and there was no soap, shirts and pants usually felt better after a day working in the rain than they did after wash day.

By now, everyone knew his responsibilities and could perform them reasonably well. Hadrian and Royce were pleased to discover they were not the only novices aboard. Recently pressed men composed nearly a quarter of the crew. Many came from as far away as Alburn and Dunmore, and most had never seen the ocean before. The other men's bumbling presence, and Wyatt's assistance, masked Hadrian's and Royce's lack of experience. Now both knew the routine and their tasks well enough to pass on their own.

The *Emerald Storm* continued traveling due south, with the wind on its port quarter laying it over elegantly as it charged the following sea. It was a marvelously warm day. Either they had run so far south that the season had yet to change, or autumn had blessed them with one last breath of perfect weather. The master's mate and a yeoman of the hold appeared on deck at the ringing of the first bell to dispense the crew's grog.

About four days into the voyage, Royce finally found his sea legs. His color returned, but even after more than a week, his temper remained sour. One contributing factor was Jacob Derning's constant accusations about his culpability in Drew's death.

"After I slit his throat, I can just drop the body into the sea," Royce casually told Hadrian. They had collected their grog and the crew lay scattered about the top decks, relaxing in the bright sunshine. Royce and Hadrian found a cozy out-of-the-way space on the waist deck between the longboat and the bulkhead where the sailmaker and his mates had left a pile of excess canvas. It made for a luxurious deck bed from which to watch the clear blue sky with its decorative puffs of clouds.

"I'll dump him at night and he's gone for good. The body won't even wash up onshore, because the sharks will eat it. It's better than having your own personal vat of lye."

"Okay, one more time." Hadrian had become exhausted from the conversation. "You can't kill Jacob Derning. We have no idea what's going on yet. What if he's Merrick's contact? So until we know something—anything—you can't kill anyone."

Royce scowled and folded his arms across his chest in frustration.

"Let's get back to what we know," Hadrian went on.

"Like the fact that Bernie Defoe was once in the Black Diamond?" Royce replied.

"Really? Well, that's interesting. So let's see . . . We've got a cargo hold full of elves, enough weapons to outfit an army, a sentinel with a company of seret, a Tenkin, and an ex-Diamond. I think Thranic must be part of this. I doubt a sentinel is just taking a pleasure cruise."

"He does stand out like a knife in a man's back, which is why I doubt he's involved."

"Okay, let's put him in the maybe category. That leaves Bernie at the top of the list. Was he in the guild at the same time as you and Merrick?"

Royce nodded. "But we never worked with him—hardly even saw him. Bernie was a digger—specialized in robbing crypts mostly, and then he got into looking for buried treasure. Taught himself to read so he could search old books for clues. He found Gable's Corner and the Lyrantian Crypt, apparently buried somewhere out in Vilan Hills. Came back with some nice stuff and all these tall tales about ghosts and goblins. He ended up having some disagreement with the Jewel, and it wasn't long before he went independent. Never heard of him after that."

"But Merrick knew him, right?"

"Yeah."

"Think he recognized you?"

"I don't know. Maybe. He wouldn't let on if he had. He's no fool."

"Any chance he's turned a new leaf and taken up sailing for real?"

"About as likely as me doing it."

Hadrian eyed Royce for a heartbeat. "I put him at the top of the list."

"What about the Tenkin?"

"That's another strange one. He—"

"Land ho!" the lookout on the foremast shouted while pointing off the port bow. Royce and Hadrian got up and looked in the direction indicated. Hadrian could not make out much, just a thin gray line, but he thought he could see twin towers rising in the distance. "Is that..."

"Drumindor," Royce confirmed, glancing over his shoulder before sitting back down with his rum.

"Oh yeah? We're that far south? Been a while since we've been around here."

"Don't remind me."

"Okay, so the fortress wasn't the best of times, but the city was nice. You have to admit Tur Del Fur is better than Colnora, really. Beautiful climate, brightly painted buildings on an aqua sea, and it's a republic port. You've got to love an open city."

"Oh? Remember how many times you banged your head?"

Hadrian frowned at him. "You really do hate dwarves, don't you? Honestly, I'm surprised you let Magnus stay at the abbey. All right, so there's a bit too much dwarven architecture there, but it sure is built well. You've got to admit that, and you liked the wine, remember?"

Royce shrugged. "What were you going to say about the Tenkin?"

"Oh yeah. His name is Staul."

"Doesn't seem like the sailor type."

"No." Hadrian shook his head. "He's a warrior. Most Tenkin men are. Thing is, Tenkins never leave the Gur Em."

"The what?"

"You've never been to Calis, have you? The whole eastern half is a tropical forest, and the thickest part is a jungle they call the Gur Em. This is the first time I've ever seen a Tenkin outside of Calis, which makes me think Staul is an outcast."

"Doesn't sound like the type Merrick would be doing business with."

"So Bernie remains our number one." Hadrian thought a moment. "You think he had anything to do with Drew's death?"

"Maybe," Royce replied, taking a sip of rum. "He was on the mainmast that night, but I was too sick to pay attention. I wouldn't put it past Bernie to give him a little push. He'd need a reason, though."

"Drew and Bernie were both at a card game earlier that night. Drew won the pot and if Bernie is a thief..."

Royce shook his head. "Bernie wouldn't kill him over a gambling dispute. Not unless it was really big money. The coppers and silvers they were likely playing for wouldn't qualify. That doesn't mean he didn't kill him. It just wasn't about gambling. Anything else happen at the game?"

"Not really, although Drew did mention he was going to talk to Grady the next morning at breakfast about someone coming aboard to help find a horn. Drew thought it was kinda funny, actually. He seemed to think the horn was easy to find. He was going to go into more detail at breakfast."

"Maybe Drew overheard something Defoe preferred he hadn't. That's a more likely reason. But a horn?"

⁂

They came across Wyatt at the ship's wheel. His plumed hat was off and his white linen shirt fluttered about his tan skin like a personal sail. He had the *Storm* tight over, playing the pressure of the rudder against the press of the wind. He was staring out at the headland with glassy eyes as they approached, but when he spotted them, he abruptly cast his head down at the binnacle and quickly wiped his face with the sleeve of his forearm.

"You all right?" Hadrian asked.

"Y-yeah," Wyatt croaked, then coughed to clear his throat. "Fine." He sniffed and wiped his nose.

"There's a good chance you'll find her," Royce assured him.

"See?" Hadrian said. "You've even got Mr. Cynical feeling optimistic about your chances. That's gotta count for something."

Wyatt forced a smile.

"Hey, we've got a question for you," Royce said. "Do you have any idea what the *horn* is?"

"Sure, you're looking right at it," Wyatt declared, gesturing toward the point. "That's the Horn of Delgos. As soon as we clear it, the captain will likely order the ship to weather round the point and then tack windward."

Royce frowned. "Let's assume for just a moment that I'm not an experienced sailor, shall we?"

Wyatt chuckled. "We're gonna make a left turn and head east."

"How do you know?"

Wyatt shrugged. "The horn is the farthest spit of land south. If we stay on this course, we'll sail into the open sea. There's nothing out there but whirlpools, Dacca, and sea serpents. If we weather round—er—turn left, we'll sail up the eastern coast of Delgos."

"And what's up that way?"

"Not much. These cliffs you see continue all the way round to Vandon, the only other sea port in Delgos. Besides being the headquarters for the Vandon Spice Company, it's also a haven for pirates, or more accurately *the* haven for pirates. We aren't going there either. The *Storm* is as fine a ship as they come, but the jackals would gather like a pack of wolves and dog her until we surrender, or they sink us."

"How does the spice company manage any trade, surrounded by pirates?"

"Who do you think runs the spice company?"

"Oh."

"Beyond that?" Royce asked.

"Dagastan Bay and the whole coast of Calis, with ports at Wesbaden and Dagastan. Then you drift out of civilization and into the Ba Ran Archipelago, and no one goes there, not even pirates."

"And you're sure this here is the horn?"

"Yep, every sailor who's ever been in the Sharon knows it. It'd be impossible to miss old Drumindor."

Though the coast was still many leagues off, the ancient dwarven edifice was clearly visible now, standing taller than anything Hadrian had ever seen. He smiled at the irony, knowing dwarves had built it. The massive towers were close to eight hundred feet from the raw rocky base, where waves crashed, to the top of the dome. It appeared to be equal parts fortification and monument. In some respects, it resembled two massive gears laid on their sides, huge cylinders with teeth jutting seaward. From the top of each tower, smoke rose. Midway up were fins—arced openings like gigantic teapot spouts that pointed toward the ocean. Between the twin towers was a single-span stone bridge connecting them like a lintel over the entrance of the harbor.

"Can't even miss her at night, the way she lights up. You should see her during a full moon when they blow the vents. It puts on quite a show. She's built on a volcano, and the venting prevents too much pressure from building up. Ships in the area often arrange to pass the point at the full moon just for the entertainment. But they also keep their distance. The dwarves that built that fortress sure knew what they were doing. No ship can enter Terlando Bay if the masters of Drumindor don't want them to. They can spew molten rock for hundreds of feet and burn a fleet of ships to drifting ash in minutes."

"We're familiar with how that works," Royce said coldly.

Wyatt cocked an eyebrow. "Bad experience?"

"We had a job there once," Hadrian replied. "A dwarf named Gravis was angry about humans desecrating what he considered a dwarven masterpiece. We had to get in to stop him from sabotaging it."

"You broke into Drumindor?" Wyatt looked impressed. "I thought that was impossible."

"Just about," Royce answered, "and we didn't get paid enough for the trouble it gave me."

Hadrian snorted. "*You?* I was the one who nearly died making that leap. You just hung there and laughed."

"How'd you get in? I heard that place is kept tighter than Cornelius DeLur's purse," Wyatt pressed.

"It wasn't easy," Royce grumbled. "I learned to hate dwarves on that job. Well, there and..." He trailed off, rubbing his left shoulder absently.

"It will be the harvest moon in a few weeks. Maybe we'll catch the show on the way back," Wyatt said.

The lookout announced the sighting of sails. Several ships clustered under the safety of the fort, but they were so far out that only their topsails showed.

"I would have expected the captain to have ordered a course change by now. He's letting us get awfully close."

"Drumindor can't shoot this far, can she?" Hadrian asked.

"No, but the fortress isn't the only danger," Wyatt pointed out. "It isn't safe for an imperial vessel to linger in these waters. Delgos isn't officially at war with us, but everyone knows the DeLurs support the Nationalists and—well—accidents can happen."

They continued sailing due south. Not until the point was well astern and nearly out of sight did the captain appear on the quarterdeck. Now they would discover which direction the *Emerald Storm* would go.

"Heave to, Mr. Bishop!" he ordered.

"Back the mains'l!" the lieutenant shouted, and the men sprang into action.

This was the first time Hadrian had heard these particular orders and he was glad that, as ship's cook, he was not required to carry them out. It did not take long for him to see what was happening. Backing the mainsail caused it to catch the wind on its forward side. If the foremast and mizzenmast were also backed, the ship would sail in reverse. Since they remained trimmed as they were, the force of the wind lay balanced between them, leaving the ship stationary on the water.

Once the ship was heaved to, the captain ordered a reading

on the ship's position, then disappeared once more into his cabin, leaving Lieutenant Bishop on the quarterdeck.

"So much for picking a direction," Hadrian muttered to himself.

They remained stationary for the rest of that day. At sunset, Captain Seward ordered lights hauled aloft, but nothing further slipped his lips.

Hadrian served supper, boiled salt pork stew again. Even he was tired of his menu, but the only complaints came from the recently pressed, who were not yet hardened to the conformities of life at sea. Hadrian suspected most of the veterans on board would demand salt pork and biscuits even on land, rather than break the routine.

"He is a murderer, that's why!"

Hadrian heard Staul shout as he entered the below deck with the last of the evening meals. The Tenkin was standing slightly crouched in the center of the crew's quarters. His dark tattooed body and rippling muscles were revealed as he removed his shirt. In his right hand he held a knife. A cloth wrapped his left fist. His chest heaved with excitement, a mad grin on his face and a sinister glare in his eyes.

In front of Staul stood Royce.

"He killed Edgar Drew. Everyone knows it. Now he'll be the one to die, eh?"

Royce stood casually, his hands loosely clasped before him as if he were just one of the bystanders—except his eyes never left the knife. Royce followed it as a cat might watch the movement of a string. It took Hadrian only a second to see why. Staul was holding the knife by the blade. On a hunch, Hadrian scanned the room and found Bernie Defoe standing behind and to Royce's left, a hand hidden behind his back.

Staul took his attention off Royce for a moment, but Hadrian noticed his weight shift to his rear foot and hoped his friend noticed as well. An instant later Staul threw the knife. The blade flew with perfect accuracy, only when it arrived, Royce was not there and the tip buried itself in a deck post.

All eyes were on Staul as he bristled with rage, shouting curses. Hadrian forced himself to ignore the Tenkin and searched for Bernie. He had moved. Spotting the glint of a blade in the crowd, he found him again. Bernie had slipped up behind Royce and lunged. Royce spun. Not taken in by the plot, he faced his old guild mate with the blade Staul had provided. Bernie halted mid-step, hesitated, and then backed away, melting into the crowd. Hadrian doubted anyone else noticed his involvement.

"Ah! You dance well!" Staul shouted, and laughed. "That is good. Perhaps next time you trip, eh?"

The excitement over, the crowd broke up. As they did, Jacob Derning muttered loud enough for everyone to hear, "Good to see I'm not the only one who thinks he killed poor Drew."

"Royce," Hadrian called, keeping his eyes focused on Jacob. "Perhaps you should take your meal up on the deck, where it's cooler."

"That was pleasant," Hadrian said after the two had safely reached the galley and closed the door behind them.

"What was?" Poe asked, dishing out the last of the stew for the midshipmen.

"Oh, nothing really. A few crewmen just tried to murder Royce."

"What?" Poe almost dropped the whole kettle.

"Now can I kill people?" Royce asked, stepping into the corner and putting his back against the wall. He had an evil look on his face.

"Who tried to murder him?"

"Bernie," Royce replied. "So what am I supposed to do now? Lie awake at night waiting for him and his buddies—I'm sorry, his *mates*—to knife me?"

"Poe, would it be possible for me and Royce to sleep in here at night?"

"In the galley? I suppose. Won't be too comfortable, but if Royce is always on time for his watch, and if you tell Mr. Bishop you want him to help with the nighttime boils, he might allow it."

"Great, I'll do that. While I'm gone, Poe, can you go below and get us a couple of hammocks that we can hang in here? Royce, maybe you can rig a lock for the door?"

"It's better than being bait."

ঌ

Royce worked both the second dogwatch and the first watch, which kept him aloft from sunset until midnight. By the time he returned, Hadrian had obtained permission for Royce to sleep in the galley. Poe had moved up what little gear they had and strung two hammocks between the walls of the narrow room.

"How is it?" Royce asked, entering the darkened galley and finding Hadrian hanging in the netting.

"Hmm?" he asked, waking up. "Oh, okay, I guess. The room is too narrow for me. I feel like I'm being bent in half, but it should be fine for you. How was your watch? Did you see Defoe?"

"Never took my eyes off old *Bernie*," he said, grinning and dodging a pot that hung from the overhead beam. Hadrian knew Royce must have enjoyed a bit of revenge on Bernie. If there was ever a place where Royce held an advantage, it was a hundred feet in the air, dangling from beams and ropes in the dark of night.

Hadrian shifted his weight, causing his hammock to swing. "What did you do?"

"Actually, I didn't do anything, but that was what drove him crazy. He's still sweating."

"So he did recognize you."

"Oh yeah, and it was like there were two moons out tonight, his face was so pale."

Royce checked the lines and the mountings of the hammock Poe had installed for him, and looked generally pleased with the work.

"To be honest, I'm surprised Bernie didn't suffer an accidental fall," Hadrian said.

Royce shook his head. "Two accidents off my mast is just bad planning. Besides, Bernie wasn't trying to kill me."

"Sure looked that way from where I was standing. And it seemed pretty organized too."

"You think so?" he asked, sitting on the crate of biscuits Poe had brought up for the morning's breakfast. "It's not how I would do it. First, why stage the fight in a room full of witnesses? If they had killed me, they would hang. Second, why attack me below? Like I said, the sea is the perfect place to dispose of a body, and the closer to the rail you get your victim, the easier it is."

"Then what do you think they were up to?"

Royce pursed his lips and shook his head. "I have no idea. If it's a diversion to rifle our belongings, why not hold it topside? For that matter, why bother with a diversion at all? There have been plenty of times while we were on deck to go through our stuff."

"You think it was just to intimidate us?"

"If it was, it wasn't Bernie's idea. Threatening to kill me but not finishing the job is famously fatal. He would know that."

"So Derning put them up to it?"

"Maybe, but...I don't know. Derning doesn't seem like someone Bernie would take orders from—especially not such stupid orders."

"Makes sense. So then—"

A muffled thump, like another body hitting the deck, brought them to their feet. Hadrian threw open the door of the galley and cautiously looked out.

The larboard watch was on duty, but rather than the typical watch-and-snooze routine, they were hard at work, running a boat drill. They had hoisted the longboat from the yard and had it over the side, where it bumped the gunwale once more before being lowered into the sea.

"Odd time for a lifeboat drill," Wyatt said, walking toward them from the shelter of the forecastle.

"Trouble sleeping?" Royce asked.

Wyatt beamed a grin. "Look who else is on duty," he told them, pointing at the quarterdeck, where Sentinel Thranic, Mr. Beryl, Dr. Levy, and Bernie Defoe stood talking.

They slipped around the forecastle, moving quickly to the bow. Looking over the rail, Hadrian saw six men rowing toward a nearby light.

"Another ship," Royce muttered.

"Really?"

"A small single-mast schooner. No flag."

"Is there anything in the longboat?" Hadrian asked. "If that's payment going to—"

Royce shook his head. "Just the crew."

They watched as the sound of the oars faded, then waited. Hadrian strained, peering into the darkness, but all he could see were the bobbing light of the little boat and the one marking its destination.

"Boat's coming back," Royce announced, "and there's an extra head now."

Wyatt squinted. "Who would they be picking up in the middle of the night from Delgos?"

They watched as the longboat returned. Just as Royce had said, there was an additional man—a passenger. Wrapped in ship's blankets, he was small and thin, with a long pasty face and wild, white hair. He looked to be very old, far too old to be any use as a sailor. He came aboard and spoke to Thranic and Dr. Levy at length. The old man's things were gathered and deposited beside him. One of the bags came loose and two weighty leather-bound books spilled onto the bleached deck. "Careful, my boy," the old man cautioned the sailor. "Those are one of a kind and, like me, are very old and sadly fragile."

"Gather his things and take them to Dr. Levy's quarters," Thranic ordered. Glancing toward the bow, he stopped abruptly. He glared at them, licking his thin lips in thought, then slowly approached. As he did, he held his dark cloak tight, his shoulders raised to protect his neck from the cold wind. Between this and his stooped back, he resembled a scavenger bird.

"What are all of you doing on deck? None of you are part of the larboard watch."

"Off duty, sir," Wyatt answered for them. "Just getting a bit of fresh air."

Thranic peered at Hadrian and took a step toward him. "You're the cook, aren't you?"

Without thinking, Hadrian felt at his side for the hilt of his absent sword. Something about the sentinel made him flinch. Sentinels were always scary, but this one was absolutely chilling. Returning his gaze was like staring into the eyes of restrained madness.

"You joined this voyage along with..." Thranic's eyes shifted to Royce. "This one—yes, the nimble fellow—the one so good at climbing. What's your name? Melborn, isn't it? Royce Melborn? I heard you were seasick. How odd."

Royce remained silent.

"Very odd, indeed."

"Sentinel Thranic?" the old man called, his weak voice barely making the trip across the deck. "I would rather like to get out of the damp wind, if I could." He coughed.

Thranic stared a moment longer at Royce, then pivoted sharply and left them.

"Not exactly the kind of guy you want taking an interest in you, is he?" Wyatt offered.

With the longboat back aboard, the captain appeared on the quarterdeck and ordered a new course—due east, into the wind.

CHAPTER 9

ELLA

"Another dispatch from Sir Breckton, sir," the clerk announced, handing a small scroll to the imperial chancellor. The elderly man returned to the desk in his little office and read the note. A scowl grew across his face.

"The man is incorrigible!" the chancellor burst out to no one, then pulled a fresh sheet of parchment and dipped his quill.

The door opened unexpectedly and the chancellor jumped. "Can't you knock?"

"Sorry, Biddings, did I startle you?" the Earl of Chadwick asked, entering with his exquisite floor-length cape trailing behind him. He had a pair of white gloves draped over one forearm as he bit into a bright red apple.

"You're always startling me. I think you get a sadistic pleasure from it."

Archibald smiled. "I saw the dispatch arrive. Is there any word from the *Emerald Storm*?"

"No, this is from Breckton."

"Breckton? What does he want?" Archibald sat in the armchair opposite the chancellor and rested his booted feet on a footstool.

"No matter how many times I tell him to wait and be patient, he refuses to grasp that we know more than he does. He wants permission to attack Ratibor."

Archibald sighed. "Again? I suppose you see now what I've had to put up with all these years. He and Enden are so headstrong I—"

"Were," the chancellor said, correcting him. "Sir Enden died in Dahlgren."

Ballentyne nodded. "And wasn't that a waste of a good man?" He took another bite and, with his mouth still full, went on. "Do you need me to write him personally? He's my knight, after all."

"What would help is to be able to tell him *why* he doesn't need to attack."

Archibald shook his head. "Saldur and Ethelred are still insisting on secrecy regarding the—"

The chancellor raised a hand, stopping him. Archibald looked confused and the chancellor pointed at the chambermaid on her knees scrubbing the floor near the windows of his office.

Archibald rolled his eyes. "Oh please. Do you really think the scrub girl is a spy?"

"I've always found it best to err on the side of caution. She doesn't have to be a spy to get you hanged for treason."

"She doesn't even know what we're talking about. Besides, look at her. It isn't likely she'll be bragging in some pub. You don't go out at night boasting in bars, do you, lass?"

Ella shook her head and refused to look up, so that her brown sweat-snarled hair continued to hang in her face.

"See!" Archibald said in a vindicated tone. "It's like censoring yourself because there is a couch or a chair in the room."

"I was referring to a more subtle kind of danger," Biddings

told him. "Should something happen. Something unfortunate with the plan, such that it fails—someone always has to be blamed. How fortunate it would be to discover a loquacious earl who had boasted details to even a mindless chambermaid."

Archibald's smirk faded immediately.

"The third son of a dishonored baron doesn't rise to the position of imperial chancellor by being stupid," Biddings said.

"Point taken." Archibald glanced back at the scrub girl with a new expression of loathing. "I had best return to Saldur's office or he'll be looking for me. Honestly, Biddings, I'm really starting to detest staying in this palace."

"She still won't see you?"

"No, I can't get past her secretary. That Lady Amilia is a sly one. Plays all innocent and doe-eyed, but she guards the empress with ruthless determination. And Saldur and Ethelred are no help at all. They insist she plans to marry Ethelred. It has to be a lie. I simply can't imagine Modina wanting that old moose."

"Particularly when she could choose a young buck like yourself?"

"Exactly."

"And your desire is true love, of course. You've given absolutely no thought about how marrying Modina would make you emperor?"

"For a man who went from third baron's son to chancellor, I'm surprised you can even ask me that."

"Archie!" bellowed the voice of Regent Saldur, echoing down the hall outside the office.

"I'm in with Biddings!" Archibald shouted back through the open door. "And don't call me—" He was interrupted by the sudden rush of the scrub girl running, bucket in hand, from the office. "Looks like she doesn't like Saldur any more than I do."

☙

Arista had spilled scrub water onto her skirt, causing it to plaster the rough material to her legs. Her thin cloth shoes made a disagreeable slapping noise as she ran down the corridor. The sound of Saldur's voice made her run faster.

That had been close, yet she wondered if even Saldur, who had known her since birth, would recognize her now. There was nothing magical about her transformation, but that did not make it any less impenetrable. She wore dirty rags, she lacked makeup, and her once lustrous hair was now a tangled mess. It had lightened, bleached by the same sun that had tanned her skin. Still, it was more than just her appearance. Arista had changed. At times, when she caught her own reflection, it took a moment to register that she was seeing herself and not some poor peasant woman. The bright-eyed girl was gone, and a dark, brooding spirit possessed her battered body.

More than anything else, the sheer absurdity of the situation provided the greatest protection. No one would believe that a sheltered, self-indulgent princess would willingly scrub floors in the palace of her enemy. She doubted even Saldur's mind would grant enough latitude to penetrate the illusion. Even if some people thought she looked familiar—and several seemed to—their minds simply could not bend that far. To conceive of the thought that Ella the scrub girl was the Princess of Melengar was as ridiculous as the idea that pigs could talk or that Maribor was not god. To entertain such a notion would require a mind open to new possibilities, and no one at the palace fit that description.

The only one she worried about, besides Saldur, was the

empress's secretary. She was not like the others—she noticed Arista. Amilia saw through her veneer with suspicious eyes. Saldur clearly surrounded the empress with his best and brightest, and Arista did all she could to avoid her.

On the road north from Ratibor, Arista had fallen in with a band of refugees fleeing to Aquesta, and they had arrived nearly a month earlier. The location spell had led her to the palace itself. Things grew more complicated after that. If she had been more confident in the magic, and her ability to use it, she might have returned to Melengar right away with the news that Gaunt was a prisoner in the imperial palace. As it was, she felt the need to see Degan for herself. She managed to obtain a job as a chambermaid, hoping to repeat the location spell inside the castle walls at various locations, only that was not working out. Closely watched by the headmistress, Edith Mon, she rarely found enough free time and privacy to cast the spell. On the few occasions she succeeded, the smoke indicated a direction, but the maze of corridors blocked any attempt to follow. Magically stymied, Arista sought to determine Gaunt's whereabouts by eavesdropping while at the same time learning her way around the grounds.

"What have ya done now?" Edith Mon shouted at Arista as she entered the scullery.

Arista had no idea what a hobgoblin looked like, but she guessed it probably resembled Edith Mon. She was stocky and strong. Her huge head sat on her shoulders like a boulder, crushing whatever neck she might have once had. Her face, pockmarked and spotted, provided the perfect foundation for her broad nose with its flaring nostrils, through which she breathed loudly, particularly when angry, as she was now.

Edith yanked the bucket from her hands. "Ya clumsy little wench! Ya best pray you spilled it only on yerself. If I hear ya left a dirty puddle in a hallway..."

Edith had threatened to cane her on three occasions but had been interrupted each time—twice by the head cook. Arista was not sure what she would do if it came to that. Scrubbing floors was one thing, but allowing herself to be beaten by an old hag was something else. If tried, she might discover there was more to her new chambermaid than she had thought. Arista often amused herself by contemplating which curse might be best for old Edith. At that moment, she was considering the virtues of skin worms, but all she said was "Is there anything else today?"

The older woman glared. "Oh! Ya think yer something, don't ya? Ya think yer better than the rest of us, that yer arse shines of silver. Well, it don't! Ya don't even have a family. I know you live in that alley with the rest of them runners. Yer one dodgy smile away from making yer meals whoring, so I'd be careful, sweetie!"

There were several snickers from the other kitchen workers. Some risked Edith's wrath by pausing in their work to watch. The scullery maids, charwomen, and chambermaids all reported to Edith. The others, like the cook, butcher, baker, and cupbearer, reported to Ibis Thinly but they sided with Edith—after all, Ella was the *new* girl. In the lives of those who lived in the scullery, seeing punishment administered was what passed for entertainment.

"Is that a yes or a no?" Arista asked calmly.

Edith's eyes narrowed menacingly. "No, but tomorrow ya start by cleaning every chamber pot in the palace. Not just emptying them, mind ya. I want them scrubbed clean."

Arista nodded and started to walk past her. As she did, cold water rained down as Edith emptied the bucket on her.

The room burst into laughter. "A shame it wasn't clean water. Ya could use a bath." Edith cackled.

The uproar died abruptly as Ibis appeared from out of the cellar.

"What's going on here?" The chief cook's booming voice drew everyone's attention.

"Nothing, Ibis," Edith answered. "Just training one of my girls is all."

The cook spotted Arista standing in a puddle, drenched from head to foot. Her hair hung down her face, dripping filthy water. Her entire smock was soaked through and the thin material clung indecently to her skin, causing her to fold her arms across her breasts.

Ibis scowled at Edith.

"What is it, Ibis?" Edith grinned at him. "Don't like my training methods?"

"No, I can't say I do. Why do you always have to treat them like this?"

"What are ya gonna do? Ya gonna take Ella under your wing like that tramp Amilia? Maybe this one will become archbishop!"

There was another round of laughter.

"Cora!" Ibis barked. "Get Ella a tablecloth to wrap around her."

"Careful, Ibis. If she ruins it, the chamberlain will have at you."

"And if Amilia hears you called her a tramp, you might lose your head."

"That little pretender doesn't have the piss to do anything against me."

"Maybe," the chief cook said, "but she's one of *them* now, and I'll bet that any noble who heard that you insulted one of their own—well, they might take it personally."

Edith's grin disappeared and the laughter vanished with it.

Cora returned with a tablecloth, which Ibis folded twice before wrapping around Arista's shoulders. "I hope you have another kirtle at home, Ella. It's gonna be cold tonight."

Arista thanked him before heading out the scullery door. It was already dark and, just as Ibis had predicted, cold. Autumn was in full swing, and the night air shocked her wet body. The castle courtyard was nearly empty, with only a few late carters dragging their wagons out through the main gate. A page raced between the stables and the keep, hauling armloads of wood, but most of the activity that usually defined the yard was absent. She passed through the great gates, where the guards ignored her, as they had done each evening. The moment she reached the bridge and stepped beyond the protection of the keep's walls, the full force of the wind struck her. She clenched her jaw to stifle a cry, hugged her body with fingers that were already turning red, and shivered so badly it was hard to walk.

Not skin worms. No. Not nearly bad enough.

"Oh dear!" Mrs. Barker exclaimed, rushing over as Arista entered Brisbane Alley. "What happened, child? Not that Edith Mon again?"

Arista nodded.

"What was it this time?"

"I spilled some wash water."

Mrs. Barker shook her head and sighed. "Well, come over to the fire and try and dry off before you catch your death."

She coaxed Arista to the communal fire pit. Brisbane Alley was literally the end of the road in Aquesta, a wretched little dirt patch behind Brickton's Tannery where the stench from the curing hides kept away any except the most desperate. Newcomers without money, relatives, or connections settled here. The lucky ones lived huddled under canvas sheets, carts, and the wagons they had arrived in. The rest simply huddled against the tannery wall, trying to block the wind as they slept. So had Arista—that is, until the Barkers adopted her.

Brice Barker worked shouting advertisements through the city streets for seven coppers a day. All of that went to buy food to feed three children and his wife. Lynnette Barker took in what sewing work she could find. When the weather turned colder, they had offered Arista a place under their wagon. She had known them for only a few weeks, but already she loved them like her own family.

"Here, Ella," Lynnette said, bringing an old kirtle for her to put on. The dress was little more than a rag, worn thin and frayed along the hem. Lynnette also brought Esrahaddon's robe. Arista went around the corner and slipped out of her wet things. Lynnette's dress did nothing to keep out the cold, but the robe vanquished the wet chill instantly in uncompromising warmth.

"That's really a wonderful robe, Ella," Lynnette told her, marveling at how the firelight made it shimmer and reflect colors. "Where did you get it?"

"A...friend left it to me when he died."

"Oh, I'm sorry," she said sadly. Her expression changed then from one of sadness to one of concern. "That reminds me, a man was looking for you."

"A man?" Arista asked as she folded the tablecloth. If anything happened to it, Edith would make Ibis pay.

"Yes, earlier today. He spoke to Brice while he was working on the street, and mentioned he was looking for a young woman. He described you perfectly, although oddly enough, he didn't know your name."

"What did he look like?" Arista hoped her concern was not reflected in her voice.

"Well," Lynnette faltered, "that's the thing. He wore a dark hood and a scarf wrapped about his face, so Brice didn't get a good look at him."

Arista pulled the robe tightly about her.

Is he here? Has the assassin managed to track me down?

Lynnette noticed the change in her and asked, "Are you in trouble, Ella?"

"Did Brice tell him I lived here?"

"No, of course not. Brice is many things, but he's no fool."

"Did he give a name?"

Lynnette shook her head. "You can ask Brice about him when he returns. He and Wery went to buy flour. They should be back soon."

"Speaking of that," Arista said, fishing coins out of her wet dress, "here's three copper tenents. They paid me this morning."

"Oh no. We couldn't—"

"Of course you can! You let me sleep under your wagon, and you watch my things when I'm at work. You even let me eat with you."

"But three! That's your whole pay, Ella. You won't have anything left."

"I'll get by. They feed me at the palace sometimes, and my needs are pretty simple."

"But you'll want a new set of clothes, and you'll need shoes come winter."

"So will your children, and you won't be able to afford them without an extra three coppers a week."

"No, no—we can't. It's very nice of you, but—"

"Ma! Ma! Come quick! It's Wery!" Finis, the Barkers' eldest son, raced down the street, shouting as he came. He looked frightened, his eyes filled with tears.

Lynnette lifted her skirt and ran, Arista chasing after her. They rushed to Coswall Avenue, where a crowd formed outside the bakery. Pushing past the crowd, they saw a boy lying unconscious on the cobblestone.

"Oh sweet Maribor!" Lynnette cried, falling to her knees beside her son.

Brice knelt on the stone, holding Wery in his arms. Blood soaked his hands and tunic. The boy's eyes were closed, his matted hair slick as if dipped in red ink.

"He fell from the baker's loft." Finis answered their unasked question, his voice quavering. "He was pulling one of them heavy flour bags down 'cause the baker said he'd sell us two cups for the price of one if he did. Pa and I told him to wait fer us, but he ran up, like he's always doing. He was pulling *real* hard. As hard as he could, and then his hands slipped. He stumbled backward and..." Finis was talking fast, his voice rising as he did until it cracked and he stopped.

"Hit his head on the cobblestones," declared a stranger who wore a white apron and held a lantern. Arista thought he might be the baker. "I'm real sorry. I didn't think the boy would hurt himself like this."

Lynnette ignored the man and pried her child from her husband, pulling Wery to her breast. She rocked him as if he were a newborn. "Wake up, honey," she whispered softly. Tears fell on Wery's blood-soaked cheeks. "Please, baby, oh for the love of Maribor, please wake up! Please, oh please..."

"Lynn, honey..." Brice started.

"*No!*" she shouted at him, and tightened her grip on the boy.

Arista stared at the scene. Her throat was tight, and her eyes were filling so quickly that she could not see clearly. Wery was a wonderful boy, playful, friendly. He reminded her of Fanen Pickering, which only made matters worse. But Fanen had died with a sword in his hand, and Wery was only eight and likely had never touched a weapon in his short life. She could not understand why such things happened to good people. Tears slipped down her cheeks as she watched the small figure of the boy dying in his mother's arms.

Arista closed her eyes, wiping the tears. When she opened them again, she noticed several people in the crowd backing away.

Her robe was glowing.

Giving off a pale light, the shimmering material illuminated those around her with an eerie white radiance. Lynnette saw the glow, and hope flooded her face. She looked up at Arista, her eyes pleading. "Ella, can...can you save him?" she asked with trembling lips and desperate eyes. Arista began to form the word *no*, but Lynnette quickly spoke again. "You can!" she insisted. "I know you can! I've always known there was something different about you. The way you talk, the way you act. The way you forget your own name, and that—*that robe*! You can save him. I know you can. Oh please, Ella." She paused and swallowed, shaking so hard it made Wery's head rock. "Oh, Ella, I know—I know it's so much more than three coppers, but he's my baby! You'll help him, won't you? Please, oh please, Ella."

Arista could not breathe. She felt her heart pounding in her ears and her body trembled. Everyone silently watched her. Even Lynnette stopped her pleading. Arista found herself saying through quivering lips, "Lay him down."

Lynnette gently lowered Wery's body, his limbs lifeless, his head tilted awkwardly to one side. Blood continued to seep from the boy's wound.

Arista knelt beside him and placed a hand on the boy's chest. He was still breathing, but it was so shallow, so weak. Closing her eyes, she began to hum. She heard the concerned mutterings of those in the crowd, and one by one, she tuned them out. Arista could sense the heartbeats of the men and women surrounding her, and she forced them out as well. She focused on the sound of the wind. Soft and gentle it blew, swirling between the buildings, across the street, skipping over stones. Above her she felt the twinkle of the stars and the smile of the moon. Her hand was on the body of the boy, but her fingers felt the strings of the instrument she longed to play.

The gentle wind grew stronger. The swirl became an eddy; the eddy, a whirlwind; and the whirlwind, a vortex. Her hair whipped madly, but she hardly noticed. Before her lay a void, and beyond that was a distant light. She could see him in the darkness, a dull silhouette before the brilliance, growing smaller as he traveled away. She shouted to him. He paused. She strummed the chords and the silhouette turned. Then, with all her strength, she clapped her hands together and the sound was thunder.

When she opened her eyes, the light from the robe had faded and the crowd was cheering.

CHAPTER 10

FALLEN STAR

"Sail ho!" the lookout shouted from the masthead.

The *Emerald Storm* was now two weeks out of Aquesta, slipping across the placid waters of the Ghazel Sea. The wind remained blowing from the southwest. Since rounding the Horn of Delgos, they made slow progress. The ship was close hauled, struggling to gain headway into the wind. Mr. Temple kept the top crews busy tacking the ship round, wearing windward, and keeping their course by crossing back and forth, but Hadrian guessed that a quickly walking man could make faster progress.

It was midmorning, and seamen who were not in the rigging or otherwise engaged in the ship's navigation were busy scrubbing the deck with sandstone blocks or flogging it dry. All the midshipmen were on the quarterdeck taking instruction in navigation from Lieutenant Bishop. Hadrian heard the lookout's call as he returned to the galley after delivering the previous evening's pork grease. Making his way to the port side, he spotted a small white square on the horizon. Bishop immediately suspended class and took an eyeglass to see for himself, then sent a midshipman to the captain's cabin. The captain emerged so quickly that he was still adjusting his hat as he appeared on the quarterdeck. He paused for a moment, tugged on his uniform, and sniffed the air with a wrinkle of his nose.

"Lookout report!" he called to the masthead.

"Two ships, off the port bow, sir!"

Hadrian looked again, and just as the lookout had reported, he spotted a second sail now visible above the line of the water.

"The foremost is showing two squares—appears to be a lugger. The farther ship...I'm seeing two red lateen sails, single-decked, possibly a tartane. They're running with the wind and closing fast, sir."

"What flag are they flying?"

"Can't say, sir, the wind has them blowing straight at us."

Hadrian watched the ships approach, amazed at their speed. Already he could see them clearly.

"This could be trouble," Poe said.

Hadrian had been so intent on the ships that he had failed to notice his assistant appear beside him. The thin rail of a boy was busy tying the black ribbon in his ponytail as he stared out at the vessels.

"How's that?"

"Those red sails."

Hadrian looked back out across the water. "And why's that a problem?"

"Only the Dacca use them, and they're worse than any pirates you'll run across."

"Beat to quarters, Mr. Bishop," the captain ordered.

"All hands on station!" the lieutenant shouted. "Beat to quarters!"

Hadrian heard a drumroll as the boatswain and his mates cleared the deck. The midshipmen, dispersed to their stations, shouted orders to their crews.

"Come on!" Poe told him.

There was a pile of briquettes at the protected center of the forecastle. Hadrian ignited them with hot coals from the galley stove as soon as the surrounding deck had been soaked with seawater. Around it, archers prepped their arrows with oil. Seamen brought dozens of buckets of seawater, along with buckets of sand, and positioned them around the ship. It took only minutes to secure for battle, and then they waited.

The ships were closer and larger now, but still the flags they flew were invisible. The *Storm* remained deathly silent, the only sounds coming from the wind, the waves, and the creaking hull. A random gust fluttered the lugger's flag.

"They're flying the Gribbon of Calis, sir!" the lookout shouted.

"Mr. Wesley," the captain addressed the midshipman stationed on the quarterdeck. "You've studied signals?"

"Aye, sir."

"Take a glass and get aloft. Mr. Temple, run up our name and request theirs."

"Aye, aye, sir."

Still no one else moved or spoke. All eyes were on the approaching vessels.

"Lead vessel is the *Bright Star*. Aft vessel is..." Wesley hesitated. "Aft vessel isn't responding, sir."

"Two points aport!" the captain shouted abruptly, and Wyatt spun the wheel, weathering the ship as close to the wind as possible, heading them directly toward the lugger. The topmen went into action like a hundred spiders, crawling along the shrouds, working to grab every bit of wind possible.

"New signal from the *Bright Star*," Wesley shouted. "Hostile ship astern!"

Small streaks of smoke flew through the otherwise clear sky. The tartane was firing arrows at the *Bright Star*, but the shots fell short, dropping into the sea a good two hundred yards astern.

"Ready the forward ballista!" the captain ordered. A squad of men on the forecastle began to crank a small capstan, which ratcheted the massive bowstring into firing position. They lighted another brazier in advance of the stanchion as an incendiary bolt was loaded. Then they waited, once more watching the ships sail closer.

Everything about the Dacca ship was exotic. Made of dark wood, the vessel glittered with gold swirls artfully painted along the hull. It bore long decorative pendants of garish colors. A stylized image of a black dragon in flight adorned the scarlet mainsail, and on the bowsprit was the head of a ghoulish beast with bright emerald eyes. The sailors appeared as foreign as the ship. They were dark-skinned, powerful brutes wearing only bits of red cloth wrapped around their waists.

Poorly handled, the *Bright Star* lost the wind and its momentum. Behind it, the tartane descended. Another volley of arrows from the Dacca smoked through the air. This time several struck the *Bright Star* in the stern, but one lucky shot made it to the mainsail, setting it aflame.

Although victorious over the lugger, the tartane chose to flee before the approaching *Emerald Storm.* It came about and Hadrian watched Captain Seward ticking off the distance as the *Storm* inched toward it. Even after the time lost during the turn, the Dacca ship was still out of ballista range.

"Helm alee. Bring her over!" the captain shouted. "Tacks and sheets!"

The *Emerald Storm* swung round to the same tack as the tartane, but the *Storm* did not have the momentum under it, nor the nimbleness of the smaller ship. The tartane was the faster vessel, and all the crew of the *Emerald Storm* could do was watch as the Dacca sailed out of reach.

Seeing the opportunity lost, Captain Seward ordered the *Storm* heaved to and the longboats launched. The *Bright Star's* mainsail and mast burned like a giant torch. Stays and braces snapped and the screams of men announced the fall of the flaming canvas to the deck. Still, the ship's momentum carried it astern of the *Storm*. As it passed, they could see the terrified sailors struggling hopelessly to put out the flames that enveloped the deck. Before the longboats were in the water, the *Bright Star* was an inferno, and most of the crew were already in the sea.

The boats returned laden with frantic men. Nearly all were tawny-skinned, dark-eyed sailors dressed in whites and grays. They lay across the deck coughing, spitting water, and thanking Maribor, as well as any nearby crew member.

❧

The *Bright Star* was an independent Wesbaden trader from Dagastan heading home to western Calis with a load of coffee, cane, and indigo. Despite the *Storm's* timely intervention, more than a third of the small crew perished. Some passed out in the smoke while fighting the flames, and others remained trapped below deck. The captain of the *Bright Star* perished, struck by one of the fiery arrows the Dacca had rained on his vessel. This left only twelve men, five of whom lay in Dr. Levy's care with burns.

Mr. Temple sized up the able-bodied survivors and added them to the ship's complement. Royce was back at work aloft as Hadrian finished serving dinner to the crew. Hadrian's easygoing attitude and generosity with the galley grease had won him several friends. There had been no more attempts on Royce's life, but they still did not know why Royce had been targeted, or by whom. For the moment, it was enough that Bernie, Derning, and Staul remained at a safe distance.

"Aye, this is Calis, not Avryn," Hadrian heard one of the new seamen say in a harsh, gravelly voice, as he brought down the last messkid. "The light of civilization grows weak like a candle in a high easterly wind. The farther east you go, the stronger the wind blows, till out she goes, and in the darkness ye stand!"

A large number of the off-watch clustered around an aft table, where three of the new sailors sat.

"Then there you are in the world of the savage," the Calian sailor went on. "A strange place, me lads, a strange place indeed. Harsh, violent seas and jagged inlets of black-toothed rock, gripped tight by dense jungle. The netherworld of the Ba Ran Ghazel, the heart of darkness is a place of misery and despair, the prison where Novron drove the beasties to their eternal punishment. They can't help but try to get out. They look at the coasts of Calis with hungry eyes and they find footholds. Like lichen, they slip in and grow everywhere. The Calians try to push them back, but it be like trying to swat a sky of flies or hold water in yer hands." He cupped his palms, pretending to lose something between his fingers.

"Goblin and man living so close together ain't natural," another said.

The first sailor nodded gravely. "But nothing in them jungles be natural. They have been linked for too long. The sons of Maribor and the spawn of Uberlin be warring one moment, then trading the next. Just to survive, the Calian warlords took to the ways of the goblins and spread the cursed practices of the Ba Ran to their own kin. Some of them are more goblin now than men. They even worship the dark god, burning tulan leaves and making sacrifices. They live like beasts. At night, the moon makes them wild, and in the darkness their eyes glow red!"

Several of the men made sounds of disbelief.

"It's the truth, me lads! Centuries ago, when the Old Empire fell, the eastern lords were abandoned to their fate. Left alone in the deep dark of the Calian jungles, they lost their humanity. Now the great stone fortresses along the Goblin Sea that once guarded the land from invasion be the home of Tenkin warlords—half-human, half-goblin monsters. They've turned their backs on the face of Maribor and embraced the ways of the Ghazel. Aye, me fellows, the state of Calis is a fearful one. So thankful we be for your daring act of kindness, for we'd be at the mercy of fate if ya hadn't pulled us from the sea. If it wasn't for your bravery, we'd surely be dead now...or worse."

"Wasn't much bravery needed," Daniels said. "The *Storm* could have whipped those buggers in a dead calm with half the crew drunk and the other half sick with the fever."

"Is that what you think?" Wyatt asked. Hadrian had not noticed him sitting silently in the gloom beyond the circle of the candle's light. "Is that what you *all* think?" His tone was oddly harsh—challenging. Wyatt sighed and, with an exasperated shake of his head, got up and climbed the ladder to the deck.

Having finished with the messkids, Hadrian followed. He found the helmsman on the forecastle. His hands gripped the rail as he stared at the shimmer of the new moon rolling on the back of the black sea.

"What's that all about?"

"We're in trouble and—" He paused, angrily motioning at the quarterdeck. Catching himself, he clenched his teeth, as if by doing so he could trap the words inside his mouth.

"What kind of trouble?" Hadrian glanced at the quarter-deck.

"The captain doesn't want me to say anything. He's a damn fool who won't listen to reason. I should disobey him and alter the ship's course right now. I could relieve Bliden on the wheel early and take us off course. No one would know until the reckoning is taken tomorrow at noon."

"Wesley would know." Hadrian pointed to the young man climbing to the quarterdeck on his nightly round as officer of the first watch. "He'd have you hauled to Mr. Bishop before you could blink."

"I could deal with Wesley if I had to. The deck is slippery, you know?"

"Now you're starting to sound like Royce. What's going on?"

"I suppose if I'm contemplating killing a midshipman, it hardly matters if I break captain's orders to keep quiet." Wyatt looked once again at the sea. "They're coming back."

"Who?"

"The Dacca. They didn't run. They're regrouping." He looked at Hadrian. "They dye their sails with the blood of their enemies. Did you know that? Hundreds of small ruddy boats line the coves and ports of their island. They know we're hugging the coast and sailing against the wind. Like wolves, they'll chase us down. Ten, twenty lateen-rigged tartanes will catch the wind that we can't. The *Storm* won't stand a chance."

"What makes you so sure? You could be wrong. The captain must have a good reason to stay on course."

"I'm not wrong."

CHAPTER 11

THE HOODED MAN

The hooded man walked away again.

Arista cowered deeper into the shadows under the tavern steps. She wanted to disappear, to become invisible. Her robe had turned a dingy brown, blending with the dirty wood. Drawing up the hood, she waited. It was *him*—the same man Lynnette had described. He was looking for her. She heard the sound of his boots on the cobblestone. They slowed, hesitated, and then grew louder.

He's coming back again!

The tall, dark figure appeared at the end of the alley for the third time. He paused. She held her breath. The streetlamps revealed a frightening figure dressed in a black hooded cloak and a thick scarf hiding his face. He wore an unseen sword—she could hear the telltale clap.

He took a tentative step toward her hiding place, then another, and then paused. The light's glare exposed white puffs issuing from his scarf. His head turned from side to side. He stood for several seconds, then pivoted so sharply his boot heel dug a tiny depression in the gravel, and walked away. After several tense minutes, Arista carefully crept out.

He was gone.

The first light of dawn rose in the east. If only she could make it back to the palace. At least there she would be safe from the assassin and away from the inevitable questions: "Who is she? How did she do it? Is she a witch?"

She had left Brisbane Alley before anyone thought to ask, but what about after? She had drawn too much attention, and—although she doubted anyone would connect the dots—the unabashed use of magic would cause a stir.

She removed the robe, carefully tucked it under the tavern steps, and set off toward the palace. The guards ignored her as usual, and she went about her tasks without incident. Throughout the day she had the good fortune to work relatively unnoticed, but by midday, news of the events of the night before had reached the palace. Everyone buzzed about the disturbance on Coswall Avenue. A boy had been brought back to life. By evening, rumors named the Witch of Melengar as the culprit. Luckily, no one suspected the scrub girl Ella of any more wrongdoing than failing to return the borrowed tablecloth.

Arista was exhausted and not merely from losing a night's sleep while avoiding the assassin. Saving Wery had drained her. After the day's work was over, she returned to the alley and retrieved the wizard's robe. She did not dare put it on, for fear someone might recognize it. Rolling it up and clutching it to her chest, she made her way to the edge of the broad avenue, unable to decide what to do next. Staying would be sheer stupidity. Looking down the broad length of Grand Avenue, she could see the front gates of the city. It felt like a lifetime since she had been home, and it would be so good to see a familiar face, to hear her brother's voice—to rest.

She knew she should leave. She should go that very minute, but she was so tired. The idea of setting out into the cold dark, alone and hungry, was too much to bear. She desperately needed a safe place to sleep, a hot meal, and a friendly face—

which meant just one thing: the Barkers. Besides, she could not leave without retrieving her pearl-handled hairbrush, the last remaining keepsake from her father.

Nothing had changed at the end of Brisbane Alley. The length was still dotted with small campfires and littered with bulky shadows of makeshift tents, carts, wagons, and barrels. People moved about in the growing dark. Some glanced at her as she passed, but no one spoke or approached her. She found the Barkers' wagon and, as always, a great tarp stretched out from it like a porch awning. One of the boys spotted her, and a moment later Lynnette rushed out. Without a word, she threw her arms around Arista and squeezed tightly.

"Come, have something to eat," she said, wiping her cheeks and leading Arista by the hand. Lynnette laid a pot on the fire. "I saved some just in case. I had to hide it, of course, or the vultures would have gobbled it all down. I wasn't sure you'd be back…"

The rest of the Barkers gathered around the fire. Finis and Hingus sat on the far side. Brice Barker, dressed in his usual white shirt and gray trousers, sat on an upturned crate, whittling a bit of wood. No one spoke. Arista took a seat on a wooden box, feeling awkward.

Is that apprehension in their eyes, or outright fear?

"Ella?" Lynnette finally asked in a small tentative voice. "Who are you?"

"I can't tell you that," she said after a long pause. She expected them to complain or press further. Instead, they all nodded silently, as if they had expected her answer, just as she had expected their question.

"I don't care who you are. You're always welcome at this fire," Brice said. He kept his eyes on the flames, but his words betrayed an emotion she had not expected. Brice, who made his living shouting in the streets all day, hardly ever spoke.

Lynnette dished out the bit of stew she had warmed up. "I wish there was more. If I had only known you'd be back."

"How is Wery?" Arista asked.

"He slept all night but was up most of the day running around, causing a nuisance as usual. Everyone who's seen him is saying the same thing—it was a miracle."

"Everyone?" Arista asked with concern.

"Folks been stopping by all day to see him and asking about you. Many said they had sick children or loved ones who are dying. One got so angry he knocked down the canvas and nearly upset the wagon before Finis brought Brice home to clear him out."

"I'm sorry."

"Oh, don't be! Please—no—don't ever be sorry," Lynnette pleaded. She paused, her eyes tearing again. "You won't be able to stay with us anymore, will you?"

Arista shook her head.

"The hooded man?"

"And others."

"I wish I could help," Lynnette said.

Arista leaned over and hugged her. "You have... more than you'll ever know. If I could just get a good night's sleep, then I—"

"Of course you can. Sleep in the wagon. It's the least we can do."

Arista was too exhausted to argue. She climbed up and, in the privacy of the cart, put the robe on to fight away the night's cold. She crawled across a lumpy bedding of coarse cloth that smelled of potatoes and onions, and laid her head down at last. It felt so good to close her eyes and let her muscles and mind go. She could hear them whispering outside, trying not to disturb her.

"She's a servant of Maribor," one of the boys said. She

could not tell which. "That's why she can't say. The gods never let them say."

"Or she could be Kile—a god disguised and doing good deeds," the other added. "I heard he gets feathers from Muriel's cloak for each one he does."

"Hush! She'll hear you," Lynnette scolded. "Go clean that pot."

Arista fell asleep to their whispers and woke to loud voices.

"I told you, I don't know what you're talking about! I don't know anything about a witch." It was Brice's voice, and he sounded frightened.

Arista peered out from the wagon. An imperial soldier stood holding a torch, his way blocked by Brice. Behind him, farther up the alley, other soldiers pounded on the door to the tannery and forced their way into the other tents.

"Sergeant," the man in front of Brice called, "over here!"

Three soldiers walked fast, their armor jangling, hard boots hammering the cobblestone.

"Tear down this hovel and search it," the sergeant ordered. "Continue to do the same for all these places. They're an eyesore and should be removed anyway."

"Leave them alone," Arista said, stepping out of the wagon. "They haven't done anything."

"Ella!" Brice snapped. "Stay out of this."

The sergeant moved briskly toward Arista, but Brice stepped in the way.

"Leave my daughter alone," he threatened.

"Brice, no," Arista whispered.

"I'm only here for the witch," the soldier told them. "But if you insist, I'll be happy to torch every tent in this alley."

"She's no witch!" Lynnette cried, clutching Wery to her side. "She saved my baby. She's a servant of Maribor!"

The sergeant studied Arista briefly, sucking on his front teeth.

"Bind her!" he ordered.

Two of his men stepped forward with a length of rope and grabbed hold of Arista by her arms. They immediately cried out in pain, let go, and stumbled backward. Esrahaddon's robe glowed a deep pulsating red. The guards glared at her in fear, shaking their injured hands.

Seeing her chance, Arista closed her eyes and began to concentrate. She focused on blocking out the sounds of the street and on—

Pain exploded across her face.

She fell backward to the ground, where she lay dazed. Her eyesight darkened at the edges. A ringing wailed in her ears.

"We'll have none of that!" the sergeant declared.

She looked up through watery eyes, seeing him standing over her, rubbing his knuckles. He drew his sword and pointed it at Brice.

"I know better than to let you cast your spells, witch. Don't make another sound, and remove that robe. Do it now! I'll strip you naked if needed. Make no sudden moves or sounds, or I'll cleave off this man's head here and now."

Lynnette was somewhere to her right, and Arista heard her gasp in horror.

"The robe. Take it off!"

Arista wiggled out of the robe, leaving herself clothed only in Lynnette's thin kirtle. The sergeant sucked on his teeth again and stepped closer. "Are my men going to have any more trouble with you?" He lifted the point of his sword toward Brice once again.

Arista shook her head.

"Good. Bind her tightly. Wrap her wrists and fingers and find something to gag her with." The guards approached again and jerked her arms so roughly behind her back that she cried out.

"Please don't hurt her," Lynnette begged. "She didn't do anything wrong!"

They tied her wrists, wrapping the rope around her fingers, pulling until the skin pinched painfully. As they did, the sergeant ordered Lynnette to pick up the robe and hand it to him. One of the soldiers grabbed Arista by the hair, dragging her to her feet. Another took hold of one of her sleeves and ripped it off.

"Open yer mouth," he ordered, pulling Arista's head back. When she hesitated, the soldier slapped her across the face. Again she staggered, and might have fallen if not for the other guard, still holding her hair. The slap was not nearly as painful as the blow the sergeant had given, but it made her eyes water again. "Now open!"

He stuffed the material into her mouth, jamming it in so far Arista thought she would choke. He tied it in place by wrapping more rope around her head and wedging it between her lips. When they tied one final length around her neck, Arista feared they might hang her right there.

"Now, that should keep us safe," declared the sergeant. "We'll cut those hands off when we get to the palace, and after you've answered questions, I expect we'll take that tongue as well."

A crowd gathered as they dragged her away, and Arista could hear Lynnette weeping. As they reached Coswall, the patrons of the Bailey turned out to watch. The men stood on the porch, holding mugs. She heard the word *witch* muttered more than once as she passed by.

By the time they reached the square, she was out of breath and choking on the gag. When she lagged behind, the guard holding the leash jerked hard and she fell. Her left knee struck the cobblestone of Bingham Square and she screamed, but the sound came out as a muffled grunt. Twisting, she landed on her shoulder to avoid hitting her face. Lying on her side, Arista cried in agony from the pain shooting up her leg.

"Up!" the soldier ordered. The rope tightened on her throat, the rough cord cutting her skin. The guard growled, "Get up, you lazy ass!" He pulled harder, dragging her a few inches across the stones. The rope constricted. She heard the pounding of blood in her ears. "Up, damn you!"

She felt the rope cut into her neck. She could barely breathe. The pounding in her ears hammered like drums, pressure building.

"Bruce?" one of the guards called. "Get her up!"

"I'm trying!"

There was another tug and Arista managed to sit up, but she was light-headed now. The street tilted and wobbled. As darkness grew at the edges of her vision, it was becoming difficult to see. She tried to tell them she was choking. All that came out was a pitiful moan.

She struggled to reach her knees, but the dizziness worsened. The ground shifted and dipped. She fell, hitting her shoulder again, and rolled to her back. She looked up at the soldier holding the leash and pleaded with her eyes, but all she saw in reply was anger and disgust.

"Get up or—" He stopped. The soldier looked abruptly to his right. He appeared puzzled. He let go of the rope and took a step backward.

The cord loosened, the pounding eased, and she could breathe again. She lay in the street, her eyes closed, happy to be alive. The clang of metal and the scuffle of feet caught her attention. Arista looked up to see the would-be strangler collapse to the street beside her.

Standing an arm's length away, the hooded man loomed with a blood-coated sword. From his belt he drew a dagger and threw it. Somewhere behind her there was a grunt and then a sound like a sack of flour hitting the ground.

The hooded man bolted past her. She heard a cry of pain. Metal struck metal, then another grunt, this one followed by a gurgling voice speaking garbled words. Another clash, another cry. She twisted around, rolling to her knees. She found him again. He stood in the center of Bingham Square, holding his sword in one hand and a dagger in the other. Three bodies lay on the ground. Two soldiers remained.

"Who are you?" the sergeant shouted at him. "We are imperial soldiers acting on official orders."

The hooded man said nothing. He rushed forward, swinging his blade. He dodged to the right, and catching the sergeant's sword high, he stabbed the man in the neck with his dagger. As he did, the remaining soldier swung at him. The hooded man cried out, then whirled in rage. He charged the last soldier, striking at him, his overwhelming fury driving the guard back.

The soldier turned and ran. The hooded man gave chase. The guard nearly made it to the end of the street before he was cleaved in the back. Once the soldier collapsed, the man continued attacking his screaming victim, stabbing him until he fell silent.

Arista sat helpless, bound in the middle of the square as the hooded man turned. With his sword and cloak dripping blood, he came for her. He pulled Arista to her feet and into a narrow alley.

He was breathing hard, sucking wetly through the scarf. No longer having the strength, physical or mental, Arista did not resist. The world was spinning and the night slipped into the unreal. She did not know what was happening or why, and she gave up trying to understand.

He dragged her into a stable and pushed her against the rough-hewn wall. A pair of horses shifted fearfully, spooked by the smell of blood. He held her tightly and brought his knife to her throat. Arista closed her eyes and held her breath. She felt the cold steel press against her skin as he drew it, cutting the cord away. He spun her around, cut her wrists loose, and then the cord holding the gag fell free.

"Follow me, quickly," he whispered, pulling her along by the hand. Confused, she staggered after him. Something was familiar in that voice.

He led her through a dizzying array of alleys, around dark buildings, and over wooden fences. Soon she had no idea where they were. He paused in a darkened corner, holding a finger to his scarf-covered lips. They waited briefly, then moved on. The wind picked up, carrying an odor of fish, and Arista heard the sound of surf. Ahead she could see the naked masts of ships bobbing at anchor along the wharf. When he reached a particularly dilapidated building, he led her up a back stair into a small room and closed the door behind them.

She stood rigid near the door, watching him as he started a fire in an iron stove. Seeing his hands, his arms, and the tilt of his head—something was so familiar. With the fire stoked, he turned and took a step toward her. Arista shrank until her back was against the door. He hesitated and then nodded. She recognized something in his eyes.

Reaching up, he drew back his hood and unwrapped the scarf. The face before her was painful to look at. Deformed and horribly scarred, it appeared to have melted into a patchwork of red blotches. One ear was missing, along with his eyebrows and much of his hair. His mouth lacked the pale pink of lips. His appearance was both horrid and so welcome she could find no words to express herself. She broke into tears of joy and threw her arms around him, hugging as tightly as her strength allowed.

"I hope this will teach you not to run off without me, Your Highness," Hilfred told her.

She continued to cry and squeeze, her head buried in his chest. Slowly his arms crept up, returning her embrace. She looked up and he brushed strands of tear-soaked hair from her face. In more than a decade as her protector, he had never touched her so intimately. As if realizing this, Hilfred straightened up and gently escorted her to a chair before reaching for his scarf.

"You're not going back out?" she asked fearfully.

"No," he replied, his voice dropped a tone. "The city will be filled with guards. It won't be safe for either of us to venture in public for some time. We'll be all right here. There are no occupied buildings around, and I rented this flat from a blind man."

"Then why are you covering up?"

He paused a moment, looking at the scarf. "The sight of my face—it makes people...uncomfortable, and it's important that you feel safe and at ease. That's my job, remember?"

"And you do it very well, but your face doesn't make me uncomfortable."

"You don't find me...unpleasant to look at?"

Arista smiled warmly. "Hilfred, your face is the most beautiful thing I've ever seen."

❧

The flat Hilfred stayed in was very small, just a single room and a closet. The floor and walls were rough pine planks weathered gray and scuffed smooth from wear. There were a rickety table, three chairs, and a ship's hammock. The single window was hazy from the buildup of ocean salt, admitting only a muted gray light. Hilfred refused to burn a single candle after dark, for fear of attracting attention. The small stove kept the drafty shack tolerably warm at night, but before dawn it was extinguished to avoid the chance of someone seeing the smoke.

For two days they stayed in the shack, listening to the wind buffet the roof shingles and howl over the stovepipe. Hilfred made soup from clams and fish he bought from the old blind man. Other than that, neither of them left the little room. Arista slept a lot. It seemed like years since she had felt safe, and her body surrendered to exhaustion.

Hilfred kept her covered and crept around the flat, cursing to himself whenever he made a noise. On the night of the second day, she woke when he dropped a spoon. He looked at her sheepishly and cringed at the sight of her open eyes.

"Sorry, I was just warming up some soup. I thought you might be hungry."

"Thank you," she told him.

"Thank you?"

"Yes, isn't that what you say when someone does something for you?"

He raised what would have been his eyebrows. "I've been your servant for more than ten years, and you've never once said *thank you*."

It was the truth, and it hurt to hear it. What a monster she had been. "Well overdue, then, don't you think? Let me check your bandage."

"After you eat, Your Highness."

She looked at him and smiled. "I've missed you so," she said. Surprise crossed his face. "You know, there were times growing up that I hated you. Mostly after the fire—for not saving my mother—but later I hated the way you always followed me. I knew you reported my every move. It's a terrible thing for a teenage girl to have an older boy silently following her every step, watching her eat, watching her sleep, knowing her most intimate secrets. You were always silent, always watchful. Did you know I had a crush on you when I was fourteen?"

"No," he said curtly.

"You were, what, a dashing seventeen? I tried everything to make you jealous. I chased after all the squires at court, pretending they wanted me, but none of them did. And you… you were such the loathingly perfect gentleman. You stood by stoically, and it infuriated me. I would go to bed humiliated, knowing that you were standing just outside the door.

"When I was older, I treated you like furniture—still, you treated me as you always had. During the trial—" She noticed Hilfred flinch and decided not to finish the thought. "And afterward, I thought you believed what they said and hated me."

Hilfred put down the spoon and sighed.

"What?" she asked, suddenly fearful.

He shook his head and a small sad laugh escaped his lips. "It's nothing, Your Highness."

"Hilfred, call me Arista."

He raised his brow once more. "I can't. You're my princess, and I'm your servant. That's how it's always been."

"Hilfred, you've known me since I was ten. You've followed me day and night. You've seen me early in the morning. You've seen me drenched in sweat from fevers. I think you can call me by my first name."

He looked almost frightened and resumed stirring the pot.

"Hilfred?"

"I'm sorry, Your Highness. I cannot call you by your given name."

"What if I command you to?"

"Do you?"

"No." Arista sighed. "What is it with men who won't use my name?"

Hilfred glanced at her.

"I only knew him briefly," she explained, not knowing why. She had never spoken about Emery to anyone before. "I've lived so much of my life alone. It never used to bother me and there's never been anyone—until recently."

Hilfred looked down and stirred the soup.

"He was killed. Since then, I've felt this hole. The other night I was so scared. I thought—no, I was certain—I was going to my death. I lost hope and then you appeared. I could really use a friend—and if you called me by—"

"I can't be your friend, Your Highness," Hilfred told her coldly.

"Why not?"

There was a long pause. "I can't tell you that."

A loud silence filled the room.

Arista stood, clutching the blanket around her shoulders. She stared at Hilfred's back until it seemed her stare caused him to turn and face her. When he did, he avoided looking in her eyes. He set out bowls on the table. She stood before him, blocking his way.

"Hilfred, look at me."

"The soup is done."

"I'm not hungry. Look at me."

"I don't want it to burn."

"Hilfred."

He said nothing and kept his eyes focused on the floor.

"What have you done that you can't face me?"

He did not answer.

The realization dawned on her and devastated Arista. He was not there to save her. He was not her friend. The betrayal was almost too much to bear.

"It's true." Her voice quavered. "You do believe the stories they say about me: that I'm a witch, that I'm evil, that I killed my father over my lust for the throne. Are you working for Saldur, or someone else? Did you steal me from the palace guards for some political advantage? Or is this all some plan to—to control me, to get me to trust you and lure me into revealing something?"

Her words had a profound effect on him. He looked pained, as if rained on by blows. His face was strained, his jaw stiff.

"You could at least tell me the truth," she said. "I should think you owe that much to my father, if not to me. He trusted you. He picked you to be my bodyguard. He gave you a chance to make something of yourself. You've enjoyed the privilege of court life because of his faith in you."

Hilfred was having trouble breathing. He turned away from her and, grabbing his scarf, moved toward the door.

"Yes, go—go on!" she shouted. "Tell them it didn't work. Tell them I didn't fall for it. Tell Sauly and the rest of those bastards that—that I'm not the stupid little girl they thought I was! You should have kept me tied and gagged, Hilfred. You're going to find it harder to haul me off to the stake than you think!"

Hilfred slammed his hand against the doorframe, making Arista jump. He spun on her, his eyes fierce and wild in a way she had never seen before, and she stepped back.

"*Do you know why I saved you?*" he shouted, his voice broken and shaking. "Do you? Do you?"

"To—to hand me over and get—"

"No! No! Not now. Back *then*," he cried, waving his arm. "Years ago, when the castle was burning. Do you know why I saved you back then?"

She did not speak. She did not move.

"I wasn't the only one there, you know. There were others.

Soldiers, priests, servants, they all just stood watching. They knew you were inside, but not a single person did anything. They just watched the place burn. Bishop Saldur saw me running for the castle and actually ordered me to stop. He said it was too late, that I would die. I believed him. I truly did, but I went in anyway. Do you know why? *Do you?*" he shouted at her.

She shook her head.

"Because I didn't care! I didn't want to live...not if you died." Tears streamed down his scarred face. "But don't ask me to be your friend. That is far too cruel a torture. As long as I can maintain a safe distance, as long as...as long as there is a wall between us—even if it's only one of words—I can tolerate—I can *bear* it." Hilfred wiped his eyes with his scarf. "Your father knew what he was doing—oh yes, he knew *exactly* what he was doing when he appointed me your bodyguard. I would die a thousand times over to protect you. But don't ask me to be grateful to him for the life he's given me, for it's been one of pain. I wish I had died that night so many years ago, or at least in Dahlgren. Then it would be over. I wouldn't have to look at you. I wouldn't have to wake up every day wishing I had been born the son of a great knight, or you the daughter of a poor shepherd."

He covered his eyes and leaned his head against the threshold. Arista did not recall doing it, but somehow she had crossed the room. She took Hilfred's face in her hands, and rising up on her toes, she kissed his mouth. He did not move, but he trembled. He did not breathe, but he gasped.

"Look at me," she said, extending her arms to display her stained and torn kirtle. "A shepherd's daughter would pity me, don't you think?" She took his hand and kissed it. "Can you ever forgive me?"

He looked at her, confused. "For what?"

"For being so blind."

Chapter 12

Sea Wolves

As it had for days, the *Emerald Storm* remained on its easterly course, making slow progress against a headwind that refused to shift. Maintaining direction required frequent tacking, which caused the top crews to work all night. Royce, as usual, had drawn the late shift. Getting this assignment was not Dime's fault. Royce had concluded that the mainmast captain was a fair man, but Royce was the newest member of a crew that rewarded seniority. He did not mind the shift. He enjoyed the nights he spent aloft. The air was fresh, and in the dark among the ropes, he was as comfortable as a spider in its web. This afforded Royce the opportunity to relax, think, and occasionally amuse himself by tormenting Bernie, who panicked anytime his old guild mate lost track of Royce.

Royce hung in the netting of the futtock shroud, his feet dangling over the open space—a drop of nearly a hundred feet. Above lay the dust of stars, while on the horizon the moon rose as a sliver—a cat's eye peering across the water at him. Below, lanterns flickered on the bow, quarterdeck, and stern, outlining the *Emerald Storm*. To his left, he could just make out the dark coast of Calis. Its thick vegetation was occasionally punctuated by a cliff or the brilliant white plume of a waterfall catching moonlight.

The seasickness was gone. He could not recall a more miserable time than his first week on board. The nausea and dizziness reminded him of being drunk—a sensation he hated. He had spent most of the first night hugging the ship's figurehead and vomiting off the bow. After four days, his stomach had settled, but he remained drained, and he tired easily. It had taken weeks to dull the memory of that misery, but nested in the rigging, looking out at the dark sea, he forgot it all. It surprised him just how beautiful the black waves could be, the graceful undulating swells kissed by the barefaced moon, all below a scattering of stars. Only one sight could surpass it.

What's she doing right now? Is she looking at the same moon and thinking of me?

Royce reached inside his tunic, pulled out the scarf, and rubbed the material between his fingers. He held it to his face and breathed deep. It smelled like her. He kept it hidden—his tiny treasure, soft and warm. On the nights of his sickness, he had lain in the hammock clutching it to his cheek as if it were a magic talisman to ward off misery. Only because of it had he been able to fall asleep.

The officers' deck hatch opened, and Royce spotted Beryl stepping out into the night air. Beryl liked his sleep and, being senior midshipman, rarely held the late watch. He stood glancing around, taking in the lay of the deck. He cast an eye up at the maintop, but Royce knew he was invisible in the dark tangles. Beryl spotted Wesley making his rounds on the forecastle and crossed the waist and headed up the stair. Wesley looked concerned at his approach but held his ground. Perhaps the boy would get another beating that night. Whatever torments Beryl had planned for Wesley were no concern of Royce's, and he thought it might be time to scare Bernie again.

"I won't do it," Wesley declared, drawing Royce's attention. Once more Beryl nervously looked upward.

Who are you looking for, Mr. Beryl?

Royce unhooked himself from the shrouds and rolled over for his own glance upward. As usual, Bernie was keeping his distance.

No threat there.

Royce climbed to the yard, walked to the end, and, just as he had done during the race with Derning, slid down the rope so he could hear them.

"I can make life on this ship very difficult for you," Beryl said, threatening Wesley. "Or have you forgotten your two days without sleep? There is talk that I'll be made acting lieutenant, and if you think your life is hard with my current rank, after my promotion it'll be a nightmare. And I'll see to it that any transfer is refused."

"I don't understand."

"You don't have to. In fact, it's better if you don't. That way you can sound sincere if the captain questions you. Just find him guilty of something. Misconduct, disrespect, I don't care. You put his buddy the cook on report for not saluting. Do something like that. Only this time it needs to be a flogging offense."

"But why me? Why can't *you* invent this charge?"

"Because if the accusation comes from you, the captain and Mr. Bishop will not question it." He grinned. "And if they do, it's your ass, not mine."

"And that's supposed to entice me?"

"No, but I'll get off your back. If you don't, you won't eat, you won't sleep, and you'll become very accident-prone. The sea can be dangerous. Midshipman Jenkins lost both thumbs on our last voyage when he slipped with a rope, which is strange, 'cause he didn't handle ropes that day. Invent a charge, make it stick, and get him flogged."

"And why do you want him whipped?"

"I told you. My friends want blood. Now do we have a deal?"

Wesley stared at Beryl and took a deep breath. "I can't misrepresent a man, and certainly not one under my command, simply to avoid personal discomfort."

"It will be a great deal more than discomfort, you little git!"

"The best I can do is to forget we had this conversation. Of course, should some unusual or circumstantial accusation be leveled against Seaman Melborn, I might find it necessary to report this incident to the captain. I suspect he will take a dim view of your efforts to advance insubordination on his vessel. It could be viewed as the seeds of mutiny, and we both know the penalty for that."

"You don't know who you're playing with, boy. As much as you'd like to think it, you're no Breckton. If I can't use you, I'll lose you."

"Is that all, Mr. Beryl? I must tack the ship now."

Beryl spat at the younger man's feet and stalked away. Wesley remained standing rigidly, watching him go. Once Beryl had disappeared below, Wesley gripped the rail and took off his hat to wipe the sweat from his forehead. He took a deep breath, replaced his hat, straightened his jacket, and then shouted in a clear voice, "Hands to the braces!"

Royce had dealt with many people in his life, from serfs to kings, and few surprised him. He knew he could always depend on their greed and weakness, and he was rarely disappointed. Wesley was the first person in years to astonish him. While the young midshipman could not see it, Royce offered him the only sincere salute he had bestowed since he had stepped aboard.

Royce ascended to the topsail to loose the yard brace in

anticipation of Wesley's next order when his eye caught an irregularity on the horizon. At night, with only the suggestion of a moon, it was hard for anyone to tell where the sky ended and the sea began. Royce, however, could discern the difference. At that moment, he noticed a break in the line. Out to sea, ahead of the *Storm*, a black silhouette broke the dusty star field.

"Sail ho!" he shouted.

"What was that?" Wesley asked.

"Sail off the starboard bow," he shouted, pointing to the southeast.

"Is there a light?"

"No, sir, a triangle-shaped sail."

Wesley moved to the starboard rail. "I don't see anything. How far out?"

"On the horizon, sir."

"The horizon?" Wesley picked up the eyeglass and panned the sea. The rest of the ship was silent except for the creaking of the oak timbers as they waited. Wesley muttered something as he slapped the glass closed and ran to the quarterdeck to pound on the captain's cabin. He paused and then pounded again.

The door opened to reveal the captain, barefoot in his nightshirt. "Mr. Wesley, have we run aground? Is there a mutiny?" The captain's steward rushed to him with his robe.

"No, sir. There's a sail on the horizon, sir."

"A what?"

"A triangular sail, sir. Over there." Wesley pointed while handing him the glass.

"On the horizon, you say? But how—" Seward crossed to the rail and looked out. "By Mar! But you've got keen eyes, lad!"

"Actually, the maintop crew spotted it first, sir. Sounded like Seaman Melborn, sir."

"I'll be buggered. Looks like *three* ships, Mr. Wesley. Call all hands."

"Aye, aye, sir!"

Wesley roused Bristol, who woke the rest of the crew. In a matter of minutes men ran to their stations. Lieutenant Bishop was still buttoning his coat when he reached the quarterdeck, followed by Mr. Temple.

"What is it, sir?"

"The Dacca have returned."

Wyatt, who was taking the helm, glanced over. "Orders, sir?" he asked coldly.

"Watch your tone, helmsman!" Temple snapped.

"Just asking, sir."

"Asking for a caning!" Mr. Temple roared. "And you'll get one if you don't keep a civil tongue."

"Shut up, the both of you. I need to think." Seward began to pace the quarterdeck, his head down. One hand played with the tie to his robe; the other stroked his lips.

"Sir, we only have one chance and it's a thin one at that," Wyatt said.

Mr. Temple took hold of his cane and moved toward him.

"Belay, Mr. Temple!" the captain ordered before turning his attention back to Wyatt. "Explain yourself, helmsman."

"At that range, with the land behind us, the Dacca can't possibly see the *Storm*. All they can see are the lanterns."

"Good god! You're right, put out those—"

"No, wait, sir!" Wyatt stopped him. "We *want* them to see the lanterns. Lower the longboat, rig it with a pole fore and aft, and hang two lanterns on the ends. Put ours out as you light those, then cast off. The Dacca will focus on it all night. We'll be able to bring the *Storm* about, catch the wind, and reach the safety of Wesbaden Bay."

"But that's not our destination."

"Damn our orders, sir! If we don't catch the wind, the Dacca will be on us by tomorrow night."

"*I'm* the captain of this ship!" Seward roared. "Another outburst and I'll not hold Mr. Temple's hand."

The captain looked at the waiting crew. Every eye was on him. He returned to pacing with his head down.

"Sir?" Bishop inquired. "Orders?"

"Can't you see I'm thinking, man?"

"Yes, sir."

The wind fluttered the sails overhead as the ship began to lose the angle on the wind.

"Lower the longboat," Seward ordered at last. "Rig it with poles and lanterns."

"And our heading?"

Seward tapped his lips.

"I shouldn't need to remind you, Captain Seward," Thranic said as he joined them on the quarterdeck, "that it's imperative we reach the port of Dagastan without delay."

Seward tapped his lips once more. "Send the longboat aft with a crew of four, and have them stroke for their lives toward Wesbaden. The Dacca will think we've seen them and will expect us to head that way, but the *Storm* will maintain its present course. There is to be no light on this ship without my order, and I want absolute silence. Do you hear me? Not a sound."

"Aye, sir."

Seward glanced at Wyatt, who shook his head with a look of disgust. The captain ignored him and turned to his lieutenant. "See to it, Mr. Bishop."

"Aye, aye, sir."

"You should have tried for the longboat's crew," Wyatt whispered to Hadrian. "We all should have."

It was still dark, and the crescent moon had long since

fallen into the sea. As per the captain's orders, the ship was quiet. Even the wind had died, and the ship rocked, motionless and silent, in the darkness.

"You don't have a lot of faith in Seward's decision?" Hadrian whispered back.

"The Dacca are smarter than he is."

"You've got to at least give him the benefit of the doubt. They might think we turned and ran."

Wyatt muffled a laugh. "If you were captain and decided to make a run for it against faster ships in the dead of night, would you have left the lanterns burning? The lantern ruse only works if they think we *haven't* seen them."

"I hadn't thought of that," Hadrian admitted. "We'll know soon enough if they took the bait. It's getting lighter."

"Where's Royce and his eagle eyes?" Wyatt asked.

"He went to sleep after his shift. We've learned over the years to sleep and eat when you can, so you don't regret not doing so later."

They peered out across the water as the light increased. "Maybe the captain was right," Hadrian said.

"How do you mean?"

"I don't see them."

Wyatt laughed. "You don't see them because you can't see anything, not even a horizon. There's fog on the water. It happens this time of year."

It grew lighter, and Hadrian could see Wyatt was right. A thick gray blanket of clouds surrounded them.

Lieutenant Bishop climbed to the quarterdeck and rapped softly on the captain's door. "You asked to be awakened at first light, sir," he whispered.

The captain came out, fully dressed this time, and proudly strode to the bridge.

"Fog, sir."

The captain scowled at him. "I can see that, Mr. Bishop. I'm not blind."

"No, sir."

"Send a lad with a glass up the mainmast."

"Mr. Wesley," Bishop called softly. The midshipman came running. "Take this glass to the masthead and report."

"Aye, sir."

Captain Seward, rocking on his heels and staring out at the fog, stood with his hand fidgeting behind his back. "It looks promising so far, doesn't it, Mr. Bishop?"

"It does indeed, sir. The fog will help hide us all the more."

"What do you think now, helmsman?" the captain asked Wyatt.

"I think I'll wait for Mr. Wesley's report. If you don't mind, sir."

Seward folded his arms in irritation and began to pace, his short legs and plump belly doing little to impart the vision of a commanding figure.

Wesley reached the masthead and extended the glass.

"Well?" Seward called aloud, his impatience getting the better of him.

"I can't tell, sir. The fog is too thick."

"They say the Dacca can use magic to raise a fog when they want," Poe whispered to Hadrian as they watched. "They're likely using it to sneak up on us."

"Or maybe it's just because the air is cooler this morning," Hadrian replied.

Poe shrugged.

The crew stood around, silent and idle, for an hour before Mr. Temple ordered Hadrian to serve the morning meal. The men ate, then wandered the deck in silence, like ghosts in a misty world of white. The midday meal came and went as well, with no break in the mist that continued to envelop them.

Hadrian had just finished cleaning up when he heard Wesley's voice from the masthead shout, "Sail!"

Emerging from the hold, Hadrian felt a cool breeze as a wind moved the fog, parting the hazy white curtains veil after veil.

The single word left everyone on edge.

"Good Maribor, man!" Seward shouted up. "What kind of sail?"

"Red lateen sails, sir!"

"Damn!" Seward cursed. "How many?"

"Five!"

"Five? Five! How could there be five?"

"No, wait!" Wesley shouted. "Six to windward! And three more coming off the port bow."

The captain's face drained of color. "Good Maribor!"

Even as he spoke, Hadrian spotted the sails clustered on the water.

"Orders, Captain?" Wyatt asked.

Seward glanced around him desperately. "Mr. Bishop, lay the ship on the port tack."

Wyatt shook his head defiantly. "We need to grab the wind."

"Damn you!" Seward hesitated only a moment, then shouted, "So be it! Hard aport, helmsman. Bring her around, hard over!"

Wyatt spun the wheel, the chains cranking the rudder so that the ship started to turn. Mr. Temple barked orders to the crew. The *Emerald Storm* was sluggish, stalling in the futile wind. The ship slowed to a mere drift. Then the foresail fluttered, billowed, and started to draw, coming around slowly. The yards turned as the men ran aft with the lee braces. The mainsail caught the breeze and blew full. The ship creaked loudly as the masts took up the strain.

The *Storm* picked up speed and was halfway round and pointed toward the coast. Still, Wyatt held the wheel hard over. The wind pressed the sails and leaned the ship, dipping the beam dangerously low. Spray broke over the rail as men grabbed hold of whatever they could to remain standing as the deck tilted steadily upward. The captain glared at Wyatt as he grabbed hold of the mizzen shroud, yet he held his tongue.

Letting the wind take the ship full on with all sails set, Wyatt pressed the wheel, raising the ship on its edge. Bishop and Temple glanced from Wyatt to the captain and back again, but no one dared give an order in the captain's presence.

Hadrian also grabbed hold of a rail to keep from slipping down the deck. Holding tight, he worried that Wyatt might capsize the ship. The hull groaned from the strain, the masts creaked with the pressure, but the ship picked up speed. At first it bucked through the waves, sending bursts of spray over the deck, then faster it went until the *Storm* skipped the waves, flying off the crests with the wind squarely on its aft quarter. The ship made its tight circle and at last Wyatt let up, leveling the deck. The ship fell in direct line with the wind and the bow rose as the *Storm* ran with it.

"Trim the sails," the lieutenant ordered. The men set to work once more, periodically glancing astern to watch the approach of the ships.

"Mr. Bishop," Seward called. "Disburse weapons to the men and issue an extra ration of grog."

Royce was on his way aloft as the larboard crew came off duty. "How long do you think before they catch us?" he asked Hadrian, looking aft at the tiny armada of red sails chasing their wake.

"I don't know. I've never done this before. What do you think?"

Royce shrugged. "A few hours maybe."

"It's not looking good, is it?"

"And you wanted to be a sailor."

&

Hadrian went about the business of preparing for the evening meal, mindful that it might be the last the men would have. Poe, conspicuously absent, hastily entered the galley.

"Where you been?"

Poe looked sheepish. "Talking to Wyatt. Those Dacca ships are gaining fast. They'll be on us tonight for sure."

Hadrian nodded grimly.

Poe moved to help cut the salted pork, then added, "Wyatt has a plan. It won't save everyone—only a handful, really—and it might not work at all, but it's something. He wants to know if you're in."

"What about Royce?"

"Him too."

"What's the plan?"

"Sail!" they heard Mr. Wesley cry even from the galley. "Two more tartanes dead ahead!"

Poe and Hadrian, like everyone else aboard, scrambled to the deck to see Mr. Wesley pointing off the starboard bow. Two red sails were slipping out from hidden coves along the shore to block their retreat. Sailing nimbly against the wind, they moved to intercept the *Storm*.

"Clear the deck for action!" Seward shouted from the quarterdeck, wiping the sweat from his head.

Men scrambled across the ship, once more hauling buckets of sand and water. Archers took their positions on the forecastle, stringing their bows. Oil and hot coals were placed at the ready.

"We need to steer clear," the captain said. "Helm, bring her—"

"We need speed, *sir,*" Wyatt interrupted.

The captain winced at the interruption. "Be mindful, Deminthal, or I'll skip the flogging I owe you and have you hanged!"

"With all due respect, you abdicated that privilege to the Dacca last night. All the sooner if I alter course now."

"By Maribor! Mr. Temple, take—" The captain stopped as he spotted the tartanes beginning to turn.

"See! They expected us to break," Wyatt told him.

Realizing their mistake, the Dacca fought to swing back, but it was too late. A hole had been created.

Seward grumbled and scowled at Wyatt.

"Sir?" Temple asked.

"Never mind. Steady as she goes, Mr. Bishop. Order the archers to take aim at the port-side ship! Perhaps we can slow them down if we can manage to set one afire."

"Aye, aye, sir!"

Hadrian rushed to the forecastle. Having proved himself one of the best archers on the ship, he was stationed at the center of the port side. He picked a strong, solid bow and tested the string's strength.

"The wind will set the arrows off a bit toward the bow," Poe mentioned, readying a bucket of glowing hot coals. "Might want to lead the target a bit, eh?"

"You're my squire now as well?"

Poe smiled and shook his head. "I've seen you in practice. I figure the safest place on this ship right now is here. I'll hand you the oiled arrows. You just keep firing."

The Dacca tartanes slipped through the waves, their red triangular sails billowing out sideways as they struggled on a tight tack to make the best use of the headwind. Dark figures scurried like ants across the decks and rigging of the smaller ships.

"Ready arrows!" Lieutenant Bishop shouted.

Hadrian fitted his first shaft in the string.

As the Dacca closed in on the *Storm*, they began to turn. Their yards swept round and their tillers cranked, pivoting much as Wyatt had, the action all the more impressive as both ships moved in perfect unison, like dancers performing simultaneous pirouettes.

"Light arrows!"

Hadrian touched the oil-soaked wad at the tip of the shaft to the pot of coals and it burst into flame. A row of men on the port side stood ready, a trail of soot-black smoke wafting aft.

"Take aim!" Bishop ordered as the Dacca ships came into range. On the deck of the tartanes, a line of flaming arrows mirrored their own. "Fire!"

Into the blue sky flew a staggered arc of fire trailing black smoke. At the same time, the Dacca launched their volley, and the arrows passed each other in midair. All around him, Hadrian heard pattering as they struck. The bucket brigade was running to douse the flames, and above them Royce dropped along a line to kick free one lodged in the masthead before it could ignite the mainsail.

Poe had another arrow ready. Hadrian fitted it, lit it with the pot, took aim, and sent it into the lower yard of their mainsail. To his right, he heard the loud *thwack* of the massive ballista, which sent forth a huge flaming missile. It struck the side of the tartane, splintering the hull and lodging there.

Hadrian heard a hissing fly past his ear. Behind him, the oil bucket splashed and the liquid ignited. Poe jumped backward as his trousers flamed. Grabbing a nearby bucket, Hadrian smothered the fire with sand.

Another volley rained, peppering the deck. Boatswain

Bristol, in the process of cranking the ballista for a second shot, fell dead with an arrow in his throat, his hair catching fire. Basil, the officers' cook, took one in the chest, and Seaman Bliden screamed as two arrows hit him, one in the thigh, and the other through his hand. Looking up, Hadrian saw this second volley came from the other ship.

Shaken but not seriously harmed, Poe found another oil bucket and brought it to Hadrian. As the two ships came closer, Hadrian found what he was looking for—a bucket at the feet of the archers. Leading his target, he held his breath, took aim, and released. The tartane's bucket exploded. Hadrian spotted a young Dacca attempt to douse the flames with water. Instantly the fire washed the deck. At that moment, the *Storm's* ballista crew, having loaded the weapon with multiple bolts this time, released a cruel hail on the passing Dacca. Screams bridged the gap between the ships as the *Storm* sailed on, leaving the burning ships in its wake.

Once more the crew cheered their victory, but it was hollow. Amid the blackened scorch marks left by scores of arrows, a dozen men lay dead on the deck. They had not slipped through the trap unscathed, and the red sails behind them were closer now.

When night fell, the captain ordered the off-crew, including Hadrian and Royce, below deck to rest. On the way they grabbed their old gear from the galley, and the two took the opportunity to change into their cloaks and tunics. Hadrian strapped on his swords. It brought a few curious looks, but no one said a word.

Not a single man slept, and few even sat. Most paced with their heads bowed to avoid the short ceiling, but perhaps this time they were also praying. Many of the crew had appeared superstitious, but none religious—until now.

"Why don't we put inland?" Seaman Davis asked his fellow sailors. "The coast's only a few miles off. We could put in and escape into the jungle."

"Coral shoals ring the shores of Calis," Banner said, scraping the surface of the table with a knife. "We'd rip the bottom of the *Storm* a mile out, and the Dacca would have it. Besides, the captain ain't gonna abandon his ship and run."

"Captain Seward is an arse!"

"Watch yer mouth, lad!"

"Why? What's he gonna do that can be worse than the Dacca?"

To that, Banner had no answer. No one did. Fear spread through the crew—fear of certain death and the poison that comes from waiting idly for it. Hadrian knew from countless battles the folly of leaving men to stagnate with nothing else to occupy their thoughts.

The hatch opened and everyone looked up to see Wyatt and Poe.

"What's the word?" Davis asked.

"It won't be long now, men. Make ready what you need to. The captain will call general quarters soon, I expect."

Wyatt paused at the bottom of the ladder and spoke quietly with Grady and Derning. They nodded, then went aft. Wyatt motioned with his eyes for Hadrian and Royce to follow him forward. Only empty hammocks filled the cramped space, leaving them enough privacy to speak.

"So, what's this plan?" Royce whispered.

"We can't win a fight," Wyatt told them. "All we can hope to do is run."

"You said the *Storm* can't outrun them," Hadrian reminded him.

"I wasn't planning on outrunning them in the *Storm*."

Hadrian and Royce exchanged glances.

"The Dacca will want her and the cargo. That's why we made it through the blockade so easily. They were trying to slow us, not stop us. If I had followed Seward's orders, we'd all be dead now. As it is, I only bought us a few hours, but they were needed."

"Needed for what, exactly?" Royce asked.

"For darkness. The Dacca can't see any better at night than we can, and while they take the *Storm*, we'll escape. They'll bring as many of their ships alongside as they can to overwhelm our decks by sheer numbers. When they board us, a party of men I've handpicked will take one of the tartanes. We'll cut the ship free and, with luck, get clear of the *Storm* before they see us. In the darkness and the confusion of battle, it might work."

They both nodded.

Wyatt motioned to Hadrian. "I want you to lead the boarding party. I'll signal you from the quarterdeck."

"What are you going to be doing?" Royce asked.

"You mean what are *we* going to be doing? I didn't come all this way not to find Allie. You and I will use the distraction to break into the captain's quarters and steal any orders or parchments we find. Just watch me. You'll know when."

"What about the elves below?" Royce asked.

"Don't worry about them. The Dacca want the ship intact. In all likelihood, they will treat them better than the New Empire has."

"Who's in this team of yours?" Hadrian asked.

"Poe, of course, Banner, Grady—"

"All hands on deck!" Temple shouted from above as drums thundered.

"See you above, gentlemen," Wyatt said while heading for the hold.

The sky was black. Invisible clouds covered the stars and shrouded the sliver of moon. Darkness wrapped the sea, a shadowy abyss where only the froth at the bow revealed the presence of water. Behind them, Hadrian saw nothing.

"Archers to the aft deck!"

Hadrian joined the others at the railing, where they lined up, shoulder to shoulder, looking out across the *Emerald Storm's* wake.

"Light arrows!" came the order.

From across the water they heard a sound, and a moment later men around Hadrian screamed as arrows pelted the stern.

"Fire!" Bishop ordered.

They raised their bows and fired as one, launching their burning shafts blindly into the darkness. A stream of flame flew in a long arch, some arrows dying with a hiss as they fell into the sea, others striking wood, their light outlining a ship about three hundred yards behind them.

"There," Bishop shouted. "There's your target, men!"

They exchanged volley after volley. Men fell dead on both ships, thinning the ranks of archers. Small fires broke out on the tartane, illuminating it and its crew. The Dacca were short, stocky, and lean, with coarse long beards and wild hair. The firelight cast on them a demonic glow that glistened off their bare sweat-soaked skin.

When the tartane lay less than fifty yards astern, its mainmast caught fire and burned like a dead tree. The brilliant light exposed the sea in all directions and stifled the cheers of the *Storm's* crew when it revealed the positions of the rest of the Dacca fleet. Four ships had already slipped alongside them.

"Stand by to repel boarders!" shouted Seward. He drew his sword and waved it over his head as he ran to the safety of the forecastle walls.

"Raise the nets!" ordered Bishop. The rigging crew drew up netting on either side of the deck, creating an entangling barrier of rope webbing. Under command of their officers, men took position at the waist deck, cutlasses raised.

"Cut the tethers!" Mr. Wesley cried as hooks caught the rail.

The deck shook as the tartanes slammed against the *Emerald Storm's* hull. A flood of stocky men wearing only leather armor and red paint stormed over the side. They screamed in fury as swords met.

"Now!" Hadrian heard Wyatt shout at him.

He turned and saw the helmsman pointing to the tartane tethered to the *Storm's* port side near the stern, the first of the Dacca's ships to reach them. Most of its crew had already boarded the *Storm.* Poe, Grady, and others in Wyatt's team held back, watching Hadrian.

"Go!" Hadrian shouted and, grabbing hold of the mizzen's port-side brace, cut it free and swung out across the gulf, landing on the stern of the tartane.

The stunned Dacca helmsman reached for his short blade as Hadrian cut his throat. Two more Dacca rushed him. Hadrian dodged, using the move to hide the thrust. His broadsword drove deep into the first Dacca's stomach. The second man, seeing his chance, attacked, but Hadrian's bastard sword was in his left hand. With it he deflected a wild swing. Drawing the broadsword from the first Dacca's stomach, Hadrian brought it across, severing the remaining man's head.

With three bodies on the aft deck, Hadrian looked up to see Poe and the rest already in possession of the ship and in the process of cutting the tethers free. With the last one cut, Poe used a pole and pushed away from the *Storm.*

"What about Royce and Wyatt?" Hadrian asked, climbing down to the waist deck.

"They'll swim for it and we'll pick them up on the far side," Poe explained as he ran past him, heading aft. "But we need to get into the shadows now!"

Poe climbed the short steps to the tartane's tiny quarterdeck and took hold of the tiller. "Swing the boom!" he shouted in a whisper. "Trim the sails!"

"We know our jobs a lot better than you, boy!" Derning hissed at him. He and Grady were already hauling on the mainsail sheet, trying to tame the canvas that snapped above like a serpent, jangling the rigging rings against the mast. "Banner, Davis! Adjust the headsail for a starboard tack."

Hadrian had never learned the ropes, and he stood by uselessly while the others raced across the deck. Even if he had picked up anything about rigging, it would not have helped. The Dacca tartane was quite different in design. Besides being smaller, the hull was sloped like a fishing vessel, but with two decks. It had just two sails: a headsail supported on a forward-tilting mast and the mainsail. Both were triangular and hung from long curved yards that crossed the masts at angles so that the vessel's profile appeared like the heads of two axes cleaving through the air. The deck was dark wood. Glancing around, Hadrian wondered if the Dacca stained it with the same blood as the sails. After seeing the rigging ornamented with human skulls, it was an easy conclusion to make.

On the *Storm*, the battle was going badly. At least half the crew lay dead or dying. No canvas was visible, as the boarding party had made striking the sails a priority. The deck was awash in stocky, half-naked men who circled the forecastle with torches, dodging arrows as they struggled to breach the bulwark.

Poe pushed the tartane's tiller over, pointing the bow away from the *Storm*. The wind caught the canvas and the little ship glided gently away. With the sails on the *Emerald Storm* struck, the ship was dead in the water, and it was easy for them to circle it. Equally small crews remained to operate the other Dacca boarding ships, but that hardly mattered, as all eyes were on the *Storm*. As far as Hadrian could tell, no one noticed them.

"I'm bringing her around," Poe said. "Hadrian, stand by with that rope there, and everyone watch the water for Wyatt and Royce."

"Royce?" Derning questioned with distaste. "Why are we picking up the murderer? I can handle the rigging just fine."

"Because Wyatt said so," Poe replied.

"What if we can't find them? What if they die before they can get off the ship?" Davis asked.

"I'll decide that when it happens," Poe replied.

"You? You're barmy, boy. I'll be buggered if I'll take orders from a little sod like you! Bloody Davis here's got more years at sea than you and he's a git if there ever was one. If we don't find Deminthal after the first pass, you'll be taking orders from me."

"Like I said," Poe repeated, "I'll decide that when it happens."

Derning grinned menacingly, but Hadrian did not think Poe, being at the stern, could have seen it in the darkness.

*

Royce wasted no time hitting the deck at the signal.

"We haven't got long," Wyatt told him. "The captain's quarters will be a priority."

He kicked the door open, shattering the frame.

Fully carpeted, the whole rear of the ship was one luxurious suite. Silk patterns in hues of gold and brown covered the walls, with matching upholstered furniture and a silk bedcover. A painting hung on one wall, showing a man bathed in sunlight, his face filled with rapture as a single white feather floated into his upraised hands. Silver lanterns swayed above vast stern windows that banked the far wall. The bed stood to one side with a large desk across from it.

Wyatt scanned the room quickly, then moved to the desk. He rifled the drawers. "He'll have put the orders in a safe place."

"Like a safe?" Royce asked, pulling a window drape aside to reveal a porthole-size compartment with a lock. "They always put them behind the drapes."

"Can you open it?"

Royce smirked. He pulled a tool from his belt and within seconds the little door swung open. Wyatt reached inside, grabbed the entire stack of parchments, and stuffed them into a bag.

"Let's get out of here," he said, making for the door. "Jump off the starboard side. Poe will pick us up."

They came out of the cabin into a world of chaos. Stocky men painted in red poured over the sides of the vessel. Each wielded short broad blades or axes that cut down everything before them. Only a handful of men stood on the waist deck. The rest had fallen back to the perceived safety of the forecastle. Those who tried to hold their ground died. Royce stepped out on the deck just in time to see Dime, his topsail captain, nearly cut in half by a cleaving blow from a Dacca axe.

Lieutenant Bishop and the other officers had been slow in reaching the castle, but now, as the Dacca flooded the deck, they were running full out to reach its walls. Stabbed in the back, Lieutenant Green collapsed. As he fell, he reached out, grabbing at anything. His hands found Midshipman Beryl running past and dragged him down as well. Beryl cursed and kicked Green off but got to his feet too late. The Dacca circled him.

"Help me!" he cried.

Royce watched as the crew ignored him and ran on—all but one. Midshipman Wesley ran back just in time to stab the nearest Dacca caught off guard by the sudden change in his fleeing prey. Wielding his sword with both hands, Wesley sliced horizontally across the chest of the next brute and kicked him aside.

"Beryl! This way, run!" he shouted.

Beryl lashed out at the Dacca, then ran to Wesley. They were quickly surrounded, and the Dacca drove them farther and farther away from the forecastle. An arrow from the walls saved Wesley from decapitation as the two struggled to defend themselves. Pushed by the overwhelming numbers, they retreated until their backs hit the rail.

A Dacca blade slashed Beryl's arm and then across his hip. He screamed, dropping his sword. Wesley threw himself between Beryl and his attacker. The young midshipman slashed wildly, struggling to defend the older man. Then Wesley was hit. He stumbled backward and reached out for the netting chains but missed them and fell overboard. Alone and unarmed, Beryl screamed as the Dacca swarmed him until they sent his head from his body.

No one noticed Wyatt or Royce creeping in the shadows around the stern, seeking a clear place to jump. They crouched just above the captain's cabin windows. Royce was about to leap when he spotted Thranic stepping out from the hold. The sentinel exited, a torch in hand, as if he merely wondered what all the noise was about. He led the seret to the main deck, where they quickly formed a wall around the sentinel. Seeing reinforcements, the Dacca rallied to an attack. They charged, only to die upon the serets' swords. The Knights of Nyphron were neither sailors nor galley slaves. They knew the use of arms and how to hold formation.

Gripping his bag to his chest, Wyatt leapt from the ship.

"Royce!" Wyatt shouted from the sea below.

Royce watched, impressed by the knights' courage and skill, as they battled the Dacca. It looked as if they might just turn the tide. Then Thranic threw his flaming brand into the ship's hold. A rush of air sounded, as if the ship were inhaling a great breath. A roar followed. A deep, resonating growl shook the timber beneath Royce's feet. Tongues of flame licked out of every hatch and porthole, the air filling with screams and cries. And in the flickering glow of burning wood and flesh, Royce saw the sentinel smile.

❧

Hadrian and the tiny crew of the stolen Dacca ship had only just reached the starboard side of the *Storm* when the area grew bright. The *Emerald Storm* was ablaze. Within little more than a minute, the fire had enveloped the deck. Men in the rigging had no choice but to jump. From that height, their bodies hit the water with a cracking sound. The rigging ignited, ropes snapped, and yards broke free, falling like flaming tree trunks. The darkness of the starless sea fell away as the *Emerald Storm* became a floating bonfire. Those near the rail leapt into the sea. Screams, cries, and the crackle and hiss of fire filled the night.

Looking over the black water, whose surface was alive with wild reflections, Hadrian spied a bit of sandy hair and a dark uniform. "Mr. Wesley, grab on!" Hadrian called, throwing a rope.

Hearing his name, Wesley turned, his face showing the same dazed expression as a man waking from a dream until he spotted Hadrian reaching out. He took the rope thrown and was reeled in like a fish and hoisted on deck.

"Nice to have you aboard, sir," Hadrian told him.

Wesley gasped for air and rolled over, vomiting seawater.

"From that, I assume you're happy to be here."

"Wyatt!" Poe shouted.

"Royce!" Hadrian called.

"Over there!" Derning said, pointing.

Poe turned the tiller and they sailed toward the sound of splashing.

"It's Bernie and Staul," Grady announced from where he stood on the bow.

The two wasted no time scrambling up the ship's ropes.

"More splashing over there!" Davis pointed.

Poe did not have to alter course, as the swimmers made good progress to them. Davis was the first to lend a hand. He reached out to help and a blade stabbed him in the chest before he was pulled overboard.

Hadrian saw them now—swarthy, painted brutes with long daggers, their wet, glistening skin shimmering with the light of the flames. They grabbed at the netting and scrambled like rats up the side of the tartane.

Hadrian drew his sword and lashed out at the nearest one, who dodged and stubbornly continued to climb. The Tenkin warrior, Staul, stabbed another in the face and the Dacca dropped backward with a cry and a splash. Bernie and Wesley joined in, thrashing wildly until the Dacca gave up and fell away into the darkness.

"Watch the other side!" Wesley shouted.

Staul and Bernie took positions on the starboard rail, but nothing moved.

"Any sign of Davis?" Hadrian asked.

"The man be dead now," Staul said. "Be more careful who you sail to, eh?"

"Bulard!" Bernie said, pointing ahead to more swimmers.

"And three more over there," Wesley announced, picking out faces in the tumultuous water. "One is Greig, the carpenter, and that's Dr. Levy, and there is..."

Hadrian did not need Royce's eyes to identify the other man. The infernal light coming off the burning ship suited the face. Sentinel Thranic swam toward them, his hood thrown back and his pale face gleaming. Derning, Bernie, and Staul were bad enough. Now they had Dovin Thranic, of all people.

Thranic needed no help as he climbed nimbly up the side of the little ship, his cloak soaked, his face angry. If he were a dog, Hadrian knew he would be growling, and for that he was pleased. Bulard, the man who had come aboard in the middle of the night, looked even paler than before. The reason became obvious the moment he hit the deck and blood mingled with seawater. Levy went to him and applied pressure to the wound.

"Hadrian...Poe!" Wyatt's voice carried from the sea below.

Poe steered toward the sound as the rest stood on their guard. This time there was no need. Wyatt and Royce were alone swimming for the boat.

"Where were you?" Wyatt asked, climbing aboard.

"Sorry, boss, but it's a big ocean."

"Not big enough," Derning said, looking over at what remained of the *Storm*, his face bright with the glow. "The Dacca are finally taking notice of us."

The mainmast of the *Emerald Storm*, burning like a tree-sized torch, finally cracked and fell. The forecastle walls blazed. Seward, Bishop, and the rest had either been lost to blades or burned alive. The *Storm* had blackened and cracked, allowing the ship to take on water. The hull listed to one side, sinking from the bow. As it did, the fire was still bright enough to see several of the Dacca on the nearest vessel pointing in their direction and shouting.

"Wheel hard over!" Wyatt shouted, running for the tiller. "Derning, Royce, get aloft! Hadrian, Banner—the mainsail braces. Grady to the headsail braces! Who else do we have here? Bernie, join Derning and Royce. Staul, help with the mainsail. Mr. Wesley, if it wouldn't be too much trouble, perhaps you could assist Grady on the forward braces. Bring her round east-nor'east!"

"That will put us into the wind again!" Grady said even as Wyatt brought the ship round.

"Aye, starboard tack. With fewer crew, and the same ship, we'll be lighter and faster."

They got the ship around and caught what wind they could.

"Here, Banner, take the tiller," Wyatt said as he scanned the deck. "We can dump some gear and lighten the load further. Who's that next to you?"

Wyatt stopped abruptly when he saw Thranic look up.

"What's he doing on board?" Wyatt asked.

"Is there a problem, helmsman?" Thranic addressed him.

"You fired the ship!" Wyatt accused. "Royce told me he saw you throw a torch in the hold. How many oil kegs did you break to get it to go up like that?"

"Five, I think. Maybe six."

"There were elves—they were locked in the hold—trapped down there."

"Precisely," Thranic replied.

"You bastard!" Wyatt rushed the sentinel, drawing his cutlass. Thranic moved with surprising speed and dodged Wyatt's attack, throwing his cloak around Wyatt's head and shoving the helmsman to the deck as he drew a long dagger.

Hadrian pulled his swords and Staul immediately moved to intercept him. Poe drew his cutlass, as did Grady, followed quickly by Defoe and Derning.

From the rigging above, Royce dropped abruptly into the

midst of the conflict, landing squarely between Thranic and Wyatt. The sentinel's eyes locked on him and smoldered.

"Mr. Wesley!" Royce shouted, keeping his eyes fixed on Thranic. "What are your orders, sir?"

At this everyone stopped. The ship continued to sail with the wind, but the crew paused. Several glanced at Wesley. The midshipman stood frozen on the deck, watching the events unfold around him.

"*His* orders?" Thranic mocked.

"Captain Seward, Lieutenants Bishop and Green, and the other midshipmen are dead," Royce explained. "Mr. Wesley is senior officer. He is, by rights, in command of this vessel."

Thranic laughed.

Wesley began to nod. "He is right."

"Shut up, boy!" Staul snapped. "It's time we took care of this business here."

Staul's words brought Wesley around. "I am no boy!" Turning to Thranic, he added, "What I am, *sir*, is the acting captain of this ship, and as such, you, and everyone else"—he glanced at Staul—"*will* obey my orders!"

Staul laughed.

"I assure you this is no joke, seaman. I also assure you that I will not hesitate to see you cut down where you stand, and anyone else who fails to obey me."

"And how do you plan to do that?" Staul asked. "This is not the *Emerald Storm*. You command no one here."

"I wouldn't say that." Hadrian flashed his familiar smile at Staul.

"Neither would I," Royce added.

"Me neither," Derning joined in, his words quickly echoed by Grady.

Wyatt got to his feet slowly. He glared at Thranic but said, "Aye, Mr. Wesley is captain now."

Poe, Banner, and Greig acknowledged with a communal "Aye."

What followed was a tense silence. Staul and Bernie looked at Thranic, who never took his gaze off Royce. "Very well, *Captain*," the sentinel said at length. "What are your orders?"

"I hereby promote Mr. Deminthal to acting lieutenant. Everyone will follow his instructions to the letter. Mr. Deminthal, you will confine your orders to saving this vessel from the Dacca and maintaining order and discipline. There are to be no executions and no disciplinary actions of any kind without my authorization. Is that clear?"

"Aye, sir."

"Petty Officer Blackwater, you are hereby appointed master-at-arms. Collect the weapons, but keep them at the ready. See to it Mr. Deminthal's and my orders are carried out. Understood?"

"Aye, sir."

"Mr. Grady, you are now boatswain. Dr. Levy, please take Mr. Bulard below so that he can be properly cared for. Let me know if there is anything you need. Mr. Derning will be top captain. Seamen Defoe and Melborn, report to him for duties. Mr. Deminthal, carry on."

"Your sword." Hadrian addressed Staul. The Tenkin hesitated but, after a nod from Thranic, handed the blade over. As he did, he laughed and cursed in the Tenkin language.

"You'd have found that a bit harder than you think," Hadrian replied to Staul, and he was rewarded with the Tenkin's shocked expression.

Wyatt had everything nonessential and not attached to the ship thrown overboard. Then he ordered silence and whispered the order to change tack. The boom swung over, catching the wind and angling the little ship out to sea. Well behind them, the last light of the *Emerald Storm* disappeared, swallowed by the waves. Not quite so far away, they could see lanterns bobbing on the following ships. From the shouts, it was clear they were displeased at losing their prize. All eyes faced astern, watching the progression of lanterns as the Dacca continued following their previous tack. After a while, two ships altered course but guessed incorrectly and turned westward. Eventually all the lanterns disappeared.

"Are they gone?" Hadrian heard Wesley whisper to Wyatt.

He shook his head. "They just put out the lanterns, but with luck they will think we're running for ground. The nearest friendly port is Wesbaden back west."

"For a helmsman, you're an excellent commander," the young man observed.

"I was a captain once," Wyatt admitted. "I lost my ship."

"Really? In whose service, the empire or a royal fleet?"

"No service. It was *my* ship."

Wesley looked astonished. "You were . . . a pirate?"

"Opportunist, sir. Opportunist."

Hadrian awoke to a misty dawn. A steady breeze pushed the tartane through undulating waves. All around them lay a vast and empty sea.

"They are gone," Wesley said, answering the unasked question. "We have lost them."

"Any idea where we are?"

"About three days' sail from Dagastan," Wyatt answered.

"Dagastan?" Grady muttered, looking up. "We're not headed there, are we?"

"That was my intention," Wyatt replied.

"But Wesbaden is closer."

"Unfortunately, I confess no knowledge of these coasts," Wesley said. "Do you know them well, Mr. Deminthal?"

"Intimately."

"Good. Then tell us, is Mr. Grady correct?"

Wyatt nodded. "Wesbaden is closer, but the Dacca know this and will be waiting in that direction. However, since it's impossible for them to be ahead of us, our present course is the safest."

"Despite our earlier differences, I agree with Mr. Deminthal," Thranic offered. "As it turns out, Dagastan was the *Storm's* original destination, so we must continue toward it."

"But Dagastan is much farther away from Avryn," Wesley said. "The *Storm's* mission was lost with her sinking. I have no way of knowing her original destination, and even if I did, I have no cargo to deliver. Going farther east only increases our difficulties. I need to be mindful of provisions."

"But you do have cargo," Thranic announced. "The *Storm's* orders were to deliver myself, Mr. Bulard, Dr. Levy, Bernie, and Staul to Dagastan. The main cargo is gone, but as an officer of the realm, it's your duty to fulfill what portion you can of Captain Seward's mission."

"With all due respect, Your Excellency, I have no way to verify what you say."

"Actually, you do." Wyatt pulled a bent and battered scroll from his bag. "These are Captain Seward's orders."

Wesley took the damp scroll and asked, "But how did you come by this?"

"I knew we'd need charts to sail by. Before I left the *Storm*, I entered the captain's cabin, and being in a bit of a hurry, I just grabbed everything on his desk. Last night I discovered I had more than just charts."

Wesley nodded, accepting this and, Hadrian thought, perhaps choosing not to inquire further. He paused a second before reading it. Most men were awake now and, having heard the conversation, watched Wesley with anticipation. When he finished, he looked over at Wyatt.

"Was there a letter?"

"Aye, sir," he said while handing over a sealed bit of parchment.

Wesley slipped it carefully into his coat without opening it. "We will maintain course to Dagastan. Being bound by imperial naval laws, I must do everything in my power to see the *Storm's* errand is fulfilled."

CHAPTER 13

THE WITCH OF MELENGAR

Modina stared out her window as usual, watching the world with no real interest. It was late and she feared sleep. It always brought the dreams, the nightmares of the past, of her father, and of the dark place. She sat up most nights, studying the shadows and the clouds as they passed over the stars. A line of moonlight crossed the courtyard below. She noted how it climbed the statues and the far gate wall, just like the creeping ivy. Once green, the plant was now a dreary red. It would go dormant, appearing to die, but would still hang on to the wall. It would continue its desperate grip on the stone even as it withered. For it, at least, there would be a spring.

The hammering at her chamber door roused her. She turned, puzzled. No one ever knocked except for Gerald, who always used a light tap. Amilia came and went frequently but never knocked. Whoever it was, they beat the door with a fury.

The pounding landed harder and with such violence that the door latch bounced with a distinct metallic clank as it threatened to break. It never occurred to her to ask who was there. It never crossed her mind to be fearful. She slid back the bolt, letting the door swing inward.

Standing outside was a man she vaguely recognized. His face was flushed, his eyes glassy, and the collar to his shirt lay open.

"There you are," he exclaimed. "At long last I am rewarded with your presence. Permit me to introduce myself again, in case you've forgotten me. I am Archibald Ballentyne, twelfth Earl of Chadwick." He bowed low, taking an awkward step when he lost his balance. "May I come in?"

The empress said nothing, and the earl took this as an invitation, pushing his way into the chamber. He held a finger to his lips. "Shh, we need to be quiet, lest someone discover I'm here." The earl stood wavering, his glazed eyes canvassing the full length of Modina's small body. His mouth hung partially open and his head moved up and down, as if trying to save his eyes the effort.

Modina was dressed only in her thin nightgown but did not think to cover herself.

"You're beautiful. I thought so from the first. I wanted to tell you before this, but they wouldn't let me see you." The earl pulled a bottle of liquor from his breast pocket and took a swallow. "After all, I'm the hero of your army, and it isn't fair that Ethelred gets to have you. You should be mine. I earned you!" the earl shouted, raising his fist.

Pausing, he looked toward the open door. After a moment, he continued, "What has Ethelred ever done? It was my army that saved Aquesta and would have crushed Melengar if they had let me. But they didn't want me to. Do you know why? They knew if I took Melengar, then I would be too great to hold back. They're jealous of me, you know. And now Ethelred is planning to take you, but you're mine. *Mine*, I say!" He shouted this last bit, then cringed. Once more he placed a finger to his lips. "Shh."

Modina watched the earl with mild curiosity.

"How can you want *him*?" He slammed his fist against his chest. "Am I not handsome? Am I not young?" He twirled around with his arms outstretched until he staggered. He steadied himself on the bedpost. "Ethelred is old, fat, and has pimples. Do you really want that? He doesn't care about you. He's only after the crown."

The earl took a moment to glance around the empty room. "Don't get me wrong," he said in a harsh whisper. He leaned in so close he had to put a hand on her shoulder to steady himself. "I want the crown, too—anyone saying different is a liar. Who wouldn't want to be emperor of the world, but"—he held up a wavering finger—"*I* would have loved you."

He paused, breathing hotly into her face. He licked his lips and caressed her skin through the thin nightgown. His hand left her shoulder and inched up her neck, his open fingers slipping into her hair. "Ethelred will never look at you like this." Archibald took her hand and placed it against his chest. "His heart will never pound like mine just by being near you. I want power. I want the throne, but I also want you." He looked into her eyes. "I love you, Modina. I love you and I want you for my own. You should be *my* wife."

He pulled her to him and kissed her on the mouth, pressing hard, pinching her lips to her teeth. She did not struggle—she did not care. He pulled back and searched her face. She did not respond except to blink.

"Modina?" Amilia called, entering the room. "What's going on?"

"Nothing," Ballentyne said sadly. He looked at Modina. He searched her face again. "Absolutely nothing at all."

He turned and left the room.

"Are you all right?" Amilia rushed to the empress, brushing her hair back and looking her over. "Did he hurt you?"

"Am I to marry Regent Ethelred?"

Amilia held her breath and bit her lip.

"I see. When were you going to tell me? On my wedding night?"

"I—I just learned about it recently. You had that incident in the kitchen and I didn't want to upset you."

"It doesn't upset me, Amilia, and thank you for stopping by."

"But I—" Amilia hesitated.

"Is there something else?"

"Ah—no, I just—You're different suddenly. We should talk about this."

"What is there to talk about? I'll marry Ethelred so he can be emperor."

"You'll still be empress."

"Yes, yes, there's no need to worry. I'm fine."

"You're never *fine*."

"No? It must be the good news that I'm to become a bride."

Amilia looked terrified. "Modina, what's going on? What's happening in that head of yours?"

Modina smiled. "It's okay, Amilia. Everything will be *fine*."

"Stop using that word! You're really frightening me," Amilia said, reaching toward her.

Modina pulled away, moving to the window.

"I'm sorry I didn't tell you myself. I'm sorry there was no guard at the door. I'm sorry you had to hear such a thing from the brandy-soaked breath of—"

"It's not your fault, Amilia. It's important to me that you know that. You're all that matters to me. It's amazing how worthless a life feels without someone to care for. My father understood that. At the time, I didn't, but now I do."

"Understand what?" Amilia asked, shaking.

"That living has no value—it's what you do with life that gives it worth."

"And what are you planning to do with your life, Modina?"

Modina tried to force another smile. She took Amilia's head in her hands and kissed her gently. "It's late. Goodbye, Amilia."

Amilia's eyes went wide with fear. She began shaking her head faster and faster. "No, no, no! I'll stay here. I don't want you left alone tonight."

"As you wish."

Amilia looked pleased for a moment, then fear crept back in. "Tomorrow I'll assign a guard to *watch* you."

"Of course you will," Modina replied.

❧

True to her word, Amilia remained in Modina's chamber all night, but slipped out before dawn while the empress still slept. She went to the office of the master-at-arms and burst in on the soldier on duty, unannounced.

"Why wasn't there a guard outside the empress's door last night? Where was Gerald?"

"We couldn't spare him, milady. The imperial guard is stretched thin. We're searching for the witch, the Princess of Melengar. Regent Saldur has commanded me to use every man I have to find her."

"I don't care. I want Gerald back watching her door. Do you understand?"

"But, milady—"

"Last night the Earl of Chadwick forced his way into the empress's room. In her room! And has it occurred to you—to anyone—that the witch might be coming to kill the empress?"

A long pause.

"I didn't think so. Now, get Gerald back on his post at once."

Leaving the master-at-arms, Amilia roused Modina's chambermaid from her bunk in the dormitory. After the girl had dressed, she hurried her along to Modina's room.

"Anna, I want you to stay with the empress and watch her."

"Watch her, what for? I mean, what should I be watching for, milady?"

"Just make certain the empress doesn't hurt herself."

"How do you mean?"

"Just keep an eye on her. If she does anything odd or unusual, send for me at once."

❧

Modina heard Anna enter the room quietly. She continued pretending to sleep. Near dawn she stretched, yawned, and walked over to the washbasin to splash water on her face. Anna was quick to hand her a towel and grinned broadly to have been of assistance.

"Anna, is it?" Modina asked.

The girl's face flushed, and her eyes lit up with joy. She nodded repeatedly.

"Anna, I'm starved. Would you please run to the kitchen and see if they can prepare me an early breakfast? Be a dear and bring it up when it's ready."

"I—I—"

Modina put on a pout and turned her eyes downward. "I am sorry. I apologize for asking so much of you."

"Oh no, Your Gloriousness, I'll get it at once."

"Thank you."

"You are most welcome, Your Worship."

Modina wondered if she kept her longer how many elaborate forms of address she might come up with. As soon as Anna left the room, Modina walked to the door, closed it, and slid the dead bolt. She walked toward the tall mirror that hung on the wall, picking up the pitcher from the water basin as she passed. Without hesitation, she struck the mirror, shattering both. She picked up a long shard of glass and went to her window.

"Your Eminence?" Gerald called from the other side of the door. "Are you all right?"

Outside, the sun was just coming up. The autumn morning light angled in sharp, slanted shafts across the courtyard below. She loved the sun and thought its light and warmth would be the only thing besides Amilia that she would miss.

She wrapped her gown around the end of the long jagged piece of glass. It felt cold. Everything felt cold to her. She looked down at the courtyard and breathed in a long breath of air scented with the dying autumn leaves.

The guard continued to bang on the door. "Your Eminence?" he repeated. "Are you all right?"

"Yes, Gerald," she said, "I'm *fine.*"

Arista entered the palace courtyard, walking past the gate guards, hoping they could not hear the pounding of her heart.

This must be how Royce and Hadrian feel all the time. I'm surprised they don't drink more.

She shook from both fear and the early-morning chill. Esrahaddon's robe had been lost the night of Hilfred's rescue, leaving her with only Lynnette's kirtle.

Hilfred. He'll be furious if he reads the note.

It hurt her heart just to think of him. He had stood in her shadow for years, serving her whims, taking her abuse, trapped in a prison of feelings he could never reveal. Twice he had nearly died for her. He was a good man—a great man.

She wanted to make him happy. He deserved to be happy. She wanted to give him what he never thought possible, to fix what she had broken.

For three nights they had hid together, and every day Hilfred had tried to convince her to return to Melengar. At last she had agreed, telling him they would leave the next day. Arista had slipped out when Hilfred went to get supplies. If all went well, she would be back before he returned and they could leave as planned. If not—if something happened—the note would explain.

It had occurred to her, only the night before, that she had never cast the location spell in the courtyard. From there, the smoke would certainly locate the wing, and if lucky enough, she might even pinpoint Gaunt's window. The information would be invaluable to Royce and Hadrian and could mean the difference between a rescue and a suicide mission. And as much as she did not want to admit it, she owed Esrahaddon as well. If doing this small thing could save Degan Gaunt, a good man wrongly imprisoned; ease the wizard's passing; and vanquish her guilt, it would be worth the risk.

The gate guards paid little attention when she had entered. She took this as a good sign that no one had connected Ella the scrub girl to the Witch of Melengar. All she needed to do now was cast the spell and walk out again.

She crossed the inner ward to the vegetable garden. The harvest had come and gone, the plants were cleared, and the soil had been turned to await the spring. The soft earth would allow her to draw the circle and symbols required. She clutched the pouch of hair still in the pocket of her kirtle as she glanced around. Nothing looked amiss. The few guards on duty ignored her.

As casually as she could, she began drawing a circle by dragging her foot in the dirt. When she had finished, she moved on to the more tedious task of the runes, which was more time-consuming to do with her toe than with her hand and a bit of chalk. All the while, she worried that her drawing would be obvious from any number of upper-story windows.

She was just finishing the second to last rune when a guard exited the palace and walked toward her. Immediately she crouched, pretending to dig. If he questioned her, she could say that Ibis sent her to look for potatoes, or that she thought she might have dropped the pantry key when she was in the courtyard. She hoped he would just walk by. She needed to be the invisible servant this one last time. It quickly became apparent that he was specifically coming for her. As he closed the distance, her only thought was of Hilfred and how she wished she had kissed him goodbye.

❧

Amilia was in her office, quickly going over instructions with Nimbus. They had ticked off only a few items for the wedding preparations. If she could give him enough to keep busy, she could return to Modina. The urgency pulled at her every minute she was away.

"If you get done with that, then come see me and I'll give you more to do," she told him curtly. "I have to get back to the empress. I think she might do something stupid."

Nimbus looked up. "The empress is a bit eccentric certainly, but, if I may, she has never struck me as stupid, my lady."

Amilia narrowed her eyes at him suspiciously.

Nimbus had been a good and faithful servant, but she did not like the sound of that. "You notice too much, I think, Nimbus. That's not such a good trait when working in the imperial palace. Ignorance is perhaps a better choice for survival."

"I am just trying to cheer you up," he replied, sounding a little hurt.

Amilia frowned and collapsed in her chair. "I'm sorry. I am starting to sound a bit like Saldur, aren't I?"

"You still have to work on making your veiled threats sound more ominous. A deeper voice would help, or perhaps toying with a dagger or swishing a glass of wine as you say it."

"I wasn't threatening you. I was—"

He cut her off. "I am just joking, my lady."

Amilia scowled, then pulled a parchment off her desk, crumpled it into a ball, and threw it at him. "Honestly, I don't know why I hired you."

"Not for my comedy, I sense."

Amilia gathered a pile of parchments, a quill, and a bottle of ink and headed for the door. "I'm going to be working from Modina's room today. Look there if you need me."

"Of course," he said as she left.

Not far down the hall, Amilia saw Anna walking by with a tray of food. "Anna," she called, rushing toward her. "I told you to stay with the empress!"

"Yes, milady, but..."

"But what?"

"The empress asked me to fetch her some breakfast."

A cold chill shot up Amilia's spine. The empress had *asked* her. "Has the empress ever spoken to you before?"

On the verge of tears, Anna shook her head. "No, milady, I was very honored. She even knew my name."

Amilia raced for the stairs, her heart pounding. Reaching the top and nearing the bedchamber, she feared what she would find. Nimbus was right, perhaps more than he knew. Modina was not stupid, and Amilia's mind filled with the many terrible possibilities. Arriving at the door, she pushed

Gerald aside and burst into the empress's room. She steeled herself, but what she saw was beyond her wildest imaginings.

Modina and Ella sat together on the empress's bed, hand in hand, chatting.

Amilia stood still, shocked. Both glanced up as she entered. Ella's face was fearful, but Modina's expression was calm as usual, as if expecting her.

"Ella?" Amilia exclaimed. "What are you doing—"

"Gerald," Modina interrupted, "from now on, no one—and I mean *no one*—is to enter without my say-so. Understood?"

"Of course, Your Eminence." Gerald looked down guiltily.

Modina waved her hand. "It's not your fault. I didn't tell you. Now please close the door."

He bowed and drew the door shut.

Amilia meanwhile stood silent. Her mouth was agape but no words came out.

"Sit down before you fall down, Amilia. I want to introduce you to a friend of mine. This is Arista, the Princess of Melengar."

Amilia tried to make sense out of the senselessness. "No, Modina, this is Ella—a scrub girl. What's going on?" Amilia asked desperately. "I thought—I thought you might be—" Her eyes went to the broken pitcher and shards of mirrored glass scattered across the corner of the room.

"I know what you thought," the empress said, looking toward the window. "That's another reason you should be welcoming Arista. If I hadn't seen her in the courtyard and realized—well—anyway, I want you two to be friends."

Amilia's mind was still whirling. Modina appeared more lucid than ever, yet she made no sense. Maybe she only sounded rational. Maybe the empress had cracked altogether. At any moment, she might introduce Red, the elkhound from the kitchen, as the Ambassador of Lanksteer.

"Modina, I know you think this girl is a princess, but just a week ago you also thought you were dead and buried, remember?"

"Are you saying you think I'm crazy?"

"No, no, I just..."

"Lady Amilia"—Ella spoke for the first time—"my name is Arista Essendon, and I *am* the Princess of Melengar. Your empress isn't crazy. She and I are old friends."

Amilia stood staring at the two of them, confused. Were they both insane? How could—*Oh sweet Maribor. It's her!* The long fingernails, the way she met Amilia's stare, the bold inquiries about the empress. Ella was the Witch of Melengar. "Get away from her!" Amilia yelled.

"Amilia, calm down."

"She's been posing as a maid to get to you."

"Arista's not here to harm me. You're not, are you?" she asked Ella, who shook her head. "There, you see? Now come here and join us. We have much to do."

"Thrace." Ella spoke, looking nervously at Modina. The empress raised a hand to stop her.

"The both of you need to trust me," Modina said.

Amilia shook her head. "But how can I? Why should I? This—this woman—"

"Because," the empress interrupted, "we have to help Arista."

Amilia would have laughed at the absurdity if Modina had not looked so serious. In all the time she had taken care of her, Amilia had never seen her so focused, so clear-eyed. She felt out of her element. The hazy Modina was gone, but she was still speaking nonsense. She had to make her understand, for her own good. "Modina, guards are looking for this woman. They've been combing the city for days."

"That's why she's going to stay here. It's the safest place.

Not even the regents will look for her in my bedroom. And it'll make helping her that much easier."

"Helping her? Helping her with what?" Amilia was nearly at the end of her own sanity just trying to follow this absurd conversation.

"We're going to help her find Degan Gaunt, the true Heir of Novron."

Chapter 14

Calis

The port of Dagastan surprised first-time visitors from Avryn, who thought of everywhere else as less civilized or uncultured. Calis was generally held, by those who had never been there, to be a crude, ramshackle collection of tribal bands living in mud or wooden huts within a dense and mysterious jungle. It shocked most when they first laid eyes on the massive domes and elegant spires rising along the coast. The city was astonishingly large and well developed. Stone and gray-brick buildings sat densely packed on a graduated hillside rising from the elegant harbor that put Aquesta's wooden docks to shame. Here four long stone piers stretched into the bay, along which stately towers rose at regular intervals, facilitating the needs of the bustling trade center. Masts of more than a hundred ships, nearly all of them exotic merchant vessels, lined the harbor.

Hadrian remembered the city the moment it came into view. The heat of the ancient stones, the spice-scented streets, the exotic women—all memories of an impetuous youth that he preferred to forget. He had left the east behind without regret, and it was not without reservations that he found himself returning.

No bells rang in the towers along the harbor as they

entered. No alarm signaled as the bloodred sails of their Dacca-built tartane entered port. A pilot boat merely issued out and hailed them at their approach.

"*En dil dual lon duclim?*" the pilot called to them.

"I can't understand you," Wesley replied.

"What's name of your vessel? And name of captain?" the pilot repeated.

"Oh, ah—it doesn't have a name, I'm afraid, but my name is Wesley Belstrad."

The pilot jotted something on a handheld tablet, frowning. "Where you outing from?"

"We are the remaining crew of the *Emerald Storm*, Her Imperial Eminence's vessel out from the capital city of Aquesta."

"What your business and how long staying will you be?"

"We are making a delivery. I am not certain how long it will take."

The pilot finished asking questions and indicated they should follow him to a berth. Another official was waiting on the dock and asked Wesley to sign several forms before he would allow anyone to set foot on land.

"According to Seward's orders, we are to contact a Mr. Dilladrum. I will go ashore and try to locate him," Wesley announced. "Mr. Deminthal, you and Seaman Staul will accompany me. Seaman Blackwater, you will be in charge here until my return. See to it that the stores are secured and the ship buttoned down."

"Aye, sir." Hadrian saluted. The three disembarked and disappeared into the maze of streets.

"Wonderful luck we've had in picking up survivors, eh?" Hadrian mentioned to Royce as he met his partner on the raised aft deck of the ship.

The others remained at the waist or the bow, staring in fascination at the port around them. There was a lot to take in.

Unusual sounds drifted from the urban landscape. The jangle of bells, the ringing of a gong, shouts of merchants in a strange musical language, and above it all the haunting voice of a man singing in the distance.

Dockworkers moved cargo to and from ships. Most were dressed in robes with vertical stripes, their skin a tawny brown, their faces bearded. Bolts of shimmering silks and sheer cloth waited to be loaded, as did urns of incense and pots of fragrant oil, whose scents drifted on the harbor breeze. The stone masonry of the buildings was impressive. Intricate designs of flowers and geometric shapes adorned nearly all the constructions. Domes were the most common architectural style, some inlaid in gold, others in silver or in colorful tiles. The larger buildings displayed multiple domes, each featuring a central spire pointing skyward.

For the first time in three days they had found an opportunity to speak alone. "I thought you showed great restraint, and I was impressed with your diplomatic solution to our little civil war," Hadrian told Royce.

"I'm just watching your back, like Gwen asked." Royce took a seat on a thick pile of netted ropes.

"It was a stroke of brilliance appointing Wesley," Hadrian remarked. "I wish I had thought of it. I like that boy. Did you see the way he picked Staul and Wyatt to go with him? Wyatt knows the docks, and Staul knows the language and possibly the city. Perfectly sensible choices, but they're also the two who would make the most trouble out of his sight. He's a lot more like his brother than he thinks. It's a shame they were born in Chadwick. Ballentyne doesn't deserve them."

"It's not looking good. You know that, right?" Royce asked. "What with the weapons and Merrick's payment going down with the *Storm*, and everyone in charge now dead. I don't see where we go from here."

Hadrian took a seat on the railing beside Royce. Water lapped against the wooden hull of the tartane and seagulls cried overhead.

"But we still have Merrick's orders and that letter. What did it say?"

"I didn't read it."

"Weren't you the one who called me stupid because—"

"I never had a chance. Wyatt grabbed them first. Then there was this little incident with a burning ship and lots of swimming. Now Wesley has them and he's hardly slept. I've not had an opportunity."

"Then we'll have to stick to that letter until either you get a chance to take a peek or we solve this riddle. I mean, what is the empire doing sending weapons to Calis when they need them to fight the Nationalists?"

"Maybe bribing Calis to join the fight on their side?"

Hadrian shook his head. "Rhenydd could beat them in a war all by itself. There's no organization down here, no central authority, just a bunch of competing warlords. The whole place is corrupt, and they constantly fight each other. There is no way Merrick could convince enough leaders to go fight for the New Empire—most of these warlords have never even heard of Avryn. And what's with the elves? What were they doing with them?"

"I have to admit, I'd like to know that myself," Royce said.

Hadrian's glance followed Thranic as he came topside and lay among the excess canvas at the bow, his hood pulled down to block the light, his arms folded across his chest. He almost looked like a corpse in need of a coffin.

Hadrian gestured toward the sentinel. "So, what's going on between you and Thranic, anyway? He appears to *really* hate you—even more than most people."

Royce did not look in his direction. He sat nonchalantly,

pretending to ignore the world, as if they were the only two aboard. "Funny thing, that. I never met him, never heard of him until this voyage, and yet I know him rather well, and he knows me."

"Thank you, Mr. Esrahaddon. Can you provide me with perhaps a more cryptic answer?"

Royce smiled. "I see why he does it now. It's rather fun. I'm also surprised you haven't figured it out yet."

"Figured what out?"

"Our boy Thranic has a nasty little secret. It's what makes him so unpleasant and at the same time so dangerous. He would have killed Wyatt, might even have given you a surprise or two. With Staul added to the mix and Bernie slinking about, it wasn't a battle I felt confident in winning, even if I didn't have Gwen's voice echoing in my head."

"You aren't going to tell me, are you?"

"What would be the fun in that? This will give you something to do. You can try to guess, and I can amuse myself by insulting your intelligence. I wouldn't take too long, though. Thranic is going to die soon."

❧

Wesley returned and trotted up the gangway to address them. "I want volunteers to accompany me, Sentinel Thranic, Mr. Bulard, Dr. Levy, and Seamen Staul and Defoe inland. We will be traveling deep into the Calian jungles. The journey will not be without significant risks, so I won't order anyone to follow me who doesn't want to go. Those who choose to stay behind will remain with the ship. Upon my return, we will sail for home, where you will receive your pay."

"Where in the jungle are you headed, Mr. Wesley?" Banner asked.

"I must deliver a letter to Erandabon Gile, who I am informed is a warlord of some note in these parts. I have met with Mr. Dilladrum, who has been awaiting our arrival and has a caravan prepared and ready to escort us. Gile's fortress, however, is deep in the jungles, and contact with the Ba Ran Ghazel is likely. Now, who is with me?"

Hadrian, who was one of the first to raise his hand, found it strange that he was among the majority. Wyatt and Poe did not surprise him, but even Jacob and Grady joined in after seeing the others. Only Greig and Banner abstained.

"I see," Wesley said with a note of surprise. "All right then, Banner, I'll leave you in charge of the ship."

"What are we to do while yer gone, sir?" Banner asked.

"Nothing," he told them. "Just stay with the ship and out of the city. Don't cause any trouble."

Banner smiled gleefully at Greig. "So we can just sleep all day if we want?"

"I don't care what you do, as long as you protect the ship and don't embarrass the empire."

Both of them could hardly contain their delight. "I'll bet the rest of you are wishing you hadn't raised your hands now."

"You realize there's only about a week's worth of rations below, right?" Wyatt mentioned. "You might want to eat sparingly."

A worried look crossed Banner's face. "You're gonna hurry back, right?"

⁂

Wesley led them off the ship and into the city, setting a brisk pace and keeping a sharp eye on the line of men. The old man, Antun Bulard, was the only straggler, but this had more to do with his age than his wounds, which had turned out to be only superficial cuts.

Loud-colored tents and awnings lined the roads of Dagastan from the harbor to the square. Throngs filled the paved pathways as merchants shouted to the crowds, waving banners with unrecognizable symbols. Old men smoked pipes beneath the shelter of striped canopies as scantily dressed women with veiled faces stood provocatively on raised platforms, gyrating slowly to the beat of a dozen drummers, bell ringers, and cymbal players. There was too much happening to focus on any single thing. Everywhere one looked there were dazzling colors, tantalizing movements, intoxicating scents, and exciting music. Overwhelmed, the little parade of sailors marched in step with Mr. Wesley as he led them to their promised guide. He and his team were waiting along a paved avenue not far from the city's Grand Bazaar.

Dilladrum looked like an overweight beggar. His coat and dark britches were faded and poorly patched. Long, dirty hair burst out from under a formless felt hat as if in protest. His beard, equally mismanaged, showed bits of grass nested in its snarls. His face was dusky, and his teeth yellow, but his eyes sparkled in the afternoon sun. He stood on the roadside before a train of curious beasts. They appeared to be shrunken, shaggy horses. The animals were loaded with bundles and linked together by leads from one to the next. Six short, half-naked men helped Dilladrum keep the train under control. They wore only breechcloths of loose linen and clattering necklaces of colored stones. Like Dilladrum, they grinned brightly at the sailors' approach.

"Welcome, welcome, gentlemen," he warmly addressed them. "I am Dilladrum, your guide. Before we leave our fair city, perhaps you would like some time to peruse our fine shops? As per previous arrangements, I and my Vintu friends will be providing you with food, water, and shelter, but we'll be many days afield, and as such, some comforts as could be obtained in the bazaar might make your trek more pleasant. Consider our fine wines, liquors, or perhaps an attractive slave girl to make the camps more enjoyable."

A few eyes turned appraisingly toward the shops, where dozens of colorful signboards advertised in a foreign tongue. Music played—strange twanging strings and warbling pipes. Hadrian could smell lamb spiced with curry, a popular dish as he recalled.

"We will leave immediately," Wesley replied, louder than was necessary for merely Dilladrum to hear him.

"Suit yourself, good sir." The guide shrugged sadly. He made a gesture to his Vintu workers and the little men used long switches and yelping cries to urge the animals of the caravan forward.

As they did, one spotted Hadrian and paused in his work. His brows furrowed as he stared intently until a shout from Dilladrum sent him back to herding.

"What was that all about?" Royce asked. Hadrian shrugged, but Royce looked unconvinced. "You were here for what—five years? Anything happen? Anything you want to share?"

"Sure," he replied with a sarcastic grin. "Right after you fill me in on how you escaped from Manzant Prison and why you never killed Ambrose Moor."

"Sorry I asked."

"I was young and stupid," Hadrian offered. "But I can tell you that Wesley is right about the jungle being dangerous. We'll want to watch ourselves around Gile."

"You met him?"

Hadrian nodded. "I've met most of the warlords of the Gur Em, but I'm sure everyone's forgotten me by now."

As if overhearing, the train worker glanced over his shoulder at Hadrian once more.

⁂

"Everywhere landward from Dagastan is uphill," Dilladrum was saying as the troop walked along the narrow dirt path through farmlands dotted by domed grass huts. "That is the way of the world everywhere, is it not? From the sea, we always need to go up. It makes the leaving that much harder, but the returning that much more welcome."

They walked two abreast, with Wesley and Dilladrum, Wyatt and Poe, Royce and Hadrian in front while Thranic's group followed behind the Vintu and the beasts. Having Thranic and his crew behind them was disconcerting, but it was better than walking with them. Dilladrum set a brisk pace for a portly little man, stepping lively and thrusting his bleached walking stick out with practiced skill. He bent the brim down on his otherwise shapeless hat to block the sun, making him look comical even while Hadrian wished he had a silly-looking hat of his own.

"Mr. Dilladrum, what exactly are your instructions concerning us?" Wesley inquired.

"I am contracted to safely deliver officers, cargo, and crew of the *Emerald Storm* to the Palace of the Four Winds in Dur Guron."

"Is that the residence of Erandabon Gile?"

"Ah yes, the fortress of the Panther of Dur Guron."

"Panther?" Wyatt asked.

Dilladrum chuckled. "It's what the Vintu call the warlord. They're a very simple folk, but very hard workers, as you can see. The Panther is a legend among them."

"A hero?" Wesley offered.

"A panther is not a hero to anyone. A panther is a great cat that hides himself in the jungle. He's a ghost to those who seek him, deadly to those he hunts, but to those he doesn't, he's merely a creature deserving of respect. The Panther does not concern himself with the Vintu, but stories of his valor, cruelty, and cunning reach them."

"You are not Vintu?"

"No. I'm Erbonese. Erbon is a region to the northwest, not far from Mandalin."

"And the Tenkin?" Wesley asked. "Is the warlord one of them?"

Dilladrum's expression turned dark. "Yes, yes. The Tenkin are everywhere in these jungles." He pointed to the horizon ahead of them. "Some tribes are more welcoming than others. Not to worry, my Vintu and I know a good route. We'll pass through one Tenkin village, but they're friendly and familiar to us, like the one you call Staul, yes? We'll make it safely."

As they climbed higher, they entered a great plain of tall grass that swayed enchantingly with the breeze. Climbing a large rock, they could see for miles in all directions except ahead, where a tall, forested ridge rose several hundred feet. They made camp just before sundown. Hardly a word passed between Dilladrum and the Vintu, but they immediately went to work setting up decorative tents with embroidered geometric designs and neatly bordered canopies. Cots and small stools were put out for each, along with sheets and pillows.

Cooked in large pots over an open fire, the evening meal was strong and spicy enough to make Hadrian's eyes water. He found it tasty and satisfying after weeks of eating the same tired pork stew. The Vintu took turns entertaining. Some played stringed instruments similar to a lute, others danced, and a few sang lilting ballads. The words Hadrian could not understand, but the melody was beautiful. Animal calls filled the night. Screeches, cries, and growls threatened in the darkness, always too loud and too close.

⁂

On their third day out, the landscape began to change. The level plains tilted upward and trees appeared more frequently. The forests that had lined the distance were upon them, and soon they were trudging under a canopy of tall trees whose massive roots spread out across the forest floor like the fingers of old men. At first it was good to be out of the sun, but then the path became rocky, steep, and hard to navigate. It did not last long, as they soon crested a ridge and began a sharp descent. On the far side of the ridge, they could see a distinct change in the flora. The undergrowth thickened, turning a deeper green. Larger leaves, vines, thickets of creepers, and needle-shaped blades encroached on the track, causing the Vintu to occasionally move ahead to chop a path.

The next day it began to rain, and while at times it poured and at others it only misted, it never ceased.

"They always seem content, don't they?" Hadrian mentioned to Royce as they sat under the canopy of their tent watching the Vintu preparing the evening meal. "It could be blazingly hot or raining like now, and they don't seem to care one way or the other."

"Are you now saying we should become Vintu?" Royce asked. "I don't think you can just apply for membership into their tribe. I think you need to be born into it."

"What's that?" Wyatt asked, coming out of the tent the three shared, wiping his freshly shaved face with a cloth.

"Just thinking about the Vintu and living a simple existence of quiet pleasures," Hadrian explained.

"What makes you think they're content?" Royce asked.

"I've found that when people smile all the time, they're hiding something. These Vintu are probably miserable—economically forced into relative slavery, catering to wealthy foreigners. I'm sure they would smile just as much while slitting our throats to save themselves another day of hauling Dilladrum's packs."

"I think you've been away from Gwen too long. You're starting to sound like the *old Royce* again."

Across the camp they spotted Staul, Thranic, and Defoe. Staul waved in their direction and grinned.

"See? Big grin," Royce mentioned.

"Fun group, eh?" Hadrian muttered.

"Yeah, they are a group, aren't they?" Royce nodded thoughtfully. "Why would a sentinel, a Tenkin warrior, a physician, a thief, and...whatever the heck Bulard is go into the jungles of Calis to visit a Tenkin warlord? And what's Bulard's deal?"

Wyatt and Hadrian shrugged in unison.

"Isn't that a bit odd? We were all on the same ship together for weeks, and we don't know anything about the man beyond the fact that he doesn't look like he's seen the sun in a decade. Perhaps if we found out, it would provide the common connection between the others and this Erandabon fellow."

"Bernie and Bulard share a tent," Hadrian pointed out.

"Hadrian, why don't you go chat with Bulard?" Royce said. "I'll distract Bernie."

"What about me?" Wyatt asked.

"Talk with Derning and Grady. They don't seem as connected to the others as I first thought. Find out why they volunteered."

The Vintu handed out dinner, which the *Storm's* crew ate sitting on stools the Vintu provided. Dinner consisted mostly of what appeared to be shredded pork and an array of unusual vegetables in a thick, hot sauce that needled the tongue.

After the meal, darkness descended on the camp and most retired to their tents. Antun Bulard was already in his, just like he always stayed in his cabin aboard ship. The light in Bulard and Bernie's tent flickered and the silhouettes of their heads bobbed about, magnified on the canvas walls. A few hours after dark, Bernie stepped out. An instant later, Royce swooped in.

❧

"How you been, *Bernie*?" Royce greeted him. "Going for a walk?"

"Actually, I was about to find a place to relieve myself."

"Good, I'll go with you."

"Go with me?" he asked nervously.

"I've been known to help people relieve themselves of a great many things." Royce put an arm around Bernie's shoulder as he urged him away from the tents. Once more Bernie flinched. "A little jumpy, aren't we?" Royce asked.

"Don't you think I have good reason?"

Royce smiled and nodded. "You have me there. I honestly still can't figure out what you were thinking."

The two were outside the circle of tents, well beyond the glow of the campfire, and still Royce urged him farther away.

"It wasn't my idea. I was just following orders. Don't you think I'd know better than to—"

"Whose idea was it?"

Bernie hesitated only a moment. "Thranic," he said, then hastily added, "but he just wanted you bloodied. Not dead, just cut."

"Why?"

"Honestly, I don't know."

They stopped in a dark circle of trees. Night frogs croaked

hesitantly, concerned by their presence. The camp was only a distant glow.

"Care to tell me what all of you are doing here?"

Bernie frowned. "You know I won't, even to save my life. It wouldn't be worth it."

"But you told me about Thranic."

"I don't like Thranic."

"So he's not the one you're afraid of. Is it Merrick?"

"Merrick?" Bernie looked genuinely puzzled. "Listen, I never faulted you for Jade's death or the war you waged on the Diamond. Merrick should have never betrayed you like that, not without first hearing your side of it."

Royce took a step forward. In the darkness of the canopy, he was certain Bernie could barely see him. Royce, on the other hand, could make out every line on Bernie's face. "What's Merrick's plan?"

"I haven't seen Merrick in years."

Royce drew out his dagger and purposely allowed it to make a metal scraping sound as it came free of its scabbard. "So you haven't seen him. Fine. But you're working for him, or someone else who's working for him. I want to know where he is and what he's up to, and you're going to tell me."

Bernie shook his head. "I—I really don't know anything about Marius or what he's doing nowadays."

Royce paused. Every line of Bernie's face revealed he was telling the truth.

"What have we here?" Thranic asked. "A private meeting? You've strayed a bit far from camp, dear boys."

Royce turned to see Thranic and Staul. Staul held a torch, and Thranic carried a crossbow.

"It's not safe to venture too far away from your friends, or didn't you think about that, Royce?" Thranic said, then fired the crossbow at Royce's heart.

❧

"Antun Bulard, isn't it?" Hadrian asked, sticking his head in the tent.

"Hmm?" Antun looked up. He was lying on his stomach, writing with a featherless quill worn to only a few inches in length. He had on a pair of spectacles, the top of which he peered over. "Why, yes, I am."

The old man was more than just pale—he was white. His hair was the color of alabaster, while his skin was little more than wrinkled quartz. He reminded Hadrian of an egg, colorless and fragile.

"I wanted to introduce myself." Hadrian slipped fully inside. "All this time at sea and we never had the opportunity to properly meet. I thought that was unfortunate, don't you?"

"Why, I—Who are you again?"

"Hadrian. I was the cook on the *Emerald Storm*."

"Ah, well, I hate to say it, Hadrian, but I was not impressed with your cooking. Perhaps a little less salt and some wine would have helped. Not that this is any great feast," he said, gesturing toward his half-eaten meal. "I'm too old for such rich foods. It upsets my stomach."

"What are you writing?"

"Oh, this? Just notes, really. My mind isn't what it once was, you see. I'll forget everything soon, and then where will I be? A historian who can't remember his own name. It really could come to that, you know. Assuming I live that long. Bernie keeps reassuring me I won't live out this trip. He's probably right. He's the expert on such things, after all."

"Really? What kind of things?"

"Oh, spelunking, of course. I'm told Bernie is an old hand at it. We make a good team, he and I. He digs up the past and I put it down, so to speak." Antun chuckled to himself until he coughed. Hadrian poured the man a glass of water, which he gratefully accepted.

After he had recovered, Hadrian asked, "Have you ever heard of a man called Merrick Marius?"

Bulard shook his head. "Not unless I have and then forgotten. Was he a king or a hero, perhaps?"

"No, I actually thought he might have been the man who sent you here."

"Oh no. Our mandate is from the Patriarch himself, though Sentinel Thranic doesn't tell me much. I'm not complaining, mind you. How often does a priest of Maribor have the opportunity to serve the Patriarch? I can tell you precisely—twice. Once when I was so much younger, and now that I'm nearly dead."

"I thought you were a historian. You're also a priest?"

"I know I don't look much like one, do I? My calling was the pen, not the flock."

"You've written books, then?"

"Oh yes, my best is still *The History of Apeladorn*, which I'm constantly having to append, of course."

"I know a monk at the Winds Abbey who'd love to meet you."

"Is that up north in Melengar? I passed through there once about twenty years ago." Antun nodded thoughtfully. "They were very helpful, saved my life if I recall correctly."

"So, you're on this trip to record what you see?"

"Oh no, that's only what I've been doing so far. As you can imagine, I don't get out much. I do most of my work in libraries and stuffy cellars, reading old books. I was in Tur Del Fur before setting off on this wonderful trip. This has been an excellent opportunity to record what I see firsthand. The Patriarch knows about my research on ancient imperial history, and that's why I'm here. Sort of a living, breathing version of my books, you see. I suppose they think that if they put in the right questions, out will pop the correct answers, like an oracle."

Hadrian was about to ask another question when Grady and Poe poked their heads in.

"Hadrian." Poe caught his attention.

"Well, isn't my tent the social center tonight?" Antun remarked.

"I'm kinda busy at the moment. Can this wait?" Hadrian asked.

"I don't think so. Thranic and Staul just followed Royce and Bernie into the jungle."

❧

Royce heard the click of the release and began to move even before the hiss of the string indicated the missile's launch. Still, his reflexes could not move faster than a flying bolt. The metal shaft pierced his side below the rib cage. The impact thrust him backward, where he collapsed in pain.

"Lucky we found you, Bernie," Thranic told the startled thief as he moved away from Royce's body. "He would have killed you. Isn't that what you said bucket men do? Now, don't you feel foolish for saying I couldn't protect you?"

"You could have hit me!" Bernie snapped.

"Stop being so dramatic. You're alive, aren't you? Besides, I heard the conversation. It didn't take much for you to give me up. In my profession, lack of faith is a terrible sin."

"In mine, it's all too often justified," Bernie snarled back.

"Get back to the camp before you're missed."

Bernie grumbled as he trotted back up the path. Thranic watched his retreat.

"We might have to do something about him," the sentinel

told the Tenkin. "Funny that you, my heathen friend, should be my stalwart ally in all this."

"Bernie, he thinks too much. Me? I am just greedy, and therefore trustworthy. We going to just leave the body?"

"No, it's too close to the path we'll be taking tomorrow, and I can't count on the animals eating him before we break camp. Drag him away. A few yards should be enough."

"Royce?" Hadrian shouted from behind them on the trail.

"Quickly, you idiot. They're coming!"

Staul rushed forward and, planting his torch in the ground, lifted Royce and ran with him into the jungle. He had traveled only a few dozen yards when he cursed.

Royce was still breathing.

"*Izuto!*" the Tenkin hissed, drawing his dagger.

"Too late," Royce whispered.

⁂

Hadrian led them into the trees the way Royce had gone earlier. Ahead he spotted the glow of a torch and ran toward it. Behind him Wyatt, Poe, Grady, and Derning followed.

"There's blood here," Hadrian announced when he got to the burning torch thrust in the ground. "Royce!"

"Spread out!" Wyatt ordered. "Sweep the grass and look for more blood."

"Over here!" Derning shouted, moving into the ferns. "There, up ahead. Two of them, Staul and Royce!"

Hadrian cut his way through the thick undergrowth to where they lay. Royce was breathing hard, holding his blood-soaked side. His face was pale, but his eyes remained focused.

"How ya doing, buddy?" Hadrian asked, dropping to his knees and carefully slipping an arm under his friend.

Royce didn't say anything. He kept his teeth clenched, blowing his cheeks out with each breath.

"Get his feet, Wyatt," Hadrian ordered. "Now lift him gently. Poe, get out front with the torch."

"What about Staul?" Derning asked.

"What about him?" Hadrian glanced down at the big Tenkin, whose throat lay open, slit from ear to ear.

When they returned to camp, Wesley ordered Royce to be taken to his tent, which was the largest, originally reserved for Captain Seward. He started to send Poe for Dr. Levy, but Hadrian intervened. Wesley appeared confused, but as Hadrian was Royce's best friend, he did not press the issue. The Vintu were surprisingly adept at first aid, and under Hadrian's watchful eye they cleaned and dressed the wound.

The bolt aimed at Royce's heart had entered and exited cleanly. He suffered significant blood loss, but no organ damage, nor broken bones. The Vintu sealed the tiny entry hole without a problem. The larger tearing of his flesh at the exit was another matter. It took a dozen bandages and many basins of water before they got the bleeding under control and Royce lay, sleeping calmly.

"Why wasn't I notified about this? I'm a physician, for Maribor's sake!"

Hadrian stepped outside the tent flap to find Levy arguing with Wyatt, Poe, Grady, and Derning, who, at Hadrian's request, guarded the entrance.

"Ah, Dr. Levy, just the man I wanted to see," Hadrian addressed him. "Where's your boss? Where's Thranic?"

Levy did not need to answer, as across the camp Thranic walked toward them alongside Wesley and Bernie.

Hadrian drew his sword at their approach.

"Put away your weapon!" Wesley ordered.

"This man nearly killed Royce tonight," Hadrian declared, pointing at Thranic.

"That's not the way he tells it," Wesley replied. "He said Seaman Melborn attacked and murdered Seaman Staul over accusations regarding Seaman Drew's death. Mr. Thranic and Seaman Defoe claim they were witnesses."

"We don't *claim* anything. We saw it," Thranic said coolly.

"And how do you *claim* this took place?" Hadrian asked.

"Staul confronted Royce, telling him he was going to Wesley with evidence. Royce warned him that he would never live to see the dawn. Then, when Staul turned to walk back to camp, Royce grabbed him from behind and slit his throat. Bernie and I expected such treachery from him, but we couldn't convince Staul not to confront the blackguard. So we followed. I brought a crossbow, borrowed from Mr. Dilladrum's supplies, for protection. I fired in self-defense."

"He's lying," Hadrian declared.

"Oh, were you there?" Thranic asked. "Did you see it happen as we did? Funny, I didn't notice your presence."

"Royce left the camp with Bernie, not Staul," Hadrian said.

Thranic laughed. "Is that the best you can come up with to save your friend from a noose? Why not say you saw Staul attack him unprovoked, or me, for that matter?"

"I saw Royce leave with Bernie too, and Thranic and Staul followed after them," Wyatt put in.

"That's a lie!" Bernie responded, convincingly offended. "I watched Royce leave with Staul. Thranic and I followed. I worked the topmast with Royce. I was there the night Edgar Drew died. Royce was the only one near him. They were having an argument. You all saw how agile he is. Drew never had a chance."

"Why didn't you report it to the captain?" Derning asked.

"I did," Bernie declared. "But because I didn't actually see him push poor Drew off, he refused to do anything."

"How convenient that Captain Seward is too dead to ask about that," Wyatt pointed out.

Thranic shook his head with a pitiful smile. "Now, Wesley, will you actually take the word of a pirate and a cook over the word of a sentinel of the Nyphron Church?"

"Your Excellency," Wesley said, turning to face Thranic. "You will address me as *Mr.* Wesley or *sir.* Is that understood?" Thranic's expression soured. "And *I* will decide whose word I will accept. As it happens, I am well aware of your personal vendetta against Seaman Melborn. Midshipman Beryl tried to convince me to bring false charges. Well, sir, I did not buckle to Beryl's threats, and I'll be damned if I will be intimidated by your title."

"*Damned* is a very good choice of words, *Mr.* Wesley."

"Sentinel Thranic," Wesley barked at him. "Be forewarned that if any further harm befalls Seaman Melborn that is even remotely suspicious, I will hold you responsible and have you executed by whatever means are at hand. Do I make myself clear?"

"You wouldn't dare touch an ordained officer of the Patriarch. Every king in Avryn—why, the regents themselves—would not oppose me. It's you who should be concerned about execution."

Wyatt, Grady, and Derning drew their blades and Hadrian took a step closer to Thranic.

"Stand down, gentlemen!" Wesley shouted. At his order, they paused. "You are quite correct, Sentinel Thranic. Your office does influence how I treat you. Were you an ordinary seaman, I would order you flogged for your disrespect. I am well aware that upon our return to Aquesta you could ruin my career, or perhaps have me imprisoned or hanged. But let me point out, sir, that Aquesta is a long way from here, and a dead man has difficulty requesting anything. It would be in my best interest, therefore, to see you executed here and now. It would be a simple matter to report you and Seaman Defoe lost to the dangers of the jungle."

Bernie looked worried and took a subtle step away from Thranic's side.

"I would have thought I could rely on your family's famous code of honor," Thranic said in a sarcastic tone.

"You can, sir, and you are, as indeed that is all that keeps you alive at this moment. It is also what you can count on to have you executed should you threaten Seaman Melborn again. Do I make myself clear?"

Thranic fumed but said nothing. He simply turned and walked away with Bernie following.

Wesley exhaled loudly and straightened his vest. "How is he doing?" he asked Hadrian.

"Sleeping at the moment, sir. He's weak, but should recover. And thank you, sir."

"For what?" Wesley replied. "I have a mission to accomplish, Seaman Blackwater. I cannot have my crew killing one another. Seamen Derning and Grady, take a few others and bring Mr. Staul's body back to camp. Let us not leave him to the beasts of this foul jungle."

CHAPTER 15

THE SEARCH

"I think I saw him."

Arista woke at the sound. Disoriented, she did not know where she was at first. Turning over, she found Thrace illuminated by a streak of moonlight. The empress was dressed in her wispy, thin nightgown, which fluttered in the draft. She stood straight, hair loose, eyes lost to a vision beyond the window's frame.

Nearly a week had passed since Gerald had invited Arista to the empress's bedroom, and she wondered if being here was a sign that she was on the right path. If fate could speak, surely this would be how it would sound.

Thrace saw to her safety, guarding her like the mother of a newborn. Soldiers stood outside her door at all times, now in pairs, with strict orders to prevent the entry of anyone without permission. Only Amilia and Nimbus ever entered the chamber, and even they knocked. At Thrace's urging, Nimbus carried messages to Hilfred.

In her nightgown, Thrace looked almost like the girl from Dahlgren, but there was something different about her—akin to sadness, yet lacking even the passion for that. Often she would sit and stare at nothing for hours, and when she spoke, her words were dull and emotionless. She never laughed, cried, or smiled. In this way, she appeared to have successfully transformed from a lively peasant girl into a true empress—serene and unflappable.

Yet at what cost?

"It was late like this," Thrace said, looking out the window. Her voice sounded disconnected, as if she was in a trance. "I was having a dream, but a squeaking noise woke me. I came to the window and I saw them. They were in the courtyard below. Men with torches, as many as a dozen, wheeled in a sealed wagon. They were knights, dressed in black-and-scarlet armor, like those we saw in Dahlgren. They spoke of the man inside the box as if he were a monster, and even though he was hooded and chained, they were afraid. After they took him away, the wagon rolled back out of the courtyard." Thrace turned to face her. "I thought it was a dream until just now. I have a lot of unpleasant dreams."

"How long ago did this happen?"

"Three months, perhaps more."

Shivering, Arista sat up. The fire had long since died and the stone walls did nothing to keep the chill out. The window was open again. Regardless of what time of day it was, or how cold the temperature, Thrace insisted. Not with words—she rarely spoke—but each time Arista closed the window, the girl opened it again.

"That would coincide with Gaunt's disappearance. You never heard anything else about this prisoner?"

"No, and you would be surprised how much you hear when you're very quiet."

"Thrace, come—" The sudden tilt of Modina's head and the curious look on her face stopped Arista.

"No one calls me that anymore."

"A shame. I've always liked the name."

"Me too."

"Come back to bed. You'll catch a cold."

Thrace walked toward her, looking at where the mirror had once hung. "I'll need to get a new mirror before Wintertide."

❧

Dawn brought breakfast and morning reports from Amilia and Thrace's tutor. Nimbus was bright-eyed and cheery, bowing to both—a courtesy Amilia refused to extend to Arista. The chief imperial secretary looked haggard. The dark circles under her eyes grew deeper each day. Holding her jaw stiff and her fists clenched, she glared at Arista eating breakfast in Thrace's bed. Despite Amilia's obvious contempt, Arista could not help liking her. She recognized the same fierce protectiveness that Hilfred exhibited.

"They've stopped the search for the Witch of Melengar," Amilia reported, looking coldly at Arista. "They think she's headed to either Melengar or Ratibor. Patrols are still out, but no one really expects to find her."

"What about where Degan Gaunt might be held?" Arista asked.

Amilia glanced at Nimbus, who stepped up. "Well, my research at the Hall of Records is inconclusive. In ancient imperial times, Aquesta was a city called Rionillion, and a building of some significance stood on this site. Ironically, several parchments refer to it as a prison, but it was destroyed during the early part of the civil wars that followed the death of the last emperor. Later, in 2453, Glenmorgan the First built a fortress here as a defense against rebellions. That fortress is the very palace in which we now stand.

"None of the histories mention anything about a dungeon—odd, given the unrest. I've made a detailed search of nearly every section of the palace, interviewed chambermaids, studied old maps and plans, but I haven't uncovered a single mention of any kind."

"What does Aquesta do with criminals?" Arista asked.

"There are three jails in the city that deal with minor offenses and the Warric prison in Whitehead for harsher cases that don't result in execution. And then there is the infamous Manzant Prison and Salt Mine in Maranon for the most severe crimes."

"Perhaps it's not a dungeon or prison at all," Arista said. "Maybe it's merely a secret room."

"I suppose I could make some inquiries along those lines."

"What is it, Amilia?" Thrace asked, catching a thoughtful look on her secretary's face.

"What? Oh, nothing..." Amilia's expression switched to one of annoyance. "This is very dangerous. Asking all these questions and nosing about. It's risky enough ordering extra food with each meal. Someone will notice. Saldur is not a fool."

"But what were you thinking just now, Amilia?" Thrace repeated.

"Nothing."

"Amilia?"

The secretary frowned. "I just—Well, a few weeks ago you talked about a dark hole..."

"You think I was there—in this dungeon?"

"Don't, Modina. Don't think about it," Amilia begged. "You're too fragile."

"I have to try. If I can remember—"

"You don't *have* to do anything. This woman—she comes here—she doesn't care about you—or what might happen. All she cares about is herself. You've done more than enough.

If you won't turn her in, at least let me get her out of here and away from you. Nimbus and I—"

"No," Thrace said softly. "She needs us...and I need her."

⁂

"Dirt," Thrace said, and shivered.

Arista looked over. She was in the midst of trying to determine how to finish her latest letter to Hilfred when she heard the word. The empress had knelt before the open window since Amilia and Nimbus had left, but this was the first she had spoken.

"Damp, cold—terrible cold, and voices, I remember them—cries and weeping, men and women, screams and prayers. Everything was dark." Thrace wrapped her arms around herself and began to rock. "Splashing, I remember splashing, a hollow sound, creaking, a whirl, and the splash. Sometimes there were distant, echoing voices coming from above, falling out of a tunnel. The walls were stone, the door wood. A bowl—yes, every day a bowl—soup that smelled bad. There was so little to eat."

Thrace rocked harder, her voice trembling, her breath hitching.

"I could hear the blows and cries, men and women, day and night, screaming for mercy. Then I heard a new voice added to the wailing, and realized it was my own. I killed my family. I killed my brother, his wife, and little Hickory. I destroyed my whole village. I killed my father. I was being punished."

Thrace began to cry.

Arista moved to her, but the girl jumped at her touch and cowered away. Crawling against the wall and sobbing, she rubbed the stone with her hands, wetting it with her tears.

Fragile? Arista thought. Thrace had taken a blow that would have killed most people. No matter what Amilia believed, Thrace was not fragile. Yet even granite would crack if you hit it with a big enough hammer.

"Are you all right?" Arista asked.

"No, I keep searching but I can't find it. I can't understand the sounds. It's so familiar and yet..." She trailed off and shook her head. "I'm sorry, I wanted to help. I wanted—"

"It's okay, Thrace. It's okay."

The empress frowned. "You have to stop calling me that." She looked up at her. "Thrace is dead."

Chapter 16

The Village

It was perpetually twilight. The jungle's canopy blocked what little sunlight managed to penetrate the rain clouds. A hazy mist shrouded their surroundings and intensified the deeper they pressed into the jungle. Exotic plants with stalks the size of men's legs towered overhead. Huge leaves adorned with intricate patterns and vibrant flowers of purple, yellow, and red surrounded the party. It all left Hadrian feeling small, shrunken to the size of an insect or crawling across the floor of a giant's forest.

Rain constantly plagued them. Water danced on a million leaves, sounding like thunder. When actual thunder cracked, it was the voice of a god. Everything was wet. Clothes stuck to their skin and hung like weights. Boots squished audibly with every step. Their hands were wrinkled like those of old men.

Royce rode on the back of a *gunguan*, what the Vintu called the pack ponies. He was awake but weak. A day had passed since the attack, because Wesley had insisted on burying Staul. Their new captain had proclaimed he would not allow the beasts to have a taste of any of his crew, and he insisted on a deep grave. No one had complained about the strenuous work of cutting through the thick mat of roots.

Hadrian doubted Wesley really cared about the fate of Staul's carcass, but the work granted Royce time to rest, kept the crew busy, and affirmed Wesley's commitment to them. Hadrian thought once again about the similarities between the midshipman and his famous brother.

Royce traveled wrapped in his cloak with the weight of the rain collapsing the hood around his head—not a good sign for Thranic and Bernie. Until then, Royce had played the part of the good little sailor, but with the reemergence of the hood, and the loss of his white kerchief, Hadrian knew that role had ended. They had not spoken much since the attack. Not surprisingly, Royce was in no mood for idle discussion. Hadrian guessed that by now his friend had imagined killing Thranic a dozen times, with a few Bernies thrown in here and there for variety. Hadrian had seen Royce wounded before and was familiar with the cocooning—only what would emerge from that cloak and hood would not be a butterfly.

Thranic, Defoe, and Levy traveled at the end of the train and Hadrian often caught them whispering. They wisely kept their distance, avoiding attention. Wesley led the party along with Dilladrum, who made a point of not taking sides or venturing anything remotely resembling an opinion. Dilladrum remained jolly as always and focused his attention on the Vintu.

Hadrian was most surprised with Derning. When Royce had been most vulnerable, his shipboard nemesis had come to his aid rather than taking advantage. Hadrian would have bet money that on the subject of Royce's guilt, Derning would have sided with Thranic. Wyatt had never had the chance to find out his reason for volunteering, but now more than ever Hadrian was convinced Derning was not part of Thranic's band. There was no doubt that Antun Bulard was a member of Thranic's troop, but the old man lacked the ruthlessness of the others. He was merely a resource. After showing an interest, Hadrian became Bulard's new best friend.

"Look! Look there." Bulard pointed to a brilliant flower blooming overhead. The old man took to walking beside Hadrian, sharing his sense of discovery along the way. "Gorgeous, simply gorgeous. Have you ever seen the like? I daresay I haven't. Still, that isn't saying much, now is it?"

Bulard reminded Hadrian of a long-haired cat, with his usually billowing robe and fluffy white hair deflated in the rain, leaving a remarkably thin body. He held up a withered hand to protect his eyes as he searched the trees.

"Another one of those wonderful long-beaked birds," the historian said. "I love the way they hover."

Hadrian smiled at him. "It's not that you don't mind the rain that amazes me. It's that you don't seem to notice it at all."

Bulard frowned. "My parchments are a disaster. They stick together, the ink runs, I haven't been able to write anything down, and as I mentioned at our first meeting, my head is no place to store memories of such wonderful things. It makes me feel like I've wasted my life locked in dusty libraries and scriptoriums. Don't do what I did, Hadrian. You're still a young man. Take my advice: live your life to the fullest. Breathe the air, taste the wine, kiss the girls, and always remember that the tales of another are never as wondrous as your own. I'll admit I was, well, concerned about this trip. No, I'll say it truthfully—I was scared. What does a man my age have to be afraid of, you wonder? Everything. Life becomes more precious when you have less of it to spare. I'm not ready to die. Why, look at all that I've never seen."

"You have seen horses before, and known women, right?" Hadrian asked with a wry grin.

Bulard looked at him curiously. "I'm a historian, not a monk."

Hadrian nearly tripped.

"I realize I don't look it now, but I was quite handsome once. I was married three times, in fact. Outlived all of them, poor darlings. I still miss them, you know—each one. My silly little mind hasn't misplaced their faces, and I can't imagine it ever will. Have you ever been in love, Hadrian?"

"I'm not sure. How do you tell?"

"Love? Why, it's like coming home."

Hadrian considered the comment.

"What are you thinking?" Bulard asked.

Hadrian shook his head. "Nothing."

"Yes, you were. What? You can tell me. I'm an excellent repository for secrets. I'll likely forget, but if I don't, well, I'm an old man in a remote jungle. I'm sure to die before I can repeat anything."

Hadrian smiled, then shrugged. "I was just thinking about the rain."

The trail widened, revealing a great, cascading waterfall and a dozen grass-thatched buildings clustered at the center of a small clearing. The domed-roof huts rested on high wooden stilts and were accessed by short stairs or ladders, depending on the size and apparent prestige of the structure. Occupying the very center of the clearing was a fire pit, surrounded by a ring of colorfully painted stones and wooden poles decorated in animal skins, skulls, and strings of bones, beads, and long vibrant feathers. The inhabitants were dark-haired, dark-eyed, umber-skinned men and women dressed in beautifully painted cloths and silks. They paused as Dilladrum advanced respectfully. Elder men met him before the fire ring, where they exchanged bows.

"Who are these people, do you suppose?" Bulard asked.

"Tenkins," Hadrian replied.

Bulard raised his eyebrows.

The village was familiar to Hadrian, though he had never been there. Hundreds of similar ones were scattered across the peninsula, mirror images of each other. The rubble of eastern Calis was the last standing residue of the Old Empire. After civil wars had torn apart the west, Calis still flew the old imperial banners and for centuries formed the bulwark against the advancing Ghazel horde. Time, however, was on the Ghazel's side. The last of the old world died when the ancient eastern capital, Urlineus, fell to the goblin hordes sweeping through the jungles. They might have overrun all of Avryn if not for Glenmorgan III.

Glenmorgan III had rallied the nobles and defeated the goblins at the Battle of Vilan Hills. The Ghazel fell back but were never driven off the mainland. Betrayed shortly after his victory, Glenmorgan III never finished his work of reestablishing the kingdom's borders. This task fell to lesser men, who squabbled over the spoils of war and were too distracted to stop the Ghazel from digging in. Urlineus, the last great city of the Old Empire, remained in the hands of the Ghazel, and Calis had never been the same.

Fractured and isolated, the eastern half of the country struggled against the growing pressure of the Ghazel nation in a maelstrom of chaos and confusion. Self-appointed warrior-kings fought against each other. Out of desperation, some enlisted the aid of the Ghazel to vanquish a rival. Ties formed, lines blurred, and out of this tenuous alliance were born the Tenkin—humans who had adopted the Ghazel's ways, traditions, and beliefs. For this, Calians ostracized the Tenkin, forcing their kind deeper into the jungles, where they lived on the borderlands between the anvil and the hammer.

Dilladrum returned. "This is the village of Oudorro. I've been here many times. Although Tenkin, they're a friendly and generous people. I've asked them to let us rest here for the night. Tomorrow morning we'll push on toward the Palace of the Four Winds. Beyond this point, travel will be much harder and unpleasant, so we'll need a good night's rest. I must caution you, however: please do nothing to offend or provoke these people. They're courteous but can be fierce if roused."

The physical appearance of the Tenkin always impressed Hadrian. Staul was a crude example of his kin, and these men were more what he remembered. Lean, bronzed muscles and strong facial features that looked hewn from blocks of stone were the hallmarks of the Tenkin warrior. Like the great cats of the jungle, they had bodies graceful in their strength and simplicity. The women were breathtaking. Long, dark hair wreathed sharp cheekbones and almond eyes. Their satin-smooth skin enveloped willowy curves. The "civilized" world never saw Tenkin women. A closely guarded treasure, they never left their villages.

The inhabitants showed neither fear nor concern at the procession of the foreigners. Most observed their arrival with silent curiosity. The women showed more interest, pressing forward to peer and talking among themselves.

"I thought Tenkins were grotesque," Bulard said with the casual manner and volume of a man commenting on animals. "I had heard they were abominations of nature, but these people are beautiful."

"A common misconception," Hadrian explained. "People tell tales that Tenkin are the result of interbreeding between Calians and Ghazel, but if you ever saw a goblin, you'd understand why that's not possible."

"I guess you can't believe everything you read in books. But don't spread that around, or I'll be out of a job."

When they reached the village center, the Vintu went about their work and began unpacking. They moved with stoic familiarity. The party waited, listening to the hiss of rain on the fire and the murmur of the crowd gathering around them. With an expectant expression, Dilladrum struggled to see over their heads. He exchanged looks with Wesley but said nothing. Soon a small elderly Tenkin dressed in a leopard wrap entered the circle. His skin was like wrinkled leather, and his hair like gray steel. He walked with a slow dignity and an upturned chin. Dilladrum smiled and the two spoke rapidly. Then the elderly Tenkin clapped his hands and shouted. The crowd fell back and he led the crew of the *Emerald Storm* into the largest of the buildings. It had four tree-sized pillars holding up a latticework of intertwined branches overlaid with thatch. The interior lacked partitions and stood as an open hall lined with tanned skins and pillows made from animal hides.

Waiting inside were four Tenkins. Three men and a woman sat upon a raised mound covered in luxurious cushions. Their leopard-clad guide bowed deeply to the four, then left. Outside, the rain increased and poured off the thatched roof.

Dilladrum stepped forward, bowed with his hands clasped before him, and spoke in Tenkin, which was a mix of the old imperial tongue and Ghazel. Hadrian had mastered a working knowledge of the language, but the isolation between villages had caused each to develop a slightly different dialect. While Hadrian missed a number of Dilladrum's words, he recognized that formal introductions were being made.

"This is Burandu," Dilladrum explained to the *Emerald Storm's* crew in Apelanese. "He is Elder." Dilladrum paused to think, then added, "Similar to the lord of a manor, but not quite. Beside him is Joqdan, his warlord—chief knight, if you will. Zulron is Oudorro's oberdaza." He gestured at a stunted, misshapen Tenkin, the only deformed one Hadrian had ever seen. "The closest thing to his office in Avryn might be a chief priest as well as doctor, and next to him is Fan Irlanu. You have no equivalent position for her. She's a seer, a visionary."

"Welcome, peoples of great Avryn." Burandu spoke haltingly in Apelanese. Despite his age, betrayed only by a head of startling white hair, he looked as strong and handsome as any man in the village. He sat adorned in a silk waistcloth and kilt, a broad necklace of gold, and a headdress formed from long, brightly colored feathers. "We are pleased to have you in our home."

"Thank you, sir, for granting us an invitation," Wesley replied.

"We enjoy company of those Dilladrum brings. Once brothers in ancient days—is good to sit, to listen, to find each other. Come, drink, and remember."

Zulron cast a fine powder over a brazier of coals. Flames burst forth, illuminating the lodge.

They all sat amid the pillows and hides. Royce found a place within the shadows against the rear wall. As always, Thranic and Bernie kept their distance from the rest of the party. They sat close to the four Tenkins, where the sentinel watched Zulron with great interest. Bulard invited Hadrian to sit beside him.

"This explains a great deal," said the old man, pointing to the decorations in the hut. "These are people lost in time. Do you see those decorated shields hanging from the rafter with the oil lamps? They used to do that in the ancient imperial throne room, and the leaders mirror the imperial body, represented by a king and his two councilors, always a wizard and a warrior. Although the seer is probably an addition of the Ghazel influences. She's lovely."

Hadrian had to agree: Fan Irlanu was stunning, even by

Tenkin standards. Her thin silk gown embraced her body with the intimacy of liquid.

Food and wine circulated as men carried in jugs and platters. "After eating," Burandu said to Wesley, "I ask you, Dilladrum, and your second to meet at my *durbo*. I discuss recent news on the road ahead. I fear the beasts are loose and you must be careful. You tell me of road just traveled."

Wesley nodded with a mouthful of food, then, after swallowing, added, "Of course, Your, ah..." He hesitated before simply adding, "Sir."

Bulard looked with suspicion at the sliced meat set before him. Hadrian chuckled, watching the old man push it around his plate. "It's pork. Wild pigs thrive in these jungles and the Tenkin hunt them. You'll find it a little tougher and gamier than what you're used to back home, but it's good—you'll like it."

"How do you know so much about them?" the old man asked.

"I lived in Calis for several years."

"Doing what?"

"You know, I still ask myself that." Hadrian stuffed a hunk of pork in his mouth and chewed, but Bulard's expression showed he did not understand. At last Hadrian gave in. "I was a mercenary. I fought for the highest bidder."

"You seem ashamed." Bulard tried a bit of fruit and grimaced. "The mercenary profession has a long and illustrious history. I should know."

"My father never approved of me using my training for profit. In a way, you might say he thought it sacrilegious. I didn't understand then, but I do now."

"So were you any good?"

"A lot of men died."

"Battles are sometimes necessary and men die in war—it

happens. You have nothing to be ashamed of. To be a warrior and live is a reward Maribor bestows on the virtuous. You should be proud."

"Except there was no war, just battles. No cause, just money. No virtue, just killing."

Bulard wrinkled his brows as if trying to decipher this and Hadrian got up before he could think of anything else to ask.

When the meal was over, three Tenkin boys held large palm branches over the heads of Burandu, Wesley, Dilladrum, and Wyatt as they ventured out into the rain. With the Elder gone, formalities relaxed. The Vintu headed out to resume camp preparations before all daylight was lost. Across the hall, Thranic and Levy spoke quietly with the oberdaza, Zulron, and all three left together. Poe, Derning, and Grady helped themselves to a jug of wine and reclined casually on the pillows.

Hadrian went over to sit beside Royce. "Wanna try the wine?"

"It's not time for drinking yet," the hood replied.

"How you feeling?"

"Not good enough."

"You need to get the dressing on your wound changed?"

"It can wait."

"Wait too long and it'll fester."

"Leave me alone."

"You should at least eat. The pork is good. Best meal you'll have for a while, I think. It'll help you heal."

There was no reply. They sat listening to the wind and rain on the grassy roof and low conversations punctuated by the occasional laugh and clink of ceramic cups.

"Are you aware you're being watched?" Royce asked. "The Tenkin on the dais, the one Dilladrum called Joqdan, the warlord. He's been staring at you since we entered. Do you know him?"

Hadrian looked at the bald, muscular man wreathed in a dozen bone necklaces. "Never seen him before. The woman next to him—she looks oddly familiar."

"She looks like Gwen."

"That's it. You're right. She does look just like her. Is Gwen from—"

"I don't know."

"I just assumed she was from Wesbaden. Everyone in Avryn who's from Calis is from there, but she could be from a village like this, huh?" Hadrian chuckled. "What an odd pairing you two make. Maybe Gwen's from this very village. That could be her sister up there, or cousin. You might be meeting the bride's family before the wedding, just like a proper suitor. You should brush your hair and take a bath. Make a good enough impression, and the two of you could settle down here. You'd look good bare-chested in one of those kilts."

Hadrian expected a cutting retort. All he heard from his friend was a harsh series of breaths. Looking over, he noticed the hood was drooping.

"Hey, you're really not doing too good, are you?"

The hood shook.

Hadrian placed a hand on Royce's back. His cloak was soaked and hot. "Damn it. I'll convince Wesley to extend our stay. In the meantime, let's get you dry and in a bed."

❧

With a flaming brand, the oberdaza led Thranic and Levy toward a cliff wall at the edge of the village, where the great waterfall thundered. Somehow even the plunging water felt foul as it splattered against rocks, casting a damp mist. Thranic continually wiped the tainted wet from his face. Everything about the village was evil. Everywhere stood signs that these humans had turned their backs on Novron and embraced his enemy—the hideous feathers they wore, the symbolic designs in the pillows, the tattoos on their bodies. They did not whisper, but rather shouted, their allegiance to Uberlin. Thranic could not imagine a greater blasphemy, and yet the others were blind to their transgressions. Given the opportunity, Thranic would burn the whole village to ash and scatter the remains. He had tried to prepare himself for what to expect even before the *Emerald Storm* set sail, but now, surrounded by their poison, he longed to strike a blow for Novron. While he could not safely put a torch to this nest of vipers, there was another profanation he could rectify, one that these worshipers of Uberlin might even assist him with.

The powder the oberdaza used to ignite the braziers had caught his attention. The Tenkin witch doctor was also an alchemist. Zulron was not like the rest of the heathens. He lacked their illusionary facade, their glimmer of false beauty. One leg was shorter than its partner, causing Zulron to shuffle with a noticeable limp. One shoulder rode up, hugging his chin, while the other slipped low, dangling a weak and withered arm. He was singular in his wretched appearance, and this honest display of his evil made him more trustworthy than the rest.

As they reached the waterfall, Zulron led them along a narrow path around the frothing pool to a crack in the cliff face. Within the fissure was a cave. Its ceiling teemed with chattering bats and its floor was laden with guano.

"This is my storeroom and workshop," Zulron explained as he pushed deeper into the cavern. "It stays cooler here and is well protected from wind and rain."

"And what prying eyes can't see..." Thranic added, guessing at the truth of the matter. Years of dealing with tainted souls had left him with an understanding of evil's true nature.

Zulron paused only briefly, to cast a glance over his low-slung shoulder at the sentinel. "You see more clearly than the rest of your brethren."

"And you speak Apelanese better than yours."

"I'm not built for hunting. I rely on study and have learned much about your world."

"This is disgusting." Levy grimaced, carefully picking his path.

"Yes," the oberdaza agreed. He walked through the guano as if it were a field of spring grass. "But these bats are my gatekeepers, and their soil, my moat."

Soon the cave grew wide and the floor cleared of filth. In the center of the cavern was a domed oven built of carefully piled stones. Surrounding it were dozens of huge clay pots, bundles of browned leaves, and a vast pile of poorly stacked wood. On shelves carved from the stone walls rested hundreds of smaller ceramic jars and a variety of stones, crystals, and bowls.

Zulron reached into one of the pots and threw a handful of dust into the mouth of the oven. He thrust his torch at the base, and a fire roared to life, which he then fed with wood. When the oven was sated and he had finished lighting a number of oil lamps, he turned to Levy. "Let me see it."

The doctor set his pack on the floor and withdrew the bundle of bloody rags. Zulron took the bandages and studied each, even holding them to his nose and sniffing. "And you say these belong to the hooded one among you? It's his blood?"

"Yes."

"How was he wounded?"

"I shot him with a crossbow."

Zulron showed no surprise. "Did you not wish him dead? Or are you a poor hunter?"

"He moved."

Zulron raised a dark brow. "He is quick?"

"Yes."

"Sees well in the dark?"

"Yes."

"And you came by ship, yes? How did he fare on the water?"

"Poorly—very sick for the first four days, I hear."

"And his ears, are they pointed?"

"No. He has no elven features. This is why we need you to test the blood. You know the method?"

The oberdaza nodded.

Thranic felt a twinge of regret that this creature was so unworthy to Novron. He sensed a kinship of minds. "How long?"

Zulron rubbed the crusted bandages between his fingers. "Days with this. It is too old. If we had a fresh sample, it could be quick."

"Getting blood from him is nearly impossible," Levy grumbled.

"I will start the test with these, but I'll also see what I can do to get fresh blood. He will need treatment soon."

"Treatment?"

"The jungle does not abide the weak or the wounded for long. He will summon me or die."

"How much gold will you want?" Thranic asked.

Zulron shook his head. "I have no need for gold."

"What payment, then?"

"My reward will not come from you. I will reap my own reward, and it is no concern of yours."

The Tenkin granted them the use of three sizable huts and Wesley divided his crew accordingly. The accommodations were surprisingly luxurious, subdivided by walls of wide woven ribbons that gave the impression of being inside a basket. Carpets of tight-threaded fibers inlaid with beautiful designs covered the floor. Peanut-shaped gourds hung from the rafters, burning oil that provided more than enough light.

Having convinced Wesley to linger in the village, Hadrian watched over Royce, who looked worse with each passing hour. Royce's skin burned and sweat poured down his forehead even as he shivered beneath two layers of blankets.

"You need to get better, pal," Hadrian told him. "Think of Gwen. Better yet, think what she'll do to me if I come back without you."

There was no reaction. Royce continued to shiver, his eyes closed.

"May enter?" a soft voice asked. Hadrian could see only the outline in the doorway, and for an instant he thought it was Gwen. "He grows worse, but you refused Zulron to see him."

"Your oberdaza has been keeping close company with the man who nearly killed my friend. I don't feel comfortable letting Zulron treat him."

"Will allow me? Am not skilled like Zulron, but know some things."

Hadrian nodded and waved her in.

"Am Fan Irlanu," she said, dipping her head into the hut while, outside, two other women waited in the rain with covered baskets.

"I'm Hadrian Blackwater, and this is my friend Royce."

She nodded, then knelt beside Royce and placed a hand to his forehead. "He has fever."

She motioned for the oil lamp and Hadrian pulled it down, then helped her open Royce's cloak and pull back his tunic to reveal the stained bandage, which she carefully removed.

Irlanu grimaced as she peeled back the cloth and studied the wound.

She shook her head. "It is the *shirlum-kath*," she said, pressing lightly on the skin around the wound, causing Royce to flinch in his sleep. "See here?" She scraped a long nail along the edge of the bloody wound and drew away a squirming parasite the size of a coarse hair. It twisted and curled on her fingertip. "They are eating him."

Fan Irlanu waved to the women outside, who entered and deposited their baskets beside her. She spoke briefly in Tenkin, ordering them to fetch other items, which Hadrian was unfamiliar with, and the two dashed from the hut.

"Can you help him?"

The woman nodded as she took out a stone mortar and began crushing bits of what looked to be dirt, leaves, and nuts with a pestle. "They common here with open wounds. Left alone, *shirlum-kath* will devour him. He die soon without help. I make poison for the *shirlum-kath*."

One of the women returned with a gourd and an earthen pot, in which Fan Irlanu mixed the contents of her mortar with oil, beating it until she had a thick, dark paste, which she spread over Royce's wound, packing it into the puncture. They turned him over and did the same to the exit wound. Then she placed a single large foul-smelling leaf over each and together they wrapped him in fresh cloth. Royce barely woke during the procedure. Groggy and confused, he soon passed out once more.

Fan Irlanu covered Royce back up with the blankets and nodded approvingly. "He will get better now, I think. I brew drinks—more poison for *shirlum-kath* and a tea for strength. When he wakes, make him drink both, eh? Then he feel better much faster."

Hadrian thanked her. As she left, he wondered why Royce always attracted beautiful women when he was near death.

❧

When Royce woke the next morning, the fever was gone, and he was strong enough to curse. According to him, the draft Fan Irlanu had provided tasted worse than fermented cow dung, but he actually liked the tea. The following day, he was sitting up and eating. By the third, he was able to walk unassisted to the communal *ostrium* for his meals.

No one complained about the delay because the rain continued. Seeing Royce in the *ostrium* that morning, Grady winked and asked Hadrian if it might be possible for Royce to have a relapse.

"He is good?" Fan Irlanu asked, coming to them after the evening meal had concluded. Her movement was entrancingly graceful, her dress glistening like oil in the lamplight. All eyes followed her.

"No—but he's feeling a lot better," Hadrian replied. His mischievous grin left a puzzled expression on her face.

"My language is perhaps not—"

"I'm very good, thank you," Royce told her. "Apparently I owe you my life."

She shook her head. "Repay me by getting strong—ah, but I do have a favor to ask of your friend Hay-dree-on. Joqdan, warlord of the village, asks that he speak with you at the *sarap*."

"Me?" Hadrian asked, looking across to where the man in the bone necklaces sat. "Is it all right if Royce joins us? I'd like to keep an eye on him."

"But of course, if he is up to it."

Hadrian helped Royce to his feet, and as the rest watched with envious stares, the two followed Fan Irlanu out of the *ostrium*. The sun had not yet set, but for what little light the jungle permitted, it might just as well have. Oil lamps hung from branches, illuminating the path, decorating the village like a Summersrule festival. The rain still poured, so they left the lodge under the protection of palm branches. Hadrian knew *sarap* translated to "meeting place," or "talking place." In this case, it was a giant oudorro tree, from which, he had recently learned, the village took its name.

The tree was not as tall as it was round. Great green leaves thrived on many of its branches despite the center of the trunk's being completely hollow. The space within provided shelter from the rain and was large enough for the four of them. A small ornately decorated fire pit dominated the center of the floor and glowed with red coals. Around this they took seats on luxurious pillows of silk and satin. The interior walls were painted with various ocher and umber dyes smeared into the wood, apparently by stained fingers. The images depicted men and animals—twisted shapes of strange visions. There were also mysterious symbols and swirling designs. Illuminated by the glowing coals, the interior of the tree was eerily talismanic, creating a sensation that left Hadrian on edge.

Joqdan was already there. He had not waited for a boy with the palms, and his bare head and chest were slick with rain. They all exchanged bows respectfully.

"Pleased am I," Joqdan greeted them. "Mine speech...is, ah...not good as the learned. I warrior—do not speak to outsiders. You are"—he paused for a moment, thinking hard—"special. Am honored. Welcome you to Oudorro, Galenti. I..." He paused, thinking again, and quickly became frustrated and turned to Fan Irlanu.

"The warlord Joqdan regrets that language skills are not good enough to honor you, and he asks that I speak words," Fan Irlanu told them as she removed her wet wrap. "He says that he saw you fight in the arena at Drogbon. He has never forgotten it. To have such a legend here is great honor. You do not wear the laurel, so he thinks you do not wish be recognized. He has asked you here to pay proper respect in private."

Hadrian glanced briefly at Royce, who remained silent but attentive. "Thank you," he told Joqdan. "And he's right—I would prefer not to be recognized."

"Joqdan begs permission to ask a question of the great Galenti. He would like to know why you left."

Hadrian paused only a moment, then replied, "It was time to seek new battles."

The warlord of Oudorro nodded as Fan Irlanu translated his words.

At that moment, something about Fan Irlanu caught Royce's attention and he rapidly approached her. She did not move, although given the ominous manner of his advance, Hadrian guessed that most anyone else would have taken a step back.

"Where did you get that mark on your shoulder?" Royce asked, indicating a small swirling tattoo.

"That is the mark of a seer," Zulron declared, startling all of them as he entered.

Unlike the other men of the village, Zulron wore a full robe. Made from a shimmering cloth, it was open enough for them to see his misshapen body, covered in strange tattoos. The one that spread across his face resembled the web of a spider.

"Fan Irlanu is a vision-walker," he explained, staring admiringly at her. "It is a talent and a gift bestowed by Uberlin upon those endowed with the hot blood of the Ghazel. Few are born each age, and she is very powerful. She can see the depths of a heart and the future of a nation." He paused to run his fingers gingerly down the side of her cheek. "She can see all things except her own destiny."

"You don't suffer from a language barrier, I see," Hadrian said.

Zulron smiled. "I am the oberdaza. I know the movement of the stars in the Ba Ran and the books of your world. All mysteries are revealed to me."

"Is it true that you are a visionary?" Royce asked Fan Irlanu.

She nodded. "With the burning of the tulan leaves, I—"

"Give him a demonstration," Zulron interrupted, causing her to look sharply at him. "Read this one's future," he said, gesturing toward Royce.

A puzzled look crossed her face, but she nodded.

Joqdan put a firm hand to Zulron's shoulder and spun him around, but he spoke too quickly for Hadrian to understand. The two argued briefly, but all he caught was one word of Zulron's reply: *important*.

When Zulron turned back, his eyes fell on Hadrian, who he openly studied. "So, you are the legendary Galenti." He raised an eyebrow. "Looking at you, I would say Joqdan is mistaken, but I know Joqdan is never mistaken. Still, you don't look like the Tiger of Mandalin. I'd thought you would be much bigger." He turned abruptly back to Fan Irlanu. "The leaves, burn them."

As Fan Irlanu moved to a stone box, Zulron asked them to take seats around the glowing coals of the fire ring.

Hadrian took Royce aside. "Perhaps we should go. I can't say I like Mr. Witch Doctor's attitude much. Seems like he's up to something. The fact that he's been spending time with Thranic doesn't help."

Royce glanced at Fan Irlanu. "No, I want to stay."

"What's all this about?"

"The tattoo—Gwen has the same one."

Reluctantly, Hadrian sat.

Fan Irlanu returned with several large dry leaves. Even withered and brittle, they were a brilliant shade of red. She held them over the coals and muttered something while crushing the leaves and letting them fall onto the embers. Instantly a thick white smoke billowed. It did not rise, but pooled and drifted. Fan Irlanu used her hands to contain the smoke, wafting it, scooping it, swirling it into a cloud before her. Then she bent and breathed in the ashen mist. Repeatedly, she swept the smoke and inhaled deeply.

The last of the leaves burned away and the smoke faded. Fan Irlanu's eyes closed and she began swaying on her knees, humming softly. After a few minutes, she reached out her hands.

"Touch her," Zulron instructed Royce.

Royce hesitated briefly. He looked at her the way Hadrian had seen him eye an elaborate lock. The greater the potential treasure behind the door, the more tension showed in Royce's eyes, and at that moment he looked as if Fan Irlanu might hold the secret to a fortune. He reached out his fingers. At his touch, she took hold of him.

There was a pause, and then Fan Irlanu began to moan and finally shake her head, slowly at first but faster and faster the longer she held on. Her mouth opened and she groaned the way one might in a nightmare, struggling to speak but unable to form words. She jerked, her eyes shifting wildly under closed lids, her voice louder but saying nothing distinguishable.

Joqdan's face was awash with concern, making Hadrian wonder if something was wrong. Fan Irlanu continued to struggle. Joqdan started to move, but a quick glare from Zulron held him back. At last, the woman screamed and collapsed on the pillows.

"*Leave her alone!*" Zulron shouted in Tenkin.

Joqdan ignored him, rushing to her side. Fan Irlanu lay on the ground thrashing. She cried out and then became still.

Joqdan clutched her, whispering in her ear. He held her head and placed a hand near her mouth to feel for breath. "*You've killed her!*" he shouted at Zulron. Without another word, he lifted the seer in his arms and ran out into the rain.

"What's going on? What's happening?" Hadrian asked.

"Your friend is not human," the oberdaza declared. Zulron stepped up to face Royce. "Why are you here?"

"We're part of the crew of the *Emerald Storm*, on our way to deliver a message to the Palace of the Four Winds," Hadrian answered for him.

Zulron did not take his eyes off Royce. "For three thousand years the ancient legends have told of the Day of Reckoning, when the shadow from the north will descend to wash over our lands."

Derning, Grady, Poe, and Bulard entered. "What's going on?" Derning asked. "We heard a woman scream and saw the big guy carrying her away."

"There was an accident," Hadrian explained.

Both Derning and Grady immediately looked at Royce.

"We don't know what happened to her," Hadrian continued. "She was doing a kind of spiritual demonstration—reading Royce's fortune or something—and she collapsed."

"She collapsed?" Derning said.

"She was breathing tulan leaf smoke. Maybe it was a bad batch."

Zulron ignored their conversation and continued to glare at Royce. "The Ghazel legend, preserved by oral memory from the time of the first Ghazel-Da-Ra, tells of death and destruction, revenge unleashed, the Old Ones coming again. I have seen the signs myself. I watch the stars and know. To the north, there have been rumblings. Estramnadon is active, and Avempartha has been opened. Now here is an elf in my village, where one has never walked before."

"An elf?" Derning asked, puzzled.

"That is what killed Fan Irlanu," Zulron told them. "Or at the very least has driven her insane."

"What?" Hadrian exclaimed.

"It's not possible to use the sight on an elf. The lack of a soul offers up only infinity. For her it was like walking off a bottomless cliff. If she lives, she will never be the same."

"You're the village healer. Shouldn't you be trying to help her?"

"He wants her dead." Royce finally spoke. Then, looking at Zulron, he added, "You knew."

"What did he know?" Bulard asked, tense but fascinated. Grady and Derning also leaned forward.

"You knew I was elven, didn't you? But you told her—no, coerced her—to do a reading," Royce said.

Outside, there were sounds of commotion, running feet and raised voices. Hadrian heard Wesley saying something over the heated shouts of Tenkins.

"Why did you want her dead?"

"I did nothing. You are the one that killed her. And killing a member of the village, especially a seer, is an unpardonable crime. The punishment is death." Zulron gave a smile before stepping outside.

The rest of them followed to find a gathering crowd.

"There he is!" Thranic shouted the moment Royce stepped out of the tree. He pointed and said, "There's your *elf*! I warned you about him."

"He has slain our seer, Fan Irlanu!" Zulron announced, and repeated it in Tenkin.

Burandu, Wesley, and Wyatt pushed their way through the mob.

"Is this true?" Wesley asked quickly, his voice nervous.

"Which?" Royce asked.

"Are you an elf, and did you just kill Fan Irlanu?"

"Yes, and I'm not sure."

The crowd grew and Hadrian could pick out words such as *justice*, *revenge*, and *kill* among the many Tenkin shouts.

"By Mar, man!" Wesley said fiercely but quietly to Royce. "What is it with you? I should let you hang just for the amount of trouble you've caused." He took a breath. The crowd pressed in. Lightning flashed overhead while thunder boomed. "What do you mean when you say you're not sure?" Wesley asked. He was speaking quickly, wiping the rain from his face.

"*The murderer must pay for his crime, Burandu,*" Zulron declared in Tenkin. "*His soullessness has killed our beloved Fan Irlanu. The law demands justice!*"

"*Where is Joqdan?*" Burandu asked.

"*Paying his last respects to his dead would-be wife. If he was here, he would agree.*"

"*He lies! Zulron is to blame.*" Hadrian spoke in Tenkin, which drew surprised looks from everyone.

"What are they saying?" Wesley asked Hadrian.

"The oberdaza is pushing for our deaths and Burandu is buying it."

"*Bring them all!*" Burandu shouted.

The warriors of the village descended. Hadrian considered for a moment whether he should draw his swords, but decided against it. He shot a look at Royce to indicate he should not resist.

They were driven to the village center, where Dilladrum was shouting, "Let go of me! What are you doing?" When he saw Wesley, he asked, "What did you do? I told you not to offend them!"

"We didn't offend them," Hadrian explained. "We killed their beloved seer."

"What!" Dilladrum looked as if he was about to faint.

"Actually, it is a misunderstanding, but I am not sure we will get the chance to explain," Wesley put in.

"At least Thranic will die with us," Royce said loud enough for the sentinel to hear.

"A martyr's death is a fair price to rid the world of you and your kind."

Lightning flashed again, revealing the pallid faces of the crew in its stark light.

Grady was shoved to the ground, and he moved his hand toward his sword.

"Grady, don't!" Hadrian said.

"That is right," Wesley shouted. "No one draw weapons. They will slaughter us."

"They will anyway," Derning replied.

Poe and Hadrian pulled Grady back to his feet. All around them the ring of warriors formed a wall, behind which churned a crowd of shouting faces and raised fists. The rain-drenched mob pushed and cried, its words lost in a roar of hatred. Lightning flashed once more, and a single voice rang out, "*You knew!*"

Instantly the crowd fell silent and parted. Only the sound of rain disturbed the stillness as Fan Irlanu entered the circle. Joqdan, at her side, carried a deadly-looking spear, his eyes grim and focused on Zulron.

"*Burandu, it is not the stranger's fault. It was Zulron who asked that I do the reading. He knew this one had elven blood. But I am still alive!*"

"*But—no...How could you...*" Zulron stammered.

"*He is not an Old One,*" Fan Irlanu said. "*He is a* kaz*! There is humanity in him—footholds, Zulron, footholds!*"

"What's going on?" Wesley asked Hadrian. "Isn't she the one Royce killed? What's she saying?"

"She seems a mite upset," Grady said.

"But not at Royce," Poe remarked.

"Who, then?" Grady asked.

"Zulron has tried to kill me. I have known for some time his ambitions were great. I saw the treachery in his heart, but I never expected he would go so far."

"Joqdan, what say you? Is what Fan Irlanu says true?" Burandu addressed his warlord.

Joqdan thrust his spear into the chest of Zulron.

The long blade passed fully through the oberdaza's body. Those nearby jostled backward, everyone moving away. Joqdan advanced the length of his spear's shaft and gripped Zulron by the throat. Holding him with strong arms, he spat in the witch doctor's face. The light faded from the oberdaza's eyes, and Joqdan withdrew his spear as Zulron fell dead.

"I think that answers your question," Poe remarked.

Burandu looked down at the body, then up at Joqdan, and nodded. *"Joqdan is never wrong. I am pleased you are safe, Fan Irlanu,"* he said to her. Then the Elder addressed Wesley and the others. "Forgive the dishonor of evil Zulron. Judge us not by his actions. You too have such men in your world, eh?"

Wesley glanced at Thranic and Royce.

Burandu shouted to his warriors and they dispersed the crowd. Many paused to kiss Fan Irlanu, who stood weakly, leaning against Joqdan. She offered a strained smile, but Hadrian could see the paleness of her face and the effort in her breathing.

The Elder spoke briefly with Joqdan and Fan Irlanu, and then Joqdan lifted the seer once more and carried her to one of the smaller dwellings. Zulron's body was dragged away and with him went most of the Tenkin.

"That's it?" Grady asked.

"Wait," Dilladrum said as the leopard-skinned man approached. They spoke for a moment, and then Dilladrum returned. "The village of Oudorro asks our forgiveness for the misunderstanding and begs the honor to continue as our host."

They looked at one another skeptically.

"They are sincere."

Wesley sighed and nodded. "Thank them for their kindness, but we will be leaving in the morning."

"Kindness?" Derning muttered. "They nearly skinned us alive. We should get out now while we can."

"I see no advantage in venturing into these jungles at night," Wesley affirmed. "We will leave at first light."

"And what about Melborn?" Thranic said.

"You, Dr. Levy, and Seamen Blackwater and Melborn will come with me. The rest I order to quarters to get as much sleep as possible."

A young Tenkin trotted up to them and spoke to Dilladrum, his eyes watching Royce.

"What is it?" Wesley asked.

"Fan Irlanu has requested Royce and Hadrian."

Wesley nodded at them, but added, "Try not to start a war this time. You are to report to me directly after—by your honor, gentlemen."

Before Thranic could object, they both nodded and offered an "Aye, aye, sir."

Fan Irlanu lay on a bed beneath a thin white sheet as a young girl patted her forehead with a damp cloth, rinsed repeatedly in a shallow basin. Joqdan remained at her side. His great spear, still covered in Zulron's blood, stood by the door.

"Is she really all right?" Hadrian asked.

"I be fine," Fan Irlanu replied. "It was terrible shock. Will take time."

"I'm sorry," Royce offered.

"I know," she told him. Her face was sympathetic to the point of sadness. "I *know* you are."

"You saw something?"

"Were I to touch Joqdan's hand with the tulan smoke in me, I could tell what he ate for his midday meal yesterday and what he eat tomorrow. If I touched Galenti's hand, I could name the woman he will marry and who will outlive the other. I could also tell the precise events that will surround his death. So clear is my sight that I can see a life in detail, but not you. You are mystery, a cloud. Looking into you is seeing a mountain range in thick fog—I can only see the high points with no means of connecting them. You are *kaz* in the Ghazel tongue—in your language a *mir*, yes?—mix of human and elven blood. This gives you long life." She paused to gather some strength, and Joqdan's brow furrowed further.

"Imagine looking down road, you see most things well, the trees, the rocks, the leaves. But with you, it is as if standing high in air, staring out at horizon—very few details. My sight can only span so far, and that not include life span of a *kaz*. There is too much."

"But you saw something."

"I saw many things. Too many," she told him. Her eyes were soft and comforting.

"Tell me," Royce said. "Please, I know a woman. She's very much like you, but something troubles her. She won't speak of it, and I think she has seen things like you have—things that trouble her."

"She is Tenkin?"

"I'm not sure, but she bears the same mark as you."

Fan Irlanu nodded. "I sent for you because of what I saw. I will tell you what I know and then I rest. I sleep for long time, and Joqdan will not let any disturb me. So I speak now. Am certain I will not see you again. I saw much but understood little—too much distance, too much time. Most are vague feelings that are hard to put in words, but what I sensed was powerful."

Royce nodded.

She paused a moment, thinking, then said, "Darkness surrounds you, death is everywhere, it stalks you, hunts you, and you feed upon it—blood begets blood—the darkness consumes you. In this darkness, I saw two lights beside you. One will blow out. The other flickers, but it must not go out. You must protect the flame against the storm.

"I saw a secret—it is, ah...it is hidden. This great treasure is covered. A man hides it, but a woman knows—she alone knows and so she prepares. She speaks in riddles that will be revealed—truth disguised for now. You will remember when the time comes. The path is laid out for you—in the dark."

Joqdan spoke something in Tenkin, but Fan Irlanu shook her head and pushed on.

"I saw great journey. Ten upon the road. She who wears the light will lead the way. The road goes deep into the earth and into despair. The voice of the dead guide your steps. You walk back in time. The three-thousand-year battle begins again. Cold grips the world, death comes to all, and a choice is before you. Alone stand you in the balance. Your weight will tilt the scales, but to which side is unclear. You must choose between darkness and light, and your choice will affect many." She paused, shaking her head slowly. "Like trees in a forest, like blades of grass—too many to count. And I fear that in the end you will choose the darkness and turn your back to the light."

"You said *she*. Who did you mean? Is it Gwen?" Royce questioned.

"I not know names. They mere feelings, glimpses of a dream."

"What is this secret?"

"I not know. It is hidden."

"When you say there are two lights and one blows out, does that mean someone will die?"

She nodded. "Think so—yes, feels that way. I sensed a loss, so great I still feel it." She reached out and touched Royce's hand and a tear slipped down her cheek. "Your road is one of great anguish."

Royce said nothing for a moment and then asked, "What is this great journey?"

She shook her head. "I wish knew more. Your life—whole life been pain and so much more lies ahead. Am sorry, but cannot tell more than that."

"She rests now," Joqdan told them. From his firm tone they knew it was time to go.

They walked out of the hut and found Wyatt watching out for them.

"Waiting up?" Hadrian asked.

"Didn't want you to step into the wrong hut by accident." He gave a wink.

"The rest bunked down?"

He nodded. "So, you're an elf," Wyatt said to Royce. "That explains a lot. What did the lady want?"

"To tell me my future."

"Good news?"

"It nearly killed her. What do you think?"

Chapter 17

The Palace of the Four Winds

Thranic was furious. Wesley refused to take any action against Royce, and the sentinel railed that under imperial law all elves were subject to arrest. Wesley had little choice but to acknowledge this, but added that given their circumstances, he had neither a prison nor chains. He also pointed out that they were not within the bounds of the New Empire, and until they were, he was the sole judge of the law.

"It is my duty to see this mission to completion," Wesley told the sentinel. "A bound man will only be a hindrance to this effort, particularly when he is injured and exhibits no desire to flee."

Royce watched all this with an expression of mild amusement. Thranic went on relentlessly until finally Wesley gave in and approached Royce. "Will you give me your word you will not attempt to escape me or Sentinel Thranic before this mission is over?"

"On my word, sir," Royce replied. "There is nothing that could make me willingly leave Sentinel Thranic's side."

"There you have it," Wesley concluded, satisfied.

"He's an elf! What good is the word of an elf?" As Thranic straightened and rose above Wesley, the look on the sentinel's face caused him to take a step back. "As secretary of Erivan affairs, appointed by the Patriarch, it's my duty to purge the empire of their foul influence. I demand you place the elf under my authority at once!"

Wesley hesitated. The challenge of a sentinel broke the nerve of many kings, and Thranic was more intimidating than any other Hadrian had encountered. His hunched-vulture demeanor and piercing glare were more than daunting.

Hadrian was tense. He knew the sentinel was already dead, but would prefer his partner got to pick his own time and place. If Wesley agreed to surrender Royce, there would be a battle that would see one of them dead. Hadrian let his fingers slip slowly to the pommels of his swords and he marked the position of Bernie in anticipation.

Wesley locked his jaw and returned Thranic's glare. "He might be an elf, sir, but he is also one of *my* crew."

"Your crew? You no longer have a ship. You're nothing but a boy playing pretend captain!" the sentinel bellowed angrily.

Wesley stiffened.

"And what were you playing at in the hold of the ship, sir? Was that what you call administering your authority?"

This took Thranic by surprise.

"Oh yes, the officers knew of your nightly visits to the *cargo*. It is a small ship, sir, and the officers' bunks were just above. We heard you every night torturing them, and I fear a good deal more than that. I am no great fan of elves, but by Maribor, there are limits to the abuses conscience permits! No, sir, I do not think I will be turning Seaman Melborn over to your authority anytime soon. Even should I trust you to treat him honorably, I need all the hands I can get, and as we both know, you are not an honorable man."

"It's a pity to see such a young, promising lad throw his life away," Thranic fumed. "I'll see that you are executed for this."

"To do so, we must return to Avryn. Let us hope we both live to see that day."

❧

At dawn the crew of the *Emerald Storm* left the village and once more plunged into the jungle, traveling northeast of the Oudorro Valley by a narrow, barely visible path. The rain had left the ground swamped, but it had stopped at last. On the third day, cliffs and chasms barred their path. They followed ridgelines where a stumble could send a man falling hundreds of feet, walked perilous rope bridges that spanned raging rivers, and followed rocky clefts down into dark valleys. In the lower ravines it was dark, even at midday. Trees created phantom images. Rocks looked like crouching animals, and stunted, gnarled bushes appeared like monsters in the mist.

Royce's health steadily improved, though his disposition remained unchanged. He was able to walk on his own most of the day, and thanks to Fan Irlanu's balm, his wounds no longer required a bandage.

They found the bodies on the fourth day out of Oudorro. Corpses, dressed in clothes similar to those of Dilladrum and the Vintu, lay on the path. Flies hovered, and the stench of decay lingered in the air. They had been dead for some time, and many were missing limbs or showed evidence of bites.

"Animals?" Wesley asked.

"Maybe." Dilladrum looked off toward the east. "But perhaps the Panther is not able to contain his beasts, just as Burandu told us."

"You're saying the Ghazel did this?"

Dilladrum paused to study the jungle around them. "Impossible to say, yet these bodies are weeks old and it's not like the jungle to let them rot. Animals don't like Ghazel and will avoid an area with their smell, even if it means passing up a free meal.

"This man is Hingara." Dilladrum pointed to the body of a swarthy little man in a red cap. "He's a guide, like me. He set out for the Palace of the Four Winds with a party like ours weeks ago. He was a good man. He knew the jungle well, and as you can see, his group was large—as many as thirty men in all. What kind of animal do you think would attack so large a company? A pack of wolves, perhaps? A pride of lions? No, they would never attack a party this large. And what animal could kill without leaving a single body of their own behind? Ghazel, on the other hand..."

"What about them?" Wesley asked.

"They're like ghosts. Hingara could not have seen them coming. Imagine beings as nimble and at ease in these jungles as monkeys, but possessing the strength and ferocity of tigers. They have the instinct of beasts but the intelligence of men. On a rainy day they can smell a human three leagues away. This was a safe path, but I fear things have changed."

"There are only about eighteen bodies here," Wesley observed. "If he set out with thirty men, where are the rest?"

Dilladrum let his sight settle on the naval officer. "Where, indeed."

Wesley grimaced as he looked at the dead. "Are you saying they took them to eat?"

"That's what they do." Dilladrum pointed to the torn and mutilated bodies. "They ate some on the spot in the fever following the battle, but I think they carried the rest back to their den, where I can only guess they feasted by barbecuing them on spits and drinking warmed blood from the men's skulls."

"You don't know that!" Wesley challenged.

Dilladrum shook his head. "As I said, I'm guessing. No one

truly knows what goes on in their camps any more than a deer knows what goes on in the dining halls of a king."

"You make it sound as if they're our betters."

"In these jungles, they are. Here they're the hunters and we're the prey. I told you the trip would be harder from now on. We'll burn no fire, cook no food, and pitch no tent. Our only hope of survival lies in slipping through unnoticed."

"Should we bury them?" Wesley asked.

"What the animals do not touch, neither should we. It would announce our presence to the whole jungle. It's also not wise to linger. We should press on with all haste."

⁂

They traveled steadily downward now, following a rapidly flowing river through a cleft in the mountains. The lower they went, the higher the canopy rose, and the darker their world became. They camped along a bank where the river swirled around a break of boulders. With no fire or tent, it was not much of a camp. They huddled on a bare sandy patch exposed by a shift in the river's bend, eating cold salted meat. Royce sat at the edge of the camp and watched Thranic watching him.

They had played this game each night since the village. Royce was certain Bernie had filled Thranic's head with numerous stories about his reign of terror against the Diamond. Thranic appeared aloof, but Royce was certain Bernie's words had wormed in nonetheless. Without Staul, and with Bernie no longer a trusted ally, Thranic was dramatically weakened. The sentinel's confrontation with Wesley had revealed Thranic's growing desperation—his failure another setback. The balance had shifted, he slipped from the hunter to the hunted, and with each day Royce grew stronger.

Royce enjoyed the game. He liked watching the shadows growing under Thranic's eyes as he got less and less sleep. He savored the way Thranic spun, his eyes searching rapidly for Royce, whenever an animal rustled branches behind him on the trail. Mental torture was never something Royce aimed for, but in Thranic's case he was making an exception.

Royce's quick turn had saved his life. Although he might have bled to death if Hadrian and the others had not found him, or died from fever if the Tenkin woman had not helped, the wound itself was relatively superficial. For several days he had portrayed being weaker than he was. He had pain when pressing on his side and was still experiencing some lack of movement, but for the most part he was his old self again.

Royce might have continued the game longer, but it was becoming too dangerous. Wesley's defiance had changed the playing field. The sentinel's options were diminishing. The ploy to force Wesley's hand had been his last civil gambit. As long as Wesley remained a legitimate leader, those like Wyatt, Grady, Derning, and Poe would side with him. Royce knew Thranic saw Wesley as a pawn blocking his forward movement, one that he would need removed. It was time to deal with the sentinel.

Royce curled up to sleep with the rest of them, but selected a place hidden by a small thicket of plants. In the darkness he lay there only briefly before leaving his blanket filled with brush and melted into the jungle.

Thranic had chosen to bed down near the river, which Royce thought considerate, since he intended to dispose of the sentinel's body in the strong current. Royce slipped around the outside of the camp until he came to where Bernie and Levy slept, but Thranic was missing.

Thwack! A narrow tree trunk splintered.

At the last moment, Royce had moved. A crossbow bolt lodged itself in the wood where a second before he had been crouching.

Thranic struggled desperately to crank back the string on his weapon. "Did you think to find me in my bed?" he said. "Did you really think killing me would be that easy—*elf*?"

He cranked back on the gear.

"You shouldn't fear me so much. I'm here to help you. It's my responsibility to help all of you. I'll cleanse the darkness in your hearts. I'll free you of the burden of your disgusting, offensive life. You no longer need to be an affront to Maribor. I'll save you!"

"And who will save you?" Royce replied.

He was just a few feet from where he had been. Thranic glanced down to set the bolt in the track. He lifted the bow, but when he looked up, Royce was gone.

"What do you mean?" Thranic asked, hoping Royce would reveal his position.

"You see awfully well in the dark, Thranic," Royce said from his right.

Thranic turned and fired, but the bolt merely ripped through an empty thicket.

"Well, but not perfectly," Royce observed, appearing once more, but much closer. Thranic immediately began ratcheting back his bow.

He had two more bolts.

"You also managed to slip into the trees without me seeing you. And you crept up behind me. That's indeed remarkable. How old are you, Thranic? I'll bet you're older than you look."

The sentinel loaded the bolt and looked up, but once more Royce was gone.

"What are you driving at, elf?" Thranic asked, holding his crossbow at his hip. Backing against a tree, he peered around the jungle.

"We're alike, you and I," Royce said from behind him.

Thranic spun around. He saw movement slipping through the brush and fired. The shot went wide and he cursed. Thranic began cranking back the string once more.

"Is that why you do it?" Royce asked. "Is that why you torture elves? Tell me, are you purging them—or yourself?"

"Shut up!" Thranic's hand slipped on the gear and the string snapped back, slashing his fingers. He was shaking now.

"You can't kill the elf inside, so you torture and murder all those you find."

He was closer.

"I said shut up!"

"How much elven blood does it take to wash away the sin of *being* one yourself?"

Closer still.

"Damn you!" he screamed, fighting with the bow, which refused to cooperate with his shaking fingers.

He drew the string back again only to have it jump the track and snap free. He put a foot through the loop at the bow's nose and pulled. Now it was stuck. He pressed desperately on the ratchet handle. It refused to move. *Crack!* The winch snapped.

In horror, Thranic stopped breathing as he looked down. He struggled to pull the bowstring back with just the strength of his arms. He pulled with all his might, but he could not get it to the catch. He was giving Melborn too much time. He let the bow fall to the grass and drew his dagger.

He waited. He listened. He spun. He looked.

He was alone.

❧

"Get up." Hadrian woke to Royce's voice as his friend moved through the camp. He knew the tone and instantly got to his feet.

"What is it?"

"Company," Royce told him. "Wake everyone."

"What's happening?" Wesley asked groggily as the camp slowly came alive.

"Quiet," Royce whispered. He crouched with his dagger drawn, staring out into the darkness.

"Ghazel?" Grady asked.

"Something," Royce replied. "A lot of somethings."

The rest of them heard it now, twigs snapping and leaves rustling. They were all on their feet with weapons drawn.

"Backs to the river!" Wesley shouted.

Ahead of them a light appeared, then disappeared, and then another blinked. Two more flickered off to the right and left and sounds of movement grew louder and closer. Dovin Thranic stumbled back into camp, causing a brief alarm. Several people looked at him oddly but said nothing.

Everyone's attention remained on sounds from the trees.

Shadowy figures carried torches within the thick weave of the jungle. Slowly they climbed out of the brush and into the clearing around the riverbank. Twenty approached from all sides at once. At first, they appeared to be strange, monstrous beasts. When they fully entered the clearing, Hadrian saw that they were men: stocky, bull-necked brutes with white-painted faces, bone armor, and headdresses of long feathers. They moved with ease through the dense brush. In their hands were crude clubs, axes, and spears. The men circled in silence, creeping forward.

"*We come in peace!*" Hadrian heard Dilladrum shout in

Tenkin, his voice sounding weak. "*We have come to see Warlord Erandabon. We bear a message for him.*"

As they grew nearer, the men began hooting and howling, shaking their weapons. Some brandished teeth, while others beat their chests or stomped naked feet.

Dilladrum repeated his statement.

One of the larger men, who carried a decorated war axe, stepped forward and approached Dilladrum. "*What message?*" the Tenkin asked in a harsh, shallow voice.

"*It is a sealed letter,*" Dilladrum replied. "*To be given only to the warlord.*"

The man eyed each of them carefully. He grinned and then nodded. "*Follow.*"

Although it was the best they could expect, Dilladrum mopped his forehead with his sleeve as he explained the conversation to the party.

The Tenkin howled orders. Torches went out and the rest melted back into the jungle. The leader remained as they quickly broke camp. Then, with a motion for them to follow, he ran back into the trees, his torch lighting the way. He led them at a brisk pace that had everyone panting for breath—and Bulard near collapse. Dilladrum shouted forward for a rest or at least a slower pace. The only response was laughter.

"Our new friends aren't terribly considerate of an old man." Bulard panted in between wheezing inhales.

"That's enough!" Wesley shouted, and raised a hand for them to stop. The crew of the *Emerald Storm* needed little persuasion to take a break. The Tenkin and his torch continued forward, disappearing into the trees. "If he wants to keep jogging on without us, let him!"

"He's not," Royce commented. "He's hiding in the trees up ahead with his torch out. There are also several on either side of us, and more than a few to our rear."

Wesley looked around, then said, "I don't see anything at all."

Royce smiled. "What good is it having an elf in your crew if you can't make use of him?"

Wesley raised an eyebrow, looked back out into the trees, then gave up altogether. He pulled the cork from his water bag, took a swig, and passed it around. Turning his attention to the historian, who sat in the dirt doubled over, he asked, "How you doing, Mr. Bulard?"

Bulard's red face came up. He was sweating badly, his thin hair matted to his head. He said nothing, his mouth preoccupied with the effort of sucking in air, but he managed to offer a smile and a reassuring nod.

"Good," Wesley said, "let's proceed, but *we* will set the pace. Let's not have them exhausting us."

"Aye," Derning agreed, wiping his mouth after his turn at the water. "It would be just the thing for them to run us in circles until we collapse, then fall on us and slit our throats before we can catch our breaths."

"Maybe that's what happened to the others we spotted. Perhaps it was these blokes," Grady speculated.

"We're going somewhere," Royce replied. "I can smell the sea."

Hadrian had not noticed it until that moment, but he could taste the salt in the air. What he had assumed was wind in the trees he now realized was the voice of the ocean.

"Let's continue, shall we, gentlemen?" Wesley said, moving them out. As they started, the Tenkin's torch appeared once more and moved on ahead. Wesley refused to chase it, keeping them at a comfortable pace. The torch returned, and after a few more attempts to coax them, gave up. Instead, the man carrying it matched their stride.

Travel progressed sharply downward. The route soon

became a rocky trail that plummeted to the face of a cliff. Below they could hear the crashing of waves. As dawn approached, they could see their destination. A stone fortress rose high on a rocky promontory that jutted into the ocean and guarded a natural harbor hundreds of feet below. The Palace of the Four Winds looked ancient, weathered by wind and rain until it matched the stained and pitted face of the dark granite upon which it sat. The palace was built of massive blocks, and it was inconceivable that men could have placed such large stones. Displaying the same austerity as the Tenkin, it lacked ornamentation. Ships filled the large sheltered bay on the lee side of the point. There were hundreds, all with reefed black sails.

When they approached the great gate, their guide stopped. "*Weapons are not allowed past this point.*"

Wesley scowled as Dilladrum translated, but he did not protest. This was the custom even in Avryn. One did not expect to walk armed into a lord's castle. They presented their weapons and Hadrian noted that neither Thranic nor Royce surrendered any.

Thranic had been acting oddly ever since stumbling into camp. He had not said a word and his eyes never left Royce.

They entered the fortress, where a dozen well-equipped guards looked down from ramparts and many more lined their route. The exterior looked nearly ruined. Stone blocks had fallen and were left broken on the ground.

Inside, the castle decor was no more cheerful. Here, too, the withering decay of centuries of neglect had left the once-great edifice little more than a primordial cave. Roots and fungi grew along the corridor crevices, and dead leaves clustered in corners where the swirl of drafts deposited them. Dust, dirt, and cobwebs obscured the ancient decorative carvings, sculptures, and chiseled writings.

Over the walls, the Tenkin had strung crude banners, long pennants that depicted a white Tenkin-style axe on a black field. Just as in Oudorro, row upon row of shields hung from the ceiling like bats in a cavern. A huge fireplace occupied one whole side of the great chamber, a massive gaping maw of a hearth, in which an entire tree trunk smoldered. Upon the floor lay the skin of a tiger, whose head stared with gleaming emerald eyes and yellowing fangs. A stone throne stood at the far end of the hall. The base of the chair had cracked where a vine intertwined the legs, making it list. Its seat was draped in a thick piling of animal skins and on it sat a wild-eyed man.

His head sported a tempest of hair, long and black with streaks of white, jutting in all directions. Deep cuts and burns scarred his face. Thick brows overshadowed bright, explosive eyes, which darted about rapidly, rolling in his skull like marbles struggling to free themselves from the confines of his head. He was bare-chested except for an elaborate vest of small laced bones. His long fingers absently toyed with a large bloodstained axe lying across his lap.

"*Who is this?*" the warlord asked in Tenkin, his loud, disturbing voice echoed from the walls. "*Who is this that enters the hall of Erandabon unannounced and unheralded? Who treads Erandabon's forest like sheep to be gathered? Who dares seek Erandabon in his den, his holy place?*"

A strange assortment of people surrounded him, and all eyes were on the party as they entered. Toothless, tattooed men spilled drinks while women with matted hair and painted eyes swayed back and forth to unheard rhythms. One lounged naked upon a silk cushion, with a massive snake coiled about her body as she whispered to it. Beside her an old hairless man with yellow nails as long as his fingers painted curious designs on the floor, and everywhere the hall was choked with the smoke of burning tulan leaves, which smoldered in a central brazier.

In the darkest shadows were others. Hadrian could barely make them out through the fog of smoke and the flickering firelight. They clustered in the dark, making faint staccato chattering sounds like the whine of cicadas. Hadrian knew that sound well. He could not see them, merely the suggestion of movement cast in shadows upon stone. They shifted nervously, anxiously, like a pack of hungry dogs, their motions jittery and too fast to be human.

Dilladrum shooed Wesley forward. Wesley took a breath and said, "I am Midshipman Wesley Belstrad, acting captain of what remains of the crew of Her Imperial Eminence's ship the *Emerald Storm*, out of Aquesta. I have a message for you, Your Lordship." He bowed deeply. Hadrian found it comical that a lad of such noble bearing bowed before the likes of Erandabon Gile, who was just shy of a madman.

"Long Erandabon has waited for word." The man upon the throne spoke in Apelanese. "Long Erandabon has counted the moons and the stars. The waves crash, the ships approach and gather, the darkness grows, and still Erandabon waits. Sits and waits. Waits and sits. The great shadow is growing in the north. The gods come once more, bringing death and horror to all. The undying will crush the world beneath their step, and Erandabon is made to wait. Where is this message? Speak! Speak!"

Wesley took a step forward as he pulled the letter from his coat, but paused after noticing the broken seal. As he hesitated, an overly thin man dressed in feathers and paint snatched the letter away. He growled at Wesley like a dog showing his teeth. "Not approach the great Erandabon with unclean hands!"

The feathered man handed the message to the warlord,

who studied it for a moment, his eyes racing madly back and forth. A terrible grin grew across his face, and he tore the note into pieces and began eating them. It did not take long, and while he ate, no one said a word. With his final swallow, the warlord raised his hand and said, "*Lock them away.*"

Wesley looked stunned as Tenkin guards approached and grabbed him. "What's happening?" he protested. "We are officials of the Empire of Avryn! You cannot—"

Erandabon laughed as the guard dragged them down the hall.

"Wait!" another voice bellowed. "It was arranged!" Thranic deftly dodged the guards, advancing angrily on the warlord. "My team and I are to be given safe passage. I'm here to pick up a Ghazel guide to take us safely through Grandanz Og!"

Erandabon rose to his feet and raised his axe, halting Thranic mid-step. "Weapons did you bring? Food for the Many did you deliver to Erandabon?" the warlord shouted at him.

"It sank!" Thranic yelled back. "And the deal wasn't based on the weapons or the elves."

The chattering sounds from the darkness grew louder. The noise appeared to disturb even the Tenkin. The hairless man stopped drawing his designs and shuddered. The woman with the snake gasped.

Erandabon remained oblivious to the rise in their tenor as he gibbered in glee. "No! Based on the open gates of Delgos! What proof of this? What proof does Erandabon have? You wait here. You stay sealed and if Drumindor does not fall, *you* will be food for the Many! Erandabon decrees it! Who are you to defy Erandabon?"

"*Who are you to defy Erandabon?*" chanted the crowd. The warlord waved his hand in the air and the chattering grew loud again. The guards moved in with spears.

❧

"Now we know what the empire has been doing with the elves they've been rounding up," Royce muttered as he ran his fingers lightly along the length of the doorjamb.

The Tenkin had locked them in cells buried in the foundation of the fortress. There were no windows. The only light came from the small barred opening of the door, beyond which torches mounted in iron sconces flickered intermittently. Hadrian and Royce were fortunate enough to share a cell with Wyatt and Wesley, while the others were in similar cells within the same block. The sounds of their independent conversations echoed as indiscernible whispers.

"It's ghastly," Wesley said, collapsing on the stone floor and dropping his head in his hands. "Admittedly, I've never held any love for those of elven blood"—he gave Royce an apologetic glance—"but this—this is loathsome beyond human imagining. That the empire could sanction such a vile and dishonorable act is...is..."

"And now we also know what that fleet of ships in the bay is for," Hadrian said. "They're planning to invade Delgos, and it would appear we delivered the orders for them to attack."

"But Drumindor is impregnable from the sea," Wesley said. "Do you think this Erandabon fellow knows that? All those ships will be burned to cinders the moment they enter the bay."

"No, they won't," Royce said. "Drumindor has been sabotaged. When they vent at the next full moon, there will be an explosion, destroying it, and I suspect Tur Del Fur as well. After that, the armada can sail in unopposed."

"What?" Wesley asked. "You can't possibly know that."

Royce said nothing.

"Yes, he does," Hadrian said.

Realization crossed Wesley's face. "The seal was broken. You read the letter?"

Royce continued exploring the door.

"How is it going to explode?" Hadrian asked.

"The vents have been blocked."

"No..." Hadrian shook his head. "Only Gravis knew how to do that and he's dead."

"Merrick found out somehow. He's doing the same thing Gravis tried. He's blocked the portals. When they try to vent during the harvest moon, the gas and molten rock will have nowhere to go. The whole mountain will blow. And that's what Merrick meant about turning the tide of war for the empire. Delgos supports the Nationalists, funded largely by Cornelius DeLur. When they eliminated Gaunt, they cut off the rebellion's head. Now they will cut off its legs. Destroying Delgos will mean the New Empire will only need to deal with Melengar."

"But those ships we saw in the harbor were not just Tenkin. The vast majority were Ghazel," Hadrian pointed out. "Gile thinks he can use them as muscle, as his attack dogs, but goblins can't be tamed. He can't control them. The empire is handing Delgos over to the Ba Ran Ghazel. Once they entrench themselves, the goblins will become a greater threat to the New Empire than the Nationalists ever were."

"I doubt Merrick cares," Royce said.

"You stole the letter from me and read it?" Wesley asked Royce. "And you had us deliver it to the warlord knowing it would launch an invasion?"

"Are you saying you wouldn't have? Those were your orders, sanctioned by the regents themselves."

"But giving Delgos to that...that...insane man and the Ghazel, it's...it's..."

"It's your sworn duty as an officer of the New Empire."

Wesley stared, aghast. "My father used to say, 'A knight draws his sword for three reasons: to defend himself, to defend the weak, and to defend his lord,' but he always added, 'Never defend yourself against the truth, never defend the weakness in others, and never defend a lord without honor.' I don't see how anyone can find honor in feeding a child to goblins or handing over a nation of men to the Ghazel horde."

"Why did you let him deliver the letter?" Hadrian asked.

"I just read it tonight during the water break. It was my last chance to get a look. I figured if we showed up completely empty-handed, we'd be killed."

"I won't be party to this... this... atrocity! We must prevent Drumindor's destruction," Wesley announced.

"You realize interfering with this would be treason?" Royce told Wesley.

"By ordering the delivery of every man, woman, and child in Tur Del Fur into the bloodthirsty hands of the Ba Ran Ghazel, the empress has committed treason to her people. It is I who remain loyal... loyal to the cause of honor."

"It might comfort you to know that it's highly unlikely that Empress Modina gave this order," Hadrian told him. "We know her—met her before she became empress. She would never sanction anything like this. I was in the palace the day before we sailed from Aquesta, and she's not in charge. The regents are the ones behind this."

"One thing's for sure: if we foil Merrick's plan, we won't have to look for him anymore. He'll find us," Royce added.

"This is all my fault." Wesley sighed. "My first command, and look where it has led."

"Don't beat yourself up. You did fine." Hadrian patted him on the shoulder. "But your duty is done now. You completed the task your lord set for you. Everything after this is of your own choosing."

"Not much of a choice, I'm afraid," Wesley said, looking around their cell.

"How long before the harvest moon?" Hadrian asked.

"About two weeks, I would guess," Royce replied.

"It would take us too long to travel back by land. How long would it take us to get there by sea, Wyatt?" Hadrian asked.

"With the wind at our backs, we'd make the trip in a fraction of the time it took us to come out. Week and a half, maybe two."

"Then we still have time," Hadrian said.

"Time for what?" Wesley asked. "We are locked in the dungeon of a madman at the edge of the world. Merely surviving will be a feat."

"You are far too pessimistic for one so young," Royce told him.

Wesley let out a small laugh. "All right, Seaman Melborn, how do you propose we sneak down to the harbor, capture a ship loaded with Ghazel warriors, and sail it out of a bay past an armada when we can't even get out of this locked cell?"

Royce gave the door a gentle push and it swung open. "I unlocked it while you were ranting," he said.

Wesley's face showed his astonishment. "You're not just a seaman, are you?"

"Wait here," Royce said, slipping out.

He was gone for several minutes. They heard no sound. When he returned, Poe, Derning, Grady, Dilladrum, and the Vintu followed. Royce had blood on his dagger and a ring of keys in his hand.

"What about the others?" Wesley asked.

"Don't worry, I won't forget about them," Royce said with a devilish grin. When he left, the others followed. A guard lay dead in a pool of blood and Royce was already at the door of the last cell.

"We don't need to be released," Defoe said from behind the door. "I could open it myself if I wanted to get out."

"I'm not here to let you out," Royce said, opening the door.

Bernie backed up and drew his dagger.

"Stay out of this, Bernie," Royce told him. "So far you've just been doing a job. I get that, but stand between me and Thranic and it gets personal."

"Seaman Melborn!" Wesley snapped. "I can't let you kill Mr. Thranic."

Royce ignored him and Wesley appealed to Hadrian, who shrugged in response. "It's a policy of mine not to get in his way, especially when the other guy deserves it."

Wesley turned to Wyatt, whose expression showed no compassion. "He burned a shipload of elves and, for all I know, was responsible for taking my daughter. Let him die."

Dr. Levy stepped aside, leaving Thranic alone at the back of the cell with only his dagger for protection. By his grip and stance, Hadrian knew the sentinel was not a knife fighter. Thranic was sweating, his eyes tense as Royce moved in.

"Might I ask why you're killing Mr. Thranic?" Bulard asked suddenly, stepping between them. "Those of you intent on fleeing could make better use of your time than butchering a man in his cell, don't you think?"

"Won't take but a second," Royce assured him.

"Perhaps, perhaps, but I'm asking you not to. I'm not saying he doesn't deserve death, but who are you to grant it? Thranic will die, and quite soon, I suspect, given where we're headed. Regardless, our mission is vital not just to the empire, but to all of mankind, and we'll need him if we're to have any hope to complete it."

"Shut up, you old fool," the sentinel growled.

This caught Royce's attention, though he kept his eyes on Thranic. "What mission?"

"To find a very old and very important relic called the Horn of Gylindora that will be needed very soon, I'm afraid."

"The horn?" Hadrian repeated.

"Yes. Given our precarious situation, I don't think it wise to give you a history lesson just now, but suffice to say it's in all of our best interests to leave Thranic alive—for now."

"Sorry," Royce replied, "but you'll just have to make do without—"

The door to the cellblock opened and a pair of soldiers with meal plates stepped in. A quick glance at the dead guard and they ran.

Royce sprinted after them. Bernie quickly closed his cell door again.

"Go, all of you!" Bulard urged.

The party ran out of the cellblock and up the stairs. By the time they reached the top, the hallway was filled with loud voices.

"They got away," Royce grumbled.

"We gathered that from the shouting," Hadrian said.

They faced a four-way intersection of identical narrow stone corridors. Wall-mounted flames burned from iron cradles staggered at long intervals, leaving large sections of shifting shadows.

Royce glanced back toward the cellblock and cursed under his breath. "That's what I get for hesitating."

"Any idea which way now?" Wyatt asked.

"This way," Royce said.

He led them at a rapid pace, then stopped abruptly and motioned everyone into a doorway. Moments later a troop of guards rushed by. Wesley started forward and Royce hauled him back. Two more guards passed.

"*Now* we go," he told them, "but stay *behind* me."

Royce continued along the multitude of corridors and

turns, pausing from time to time. They climbed two more sets of stairs and dodged another group of soldiers. Hadrian saw the wonderment reflected in the party's faces at Royce's skill. It was as if he could see through walls or knew the location of every guard. For Hadrian it was nothing new, but even he was impressed at their progress, given that Royce was towing a parade.

A door unexpectedly opened and several Tenkins literally bumped into Dilladrum and one of the Vintu. Terrified, Dilladrum fled down a corridor, the Vintu following. The stunned Tenkins were not warriors and were just as scared as Dilladrum. They retreated inside. Royce shouted for Dilladrum to stop, but it was no use.

"Damn it!" Royce cursed, chasing after them. The rest of the crew raced to keep up as they ran blindly through corridor after corridor. Rounding a corner, Hadrian nearly ran into Royce, whose way was blocked by Tenkin warriors. The dead bodies of Dilladrum and the Vintu lay on the floor, blood pooling across the stone. Behind them, a small army cut off their retreat.

"*Who are you to defy Erandabon?*" chanted the crowd of Tenkin warriors.

"Get back!" Hadrian ordered, pushing Wesley and the others into a niche that afforded a small amount of defense. He pulled a torch from the wall and together with Royce formed a forward defense.

The Tenkin soldiers charged, screaming as they attacked.

Royce appeared to dodge the advance, but the foremost warrior fell dead. Hadrian drove the flame of his torch into the second Tenkin's face. Using his feet, Royce flipped the dead man's sword to Hadrian, who caught it in time to decapitate the next challenger.

Two Tenkins charged Royce, who simply was not where

they expected him to be when they arrived. His movements were a blur, and two more collapsed. Hadrian advanced as Royce kicked the dead men's weapons behind them to Wyatt, Derning, and Wesley. Hadrian stood at the center now.

Three attacked. Three fell dead.

The rest retreated, bewildered, and Hadrian picked up a second blade.

Clap! Clap! Clap!

The warlord walked toward them, applauding and grinning. "Galenti, it is you. So good to have you back!"

Chapter 18

The Pot of Soup

Amilia sulked in the kitchen, head in her hands, elbows resting on the baker's table. This was where it had all started, when Modina's former secretary had brought her to the kitchen for a lesson in table manners. Remembering the terror of those early days, she was staggered to realize those had been better times.

Now a witch hid in Modina's room, filling the empress's head with nonsense. She was a foreigner, the princess of an enemy kingdom, and yet she spent more time with Modina than Amilia did. She could be manipulating the empress in any number of ways. Amilia had tried to reason with Modina, but no matter what Amilia said, the girl remained adamant about helping the witch find Degan Gaunt.

Amilia preferred the old days, when Modina had left everything to her. Sitting there, she wondered what she should do. She wanted to go to Saldur and report the witch but knew that would hurt Modina. The empress might never recover from such a betrayal, especially by Amilia, whom she trusted implicitly. The loss would surely crush her fragile spirit, and Amilia saw disaster at the end of every path. She felt as if she were in a runaway carriage racing toward a cliff, with no way to reach the reins.

"How about I make you some soup?" Ibis Thinly asked her. The big man stood in his stained apron, stirring a large steaming pot, into which he threw bits of celery.

"I'm too miserable to eat," she replied.

"It can't be as bad as all that, can it?"

"You have no idea. She's become a handful and then some. I'm actually afraid to leave her alone. Every time I walk out of her room, I'm frightened something terrible will happen."

It was late and they were the only two in the scullery. Long shadows, cast by the flames of the cook's hearth, traced up the far wall. The kitchen was warm and pleasant, except for a foul smell coming from the bubbling broth Ibis cooked on the stove.

"Oh, it can't be as bad as all that. Come on, can't I interest you in some soup? I make a pretty mean vegetable barley, if I do say so myself."

"You know I love your food. It's just that my stomach is in knots. I noticed a gray hair in the mirror the other day."

"Oh please, you're still just a girl," Ibis laughed, then caught himself. "I guess I shouldn't speak to you that way, you being noble and all. I should be saying, 'Yes, Your Ladyship,' or in this case, 'No, no, Your Ladyship! If you'll allow me to be so bold as to speak plainly in your presence, I beg to differ, for I think you're purty as a pot!' That would be a more proper response."

Amilia smiled. "You know, I never have understood that saying of yours."

Ibis drew himself up in feigned offense. "I'm a cook. I like pots." He chuckled. "Have some soup. Something warm in your belly will help untie some of those knots, eh?"

She glanced at the pot he was stirring and grimaced. "I don't think so."

"Oh no, not this. Great Maribor, no! I'll make you something good."

Amilia looked relieved. "What is that you're making? It smells like rotten eggs."

"Soup, but it's barely fit for animals, made with all the worst parts of old leftovers. The smell comes from this horrid yellow powder I have to use. I try to dress it up as best I can. I throw some celery and spices in, just to ease my conscience."

"Who's it for?"

"I've no idea but in a little while a couple of guards will come by and take it. To be honest...I'm afraid to ask where it goes." He paused. "Amilia, what's wrong?"

Amilia stared at the big pot, her mouth partially open. Noise on the stairs caught her attention. Two men entered the kitchen. She knew them by sight. They were guards normally assigned to the east wing's fourth-floor hall—the administration corridor, where she and Saldur worked. They recognized her as well and took a moment to bow. Amilia graciously inclined her head in response. Their looks revealed they found this courtesy odd but appreciated it. Then they turned to Ibis.

"All done?"

"Just a sec, just a sec," he muttered. "You're early."

"We've been on duty since dawn," one of the guards complained. "This is the last job of the night. Honestly, I don't know why you put such effort into it, Thinly."

"It's what I do, and I want it done right."

"Trust me, no one is going to complain. Nobody cares."

"*I* care," Ibis remarked, his voice sharp enough to end the subject.

The guard shrugged his shoulders and waited.

"Who's the soup for?" Amilia asked.

The guard hesitated. "Not really supposed to talk about that, milady."

The other guard gave him a rough nudge. "She's the bloody secretary to the empress."

The first one blushed. "Forgive me, milady. It's just that Regent Saldur can be a little scary sometimes."

Amilia agreed in her head but externally remained aloof.

His friend slapped himself in the forehead, rolling his eyes. "Blimey, James, you're a fool. Forgive him, milady."

"What?" James looked puzzled. "What'd I say?"

The guard shook his head sadly. "You just insulted the regent and admitted you don't respect Her Ladyship all in one breath."

James's face drained of color.

"What's your name?" she asked the other guard.

"Higgles, milady." He swallowed hard and bowed again.

"Why don't *you* answer my question, then?"

"We takes the soup to the north tower. You know, the one 'tween the well and the stables."

"How many prisoners are there?"

The two guards looked at each other. "None that we know of, milady."

"So who is the soup for?"

He shrugged. "We just leave it with the Seret Knight."

"Soup's done," Ibis declared.

"Is that all, milady?" Higgles asked.

She nodded and the two disappeared out the door to the courtyard, each holding one of the pot's handles.

"Now, let me make *you* something," Ibis said, wiping his big hands on his apron.

"Huh?" Amilia asked, still thinking about the two guards. "No thanks, Ibis," she said, getting up. "There's something I need to do, I think."

⁂

The lack of a cloak became painfully uncomfortable when Amilia was halfway across the inner ward. The weather had jumped from a friendly autumn of brightly colored leaves, clear blue skies, and crisp nights to the gray, icy cold of pre-winter. A half-moon glimmered through hazy clouds as she stepped through the vegetable garden, now no more than a graveyard of brown dirt. She approached the chicken coop carefully, trying to avoid disturbing the hens. There was nothing wrong with being out, no rules against wandering the ward at night, but at that moment she felt sinister.

She ducked into the woodshed just as James and Higgles passed by on their return journey. After several minutes, Amilia crept forward, slipped around the well, and entered the north tower—the *prison tower* as she now dubbed it.

Just as described, a Seret Knight, dressed in black armor with the red symbol of a broken crown on his chest, stood at attention. Decorated with a red feather plume, the helm he wore covered his face. He appeared not to notice her, which was odd, as all guards bowed to Amilia now. The seret said nothing as she stepped around him toward the stairs. She was shocked when he made no move to stop her.

Up she went, periodically passing cells. None of the doors were locked, and she pushed some open and stepped inside. Each room was small. Old, rotted straw lay scattered across the ground. Tiny windows allowed only a fraction of moonlight to enter. There were heavy chains mounted to the walls and the floor. Some rooms had a stool or a bucket, but most were bare of any furniture. Amilia felt uncomfortable while in the rooms—not just because of the cold, but because she feared she might end up in just such a place.

James and Higgles had been correct. The tower was empty.

She returned down the steps to the seret. "Excuse me, but what are you guarding? There is no one here."

He did not respond.

"Where did the soup go?"

Again, the seret stood mute. Unable to see his eyes through the helm, and thinking perhaps he was asleep while standing up, she took a step closer. The seret moved, and as fast as a snake, his hand grabbed hold of his sword and drew it partway from its scabbard, allowing the metal to hiss, a sound that echoed ominously in the stone tower.

Amilia fled.

"Are you going to tell her?" Nimbus asked.

The two were in Amilia's office, finishing the last of the invitation lists for the scribes to begin working on. Parchments were everywhere. On the wall hung a layout of the great hall, perforated with countless pinholes from the shifting of guest positions.

"No, I'll not add to that witch's arsenal of insanity with tales of mysterious disappearing pots of soup! I've worked for months to put Modina back together. I won't allow her to be broken again."

"But what if—"

"Drop it, Nimbus." Amilia shuffled through her scrolls. "I should never have told you. I went. I looked. I saw nothing. I can't believe I even did that much. Maribor help me. The witch even had me out in the dark chasing her phantoms. What are you grinning at?"

"Nothing," Nimbus said. "I just have this impression of you slinking around the courtyard."

"Oh, stop it!"

"Stop what?" Saldur asked as he entered unannounced.

The regent swept into her office and looked at each of them with a disarming smile.

"Nothing, Your Grace, Nimbus was merely having a little joke."

"Nimbus? Nimbus?" Saldur repeated while eyeing the man, trying to recall something.

"He's my assistant, and Modina's tutor, a refugee from Vernes," Amilia explained.

Saldur looked annoyed. "I'm not an idiot, Amilia, I know who Nimbus is. I was thinking about the name. The word is from the old imperial tongue. *Nimbus*, unless I'm mistaken, means 'mist' or 'cloud,' isn't that right?" He looked at Nimbus for acknowledgment, but Nimbus merely shrugged apologetically. "Well, anyway," Saldur said, addressing Amilia. "I wanted to know how things were proceeding for the wedding. It's only a few months away."

"I was just sending these invitations to the scribes. I've ordered them by distance, so those living the farthest away should have couriers leaving as early as next week."

"Excellent, and the dress?"

"I finally got the design decided. We're just waiting for material to be delivered from Colnora."

"And how is Modina coming along?"

"Fine, fine," she lied, smiling as best she could.

"She took the news of her wedded bliss well, then?"

"Modina receives all news pretty much the same way."

Saldur nodded at her pleasantly. "Yes, true... true." He appeared so grandfatherly, so kind and gentle. It would be easy to trust him if she had not seen firsthand the volcano that lurked beneath that warm surface. He brought her back to reality when he asked, "What were you doing in the north tower last night, my dear?"

She bit her tongue just in time to stop herself from replying with total honesty. "I bumped into some guards delivering soup there in the middle of the night, which I thought odd, because..."

"Because what?" Saldur pressed.

"Because there's no one in the tower. Well, besides a seret, who appears to be standing guard over nothing. Do you know what that's all about?" she asked, pleased with how she had managed to reinforce her innocence by casually turning the tables on the old man. She even considered batting her eyes but did not want to push it. Memories of Saldur ordering the guard to take her out of his sight still rang in her head. She did not know what that order had really meant, but she remembered the regret in the guard's eyes as he had approached her.

"Of course I do. I'm regent—I know *everything* that goes on."

"The thing is... that was quite a lot of soup for one knight. And it vanished, pot and all, in just a few minutes. But since you already know, I suppose it doesn't matter."

Saldur studied her silently for a moment. His expression was no longer the familiar one of condescension. She detected a faint hint of respect forming beneath his wrinkled brows.

"I see," he replied at length. He glanced over his shoulder at Nimbus, who was smiling back, as innocent as a puppy. To her chagrin, Amilia noticed that he did bat his eyes. Saldur took no apparent notice of his antics, then reminded her not to seat the Duke and Lady of Rochelle next to the Prince of Alburn before withdrawing from her office.

"That was creepy," Nimbus mentioned after Saldur left. "You poke your head in the tower and the next morning Saldur knows about it?"

Amilia paced the length of her office, which allowed her only a few steps each way before she had to turn, but it was better than standing still. Nimbus was right. Something strange was going on with the tower, something that Saldur himself kept careful watch over. She struggled to think of alternatives, but her mind kept coming back to one name—Degan Gaunt.

Chapter 19

Galenti

The corridor outside the great hall in the Palace of the Four Winds was deathly silent as the small band remained huddled in the niche. All of the *Emerald Storm's* party now held swords salvaged from slain Tenkins, each one made from Avryn steel. Warriors took strategic positions, armed with imperial-crafted crossbows, while the bulk of the Tenkin fighters moved back to allow them clear lines of sight. Clustered in a tight group, Hadrian's party made an easy target.

Erandabon stepped forward, but not so far as to block the path of the archers. "Erandabon did not recognize you, Galenti! Many years it has been, but you have not lost your skill," he said, looking down at the bodies of his fallen warriors. "Why travel with such creatures as these, Galenti? Why suffer the humiliation? It would be the same for Erandabon to slither on the forest floor with the snakes or wallow with the pigs. Why do you do this? Why?"

"I came to see you, Gile," Hadrian replied. Instantly there was a gasp in the hall.

"Ha-ha!" the warlord laughed. "You use my Calian name, a crime for which the punishment is death, but I pardon you,

Galenti! For you are not like these." He waved his hand, gesturing vaguely. "You are in the cosmos with Erandabon. You are a star in the heavens shining nearly as bright as Erandabon. You are a brother and I will not kill you. You must come and feast with me."

"And my friends?"

Erandabon's face soured. "They have no place at the table of Erandabon. They are dogs."

"I'll not eat with you if they are ill-treated."

Erandabon's eyes moved about wildly in random circles, then stopped. "Erandabon will have them locked up again—safely this time—for their own good. Then you will eat with Erandabon?"

"I will."

He clapped his hands and warriors tentatively moved forward.

Hadrian nodded, and Royce and the others laid down their weapons.

❧

The balcony looked out over the bay from a dizzying height. Moonlight revealed the vast fleet of Ghazel and Tenkin ships anchored in the harbor. Dotted with lights, the vessels bobbed on soft swells. Distant shouts rose with the cool breeze and arrived as faint whispers. Like the rest of the castle, the balcony was a relic of a forgotten time. While perhaps beautiful long ago, the stone railing had weathered over centuries to a dull, vague reminder of its previous glory. A lush covering of vines blanketed it with blooming white flowers the way a cloth might disguise a marred table. Beneath their feet, once-stunning mosaic tiles lay dirty, chipped, and broken. Several oil lanterns circled the balcony but appeared to be more for decoration than illumination. On a stone table lay a massive feast of wild animals, fruits, and drink.

"Sit! Sit and eat!" Erandabon told Hadrian as several Tenkin women and young boys hurried about, seeing to their every need. Aside from the servants, the two were alone. Erandabon tore a leg from a large roasted bird and gestured with it toward the bay. "A beautiful sight, eh, Galenti? Five hundred ships, fifty thousand soldiers, and all of them under Erandabon's command."

"There are not fifty thousand Tenkin in all of Calis," Hadrian replied. He looked at the food on the table dubiously, wondering if elf was somewhere on the menu. He selected a bit of sliced fruit.

"No," the warlord said regretfully. "Erandabon must make do with the Ghazel. They are like ants spilling out of their island holes. Erandabon cannot trust them any more than Erandabon can trust a tiger, even if Erandabon raised it from a cub. They are wild beasts, but Erandabon needs them to reach the goal."

"And what is that?"

"Drumindor," he said simply, and followed the word with a swallow of wine, much of which spilled unnoticed down the front of his chin. "Erandabon needs a shelter from the storm, Galenti, a strong place, a safe place. For many moons the ants fight for Drumindor. They know it can stand against the coming wind. Time is running out, the sand spills from the glass, and they are desperate to flee the islands. Erandabon promises he can help them get it. He could have fifty thousand, perhaps a hundred thousand ants, Galenti. They are everywhere in the islands, but Erandabon will make do with these. Too many ants spoil a picnic, eh, Galenti?" He laughed.

A servant refilled the wineglass Hadrian had barely touched.

"What do you know about Merrick Marius?" Hadrian asked.

Erandabon spat. "He is dirt. He is pig. He is pig in dirt. He promise weapons...there is none. He promise food for the Many...and there is none. He makes it hard for Erandabon to control the ants. Erandabon wish he was dead."

"I might be able to help you with that, if you tell me where he is."

The warlord laughed. "Oh, Galenti, you do not fool Erandabon. You would do this for you, not for Erandabon. But it matters not. Erandabon does not know where he is."

"Do you expect him to visit again?" Hadrian pressed.

"No, there be no need. Erandabon will not be here long. This place is old. This is not good place for storm." He rolled a fallen block of granite from the balcony. "Erandabon and his ants will go to the great fortress, where even the Old Ones cannot reach us. Erandabon will watch the return of the gods and the burning of the world. You could have a seat beside Erandabon. You could lead the ants."

Hadrian shook his head. "Drumindor will be destroyed. There will be no fortress for you and your ants. If you release me and my friends, we can stop this from happening."

Erandabon roared a great laugh. "Galenti, you make big joke. You think Erandabon is dumb like the ants? Why do you try to tell Erandabon such lies? You will say anything to leave here with your dog friends."

He finished off the leg by ripping the meat from the bone and chewed it with an open mouth, spitting out bits of gristle. "Galenti, you offer Erandabon so much help. You must see how great Erandabon is and wish to please. Erandabon likes this. Erandabon knows of something you can do."

"What is that?"

"There is a Ghazel chieftain—Uzla Bar." He spat on the

ground. "He defies Erandabon. He challenge Erandabon for control of the ants. Now, with no food for the Many, he be big problem. Uzla Bar attacks caravans from Avryn, stealing the weapons and the Many's food. He do this to weaken Erandabon in the eyes of the ants. Uzla Bar challenge Erandabon to fight. But Erandabon is no fool. Erandabon knows none of his warriors can win against the speed and strength of the Ba Ran Ghazel. But then the stars shine on Erandabon and bring you here."

"You want me to fight him?"

"The challenge is by Ghazel tradition. Erandabon has seen you fight this way. Erandabon think you can win."

"Who will I be fighting with? You?"

He shook his head and laughed. "Erandabon does not dirty his hands so."

"Your warriors?"

"Why should Erandabon risk his warriors? Erandabon need them to control the ants. Erandabon saw those dogs with you. They fight good. When choice is death, all dogs fight. If you lead the dogs, they will fight well. Erandabon has seen you win in the arena with worse dogs. And if you lose—Erandabon is same as before."

"And why would I do this?"

"Did you not offer to help Erandabon twice already?" He paused. "Erandabon can see you like your dogs. But you and them kill many of Erandabon's men. For that you must die. But...if you do this...Erandabon will let you live. Do this, Galenti. The heavens would be less bright without all its stars."

Hadrian pretended to consider the proposal in silence. He waited so long that Erandabon became agitated. It was obvious the warlord had nearly as much riding on this fight as Hadrian did.

"You answer Erandabon now!"

Hadrian remained quiet for a few moments longer and then said, "If we win, I want our immediate release. You won't hold us until the full moon. I want a ship—a small, fast ship—fully provisioned and waiting the moment the battle is won."

"Erandabon agrees."

"I also want you to look into finding an elven girl who is called Allie. She may have been brought with the last shipment from Avryn. If she's alive, I want her brought here."

Erandabon looked doubtful but nodded.

"I want my companions freed, treated well, and all of our weapons and gear returned to us immediately."

"Erandabon will have the dogs you fought with brought here so you can eat with them when Erandabon is done. Erandabon also give other weapons you might need."

"What about the others? The men that did not fight with me in the hall."

"They no kill Erandabon's men, so they no die. Erandabon have deal with them. They stay until deal is done. Deal goes good, they be let go. Deal no good, they be food for the Many. Is good?"

"Yes. I agree."

"Excellent, Erandabon is very happy. Erandabon get to see Galenti fight in arena once more." Erandabon clapped twice and warriors appeared on the balcony, each reverently carrying one of Hadrian's three swords. More approached with the rest of their gear. Erandabon took Hadrian's spadone and lifted it.

"Erandabon has heard of Galenti's famous sword. It is weapon of the ancient style."

"It's a family heirloom."

He gave it to Hadrian. "This..." the warlord said, picking

up Royce's dagger, "Erandabon has never seen such a weapon. Does it belong to the small one? The one who fought next to you?"

"Yes." Hadrian saw the greed in Erandabon's eyes. "That's Alverstone. You don't want to think of keeping *that* weapon."

"You no fight if Erandabon keeps?"

"That too," Hadrian told him.

"That one is a *kaz*?"

"Yes, and as you saw, he's a good fighter. I need him and his weapon." Hadrian strapped his swords back on, feeling more like himself again.

"So, the Tiger of Mandalin will fight for Erandabon."

"It looks that way," Hadrian said, then sighed.

"So how does this work?" Royce asked, checking over his dagger.

The sun had risen on a gray day. The seven of them ate together on the balcony. The food—leftovers from the warlord—was now suitable for the dogs.

Hadrian said, "The battle will be five against five. I was thinking Wesley and Poe ought to be the ones to sit out. They're the youngest—"

"We will draw lots," Wesley declared firmly.

"Wesley, you've never fought the Ba Ran Ghazel before. They're extremely dangerous. They're stronger than men—faster too. To disarm them you literally have to, well, disarm them."

"We will draw lots," Wesley repeated, and finding a dead branch he snapped seven twigs—two shorter than the others.

"I have to fight. It's part of the deal," Hadrian said.

Wesley nodded and tossed one of the long twigs away.

"I'm fighting too," Royce told him.

"We need to do this fairly," Wesley protested.

"If Hadrian fights, so do I," Royce declared.

Hadrian nodded. "So it will be between you five."

Wesley hesitated, then threw aside another twig and held his fist out. Wyatt pulled the first stick, a long one. Poe drew next and got the first short twig. He showed no emotion and simply stepped back. Grady drew—a long one. Derning drew last, receiving the other short stick, leaving the last long twig in Wesley's fist.

"When do we fight?"

"At sunset," Hadrian replied. "Ghazel prefer to fight in the dark. That gives us the day to plan, practice a few things, and take a quick nap before facing them."

"I don't think I can sleep," Wesley told them.

"Best give it a try anyway."

"I've never even seen a Ghazel," Grady admitted. "What are we talking about here?"

"Well," Hadrian began, "they have deadly fangs, and if given the chance, they will hold you down and rip with their teeth and claws. The Ghazel have no qualms about eating you alive. In fact, they relish it."

"So they're animals?" Wyatt asked. "Like bears or something?"

"Not really. They're also intelligent and proficient with weapons." He let this sink in a moment before continuing. "They're usually short-looking, but that's misleading. They walk hunched over and can stand up to our height, or taller. They are strong and fast and can see well in the dark. The biggest problem—"

"There's a bigger problem?" Royce asked.

"Yeah, funny that, but you see, the Ghazel are clan fighters, so they're organized. A clan is a group of five made up of a chief, a warrior, an oberdaza, a finisher, and a range. The chief is usually not as good of a fighter as the warrior. And don't confuse a Ghazel oberdaza with a Tenkin. The Ghazel version wields real magic, dark magic, and he should be the first one we target to kill. They won't know we're aware of his importance, so that might give us an edge."

"Leave him to me," Royce announced.

"The finisher is the fastest of the group, and it'll be his job to kill us while the warriors and oberdaza keep us busy. The range will be armed with a trilon—the Ghazel version of a bow—and maybe throwing knives as well. He'll likely stay near the oberdaza. The trilon isn't terribly accurate, but it's fast. His job won't be so much to kill us as to distract. You'll want to keep your shield arm facing him."

"Will we have shields?" Grady asked.

"Good point." Hadrian looked over the weapons provided. "No, I don't see any. Well, look at it this way: that's one less thing to worry about, right? The clan is well organized and experienced. They will communicate through clicks and chattering that will be gibberish to us, but they can understand everything we say. We'll use that to our advantage."

"How do we win?" Wyatt asked.

"By killing all of them before they kill all of us."

They spent the morning hours sparring and practicing. Luckily, they were all adept with basic combat. Wesley had trained with his brother and as a result was a far better swordsman than Hadrian had expected. Grady was tough and surprisingly fast. Wyatt was the most impressive. His ability with a cutlass showed real skill, the kind Hadrian recognized instantly as something he called *killing experience*.

Hadrian demonstrated some basic moves to counter likely scenarios. Most dealt with parrying multiple attacks, like those from both mouths and claws, something none of them had any training in. He also showed them how to use the trilon Erandabon had provided, and each took his turn, with Grady showing the most promise.

Hungry after the morning's practice, they sat to eat once more.

"So, what's our battle plan?" Wyatt asked.

"Wesley and Grady will stay to the rear. Grady, you're on the trilon."

He looked nervous. "I'll do the best I can."

"That's fine. Just don't aim anywhere near the rest of us. Ignore the battle in the center of the arena and concentrate your arrows on the oberdaza and the range. Keep them off balance as much as possible. You don't have to hit them, just keep them ducking.

"Wesley, you protect Grady. Wyatt, you and I will form the front and engage the warrior and chief. Just remember to say what I told you and stay away from him. Questions?"

"What about Royce?" Wyatt asked.

"He knows what to do," Hadrian said, and Royce nodded. "Anything else?"

If there was anything, no one spoke up, so they all bedded down for a nap. After the workout even Wesley managed to fall asleep.

⁂

The arena was a large oval open-air pit surrounded by a stone wall, behind which tiers of spectators rose. Two gates at opposite ends provided entrance to opposing teams. Giant braziers mounted on poles illuminated the area. The dirt killing field, like everything else at the Palace of the Four Winds, had suffered from neglect. Large blocks of stone had fallen and small trees grew around them. Near the center a shallow muddy pool formed. A partially hidden rib cage glimmered eerily in the firelight, and a skull hung from a pike that protruded from the earth.

As Hadrian walked out, his mind reeled with memories. The scent of blood and the cheering crowd opened a door he had thought locked forever. He had been only seventeen the first time he had entered an arena, yet his training had made victory a certainty. He had been the more knowledgeable, the more skilled, and the crowds loved him. He had defeated opponent after opponent with ease. Larger, stronger men had challenged him and died. When he had fought teams of two and three, the results were always the same. The crowds had begun to chant his new name, Galenti—*killer.*

He had traveled throughout Calis, meeting with royalty, eating at banquets held in his honor, and sleeping with women who had been given in tribute. He had entertained his hosts with displays of skill and prowess. Eventually the battles had become macabre. Multiple strong men had not been enough to defeat him. They had tested him against Ghazel and wild animals. He had fought boars, a pair of leopards, and finally the tiger.

He had killed scores of men in the arena without a thought, but the tiger in Mandalin had been his last arena fight. Perhaps the blood he had spilled had finally soaked in, or he had grown older and had matured beyond his desire for fame. Even now he was unsure what was the truth and what he merely wanted to believe. Regardless, everything changed when the tiger died.

Each man he had battled had chosen to fight, but not the cat. As he had watched the regal beast die, for the first time he had felt like a murderer. In the stands above, the crowd had shouted, *Galenti!* The meaning had never sunk in until that moment. His father's words had reached him at last, but Danbury would die before Hadrian could apologize. Like the tiger, his father had deserved better.

Now, as he entered the arena, the crowd once again shouted the name—*Galenti!* They cheered and stomped their feet like thunder. "Remember, Mr. Wesley, stay back and guard Grady," Hadrian said as they gathered not far from where the skull hung.

The far gate opened and into the arena came the Ba Ran Ghazel. Hadrian could tell from his friends' shocked expressions that even after his description, they had never expected what now came toward them. Everyone had heard tall tales of hideous goblins, but no one really expected to see one—much less five, scurrying in full battle regalia illuminated by the flickering red glow of giant torch fires.

They were not human, not animal, nor anything at all familiar. They did not appear to be of the same world. Movements defied eyesight, and muscles flexed unnaturally. They drifted across the ground on all fours. Rather than walk, they skittered, their claws clicking on the stones in the dirt. Their eyes flashed in the darkness, lit from within, a sickly yellow glow rising behind an oval pupil. Muscles rippled along hunched backs and arms as thick as a man's thigh. Their mouths were filled with row upon row of needle-sharp teeth that spilled out each side as if there was not enough room to contain them.

The warrior and the chief advanced to the center. They were large, and even hunched over, they still towered above Hadrian and Wyatt. Behind them the smaller oberdaza, decorated in dozens of multicolored feathers, danced and hummed.

"I thought they were supposed to be smaller," Wyatt whispered to Hadrian.

"Ignore it. They're puffing themselves up like frogs—trying to intimidate you—make you think you can't win."

"They're doing a good job."

"The warrior is on the left, and the chief is on the right," Hadrian told him. "Let me take the warrior. You have the chief. Try to stay on his left side, swing low, and don't get too close. He'll likely kill you if you do. And watch for arrows from the range."

From the walls a flaming arrow struck the center of the field, and the moment it did, drums began to beat.

"That's our cue," Hadrian said, and walked forward along with Royce and Wyatt.

The Ghazel chief and warrior waited for them in the center. Each held a short curved blade and a small round shield. They hissed at Hadrian and Wyatt as they approached. Wyatt had his cutlass drawn, but Hadrian purposely walked to meet them with his weapons sheathed. This brought a look from Wyatt.

"It's my way of puffing up."

Before they reached the center of the arena, Hadrian had lost track of Royce, who veered away into a shadow beyond the glow of bonfires.

"When do we start?" Wyatt asked.

"Listen for the sound of the horn."

This comment was overheard by the chief, causing him to smile. He chattered to the warrior, who chattered back.

"They can't understand us, right?" Wyatt recited his line.

"Of course not," Hadrian lied. "They're just dumb animals. Remember, we want to draw them forward so Royce can slip up behind the chief and kill him. He's the one we need to kill first. He's their leader. Without him, they will all fall apart. Just step back as you fight, and he will follow you right into the trap."

More chattering.

Two more flaming arrows whistled and struck the ground.

"Get ready," Hadrian whispered, then very slowly he drew both swords.

❧

A horn sounded from the stands.

Wesley watched as Hadrian and the warrior slammed into each other, metal clanging. Wyatt, however, shuffled back like a dancer, his cutlass held up and ready. The chief stood still, sniffing the air.

Grady let loose the first of his arrows. He aimed at the distant pile of dancing feathers but greatly overshot. "Damn," he cursed, working to fit another in the string.

"Lower your aim," Wesley snapped.

"I never said I was a marksman, did I?"

Something hissed, unseen, by Wesley's ear. Grady fired a second shot. It landed too short, coming close to where Wyatt feinted, trying to persuade the chief to follow him.

Hissing whistled by again.

"I think they are shooting their arrows at us," Wesley said, turning just in time to see Grady collapse with a black shaft buried in his chest. He hit the ground, coughing and kicking. His hands struggled to reach the arrow. His fingers went limp, and his hands flapped on the ends of his wrists. He flailed on the dirt, spitting blood, struggling to breathe. A third arrow hissed and struck Grady in his boot. His leg struggled to recoil, but his foot was pinned to the ground.

Wesley stared in horror as Grady shuddered, then fell still.

⁂

Royce was already close to the oberdaza when the horn sounded. The clash of steel let him know the fight was on. He had slipped around one of the shattered stone blocks, trying to find a position behind the witch doctor, when the air felt wrong. It was no longer blowing, but bouncing—hitting something unseen. A quick glance at the field revealed only four Ghazel: the chief, the warrior, the oberdaza, and the range. Royce ducked just in time to avoid a slit throat. He spun, cutting air with Alverstone. Turning, he found himself alone. On instinct, he dodged right. Something cut through his cloak. He thrust back his elbow and was rewarded with a solid, meaty thump. Then it was gone again.

Royce spun completely around, but he could see nothing.

In the center of the arena, Hadrian battled with the warrior while Wyatt taunted the chief, who was still reluctant to engage. The range fired arrow after arrow. Beside him, the oberdaza danced and sang.

Intuition told Royce to move again, only he was too late. Thick, heavy arms gripped him as the weight of a body drove him forward. His feet slipped and he fell, pulled down to the bloodstained earth. He turned his blade and stabbed, but it passed through thin air. He could feel clawed hands trying to pin him. Royce twisted like a snake, depriving his attacker of a firm grip. He repeatedly cut at the shadowy thing, but nothing connected. Then he felt the hot breath of the Ghazel finisher.

⁂

Hadrian's stroke glanced off the Ghazel's shield. He thrust with his other sword but found it blocked by an excellent parry. The warrior was good. Hadrian had not anticipated his skill. He was strong and fast, but more importantly, more frighteningly, the Ghazel anticipated Hadrian's moves perfectly. The warrior stabbed and Hadrian dodged back and to the left. The Ghazel bashed his face with his shield, having started his swing even before Hadrian turned. It was as if his opponent were reading his mind. Hadrian staggered backward, putting distance between them to catch his breath.

Above, the crowd booed their displeasure with Galenti. Beside him, Wyatt was still playing with the chief. His ruse had bought the helmsman time. The chief was too afraid of Royce to engage, but it would not last long. Hadrian needed to finish his opponent quickly, only now he was not even certain he could win.

The warrior advanced and swung. Hadrian spun to the left. Once more the Ghazel anticipated his move and cut Hadrian across the arm. He staggered back and dodged behind a large fallen block, keeping it between him and his opponent.

The crowd booed and stomped their feet.

Something was very wrong. The warrior should not be this good. His form was bad, his strokes lacking expertise, yet he was beating him. The warrior attacked again. Hadrian took a step back and his foot caught on a rock and he stumbled. Once more the Ghazel appeared to foresee this and was ready with a kick that sent Hadrian into the dirt.

He lay flat on his back. The warrior screamed a cry of victory and raised his sword for a downward penetrating kill. Hadrian started to twist left to dodge the thrust, but at the last minute, while still concentrating his thoughts on turning left, he pulled back to center. The stroke of the warrior pierced the turf exactly where Hadrian would have been.

Grady was dead and the arrows were still coming.

Wesley was shaken. He had already failed in his duty. Not knowing what else to do, he picked up the trilon, fitted an arrow, and let it loose. Wesley was no archer. The arrow did not even fly straight, but spun wildly, falling flat on the ground not more than five yards ahead of him.

In the center of the field, Hadrian was avoiding his opponent and the chief had finally decided to engage Wyatt. Royce was in the distance, on the ground, wrestling with something invisible not far from where the oberdaza danced and chanted.

This was not going as planned. Grady was dead and Hadrian... Wesley saw the warrior raise his sword for the killing blow.

"No!" Wesley shouted. Just then, the sharp exploding pain from an arrow pierced his right shoulder, and he fell to his knees.

The world spun. His eyes blurred. He gasped for air and gritted his teeth as darkness threatened at the edges of his eyesight. In his ears, a deafening silence grew, swallowing the sounds of the crowd.

The oberdaza! The memory of Hadrian's instructions surfaced. *The Ghazel version wields real magic, dark magic, and he should be the first one we target to kill.*

Wesley clutched the hilt of his sword, fighting back, willing himself not to pass out. He ordered his legs to lift him. Shaking, wobbling, they slowly obeyed. His heart calmed, and his breathing grew deeper. The world came into focus once more and the roar of the crowd returned.

Wesley looked across the field at the witch doctor. He glanced at the trilon and knew he could never use it. He tried to raise the sword, but his right arm did not move. He shifted the pommel to the left. It felt awkward and clumsy, but it had strength. Listening to the sound of his heart pounding, he walked forward, slowly at first, but faster with each step. Another arrow hissed. He ignored it and began to jog. His feet pounded the moist, muddy ground. Wesley held his sword high like a banner. His hat flew off, his hair flowing in the breeze.

Another arrow landed just a step ahead of him and he snapped it as he ran. He felt a strange painful pulling and realized the wind was blowing against the feathers of the arrow that still protruded from his shoulder. He focused on the dancing witch doctor.

Out of the corner of his eye he saw the range put down his bow and run at him, drawing a blade. He was too late. Only a few more strides. The oberdaza danced and sang with his eyes closed. He could not see Wesley's charge.

Wesley never checked his pace. He never bothered to slow down. He merely lowered the point of his blade as if it were a lance and put on a last burst of speed—jousting like his famous brother—jousting on foot. Already the darkness was creeping in, tunneling his vision once more. His strength was running out, flowing away with his blood.

Wesley plowed into the oberdaza. The two collided with a loud *thrump!* They skidded together, then rolled apart. Wesley's sword was gone from his hands. The arrow in his shoulder had snapped. The taste of blood was in his mouth as he lay facedown, struggling to push himself up. A hot pain burst across his back, but it faded quickly as darkness swallowed him.

Royce twisted but could not break free of the claws that cut into his flesh, struggling to break his grip on Alverstone. He could not grab the shadow. Its body felt loose and slippery, as if it existed only where it wanted. Royce would get a partial grip and then it would dissolve.

Teeth grazed him as the Ghazel snapped, trying to rip his throat out. Each time, Royce knew to move. On the third attempt, he gambled and butted forward with his own head. There was a *thunk* and pain, but he was able to break free.

He looked around and once more the finisher was invisible.

Royce caught a glimpse of Wesley running across the field with his sword out in front of him, then dodged another attack. He avoided the blow but fell to the ground. Weight hit him once more. This time the claws got a better grip. Rear claws scraped along Royce's legs, pinning him, stretching him out, holding him helpless. He felt the hot breath again.

There was a noise of impact not far away and a burst of feathers.

Suddenly Royce saw yellow eyes, bright glowing orbs, inches away from his own. Fangs drenched with spit drooled on him.

"*Ad haz urba!*" the creature said, gibbering.

Alverstone was still in Royce's hand. He just needed a little movement from his wrist. He spat in the Ghazel's eye and twisted. Like cutting through ripe fruit, the blade severed the hand of the Ghazel at the wrist. With a howl, the finisher lost support and fell forward. Royce rolled him over, using two hands to restrain his remaining claw, pinning the Ghazel with his knees. The finisher continued to snap, snarl, and rake. Royce severed the goblin's other hand, and the beast shrieked in pain until Royce removed its head.

❧

The Ghazel warrior staggered suddenly, though Hadrian had not touched him. Trying to keep his distance, Hadrian was a good two sword lengths away, but the warrior clearly rocked as if struck. The Ghazel paused, confidence faded from his eyes, and he hesitated.

Hadrian looked over his shoulder to the hill and spotted Grady's body, but Wesley was gone. He looked over his opponent's shoulder and found Wesley on the ground. At his side, the oberdaza lay with the midshipman's cutlass buried in his chest. As Hadrian watched, the range stabbed Wesley in the back.

"Wesley! No!" he shouted.

Then Hadrian's eyes locked sharply on the warrior before him. "I only wish you could read my thoughts now," he said, sheathing both swords.

Confusion crossed the warrior's face until he saw Hadrian draw forth the large spadone from his back. Seizing the chance, the warrior swung. Hadrian blocked the stroke, which made the spadone sing. He followed this with a false swing, which the Ghazel nevertheless moved to dodge, setting himself off balance. Hadrian continued to spin, carrying the stroke round in a full circle. He leveled the blade at waist height. There was nowhere for the Ghazel to go, and the great sword cut the warrior in half.

Wyatt was fighting the chief now, their swords ringing like an alarm bell as they repeatedly clashed. Blow after blow drove Wyatt farther and farther backward until Hadrian thrust the spadone through the chief's shoulder blades.

With a roar like a violent wind, the crowd jumped to its feet, cheering and applauding.

Turning, Hadrian saw Royce kneeling beside Wesley's prone body. The range lay beside him. Hadrian ran to them as Wyatt checked on Grady.

Royce shook his head in silent reply to Hadrian's look.

"Grady is dead too," Wyatt reported when he reached them.

Neither said a word.

The gates opened and Erandabon entered with a bright smile. Poe and Derning followed him. Derning stared at Grady's body. Erandabon lifted his arms to the stands like a conquering hero as the crowd cheered even louder. He approached them, exuberant and delighted.

"Excellent! Excellent! Erandabon is very pleased!"

Hadrian strode forward. "Get us to that ship now. Give me time to think, and I swear I'll introduce you to Uberlin myself!"

Chapter 20

The Tower

Modina watched as Arista sat within the chalk circle on the floor of her bedroom, burning the hair. Together they watched the smoke drift.

"What's that awful smell?" Amilia said, entering and waving a hand in front of her face while Nimbus trailed behind her.

"Arista was performing a spell to locate Gaunt," Modina explained.

"She's doing magic—in here?" Amilia looked aghast, then added, "Did it work?"

"Sort of," Arista said with a decidedly disappointed tone. "He's somewhere directly northeast of here, but I can't pinpoint the exact location. That's always been the problem."

Amilia stiffened, her eyes glancing at Nimbus accusingly.

"I didn't say a word," he told her.

Amilia asked Arista, "If you find Degan Gaunt, what are you planning to do?"

"Help him escape."

"He's the general of an army poised to attack us." She turned to Modina. "I don't see why you're helping her—"

"I'm not trying to return him to his army," Arista cut in. "I need him to help me find something—something only the Heir of Novron can locate."

"So you... and Gaunt... will leave?"

"Yes," Arista told her.

"And what if you are caught? Will you betray the empress by revealing the aid she has provided you?"

"No, of course not. I would never do anything to harm her."

"Why are you asking this, Amilia?" Modina looked from her to Nimbus and back again. "What do you know?"

Amilia hesitated for only a moment, then spoke. "There is a Seret Knight standing guard in the north tower."

"I'm not familiar with your palace. Is that unusual?" Arista asked.

"There's nothing to guard there," Amilia explained. "It's a prison tower, but none of the cells hold prisoners. Yet last night I watched two fourth-floor guards deliver a pot of soup there."

"To the guard?"

"No," Amilia said, "they delivered the soup to the tower. Less than five minutes later, I arrived. The soup was gone, pot and all."

Arista stood. "They were feeding a prisoner, but you say there are no occupied cells in the tower? Are you sure?"

"Positive. Every door was open, and every cell vacant. It looked to have been that way for some time."

"I need to get in that tower," Arista declared. "I could burn a hair in one of the empty cells. If he's nearby, that could really tell us something."

"There is no way you are getting in that tower," Amilia told her. "You'd have to walk right past the knight. While the chief imperial secretary to the empress might get away with such a thing, I highly doubt the fugitive Witch of Melengar will."

"I bet Saldur could walk in and out of there without question, couldn't he?"

"Of course, but you aren't him."

Arista smiled.

She turned to the tutor. "Nimbus, I have a letter for Hilfred and another for my brother. I wrote them in the event something happened to me. I want to give them to you now, just in case. Don't deliver them unless you know I'm not coming back."

"Of course." He bowed.

Amilia rolled her eyes.

Arista handed the letters to Nimbus and, for no particular reason, gave him a kiss on the cheek.

"Just make certain when you are caught that you don't drag Modina into it," Amilia said, leaving with Nimbus.

"What are you planning to do?" Modina asked.

"Something I've never tried before, something I'm not even certain I can do. Modina, I don't know what will happen. I might do some strange things. Please ignore them and don't interfere, okay?"

Modina nodded.

Arista knelt and spread her gown out around her. She took a deep breath, closed her eyes, and tilted her head back. She took another deep breath, then sat still. She did not move for a long time. She sat breathing very slowly, very rhythmically. Her hands opened. Her arms lifted, as if floating on their own—pulled by invisible strings or rising on currents of air. She began to sway gently from side to side, her hair flowing back and forth. Soon she began to hum. The humming took on a melody, and the melody produced words Modina did not understand.

Then Arista began to glow. The light grew brighter with each word. Her dress turned pure white, her skin luminous. It soon hurt Modina's eyes to look at her, so she turned away.

The light went out.

"Did it work?" Modina asked. She turned back to face Arista and gasped.

❧

When Arista opened the door, the guard stared at her, stunned. "Your Grace! I didn't see you come in."

"You should be more watchful, then," Arista said, frightened by the sound of her own voice—so familiar and yet so different.

The guard bowed. "Yes, Your Grace. I will. Thank you, Your Grace."

Arista hurried down the stairs, self-conscious and fearful as she clutched three strands of hair in her left hand and a chunk of chalk in her right. She felt exposed, walking openly in the hallways after hiding for so long. She did not feel any different. Only by looking at her hands and clothing could she see evidence that the spell had worked. She was wearing imperial robes and her hands were those of an old man, with thick gaudy rings. Each servant or guard she passed nodded respectfully, saying softly, "Good afternoon, Your Grace."

Growing up with Saldur practically as her uncle had one advantage—she knew every line of his face, his mannerisms, and his voice. She was certain she could not perform a similar illusion with Modina, Amilia, or Nimbus, even if she had them in front of her for reference. This took more—she *knew* Saldur.

By the time she reached the first floor of the palace, she was gaining confidence. Only two concerns remained. What if she ran into the real Saldur, and how long would the spell last? Stumbling through what had to be an advanced magical technique, she had worked solely by intuition. She had known what she wanted and had a general idea how to go about it, but the result had been more serendipity than skill. So much of magic was guesswork and nuance. She was starting to understand that now and could not help being pleased with herself.

Unlike what she had managed in the past, this was completely new, something she had not even known was possible. Casting an enchantment on herself was a frightening prospect. What if there were rules against such things? What if the source of the Art forbade it and imposed harm on those who tried? She never would have attempted it under different circumstances, but she was desperate. Still, having done so, and succeeded, she felt thrilled. She had invented it. Perhaps no wizard had ever managed such a thing!

"Your Grace!" Edith Mon was caught by surprise, coming around a corner where they nearly collided. She carried a stack of sheets in her arms and nearly lost them. "Forgive me, Your Grace! I—I—"

"Think nothing of it, my dear." The *my dear* at the end of the sentence came out unconsciously—it just felt right. Hearing it sent a chill through her, which proved it was pitch-perfect. This might be fun if not for the mortal fear.

A thought popped into her head. "I've heard reports that you've been treating your staff poorly."

"Your Grace?" Edith asked, looking nervous. "I—I don't know what you mean."

Arista leaned toward her with a smile that she knew from experience would appear all the more frightening for its friendly, disarming quality. "You aren't going to lie to my face, are you, Edith?"

"Ah—no, sir."

"I don't like it, Edith. I don't like it at all. It breeds discontent. If you don't stop, I'll need to find a means of correcting your behavior. Do you understand me?"

Edith's eyes were wide. She nodded as if her head were hinged too tight.

"I'll be watching you. I'll be watching *very* closely."

With that, Arista left Edith standing frozen in the middle of the corridor, clutching her bundle of sheets.

The guards at the front entrance bowed and opened the doors for her. Stepping outside, her senses were alert for any sign of trouble. She could smell the bread in the ovens of the bakehouse. To her left, a boy chopped wood, and ahead of her, two lads shoveled out the stable, placing manure in a cart, no doubt for use in the garden. The afternoon air was cold and the manure steamed. She could see her breath puffing in steamy clouds as she marched between the brick chicken coop and the remnants of the garden.

She reached the north tower, opened the door, and entered. A Seret Knight with a deadly-looking sword strapped to his belt stood at attention. He said nothing and she did the same while looking about.

The tower was cylindrical, with arched windows that allowed light to stream in and gleam off the polished stone floor. A tall arched frame formed the entrance to the spiral stair. Across from it, a small fireplace provided heat for the guard. Covered in cobwebs, a wooden bench stood beside a small empty four-legged table. The only unusual thing was the stone of the walls. The rough-hewn rock of the upper portion of the tower was lighter in color than the more neatly laid, darker stone beneath.

The knight appeared uncomfortable at her silence.

"Is everything all right here?" Arista asked, going for the most neutral thing she could think of.

"Yes, Your Grace!" he replied enthusiastically.

"Very good," she said, and casually shuffled to the stairs and began to climb. She glanced behind her to see if the guard would follow, but he remained where he was without even looking in her direction.

She went up one flight and stopped at the first open cell. Just as Amilia had reported, it appeared to have been long abandoned. She checked to make certain the cell door would not lock, and then carefully closed it. She got on her knees, quickly drawing the circle and the runes.

She placed the blond hairs on the floor, lining them up in rows. Picking up several pieces of straw, she twisted them tightly into a rope stalk. She repeated the phrase she had used for weeks and instantly the top of the straw caught fire, becoming a tiny torch. She recited the location spell and touched the flame to one of the hairs. It heated up like a red coil and turned to ash. Arista looked for the smoke, but there was none. She glanced around the room, confused. She looked at the smoke coming off the straw. It drifted straight up. There was no wind, no draft of any kind in the cell.

She tried again with the second hair, this time putting out the straw, thinking its smoke might be interfering. Instead, she cast the burn spell directly on the hair, followed by the location incantation. The hair turned to ash without a trace of the familiar light gray smoke.

Was something about the tower blocking her spell? Could it be like the prison where they had kept Esrahaddon? The Old Empire had placed complicated runes on the walls, blocking the use of magic. She looked around. The walls were bare.

No, she thought, *I wouldn't be able to cast the burn spell if that were the case. For that matter, my Saldur guise would have failed the moment I entered.*

Looking down, she saw that there was only one hair left. She considered moving to a different room, and then the answer dawned on her. Reciting the spell once more, she picked up the last hair, held it between her fingers, and lit it.

There it is!

The smoke was pure white now and spilled straight down between her fingers like a trickle of water. It continued to fall until it met the floor, where it immediately disappeared.

She stood in the cell, trying to figure out what it meant. According to the smoke, Gaunt was very close and directly below her, but there was nothing down there. She considered that perhaps there might be a door in the fireplace, but concluded the opening was too small. There simply was nothing else below her except—the guard!

Arista gasped.

She checked her hands, reassured to see the wrinkled skin and ugly rings, and went back down the stairs to the base of the tower. The guard remained standing statue-like with his helm covering every trace of his features.

"Remove your helm," she ordered.

The knight hesitated only briefly, then complied.

She knew exactly what Degan Gaunt looked like from his image in Avempartha. The moment he removed his helm, her hopes disappeared. This was not the man she had seen in the elven tower.

She forgot herself for a moment and sighed in a most un-Saldur-like way.

"Is there something wrong, Your Grace?"

"Ah—no, no," she replied quickly, and started to leave.

"I assure you, sir, I told her nothing of the prisoner. I refused to speak a single word."

Arista halted. She pivoted abruptly, causing her robes to sweep around her majestically. The dramatic motion had a visible impact on the guard and she finally understood why Saldur always did that.

"Are you certain?"

"Yes!" he declared, but doubt crossed his face. "Did she say differently? If she did, she's lying."

Arista said nothing but merely continued to stare at him. This was not an intentional act. She was simply trying to determine what to say next. She was not sure how to form her statement to get the knight to talk without being obvious. As she stood there, formulating her next words, the knight broke under her stare.

"Okay, I did threaten to unsheathe my sword, but I didn't. I was very careful about that. I only pulled it partway out. The tip never cleared the sheath, I swear. I just wanted to scare her off. She did not see anything. Watch." The knight pulled his sword and gestured toward the floor. "See? Nothing."

Arista's eye immediately focused on the large emerald in the pommel, and she bit her tongue to restrain herself. It all made sense. There was only one thing still to learn. To inquire was a gamble, but a good one, she thought. Arista asked, "Did Gaunt like his soup?"

She held her breath as she waited for his answer.

"He ate it, but none of them ever like it."

"Very good," she said, and left.

When Arista returned, Modina did not speak a word. After admitting her, the empress stood watching cautiously. Arista started to laugh, then rushed forward and gave her an unexpected hug. "We've found him!"

Chapter 21

Drumindor

Led by a fast-walking Tenkin warrior, the few remaining members of the *Emerald Storm's* crew made their way down from the Palace of the Four Winds through a series of damp caves to the base of the blackened cliffs where the surf attacked the rock. In a tiny cove, a little sloop waited for them. Smaller and narrower than the Dacca vessel, the ship sported two decks but only a single mast. Wyatt rapidly looked the ship over, declaring it sound, and Poe checked for provisions, finding it fully stocked for a monthlong trip.

They quickly climbed aboard. Poe and Hadrian cast off while Wyatt grabbed the wheel. Derning and Royce ran up the mast and loosed the headsail, which billowed out handsomely. The power of the wind just off the point was so strong that the little sloop lurched forward, knocking Poe off his feet. He got up and wandered to the bow.

"Look at them. They're everywhere," he said, motioning at the hundreds of black sails filling the harbor like a hive of bees.

"Let's just hope they let us through," Derning said.

"We'll get through," Hadrian told them. He was seated on a barrel, holding Wesley's hat, turning it over and over.

Hadrian had refused to leave Wesley and Grady in Erandabon's hands. Their bodies had been brought aboard for a proper burial at sea. He kept Wesley's hat. He was not sure why.

"He was a good man," Royce said.

"Yes, he was."

"They both were," Derning added.

The tiny sloop was a bit hard to manage with just the five of them, but it would be ideal once they picked up Banner and Greig in Dagastan. It was a fast ship, and they were confident they could reach Tur Del Fur in time. The armada of Tenkin and Ghazel ships looked to be still gathering.

"Jacob, trim the foresail. I'm bringing her over two points," Wyatt snapped as he gripped the slick ship's wheel. "And everyone jump lively. We're in the Ba Ran Archipelago and this is no place for slow-witted sailors."

The moment they cleared the cove they understood Wyatt's warning. Here the sea was a torrent of wave-crashed cliffs and splintered islands of jagged rock. Towering crags rose from dense fog, and blind reefs of murderous coral lay in ambush. Currents coursed without reason, rogue waves crashed without warning, and everywhere the dark water teemed with sweeping triangles of black canvas—each emblazoned with white slashes that looked vaguely like a skull. The Ghazel ships spotted them the moment they cleared the point. Five abruptly changed course and swooped in.

The black ships of the Ba Ran Ghazel made the Dacca look like incompetent ferrymen as they channeled through the surf and flew across the waves.

"Run up the damn colors!" Wyatt shouted, but Royce was already hauling the black banner with white markings that stretched out long and thin.

There was a brief moment of tension as Hadrian watched

the approaching sails. He started to curse himself for trusting Erandabon Gile. But after the colors were hoisted, the sails peeled away like a shiver of sharks, swinging around to resume their earlier paths.

Wyatt cranked the wheel until they were headed for Dagastan, and ordered Royce to the top of the masthead to watch for reefs. No one spoke after that except for Royce, who shouted out obstacles, and Wyatt, who barked orders. It took only a few hours for them to clear the last of the jagged little islands, leaving both the archipelago and the black sails behind. The little sloop rolled easily as it entered the open waters of the Ghazel Sea.

The crew relaxed. Wyatt set a steady course. He leaned back against the rail, caught the sea spray in his hand, and wiped his face as he looked out at the ocean. Hadrian sat beside him, head bowed while he turned Wesley's hat over in his hands.

Erandabon had sent a messenger to Hadrian as they had left the arena. The search for Allie had produced no results. All previous shipments had been delivered to the Ghazel weeks earlier. He knew females, especially young ones, were considered a rare delicacy. She was dead, likely eaten alive by a high-ranking goblin who would have savored the feast by keeping the girl conscious as long as possible. For Ghazel, screams were a garnish.

Hadrian sighed. "Wyatt...I've something to tell you... Allie..."

Wyatt waited.

"As part of the deal, I made Gile investigate the whereabouts of your daughter. The results weren't good. Allie is dead."

Wyatt turned to gaze once more at the ocean. "You—you made that part of the deal? Asking about my daughter?"

"Yeah, Gile was a little put out, but—"

"What if he had said no?"

"I wasn't going to accept that answer."

"But he could have killed all of us."

Hadrian nodded. "She's your daughter. If I thought she was alive, trust me, Royce and I would be on it, even if that meant heading back into the Ba Ran Islands, but...well. I'm really sorry. I wish I could have done more." He looked down at the hat in his hands. "I wish I could have done a lot more."

Wyatt nodded.

"We can still save Tur Del Fur," Hadrian told him. "And we wouldn't have that chance without you. If we succeed, she won't have died in vain."

Wyatt turned to look at Hadrian. He opened his mouth, then stopped and looked away again.

"I know," Hadrian said, once more fidgeting with Wesley's hat. "I know."

Greig and Banner were pleased to see them. Nights living on the little Dacca ship were getting cold, and provisions were dangerously low. They had already resorted to selling nets and sails to buy food in town. They made a hasty sale of the Dacca ship, since the Tenkin vessel was far faster and already loaded.

Wyatt aimed the bow homeward, catching the strong autumn trade winds. The closer they came to home, the colder it got. The southern currents that helped warm Calis did not reach Delgos, and soon the wind turned biting. A brief rainstorm left a thin coat of ice on the sheets and deck rails.

Wyatt continued at the helm, refusing to sleep until he was near collapse. Hadrian concluded that, failing to find Allie,

Wyatt placed his absolution in saving Delgos instead. In a way, he was certain that they all did. Many good people had died along the trip, and they each felt the need to make those sacrifices mean something. Even Royce, suffering once more from seasickness, managed to climb to the top of the mainsail, where he replaced the Ghazel banner with Mr. Wesley's hat.

They explained to Greig and Banner the events of the previous weeks, as well as Merrick's plan and the need to reach Drumindor before the full moon. Each night they watched the moon rise larger on the face of the sea, indifferent to their race against time. Fortune and the wind were with them. Wyatt captured every breath, granting them excellent speed. Royce spotted red sails off the port aft twice, but they remained on the horizon and each time vanished quietly in their wake.

Shorthanded, and with Royce seasick, Hadrian volunteered for mast work. Derning spent the days teaching him the ropes. He would never be very good at it. He was too big, yet he managed to grasp the basics. After a few days he was able to handle most of the maneuvers without instruction. At night, Poe cooked while Hadrian sat practicing knots and watching the stars.

Instead of hugging the coast up to Wesbaden, they took a risk and sailed due west off the tip of Calis directly across Dagastan Bay. The gamble almost proved to be a disaster, as they ran into a terrible storm producing mountainous waves. Wyatt expertly guided the little sloop, riding the raging swells with half canvas set, never leaving the wheel. Seeing the helmsman's rain-lashed face exposed in a flash of lightning, Hadrian seriously began to wonder if Wyatt had gone mad. By morning, the sky had cleared and they could all see Wesley's hat still blowing in the wind.

The gamble paid off. Two days ahead of the harvest moon they rounded the Horn of Delgos and entered Terlando Bay.

&

As they approached the harbor, the Port Authority stopped them. They did not care for the style of the ship or the black sails—Wesley's hat notwithstanding. As the ship was held directly under the terrifying smoking spouts of Drumindor, dock officers boarded and searched the vessel thoroughly before allowing them to pass below the bridge between the twin stone towers. Even then they were given an escort to berth fifty-eight, slip twenty-two of the West Harbor. Being familiar with the city and the Port Authority, Wyatt volunteered to notify the officials of the impending invasion and warn them to search for signs of sabotage.

"I'm off, mates," Derning announced as soon as they had the ship berthed. The topman had a small bundle over his shoulder.

"What about the ship and the stores?" Greig asked. "We're going to sell it—you'll get a share."

"Keep it—I've business to attend to."

"But what if we can't get..." Greig gave up as Derning trotted away into the narrow streets. "That seemed a bit abrupt—man's in a hurry to go somewhere."

"Or just glad to be back in civilization," Banner mentioned.

Tur Del Fur welcomed sailors like no other port. Brightly painted buildings with exuberant decorations welcomed them to a city filled with music and mirth. Most of the shops and taverns butted up against the docks, where loud signs fought for attention: THE DRUNKEN SAILOR — JOIN THE CREW! FRESH BEEF & POULTRY! PIPES, BRITCHES, & HATS! LADIES OF THE BAY (WE WRING THE SALT OUT!)

For recently paid sailors who might have been at sea for two or more years, they screamed *paradise*. The only oddity remained the size and shapes of the buildings. Whimsical western decorations could not completely hide the underlying history of this once-dwarven city. Above every door and threshold was the sign WATCH YOUR HEAD.

Seagulls cried above them as they crisscrossed a brilliant blue sky. Water lapped the sides of ships, which creaked and moaned like living beasts stretching after a long run.

Hadrian stepped onto the dock alongside Royce. "Feels like you're gonna fall over, doesn't it?"

"To answer your question from before... No, I don't think we should be sailors. I'd be happy never to see a ship again."

"At least you don't have to worry about land sickness."

"Still feels like the ground is pitching beneath me."

The five of them bought fresh-cooked fish from dock vendors and ate on the pier. They listened to the shanty tunes spilling out of the taverns and smelled the pungent fishy reek of the harbor. By the time Wyatt returned to the ship, he was red-faced angry.

"They're going through with the venting! They refused to listen to anything I said," he shouted, trotting up the quay.

"What about the invasion?" Hadrian asked. "Didn't you tell them about that?"

"They didn't believe me! Even Livet Glim, the port controller—and we were once mates! I shared a bunk with him for two years and the bloody bastard refuses to, as he puts it, 'Turn the entire port on its ear because one person thinks there might be an attack.' He says they haven't heard anything from any other ships, and they won't do a thing unless the armada is confirmed by other captains."

"It will be too late by then."

"I tried to tell them that, but they went on about how they *had* to regulate the pressure on the full moon. I went to every official in the city, but no one would listen. After a while, I think they became suspicious that *I* was up to something. I stopped when they threatened to lock me up. I'm sorry."

"Maybe if we all went?"

Wyatt shook his head. "It won't do any good. Can you believe this? After all we've been through, we get here and it won't change a single thing. Unless..." He looked directly at Hadrian.

"Unless what?" Poe asked.

Hadrian sighed and looked at Royce, who nodded.

"What am I missing?" Poe asked.

"Drumindor was built by dwarves thousands of years ago," Hadrian explained. "Those huge towers are packed with stone gears and hundreds of switches and levers. The Tur Del Fur Port Authority only knows what a handful of them actually do. They know how to vent the pressure and blow the spouts, and that's about it."

"We know how to shut it off," Royce said.

"Shut it off?" Poe asked. "How do you shut off a volcano?"

"Not the volcano—the system," Hadrian went on. "There's a master switch that locks the whole gearing system. Once dropped, the fortress doesn't build pressure anymore. The volcano just vents itself. It won't be able to stop the invasion, but it won't explode either."

"How does that help?"

"If nothing else, it'll prevent the instant destruction of this city. When the black sails appear, people might have time to evacuate, maybe even put up a defense. Once the system is shut down, Royce and I can crawl through the portals to find out what Merrick did. If we can get it fixed in time, we can raise the master switch and barbecue an armada of very surprised goblins."

"Can we help?" Banner asked.

"Not this time," Hadrian told him. "Can you four handle this ship alone?"

Wyatt nodded. "It will be tough with no topmen, but we'll work something out."

"Good, then you get out of here before the fleet comes in. You were a good assistant, Poe. Stick with Wyatt and you'll be a captain one day. This one we have to do alone."

⁂

Legend held that dwarves had existed centuries before man walked the face of the world. Back in an age when they and the elves had fought for supremacy of Elan, dwarves had a powerful and honorable nation governed by their own kings with their own laws and traditions. That had been a golden age of great feats, wondrous achievements, and marvelous heroes. Then the elves won the war.

The strength of the dwarves had been shattered forever, and the emergence of men had destroyed what remained. Although dwarves had never been enslaved like the remnants of the elves, men distrusted and shunned the sons of Drome. Fearful of a unified dwarven kingdom, humans had forced the dwarves out of their homeland of Delgos into a shadowy existence of nomadic persecution. Despite the dwarves' skills in crafts, humans scattered them whenever they gathered in groups too large for comfort. For their own survival, dwarves had learned to hide. Those who could, adopted human ways and attempted to fit in. Their culture had been obliterated by centuries of careful erasure, little survived of their former glory except what stone could tell. Few dwarves, and even fewer humans, possessed the imagination to recall a day when dwarves had ruled half the world—unless, like Royce and Hadrian, they were staring up at Drumindor.

The light of the setting sun bathed the granite rock, making it shine like silver. Sheer walls towered hundreds of feet, rising out of the bedrock of the burning mountain's back. The twin towers stood joined by the thin line of what appeared from that distance to be a wafer-thin bridge. The tops of the towers smoldered quietly, leaking plumes of dark smoke out of every vent, creating a thin gray cloud that hovered overhead. Up close, the scope and mammoth size were breathtaking.

They had one night and the following day to accomplish the same magic trick they had performed many years earlier. By the time they purchased the necessary supplies it was dark. They slipped through the city of Tur Del Fur and hiked up into the countryside, following goat paths into the foothills that eventually led to the base of the great fortress itself.

"Is this where it was?" Royce asked, stopping and studying the base of the tower.

"How should I know?" Hadrian replied as his eyes coursed up the length of the south tower. Up close, it blocked everything else out, a solid wall of black rising against the light of the moon. "I can never understand why such small people build such gigantic things."

"Maybe they're compensating," Royce said, dropping several lengths of rope.

"Damn it, Royce. It's been eight years since we did this. I was in better shape then. I was younger, and if I recall, I vowed I would never do it again."

"That's why you shouldn't make vows. The moment you do, fate starts conspiring to shove them down your throat."

Hadrian sighed, staring upward. "That's one tall tower."

"And if the dwarves were still here maintaining it, it would be impregnable. Lucky for us, they've let it rot. You should be happy—the last eight years would only have eroded it further. It should be easier."

"It's granite, Royce. Granite doesn't erode much in eight years."

Royce said nothing as he continued to lay out coils of rope, checking the knots in the harnesses and slipping on his hand-claws.

"Do you recall that I nearly fell last time?" Hadrian asked.

"So don't step there this time."

"Do you remember what the nice lady in the jungle village told you? One light will go out?"

"We either climb this or let the place blow. We let the place blow and Merrick wins. Merrick wins, he gets away and you never find Degan Gaunt."

"I never thought you cared all that much if I ever found Gaunt." Hadrian looked up at the tower again. "At least not *that* much."

"Honestly? I don't care at all. This whole quest of yours is stupid. So you find Gaunt—then what? You follow him around being his bodyguard for the rest of your life? What if he's like Ballentyne? Wouldn't that be fun? Granted it'll be exciting, as I'm sure anyone with a sword will want to kill him, but who cares? There's no reward, no point to it. You feel guilt—I kinda get that. You ran out on your father and you can't say you're sorry anymore. So for that, you'll spend your life following this guy around being his butler? You're better than that."

"I think there was a compliment in there somewhere—so thanks. But if you're not doing this to help me find Gaunt, why are you?"

Royce paused. From a bag he drew out Wesley's hat. He must have fetched it down before they left the ship. "He stuck his neck out for me three times. The last one got him killed. There's no way this fortress is blowing up."

❧

Even in the dark, Royce found handholds and spots to place his feet that Hadrian could never have spotted in the full light of day. Like a spider, he scaled the side of the tower, until he came to the base of the first niche. There he set his first anchor and dropped a rope to Hadrian. By the time Hadrian reached the foothold of that niche, Royce was already nailing in the next pin and sending down another coil. They continued this way, finding minute edges where several thousand years of erosion revealed the maker's seams in the rock. Centuries-old crevices and cracks allowed Royce to climb what had once been slick, smooth stone.

Two hours later, the trees below appeared like tiny bushes, and the cold, wintry winds buffeted them like barn swallows. They were only a third of the way up.

"It's time," Royce shouted over the howl of the wind. He anchored a pin, tied a rope to it, and climbed back down.

Hadrian groaned. "I hate this part!"

"Sorry, buddy, nothing I can do about it. The niches are all over that way." Royce gestured across to where the vertical grooves cut into the rock on the far side of a deep crevasse.

Royce tied the rope to his harness and linked himself to Hadrian.

"Now, just watch me," Royce told him, and taking hold of the rope, he sprinted across the stone face. Reaching the edge of the crevasse, he leapt, swinging out like a clock's pendulum. He cleared the gap by what looked like only a few inches. On the far side, he clung to the stone, dangling like a bug on a twig. He slowly pulled himself up and drove another pin. Then, after tying off the rope, he waved to Hadrian.

If Hadrian missed the jump, he would slip into the crevasse, where he would end up dangling helplessly, assuming the rope held him. The force of the fall could easily pop out the holding pin or even snap the rope. He took a deep breath of cold air, steadied himself, and began to run. On the far side, Royce leaned out for him. He reached the edge and jumped. The wind whistled past his face, blurring his vision as tears streaked across his cheeks. He struck the far side just short of the landing, bashing his head hard enough to see stars. He tasted blood and wondered if he had lost his front teeth even as his fingertips lost their tenuous hold and he began to fall. Royce tried to grab him, but was too late. Hadrian fell.

He dropped about three inches.

Hadrian dangled from the rope Royce had anchored the moment his partner landed. Hadrian groaned in pain while wiping blood from his face.

"See?" Royce shouted in his ear. "That went *much* better than last time!"

They continued scaling upward, working within the relative shelter of the vertical three-sided chimneys. They were too high now for Hadrian to see anything except the tiny lights of the port city. Everything else below was darkness. They rested for a time in the semi-sheltered niche and then climbed upward again.

Higher and higher, Royce led the way. Hadrian's hands were sore from gripping the rope and burned from the few times he had slipped. His legs, exhausted and weak, quivered dangerously. The wind was brutal. Gusting in an eddy caused by the chimney they followed, it pushed outward like an invisible hand trying to knock them off. The sun came up and

Hadrian was nearing the end of his endurance when they finally reached the bridge. They were slightly more than two-thirds of the way, but thankfully they did not need to reach the top.

What appeared from the ground to be a thin bridge was actually forty feet thick. They scrambled over the edge, hauled up their ropes, ducked into a sheltered archway, and sat in the shadows, catching their breath.

"I'd like to see Derning scale *that*," Royce said, looking down.

"I don't think anyone but you could manage it," Hadrian replied. "Nor is there anyone crazy enough to try."

Dozens of men guarded the great gates at the base of the tower, but no one was on the bridge. It was thought to be impossible for intruders to enter from the top, and the cold wind kept the workers inside. Royce gave the tall slender stone doors a push.

"Locked?" Hadrian asked.

Royce nodded. "Let's hope they haven't changed the combination."

Hadrian chuckled. "Took you eighteen hours last time, right after you told me, 'This will only take a minute.'"

"Remind me again why I brought you?" Royce asked, fanning his hands out across the embossed face of the doors. "Ah, here it is."

Royce placed his fingers carefully and pushed. A hundred tons of solid stone glided inward as if on a cushion of air, rotating open without a sound. Inside, an enormous cathedral ceiling vaulted hundreds of feet above them. Shafts of morning sunshine entered through distant skylights built into the dome overhead, revealing a complex world of bridges, balconies, archways, and a labyrinth of gears. Some gears lay flat, while others stood upright. Some were as small as a copper coin, and then there were those that were several stories tall and thicker than a house. A few rotated constantly, driven by steam created from the volcanically superheated seawater. The majority of the gears, particularly the big ones, remained motionless, waiting. Aside from the mechanisms, nothing else moved. The only sounds were the regular ratcheting rhythm and the whirl of the great machine.

Royce scanned the interior. "Nobody home," he said at length.

"Wasn't last time either. I'm surprised they haven't tightened security up more."

"Oh yeah, a single break-in after centuries is something to schedule your guards around."

"They'll be kicking themselves tomorrow."

They found the stairs—short, shallow steps built for little feet. Royce and Hadrian took them two and three at a time. Ducking under low archways, Hadrian nearly had to crawl through the entrance to the Big Room. This was the name Hadrian had given it the last time they had visited. The room itself was huge, but the name came from the master gear. It stood on edge and what they could see was as high as a castle tower, but most of its bulk sunk beneath the floor and through a wall, leaving only a quarter of the gear visible. Its edge was ringed with thick teeth like a castle battlement, only larger—much larger. It meshed with two other gears, which connected to a dozen more that joined the dwarven puzzle.

"The lock was at the top, right?" Royce asked.

"Think so—yeah, Gravis was up there when we found him."

"Okay, I'll handle this. Keep an eye out."

Royce leapt up to one of the smaller gears and walked up the teeth like they were a staircase. He jumped from one to the next until he reached the master gear. Harder to climb since the teeth were huge, but for Royce it was no problem. He was soon out of sight, and a few minutes later a loud stone-upon-stone sound echoed as a giant post of rock descended from the ceiling, settling in the valley between two teeth, locking the great gear.

When Royce returned, he was grinning happily.

"I'd love to see the look on Merrick's face when this place doesn't blow. Even if the Ghazel take the city, he'll be scratching his head for months. There's no way he can know about this master switch. Gravis only knew because it was his ancestor that designed the place."

"And we only know because we caught him in the act." Hadrian thought a moment. "Do you think Merrick might be nearby, waiting for the fireworks?"

Royce sighed. "Of course not. If it were me, I wouldn't be within a hundred miles of this explosion. I don't even want to be here now. Don't worry, I know him. The fact that this mountain doesn't explode will drive him nuts. All we have to do is drop the right hints to the wrong people and we won't have to look for him—he'll find us. Now come on. Let's see if we can find what's blocking the vents so we can put this back in place and cook some goblins."

Chapter 22

Going Home

Archibald Ballentyne stared out the window of the great hall. It looked cold. Brown grass, blowing dead leaves, clouds that looked heavy and full of snow, and geese that flew away before a veil of gray all reminded him the seasons had changed. Wintertide was less than two months away. He kicked the stone of the wall with his boot. It made a muffled thud and sent a pain up his leg, making him wince.

Why do I have to think of that? Why do I always have to think of that?

Behind him, Saldur, Ethelred, and Biddings debated something, but he was not listening. He did not care anymore. Maybe he should leave. Maybe he should take a small retinue and just go home to Chadwick and the sanctity of his Gray Tower. The palace would be a wreck by now, and he could busy himself with repairing the damage the servants had caused in his absence. Bruce had likely been dipping into his brandy store and the tax collectors would be behind in their duties. It would feel nice to be home for the holiday. He could invite a few friends and his sister over for— He stopped and considered kicking the wall again, but it had hurt enough last time.

Sleeping in a tent this time of year would be miserable.

Besides, what would the regents say? Moreover, what would they do in his absence? They treated him badly enough when he was here. How much worse would they conspire against him if he left?

He did not really want to be home. Ballentyne Castle could be a lonely place, all the more horrid in winter. He used to dream of how all that would change when he married, when he had a beautiful wife and children. He used to fantasize about Alenda Lanaklin. She was a pretty thing. He also often imagined taking the hand of King Armand's daughter, Princess Beatrice. She was certainly appealing. He had even spent many a summer evening watching the milkmaids in the field and contemplating the possibility of snatching one from her lowly existence to be the new Lady Ballentyne. How grateful she would be, how dutiful, how easily controlled. That had been before he had come to Aquesta—before he had met her.

Even sleep gave him no solace, as he dreamed about Modina now. He danced with her on their own wedding day. He despised waking up. Archibald did not even care about the title anymore. He would give up the idea of being emperor if he could have her. He even considered that he would give up being earl—but she was marrying *Ethelred*!

He refused to look at the regent. The fool cared nothing for her. How could he be so cold as to force a girl to marry him just for the political benefit? The man was a blackguard.

"Archie... Archie!" Ethelred was calling him.

He cringed at the mention of the name he hated and turned from the window with a scowl.

"Archie, you need to talk to your man Breckton."

"What's wrong with him now?"

"He's refusing to take my orders. He insists he serves only you. You need to set him straight on the lay of things. We can't have knights whose allegiance is strictly to their lords.

They have to recognize the supremacy of the New Empire and the chain of command."

"Seems to me that's what he's doing, observing the chain of command."

"Yes, yes, but it's more than that. He's becoming obstinate. I'm going to be the emperor in a couple of months and I can't have my best general requiring that I get your permission to give him an order."

"I'll speak with him," Archibald said miserably, mostly just so he could stop listening to Ethelred's voice. If the old bastard were not such an accomplished soldier, he would seriously consider challenging him, but Ethelred had fought in dozens of battles, while Archibald had engaged only in practice duels with blunt-tipped swords. Even if he wanted to commit suicide, he certainly would not give Ethelred the satisfaction.

"What about Modina?" Ethelred asked.

The mention of her name brought Archibald's attention back to the conversation.

"Will she be ready?"

"Yes, I think so," Saldur replied. "Amilia has been doing wonders with her."

"Amilia?" Ethelred tapped his forehead. "Isn't she the maid you promoted to Chief Imperial Secretary?"

"Yes," Saldur said, "and I've been thinking that after the wedding, I want to keep her on."

"We'll have no use for her *after* the wedding."

"I know, but I think I could use her elsewhere. She's proven herself to be both intelligent and resourceful."

"Do whatever you like with her. I certainly don't—"

"Queens always have need of secretaries, even when they have husbands," Archibald interrupted. "I understand you're going to assume total control of the New Empire, but she'll still need an assistant."

Ethelred looked at Saldur with a puzzled expression. "He doesn't know?"

"Know what?" Archibald asked.

Saldur shook his head. "I felt the fewer that knew, the better."

"After the wedding," Ethelred told Archibald, "once I'm crowned emperor, I'm afraid Modina will have an unfortunate accident—a fatal accident."

❧

"It's all arranged," Nimbus reported. Arista paced the room and Modina sat alone on the bed. "I got the uniform to him, and tonight the farmer will smuggle Hilfred into the gate just before sunset in the hay cart."

"Will they check that?" Arista asked, pausing in her journey across the room.

"Not anymore, not since they called off the witch hunt. Things are business as usual again. They know the farmer. He's in and out every third day of the week."

Arista nodded and resumed her pacing.

"The same wagon will cart you all out at dawn. You'll go out through the city gates. There will be three horses waiting at the crossroads for you with food, water, blankets, and extra clothing."

"Thank you, Nimbus." Arista hugged the beanpole of a man, bringing a blush to his cheeks.

"Are you sure this will work?" Modina asked.

"I don't see why not," Arista said. "I'll do just what I did last time. I'll become Saldur, and Hilfred will be a fourth-floor guard. You're sure you took the right uniform?"

Nimbus nodded.

"I'll order the guard to open the entrance to the prison.

We'll grab Gaunt and leave. I'll instruct the seret to remain on duty and tell no one. Believing I'm Saldur, no one will know he's gone for hours, maybe even days."

"I still don't understand." Modina looked puzzled. "Amilia said there was a prison in the tower, but all the cells were empty."

"There is a secret door in the floor. A very cleverly hidden door, sealed with a gemlock."

"What's a gemlock?"

"A precious stone cut to produce a specific vibration that when held near the door trips the lock open. I used a magical variation on my tower door back home, and the church used a far more sophisticated version to seal the main entrance to Gutaria Prison. They're using the same thing here, and the key is the emerald in the pommel of the sword the Seret Knight wears."

"So, you'll make your escape tonight?" the empress asked.

Arista nodded. The empress looked down, a sadness creeping into her eyes. "What's wrong?" Arista asked.

"Nothing. I'm just going to miss you."

⁂

Arista's stomach twisted as she looked out the window and watched the sun set.

Am I being foolish?

Her plan had always been to merely locate Gaunt, not break him out. Now that she knew exactly where he was, she could return home and have Alric send Royce and Hadrian to rescue him. Only that had been before—before she had found Hilfred, before she had been reunited with Thrace, and before she had known she could impersonate Saldur. It seemed like such an easy thing to do that leaving without Gaunt would be an unnecessary risk. The smoke verified that he still lived, but could she be sure that would be the case several weeks from then?

She was alone with Modina. They had not said a word to each other for hours. Something was troubling the empress—something more than usual. Modina was stubborn, and no force could move her once she decided on a course. Apparently the course she had decided on was not to talk.

The gate opened and the hay cart entered.

Arista watched intently. Nothing seemed amiss—no guards, no shouting, just a thick pile of hay and a slow-walking donkey pulling it. The farmer, an elderly man, parked the cart by the stables, unhitched his donkey, hitched it to a new cart, and led the animal out again. Staring at the cart, she could not help herself. The plan had been to wait until just before dawn, but she could not leave Hilfred lying there. She managed to restrain herself only until she saw the harvest moon begin to rise, and then she stood.

"It's time," she said.

Modina lifted her head.

Arista walked to the middle of the room and knelt.

"Arista, I..." Modina began hesitantly.

"What is it?"

"Nothing... Good luck."

Arista got up and crossed the room to hug her tightly. "Good luck to you too."

The empress shook her head. "You keep all of it—I'm not going to be needing any."

&

Disguised as Regent Saldur, Arista traveled down the stairs, wondering what Modina had almost said. The excitement of the night, however, kept her thoughts jumping from one thing to the next. She discovered that she could remain in her disguise for a long time. It broke when she slept, but it would last beyond what she would need that night. This gave her greater confidence. Although she was still concerned about bumping into the real Saldur, the thought of seeing Hilfred again was overwhelming.

Her heart leapt at just the thought of traveling home to Melengar with Hilfred once more at her side. It had been a long and tiring road, and she wanted to be home. She wanted to see Alric and Julian and to sleep in her own bed. She vowed she would treat Melissa better and planned to give her maid a new dress for Wintertide. Arista was occupied with a long list of Wintertide presents for everyone when she stepped outside. The broad face of the harvest moon illuminated the inner ward, allowing her to see as clearly as if it were a cloudy day. The courtyard was empty as she crept to the wagon.

"Hilfred!" she whispered. There was no response, no movement in the hay. "Hilfred." She shook the wagon. "It's me, Arista."

She waited.

Her heart skipped a beat when the hay moved. "Princess?" it said hesitantly.

"Yes, it's me. Just follow." She led him into the stables and to the last stall, which was vacant. "We need to wait here until it's nearly dawn."

Hilfred stared at her dubiously, keeping a distance.

"How . . . ?" he began, but faltered.

"I thought Nimbus explained I would appear like this."

"He did."

Hilfred's eyes traveled up and down her figure, a look on his face as if he had just tasted something awful.

"The rumors are true," she admitted, "at least the ones about me using magic."

"I've known that, but your hair, your face, your voice." He shook his head. "It's perfect. How do I know you're not the real Saldur?"

Arista closed her eyes, and in an instant Saldur disappeared and the Princess of Melengar returned.

Hilfred stumbled backward until he hit the rear of the stall, his eyes wide and his mouth open.

"It *is* me," she assured him. Arista took a step forward and watched him flinch. It hurt her to see this, more than she would have expected. "You need to trust me," she told him.

"How can I? How can I be certain it's really you, when you trade skins so easily?"

"Ask me a question that will satisfy you."

Hilfred hesitated.

"Ask me, Hilfred."

"I've been with you daily since I was a very young man. Give me the names of the first three women I fell in love with and the name of the one I lost because of the scars on my face."

She smiled and felt herself blush. "Arista, Arista, Arista, and no one."

He smiled. She did not wait for him. She knew he would never presume to take such a step on his own. She threw her arms around his neck and kissed him. She could feel the sudden shock in the tightening of his muscles, but he did not pull away. His body relaxed slowly and his arms surrounded her. He squeezed so that her cheek pressed against his, her chin resting on his shoulder.

"Maribor help me if you really are Saldur," Hilfred whispered in her ear.

She laughed softly and wondered if it was the first time she had done so since Emery died.

CHAPTER 23

THE HARVEST MOON

Royce and Hadrian began investigating the spouts, giant tunnels bored out of the rock through which molten lava would blast on its way to the sea. There were dozens, each one aiming in a different direction, their access to the mountain's core sealed off by gear-controlled portals. They climbed the interior until they reached the opening and the sky.

The sun was up and the sight below forced Hadrian's stomach into his mouth. They were well above the bridge level. The world looked very small and very far away. Tur Del Fur was a small cluster of petite buildings crouched in the elbow of a little cove. Beyond it rose mountains that looked like little hills. Directly below, the sea appeared like a puddle with tiny flashes of white. It took Hadrian a moment to realize they were the crests of waves. What he thought might be insects were gulls circling far below.

None of the spouts were blocked, none of the portals tampered with.

"Maybe it's in the other tower?" Hadrian asked after they had climbed out of the last tunnel.

Royce shook his head. "Even if that one is blocked, the pressure will vent here. Both have to be closed. It's not the spouts or the portals. It's something else—something we've overlooked—something that can seal all the exits at once to make the mountain boil over. There has to be another master switch, one that locks all the portals closed."

"How are we going to find that? Do you see how many gears are in here? And it could be any one. We should have brought Magnus."

"Sure, with him it would be easy to find—in a year or two. Look at this place!" Royce gestured at the breadth of the tower, where the sun's light pierced through skylights, spraying the tangled riddle of a million stone gears. Some spun, some whirled, some barely moved, and everywhere were levers. Like arrows peppering a battlefield, stone arms protruded. Just as the gears came in various sizes, so did the levers—some tiny and others the size of tree trunks. "It's a wonder they ever learned how to vent the core."

"Exactly," Hadrian said. "No one knows what most of this stuff does anymore. The Port Authority leaves it alone for fear they might destroy the world or something, right? So whatever Merrick did, it's a sure bet the folks in charge here don't know anything about it. It's got to be a lever that hasn't been moved in centuries, maybe even thousands of years. It might show signs of recent movement, right?"

"Maybe."

"So we just need to find it."

Royce stared at him.

"What?"

"We only have a few hours left, and you're talking about finding a displaced grain of sand on a beach."

"I know, and when you come up with something better, we'll try it. Until then, let's keep looking."

Hours passed and still they found nothing. Adding to the

dilemma was the interior of Drumindor itself, which was a maze of corridors, archways, and bridges. Often they could see where they wanted to go but could not determine how to get there. Luck remained on their side, however, as they saw precious few people. They spotted only a handful of workers and even fewer guards. All of them were easily avoided. The sunshine passing through the skylights shone with the brilliance of midday, then diminished as evening arrived, and they still had not achieved their goal.

Finally, they headed for the bottom of the tower.

Going there was their last resort, as the Drumindor defensive garrison fortified the first three floors. Approximately forty soldiers guarded the base, and they had a reputation for their harsh treatment of intruders. Still, whatever Merrick had done, he had most likely done it to the mechanism that controlled the lava's release. Descending yet another winding staircase, they paused in a sheltered alcove just outside a large chamber. Peering in, they saw it was similar to an interior courtyard, or a theater, with four gallery balconies ringing it stacked one upon another.

"There." Royce pointed to an opening in the room below, which radiated a yellow glow. "It has to be in there."

They crept down the stairs to the bottom. Elaborate square-cut designs of inlaid bronze and quartz lined the tiled floor. It picked up the glow coming from the open doorway on the far side. The air warmed dramatically as it blew in their faces, heavy with the smell of sulfur.

"This has to be it," Royce whispered.

They looked up at the stacked galleries of arched openings circling the walls above them, and slowly, carefully stepped forward together, crossing the shimmering tile, heading for the glowing doorway.

"Halt!" The command echoed through the chamber the moment they reached the center of the room. "Lie facedown, arms and legs spread."

They hesitated.

Twenty archers appeared, moving out from behind the pillars of the galleries with stretched bows aimed down on Royce and Hadrian from three sides. Pikemen entered the hall in an orderly march, boot heels clicking on the tile. They spread out, forming two lines. A dozen more armored men issued down the side corridor from the second-story gallery and proceeded in two-by-two formation to the bottom of the stairs, fanning out to block any retreat back the way they had come.

"Now, lie on your bellies, or we'll cut you down where you stand."

"We're not here to cause trouble. We're here—" Hadrian's words were cut short as an arrow hissed through the air and glinted off the stone less than a foot from them.

"Now!" the voice shouted.

They lay down.

The moment they did, troops from in front and behind entered, pinning them and stripping them of their weapons.

"You have to listen to us. There's an invasion coming—"

"We've heard all about your phantom armada, Mr. Blackwater, and you can give up that charade."

"It's real! They will be here tonight, and if you don't fix the tower, all of Delgos will be taken!"

"Bind them!"

They brought forth chains, tongs, and a brazier. Smiths arrived and went to work hammering manacles onto their wrists and legs.

"Listen to me!" Hadrian shouted. "At least check the pressure-release controls, see if something is wrong."

There was no reply except the smiths' hammers pounding the manacles closed.

"What's the harm in checking?" Hadrian went on. "If I'm wrong, what does it matter? If I'm right and you don't even look, you're sealing the fate of the Delgos Republic. Just humor me. If nothing else, it'll shut me up."

"Slitting your throat will do that too," the voice said. "But I'll send a worker if you two come quietly without resistance."

Hadrian was not certain what kind of resistance he expected them to give as the smith finished attaching another chain to his legs, but he nodded anyway.

The voice gave the order and the guards pulled them to their feet. Navigating stairs with hobbled legs was difficult. Hadrian nearly fell more than once, but soon they reached the main gate at the bottom of the fortress.

The gigantic doors of stone soundlessly swept open. Outside, the late-afternoon sun revealed a contingent of port soldiers waiting. The commander of the fortress guard stepped forward and spoke quietly with the Port Authority captain for some time.

"You don't think these guys are always waiting out here, do you?" Hadrian whispered to Royce. "We've been set up, haven't we?"

"It didn't tip you off when they called you by name?"

"Merrick?"

"Who else?"

"That's a bit far-fetched. How could he possibly expect us to be here? We didn't even know we would be here. He can't be that smart."

"He is."

A runner appeared, trotting up from the bottom of the tower, and reported to the commander with a sharp salute.

"Well?" the fortress commander asked.

The runner shook his head. "There is no problem with the pressure-release control—everything checked out fine."

"Take them away," the commander ordered.

❧

The Tur Del Fur City Prison and Workhouse sat back, hidden on a hillside away from the dock, the shops, and the trades. It appeared as little more than a large stone box at the end of Avan Boulevard, with few windows and a spiked iron fence. Hadrian and Royce both knew it by reputation. Most offenders typically died within the first week due to execution, suicide, or brutality. The magistrate's role was merely to determine the manner of execution. Parole was not an option. Only those known to be serious threats went there. Petty thieves, drunks, and malcontents went to the more popular and lenient Portside Jail. For those in Tur Del Fur Prison, this was the end of the road, literally as well as figuratively.

Royce and Hadrian hung by their wrists with their ankles chained to the wall of cell number three, where they had spent the past few hours. The room was smaller than those in Calis. There was no window, stool, nor pot—not even straw. The room was little more than a small stone closet with a single metal door. The only light came from the gap between the door and its frame.

"You're awfully quiet," Hadrian said to the darkness.

"I'm trying to figure this out," Royce replied.

"Figure it out?" Hadrian laughed even though his arms and wrists burned like fire from the metal cutting into his skin. "We're hanging chained to a wall, awaiting execution, Royce. There's not that much to it."

"Not *that.* I want to know why we didn't find anything wrong with the spouts."

"Because there's a million levers and switches in there and we were looking for just one?"

"I don't think so. When we got to the bridge, what was it you said? You said you didn't think anyone could scale that fortress except me. I think you're right. I know Merrick couldn't. He's a genius, not an elf. I always outdid him when it came to anything physical."

"So?"

"So a thought has been nagging me since they brought us here. How could Merrick get into Drumindor to sabotage it?"

"He figured another way in."

"We spent weeks trying to do that, remember?"

"Maybe he bribed someone on the inside, or maybe he paid someone to break in."

"Who?" Royce thought a minute. "This is too important to trust to someone who *might* be able to do it—he would need someone he *knew* could do it."

"But how do you know someone can do something until they've actually—" Hadrian stopped himself as the realization hit. "Oh, that's not good."

"Throughout this whole thing we've been following two letters, both written by Merrick. The first we thought was intercepted and delivered to Alric, but what if it was *intentionally* sent to him? Everyone knows we work for Melengar."

"Which led us to the *Emerald Storm,*" Hadrian said.

"Right. Where we got the next letter—the one to be delivered to that crazy Tenkin in the jungle, and it just happened to mention that Drumindor was set to blow."

"I'm not liking where this is heading," Hadrian muttered.

"And what if Merrick knew about the master gear?"

"That's impossible. Gravis is dead. Crushed, as I recall, under one of those big gears."

"Yes. *He* is dead, but Lord Byron isn't. He probably boasted about how he saved Drumindor by hiring two no-account thieves."

"It still seems too perfect." Hadrian tried to convince himself. "In retrospect, sure, it sounds like the pieces fall into place, but there are too many things that could have gone wrong along the way."

"Right. That's why he had someone on board the *Storm* making sure it all worked—Derning. Did you see the way he took off the moment we hit port? He knew what was coming and wanted to get away."

"I should have let you kill him."

Silence.

"You're nodding, aren't you?"

"I didn't say a word."

"Bastard," Hadrian grumbled.

"You know the worst thing?"

"I've got a pretty long list of *bad* things right now, and I'm not sure which one I would put on top. So I'll bite."

"We did exactly what Merrick *couldn't* do himself. He used us to disarm Drumindor."

"So he never sabotaged anything? That would explain why Gile laughed when I told him Drumindor was going to explode. He knew it wasn't. Merrick promised he would have it intact. Merrick's a bloody genius."

"I think I mentioned that once or twice."

"So now what?" Hadrian asked.

"Now nothing. He's beaten us. He's sitting somewhere with a warm cup of cider, smiling smugly with his feet up on the pile of money he's just been paid."

"We have to warn them to reengage the master gear."

"Go ahead."

Hadrian shouted until the little observation door opened, flooding the cell with light.

"We need to speak to someone. It's important."

"What is it?"

"We realized the mistake we made. We were tricked. You need to tell the commander at Drumindor that we locked the master gear. We can show him where it is and how to release it."

"You two never stop, do you? I'm not sure if you're really saboteurs or just plain nuts. One thing's for certain: we're going to find out how you got in, and then we're going to kill you."

The observation door closed, casting them back into darkness.

"That worked out really well," Royce said. "Feel better now?"

"Bastard."

CHAPTER 24

THE ESCAPE

Arista stayed in the corner of the stable, wrapped in Hilfred's arms most of the night. He stroked her hair and, from time to time, without any particular reason, kissed her passionately. It felt safe, and lying there, Arista realized two things. First, she was certain she could be content remaining in his arms forever. And second, she was not in love with Hilfred.

He was a good friend, a piece of home she missed so dearly that she drank him in with a desert-born thirst, but something was missing. She thought it strange that she had come to this conclusion while in his arms. Yet she knew it with perfect clarity. She did not love Hilfred and she had not loved Emery. She was not even certain what love was, what it should feel like, or if it existed at all.

Noblewomen rarely knew the men they married before their wedding day. Perhaps they grew to love their husbands in time, or merely grew to believe they did. At least she knew Hilfred loved her. He loved enough for both of them. She could feel it radiating off him like warmth from smoldering coals. He deserved happiness after waiting so long, after so much sacrifice, and she would make it up to him. Arista would return to Melengar and marry him. Alric would make him Archduke Reuben Hilfred. She laughed softly at the thought.

"What?"

"I just remembered your first name is Reuben."

Hilfred laughed, then pointed to his face. "I look like this, and you're making fun of my *name*?"

She took his face in her hands. "I wish you wouldn't do that. I think you're beautiful."

He kissed her again.

Periodically, Hilfred would peek out at the sky and check the position of the moon. Eventually he returned and said, "It's time."

She nodded, and once more Arista transformed into the morose visage of Regent Saldur.

"I still can't believe it," Hilfred told her.

"I know. I'm really starting to get the hang of this. Care to kiss me again?" she teased, and laughed at his expression. "Now remember, don't do anything. The idea is to just walk in and walk out. No fighting, understand?"

Hilfred nodded.

They stepped out of the stable. As they did, Arista looked up at Modina's window. Although it was dark, she was certain she saw her figure sitting framed within it. Once again she recalled Modina's final words, and regretted not asking her to come. Maybe she would have refused, but now it was too late. Arista wished she had at least asked.

Nipper came out of the kitchens, yawning and carrying two empty water buckets. He stopped short, surprised to see them.

She ignored him and headed directly to the tower.

Just as before, the Seret Knight stood at attention in the center of the room, his face hidden, his shoulders back, the jeweled sword at his side.

"I'm going to see Degan Gaunt. Open up."

The guard drew his sword.

There was a brief moment of terror when Arista's heart pounded so loudly she thought the seret might hear. She glanced at Hilfred and saw him flinch, his hand approaching his own weapon. Then the knight bent on one knee and lightly tapped the stone floor with the pommel. The stones immediately slid away, revealing a stair curving into the darkness.

"Shall I come with you, Your Grace?"

Arista considered this. She had no idea what was down there. It could be one cell or a maze of corridors. It might take her a long time to discover where Gaunt was. Just outside, she heard Nipper filling his buckets. The castle was already waking up.

"Yes, of course. Lead the way."

"As you wish, Your Grace." The knight pulled a torch from the wall and descended the steps.

It was dark inside. The stair was narrow and oppressive. Ahead, she could hear the sounds of faint weeping. The same heavy stones that made up the base of the tower formed the dungeon. Here, however, decorations adorned the walls. Nothing recognizable, merely abstract designs carved everywhere. Arista felt she had seen them before—not these exactly, but similar ones.

Then she felt it.

Like the snap of a twig or the crack of an egg, a tremor passed through her body—a sudden disconcerting break.

She looked down. The old man's hands were gone and she was seeing her own fingers and sleeves revealed in the flickering torchlight.

With his back turned, the knight continued to escort them. As he reached the bottom of the stairs, he began to turn, saying, "Your Grace, I—"

Before he was fully around, Hilfred shoved her aside.

He drew his sword just as the knight's eyes widened. As he drove his blade at the man's chest, the black armor turned the tip. It skipped off, penetrating the gap between the chest plate and the right pauldron, piercing the man's shoulder.

The knight cried out.

Hilfred withdrew his sword. The knight staggered backward, struggling to draw his own. Hilfred swung at the knight's neck. Blood exploded, spraying both of them. The seret made no further noise as he crumpled and fell.

"What happened?" Hilfred asked, picking up the torch.

"The walls," she said, touching the chiseled symbols. "They have runes on them like in Gutaria Prison. I can't do magic in here. Do you think anyone heard that?"

"I'm sure the kid fetching water did," he said. "Will he do anything?"

"I don't know. We should close the door," Arista said, picking up the sword with the emerald and looking up the long staircase at the patch of light at the top. What they had covered so casually minutes earlier now appeared so far—so dangerous. "I'll do it. You find Gaunt."

"No. I won't leave your side. There could be more guards. Forget the door. We'll find him together and get out of here." He took her left hand and pulled her along. Her right hand held on to the sword.

The hallways were narrow stone corridors without any light except what came from the torch they held. The ceiling arched to a peak not more than a foot above Arista's head, forcing Hilfred to stoop. Wooden doors, so short they looked more like livestock gates, began appearing on either side.

"Gaunt!" Hilfred yelled.

"Degan Gaunt!" Arista shouted.

They ran down the darkened passageways, pounding on

doors, calling his name, and peering inside. The hallway ended at a T-intersection. With only one torch, they had no option to split up, even if Hilfred could be convinced. They turned right and pressed on, finding more doors.

"Degan Gaunt!"

"Stop!" Arista stopped suddenly.

"Wha—"

"Shush!"

Very faintly—"Here!"

They trotted down the next corridor but reached a dead end.

"This place is a maze," Arista said.

They ran back and took another turn. They called again.

"Here! I'm here!" came the reply, louder now.

Running once more, they again met a solid wall. They retraced their steps, found another corridor that appeared to go in the right direction, and followed it as far as the hallway allowed.

"Degan!" she cried.

"Over here!" called a voice from the last door in the block.

When they reached it, Arista bent down and held up the torch. In the tiny grated window, she saw a pair of eyes. She grabbed the door handle and pulled—locked. She tried the gemstone but nothing happened.

"Damn it!" she cried. "The guard, he must have the key. Oh, how could I be so stupid? I should have searched him before we ran off."

Hilfred hammered the wooden door with his sword. The hard oak, nearly as solid as stone, gave up only sliver-size chips.

"We'll never get the door open this way. Your sword isn't doing anything! We have to go back for the keys."

Hilfred continued to strike the door.

"We'll be back, Degan!" Arista said before starting back down the hall, carrying the torch.

"Arista!" Hilfred shouted as he chased after her.

They rounded the corridors, turning left, then right, and then—

"Arista?" Saldur said, stunned, as they nearly ran into the regent. Around him were five Seret Knights with swords drawn and torches held high.

Hilfred pushed Arista back. "Run!" he told her.

Saldur stared at them for a moment, then shook his head. "There is nowhere to run to, dear boy. You're both quite trapped."

Saldur, his hair loose and wild, wore a white linen nightgown, over which he had pulled a red silk robe that he was still in the midst of tying about his waist. "So it was you after all. I would not have believed it. You've been very clever, Arista, but you've always been a clever girl, haven't you? Always poking your nose into places you shouldn't.

"And you, Hilfred, reunited with your princess once more, I see. It's a wonderfully gallant gesture to defend her with your life, but it's also futile, and where is the honor in futility? There's no other exit from this dungeon. These men are Seret Knights, highly skilled, brutally trained soldiers who will kill you if you resist."

Saldur took the torch from the lead seret, who now also drew a dagger. "You have wasted half your life protecting this foolish girl, whose stupidity and rash choices have dragged you through torment and fire. Put down your sword and back away."

Hilfred checked his grip and planted his feet.

"When I was fifteen, you told me I would die if I tried to save her. That night I ran into an inferno. If I didn't listen to you then, what makes you think I will now?"

Saldur sighed. "Don't make them kill you."

Hilfred stood his ground.

"Stop, please. I beg you!" Arista shouted. "Sauly, I'll do anything you ask. Please, just let him go."

"Persuade him to put down his sword and I will."

"Hilfred—"

"Not even if you order me to," he said, his voice grave. "There is no power in Elan capable of making me walk away from you—not now, not ever again."

"Hilfred..." she whispered as tears fell.

He glanced at her. In that moment of inattention, the seret saw an opening and slashed. Hilfred dodged.

Swords clashed.

"*No!*" Arista cried.

Hilfred swung for the throat again, but the knight ducked. Hilfred's blade struck the wall, kicking up sparks. The knight stabbed him in the side. Hilfred gasped and staggered but managed to lunge and thrust his sword at the knight's chest. Again the point of the blade deflected off the black armor, but this time he was not fortunate enough to connect.

Arista watched as a second knight lunged, driving his sword through Hilfred's stomach. The sword pierced his body, pushing out the back of his tunic.

"No! *No!*" she screamed, falling against the wall as her knees threatened to buckle.

With blood spilling from his lips, Hilfred struggled to raise his sword again. The foremost knight brought his own blade down, severing Hilfred's arm at the elbow with a burst of warm blood that splashed across Arista's face.

Hilfred collapsed to his knees. His body hitched.

"A-Aris..." he sputtered.

"Oh, Hilfred..." Arista whispered as her eyes burned.

The knights stood over him. One raised his sword.

"*Arista!*" he cried.

The knight's sword came down.

Arista collapsed as if the blade pierced them both. She slumped to the floor. She could not speak. She could not breathe. Her eyes locked on the dead body of Hilfred as a warm wetness pooling across the stone floor crept between her fingers.

"Hilfred." She mouthed the word. She had no breath left to speak it.

Saldur sighed. "Get him out of here."

"What about her?"

"She went through so much trouble to get in, so let's find her a nice permanent room."

Chapter 25

Invasion

"What do you think is going to happen?" Hadrian asked Royce as they hung in the dark.

"The fleet will come in and there will be no pressure to fire the spouts. The Ghazel will land without opposition and slaughter everyone. Eventually they'll reach here, break in, and butcher us."

"No," Hadrian said, shaking his head. "See, that's where you're wrong. The Ghazel will eat us alive, and they'll take their time savoring every moment. Trust me."

They hung in silence.

"What time do you think it is?" Hadrian asked.

"Close to sunset. It was pretty late when they brought us in."

Silence.

They could hear the random movements of guards on the other side of the door, muffled conversation, the slide of a chair, occasional laughter.

"Why does this always happen?" Royce asked. "Why are we always hanging on a wall, waiting to die by slow vivisection? I just want to point out that this was your idea—*again.*"

"I've been waiting for that. But I believe I told you not to come." Hadrian shifted in his chains and sighed. "I don't suppose there's much chance of a beautiful princess coming in here and saving us again."

"That card's been dealt."

"I wish I had met Gaunt," Hadrian said at length. "It would have been nice to actually meet the man, you know? My whole life was fated to protect this guy and I never even saw him."

They were quiet for a time, and then Royce made a *hmm* sound.

"What?"

"Huh? Oh—nothing."

"You're thinking something. What is it?"

"Just interesting that you think Arista is beautiful."

"Don't you?"

"She's okay."

"You're blinded by Gwen."

Hadrian heard Royce sigh. There was a silence, and then he said, "She already named our children. Elias if we had a boy—or was it Sterling? I forget—and Mercedes if a girl. She even took up knitting and made me a scarf."

"For what it's worth, I'm sorry I dragged you into this."

"She wanted me to go, remember? She said I had to protect you. I had to save your life."

Hadrian looked over at him. "Good job."

Chairs moved in the outer office, footsteps, a banging door, agitated voices. Hadrian caught snippets of the conversation.

"...black sails...a dark cloud on the ocean..."

"No, someone else..."

A chair turned over and hit the floor. More hurried footsteps. Silence.

"Sounds like the fleet is in." Hadrian waited, watching the door to their cell. "They left us for dead, didn't they? We told them this would happen. We came all this way to try and save them. You'd think they'd have the decency to let us out when they saw we were right."

"Probably think we're behind it. We're lucky they didn't just kill us."

"Not sure that's lucky. A nice, quick decapitation is kind of appealing right now."

"How long do you think before the Ba Ran find us?" Royce asked.

"You in a hurry?"

"Yeah, actually. If I have to be eaten, I would sort of like to get it over with."

Hadrian heard the sound of breaking glass.

"Ah, well, that didn't take long, did it?" Royce muttered miserably.

Footsteps shuffled in the outer room. There was a pause, and then the steps started again, coming closer. There were sounds of a struggle and a muffled cry. Hadrian braced himself and watched the door as it opened. What stood in the doorway shocked him.

"You boys ready to go?" Derning asked.

"What are *you* doing here?" they both said in unison.

"Would you prefer me to leave?" Derning smiled. Noticing the riveted manacles, he grimaced. "Thorough buggers, aren't they? Hang on. I saw some tools out here."

Royce and Hadrian looked at each other, bewildered.

"Okay, so he's not a beautiful princess. But it works for me."

There were sounds of slamming and an "Aha!" Then Derning returned with a hammer and a chisel.

"The Ghazel fleet arrived and Drumindor isn't working, but it didn't blow up either, so I guess we have you to thank for that," Derning told them as he went to work on the manacle pins.

"Don't mention it. And I'm not just saying that. I really mean...don't mention it," Hadrian said with a wince.

"Now half the folks—the smart half—are running. The others are going to try to fight. That means we don't have much time to get out of here. I have horses and provisions waiting just outside town. We'll take the mountain road north. I'll ride with you as far as Maranon and then I'll be going my own way."

"But I still don't get why you're here," Royce said as Derning finished with one of the metal bracelets. "Don't you work for Merrick?"

"Merrick Marius?" Derning laughed. "That's funny. Grady and I were convinced you two worked for Marius." Derning finished cracking open the manacles on Royce, then turned to Hadrian. "We work for Cornelius DeLur. You might know him—big fat guy, father of Cosmo. He pretty much runs this country—or owns it, depending on your viewpoint. Imagine my surprise yesterday when I checked in and found out you worked for Melengar. DeLur got a big kick out of that. The old fat man has a sick sense of humor sometimes."

"I'm confused. Why were you on the *Storm*?"

"When the Diamond found a message from Merrick, Cosmos thought it was important enough to relay to his daddy, and Cornelius sent us to check out what was going on. Grady and I started as sailors and are still well known on the Sharon. We were so sure Royce killed Drew, which is why we thought you two were mixed up with Merrick. We thought it had something to do with that horn comment that Drew made."

"Bernie killed him," Royce said simply.

"Yeah, we figured that out. And, of course, that horn thing

had nothing to do with Merrick. That was all Thranic's group. When we heard you had been arrested, it wasn't too hard to find ya."

He finished freeing Hadrian, who rubbed his wrists.

"Come on, most of your gear is out here." He pulled Alverstone out of his belt and handed it to Royce. "Took this off one of the guards. I think he thought it was pretty."

Outside their cell the tiny jail office was empty except for two guards. One looked dead but the other might have just been unconscious. They found their possessions in a series of boxes set aside in a room filled with all manner of impounded items.

Outside, dawn rose and people were running with bundles in their arms. Mothers held crying children to their breasts. Men struggled to push overfilled carts uphill. Down in the harbor they could see a forest of dark masts. Drumindor stood a mute witness to the sacking of the city.

Derning led them up refugee-choked streets. Fights broke out. Roads were blocked, and finally Derning resorted to the roofs. They scaled balconies and leapt alleys, trotting across the clay-tiled housetops until they cleared the congestion. They dropped back to the street and soon reached the city's eastern gate. Hundreds of people were rushing by with carts and donkeys—women and children mostly, traveling with boys and old men.

Derning stopped just outside the gates, looking worried. He whistled and a bird call answered in response. He led them off the road and up an embankment.

"Sorry, Jacob," said a spindly youth, emerging with four horses. "I figured it was best to wait out of sight. If anyone saw me with these, I wouldn't keep them for long."

From the crest of the hill they could see the bay far below. Smoke rose thickly from the buildings closest to the water.

"We weren't able to stop it," Derning said, looking at the refugees fleeing the city, "but between you defusing the explosion and my reporting to Cornelius so he could raise the alarm, it looks like we saved a lot of lives."

They mounted up and Hadrian took one last look at Tur Del Fur as the flames, fanned by the morning's sea breeze, swept through the streets below.

Chapter 26

Payment

Merrick entered the great hall of the imperial palace. Servants were hanging Wintertide decorations, which should have given the room a festive feel, but to Merrick it was still just a dreary chamber with too much stone and too little sunlight. He had never cared for Aquesta, and regretted that it would be the capital of the New Empire—an empire whose security he had ensured. He would have preferred Colnora. At least it had glass streetlamps.

"Ah! Merrick," Ethelred greeted him. The regents, Earl Ballentyne, and the chancellor were all gathered around the great table. "Or should I call you Lord Marius?"

"You should indeed," Merrick replied.

"You bring good news, then?"

"The best, Your Lordship—Delgos has fallen."

"Excellent!" Ethelred applauded.

Merrick reached the table and pulled off his gloves, one finger at a time. "The Ghazel invaded Tur Del Fur five days ago, meeting only a weak resistance. They took Drumindor and burned much of the port city."

"And the Nationalist army?" Ethelred asked, sitting down

comfortably in his chair with a smile stretching across his broad face.

"As expected, the army packed up and went south the moment they heard. Most have family in Delgos. You can retake Ratibor at will. You won't even need the army. A few hundred men will do. Breckton can turn his attention north to Melengar and begin plans for the spring invasion of Trent."

"Excellent! Excellent!" Ethelred cheered. Saldur and the chancellor joined in his applause, granting each other smiles of relief and pleasure.

"What happens when the Ghazel finish with Delgos and decide to march north?" the Earl of Chadwick asked. Seated at the far end of the table, he did not appear to share his companions' gaiety. "I'm told there's quite a lot of them and hear they're fearsome fighters. If they can destroy Delgos, what assurance do we have they won't attack us?"

"I'm certain the Nationalists will halt their ambitions in the short term, milord," Merrick replied. "But even if not, we face no threat from the Ba Ran Ghazel. They're a superstitious lot and expect some sort of world-ending catastrophe to beset them shortly. They want Drumindor as a refuge, not as a base for launching attacks. This will buy the time you need to take Melengar, Trent, and possibly even western Calis. By then the New Empire will be supreme and the Nationalists a memory. The remaining residents of Delgos, those once-independent merchant barons, will beg for imperial intervention against the Ghazel and eagerly submit to your absolute rule. The empire of old will be reforged."

The earl scowled and sat back down.

"You are indeed a marvel and deserving of your new title and station, Lord Marius."

"Because you already have Gaunt and Esrahaddon is dead, I believe that finishes my employment obligations."

"For now," Ethelred told him. "I won't let a man of your talents get away that easily. Now that I've found you, I want you in my court. I'll make it worth your loyalty."

"Actually, I already spoke with His Grace about the position of Magistrate of Colnora."

"Magistrate, eh? Want your own city, do you? I like the idea. Think you can keep the Diamond under your thumb? I suppose you could—certainly, why not? Consider it done, Lord Magistrate, but I insist you do not take your post until after Wintertide. I want you here for the festivities."

"Ethelred is getting married and crowned emperor," Saldur explained. "The Patriarch will be coming to perform the ceremony himself, and if that's not enough, we will be burning a famous witch."

"I wouldn't miss it."

"Excellent!" Ethelred grinned. "I trust accommodations in the city are to your liking? If not, tell the chamberlain and he'll find a more suitable estate."

"The house is perfect. You are too kind, my lord."

"I still don't see why you don't simply stay in the palace."

"It's easier for me to do business if I'm not seen here too frequently. And now, if you'll forgive me, I must—"

"You aren't leaving?" Ethelred asked, disappointed. "You just got here. With news like this, we have to celebrate. Don't doom me to merrymaking with the likes of an old cleric and a melancholy earl. I'll call for wines and beef. We'll get some entertainment, music, dancers, and women if you'd like. How do you like your women, Marius? Thin or plump, light or dark, saucy or docile? I assure you, the lord chamberlain can fill any order."

"Alas, my lord, I have some remaining business to which I must attend."

Ethelred frowned. "Very well, but you must show up for Wintertide. I insist."

"Of course, my lord."

Merrick left while the imperial rulers exchanged congratulatory accolades. Outside, a new carriage waited, complete with four white horses and a uniformed driver. On the seat rested the package from the city constable. Merrick had offered brandy in trade and the man had leapt at the opportunity. A bottle of fine liquor in return for the worthless remnants of the defunct witch hunt was the sort of good fortune that the sheriff was unaccustomed to receiving. Unwrapping the package, Merrick ran his fingers over the shimmering material of the robe.

The carriage traveled up The Hill and turned on Heath Street, one of the more affluent neighborhoods in the city. The homes, though not terribly large, were tasteful and elegant. A servant waited dutifully to remove his cloak and boots while another stood by with a warm cup of cider. Merrick no longer drank wine, ale, or spirits, and was amused to see this accommodation taken into account. He sat in the drawing room, surrounded by burgundy furnishings and dark wood paneling, sipping his drink and listening to the pop of the fireplace.

A knock sounded at the door. He nearly rose to answer when he spotted one of his new servants trotting to the foyer.

"Where is she, Merrick?" he heard an angry voice shout.

A moment later the valet led two men into the drawing room.

"Please have a seat, both of you." Merrick reclined in his soft chair, warming his hands with his cup. "Would either of you care for a drink before we conduct business? My servants can bring you whatever you like, but I must say the cider is especially good."

"I said, where is she?"

"Relax, Mr. Deminthal, your daughter is fine and I'll bring her down shortly. You fulfilled your end of the bargain brilliantly, and I always honor my commitments. I merely wish to go over a few details. Only a formality, I assure you. First, let me congratulate you, Wyatt. May I call you Wyatt? You've done an excellent job. Poe's report gave you extremely high marks.

"He tells me you were instrumental in getting Royce and Hadrian on board, and even after the unexpected sinking of the *Emerald Storm*, your quick thinking saved the ship's orders and the mission. I'm especially impressed by how you won over Royce's trust—no small feat, I might add. You must be a very convincing fellow, as demonstrated by how you persuaded the Port Authority that Royce and Hadrian were in Tur Del Fur to destroy Drumindor. I'm convinced it's only by your skill and intelligence that the operation was such a wonderful success."

Merrick took a sip from his cider and sat back with a grin. "I have just one question. Do you know where Royce and Hadrian are now?"

"Dead. By the Ghazel or the Tur Del Fur officials, whoever got them first."

"Hmm, I doubt that. Royce is not easy to kill. He has gotten out of much more difficult situations before. I would say he leads a charmed life, but I know all too well what kind of life he's lived. Still, I wouldn't even trust Death to bind him long."

"I want my daughter—now," Wyatt said quietly through clenched teeth.

"Of course, of course. Mr. Poe, would you be so kind as to run up and bring her down? Third door on the left." Merrick handed him a key. "Seriously, Wyatt, you're a very capable man. I could use you."

"Do you think I *liked* doing this? How many hundreds of people are dead because of me?"

"Don't think of it that way. Think of it as a job, an assignment, which you performed with panache. I don't see talent such as yours often, and I could find other uses of your skills. Join with me and you'll be well compensated. I'm working on another project now, for an even more lucrative employer, and I'm in a position to make a great many good things happen for you. You and your daughter can live like landed gentry. How would you like your own estate?"

"You kidnapped my daughter. The only business I'm interested in doing with you is arranging your death."

"Don't be so dramatic. Ah, see? Here she is now. Safe and sound."

Poe escorted a little girl down the steps. She was around ten years old, her light-brown hair was tied in a bow, and she wore an elegantly tailored blue dress with fine leather shoes.

"Daddy!" she shouted.

Wyatt rushed over, throwing his arms around her. "Did they hurt you, honey?"

"No, I'm okay. They bought me this pretty dress and got me these shoes! And we played games."

"That's good, honey." Turning to Merrick, Wyatt asked, "What about Elden?"

"He's fine, still in Colnora. Waiting for you, I presume. Wyatt, you really need to consider my offer, if for no other reason than your own safety."

Wyatt spun on him. "I did your job! You sat there and told me I did it *brilliantly*! Why are you still threatening us?"

Merrick looked at the girl. "Poe, take Allie in the kitchen. I think there are some cookies she might like."

Wyatt held her to him.

"Don't worry, she'll be right back."

"Do you like cookies?" Poe asked her. The little girl grinned, bobbing her head. She looked up at her father.

Wyatt nodded. "It's okay, go ahead. Hurry back, honey."

Poe and Allie left the room hand in hand.

"I'm not threatening you. As I already said, I'm very pleased with your skills. I'm merely trying to protect you. Consider for a moment, what if Royce is not dead? He'll put two and two together, if he hasn't already. You should be afraid of what he'll do to you—and your daughter. Royce will probably kill Allie first and make you watch."

"He's not like that."

Merrick released a small chuckle. "Oh, sir, you have no idea what Royce is like. I'll grant you that his association with Hadrian Blackwater has tempered him greatly. Twelve years with that idealistic dreamer have made him practically human, but I *know* him. I know what lurks beneath. I've seen things that make even my hardened heart shudder. Get his anger up, and you'll unleash a demon that no one can control. Believe me, he's *like that* and so much more. Nothing is beyond him."

Allie returned with a handful of sugar cookies. Taking her other hand, Wyatt headed for the door. He paused at the threshold and looked back. "Merrick, if what you say about Royce is true, then shouldn't *you* be the one who's afraid?" Wyatt walked out, closing the door behind him.

Merrick sipped his cider again, but it had gone cold.

GLOSSARY OF TERMS AND NAMES

ADAM: Wheeler from Ratibor

ADDIE WOOD: Mother of Thrace/Modina, wife of Theron, killed in Dahlgren

ALBERT WINSLOW: Landless viscount used by Riyria to arrange assignments from the gentry

ALBURN: Kingdom of Avryn ruled by King Armand and Queen Adeline, member of the New Empire

ALENDA LANAKLIN: Daughter of Marquis Victor Lanaklin and sister of Myron the monk

ALGAR: Woodworker in Hintindar

ALLIE: Daughter of Wyatt Deminthal

ALRIC BRENDON ESSENDON: King of Melengar, son of Amrath, brother of Arista

ALVERSTONE: \al-ver-stone\ Dagger used by Royce

AMBERTON LEE: Hill with old ruins not far from Hintindar

AMBROSE MOOR: Administrator of the Manzant Prison and Salt Works

AMILIA: Carriage maker's daughter from the small village of Tarin Vale

AMITER: Second wife of King Urith, sister of Androus

AMRATH ESSENDON: \am-wrath\ Deceased king of Melengar, father of Alric and Arista

AMRIL: \am-rill\ Countess that Arista cursed with boils

ANDROUS: Viceroy of Ratibor

ANNA: Chambermaid of Empress Modina

ANTUN BULARD: Historian and author of *The History of Apeladorn*, passenger on the *Emerald Storm*

APELADORN: \ah-pell-ah-dorn\ Four nations of man, consisting of Trent, Avryn, Delgos, and Calis

APELANESE: Language spoken throughout the four kingdoms of men

AQUESTA: \ah-quest-ah\ Capital city of the kingdom of Warric, seat of power for the New Empire

ARBOR: Baker in Hintindar, married to Dunstan, shoemaker's daughter

ARCADIUS VINTARUS LATIMER: Professor of Lore at Sheridan University

ARCHIBALD BALLENTYNE: Earl of Chadwick, commander of Sir Breckton, promised providence of Melengar for service to the New Empire

ARISTA ESSENDON: Princess of Melengar, daughter of Amrath, sister of King Alric

ARMAND: King of Alburn, married to Adeline

ARMIGIL: Brew mistress of Hintindar

ART, THE: Magic, generally feared due to superstition

ARVID MCDERN: Son of Dillon McDern from Dahlgren

AVEMPARTHA: Ancient elven tower, home of Gilarabrywn, which attacked Dahlgren

AVRYN: \ave-rin\ Central and most powerful of the four nations of Apeladorn, located between Trent and Delgos

AYERS: Proprietor of The Laughing Gnome in Ratibor

BACKING: Rigging a sail such that it catches the wind from its forward side; having both backed and regular rigged sails can render a ship motionless

BAILIFF: Officer who is employed to make arrests and administer punishments

BALDWIN: Lord whose landholdings include Hintindar

BALLENTYNE: \bal-in-tine\ Ruling family of the earldom of Chadwick

BANNER: Crew member of the *Emerald Storm*
BA RAN ARCHIPELAGO: Island of the goblins
BA RAN GHAZEL: Goblins of the sea
BARKERS: Refugee family living in Brisbane Alley of Aquesta; father Brice, mother Lynnette, sons Finis, Hingus, and Wery
BARTHOLOMEW: Carriage maker of Tarin Vale, father of Amilia
BARTHOLOMEW: Priest in Ratibor
BASIL: Officers' cook on the *Emerald Storm*
BASTION: Servant in the imperial palace
BATTLE OF MEDFORD: Skirmish that occurred during Princess Arista's witch trial
BATTLE OF RATIBOR: Skirmish between Nationalists and Imperialists
BELINDA PICKERING: Extremely attractive wife of Count Pickering, mother of Lenare, Mauvin, Fanen, and Denek
BELSTRADS: \bell-straads\ Noble family from Chadwick, including Sir Breckton and Wesley
BENTLY: Sergeant in the Nationalist army
BERNARD: Lord Chamberlain of the imperial palace
BERNICE: Former handmaid of Princess Arista, killed in Dahlgren
BERNIE DEFOE: Topsail crew member of the *Emerald Storm*, former member of the Black Diamond thieves' guild
BERNUM HEIGHTS: Wealthiest residential district in Colnora
BERNUM RIVER: Waterway that bisects the city of Colnora
BERYL: Senior midshipman on the *Emerald Storm*
BETHAMY: King reputed to have had his horse buried with him
BIDDINGS: Chancellor of the imperial palace
BISHOP: Lieutenant aboard the *Emerald Storm*
BLACK DIAMOND, THE: International thieves' guild centered in Colnora

BLACKWATER: Last name of Hadrian and his father, Danbury
BLINDEN: Quartermaster's mate on the *Emerald Storm*
BLYTHIN CASTLE: Castle in Alburn
BOATSWAIN: Petty officer who controls the work of other seamen on a ship
BOCANT: Family who built a lucrative industry from pork, second wealthiest merchants in Colnora
BOTHWICKS: Family of peasant farmers from Dahlgren
BRAGA, PERCY: See Percy Braga
BRECKTON: Sir Breckton Belstrad, son of Lord Belstrad, brother of Wesley, commander of the Northern Imperial Army, knight of Chadwick, considered by many to be the best knight of Avryn
BRIGHT STAR, THE: Ship sunk by Dacca
BRISTOL BENNET: Boatswain on the *Emerald Storm*
BRODRIC ESSENDON: Founder of the Essendon dynasty
BUCKET MEN: Term for assassin used by the Black Diamond thieves' guild
BULARD, ANTUN: See Antun Bulard
BURANDU: \bur-and-dew\ Lord of the Tenkin village of Oudorro
BYRNIE: Long (usually sleeveless) tunic of chain mail worn as defensive armor
CALIAN: \cal-lay-in\ Pertaining to the nation of Calis
CALIANS: Residents of the nation of Calis, darker in skin tone, with almond-shaped eyes
CALIDE PORTMORE: Folk song often sung while drinking
CALIS: \cal-lay\ Southern- and easternmost of the four nations of Apeladorn, considered exotic; in constant conflict with the Ba Ran Ghazel
CAPSTAN: Spoked wheel on a ship that turns to raise the anchor

CARAT: Young member of the Black Diamond thieves' guild
CASWELL: Family of peasant farmers from Dahlgren
CENZARS: \sen-zhar\ Wizards of the Old Novronian Empire
CHAMBERLAIN: Someone who manages the household of a king or nobleman
COLNORA: \call-nor-ah\ Largest and wealthiest city of Avryn, merchant-based, grew from a rest stop at a central crossroads from various major trade routes
CONSTANCE, LADY: Noblewoman, fifth imperial secretary to Empress Modina
CORA: Dairymaid at the imperial palace
CORNELIUS DELUR: Rich businessman, rumored to finance Nationalists and involved in black market, father of Cosmos
COSMOS SEBASTIAN DELUR: Son of Cornelius, also known as the Jewel, head of the Black Diamond thieves' guild
COXSWAIN: Helmsman of a racing ship
CRANSTON: Professor at Sheridan University, tried and burned for heresy
CRIMSON HAND: Thieves' guild operating out of Melengar
CROWN CONSPIRACY, THE: Play reputed to be based on the murder of King Amrath, follows the exploits of two thieves and the Prince of Melengar
CROWN TOWER: Home of the Patriarch, center of the Nyphron Church
CUTTER: Moniker used by Merrick Marius when a member of the Black Diamond thieves' guild
DACCA: Fierce seafaring people who live on the island of Dacca, south of Delgos
DAGASTAN: Major and easternmost trade port of Calis
DAHLGREN: \dall-grin\ Remote village on the bank of the Nidwalden River, destroyed by Gilarabrywn

DANBURY BLACKWATER: Father of Hadrian
DANTHEN: Woodsman from Dahlgren
DAREF, LORD: Noble of Warric, associate of Albert Winslow
DARIUS SERET: Founder of the Seret Knights
DAVENS: Squire who Arista had a youthful crush on
DAVIS: Crew member of the *Emerald Storm*
DEACON TOMAS: Priest of Dahlgren, witnessed destruction of Gilarabrywn, proclaimed Thrace Wood as the Heir of Novron
DEFOE, BERNIE: See Bernie Defoe
DEGAN GAUNT: Leader of the Nationalists, sister of Miranda
DELANCY, GWEN: See Gwen DeLancy
DELANO DEWITT: Alias used by Wyatt Deminthal when he framed Hadrian and Royce for King Amrath's death
DELGOS: One of the four nations of Apeladorn. The only republic in a world of monarchies, Delgos revolted against the Steward's Empire after Glenmorgan III was murdered and after surviving an attack by the Ba Ran Ghazel with no aid from the empire.
DELORKAN, DUKE: Nobleman from Calis
DELUR: Family of wealthy merchants
DEMINTHAL, WYATT: See Wyatt Deminthal
DENEK PICKERING: Youngest son of Count Pickering
DENNY: Worker at The Rose and Thorn
DERMONT, LORD: General of imperial army
DERNING, JACOB: Maintop captain on the *Emerald Storm*
DEVON: Monk of Tarin Vale, taught Amilia to read and write
DEWITT, DELANO: See Delano DeWitt
DIGBY: Guard at Essendon Castle
DILLADRUM: Erbonese guide, hired to take crew of the *Emerald Storm* to Palace of the Four Winds
DILLNARD LINROY: Royal Financier of Melengar

DIME: Crew member of the *Emerald Storm*

DIOYLION: \die-e-leon\ *The Accumulated Letters of Dioylion*, a very rare scroll

DIXON TAFT: Bartender and manager of The Rose and Thorn Tavern, lost an arm in the Battle of Medford

DOVIN THRANIC: Sentinel of Nyphron Church aboard the *Emerald Storm*

DREW, EDGAR: See Edgar Drew

DR. GERAND: Physician in Ratibor

DR. LEVY: Physician aboard the *Emerald Storm*

DROME: God of the dwarves

DRONDIL FIELDS: Count Pickering's castle, once the fortress of Brodric Essendon, the original seat of power in Melengar

DRUMINDOR: Dwarven-built fortress located at the entrance to Terlando Bay in Tur Del Fur, can utilize lava from nearby volcano for its defense

DRUNDEL: Peasant family from Dahlgren consisting of Mae, Went, Davie, and Firth

DUNLAP, PAUL: Former carriage driver of King Urith, dead

DUNMORE: Youngest and least sophisticated kingdom of Avryn, ruled by King Roswort; member of the New Empire

DUNSTAN: Baker in Hintindar, childhood friend of Hadrian, married to Arbor

DURBO: Tenkin dwelling

DUR GURON: Easternmost portion of Calis

DUSTER: Moniker used by Royce while a member of the Black Diamond

ECTON, SIR: Chief knight of Count Pickering and military general of Melengar

EDGAR DREW: Old seaman on the *Emerald Storm*, died in a fall

EDITH MON: Head maid in charge of the scullery and chamber servants in the imperial palace

EDMUND HALL: Professor of geometry at Sheridan University, reputed to have found Percepliquis, declared a heretic by the Nyphron Church, imprisoned in the Crown Tower

ELAN: The world

ELDEN: Large man, friend of Wyatt Deminthal

ELINYA: Esrahaddon's girlfriend

ELLA: Cook at Drondil Fields

ELLA: Maid at imperial palace

ELLIS FAR, THE: Melengarian ship

ELVEN: Pertaining to elves

EMERALD STORM, THE: Ship of the New Empire, captained by Seward

EMERY DORN: Young revolutionary living in Ratibor

EMPRESS MODINA: See Modina, Empress

ENDEN, SIR: Knight of Chadwick, considered second best to Breckton

ERANDABON GILE: Panther of Dur Guron, Tenkin Warlord, madman

ERBON: Region of Calis northwest from Mandalin

EREBUS: Father of the gods, also known as Kile

ERIVAN: \ear-ah-van\ Elven Empire

ERMA EVERTON: Alias used by Arista while in Hintindar

ERVANON: \err-vah-non\ City in northern Ghent, seat of the Nyphron Church, once the capital of the Steward's Empire as established by Glenmorgan I

ESRAHADDON: \ez-rah-hod-in\ Wizard, former member of the Cenzar, convicted of destroying the Old Empire, sentenced to imprisonment, held in Gutaria

ESSENDON: \ez-in-don\ Royal family of Melengar

ESSENDON CASTLE: Home of ruling monarchs of Melengar

ESTRAMNADON: \es-tram-nah-don\ Believed to be the capital or at least a very sacred place in the Erivan Empire

ESTRENDOR: \es-tren-door\ Northern wastes

ETCHER: Member of the Black Diamond thieves' guild

ETHELRED, LANIS: \eth-el-red\ Former king of Warric, co-regent of New Empire, Imperialist

EVERTON: Alias used by Arista, Hadrian, and later Royce

EVLIN: City along the banks of the Bernum River

FALINA BROCKTON: Real name of Emerald, waitress at The Rose and Thorn Tavern

FALQUIN: Professor at Sheridan University

FANEN PICKERING: \fan-in\ Middle son of Count Pickering, killed by Luis Guy

FAN IRLANU: Visionary of Oudorro, seer, fortune-teller

FAQUIN: Inept magician who uses alchemy rather than channeling the Art

FAULD, THE ORDER OF: \fall-ed\ Post-imperial order of knights dedicated to preserving the skill and discipline of the Teshlor Knights

FENITILIAN: Monk of Maribor, made warm shoes

FERROL: God of the elves

FINILESS: Noted author

FINISHER: Stealthy Ghazel fighter

FINLIN, ETHAN: Member of the Black Diamond, stores smuggled goods, owns windmill

FLETCHER: Maker of arrows

FORECASTLE: Raised portion in the bow of a ship containing living quarters of senior crew members

FORREST: Ratibor citizen with fighting experience, son of a silversmith

GAFTON: Imperial admiral

GALEANNON: \gale-e-an-on\ Kingdom of Avryn, ruled by Fredrick and Josephine, member of the New Empire

GALENTI: \ga-lehn'-tay\ Calian nickname attributed to Hadrian

GALEWYR RIVER: \gale-wahar\ Marks the southern border of Melengar and the northern border of Warric and reaches the sea near the fishing village of Roe

GALIEN: \gal-e-in\ Archbishop of the Nyphron Church

GALILIN: \gal-ah-lin\ Province of Melengar formerly ruled by Count Pickering

GAUNT, DEGAN: See Degan Gaunt

GEMKEY: Gem that opens a gemlock

GEMLOCK: Dwarven invention that seals a container or entrance and can only be opened with a precious gem of the right type and cut

GENTRY SQUARE: Affluent district of Melengar

GERALD BANIFF: Primary bodyguard of Empress Modina

GERTY: Midwife in Hintindar who delivered Hadrian, married to Abelard

GHAZEL: \gehz-ell\ Ba Ran Ghazel, the dwarven name for goblins, literally: Sea Goblins

GHAZEL SEA: Southern body of water east of the Sharon Sea

GHENT: Ecclesiastical holding of the Nyphron Church, member of New Empire

GILARABRYWN: \gill-lar-ah-bren\ Elven beast of war; one escaped Avempartha and destroyed village of Dahlgren before being killed by Thrace

GILL: Sentry in the Nationalist army

GINLIN: \gin-lin\ Monk of Maribor, winemaker, refused to touch a knife

GLAMRENDOR: \glam-ren-door\ Capital of Dunmore

GLENMORGAN: 326 years after the fall of the Novronian Empire, this native of Ghent reunited the four nations of Apeladorn; founder of Sheridan University; creator of the great north-south road; builder of the Ervanon palace (of which only the Crown Tower remains)

GLENMORGAN II: Son of Glenmorgan. When his father died young, the new and inexperienced emperor relied on church officials to assist him in managing his empire. They in turn took the opportunity to manipulate the emperor into granting sweeping powers to the church and nobles loyal to the church. These leaders opposed defending Delgos against the invading Ba Ran Ghazel in Calis and the Dacca in Delgos, arguing the threat would increase dependency on the empire.

GLENMORGAN III: Grandson of Glenmorgan. Shortly after assuming the stewardship, he attempted to reassert control over the realm his grandfather had created by leading an army against the invading Ghazel that had reached southeastern Avryn. He defeated the Ghazel at the First Battle of Vilan Hills and announced plans to ride to the aid of Tur Del Fur. Fearing his rise in power, in the sixth year of his reign, his nobles betrayed and imprisoned him in Blythin Castle. Jealous of his popularity and growing strength, and resentful of his policy of stripping the nobles and clergy of their power, the church charged him with heresy. He was found guilty and executed. This began the rapid collapse of what many called the Steward's Empire. The church later claimed the nobles had tricked them, and condemned many, most of whom reputedly ended their lives badly.

GLOUSTON: Province of northern Warric bordering on the Galewyr River, formerly ruled by Marquis Lanaklin, invaded and taken over by the New Empire

GNOME, THE: Nickname of The Laughing Gnome Tavern
GRADY: Seaman on the *Emerald Storm*
GRAVIS: Dwarf who sabotaged Drumindor
GREAT SWORD: Long sword designed to be held with both hands
GREEN: Lieutenant on the *Emerald Storm*
GREIG: Carpenter aboard the *Emerald Storm*
GRELAD, JERISH: See Jerish Grelad
GRIBBON: Flag of Mandalin Calis
GRIGOLES: \gry-holes\ Author of *Grigoles Treatise on Imperial Common Law*
GRIMBALD: Blacksmith in Hintindar
GRONBACH: Dwarf, fairy-tale villain
GRUMON, MASON: \grum-on\ Blacksmith in Medford, worked for Riyria, died in Battle of Medford
GUARDIAN OF THE HEIR: Teshlor, protector of the Heir of Novron
GUNGUAN: Vintu pack ponies
GUR EM: Thickest part of the jungle in Calis
GUTARIA: \goo-tar-ah\ Secret Nyphron prison designed to hold Esrahaddon
GUY, LUIS: See Luis Guy
GWEN DELANCY: Calian prostitute and proprietor of Medford House and The Rose and Thorn Tavern in Medford, girlfriend of Royce Melborn
HADDY: Childhood nickname of Hadrian
HADRIAN BLACKWATER: Mercenary, one-half of Riyria
HALBERD: Two-handed pole used as a weapon
HANDEL: Master at Sheridan University, originally from Roe, proponent to have Delgos's Republic officially recognized
HARBERT: Tailor in Hintindar, husband of Hester

HARVEST MOON: Full moon nearest the fall equinox
HEIR OF NOVRON: Direct descendant of demigod Novron, destined to rule all of Avryn
HELDABERRY: Wild-growing fruit often used to make wine
HESLON: Monk of Maribor, great cook
HIGHCOURT FIELDS: Once the site of the supreme noble judicial court of law in Avryn, location of Wintertide games
HILFRED, REUBEN: Former bodyguard of Princess Arista, severely burned in Dahlgren
HILL DISTRICT: Affluent neighborhood in Colnora
HIMBOLT: Baron of Melengar
HINGARA: Calian guide, died in jungles of Gur Em
HINTINDAR: Small manorial village in Rhenydd, home of Hadrian Blackwater
HOBBIE: Stableboy in Hintindar
HORN OF DELGOS: Landmark used by sailors to determine the southernmost tip of Delgos
HORN OF GYLINDORA: Item Esrahaddon indicates is buried in Percepliquis
HOUSE, THE: Nickname used for Medford House
HOYTE: Onetime First Officer of the Black Diamond, set up Royce to kill Jade, sent Royce to Manzant Prison, killed by Royce
IBIS THINLY: Head cook of the imperial palace
IMP: Slang for Imperialist
IMPERIALISTS: Political party that desires to unite all the kingdoms of men under a single leader who is the direct descendant of the demigod Novron
IMPERIAL PALACE: Seat of power of the New Empire
IMPERIAL SECRETARY: Caretaker of Empress Modina, charged with making her publically presentable

JACOB DERNING: See Derning, Jacob
JADE: Assassin in the Black Diamond, girlfriend of Merrick, mistakenly killed by Royce
JENKINS TALBERT: Squire in Tarin Vale
JEREMY: Guard at Essendon Castle
JERISH GRELAD: Teshlor Knight, first Guardian of the Heir, protector of Nevrik
JERL, LORD: Nobleman, neighbor of the Pickerings known for his prize-winning hunting dogs
JEWEL, THE: Head of the international Black Diamond thieves' guild, also known as Cosmos DeLur
JIMMY: Tavern worker at The Laughing Gnome
JOQDAN: \jok-dan\ Warlord of the Tenkin village of Oudorro
JULIAN TEMPEST: Chamberlain of the kingdom of Melengar
KAZ: Calian term for anyone with mixed elven and human blood
KENDELL, EARL: Nobleman of Melengar, loyal to Alric Essendon
KHAROLL: Long dagger
KILE: Name used by Erebus when sent to Elan, performs good deeds in the form of a man
KILNAR: City in the south of Rhenydd
KNOB: Baker at the imperial palace
KRINDEL: Prelate of the Nyphron Church and historian
KRIS DAGGER: Weapon with a wavy blade, sometimes used in magic rituals
LAMBERT, IGNATIUS: Chancellor of Sheridan University
LANAKLIN: Once ruling family of Glouston, currently in exile in Melengar, opposes the New Empire
LANDONER: Professor at Sheridan University, tried and burned for heresy
LANKSTEER: Capital city of the Lordium kingdom of Trent

LAUGHING GNOME, THE: Tavern in Ratibor
LAVEN: Citizen of Ratibor
LEIF: Butcher at the imperial palace
LENARE PICKERING: Daughter of Count Pickering and Belinda, sister of Mauvin, Fanen, and Denek
LINGARD: Capital city of Relison, kingdom of Trent
LINROY, DILLNARD: See Dillnard Linroy
LIVET GLIM: Port Controller at Tur Del Fur
LONGWOOD: Forest in Melengar
LOTHOMAD THE BALD: King of Lordium, Trent, expanded territory following the collapse of the Steward's Reign, pushing south through Ghent into Melengar, where Brodric Essendon defeated him in the Battle of Drondil Fields in 2545
LOWER QUARTER: Impoverished section of the city of Medford
LUGGER: Small fishing boat rigged with one or more lugsails
LUIS GUY: Sentinel of the Nyphron Church, killed Fanen Pickering
LURET: Imperial envoy to Hintindar
MAGNUS: Dwarf, killed King Amrath, sabotaged Arista's Tower, discovered entry into Avempartha, rebuilding Winds Abbey
MANDALIN: \man-dah-lynn\ Capital of Calis
MANZANT: \man-zahnt\ Infamous prison and salt mine, located in Manzar, Maranon; Royce Melborn is the only prisoner to have been released from it
MARANON: \mar-ah-non\ Kingdom in Avryn, ruled by Vincent and Regina, member of the New Empire, rich in farmland
MARES CATHEDRAL: Center of the Nyphron Church in Melengar, formerly run by Bishop Saldur
MARIBOR: \mar-eh-bore\ God of men

MARIUS, MERRICK: See Merrick Marius

MAUVIN PICKERING: \maw-vin\ Eldest of Count Pickering's sons, friends since childhood with Essendon royal family, bodyguard to King Alric

MAWYNDULË: Powerful wizard

MCDERN, DILLON: Blacksmith of Dahlgren

MEDFORD: Capital of Melengar

MEDFORD HOUSE: Brothel run by Gwen DeLancy and attached to The Rose and Thorn

MELENGAR: \mel-in-gar\ Kingdom in Avryn, ruled by the Essendon royal family, only Avryn kingdom independent of the New Empire

MELENGARIANS: Residents of Melengar

MELISSA: Head servant of Princess Arista, nickname Missy

MERCS: Mercenaries

MERCY: Young girl under the care of Arcadias

MERLONS: Solid section between two crenels in a crenellated battlement

MERRICK MARIUS: Former member of the Black Diamond, alias Cutter, master thief and assassin, former best friend of Royce, known for his strategic thinking, boyfriend of Jade

MESSKID: Container used to transport meals aboard a ship, resembles bucket

MILBOROUGH: Melengarian baron, died in battle

MILFORD: Sergeant in the Nationalist army

MILLIE: Formerly Hadrian's horse, died in Dahlgren

MIR: Person with both elven and human blood

MIRANDA GAUNT: Sister of Degan Gaunt

MIZZENMAST: Third mast from the bow in a vessel having three or more masts

MODINA, EMPRESS: Ruler of the New Empire, previously Thrace Wood of Dahlgren

MON, EDITH: See Edith Mon
MONTEMORCEY: \mont-eh-more-ah-sea\ Excellent wine imported through the Vandon Spice Company
MOTTE: Man-made hill
MOUSE: Royce's horse, named by Thrace, gray mare
MR. RINGS: Baby raccoon, pet of Mercy
MURIEL: Goddess of nature, daughter of Erebus, mother of Uberlin
MYRON LANAKLIN: Sheltered monk of Maribor with indelible memory, son of Victor, sister of Alenda
MYSTIC: Name of Arista's horse
NAREION: \nare-e-on\ Last emperor of the Novronian Empire
NARON: Heir of Novron who died in Ratibor in 2992
NATIONALISTS: Political party led by Degan Gaunt that desires rule by the will of the people
NATS: Nickname of the Nationalists
NEST, THE: Nickname of the Rat's Nest
NEVRIK: \nehv-rick\ Son of Nareion, the heir who went into hiding, protected by Jerish Grelad
NEW EMPIRE: Second empire uniting most of the kingdoms of man, ruled by Empress Modina, administered by co-regents Ethelred and Saldur
NIDWALDEN RIVER: Marks the eastern border of Avryn and the start of the Erivan realm
NIMBUS: Tutor to the empress, assistant to the imperial secretary, originally from Vernes
NIPPER: Young servant assigned primarily to the kitchens of the imperial palace
NOVRON: Savior of mankind, demigod, son of Maribor, who defeated the elven army in the Great Elven Wars, founder of the Novronian Empire, builder of Percepliquis, husband of Persephone

NOVRONIAN: \nov-ron-e-on\ Pertaining to Novron

NYPHRON CHURCH: The worshipers of Novron and Maribor

NYPHRONS: \nef-rons\ Devout members of the church

OBERDAZA: \oh-ber-daz-ah\ Tenkin or Ghazel witch doctor

OLD EMPIRE: Original united kingdoms of man, destroyed one thousand years in the past after the murder of Emperor Nareion

ORRIN FLATLY: Ratibor city scribe

OSGAR: Reeve of Hintindar

OSTRIUM: Tenkin communal hall where meals are served

OUDORRO: Friendly Tenkin village in Calis

PALACE OF THE FOUR WINDS: Home of Erandabon Gile in Dur Guron

PARKER: Quartermaster of Nationalist army

PARTHALOREN FALLS: \path-ah-lore-e-on\ The great cataracts on the Nidwalden near Avempartha

PATRIARCH: Head of the Nyphron Church who lives in the Crown Tower of Ervanon

PAULDRON: A piece of armor covering the shoulder

PERCEPLIQUIS: \per-sep-lah-kwiss\ The ancient city and capital of the Novronian Empire, named for the wife of Novron, destroyed and lost during the collapse of the Old Empire

PERCY BRAGA: Former Archduke and Lord Chancellor of Melengar, expert swordsman, uncle-in-law to Alric and Arista, killed by Count Pickering, commissioned the murder of King Amrath

PERIN: Grocer from Ratibor

PERSEPHONE: Wife of Novron

PICKERING: Noble family of Melengar and rulers of Galilin. Count Pickering is known to be the best swordsman in Avryn and believed to use a magic sword.

PICKILERINON, SEADRIC: Noble who shortened the family name to Pickering

PLESIEANTIC INCANTATION: \plass-e-an-tic\ A method used in the Art to draw power from nature

POE: Cook's assistant aboard the *Emerald Storm*

POLISH: Head of the Black Diamond thieves' guild in Ratibor

PRALEON GUARD: \pray-lee-on\ Bodyguards to the king in Ratibor

PRICE: First Officer of the Black Diamond thieves' guild

QUARTZ: Member of the Ratibor thieves' guild

RATIBOR: Capital of the kingdom of Rhenydd, home to Royce

RAT'S NEST, THE: Hideout of the Black Diamond thieves' guild in Ratibor

RED: Old elkhound, large dog frequently found in kitchen of imperial palace

REEVE: Official who supervises serfs and oversees the lands for a lord

REGAL FOX INN, THE: Least expensive tavern in affluent Hill District in Colnora

REGENT: Someone who administers a kingdom during the absence or incapacity of the ruler

RENDON, BARON: Nobleman of Melengar

RENIAN: \rhen-e-ahn\ Childhood friend of Myron the monk

RENKIN POOL: Citizen of Ratibor with fighting experience

RENQUIST: Soldier in the Nationalist army

RENTINUAL, TOBIS: History professor at Sheridan University, built catapult to fight Gilarabrywn

RHELACAN: \rell-ah-khan\ Great sword given to Novron by Maribor, forged by Drome, enchanted by Ferrol, used to defeat and subdue the elves

RHENYDD: Poor kingdom of Avryn, now part of the New Empire

RILAN VALLEY: Fertile land that separates Glouston and Chadwick

RIONILLION: \ri-on-ill-lon\ Name of the city that first stood on the site of Aquesta but was destroyed during the civil wars that occurred after the fall of the Novronian Empire

RIYRIA: \rye-ear-ah\ Elvish for *two*, a team or a bond, name used to collectively refer to Royce Melborn and Hadrian Blackwater

RONDEL: Common type of stiff-bladed dagger with a round handgrip

ROSE AND THORN, THE: Tavern in Medford run by Gwen DeLancy, used as a base by Riyria

ROSWORT: King of Dunmore

ROYALISTS: Political party that favors rule by independent monarchs

ROYCE MELBORN: Thief, one-half of Riyria

RUFUS: Ruthless northern warlord, intended emperor for the New Empire, killed by a Gilarabrywn in Dahlgren

RUFUS'S BANE: Name given to the Gilarabrywn slain by Thrace/Modina

RUSSELL BOTHWICK: Farmer from Dahlgren

SALDUR, MAURICE: Former bishop of Medford, former friend and advisor to the Essendon family, co-regent of the New Empire

SALIFAN: \sal-eh-fan\ Fragrant wild plant used in incense

SALTY MACKEREL, THE: Tavern in the shipping district of Aquesta

SARAP: Meeting place, or talking place, in the Tenkin language

SAULY: Nickname of Maurice Saldur, used by those closest to him

SENON UPLANDS: Highland plateau overlooking Chadwick

SENTINEL: Inquisitor generals of the Nyphron Church, charged with rooting out heresy and finding the lost Heir of Novron

SERET: \sir-ett\ Knights of Nyphron. The military arm of the church, first formed by Lord Darius Seret, commanded by Sentinels.

SET: Ratibor member of the Black Diamond thieves' guild

SEWARD: Captain of the *Emerald Storm*

SHARON SEA: Southern body of water west of the Ghazel Sea

SHERIDAN UNIVERSITY: Prestigious institution of learning, located in Ghent

SHIP'S MASTER: Highest non-officer, in charge of running the daily working of the ship

SHIRLUM-KATH: Small, parasitic worm found in Calis, can infect untreated wounds

SIWARD: Bailiff of Hintindar

SKILLYGALEE: \Skil`li-ga-lee\ A kind of thin, weak broth or oatmeal porridge

SPADONE: Long two-handed sword with a tapering blade and an extended flange ahead of the hilt allowing for an extended variety of fighting maneuvers. Due to the length of the handgrip and the flange, which provides its own barbed hilt, the sword provides a number of additional hand placements, permitting the sword to be used similarly to a quarterstaff, as well as a powerful cleaving weapon. The spadone is the traditional weapon of a skilled knight.

STAUL: Tenkin warrior aboard the *Emerald Storm*

SUMMERSRULE: Popular midsummer holiday celebrated with picnics, dances, feasts, and jousting tournaments

TABARD: A tunic worn over armor usually emblazoned with a coat of arms

TALBERT, BISHOP: Head of Nyphron Church in Ratibor

TARIN VALE: Hometown of Amilia

TARTANE: Small ship used for fishing and coastal trading; single mast, large sail

TEK'CHIN: One of the fighting disciplines of the Teshlor Knights, preserved by the Knights of the Fauld and handed down to the Pickerings

TEMPLE: Ship's master of the *Emerald Storm*, second in command

TENENT: Most common form of semi-standard international currency. Coins of gold, silver, and copper stamped with the likeness of the king of the realm where it was minted.

TENKIN: Community of humans living in the manner of Ghazel and suspected of having Ghazel blood

TERLANDO BAY: Harbor of Tur Del Fur

TESHLORS: Legendary knights of the Novronian Empire, greatest warriors ever to have lived

THEOREM ELDERSHIP: Secret society formed to protect the heir

THERON WOOD: Father of Thrace Wood, farmer of Dahlgren, killed by Gilarabrywn

THRACE WOOD: Daughter of Theron and Addie, name changed to Modina by regents, crowned empress of the New Empire, killed Gilarabrywn in Dahlgren

THRANIC, DOVIN: See Dovin Thranic

TIGER OF MANDALIN: Moniker given to Hadrian while in Calis

TILINER: Superior side sword used frequently by mercenaries in Avryn

TOLIN ESSENDON: Son of Brodric, moved the Melengar capital to Medford, built Essendon Castle, also known as Tolin the Great

TOPMEN: Members of a ship's crew that work high up in the rigging and sails

TORSONIC: Torque-producing, as in the cable used in crossbows
TRAMUS DAN: Guardian of Naron
TRENCHON: City bailiff of Ratibor
TRENT: Northern mountainous kingdoms not yet controlled by the New Empire
TRILON: Small, fast bow used by Ghazel
TRUMBUL, BARON: Mercenary, hired by Percy Braga to kill Prince Alric
TULAN: Tropical plant found in southeastern Calis, used in religious ceremonies, leaves are dried and burned as offerings to the god Uberlin, smoke of the leaves produce visions when inhaled
TUR: Small legendary village believed to have once been in Delgos, site of the first recorded visit of Kile, mythical source of great weapons
TUR DEL FUR: Coastal city in Delgos, on Terlando Bay, originally built by dwarves
UBERLIN: The god of the Dacca and the Ghazel, son of Erebus and his daughter, Muriel
ULI VERMAR: Obscure reference used by Esrahaddon
URITH: Former king of Ratibor, died in a fire
URLINEUS: Last of the Novronian Empire cities to fall, located in eastern Calis, constantly attacked by Ghazel. After collapse it became the gateway for the Ghazel into Calis.
UZLA BAR: Ghazel chieftain, challenging Erandabon Gile for control of Ghazel
VALIN, LORD: Elderly knight of Melengar known for his valor and courage but lacking strategic skills
VANDON: Port city of Delgos, home to the Vandon Spice Company, pirate haven, grew into a legitimate business center when Delgos became a republic
VELLA: Kitchen servant in the imperial palace

VENDEN POX: Poison impervious to magic remedies

VENLIN: Patriarch of the Nyphron Church during the fall of the Novronian Empire

VERNES: Port city at the mouth of the Bernum River

VIGAN: Sherriff of Ratibor

VILLEIN: Person who is bound to the land and owned by the feudal lord

VINCE EVERTON: Alias used by Royce Melborn while in Hintindar

VINTU: Native tribe of Calis

WANDERING DEACON OF DAHLGREN: Name that refers to Deacon Tomas

WARRIC: Kingdom of Avryn, once ruled by Ethelred, now part of the New Empire

WATCH OFFICER: Officer of the watch, in charge during a particular shift, responsible for everything that transpires during this time

WESBADEN: Major trade port city of Calis

WESLEY: Son of Lord Belstrad, brother of Sir Breckton, junior midshipman on the *Emerald Storm*

WESTBANK: Newly formed province of Dunmore

WESTERLANDS: Unknown frontier to the west

WHERRY: Light rowboat, used for racing or transporting goods and passengers on inland waters and harbors

WICEND: \why-send\ Farmer in Melengar, name of the ford that crosses the Galewyr into Glouston

WIDLEY: Professor at Sheridan University, tried and burned for heresy

WILFRED: Carter in Hintindar

WINDS ABBEY: Monastery of the Monks of Maribor, rebuilt by Myron Lanaklin after being burned

WINSLOW, ALBERT: See Albert Winslow

WINTERTIDE: Chief holiday, held in midwinter, celebrated by feasts and games of skill

WITCH OF MELENGAR: Derogatory title attributed to Princess Arista

WYATT DEMINTHAL: Quartermaster and helmsman of the *Emerald Storm*, father of Allie

WYLIN: \why-lynn\ Master-at-arms at Essendon Castle

WYMAR, MARQUIS: Nobleman of Melengar, member of Alric's council

YOLRIC: Teacher of Esrahaddon

ZULRON: Deformed oberdaza of Oudorro

extras

www.orbitbooks.net

about the author

After finding a manual typewriter in the basement of a friend's house, **Michael J. Sullivan** inserted a blank piece of paper and typed *It was a dark and stormy night, and a shot rang out*. He was just eight. Still, the desire to fill the blank page and see where the keys would take him next wouldn't let go. As an adult, Michael spent ten years developing his craft by reading and studying authors such as Stephen King, Ayn Rand, and John Steinbeck, to name just a few. He wrote ten novels, and after finding no traction in publishing, he quit, vowing never to write creatively again.

Michael discovered forever is a very long time and ended his writing hiatus ten years later. The itch returned when he decided to write books for his then thirteen-year-old daughter, who was struggling in school because of dyslexia. Intrigued by the idea of a series with an overarching story line, yet told through individual, self-contained episodes, he created the Riyria Revelations. He wrote the series with no intention of publishing it. After presenting his book in manuscript form to his daughter, she declared that it had to be a "real book," in order for her to be able to read it.

So began his second adventure on the road to publication, which included drafting his wife to be his business manager, signing with a small independent press, and creating a publishing company. He sold more than sixty thousand books as a self-published author and leveraged this success to achieve mainstream publication through Orbit (the fantasy imprint of Hachette Book Group) as well as foreign translation rights including French, Spanish, Russian, German, Polish, and Czech.

Born in Detroit, Michigan, Michael presently lives in Fair-fax, Virginia, with his wife and three children. He continues to fill the blank pages with three projects under development: a modern fantasy, which explores the relationship between good and evil; a literary fiction piece, profiling a man's descent into madness; and a medieval fantasy, which will be prequel to his best-selling Riyria Revelations series.

Find out more about Michael J. Sullivan and other Orbit authors by registering for the free monthly newsletter at www.orbitbooks.net

if you enjoyed

RISE OF EMPIRE

look out for

HEIR OF NOVRON

volume three of the Riyria Revelations

also by

Michael J. Sullivan

CHAPTER 1

AQUESTA

Some people are skilled, and some are lucky, but at that moment Mince realized he was neither. Failing to cut the merchant's purse strings, he froze with one hand still cupping the bag. He knew the pickpocket's creed allowed for only a single touch, and he had dutifully slipped into the crowd after two earlier attempts. A third failure meant they would bar him from another meal. Mince was too hungry to let go.

With his hands still under the merchant's cloak, he waited. The man remained oblivious.

Should I try again?

The thought was insane, but his empty stomach won the battle over reason. In a moment of desperation, Mince pushed caution aside. The leather seemed oddly thick. Sawing back and forth, he felt the purse come loose, but something was not right. It took only an instant for Mince to realize his mistake. Instead of purse strings, he had sliced through the merchant's belt. Like a hissing snake, the leather strap slithered off the fat man's belly, dragged to the cobblestones by the weight of his weapons.

Mince did not breathe or move as the entire span of his ten disappointing years flashed by.

Run! the voice inside his head screamed as he realized there was a heartbeat, perhaps two, before his victim –

The merchant turned.

He was a large, soft man with saddlebag cheeks reddened by the cold. His eyes widened when he noticed the purse in Mince's hand. "Hey, you!" The man reached for his dagger, and surprise filled his face when he found it missing. Groping for his other weapon, he spotted them both lying in the street.

Mince heeded the voice of his smarter self and bolted. Common sense told him the best way to escape a rampaging giant was to head for the smallest crack. He plunged beneath an ale cart outside The Blue Swan Inn and slid to the far side. Scrambling to his feet, he raced for the alley, clutching the knife and purse to his chest. The recent snow hampered his flight, and his small feet lost traction rounding a corner.

"Thief! Stop!" The shouts were not nearly as close as he had expected.

Mince continued to run. Finally reaching the stable, he ducked between the rails of the fence framing the manure pile. Exhausted, he crouched with his back against the far wall. The boy shoved the knife into his belt and stuffed the purse down his shirt, leaving a noticeable bulge. Panting amidst the steaming piles, he struggled to hear anything over the pounding in his ears.

"There you are!" Elbright shouted, skidding in the snow and catching himself on the fence. "What an idiot. You just stood there — waiting for the fat oaf to turn around. You're a moron, Mince. That's it — that's all there is to it. I honestly don't know why I bother trying to teach you."

Mince and the other boys referred to thirteen-year-old Elbright as the Old Man. In their small band only he wore an actual cloak, which was dingy gray and secured with a -tarnished metal broach. Elbright was the smartest and most accomplished of their crew, and Mince hated to disappoint him.

Laughing, Brand arrived only moments later and joined Elbright at the fence.

"It's not funny," Elbright said.

"But — he —" Brand could not finish as laughter consumed him.

Like the other two, Brand was dirty, thin, and dressed in mismatched clothing of varying sizes. His pants were too long and snow gathered in the folds of the rolled-up bottoms. Only his tunic fit properly. Made from green brocade and trimmed with fine supple leather, it fastened down the front with intricately carved wooden toggles. A year younger than the Old Man, he was a tad taller and a bit broader. In the unspoken hierarchy of their gang, Brand came second — the muscle to Elbright's brains. Kine, the remaining member of their group, ranked third, because he was the best pickpocket. This left Mince unquestionably at the bottom. His size matched his position, as he stood barely four feet tall and weighed little more than a wet cat.

"Stop it, will ya?" the Old Man snapped. "I'm trying to teach the kid a thing or two. He could have gotten himself killed. It was stupid – plain and simple."

"I thought it was brilliant." Brand paused to wipe his eyes. "I mean, sure it was dumb, but spectacular just the same. The way Mince just stood there blinking as the guy goes for his blades. But they ain't there 'cuz the little imbecile done cut the git's whole bloody belt off! Then…" Brand struggled against another bout of laughter. "The best part is that just after Mince runs, the fat bastard goes to chase him, and his breeches fall down. The guy toppled like a ruddy tree. *Wham*. Right into the gutter. By Mar, that was hilarious."

Elbright tried to remain stern, but Brand's recounting soon had them all laughing.

"Okay, okay, quit it." Elbright regained control and went straight to business. "Let's see the take."

Mince fished out the purse and handed it over with a wide grin. "Feels heavy," he proudly stated.

Elbright drew open the top and scowled after examining the contents. "Just coppers."

Brand and Elbright exchanged disappointed frowns and Mince's momentary elation melted. "It felt heavy," he repeated, mainly to himself.

"What now?" Brand asked. "Do we give him another go?"

Elbright shook his head. "No, and all of us will have to avoid Church Square for a while. Too many people saw Mince. We'll move closer to the gates. We can watch for new arrivals and hope to get lucky."

"Do ya want –" Mince started.

"No. Give me back my knife. Brand is up next."

The boys jogged toward the palace walls, following the trail that morning patrols had made in the fresh snow. They circled east and entered Imperial Square. People from all over Avryn were arriving for Wintertide, and the central plaza bustled with likely prospects.

"There," Elbright said, pointing toward the city gate. "Those two. See 'em? One tall, the other shorter."

"They're a sorry-looking pair," Mince said.

"Exhausted," Brand agreed.

"Probably been riding all night in the storm," Elbright said with a hungry smile. "Go on, Brand, do the old helpful stable-boy routine. Now, Mince, watch how this is done. It might be your only hope, as you've got no talent for purse cutting."

Royce and Hadrian entered Imperial Square on ice-laden horses. Defending against the cold, the two appeared as ghosts shrouded in snowy blankets. Despite wearing all they had, they were ill-equipped for the winter roads, much less the mountain passes that lay between Ratibor and Aquesta. The all-night snowstorm had only added to their hardship. As the two drew their horses to a stop, Royce noticed Hadrian breathing into his cupped hands. Neither of them had winter gloves. Hadrian had wrapped his fingers in torn strips from his blanket, while Royce opted for pulling his hands into the shelter of his sleeves. The sight of his own handless arms disturbed Royce as they reminded him of the old wizard. The two had learned the details of his murder while passing through Ratibor. Assassinated late one night, Esrahaddon had been silenced forever.

They had meant to get gloves, but as soon as they had arrived in Ratibor, they saw announcements proclaiming the

Nationalist leader's upcoming execution. The empire planned to publicly burn Degan Gaunt in the imperial capital of Aquesta as part of the Wintertide celebrations. After Hadrian and Royce had spent months traversing high seas and dark jungles seeking Gaunt, to have found his whereabouts tacked up to every tavern door in the city was as much a blow as a blessing. Fearing some new calamity might arise to stop them from finally reaching him, they left early the next morning, long before the trade shops opened.

Unwrapping his scarf, Royce drew back his hood and looked around. The snow-covered palace took up the entire southern side of the square, while shops and vendors dominated the rest. Furriers displayed trimmed capes and hats. Shoemakers cajoled passers-by, offering to oil their boots. Bakers tempted travelers with snowflake-shaped cookies and white-powdered pastries. And colorful banners were everywhere announcing the upcoming festival.

Royce had just dismounted when a boy ran up. "Take your horses, sirs? One night in a stable for just a silver each. I'll brush them down myself and see they get good oats too."

Dismounting and pulling back his own hood, Hadrian smiled at the boy. "Will you sing them a lullaby at night?"

"Certainly, sir," the boy replied without losing a beat. "It will cost you two coppers more, but I do have a very fine voice, I does."

"Any stable in the city will quarter a horse for five coppers," Royce challenged.

"Not this month, sir. Wintertide pricing started three days back. Stables and rooms fill up fast. Especially this year. You're lucky you got here early. In another two weeks, they'll be stocking horses in the fields behind hunters' blinds. The only lodgings will be on dirt floors, where people will be stacked like cordwood for five silvers each. I know the best places and the lowest costs in the city. A silver is a good price right now. In a few days it'll cost you twice that."

Royce eyed him closely. "What's your name?"

"Brand the Bold they call me." He straightened up, adjusting the collar of his tunic.

Hadrian chuckled and asked, "Why is that?"

"'Cuz I don't never back down from a fight, sir."

"Is that where you got your tunic?" Royce asked.

The boy looked down as if noticing the garment for the first time. "This old thing? I got five better ones at home. I'm just wearing this rag so I don't get the good ones wet in the snow."

"Well, Brand, do you think you can take these horses to The Bailey Inn at Hall and Coswall and stable them there?"

"I could indeed, sir. And a fine choice, I might add. It's run by a reputable owner charging fair prices. I was just going to suggest that very place."

Royce gave him a smirk. He turned his attention to two boys who stood at a distance, pretending not to know Brand. Royce waved for them to come over. The boys appeared hesitant, but when he repeated the gesture, they reluctantly obliged.

"What are your names?" he asked.

"Elbright, sir," the taller of the two replied. This boy was older than Brand and had a knife concealed beneath his cloak. Royce guessed he was the real leader of their group and had sent Brand over to make the play.

"Mince, sir," said the other, who looked to be the youngest and whose hair showed evidence of having recently been cut with a dull knife. The boy wore little more than rags of stained, worn wool. His shirt and pants exposed the bright pink skin of his wrists and shins. Of all his clothing, the item that fit best was a torn woven bag draped over his shoulders. The same material wrapped his feet, secured around his ankles by twine.

Hadrian checked through the gear on his horse, removed his spadone blade, and slid it into the sheath, which he wore on his back beneath his cloak.

Royce handed two silver tenents to the first boy, then, addressing all three, said, "Brand here is going to have our horses stabled at the Bailey and reserve us a room. While he's gone, you two will stay here and answer some questions."

"But, ah, sir, we can't —" Elbright started, but Royce ignored him.

"When Brand returns with a receipt from the Bailey, I will pay *each* of you a silver. If he doesn't return, if instead he runs off and sells the horses, I shall slit both of your throats and hang you on the palace gate by your feet. I'll let your blood drip into a pail, then paint a sign with it to notify the city that Brand the Bold is a horse thief. Then I'll track him down, with the help of the imperial guard and *other connections* I have in this city, and see he gets the same treatment." Royce glared at the boy. "Do we understand each other, Brand?"

The three boys stared at him with mouths agape.

"By Mar! Not a very trusting fellow, are ya, sir?" Mince said.

Royce grinned ominously. "Make the reservation under the names of Grim and Baldwin. Run along now, Brand, but do hurry back. You don't want your friends to worry."

Brand led the horses away while the other two boys watched him go. Elbright gave a little shake of his head when Brand looked back.

"Now, boys, why don't you tell us what is planned for this year's festivities?"

"Well . . ." Elbright started, "I suspect this will be the most memorable Wintertide in a hundred years on account of the empress's marriage and all."

"Marriage?" Hadrian asked.

"Yes, sir. I thought everyone knew about that. Invitations went out months ago, and all the rich folk, even kings and queens, have been coming from all over."

"Who's she marrying?" Royce asked.

"*Lard* Ethelred," Mince said.

Elbright lowered his voice. "Shut it, Mince."

"He's a snake."

Elbright growled and cuffed him on the ear. "Talk like that will get you dead." Turning back to Royce and Hadrian, he said, "Mince has a bit of a crush on the empress. He's not too pleased with the old king, on account of him marrying her and all."

"She's like a goddess, she is," Mince declared, misty-eyed. "I seen her once. I climbed to that roof for a better view when she gave a speech last summer. She shimmered like a star, she did. By Mar, she's beautiful. Ya can tell she's the daughter of Novron. I've never seen anyone so pretty."

"See what I mean? Mince is a bit crazy when it comes to the empress," Elbright apologized. "He's got to get used to Regent Ethelred running things again. Not that he ever really stopped, on account of the empress being sick and all."

"She was hurt by the beast she killed up north," Mince explained. "Empress Modina was dying from the poison, and healers came from all over, but no one could help. Then Regent Saldur prayed for seven days and nights without food or water. Maribor showed him that the pure heart of a servant girl named Amilia from Tarin Vale had the power to heal the empress. And she did. Lady Amilia has been nursing the empress back to health and doing a fine job." He took a breath, his eyes brightened, and a smile grew across his face.

"Mince, enough," Elbright said.

"What's all this about?" Royce asked, pointing at bleachers that were being built in the center of the square. "They aren't holding the wedding out here, are they?"

"No, the wedding will be at the cathedral. Those are for folks to watch the execution. They're gonna kill the rebel leader."

"Yeah, that piece of news we heard about," Hadrian said softly.

"Oh, so you came for the execution?"

"More or less."

"I've got our spots all picked out," Elbright said. "I'm gonna have Mince go up the night before and save us a good seat."

"Hey, why do I have to go?" Mince asked.

"Brand and I have to carry all the stuff. You're too small to help and Kine's still sick, so you need to —"

"But you have the cloak and it's gonna be cold just sitting up there."

The two boys went on arguing, but Royce could tell Hadrian was no longer listening. His friend's eyes scanned the palace gates, walls, and front entrance. Hadrian was counting guards.

Rooms at the Bailey were the same as at every inn — small and drab, with worn wooden floors and musty odors. A small pile of firewood was stacked next to the hearth in each room but never enough for the whole night. Patrons were forced to buy more at exorbitant prices if they wanted to stay warm. Royce made his usual rounds, circling the block, watching for faces that appeared too many times. He returned to their room confident that no one had noticed their arrival — at least, no one who mattered.

"Room eight. Been here almost a week," Royce said.

“A week? Why so early?” Hadrian asked.

“If you were living in a monastery for ten months a year, wouldn’t you show up early for Wintertide?”

Hadrian grabbed his swords and the two moved down the hall. Royce picked the lock of a weathered door and slid it open. On the far side of the room, two candles burned on a small table set with plates, glasses, and a bottle of wine. A man, dressed in velvet and silk, stood before a wall mirror, checking the tie that held back his blond hair and adjusting the high collar of his coat.

“Looks like he was expecting us,” Hadrian said.

“Looks like he was expecting someone,” Royce clarified.

“What the —” Startled, Albert Winslow spun around. “Would it hurt to knock?”

“What can I say?” Royce flopped on the bed. “We’re scoundrels and thieves.”

“Scoundrels certainly,” Albert said, “but thieves? When was the last time you two stole anything?”

“Do I detect dissatisfaction?”

“I’m a viscount. I have a reputation to uphold, which takes a certain amount of income — money that I don’t receive when you two are idle.”

Hadrian took a seat at the table. “He’s not dissatisfied. He’s outright scolding us.”

“Is that why you’re here so early?” Royce asked. “Scouting for work?”

“Partially. I also needed to get away from the Winds Abbey. I’m becoming a laughingstock. When I contacted Lord Daref, he couldn’t lay off the Viscount Monk jokes. On the other hand, Lady Mae does find my pious reclusion appealing.”

“And is she the one who . . .” Hadrian swirled a finger at the neatly arranged table.

"Yes. I was about to fetch her. I'm going to have to cancel, aren't I?" He looked from one to the other and sighed.

"Sorry."

"I hope this job pays well. This is a new doublet and I still owe the tailor." Blowing out the candles, he took a seat across from Hadrian.

"How are things up north?" Royce asked.

Albert pursed his lips, thinking. "I'm guessing you know about Medford being taken? Imperial troops hold it and most of the provincial castles except for Drondil Fields."

Royce sat up. "No, we didn't know. How's Gwen?"

"I have no idea. I was here when I heard."

"So Alric and Arista are at Drondil Fields?" Hadrian asked.

"King Alric is but I don't think the princess was in Medford. I believe she's running Ratibor. They appointed her mayor, or so I've heard."

"No," Hadrian said. "We just came through there. She was governing after the battle but left months ago in the middle of the night. No one knows why. I just assumed she went home."

Albert shrugged. "Maybe, but I never heard anything about her going back. Probably better for her if she didn't. The Imps have Drondil Fields surrounded. Nothing is going in or out. It's only a matter of time before Alric will have to surrender."

"What about the abbey? Has the empire come knocking?" Royce asked.

Albert shook his head. "Not that I know of. But like I said, I was already here when the Imperialists crossed the Galewyr."

Royce got up and began to pace.

"Anything else?" Hadrian asked.

"Rumor has it that Tur Del Fur was invaded by goblins. But that's only a rumor, as far as I can tell."

"Not a rumor," Hadrian said.

"Oh?"

"We were there. Actually, we were responsible."

"Sounds . . . interesting," Albert said.

Royce stopped his pacing. "Don't get him started."

"Okay, so what brings you to Aquesta?" Albert asked. "I'm guessing it's not to celebrate Wintertide."

"We're going to break Degan Gaunt out of the palace dungeon, and we'll need you for the usual inside work," Royce said.

"Really? You do know he's going to be executed on Wintertide, don't you?"

"Yeah, that's why we need to get moving. It would be bad if we were late," Hadrian added.

"Are you crazy? The palace? At Wintertide? You've heard about this little wedding that's going on? Security might be a tad tighter than usual. Every day I see a line of men in the courtyard, signing up to join the guard."

"Your point?" Hadrian asked.

"We should be able to use the wedding to our advantage," Royce said. "Anyone we know in town yet?"

"Genny and Leo arrived recently, I think."

"Really? That's perfect. Get in touch. They'll have rooms in the palace for sure. See if they can get you in. Then find out all you can, especially about where they're keeping Gaunt."

"I'm going to need money. I was only planning to attend a few local balls and maybe one of the feasts. If you want me inside the palace, I'll have to get better clothes. By Mar, look at my shoes. Just look at them! I can't meet the empress in these."

"Borrow from Genny and Leo for now," Royce said. "I'm going to leave for Medford tonight and return with funds to cover our expenses."

"You're going back? Tonight?" Albert asked. "You just got here, didn't you?"

The thief nodded.

"She's okay," Hadrian assured Royce. "I'm sure she got out."

"We've got nearly a month to Wintertide," Royce said. "I should be back in a week or so. In the meantime, learn what you can, and we'll formulate a plan when I return."

"Well," Albert grumbled, "at least Wintertide won't be boring."

orbit